I0788178

THE KAELANDUR SERIES

THE KAELANDUR SERIES

BOOKS 1-3

Melorka
Dyndaer
Maharia

THRICE NINE LEGENDS

Joshua Robertson

CRIMSON EDGE PRESS

Thrice Nine Legends Saga

The Blood of Dragons by Joshua Robertson & J.C. Boyd
ANAERFELL*
HESHAYOL*

The Kaelandur Series by Joshua Robertson
MELKORKA*
DYNDAER*
MAHARIA*

Other Thrice Nine Legends Saga by Joshua Robertson & J.C. Boyd
STRONG ARMED*
WHEN BLOOD FALLS*
THE NAME OF DEATH*
WARDEN OF THE ASH TREE*
THE HIGHBORN LONGWALKER*
DEATH AT DUSK**

Additional Works

Legacy Series by Joshua Robertson & J.C.Boyd
BLOOD & BILE*

THE HAWKHURST SAGA*
GRIMSDALR*
THE PRINCE'S PARISH*
JACK SPRATT*

**Published by Crimson Edge*
***Forthcoming by Crimson Edge*

Table of Contents

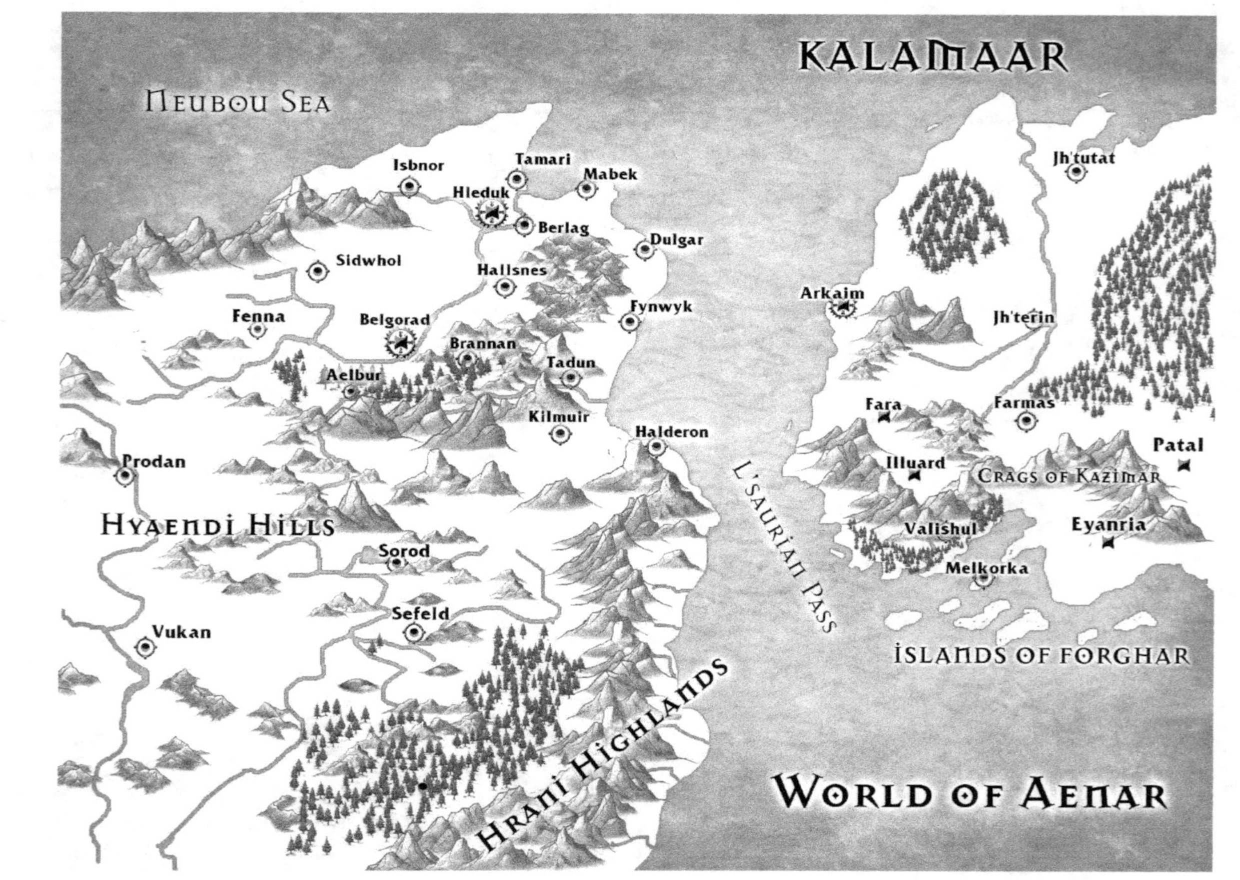

NEUBOU SEA
KALAMAAR
Isbnor
Tamari
Mabek
Hieduk
Berlag
Dulgar
Sidwhol
Hallsnes
Fynwyk
Arkaim
Jh'tutat
Jh'tefin
Fenna
Belgorad
Brannan
Tadun
Aelbur
Kilmuir
Halderon
Fara
Farmas
Patal
Prodan
Illuard
Crags of Kazimar
Valishul
Eyanria
Hyaendi Hills
Sorod
Melkorka
Vukan
Sefeld
L'Saurian Pass
Islands of Forghar
Hrani Highlands
World of Aenar

Rhian
Anaerfell
Bennect
VALARUN
Ayral
Racassi
Charreni
Echelia
MAHARIA
(THE NORTH)
Lairhein
Lonmere
Wojtek
THE SHADE FELLS
Strahil
Egis
Iriy
Gavlok
MOUNT ZYEM
WORLD OF AENAR

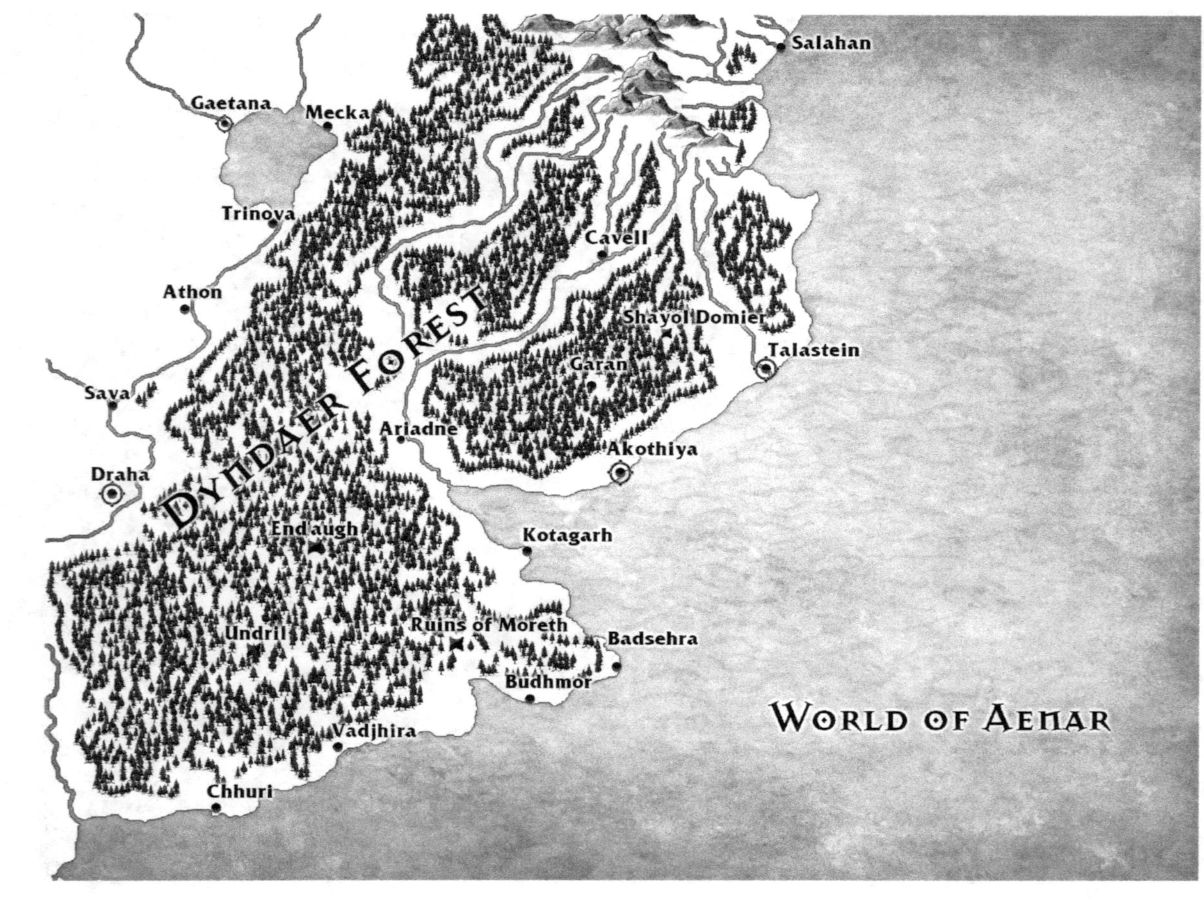

Salahan
Gaetana
Mecka
Trinova
Cavell
Athon
Shayol Domier
Garan
Talastein
Sava
Ariadne
Akothiya
Draha
DYNDAER FOREST
Endaugh
Kotagarh
Undril
Ruins of Moreth
Badsehra
Budhmor
Vadjhira
Chhuri
WORLD OF AENAR

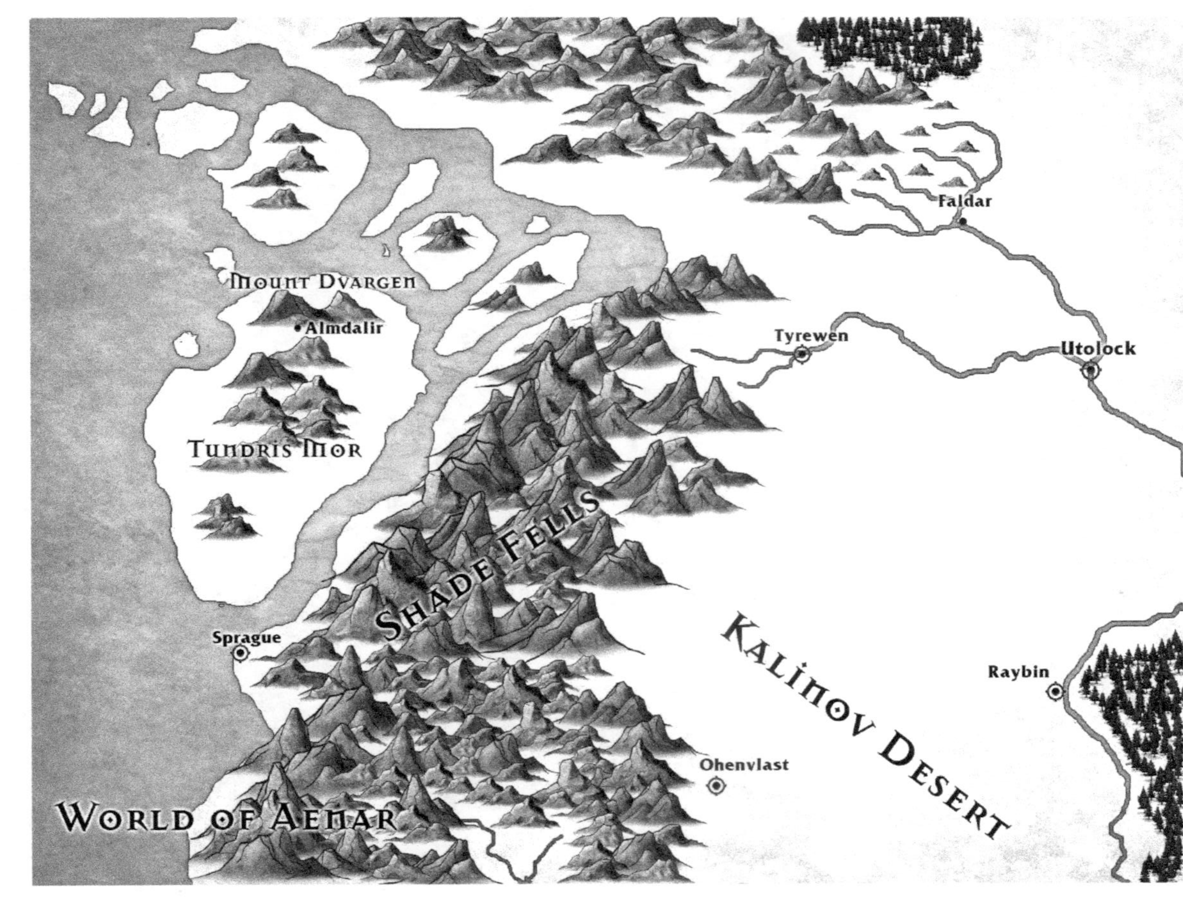

WORLD OF AENAR
Mount Dvargen
Almdalir
Tundris Mor
Shade Fells
Sprague
Tyrewen
Utolock
Faldar
Kalinov Desert
Raybin
Ohenvlast

Preface

For over a decade I steadily worked on *The Kaelandur Series,* trying to capture the essence of my epic fantasy world, Aenar, and the overall feeling of the *Thrice Nine Legends Saga.* Failure in doing so quickly became the norm. Then, in December 2013, I woke from a rich and detailed dream about a dagger with the power to return the dead back to the world of the living. I hurriedly outlined the dream, and subsequently the first book of the series, *Melkorka,* which I finished less than a month later. *Thrice Nine Legends* was alive!

My lineage is an amalgamation of many regions of the world including the Scots, the Germans, the English, and the Slavs. I grew up in a home where we routinely spoke of our ancestral roots and what it meant to be a Robertson. While my bloodline certainly aligns strongly with Clan Donnachaidh (hence the Robertson surname), my family was exceptionally fond of our Czechslovakian heritage. In fact, at a young age, my family went with my grandfather to a Czech festival in Nebraska to learn more about their culture. As you might imagine, I was hooked.

As a result, this became the building blocks of my world building. *The Kaelandur Series,* and the *Thrice Nine Legends Saga* as a whole, are mostly based on Slavic myth. Readers will discover unmistakeable parallels to the gods, the races, the legends, and the monsters of the ancient Slavic world. Without a doubt, the process of building Aenar was a delightful study of my ancestors and their dark history, but this also served as a surefire way to deliver a fantasy world, brimming with mystery and realism.

From the first pages, readers discover that *Thrice Nine Legends* holds many of the same themes as other epic sagas: heroism, the quest, magic, friendship, sacrifice, fate versus free will, and so on. Yet readers also find this is not a typical fantasy novel. For example, medieval European fantasy is gone. Every society has realistic complexities, including politics, religion, commerce, and diversity. And, well, characters are ugly.

For instance, let's consider the central character of *The Kaelandur Series*. Branimir Baran is an unsightly Kras with a long nose, pointed ears, crooked eyes, and crimson-colored skin. As one reader claimed, Branimir *looks like a creature straight from hell*; the gods know every man, woman, and child he crosses in his adventure believes him to be as much. Readers often ask why I chose such an unattractive main character. If I am being honest, I did not think too hard on it. Though, in reflection, I likely chose him for the same reasons I am questioned. As a lowly slave, with few thoughts of his own, Branimir was the most unlikely hero.

I could prattle on for pages about the many characters, the themes, or my intent as an author in writing *Thrice Nine Legends*. For the sake of brevity, let's simply say I did not only mature as a writer, but also as a human being, while writing. These stories have become my legacy and I hope they are valuable to you.

While I have carefully written the tales in *Thrice Nine Legends* to be read as either standalones or in a series form, you will find the most enjoyment by consuming the tales chronologically. The recommended order of the first ennead of books are as follows: *Anaerfell* (The Blood of Dragons #1), *Warden of the Ash Tree, The Highborn Longwalker, Melkorka* (The Kaelandur Series #1), *When Blood Falls, Dyndaer* (The Kaelandur Series #2), *The Name of Death, Maharia* (The Kaelandur Series #3), *Heshayol* (The Blood of Dragons #2).

You can get *When Blood Falls* and *The Name of Death* for free when joining my newsletter.

Lastly, my thanks to those that have crossed my path in this existence, sharing thoughts about thinking over frothy brew, who have tolerated me in all my frolicsome forays, who have whispered words of affirmation when my mind riddled in antagonism, and to my wife and brother most of all.

-Joshua Robertson

MELKORKA

BOOK 1
The Kaelandur Series

THRICE NINE LEGENDS

Joshua Robertson

There once was a time when the gods were gods without question. When men were men without example. When heroes were only the frivolous dreams of lurid mortality. It was a time when truths and untruths were indistinguishable, hatred and love were equally excusable, and life and death regaled all of humanity in the same breath. Myths of old were realized and legends were born from the very dust man was formed of, to be told and retold until the grace of time altered them beyond knowing or forgot them completely. Still, some tales were preserved deep within the hearts of mankind, for reasons that could not be fathomed. Perhaps bearing the fruit of some profound truth or kept alive merely by the strength of the men who lived them. Some tales would never be forgotten.

Month of High Grass
Third of Warmth
124 CE

Chapter I

Branimir Baran cowered away from the copper ore heating in the open hearth. He could not keep his heart from beating in his chest, knowing this would be the first weapon to ever have been crafted at Melkorka. His masters, the Highborn, had never needed a corporal weapon before this day. Even a hundred years ago when they had defended against the demonic Bukavac that bled from the Crags of Kazimir, not a single Highborn had held a weapon. Then again, there was not an *Eretik*, or an evil magus, living among them a hundred years ago.

Even at a distance, the warmth of the hearth touched Branimir's cheeks. "Why does the law say to cut off *their* heads?"

He scarcely noticed he had actually said the words until Jhar Gurov responded with a throaty growl, "It says to decapitate them, crush their skull, and blacken their carcass! The law of men is clear enough about Eretiks! You would not understand, Kras. You are not like us."

Branimir, standing at half the height of the man, turned his head away. The words struck him. It was true he was not the same as the Highborn. Many would think he had demon blood running through his veins, considering his red skin, pointed ears, and pale eyes.

He absentmindedly grinded his crooked teeth and pulled at his long, hooked nose. He supposed he was considered grotesque by human standards.

Regardless, Jhar's next words implied the man did not fully understand why they were crafting the copper blade either. "The real question is why we have to fulfill the law of the Northmen. This is not what it means to be a Highborn!"

A timeworn man, shrouded in murky robes, swayed in a wooden chair behind Branimir. The rockers of the chair creaked at every incline. The man's grey mane bobbed, including the braided tassels of the beard hanging from his pointed chin. He spoke smoothly in a strange accent, "A proper weapon for a proper beheading, so we are told, yes?"

"Weapon or not, we are not blacksmiths, Dorofej," Jhar said firmly grasping his waistband. Branimir took a slight step back toward Dorofej, as though the wrinkled Highborn could protect him. Jhar had an expression that suggested he was on the verge of strangling something.

"We are never the things we ought to be, yes?"

Jhar gained momentum with his discourse, his voice drowning out Dorofej. "How does Kinhar expect us to make a dagger by hand? The Highborn do not make daggers! Never have!" The dark-headed man snorted hard enough to suck the layered soot from the wooden floor to his nostrils.

"And yet here we are, yes?"

"Yes. Here we are!" Jhar slurred in mocking tone. "We should at least be allowed to use magic to hurry things along!"

Dorofej looked to the fire as though he might have been measuring the weight of the suggestion. The old Highborn hovered over Branimir even when sitting hunched over in his rocking chair. Branimir scooted closer to him, his own heartbeat thumping loud enough to ring his ears. With a gulp, Branimir followed Dorofej's gaze to the hearth, hoping to find whatever calm the Highborn had suddenly found.

Branimir had to admit that there was something hypnotic about the copper softening under the intense temperature of the kiln. Its glow was a cherry red with a black coating that slowly formed around its surface. It helped him breathe a bit easier.

Jhar paced around the room. He scrunched his face up, persisting in his rant. "If we must do this, would it have been that hard to find copper nuggets? Do we really have to sit here like fools watching the slag separate?"

"Found on the Seven Islands or Kalamaar, copper is not," Dorofej said. "Kinhar was lucky that he found it in Arkaim at all."

"He did not find anything! It was that new convert—that young woman—who he had fetch it for him like an inept hound."

Dorofej nodded again, his knees bending and extending, keeping rhythm with the chair. "Katerina, her name is, yes? Katerina Gajic from Arkaim. It was likely she would be sent, with her father being in the merchant trade and—"

"I don't need a story, Dorofej. It doesn't matter. He should have sent a Kras. Those little, red broods are the pawns, not the Highborn!"

"Too far a journey for a Kras, I would think. In the wake of the Crags, beyond the hills and the sea—"

"Dorofej!" Jhar said the man's name as though he were casting it into the fire with the burning copper.

The older man innocently raised his bushy eyebrows, his blue eyes widening momentarily at the younger Highborn. He seemed to finally take the hint of Jhar's irritation and mused, "Do not let my reasoning mind disturb your senseless repartee. By all means, let your tongue continue to twitch."

Jhar scowled.

Branimir watched and listened, finding a hint of hilarity in the situation. Any fear he had a moment ago finally fled as he covered his mouth to stop himself from cackling out loud.

He swallowed hard to stomach the laughter. Branimir had been brought up like every other Kras that served at Melkorka. It was their duty to serve the Highborn from birth to death, following directions without question. It was a simple way to live. In fact, it had guided his bloodline for at least the past millennium. He was smart enough to not be caught with a fit of the giggles.

Again, Branimir focused on the copper in the fire. The residue from the ore separated to be collected from the natural element and then disposed. Soon, the metal would be ready to be crafted into a blade and then delicately sharpened.

"Kras," Jhar mumbled, "tell Kinhar that *Kaelandur* will be ready by nightfall. He can have his execution then, if that is his wish."

Branimir stood up from the fire. Apparently, the Highborn had named the copper dagger to be formed. It would be called Kaelandur.

He dipped his head slightly. "At once, Lord," Branimir wheezed between his crooked teeth and cracked lips.

"Killing one of our own and with a weapon. It is madness," Jhar blathered, his fingers twisting to fists, turning white.

Branimir made no comment. The statement was not directed toward him.

Instead, Branimir straightened his wool jacket and pulled the cuffs over his crimson-colored hands. Adjusting his black cloak, he headed toward the rickety door leading to the courtyard. Rays of sunlight pierced through cracks in the wood. The fresh smell of spring pressed against his nostrils.

He grinned behind his closed lips, knowing the Season of Frost was still a quarter of a year away. He still had time to enjoy the sun. The cold was the worst.

He had just taken hold of the latch when Dorofej whispered his name.

"Branimir."

He turned on command. Dorofej was the only Highborn who ever called him by name. "Yes, my Lord."

Dorofej leaned forward in his rocker, clearing his throat while turning his head to observe the younger Highborn. Jhar paid him no attention as usual. Dorofej took a slow breath before speaking in a soft tone. "It has been many years that you have served the Highborn at Melkorka, has it not?"

"Yes, Lord. Over five decades."

With the flames dancing behind him, Dorofej's blue eyes looked like stones frozen in ice. He peered toward the slave as if weighing his next words carefully.

Branimir waited. His time was not his to measure.

"You have never known of an Eretik being beheaded here at Melkorka prior to Nedezhda, yes?"

Branimir kept himself from gasping at the sound of the Eretik's name. No one at Melkorka had said Nedezhda Mager's name in two days. Chained in the dungeons, she was already forgotten by the Highborn.

Branimir had not questioned her fate. She was considered a traitor the moment she was found meddling with death magic and worshipping dark gods. Laws about such things were for the humans, not him.

Branimir shuddered, his hand quivered against the latch with each word. "I do not understand, my Lord. Do you ask whether I have known of Eretiks among the Highborn, or whether I have known of Eretiks who have come to Melkorka, or simply knowing of Eretiks losing their head altogether?" The penalty for questioning the Highborn was not pleasant and ranged from a firm beating to missing appendages. The Highborn were not considered violent as humans were concerned, but the Kras were not regarded much more than a filthy throw rug. Beating out the crud was not only believed to be necessary, but commonplace.

The handle clicked noisily against the planks of the door. The fear churning in his belly practically bubbled.

"I mean what I ask and nothing more," Dorofej replied.

"No, Lord." Branimir gulped, choosing his words carefully. "In my lifetime, or the lifetime of my lineage, there has never been an Eretik who has lost their head at Melkorka. My father would have told me."

Dorofej harrumphed, returning to his private thoughts. Branimir waited, frozen under the gaze of the Highborn. Several moments passed before Dorofej turned back to the fire.

"Odd for it to happen this day, it is."

The statement seemed to reflect Dorofej's conversation with himself, not meant to be heard by others. It was surely not directed toward Branimir, a lowly Kras.

The Highborn did have a funny way of constantly talking to themselves.

"Do as Jhar told you, Branimir," Dorofej said.

"Yes, my Lord." Branimir dipped his head again and squeezed through the narrow door into the morning sunbeams. He sighed with a sense of relief.

The sun was high for it being only a few hours after morning meal. As was common in the Season of Warmth, the sun brightened the stronghold called Melkorka. The castle was considered great in ancient times, as well as now, even when compared to modern day manors in the cities on the mainland. Branimir had never been to the mainland, but he had overheard stories from the Highborn. He was quite sure nothing could ever be greater than Melkorka.

It was not an exceedingly large castle. In fact, it could easily be overlooked if not sought out. Melkorka did not oversee any city, village or hamlet. No monuments pinpointed its exact location. Melkorka stood alone, hidden and forlorn, like a lone warrior, dauntless and diligent.

Branimir had heard the stone structure was crafted from chiseled boulders nearly two thousand years ago. The massive rocks, the size of faerings, or long boats, were stacked in such a way that they almost appeared to have grown straight out of the hilltop. It was said that the heavy stones had been carried by an unknown means from the Crags of Kazimir to the south and east to build Melkorka. Although it was likely that the Highborn had used their magic, Branimir preferred the stories that suggested that giants had moved the chunks of rock. There was something thrilling about creatures who towered over humans.

His gaze drifted, seeing the few Highborn and fewer Kras. Of course, most of the Highborn would be in the keep, and there were not many Kras left at Melkorka. Not many at all.

The flapping tapestries atop the towers of the stronghold stole Branimir's attention. The symbol was circular with thick golden, dancing swirls strewn throughout. Such a sign was meant to represent the god, Dahz, the ruler of the golden sun and Protector of Men.

"Bran!" A comforting voice resounded as he made his way across the courtyard toward the keep. "Bran!"

Branimir turned to see another Kras come running from the guardhouse just inside the main gate. Mojmir Nok rushed across the worn path inside the walls, barely making a sound. His scarlet skin glistened against the sun rays, a head of thin, black hair bouncing over his offset mouth. Mojmir was an odd creature to look at. Not because of his traits of being a Kras, but because he was missing his left eye. This gave more attention to his right eye. Its color was dark as pitch.

Mojmir squeaked again in his shrill voice. "Bran!"

Branimir raised his hand to quiet his friend. "What is the hubbub, Mojmir?"

"Andrik sent me. Kinhar is in the dungeon with…her… he wants you."

Branimir chewed the inside of his lip. Obviously, *her* could only be Nedezhda Mager, the Eretik. "Why me?"

Mojmir shrugged his shoulders.

Branimir turned to look at the housing unit he had just exited, holding Dorofej and Jhar. Similar stone houses with thatched roofs lined the inner side of the wall. They had just replaced the straw at the beginning of the season and would have to change it again in a few months before the cold came.

He scratched his head. Being sent to Kinhar was one thing but being summoned by him was another matter entirely. "I needed to speak with Kinhar anyhow."

Branimir turned from Mojmir without a farewell and quickly climbed the stone staircase that stood adjacent to the keep. He did not hesitate and entered through the sturdy wooden door. Mojmir had gone his own way after delivering the message. Even if Branimir had the option, he would not have asked Mojmir to join him. A Kras always had their orders to attend to and could not be distracted by idle chitchat.

Branimir stepped within the hall of the keep. It gave suggestion to the skeleton of the building's framework. The walls were the same stone as most of Melkorka, but the main flooring was made of beaten earth laid between the stone walls. There were two upper floors that had planks of timber covered with light layers of dirt in many areas. He tiptoed to the dungeon to the left and then right, following no more than a dirt trail that led at a harsh angle into the depths of the earth beneath the castle. The single path to the dungeon was much like the others, smooth and even from ages of being walked upon.

Branimir glided his hand along the smooth stone as he crept down into the dungeon, careful not to slip down the crevice. He cautiously placed each of his small feet in front of one another and inched twenty feet deep toward the dilapidated door that was supposed to hold prisoners securely beneath Melkorka.

Branimir approached the poor excuse for a door. He had been enslaved to the Highborn for his entire life. Never once had he tried to make an escape, nor had any Kras within Melkorka. It was likely that the Highborn would have their heads before they could dream up a scheme for escape. Branimir could as easily claim that no prisoner had ever runaway either, but then again, there had never been a prisoner at Melkorka in his lifetime.

Nedezhda was the first.

Branimir pushed open the door, afraid that it might crumble beneath his touch. When it did not, the Kras scooted inside the narrow opening.

Kinhar Sayan's voice was easily recognizable in a hollowed wheeze, "It pains me to have to sentence you to death, but there is no other way. You know the penalty of being an Eretik. I do not have to explain the law to you, Nedezhda."

Kinhar's coarse cloth outlined his frail frame. He was easily aged beyond that of the ancient Dorofej. Kinhar stood, stooped with his hand against the stone wall for support. His white hair fell to his heels, tied in knots to keep him from tripping over it. His upper lips and chin had flimsy hair of the same color that hung wildly over his mouth and chest.

He appeared to be more hair than man.

"I know your schemes, Kinhar. Taking my head this night will not silence your wickedness."

Nedezhda was sprightly, despite the chains that bound her body to the stone wall. A small etching of an eye scraped with a moon and a cross was engraved over her head. Branimir could only guess that the symbol prevented her from touching the craft, *Koldovstvo*. There was no evidence of torture to her flesh or mind, as she stared defiantly at Kinhar. Her light blue eyes were alarming, shining in the darkness, with a hint of knowing that made Branimir shiver and turn his head away momentarily.

"The evil traces of Koldovstvo flow deep in your veins, my poor girl. Madness has enveloped your mind and has led you to paranoia and delusion and—"

"I know what was said!" The woman's nose was small, but her nostrils flared with the intensity of a horrendous beast. "You spoke of the Kadari!"

Kinhar was poised as though her shouts were the quietest of whispers. "Such faith I had in you, Nedezhda. The Highborn are the hand of the Lightbringer. We will be the deliverers of hope even when there is none to be had."

"The Highborn are to have no allegiance," she began.

"And yet, you have allied yourself with the heart of darkness, embracing its futility and uniting eternally with its acidic breath," Kinhar continued.

Nedezhda gave no sign of wavering to her elder. "Cut me down this night or the next, Kinhar Sayan, but know that my innocence will be avenged. The Highborn do not kill their own."

"The law must be upheld. It has been decreed that your actions extend beyond the privilege of breath. Dahz demands that Strega's breath be breathed by His brethren and not those that spit on righteousness."

"You speak of the gods as if they speak to you. You speak of good and evil as though it is defined by the divine. Any delusion that runs rampant in Melkorka is in your mind, Kinhar!"

"Bah!" The old man turned his crumpled face from the younger woman, taking notice of Branimir standing idly behind him.

Branimir recoiled at the man's sudden attention.

"Alas, you have come, Kras," Kinhar spoke steadily, turning his attention back to the Eretik with a snort. "See how the Kras knows their function without question, ever vigilant in their loyalty to those of exceptional power. The Kras to the Highborn is the Highborn to the Lightbringer, Nedezhda. Such simple logic you should have recognized early in your apprenticeship."

"Such loose connections are contrived by men absorbed with entitlement, taking advantage of the less fortunate," she flung back at him.

Kinhar shook his head in disbelief at the woman, returning focus to the Kras. "What news do you bring from Jhar and Dorofej?"

"My Lord, Kaelandur will be ready by nightfall."

"So, it is this night that justice will run its course in Melkorka?"

Branimir hesitated, uncertain if the question was meant for him. It was awfully difficult to know when the Highborn were speaking to one of their gods or themselves entirely. "Yes, my Lord."

Kinhar looked at Branimir, with a hint of surprise that he had spoken and then continued, "I have a task for you and the one-eyed one."

Branimir recognized the reference to Mojmir. "Speak it and consider it done, my Lord."

"Take this," Kinhar grabbed a hand full of Nedezhda's hair and tore it from her head. She screamed, blood immediately surfacing on her scalp.

Branimir winced, holding his small, red hand out to take the strands of hair from his Lord with as much eagerness as he could muster. "Yes, my Lord."

"Take this inland toward the Crags and set fire to it so that when the evening gale blows, the ashes are swept toward the shores of Strega's Deep. Make haste and do not let any Highborn go with you."

"You will bring death to the world," Nedezhda hissed.

Kinhar frowned at her.

Branimir winced at her words. He was inclined to ask Kinhar of the true purpose of the task, but he knew better than to question the Highborn.

He bowed his head in submission. "As you wish, my Lord. It will be done at once."

"By the time you return," Kinhar said with more ferocity than Branimir had ever witnessed from the old man, "the Eretik will have her neck severed and body bloodied in flame."

With the hesitation of a raindrop falling from a thatch roof, Branimir raised his pale eyes slowly to look at Nedezhda and quickly wished he had refrained. Her cold eyes were ignited with equal rage, stained with the shadow of an inescapable death, and were frozen to his own with timeless hatred.

Chapter II

In the dim light of the failing sun, the peaks of the adjacent Crags were a silhouette on the horizon, stretching toward the scattered clouds in the evening sky.

"Bran," Mojmir squeaked. "How far inland must we go before burning this hair? We've been walking for hours."

"Lord Kinhar did not say exactly," Branimir said. "I suppose this is far enough. The evening gale will be upon us shortly anyway."

Mojmir nodded, picking at the hole where his left eye should have been. "It has never been the same without it."

Branimir stared at his companion, unsure of how to respond to such a statement. "I suppose not."

Mojmir circled around in the dirt, walking without purpose as Branimir held Nedezhda's hair against the ground under his foot. He reached in his pocket for tinder, flint, and steel. In the meantime, Mojmir hopped and bounced about somewhat carelessly before finally sitting with his legs crossed. The other Kras stared toward the Crags. His hand petted the eye socket repeatedly as if mourning the loss of his full sight.

"What do you think it was like, Branimir?"

Branimir laid the tinder over the hair and clicked the flint and steel together creating a spark. "What are you talking about?"

"Farmas? Patul? Illuard? Faran? Eyanria?"

Branimir paused with his kin to look at the Crags of Kazimir. Mojmir spoke of the lost, underground cities of the Kras that once existed deep in the mountainside. They were not permitted to speak of such things around the Highborn. Branimir found himself hesitant, even now, but still said softly, "It was said that Eyanria had more gems than the Kras had pockets, with chests overflowing with trinkets, charms, and shiny stones."

"I would like to have a shiny stone."

"Me too, Mojmir."

"My father's father told me that Farmas was pretty."

"I did not know you had met your father's father."

"It was brief when I was a small child. I was surely the size of a pebble at the time."

Branimir raised an eyebrow at Mojmir, who did his best to keep a straight face before letting loose a gut-wrenching bellow of a laugh. Branimir could not help but join in with the foolish Kras.

"Don't say that around the Highborn. Their sense of humor is as keen as their taste in women!"

"Ha!" Mojmir gaped open his mouth, overly amused with himself. "In fifty years, I have yet to see one worth looking at!"

Branimir grabbed his stomach, falling backwards gleefully with an abrupt chuckle. "No wonder they never mate."

"Hold on a minute," Mojmir paused, taking a deep breath, becoming very serious. "I thought the Highborn came from lightning bolts from their gods. You mean they actually have mating rituals?"

Branimir stopped, his laughter silenced in an instant. He turned toward Mojmir. "You cannot be serious?"

Mojmir shrugged. "I've never seen a Highborn infant."

Branimir had to admit that he had never seen one either, but he knew humans did not descend from lightning. "I am not explaining to you how human pollen spreads."

"What does that mean, Bran?"

"It means…forget it."

"If you think so," Mojmir shrugged again. "Anyway, I would like to know what a Kras woman looks like."

Branimir stared blankly at Mojmir. "You had a mother."

Mojmir returned the look of absoluteness, placing a finger on his nose. "And she was a mother, not a woman. Heh?"

"You have seaweed for brains, Mojmir."

Branimir could not condemn Mojmir for having such thoughts, as Branimir had thought such things himself in the late hours, in secret. Never had he met a female Kras outside of his own mother or seen any real remnant of the Kras civilization. He had few answers and even fewer questions, because he had no basis of knowing where to begin.

The Kras would soon become extinct, forever removed from the world of men. Their underground cities were home to demons. Their riches had long ago been appropriated and traded by humans. And their fates were at the hands of the Highborn. Truly, the life of the Kras was forlorn.

As if remembering his task, Branimir struck flint against steel again, dropping spark to the tinder. The stench immediately touched his nostrils. He wiggled his hooked nose to take away the itch before giving breath to the flame. Stepping back from harm's way, the hair caught fire and singed to ash. As if prompted, the evening wind swept from east to west, picking up the scorched strands of hair and carried them toward Strega's Deep.

"What was that? Did you hear that, Bran?"

Mojmir jumped to his feet, continuing to look toward the Crags.

Branimir noticed the sun was nearly gone from the sky. It did not matter much to him. He and Mojmir could see as well in the dark as they could during the day. In fact, they did not know much difference except when the Highborn complained about it.

Branimir stepped carefully toward Mojmir with the grace of a fish in water, barely making a sound on the light pebbles beneath his feet. He was not sure he had heard anything.

Mojmir ran a thin hand through his black strands of hair, before touching the missing eye again. "Branimir! Did you hear it or not?"

Branimir grimaced. "I can't hear anything but the wind. May I add, it doesn't help with you and your hubbub, Mojmir."

In that moment, a definite howl resounded in the distance ahead of them, causing them both to drop to the ground on their stomachs, nearly simultaneously.

"That's not wind, Bran," Mojmir cried out again, attempting to scoot back the way they had come.

"Stay down, you fool!" Branimir instructed. "You aren't going to scoot all the way back to Melkorka."

Mojmir gave no argument, stopping instantly.

"We are safe if we do not move," Bran reasoned. "The light has dimmed, and our clothes are dark."

"Unless whatever it is can see as we do."

Branimir bit his cheek. He had not thought about that.

"But," Mojmir lifted his eyebrows, surprised at his own thought, "we can always disappear from sight if needed!"

Branimir grinned enthusiastically in agreement. A Kras could always disappear when needed. "Good thinking."

"Okay, I am not moving. What do you see?"

"Give me a moment," Branimir replied, taking a slow breath. Ever so slightly, he raised his body from the dirt.

Branimir scanned the low hills between Melkorka and the Crags. The skies darkened but it did not impair Branimir's vision in the slightest. He could faintly see something moving on the horizon. Blinking a couple of times, he focused on the shadows dancing at the base of the mountains.

"What is it?" Mojmir wheezed. His single eye darted to Bran's face looking for some sort of answer.

Lightning ricocheted through the colorless clouds. And Branimir knew these were not storm clouds. This lightning was unnatural.

Again, the lightning flashed, illuminating the ground around the two Kras. Mojmir squeaked again pushing his body closer to the uneven ground, covering his single eye.

"Are one of the Highborn being born?"

"No. Bukavac," Branimir said with a trembling voice, ignoring the other Kras's ignorance.

"Demons from the Netherworld..." Mojmir croaked at a whisper, throwing his head up again. "That's not funny! You have never seen a Bukavac. How would you know?"

"Hard to mistake! I have heard stories."

"What kind of stories?"

Branimir scoffed. "There aren't any good stories with Bukavac, Mojmir!"

Mojmir scrunched his nose, hesitantly keeping his eye on Branimir. His words were filled with distrust, "Well, how many are there?"

"More than I can count."

A beastly roar like no other sounded across the expanse. The ground shook beneath their feet. It was as though an army were marching on it. Mojmir's tone drastically changed with the realization that Branimir was speaking truthfully.

"They are giant." Branimir's words hung in the air for a moment before Mojmir said anything. Maybe demons had built Melkorka.

"Have... have they spotted us?"

"Not yet. Not...quite yet," Branimir said. "We must get back to Melkorka and tell the Highborn."

"If they see us, we are dead."

"Then don't get spotted!" Branimir mocked.

"But—"

"Shut it, Mojmir, and run!"

Branimir flung himself from the ground and scampered northwest toward the castle. He could hear Mojmir panting behind him. He may be a dupe for running like a three-legged mule across open land, but it was far more foolish to be discovered with his face pressed to the earth.

Legend held truth in saying the Kras were fast. Not as quick as a horse or a dog, but quicker than a human. Branimir hoped they were faster than the demonic Bukavac too.

Chapter III

Branimir was relieved when Melkorka appeared before him. His feet ached, and his legs burned from running, but he did not plan to stop until he was within the stronghold. The walls were gigantic compared to him, standing almost three times his height. The towers and keep were even grander in size. Yet Branimir was afraid that their height would be trivial when compared to the size of the Bukavac.

Melkorka was triangle-shaped, positioned on top of a narrow, flat hill. One tower provided a lookout at the gate and the other overlooked the ocean to the west and the hills to the north. Branimir was certain that no one was manning the towers. The Highborn would not waste their time idly guarding the landscape. Luckily, Melkorka was a solid structure, built to withstand the attack of small legions. The greatest defense for the castle was the steep slopes surrounding the hill. Historically, it had slowed enemies, lessening their numbers, preventing any army from overrunning the castle. In fact, he had heard stories of the Highborn defending against demons before and winning.

Branimir hoped tonight would not be any different.

The tapestries hanging from the towers were likely too dark for any human to make out in the night, but he could see them clearly. They flapped fiercely in the lurching wind. He did not understand why but seeing the sun symbol on the fabric made his gut churn.

Branimir knew the Lightbringer's crest had not always been honored at Melkorka. Before his father's death, the Highborn had held fidelity to no god.

The gods were the humans concern though; not his.

Branimir and Mojmir did not slow until they had made it through the aged wooden doors leading to the courtyard. At Melkorka's entrance stood Dorofej and Jhar. A few oil lamps lit the area to give some light to the humans. Thirty feet behind them was the outside staircase of stone that led to the keep.

Dorofej was speaking to Jhar as Branimir approached them. His robes were so thick that they easily hid his ripened body in shadows. It did not help that the attire was dyed with mixed shades of black and dark grey. Not only was the man heavily wrapped up in cloth, but also in his words. Dorofej did not show any indication of acknowledging him or Mojmir.

Jhar, on the other hand, noticed them immediately and interrupted Dorofej, "By the Nine Lands, Kras! You are back awfully fast. What is the rush?" Jhar wore similar attire as the elderly man, but strangely enough was the one that carried a walking stick. He slammed the base of the shaft against the ground as he finished speaking. Dust sprinkled into the air.

Dorofej grunted in surprise as the two tried to catch their breath. As expected, the old man spoke before either of the half-sized men had a chance. "Something is coming, yes?" Wrinkles of wisdom lined his eyes. "Look at them, Jhar. Mojmir is shaking right out of his red skin, he is!"

It was true. Mojmir's pint-size body trembled beyond control.

Lightning flashed.

"Speak to us," Jhar said in a demanding tone.

"Bukavac...from the Crags," Branimir said between heaves. "We must tell Lord Kinhar."

"It cannot be," Dorofej said, speaking over the top of Branimir's last words. He cleared his throat. "Eighty years, it has been, since any demon has come down from the mountaintops."

"Are you sure?"

Branimir nodded. "Twice your height, skin like ice, clawed and fanged like the Seamstress of Nightmares herself..."

"Enough, Kras." Jhar ordered.

Dorofej had a twinkle in his eye. "What would cause them to return to the world of the living, I wonder?"

Jhar scowled. "Her death, Dorofej. She has come for her revenge."

"Nedezhda?"

Jhar nodded as though the answer could not be more obvious. "Kaelandur took her life once already. And now, how will we defeat her when she is already dead?"

"Kinhar will know a way, yes?" Dorofej's lip curled under his white mustache.

"He better after playing with daggers." Jhar dipped his head, hitting the butt of his staff against the dirt again. The cloud of dust powdered the air over Branimir's head. Jhar peered at him. "How many Bukavac does Nedezhda bring?"

Branimir blinked, suddenly remembering his place among the humans, among the Highborn. "An army, my Lord." He watched each pinch of dust fall back to the ground. Branimir shivered under his cloak.

Dorofej licked his lips, dry and cracked. He did it carefully, meticulously—as though it were the last time to perform such a mundane task. His voice was steady. "Run along and inform Kinhar, you will. Be quick about it, yes?"

Mojmir and Branimir were well practiced in following instruction without questioning it. The Highborn had been sure of that. As Branimir scurried toward the entrance, the final words of the conversation effortlessly fell upon his ears.

"What will we do, Dorofej?"

"It is likely we will die. That will be another adventure entirely, yes?"

Branimir and Mojmir did not take any more time to scan the courtyard. It was silent, suggesting many of the Highborn were already in their beds. Branimir rushed up the staircase and through the wooden door leading into the keep.

For the second time that day, Branimir's feet fell over the beaten earth of Melkorka's halls. He headed the way carefully, avoiding the rotten timbers, with Mojmir close at his heels.

"Do you really think Nedezhda is back from the dead?" Mojmir asked.

"I know little about Koldovstvo."

"The human's craft? Me either."

"I don't think we are meant to." Branimir scrunched his shoulders. He might be able to manipulate his body to blend in with the world around him, but he could not manipulate the elements like a Highborn.

Branimir slowed his pace as they neared Lord Kinhar's chambers.

"Maybe she was not killed," Mojmir suggested. "I don't think you can return from the dead once you are…dead."

"Her head was chopped off, Mojmir." Branimir's tone was dry.

"Yeah, but maybe—"

"Shut it, Mojmir."

Kinhar's chamber was narrow and uneven, with the north wall shorter than the south. It was evident that water dripped frequently in the room, causing mold and stalactites to form on the ancient stones. The smoke from the flames in a center fire pit touched Branimir's nostrils before escaping through a hole in the wall. He suddenly found himself distracted with thoughts of burning hair.

Lightning flashed again and Branimir jerked his head to the window. The southeast tower was visible but Branimir could not see much else. Several footsteps trudged across the ground below, accompanied by frantic shouting.

"You have returned. I hope that you did not tarry in your task." Kinhar sat in his stitched robes hunched on a stone chair on a raised dais. Oil lamps sat on either side of the throne-like seat for better lighting. His hair was still knotted in the back, his beard shrouding his torso. Standing behind him was a man and two women.

Again, Branimir found it hard to look at the powerful Highborn and distracted himself by drifting his gaze throughout the chamber. Dormant tables were misplaced throughout the room, awkwardly positioned with piles of scrolls and books strewn over them. The place was a mess.

"What do you mean?" Mojmir muddled.

"When burning the hair? Did you waste time?"

"We burned..." Mojmir tried again. "We...burned it..."

Branimir interrupted, "We did not tarry, my Lord."

"Do not lie to me, Kras, or I will have your head."

Branimir squinted, unsure of how he may have failed the Highborn.

"What have you come to tell me?"

"The Bukavac are coming from the Crags. Dorofej and Jhar say that Nedezhda has returned for revenge."

Sighing, Kinhar leaned forward, gripping an ash branch that suddenly seemed to appear from the sleeve of his filthy green and white tunic. He stood as straight as he could. The stave helped him maintain balance. Carefully, the old man hobbled toward the fire.

"My Lord," Branimir raised his tone, "Nedezhda has come back from the Netherworld. She will kill us all!"

"I am aware, Branimir Baran." Kinhar shuffled closer toward the fire pit and sighed. "This should not have happened. This was only a sacrifice." The old man's voice was eerily calm at a whisper, but it was the use of Branimir's full name that gave him chills.

Branimir hung to Kinhar's words. Taking Nedezhda's head was meant to be a punishment, not a sacrifice.

"Falmagon, Katerina, Faina," Kinhar muttered to the room. "Jhar and Dorofej will need your assistance. Help rouse those who are not already awake. The Bukavac have likely reached the outer walls by now."

Branimir gawked at the familiar Highborn making their exit from the room.

Falmagon was a young man with a pointed nose over a thick mustache. Like Mojmir, this human was also missing his left eye.

The gaping hole in his skull was covered with a piece of cloth tied back under his scraggly, brown hair. He spoke with unyielding respect to the older Highborn, "As you wish, Kinhar."

The middle-aged woman, Faina, went to the window and peered out at the courtyard fifteen feet down. She glanced back to Kinhar, the firelight outlining the wrinkles at the corners of her mouth. Her gaze was undeniably filled with concern. Without a word, she leaped from the window to the ground below.

Katerina dipped her head but also held her tongue. The woman was the youngest Highborn at Melkorka, arriving only a few months ago from Arkaim. Her hair was dark brown much like her large eyes. She was too young to have ever seen one of the frozen demons, let alone battle against them. Of course, no one had fought the Bukavac in almost a century. It was no wonder Katerina stumbled over her own feet before squeezing through the door after Falmagon.

Branimir stayed with her until she faded from sight, paying less attention to Falmagon and Faina. Katerina often had shown kindness to him, even smiling in his direction from time to time. She held no smile now.

"Are you not going to join the battle, Kras? This moment will likely change the world. You may yet be recorded in the history of men."

Branimir mirrored Mojmir's blank stare. Kinhar could not be serious. Branimir would have less than nothing to offer against the giant demons of the Netherworld.

Mojmir was the first to break the silence. "Is that an order, my Lord?" The quiver in his voice was unmistakable.

Kinhar tilted his head for a moment as if hearing a whisper in his ear. "No, not at all. No, I do not command men or women, human or otherwise, to their death."

Branimir eyed the window, where the Highborn would engage in battle against the Bukavac. Victory or not, from the stories he had heard of demons, several Highborn would be die in this fight, and at the direction of their fearless leader.

With a gulp, Branimir decided to keep his mouth closed. Either the spearhead of the Highborn was speaking in jest, or he was delusional.

Mojmir was less wise. "You just chopped off Nedezhda's head."

Kinhar raised his thick brow in surprise at the Kras's boldness. A frown formed under the man's hairy face, disgruntled in trying to provide reason to a slave. Bran wondered if the explanation was for his benefit and not for Mojmir. "Nedezhda's choices led her to that fate. The command for her execution came down from Dahz the Lightbringer."

"The Sun God, the Protector of Men, told you to kill Nedezhda?" Mojmir scrunched up his face. The Kras was actually challenging the spearhead of the Highborn.

"Yes."

"What could she have—"

"Mojmir, shut it!" Branimir hissed between clenched teeth.

"If you had not killed her then the Bukavac would not have come!"

Branimir jumped at the crash of splitting wood. It sounded from outside, suggesting the wooden gates had been smashed. Shouts and cries of combat sounded through the window. Instant screams of men and roars of beasts followed.

"You will kill us all!" Mojmir cried out.

Branimir puffed out his cheeks and turned to hit Mojmir with his fist. The shorter Kras turned to look at him. Branimir hastily pointed to his good two eyes and then made a small fist.

Mojmir's mouth gaped open with confusion. He mouthed the single word. "What?"

"Who cut out your eye, Mojmir?" Branimir said just loud enough for his friend to hear.

"Uh…" He uncomfortably mumbled, twisting his neck to look back at Kinhar.

Kinhar was too old to make out their murmurs. He rambled, "Nedezhda defied the will of Dahz and used Koldovstvo as an Eretik. Any practice of death magic is an atrocity only to be punished with death. Her execution was judged correctly by the gods, as evidenced by her rise from the frozen Netherworld with these demon spawn." Kinhar's voice trailed. "This must be a test from the Lightbringer."

Mojmir bowed his head. "I see, Lord…um…Kinhar, my Lord. Forgive my stupidity."

"To forgive a fool is to be a fool!" Kinhar's voice was harsh, unbecoming of an old man. "I have no time to deal with it now. Move to the window, out of my way, and out of my sight. I have little time."

Branimir and Mojmir stepped away from the tables and fire pit, where Kinhar hurriedly began to dig through scrolls, searching for something. Branimir moved next to the single window in the room and stood up on his tippy-toes to peer outside.

Twenty of the Highborn were strategically placed across the courtyard and in the towers. Branimir could see fires from torchlight to light the grounds for the Highborn. He imagined most of Melkorka was darkened by the night, shadow on shadow. For him, he could see everything.

The wooden gates were destroyed as expected. The fallen Highborn were already speckled in heaps with dead Bukavac. Bodies littered Melkorka. The numbers of the beasts were overwhelming though, pressing through the gates like flooding waters. He could not see the end to their army across the terrain beyond the gates. The Bukavac bled out from the Crags like a wound that could not be healed.

The demonic, man-shaped creatures were truly from horror dreams. Each Bukavac stood twice as tall as any Highborn. With a simple leap, any of them could reach the window ledge leading into the chamber where Branimir hid. Fortunately, no one of their size would be able to fit through the opening without tearing out the stone wall.

"And to think I always wanted to see giants…" Branimir said to himself.

The faces of the Bukavac were etched in fanged snarls, teeth longer than Branimir's torso. Their weapons were not made from copper or bronze, but of a stronger substance that they gripped between their three fingers and thumb. These weapons had never been seen at Melkorka. Branimir did not know what they were, but they looked sharp and dangerous. He could only guess they had been forged in the Netherworld, the home of these demons.

The fires in Melkorka's courtyard reflected off the bluish-white bodies of the Bukavac, colored like snowfall on the Eve of Frost. The light illuminated their blue-grey eyes, like the precious gems of the underearth.

War cries echoed again and again across the demonic ranks. Screams of agony mixed with valiant shouts from the Highborn were nearly silenced in the uproar. Nothing was louder than the soul-shattering sound of death's undertone.

The lightening that once again ricocheted through the pastel clouds illuminated the battleground below and above. Branimir squeaked holding his body closer to the uneven wall in Kinhar's chamber. He could feel the broken rock crumble away from the aged stones as he pressed harder. His skilled ears heard them as they collided with the worn floor.

The few Highborn against hundreds of Bukavac crafted the energy of flame, stone, sky and sea. Waves from the Strega's Deep crashed into the courtyard. Fire and rock erupted from the ground. Still, the demons spread into Melkorka. Nothing could stop them. For every fallen Bukavac, three more seemed to take its place.

"Look, Bran!" Mojmir squealed, staring out the window with a pointed finger, "Lord Jhar and Lord Dorofej are still alive."

"Quiet, Mojmir," Branimir said softly, shadowing Mojmir's gesture. "You will draw attention to us."

Mojmir was right. The two Highborn were fighting against the Bukavac. Jhar and Dorofej stood with three other Highborn against the base of the east tower, facing more demons than they had fingers among the lot of them.

Jhar held the front line, wielding his wooden staff between his left and right hand with exceptional speed. He frequently slammed the stick against the ground, causing the clouds of dust to rise into the air. These small particles circled around him and whirled like a sandstorm, with some of its pieces enlarging to the size of flagstones. The larger chunks of earth were then manipulated by Jhar with a wave of his hand, thrown into the Bukavac like a stone from a sling.

Branimir screeched as bodies exploded and limbs were severed. The death was rampant, but he could not turn his eyes away. The magic was magnificent.

As more Bukavac filled the courtyard, Falmagon joined the five men, using his own crooked staff in a similar fashion. With his one eye, Falmagon peered decisively at the demons, striking his own staff into the dirt. Walls of earth erupted across the courtyard forcing the Bukavac to funnel to the tower and away from the keep where Branimir was hiding.

He could only think Falmagon tried to protect Kinhar.

Lightning zig-zagged again, but this time it struck at the ground. The bolt tore through one man near Jhar.

Branimir gasped.

The man's cry echoed above the sounds of battle as the tormenting fire ripped through his chest and out of his back. Blood sprayed from the gaping hole.

"Andrik…" Mojmir wept in recognition.

Dorofej's gritty voice was heard above the battle, echoing Mojmir's murmurs. "Andrik!" The old man sprang to the fallen Highborn burning from the lightning bolt. In a heap of his heavy enigmatic robes, he kneeled in the pool of blood.

Branimir became fixated on the scene, watching in absolute horror.

"Leave him!" It may have been Falmagon who instructed Dorofej. Branimir could not be certain.

Dorofej ignored the words. His frail hands sank deep into Andrik's flesh, blood surged over his shaking hands.

Branimir tuned into Dorofej's whispered words despite the raging battle. They sounded ancient, flowing like a song. A glow of red and yellow glowed beneath Andrik's skin as Dorofej manipulated Koldovstvo. As the spell increased in complexity, a clear difference presented itself in Dorofej. The Highborn began to show signs of increased aging. Additional wrinkles formed under his eyes, and his hair lightened and lengthened. His skin sunk against his bones, and his voice rasped and croaked. Bran would not have been surprised if his very bone was turning to ash beneath the flesh.

"Dorofej!" Jhar pulled the old man away from Andrik's body. "You'll kill yourself!"

"No." Dorofej fought against Jhar's grip but was too weak to struggle. His eyes scanned the body of Andrik. The flesh had mended considerably, but a gaping hole remained from chest to back. The damage to the body was too great.

"The man is dea—" Jhar began, before an arrow the size of his staff tore through his skull. The younger man's body collapsed on top of Dorofej, crushing the old Highborn to the ground.

"No!" Dorofej screamed.

"No!" Branimir echoed.

Mojmir grabbed him and pulled him away from the window. "Koldovstvo has its cost. Life for power."

"I know," Branimir teared up. "But, Lord Dorofej…"

"He was willing to pay the price."

Branimir pushed Mojmir off him and jumped back to the window. Dorofej was motionless under the body of Jhar. He could not believe it.

It was now that Falmagon that took charge of the Highborn and directed the battle. The Bukavac began to bust through the walls of earth with their fists instead of following the path Falmagon had formed. Branimir saw Katerina and Faina near the one-eyed Highborn. It was evident Katerina had nearly exhausted herself; her features had drastically changed from a young woman to one closer to Faina's age.

"They are all going to die." Branimir quivered.

Mojmir asked the question needing answered, "But, if she has returned, where is Nedezhda?"

"Get back." Branimir grabbed Mojmir and pulled him down from the window. A Bukavac drew near the opening in the keep.

His question was forgotten.

Branimir peaked carefully at the glimmering beast. It was seemingly made of stone, iced over, standing just short of the ledge. The sharpened sword he carried would easily split Branimir in two, maybe three. Mojmir quickly disappeared entirely, his body fading so none could see him, save Branimir.

Branimir copied Mojmir's actions, physically vanishing from sight, as was the way of the Kras.

He was surprised by the overwhelming stench of burnt flesh reeking from the demon. The Bukavac seemed to be layer on layer of frozen skin. He turned to Mojmir ever so slightly, pleased to see his friend also was discontent with the smell.

Mojmir heaved a sigh as the Bukavac marched past. Mojmir waited several seconds after the demon was out of sight before reappearing.

"That was close," Mojmir said.

Branimir nodded and became visible once more.

Mojmir sighed looking across the courtyard, "Not many Highborn left."

Kinhar, whom Branimir had nearly forgotten about, barked at them, "If you two do not keep your mouths shut, I am going to cut your tongues out."

Branimir and Mojmir exchanged a simple look. The threat did not have to be repeated. Lord Kinhar continued to move around the room from table to table, muttering under his breath.

The battle continued in the courtyard of Melkorka, ever increasing in vigor and ferocity. As the Bukavac advanced through the corridors of Melkorka, across the courtyard, and within the towers, the body count seemed incalculable. Screams and shrieks were carried throughout the air. The cream-colored blood of the Bukavac mixed with the crimson blood of the Highborn. Death painted the grass and stone of Melkorka.

The footsteps outside of Kinhar's chambers were heard by Branimir several seconds before Kinhar lifted his head toward the wooden door. Branimir vanished again, hiding himself before the door opened. Mojmir followed suit.

Kinhar, on the other hand, balanced himself with his ash branch and hobbled back to the fire pit. He waited for the door to open.

Nedezhda came through the door delicately. Her grace was unexpected, considering all that had taken place in the courtyard thus far. But the door slowly opened, barely creaking. The undead woman stepped through as though she had been personally invited and closed the door behind her.

In a moment of silence, as the living stared into the icy gaze of the dead, Branimir considered Nedezhda, a shadow of her old self. Her eyes were still bright blue, and her nose was still diminutive above her wide mouth. Yet her hair had become disheveled and discolored with the consistency of algae on a pond's surface. Though, the black stitches circling her neck are what held Branimir's gaze. Her head must have been reattached to her body in the Netherworld.

"Death comes to all of us, Kinhar," She stepped a foot closer, smiling at the old man.

Her dark robe hung loosely over her pale flesh. The blood blotching her visible skin was clearly not her own.

"Killing me will be no easy task, Nedezhda," Kinhar raised himself up as best he could, his long white hair still fastened in knots behind his head. His lie was not convincing. "I was long prepared for your return, well before your beheading this evening."

"This evening?" Nedezhda paused, flicking her tongue against her lip. "I have been dead for years upon years, waiting in the Netherworld to return to Aenar. The valleys of the dead are overflowing with legions."

Kinhar harrumphed. "Even in death, you are a fool. The Kadari will strike you down still!"

Nedezhda looked amused. "At last, you speak of your little secrets? Though, it is too late! The Kadari and all of Aenar will be dust when I am through, Kinhar." She clenched her webbed fingers into fists at her side. Nedezhda's smile faded from her pasty face. She did not wane. Never had a woman been so full of hate.

Kinhar stood with his head high, showing no sign of defending himself. "You will not succeed, Nedezhda. Why do you come back from the Netherworld? Does Marheena banish you from her sight? Return to your Seamstress of Nightmares, accept your fate, and leave the living alone. Not even the Ash Tree can save you."

Nedezhda scoffed. "Banished? My army of Bukavac grows with Marheena's blessing. I prepare the way for the Likhyi. I have defiled the roots of your petty tree, and I will cut down its girth in the Waters of Life. Humankind will suffer at my hand as I did at yours. I will steal away their breath."

"I will not allow it."

"You cannot stop the will of the gods, Kinhar."

"You are no god. You are an Eretik!"

"I am the hand of Marheena," Nedezhda said in a deadly whisper. "I am closer to the gods than you have ever been. I have done what no other has had the strength to do. You killed me because you feared my knowledge and my power." Nedezhda assailed upon Kinhar. "Now, in death, I am a Lord and you will be my slave."

She waved her right hand at Kinhar. Lightning blasted through the window, striking the ground in front of the old man. As he stepped back, Nedezhda waved her hand, using Koldovstvo to throw the frail body of Kinhar backwards near his makeshift throne. Kinhar took his time returning to his feet.

He sighed brushing himself off. "A simple spell for such a powerful Eretik," Kinhar said with amusement. He waved his own hands forward with a whisper and fire flung from the two oil lamps, raining toward Nedezhda. Yet, before a drop of fire touched her fair skin, a blue orb surrounded her and deflected the fire.

"You waste my time. Will you kill me again? I am already dead!" Nedezhda mumbled inconceivable words. A Bukavac's mighty fist slammed into the base of the window to the courtyard. The stones from Crags of Kazimir that formed the walls of Melkorka shattered.

Branimir and Mojmir flickered into sight for a brief instant before regaining their control and hiding again. The two Kras fled from the window and the Bukavac, hiding behind the powerful Highborn and his stone seat.

Kinhar smirked as he clamped his hands together firmly. The Bukavac fell back from the window, its body smashing lifelessly against the ground. "You die as a demon, Nedezhda, and your soul is erased from existence."

"Only in the Netherworld! Kill me in this world all you want; I will simply return to the Netherworld. I can come fight you for eternity."

"And, for eternity, I will murder you," his aged voice cracked.

"Unlikely, old man."

A black blade erupted from the palm of Nedezhda. With a simple word, the blade swung toward Kinhar as though wielded by an invisible swordsman. Kinhar's eyes widened only briefly before he took the defensive. Kinhar barely dodged and ducked from the sword's attacks, watching Nedezhda from the corner of his eye. Nedezhda continued to manipulate the energy of the living world and in moments ice was plummeting from the ceiling.

Kinhar grabbed his staff in a firm grip and stumbled toward the fire pit, crying out in a language never heard by any man, dead or alive. He twisted and turned, all the while staying clear of the deadly blade from the Netherworld. A ball of ice smashed against his left shoulder. He fell to a knee but pressed forward to the flames. Several scrolls from the tables were flung into the fire, turning the flames from plum and cerulean to scarlet and olive. With a final effort Kinhar fell into the colored blaze.

A light brighter than high sun at midday, a hundred times over, flashed within the room. Thunder, greater than a thousand warhorses stampeding, resounded against the walls within Kinhar's chambers. Koldovstvo was ancient, as old as the gods themselves, known by many and mastered by few. Kinhar was a master.

The ice continued to fall. The black blade continued to strike. Yet, where an old decaying man once stood, there now stood a youthful man. The ash branch that was used as his staff was gone, but Kinhar stood, nearly limitless in his power. His long white hair was gone, replaced with thick black strands. His lip and chin were clean shaven as though hair had never touched his face. Where delicate muscles once barely framed his skin, muscle on muscle now bulged from the coarse cloth. He looked to be a hundred years younger.

Without the limitations presented by old age, Kinhar effortlessly tumbled away from the falling balls of ice and spoke a word, raising three blades of his own around his body. The silver swords that he conjured defended against the black blade, giving him an opportunity to focus on his own casting, a lifetime of Koldovstvo was suddenly available to him.

Arrows of flame manifested from behind Kinhar and flew at Nedezhda swiftly. Nedezhda conjured small shields of stone and blocked the arrows. Kinhar called on the winds from the north and the waters from the sea, pulling their power into the small room, creating a storm any seafaring man would fear. Nedezhda transformed the wind into a breeze and the water to fog. Nothing could touch the dead sorceress.

She laughed, "You will kill yourself. The aging effects of magic only affect the living."

"So be it!" Kinhar said, already ten years older in a matter of minutes.

"So be it," Nedezhda repeated menacingly.

Nedezhda and Kinhar unleashed energy at one another while their swords danced about them. More lightning and fire fell along with ice and stone.

Branimir screamed among the madness.

The room was destroyed. Scrolls burned, embers floated, and the tables were overturned or in ashes. The two, one living and one dead, attacked and defended. Their war was personal. It was eternal.

In the end, Branimir found himself huddled in the corner of the room, not knowing what to do but clutch Mojmir in terror when he heard footsteps racing outside Kinhar's chamber.

Faina burst through the door with far less subtlety than Nedezhda. She had more wrinkles on her face from using Koldovstvo. The redheaded woman immediately joined the fight, raising her finger at Nedezhda, repeatedly speaking words as song.

Nedezhda, taken by surprise, flung the black sword at Faina away from the silver swords.

Faina cried out in surprise as the blade plunged deep into her right shoulder, stopping Koldovstvo from flowing off her tongue. The blade dissolved into ashes. Blood spilled.

"No!" Katerina lunged into the chamber immediately after Faina.

She tried to grab Faina to pull her to safety, but Nedezhda was ready this time. She grasped a handful of Katerina's dark hair with a greasy, webbed hand. Poor Katerina, who had been a young lady only hours before, cried out. Her round, brown eyes widened with terror.

With a fitful cry, Nedezhda flung Katerina through the gaping hole in the chamber wall toward the Bukavac who continued to crowd the courtyard. The dark-haired woman was caught midair between two Bukavac and torn in half at the waist. No scream left her innocent lips. She was forever silenced.

Kinhar hurled his three swords through the air at Nedezhda, but not quickly enough. The woman dodged them effortlessly as they hit the stone wall behind her and fell to the ground.

"You kill your own brethren, Nedezhda!" Kinhar screamed.

"You killed me, Kinhar," she said.

"You disobeyed the law!" Kinhar roared, clenching his fists.

Nedezhda's face went from calm to fury. "Your law!"

The copper dagger called Kaelandur suddenly plunged through the stitches of Nedezhda's neck, taking her life for the second time. Her head toppled to the floor, quickly obscured by her collapsing body. Pasty white blood poured across the old timber flooring.

Falmagon stood erect, holding Kaelandur firmly in his right fist, the crooked staff held by his left. He used the dagger to motion at Kinhar before replacing it at his belt. The Highborn said nothing regarding Kinhar's change in appearance. "We must flee or we will join the dead."

"We cannot flee," Faina muttered, trying to pull herself up from the ground only to fall back to her knees. "This is Melkorka and Nedezhda will return shortly from the Netherworld. We must defend Melkorka! The prophecy…"

"No. Falmagon is right," Kinhar said. "The Kadari must find a way to kill Nedezhda permanently. Until then, we must find and protect the Ash Tree. If she destroys it then the entire world will die! This is our duty now."

Branimir shuddered. He did not know what the Kadari was, but he had heard of the Ash Tree. Legends said that it gave life to the world of the living and the non-living, sitting within the Waters of Life, stretching across all worlds.

The one-eyed Highborn sniffed. "Then you must lead us there, Kinhar."

"First, we go to Arkaim to see Erzebeth for guidance."

"Come! Dorofej has horses." Falmagon grabbed a hold of Faina's robes and pulled her to her feet. She used him as support, trying to ignore the blood flowing down her front.

"I'm weak…" Faina collapsed onto Falmagon's shoulder. He caught her, sweeping her up into his arms.

"Dorofej is dead," Mojmir cried. The Kras came into view, materialized from his hiding place. Branimir joined him without a word.

"Dorofej took the tunnels north," Falmagon claimed assuredly. "He waits for our escape."

"I watched him die," Mojmir screeched in his squeaky voice. "We both did!"

"Bah!" Kinhar stormed up to Mojmir's side, grabbing him by his child-sized head. In a quick motion, he snapped the neck of the small creature.

The Kras fell to the ground dead.

Branimir froze in fear, staring at the lifeless body of his kin. He did not hear Kinhar speak to him the second time, or even third. The world spun, nearly knocking him to one knee.

"Answer me or your fate will be the same as his," Kinhar growled, obviously irritated by asking more than once. "Are you a fool, too?"

"No..." Branimir stammered, "no, my Lord." He could not bring himself to look at the face of the young Highborn, who had appeared to be only a few breaths away from death an hour ago.

"Good. Then you will continue to serve me. Say anything to Dorofej of the Kadari and it will be your death."

"Yes, Lord Kinhar," Branimir wept.

Kinhar turned his attention to his companions, "To the tunnels, Falmagon. Consider Melkorka fallen."

Branimir followed the Highborn obediently.

Chapter IV

Branimir was awakened by the red glare of the horizon against his eyelids. His body slumped against Kinhar's back as they trotted along the coastline on a brown horse. He rubbed his eyes wearily.

His first thoughts were of Mojmir. His second were of himself. Mourning the dead would not help him this day or the next; his father had told him that. Besides, Branimir was certain Mojmir's fate would prove to be one of luck compared to what he was about to endure. He was not sure how he could be so exhausted when he had not actually done any of the fighting.

Faina and Falmagon were riding to the left on their own horses. Faina was unconscious and slouched over with more blood on her robes than fabric. Falmagon led both mounts with a single hand, while keeping Faina on her horse with his other. His one eye was fixated on the sands ahead of them.

Dorofej marked the rear, still shrouded in his dark robes. The man was brittle, barely maintaining the strength to sit on his own brown horse. It was only hoped that some strength might return to the old man. The reins were wrapped repeatedly around his wrists and the horn of the saddle, assuring that he stayed atop the animal.

Branimir did not think any of the three men had slept during the night.

"When we reach Narthwich," Kinhar began, "we need to obtain a boatman to take us to Kalamaar."

"We need an herbal healer for Faina," Falmagon said. "She is fortunate to have stayed alive this long. Who knows the sorcery of the death blade that pierced her flesh? Dorofej cannot heal her with Koldovstvo. The old man is far too weak and we do not have the right bloodline."

"Even if with the strength, it is likely nothing can heal her beyond the Waters of Life, yes? And, we know not where to find such a thing, whether myth or truth is quite uncertain, it is."

Kinhar spoke over his shoulder, "It must be truth, Dorofej. Nedezhda seeks it with the purpose of destroying the Ash Tree. She said as much last night. We are charged with protecting this world and that means we must keep the Ash Tree safe! Erzebeth is in Arkaim. She will provide us the guidance needed to stop the Eretik."

"Kinhar, you do not know the way?" Dorofej wheezed. His voice was guttural, giving suggestion he barely had any life left within him.

The spearhead of the Highborn gave pause. "How could I know the way? No living man knows the way."

"Yet," Dorofej's bushy eyebrows lifted, "you have a youth about you that only the Ash Tree could provide. Only yesterday you had more wrinkles on your face than I do between my thighs, yes?"

"Watch your mouth, Dorofej," Kinhar glared threateningly under the dark locks that bespoke of the youth Dorofej perceived.

Dorofej pressed with a tilted chin. "Erzebeth is who precisely? In all my years, I have never heard her name mentioned in the halls of Melkorka."

"She is a friend. That is all you need to know."

"I see," Dorofej slumped back into his saddle in apparent defeat.

Kinhar did not seem to notice and returned to his original point. "Regardless, Faina will not make it to the Waters of Life by any means. That type of luck is unheard of in history, myth, or legend."

Falmagon pulled the woman firmly onto her saddle as she began to slip. "Tell me, what can we do, Kinhar? I cannot carry her for eternity on her saddle."

"She should stay at Narthwich and let Dahz decide her fate."

Branimir noticed Dorofej lift his hand to object before second guessing himself. The old man's eyes locked onto Branimir. The dissatisfied look on his face was unmistakable, even beneath the braided white beard shielding his thin lips.

"May Dahz look kindly upon her in this life and the next," Falmagon said.

They rode the rest of the distance in the company of the waves that crashed against the shoreline. The dark blue waters lashed against each other in an endless war.

Branimir knew a little about Narthwich. It was a worn city of few buildings against the coast that stood adjacent to the mainland of Kalamaar. The village was small, fitted for the poor fishermen residing there. Branimir could see the entire village from the hilltop, including the docks stretching into Strega's Deep. Long boats with oars and simple sails called faerings, built from the inland trees, lined either side of the wooden platforms extending over the water.

Kinhar led them down the hill at a gallop, unnecessarily demonstrating the calamity that had befallen them. There was more urgency in his actions in this moment than Branimir had witnessed in the past day, even when slinging magic against Nedezhda. The Kras held tightly onto Kinhar's robes as he raced down the hillside on the horse. Once within earshot, Kinhar raised his voice, shouting at the villagers to fetch Jarl Avar. Seeing the Highborn riding down the hillside set the people of Narthwich into action, not questioning the motives of the so-called guardians of the Seven Islands. The Highborn, although often secluded from civilization, were not strangers to the races of regular men.

Branimir had the fleeting thought that the people may think less of the Highborn if they knew the atrocities that had been committed.

It was hard to be called guardian when responsible for unleashing the dead and worse upon the world.

"Jarl!" Kinhar halted the horses in front of the great hall that marked center to Narthwich. He used the common title for the chief of small settlements. The position was respectable, generally appointed by the King.

Immediately a man bounded from the door, holding hilt in hand to the copper sword at his belt. The Kras shifted his attention quickly away from the weapon that reminded him of Kaelandur, the cause of all their problems.

The Jarl's hair was curled and wild, along with the scruffy beard that prickled his chin. The villagers that had run ahead had done well in conveying the alarm. The man looked like he had just been pulled out of bed.

"Highborn, I am Jarl Likshol Avar of Narthwich. We witnessed fires in the sky late last eve from Melkorka, knowing not what in the Nine Lands had befallen its stone walls. What has happened?"

"Bukavac have bled from the Crags and have taken Melkorka. We are all that remain."

Whispers erupted around them from the villagers who gathered around Kinhar on his horse and Jarl Avar. The seed of fear had been planted with such few words.

"Who are you exactly? Is that one of the demons on the back of your mount?" the Jarl asked cautiously, pointing at Branimir.

Branimir gasped in astonishment, keeping his hands from covering his face. Humans and Kras had shared the Seven Islands for centuries before being enslaved by the Highborn. He knew some may mistake him as a demon, but he expected those on the same island to know his kind.

"I am Kinhar Sayan of Melkorka, and—"

"Kinhar Sayan?" the Jarl pulled at his sword, "Although I know not the man, I am quite familiar with the name. Kinhar was known by my father thirty years ago, marking him a man much more aged than you."

Kinhar started again, "I—"

Dorofej interrupted, "You are as wise as your father, my Lord. I am Kinhar Sayan of Melkorka. This Highborn speaks in my stead to protect me from those who may wish an old man harm. Lies are not becoming of the Highborn, but such precautions must be taken after the loss we have experienced. You understand, yes?"

Jarl Avar released his hilt with a respectful nod. "What of the demon on the horse?"

Dorofej shook his head. "No, my Lord. That is a Kras, a loyal servant of the Highborn. You may never find a more loyal creature."

Again, whispers resounded in the crowd.

"My apologies," the Jarl faltered, sliding his hands to his waist. "I did not know the Kras were still in existence."

Dorofej nodded, taking a moment to look at Branimir, "He may very well be the last of their number."

Branimir choked at the statement. He turned from the Jarl and Dorofej, burying his face in the musty robes of Kinhar. The truth had not struck him until this moment and it made his heart hurt. He was the last of his kind.

"May your future deeds bespeak of your race as honorable and glorious, Kras," Jarl Avar stumbled for the right words.

Branimir steadied his voice as best as he was able. "My thanks, my Lord."

The Jarl dipped his head, as was custom, and turned back to Dorofej. "Demons from the mountains, you say? What numbers? Do they come this way?"

"Their numbers are unknown, Jarl. As for now, your people are safe in Narthwich. There has been no sign of pursuit through the night, but the beasts must not be allowed to cross to Kalamaar."

"What do you need from us, Kinhar?"

Dorofej licked his lips, taking a moment to reflect on the leveled gaze Kinhar gave him. There was no mystery in its meaning. "Lady Faina Zholdan will be left in your care without charge. I say, she will likely pass in the night, and we would ask for a proper burial."

The Jarl signaled for two of the villagers to take Faina from the horse as Dorofej spoke. The redheaded woman was slumped into the arms of a mid-sized man who quickly carried her into the great hall. Branimir could not help but notice the villagers shrinking back from him as though he were a demon, too. Bran swore he could hear whispers in the gathering crowd about his skin and his ears.

Branimir tried to focus on the negotiation between Dorofej and the Jarl.

"A faering is requested to cross the pass to the mainland. Our horses can be payment, if that suits you well enough, yes?"

"For what purpose?"

Dorofej was quick of tongue. "Support from Arkaim and to inform the King, of course. The people of the Seven Islands must be protected from the shade of the Netherworld."

"Of course!" the Jarl exclaimed. "We will fetch rations for the journey. Delcho and Lel can take you across Strega's Deep."

Kinhar broke in, "That will be unnecessary."

"Nonsense! It is completely necessary. It will take half a day or more, depending on the Nine Winds. Let us pray that Strega's breath is strong in such desperate times.

"Indeed," Dorofej agreed.

"It is likely you will travel on land to Arkaim or find route on ship at Valishul upland. I can spare shana to help with any cost that you may endure. As I recall, the Highborn rarely have coin in their pockets."

Branimir's jaw nearly hit the horses back. Silver pieces, or shana, were scarce on the Seven Islands.

"Your generosity is well received, Jarl Avar. You truly are your father's son," Dorofej said sincerely. "Your benevolence is to be echoed to King Merreider Kar in Arkaim, it will."

Branimir watched incredulously as Dorofej spoke like a true Highborn. The knowledge under the wrinkled skin of the old man was astonishing. The mere happenstance that Dorofej would know the name of the King of Arkaim, when, to knowledge, he had not stepped foot from Melkorka in half a century was beyond Branimir.

The Jarl said, "You just be assured that you come back. Please do not leave my people at the hands of demons and worse."

"I say, our intent is to return, Jarl," Dorofej visibly shuddered. "But send a message along the Seven Islands to the other villages, you will. Jaoarr. Geirland. Refsstaoir. As far as Mjovadalsa if you can spare it, yes?"

The Jarl raised his hand to stop Dorofej, "You frighten my people, Kinhar. What are you expecting?"

Kinhar attempted to silence Dorofej. "He is fatigued. Prepare the faering and supplies so we can be on our way."

Dorofej's blue eyes locked onto the Jarl's with certainty beyond certainty. Branimir found himself squirming in the saddle, shivering well before the words escaped the old man's lips. "I expect death. Eternal war and death."

Chapter V

The faering rocked against the deep waters somewhere between Folkmar, home to Melkorka, and Kalamaar. Three of the Seven Islands of Forghar could be viewed from the aft. With Folkmar an hour behind them, appearing as a ghastly haze of smoke on the skyline, they rushed toward Kalamaar with the wind at their backs.

Branimir sat at the stern atop one of the four slats that provided seating across the deck. Kinhar, Falmagon, and Dorofej were scattered across the boat, partially asleep.

Branimir held his stomach with one hand, wishing he could join the Highborn and find some much-needed sleep. Instead, he leaned over the boat with his other hand caressing the white oak planks that overlapped on the clinker-built faering. He had never been on a vessel before, or even on the sea, despite living next to it his entire life. He was rapidly discovering that seafaring was not in his blood.

Along with exhaustion, Branimir's perception of the world around him was thwarted. The smell of saltwater and the sounds of slopping waves against the hull were overwhelming to his sensitive nose and ears. Not to mention, it was a constant reminder that if the faering upturned, Branimir would drown.

"Have another swig, Kras," the tall man from Narthwich called Lel slurred, stretching a clay jug toward him. It was as large as Branimir's head.

"Being drunk on mead will not settle my stomach or keep me afloat, Lord." Branimir decided to keep it to himself that the first drink and the second had done nothing more but burn his insides and make his eyes water.

"It just might! Get enough in your belly and you'll be rounder than a blowfish."

Branimir waved him off, feeling spew welling up in his throat.

"Kras, it is just honey and water. It will calm your nerves. Before you know it, the ocean will be riding you."

Branimir squinted at the seafaring man, swallowing vomit, looking for some hint of humor in the man's bloodshot eyes. "Excuse me, my Lord. What does that even mean?"

"Forget him, Kras," Delcho said, taking the jug from Lel and swallowing a mouthful of the dark liquid before continuing. "Mead turned Lel's mind to mush long before you were born."

Branimir looked at the two men, who may have been in their mid-years, if not younger. He was dumbfounded, "I am fifty-six-years-old, Lord." The humans obviously knew very little about the Kras. It was likely that he was the last one of his kind, just as Dorofej had suggested.

"Ha!" Lel croaked. "Fifty-six-years-old, you say, Kras? My oldest daughter hasn't had her first bleeding and she is bigger than you!"

"Yes, Lord. All the same, it is the truth."

"Sure, it is."

"It is true!" Branimir squealed, hearing the ridicule in Lel's tone.

"Don't hold to a poor joke, Kras," Delcho belched. "The two of us hear the worst from seamen. Yury. Tyoma. Genrickh. We know lying when we hear it."

"That we do! Don't go joshing about—"

"Lord, I am not—"

Delcho hollered over the top of them both. "Spending all day working your shaft does not make you a jester, that's for sure! Every seafaring man knows that much."

"Nope. It sure does not."

"Craft, I mean," Delcho roared in laughter at himself.

"What?" Lel's eyes went crooked.

Delcho slapped his bare knee beneath his cutoff trousers. "I said working your shaft instead of craft."

Lel shrugged with a sudden gleam. "No matter. You don't become a jester either way."

Delcho laughed harder with Lel echoing his mirth.

Branimir was baffled, not sure how to respond. The two were intoxicated. Before he could say anything, he felt sick again and leaned over the side of the faering to empty what mead was left in his stomach.

Lel took the mead jug back from Delcho, "Genrickh was the worst. Remember that tale he told at Ida's about the rusalki supposedly slinking aboard his boat. Said the fish woman sang and danced and kissed him; and all sorts of rubbish. Even had the gall to say *on the mouth*! What woman, half fish or otherwise, would kiss a man as ugly as Genrickh Bershov on the mouth?"

Delcho jerked the jug back before Lel could get a drink. "Jealous, were you?"

Branimir found himself grinning at the jest as Delcho polished off the jug with a large gulp and swallow. With all that had happened, the Kras found himself feeling guilty for finding enjoyment in the company of the men, and attempted to appear more solemn.

Lel watched with longing as the mead was emptied, "Hey—"

"What are you two fools blathering about?" Kinhar pulled himself upright with the gunwale at the bow of the faering.

"Highborn," Delcho garbled, "we were just making conversation to pass the time. Did not mean to wake you."

Kinhar glowered under the thick black strands of hair that fell past his ears. His deep blue eyes seemed to be as shadowy as the waters they sailed upon. The course grey cloth of his robe clung to the muscle that bulged from his chest and arms. "You obviously do not have the sense to grasp the significance of what we are trying to accomplish here."

Delcho and Lel had blank looks about them.

Branimir watched in astonishment as Kinhar struck Falmagon upside the head to wake him. The one-eyed man grunted, sitting up quickly with his scraggly brown hair in knots.

"We cannot be to Kalamaar yet."

"No," Kinhar said. "These two half-wits have drunk themselves stupid, needlessly endangering the success of our journey."

"That is not true," Delcho muttered, suddenly very sober. "We have never sailed without mead, and we have always found our destination."

Lel grinned like a fool, speaking in turn with absolute honesty. "Yeah…eventually."

Kinhar's expression of disapproval deepened.

Branimir waited as Kinhar and Falmagon glared across the small vessel at Lel and Delcho. What felt like an eternity passed before Kinhar twisted his head to examine Dorofej. The old man did not budge in his black robes, and as if on cue, snorted in his sleep, giving sign that he was lost in a world of dreams.

"Falmagon," Kinhar spoke softly. "The faering will reach Kalamaar all the quicker if we lighten the load."

Falmagon did not say a word. Before Branimir could react, the one-eyed Highborn grabbed the two sailors with Koldovstvo and flung them into Strega's Deep, beyond the reaches of the boat, beyond the sound of their bloodcurdling screams.

Branimir squealed, jumping to his feet, witnessing the undeserved murder from the Highborn men. He had heard of mankind slaughtering their own race, but it was not the Highborn way. Mojmir was easily overlooked as a Kras, but these were of the same kin as the Highborn.

Dorofej shifted in his sleep.

"Stay seated, Branimir," Kinhar threatened between clenched teeth.

The Kras kneeled slowly back to the plank, swiftly recognizing how much was outside of his control. He had served the Highborn all his life. After that much time, Branimir's free will was practically buried in the grave. He had to remember his place in this tale, no matter how it unfolded. He was the Highborn's lackey.

"Yes, Lord," Branimir whispered.

Even in this moment, Branimir thought of Mojmir and the quick death he had received. He hoped that his foolish kin had found peace in the Beyond.

For the next two hours, Dorofej slept and Falmagon used Koldovstvo to blow the square sail in the center of the planks. The faering sped across the waves at impressive speed, with the oars staying tucked inside the hull without purpose.

Droplets of tears had come and gone from the pale eyes of Branimir. The two Highborn men ignored him in the corner of the boat as he wept with little control. Branimir desperately wanted to sleep, but was ever fearful that he may, too, be flung into the dangerous waters of the ocean. Try as he might, Branimir could find no reason as to why Kinhar would keep him living much longer.

Dorofej coughed and sat up from his resting place against the side. The man took his time scanning the boat, stroking the braided tassels of hair that formed his beard and the long stretches of his white mustache.

His eyes held all the innocence in the world as he acknowledged Falmagon and Kinhar with a dip of his head. Branimir caught a glimpse of a sliver of a smile beneath the overgrowth on his face. After several minutes, Branimir wondered if Dorofej was going to say anything at all.

When the old man finally loosened his tongue, his words were ungainly. "Dreamt of a woman with massive breasts. Barely could convince myself to wake, so enticing they were."

Falmagon hit the butt of his crooked staff against the white oak, peering eerily at Dorofej. "Keep those dirty thoughts to yourself, old man. What is wrong with you?"

"Like large buoys floating among the waves of this ocean. Must be my mind playing tricks on me, being on this boat, yes? Yet, unequivocally massive, they were! Enough of a teat to feed a throng of children, yes? I reached out to touch the nipple, to cop a feel, if you will, to receive the treasure of treasures, before waking back to this unsightly world." Dorofej shook his head miserably and let out an elongated sigh. "As fate would have it, swallowed them whole before I could fondle such splendor, the ocean did."

"He is mad, Kinhar," Falmagon said.

"Speak plainly, Dorofej," Kinhar demanded crossly.

"A good pair of breasts are hard to come by is all—and when they are found—well, plundering them triumphantly is impossible, yes?"

"I have no idea how to respond," Falmagon muttered.

"Moreover," Dorofej scrunched his nose, his lip curling slightly, "our vessel has grown lighter whilst I was inhibited, yes? Then again, I am old, and my mind has begun to wilt. By chance, two men from Narthwich were never aboard this faering, yes? By chance, I am not on a faering at all, yes? By chance, I am truthfully lying in my stone bed at Melkorka covered in sheep fur, dreading to hear Jhar's twitching tongue at daybreak, yes?" Dorofej cleared his throat. "Dream and reality are equally misleading, it seems."

"Enough, Dorofej! When Falmagon and I awoke, the men were no longer aboard," Kinhar lied dryly, finding no humor with Dorofej. "We know not what their fate was."

"Is that so?"

"It is so," Falmagon supported Kinhar's untruth. His face looked to be chiseled from the Crags themselves.

The boat rocked as Dorofej hobbled over to a bench and slumped down next to the Kras. He unexpectedly grabbed Branimir by the shoulder. "Branimir Baran has been weeping, yes?"

Branimir quickly wiped his eyes, finding that his eyes were watering once more. He could not look at the old man. He feared to look at Kinhar or Falmagon. With all his heart, Branimir kept his gaze on the ocean that surrounded them.

Dorofej's blue eyes were penetrating and unrelenting on the back of his head.

"I have not, Lord," Branimir lied, too. "Just tired, I think." He did not need the wrath of any of the Highborn upon him, including Dorofej.

Dorofej snickered.

"He has every reason to weep after what happened at Melkorka," Falmagon challenged, hitting his staff against the baseboard again. "We all do."

Dorofej settled back against the stern. "Quite right you are, Falmagon Sej. Where has my mind gone…to question irregularity, especially in a dreadful world of relentless regularity, yes? The men from Narthwich surely fell overboard by accident, or felt elated to take a midday swim, or grew bird parts and flew straight to the Lightbringer, yes!"

Branimir held his head in his hands, tormented by the situation. He tried to focus his energy on keeping his lips sealed.

"We may never know," Kinhar sarcasm was teeming like poison from a viper.

"No, I suppose not," Dorofej finished with a hint of peril in his own words. "Then again, it may have been a pair of bounteous breasts that beguiled them to take a plunge, yes? Luck had it that we were *each* asleep, lest accompany them, we *each* would have."

No one said another word the rest of the way to Kalamaar.

Chapter VI

Evening had set in over Kalamaar after they had landed along an abandoned shore. Kinhar had led them northwest along the coastline in hopes of reaching Valishul. After two hours of steady walking, they still had not seen any sign of life.

Dorofej declared the massive mountains lining the length of the shoreline were also called the Crags of Kazimir, needing no other name, and fell inland for miles. History suggested that the Seven Islands had adopted the name from the mainland centuries ago. It was a suitable explanation, as the Crags maintained the same red rock and grew to greater heights on Kalamaar.

With the frequent ups and downs in the terrain, they attempted to steer clear of entering the mountain range. Unfortunately, thick grasses full of thorns and burrs grew between the Crags and the water's edge, keeping movement restricted. As night set in, their advancement was slowed even more. None of them could see past their feet, save Branimir.

He could see perfectly as though it were daylight, but he had never stepped foot on Kalamaar. This left him with little ability to lead the Highborn anywhere sensible or safe.

"Should have stayed in the boat and sailed it along the coast instead of walking," Falmagon reasoned after the first couple of miles.

"Too many rocks along the coast," Kinhar said.

"Unfortunate the men who had nautical knowledge vanished, lest they could have maneuvered about them, yes?" Dorofej scoffed as he took another step forward on his weakened knees, trying to wedge his way through the grasses.

Falmagon turned to face Dorofej at his rear, "Drop it, Dorofej. It is only two men."

"Two men, it is," Dorofej's bushy eyebrows angled in the dark, only visible by Branimir. "Two men who you disregard as though they were untimely flatus expelled through your pinned anus."

"We lost more at Melkorka, you fool," Falmagon said with a sneer. "The Bukavac are coming. Why would you cause ruckus over simple men? Our concern is greater—"

"Because I am Highborn, Falmagon!" Dorofej's chin quivered slightly, from pain or rage was uncertain. He took a deep breath and flattened his voice. "It is our duty to protect. Our vows, Koldovstvo, and all that we have, rests on our decency, yes? If the Highborn lose their way, what way can there be? I say, for over a thousand years, goodness prevailed over the enemy."

Falmagon's crooked staff inched forward as he leaned toward the bearded Dorofej. His words lingered with his foul breath. "Olden ways for olden times, old man."

Dorofej considered Kinhar at the front. Even in the dark, it was evident that the spearhead of the Highborn had nothing to add to Falmagon's sacrilege.

"Your orations fall on deaf ears, Dorofej," Falmagon spat, saliva catching the end of his long hanging mustache. "In Narthwich, you incited fear and now deliver lectures on righteousness. Mend your own compass before piddling with mine!"

"He was trying to protect them." Branimir matched Falmagon's patronizing tone in a shrill voice.

As soon as the words were said, Branimir regretted it. His chest tightened with the sudden thumping of his heartbeat.

Falmagon abandoned the argument with Dorofej and heatedly approached Branimir with his staff raised at waist level. Branimir dropped to his knees immediately, raised his hands defensively, and dipped his head so that it barely reached Falmagon's thigh. Branimir whispered apologies and mutterings of forgiveness, ending each befuddled breath with Lord.

"The world truly is truly falling to ashes when a Kras speaks against a Highborn," Falmagon said with vehemence. The man brought the staff down across Branimir's dipped skull without hesitation.

Branimir cried out, falling forward on his face against the sharp thorns in the grass. He could already feel blood gushing from the top of his head and down over his pointed ear. He rolled over, writhing in pain. A second strike hit him across the mid-section. The thwack that reverberated was mirrored with the sound of cracking ribs.

"My...Lord..." Branimir wheezed.

Falmagon raised the staff again.

"That will be enough," Kinhar stepped over Branimir's body protectively. "I will not have the Kras harmed beyond reprieve."

Salty tears blurred Branimir's vision, as he peeked at the Highborn for a sign as to why he should be kept alive when so many others would be killed. He was most surprised when his mouth formed the same question. "Why, my Lord? Why keep me alive?"

Kinhar glimpsed at Branimir, and then lifted his eyes to the other two Highborn.

Branimir followed the gaze to look at Falmagon mid-swing, and then Dorofej, who hurriedly averted his eyes.

"We will make camp here for the night," Kinhar forestalled the question. "Dorofej, tend to the Kras."

Within the hour, Branimir was sitting under the watch of Dorofej near a crackling fire. With a flick of Falmagon's finger, and a few thrusts of his staff against the ground, rocks had surfaced for sitting, the grass was drowned with sand, and a fire was formed in the center of a stone pit.

"Lord Dorofej," Branimir started, looking to Dorofej who inspected the gashed wound above his temple. The bleeding had stopped, but the pain made his head throb against the old man's gentle touch.

Dorofej scanned the darkness outside the fire before responding, "Speak, Branimir, swiftly and softly."

"There are many things I do not understand."

"Recognizing your ignorance makes you wiser than most, it does." Again, the bearded man peered into the darkness. Perhaps, he was assuring himself that Falmagon and Kinhar were out of earshot. They had stepped away to find something more substantial to burn with the brush.

"Koldovstvo has the power to do many things, and yet we still sail on a boat, walk along the shoreline, and search for firewood. Why not just do what must be done to end this madness?" Branimir said.

"Koldovstvo must be balanced in its use or more madness there would be. The cost is frequently greater than its benefit," Dorofej paused to look at his wrinkled hands that ran through the thin hair of the Kras. As if remembering his place, he continued, "Simple tasks as lighting this campfire may cause a Highborn to lose minutes of their life, where walking across the sea would kill them."

"I have seen Highborn grow old when casting Koldovstvo," Branimir licked his cracked lips, trying to fully understand. He jerked away from Dorofej's light touch again. The pain in his head far outweighed the aching at his side. "But, I have also seen Kinhar grow young."

Dorofej grunted. "Best keep that to yourself unless you like holes in your skull, yes?"

Branimir shook his head, indicating not. Dorofej's fingers scrapping against his wound caused him to retract once more. "Can you not just mend it, Lord Dorofej? Why pick at it with your nails?"

Dorofej tilted his head at the Kras. "I am not picking, Branimir Baran. I am harvesting dirt and grass from your brains to keep you from infection. Besides, Highborn do not heal Kras, and even if it were so, I am spent. Koldovstvo would drain my life permanently if I were to mend you, yes? Favor dying, I do not. Wear these wounds you must, yes?"

Branimir exhaled, cupping his chin in his hands while Dorofej continued to work. Branimir returned to the prior conversation. "How then does Falmagon uses Koldovstvo regularly, while barely growing old, even at Melkorka against the Bukavac."

"*Habërmani* is the name of the crooked staff he clings to, yes? The inner fires of Habërmani feed on Koldovstvo; lessening the effects of aging, it does. Yet drains him to some degree, it does. While in his possession, Falmagon will steal away from the natural balance of Koldovstvo, yes?"

"Where would he get such a thing? Do all Highborn have such tools to wield Koldovstvo?"

"Be best not to ask him, yes?"

"Do you?"

The flames flickered off Dorofej's icy eyes much like they had when he had helped melt the slag to craft Kaelandur at Melkorka. "Best not to ask me either."

Branimir turned to face the fire. "My apologies, Lord Dorofej. I am not generally one to forget my place."

Dorofej cleared his throat. "I say, you will find you are not generally one to do a lot of the things in the coming months, but do them, you will."

"Months?" Branimir gasped, "Where are we going? What do you know, Dorofej?"

Dorofej's bushy eyebrows rose keenly.

Branimir stumbled with his speech. "Lord Dorofej, I mean."

"For now," Dorofej said. "We will go to Arkaim to see this Erzebeth that Kinhar speaks of, yes?"

Branimir could hear movement, indicating Kinhar and Falmagon were returning to the campfire. He quickly twisted his head toward the Highborn at his back. "You know why they are keeping me alive, don't you, Lord Dorofej?"

Dorofej placed a hand on either side of Branimir's child-sized head. The strength in his clasp was unexpected as he forcibly straightened Branimir to stare into the flames.

The Highborn then leaned down, shrouded in his ominous robes, sharing insight that Branimir would have never considered. "Alive at my request, you are."

Chapter VII

Falmagon kicked Branimir in his side harder than necessary, waking him an hour before the sun peaked over the water's edge. Despite the rough awakening, Branimir was thankful the Highborn had not connected with his sore ribcage. He did not want to check with Falmagon standing around, but he was sure the swelling and bruising had gotten worse.

He groaned and sat upright. His head ached something fierce from the thrashing with Habërmani. Before he could lift his hand to touch the tender flesh, three dead rabbits flopped in his lap. Branimir sighed, taking the hint that he was meant to clean and cook them for the morning meal.

He spent the next half hour pulling fur from flesh and turning the meat over the fire, while Falmagon watched him like a guard over a thief. Branimir was not sure what to make of the Highborn's behavior, but he felt uneasy and unwelcomed. Up until now, he had little to no interaction with Falmagon. The one-eyed man was frequently gone from Melkorka, doing only the gods knew what.

If a thousand questions had sat idle in Branimir's mind the night prior, there were ten thousand more this morning. Branimir had known each Highborn to be secretive, as was their way, but he had assumed their confusing actions were due to his lack of understanding and position. After all, they were humans and he was a Kras. They were masters and he was a slave. He had never questioned their motives, always certain to act in accordance with their commands. Though, he had never been a pawn to be played in their schemes either. Even now, he could not be certain that was the case, but Dorofej wanted him alive and Kinhar had allowed him to live. None of it made any sense.

"You keep thinking that hard, and you are liable to have your brain bleed from your ears, Kras," Falmagon said. "If the Lightbringer wanted you to be thinking, you wouldn't be a slave."

Branimir kept his expression as blank as physically possible. His pale eyes did not flinch in the slightest. "Yes, my Lord."

Falmagon scoffed with a shake of his head. After another long look, he turned his attention from Branimir, seemingly bored in watching him cook.

As the sky lightened to a teal and pink, Falmagon began to dig through his pack, holding the supplies from Narthwich. He dumped it out on the ground, taking the inventory before they set off for the day. There were several wraps of dried meat and unleavened bread as well as a fishing line with hooks. There also were two coin purses of shana, a curved blade called a kinzhal, and a case of flint and steel.

While Falmagon scattered the belongings, Kinhar and Dorofej echoed each other's snores. Branimir ignored all three of the Highborn and scanned the landscape. He was not sure what he expected, but he knew he was a better lookout than any of the humans.

The Crags were larger than those on Folkmar, towering behind them. Branimir gazed up at the mountains, covered in light green grasses until the tips suddenly reddened at the end of the tree line. He had always felt comforted by the mountains, even near Melkorka, where demons apparently crawled to the surface from the depths of the Netherworld.

He pushed the thought from his head. The camp was safe between the Crags and Strega's Deep. The coastline stretched southeast, the way they had come, to the northeast, to the village of Valishul. Branimir hoped the morning walk did not take long; although, he suspected they would be boarding another ship for Arkaim. It was not an option he was particularly thrilled about.

The rabbits were nearly done roasting when a sound caught up with his pointed red ears. Jumping to his feet, he peered to the southeast, sniffing the air and squinting.

"What is it, Kras?" Falmagon hissed, noticing Branimir's quick movement. Falmagon may have been a brute, but, at least, he was intelligent enough to recognize the signs of a startled Kras.

"Bukavac." Branimir squealed, backing up toward the fire. "The demons have crossed the water in the night."

"Impossible." Falmagon said, sweeping the belongings into the pack, and snatching up his crooked staff, Habërmani.

"My Lord," Branimir stumbled with his words, "they are moving up the coastline."

Falmagon snarled. "Speak softly or I will have your head, Kras. How many?"

"Twenty or more."

Falmagon twisted his mouth beneath his mustache. "And Nedezhda?"

Branimir scanned the frozen bodies of the demons tearing across the terrain. The large beasts seemed to move in formation, padded armor against padded armor. Each icy fist held a labrys, a double-sided axe at the end of a shaft, stretching twice the length of a human.

"Nedezhda? Is she among them?" Falmagon repeated.

"I do not see her, my Lord." Branimir shivered. "What do we do?"

Falmagon tossed Branimir the pack. "Carry this and douse the fire. We make haste to Valishul."

"We cannot outrun them!"

Falmagon raised his staff with the unspoken threat of being hit. "Do as I say, Kras."

The Highborn moved to the side of Kinhar and Dorofej, waking them in hushed voices while Branimir slung the pack over his shoulders and began kicking dirt over the flames. He was careful not to sling dirt onto the roasted rabbits.

"How could they have crossed the water? Strega would have drowned them." Kinhar spluttered, hearing the news. He stumbled about pulling on his robes and boots.

Dorofej casually slid on his first boot. "Tell me, why any god would interfere in the struggles of men, especially when facing demons?"

"For righteousness," Falmagon said bitingly.

Dorofej plucked his other boot off the ground and shook it at Falmagon mischievously. "Glory to be had, there is not, if gods relieve men of tribulations."

Falmagon angled his brow. "Don't lecture me, Dorofej."

A horn bellowed to the southeast and northeast, one after another. Branimir twisted in either direction. Fear enveloped him.

"The Bukavac come from the front and rear, my Lords," Branimir bawled. "They have found us out and are closing."

"We must fight," Falmagon declared, hitting the crooked staff against the ground.

"Three Highborn and a Kras," Dorofej shook his head. "After the numbers fallen at Melkorka? Fighting here would be fruitless, yes?"

"There is no choice!" Falmagon insisted.

"Opportunity lies in wait if you look for it, yes?"

"Bah! Stop speaking in riddles, Dorofej," Kinhar bellowed, grabbing his own pack off the ground. "Speak plainly."

"I am too feeble for fighting, and be plunging myself into the ocean to drown, I will not. I say, the Crags seem a worthwhile option."

Kinhar eyed the charging Bukavac who advanced on their position, agreeing, "We will not win a battle here. We should go through the Crags and circle around to Arkaim."

Dorofej smiled. "Go beneath, instead, I would recommend."

Falmagon curled his lip. "Who in their right mind would go under the Crags? Whatever you find in the depths of the Crags may very well contend with the Bukavacs at our backs."

Dorofej shrugged. "Battling the Bukavac will knowingly bring a close to our saga. Though, the battles yet to come have not been weighed, yes?"

"It doesn't matter, Dorofej," Falmagon argued. "Any entrance into the mountains is lost to the dead. It would take us a lifetime to find an opening, and even if we did, nothing would stop the Bukavac from pursuing."

Dorofej made his way to the dull fire pit and pulled a chunk from one of the rabbits. He peeled a piece of meat off and put it into his mouth. He chewed the meat and waited.

Falmagon glowered with hate. "I cannot take this infernal swine anymore." He slammed his stick into the ground again causing the rocks around the fire pit to rise into the air and fall again to the earth.

Branimir howled a ghastly cry as though he were on the front lines of battle. It was a sound that had not been heard from a Kras in two thousand years or more.

Branimir stormed around the fire pit, shouting, "We do not have the time to argue or to feast on rabbits. Call stone and fire down on the enemy or flee." Branimir reached out and slapped the cooked rabbit out of Dorofej's lifted hand.

Dorofej stopped chewing to catch his jaw, watching the precious meat drop to the dirt as though it were his own heart.

Branimir, realizing his tactless action, dropped his hands to his sides and swiftly added, "My Lords."

Falmagon swung Habërmani and Branimir threw himself to the ground, fearing the weapon was aimed for his skull once more.

Instead, the stones around the fireplace were thrown skillfully with Koldovstvo into the first Bukavac. The beast roared as the first struck it in the chest and the second across its frozen cheekbone. The Bukavac stumbled but continued its charge.

The demon swung the labrys with the sharpened blade in full arc toward Falmagon, who fell on his back to dodge the blow. The Bukavac raised the double-sided axe over his head, ready to slice the Highborn in half from chin to gut.

Before the bluish-white demon could complete the attack, a ray of fire burst from Kinhar's hands into the Bukavac's eyes, colored like labradorites, blinding the beast. The Bukavac thrashed with its horns wildly and let loose another thunderous boom from his throat calling the attention of every demon within miles.

Habërmani struck the Bukavac repeatedly across the thighs, neck, and gut as Falmagon danced around the demon. The Bukavac, with fire in its eyes, swung wildly to hit the Highborn, crouching at half the height. Falmagon easily dodged the beast, and then finally hit the staff against the ground again. Rocks the size of Branimir's fists formed into stone spearheads. The stone pierced through the Bukavac a hundred times over and dropped the beast to the ground.

"This way. Come!" Dorofej shouted from several feet away. He had already begun making his way through the tall grasses up to the Crags of Kazimir. Branimir was not surprised to see the old Highborn holding another rabbit from the fire in his hand, a piece of the meat already hanging out from his thin lips.

Branimir scampered to his feet and ran toward Dorofej with Falmagon's pack held securely on his back. The Kras ignored the burrs and thorns that had haunted him the night prior, finding their irritation a minor payment for surviving the Bukavac. Death by a demon's blade was not a fate he envied.

Kinhar hesitantly trailed behind with Falmagon at the far rear. The four of them said nothing as they abandoned the campsite and their destined path to Valishul. Branimir followed willingly as the Highborn forged another path. He could only guess it was fortune that pulled them down the path through the Crags with all other routes leading to death. Before long the tall grasses disappeared, and red rock and gravel was all that remained.

For half an hour, the four of them scampered like dormice dodging the deathly talons of a sparrowhawk. The sounds of the Bukavac giving chase never ceased. The echoes of their heavy footsteps and blood-hungry growls were lively upon the stone of the Crags.

Despite the Kras being quicker than humans, it soon became all Branimir could do to keep up with Dorofej, who had suddenly taken charge of their fates. The euphoric, old Highborn ran with increased urgency through the Crags, seeming to have ancient knowledge of the speed and determination of the Bukavac.

Dorofej chortled like a madman as he twisted and turned past fallen rocks, loosened pebbles, and uneven paths that had not been traveled on for ages. He jumped and skidded through the terrain, full of vigor, as though he were half a century younger than he appeared.

"Where are you leading us, Dorofej?" Falmagon asked.

Dorofej paused for a moment to glance back at the younger Highborn before sticking his tongue out. The air was light and chilled, like dew from clovers in a dampened paddock. With a gleeful shout, he again picked up the pace with a sudden earnestness, rounding another crook in the mountain.

Two sarsen stones the size of the Bukavac stood polished against the mountain side. They were peculiar next to the red rock, but likely would be passed over if not sought out. Through the stones, one offset behind the right, was a gaping hole, pitch in color, leading into the depths of the mountainside. The dwelling was meant to be secluded, meant to be overlooked, meant to be forgotten.

Dorofej scarcely squeezed through the stones, making his way to the hole, small enough that he would have to crouch significantly to make his way inside the stuffy hole.

Branimir touched the smooth rock unnervingly as he passed through the crevice in the rocks.

"Quite fortunate there are no portly men in our fellowship, yes?" Dorofej said, still full of breath, urging them with a jerk of his head to follow. "Come."

Branimir was pushed to the front by Dorofej, to lead the way in the darkened tunnel as their guide. He had only made it a couple steps before Falmagon asked the question.

"What is this place?"

Kinhar gaped at the sarsen stones in wonderment and replied, "Dorofej has found the ingress to the Kras city of Illuard."

Branimir's knees buckled.

Chapter VIII

Pushing forward as though he had dug the tunnel himself, Branimir guided the Highborn down the dark path. Dorofej held fast to Branimir's small hand while the Highborn behind him held onto one another in a similar fashion. Unlike Branimir, the humans were sightless in the underground passageway, seeing nothing but darkness bounded in darkness.

Twice, Branimir had come to junctures in the tunnel where alternative tunnels had been dug out, forking wide in opposite directions. With simple explanation, Dorofej had wasted little time in directing Branimir down each path. Branimir was certain the old man had been here before.

Branimir recalled the conversation with Dorofej around the campfire about having an inquisitorial mind, and decided it was best to keep curiosity at sword's edge for the moment. He did not need holes in his skull.

The Kras was well-fitted in the smooth tunnel, having full range to walk upright. The walkway was worn with flat walls and ceiling, covered in a thick layer of dust. The Highborn behind him were not as privileged with their backs curved and necks bent; they still collided into the solid walls of earth on either side. Their muffled complaints harmonized with their stumbled footfalls as they descended into the depths of the mountainside.

After an hour or more, a dim, cloudy light brightened the end of the burrow. Thinking they had reached the outside, Branimir continued forward through the gap into the light. As he stepped out of the tunnel, he sauntered into a cave chamber the size of Narthwich, grander than Melkorka.

"The great hall of the Kras city of Illuard," Dorofej said from behind him, "distinguished as the *Eevaltti*, Hollow of Gravels, house of Electress Arabella, daughter to Atanasius Kulmata, Ninth Emperor of *Ojanen*, it is."

Light from a narrow, curved opening in the ceiling spilled with sparkling water, falling into a basin in the center of the cavern like a waterfall from the heavens. Mist bellowed from the gurgling basin fogging the cavern considerably. The smoky light shadowed columns formed from stalactites and stalagmites throughout the expanse.

"An empire long forsaken, long torn from the songs of skalds, and long forgotten by men," Kinhar added.

"Apparently, not all men," Falmagon muttered, eyeing Dorofej suspiciously. "How do you know of this place?"

Dorofej snorted, rubbing the mustache bristles from his inner nose. "From time to time, reminisce in the sound of songs once sung, my mind does."

"You mean, there is no one here," Branimir said disappointedly. "Where are the Kras?"

"I thought I had said you were the last of your kind." Dorofej offered without emotion, moving toward the basin.

Kinhar snickered.

Branimir looked at the spearhead of the Highborn, noting the odd behavior. He did not think he had ever heard the man scoff before.

"I expected…" Branimir did not know what he had expected.

"It is a ruin," Falmagon said. "Nothing more."

Branimir ogled as the Highborn scattered across the room, like newborns opening their eyes for the first time. The great hall was surrounded in multitudes of staircases sculpted from the mountainside led into more tunnels on several different levels.

There were hundreds of them, each leading a different path, making up the city of Illuard.

The basin appeared to be naturally created, possibly from an underground waterway that flowed through the mountain, possibly creating this cavern thousands of years ago. Dorofej kneeled at the pool putting the liquid to his tongue and spitting on the ground.

"Bitter as acid, it is," he mumbled.

On the opposite side of the murky pool was a flattened surface with old stone tables thirty feet long covered with red chunks of stone and rusty pickaxes. Clay kilns were stretched around the tables, some collapsed or broken. Branimir could only assume they had been used to heat any ore found in the rocks, but there were no weapons or armor visible.

A treasure of the room was a ceremonial chair made of shiny stones, positioned inside an opening in the back wall on the opposite side of the cavern. Spinel, bloodstone, apatite, jade, and tanzanite were stacked together. The seat was clearly a masterpiece, far grander than Kinhar's stone throne back at Melkorka. The throne was built in the side of the mountain, in a cranny only large enough for a Kras to squeeze into, placed high enough in the wall to overlook the entire cavern with ease. In the depths of the edged rock, behind the grandiose throne, hung a tapestry. It was muddied and discolored beyond recognition.

Branimir found himself standing by the throne, stroking the gems gently, salivating from the lips. He had no memory of walking across the cavern or climbing the small incline to the impressed cavity in the red rock.

His small hands traced each gemstone, each jewel, and each nugget, seared to the one next to it without hope of ever being removed from the throne. If his life were measured by feelings of ecstasy or absolute joy, in this moment, Branimir had just been born.

Dorofej's voice whispered from below. "Sat and watched over his people from *Oreg'henite*, Emperor Atanasius Kulmata would have."

Branimir did not respond. He couldn't figure out what words he wanted to say. The stones were so shiny.

"Branimir." Dorofej poked him in the side. The old Highborn's bushy eyebrows peeked over the edge from the level below with a coltish gaze.

"I want one," Branimir wheezed.

"Behind Oreg'henite, you will unearth the stone of stones. Quickly, now."

Branimir did not budge, still focused on the treasure before his eyes. He felt urged to sit in it, to feel the shiny stones all around him.

"Foolish, Kras." Dorofej pushed his finger harder into Branimir, striking his tender rib purposefully. "Oreg'henite, the throne is. Dig behind it, tear down the tapestry, and make haste," he urged through clenched teeth.

Branimir squealed in pain, turning to face Dorofej feeling the madness swell in his eyes. His first instinct was to strike out at the Highborn, but five decades of conditioning prevented him from acting on his natural disposition. He suddenly realized Dorofej could not do much more but poke at him. The Highborn could not fit behind Oreg'henite.

"What have you found, Dorofej?" Kinhar called from a distance.

"Dig." Dorofej whistled at Branimir. "I say, find me the moonstone, *Ojenek*. Fit in the palm of your hand, it will. Smaller than your fist, it is!"

Branimir bobbed his head.

"Dorofej?" Kinhar said again.

"Oreg'henite, the Ojanen Throne, Kinhar," Dorofej sung out in a bard's tone, causing a distraction away from Branimir. "Magnificent, yes? The Kras were slaves to their own before the Highborn, serving the Emperor night and day to find gemstones and precious rocks for the construction of Oreg'henite from Gjetvald Meas, the First Emperor of Ojanen, to the Ninth. It took era upon era to craft the chair. Still, Gjetvald had the most prevalent contribution, being the First to rule in Eevaltti, with each subsequent ruler adding bits more, yes?"

Branimir dug frantically behind Oreg'henite in the soft, muddied soil that lined its rear. His fingernails filled with red muck as he dug deeper and deeper into the earth.

"The Kras would sit beneath their ruler at these stone tables, breaking stone from clay, gem from stone, yes? An eternal search for jewels—to match their desire—in the depths of the mountains, they had."

Branimir's fingers touched a leather pouch, damp with decay. He pulled it free from the mud, ripped loose the leather binding, and dumped the contents into his hands eagerly. There, in his palm, was the bluish moonstone, sparkling as though it were filled with an inner fire, called Ojenek.

Branimir smiled wide. Ojenek, the jewel of an emperor, the talisman of the Kras, was held firmly in his grasp.

Falmagon raised next to Kinhar, passing through the columns, his single eye always watching and wary. "What did they discover in all their digging, Dorofej?" He clutched Habërmani, clearly showing he was aware of the significance of relics and Koldovstvo found within them.

"I found it!" Branimir yelped in delight, his little voice echoing from wall to tunnel like the uplifting exclamations of a hundred Kras cutting the sediment from their first shiny stone. He stood erect by Oreg'henite, jubilantly holding Ojenek in the air between his finger and thumb.

"Doltish, imprudent, Kras!" Dorofej's palm connected with his forehead. He shook his head, the tassels from his chin bouncing in defeat.

Before Kinhar or Falmagon could question the utility of the moonstone between Branimir's crimson fingers, horrifying howls of awakened creatures reverberated into the cavern.

"The Bukavac have found us!" Falmagon cried out.

"Not likely," Kinhar said. "With their size, they would have never made it down here. This is something else entirely."

Small creatures, as large as a Highborn's forearm flew from out from the many tunnels and circled wildly about the great hall in a fit of perceived madness. The forelimbs of the creatures served as wings, with a membranous skin that was too thin to see in the hazy cavern. The demonic looking creatures closely resembled bats apart from their spindly legs and miniature horned skulls.

Branimir did not hesitate in shoving Ojenek back into the leather pouch and stuffing it into the pocket of his trousers.

The ear-piercing screech of the flying demons did not match the howling heard moments before. Branimir covered his susceptible ears to block out the mishmash of noise erupting from the fanged mouths.

"What is this?" Branimir squealed, falling to his knees.

"Skyrz!" Kinhar bellowed over the insufferable noise. "They will fetch much worse with their clamoring."

Falmagon shrieked as a Skyrz swooped down and clamped onto his cheek. The claws of its feet tore into the flesh of Falmagon's neck as it extracted blood from the face of the Highborn ravenously with its hollowed fangs. Its wings beat violently about, maintaining its grip, while Falmagon lurched, pulling at the gristly body of the beast.

Dorofej sprang to Falmagon, grabbing the Skyrz by its gangling neck. Swiftly, Dorofej squeezed, crushing the bones and nearly severing the head. As the Skyrz dropped in a heap, the sharpened teeth were expelled from Falmagon and blood decanted from the bleeding puncture wounds in the Highborn's neck.

"Hold it fast." Dorofej said, tearing at the black fabric of his robes.

Falmagon clung to his cheek, dark blood oozing over his fingertips blending with the crimson liquid bleeding from the claw marks on his throat.

Another two Skyrz plummeted through the cavern pillars toward Dorofej and Falmagon but were quickly met with fire flailing like whips from Kinhar's fingertips. As if being beckoned to war, the rest of the Skyrz about the room wheeled toward the Highborn with gnashing teeth and hollow eyes.

Dorofej shredded the end of his robe and handed Falmagon the cloth.

Falmagon took it eagerly, holding it tightly against his cheek, blood swelling in his mouth. In his free hand, he used the crooked staff to keep another Skyrz from latching onto him.

Dorofej ducked a swooping Skyrz who collided with another string of fire unleashed from Kinhar.

"I will not waste my life with these demons!" Kinhar shouted above the echoing shrieks.

"Falmagon," Dorofej directed with an extended hand. "A weapon, if you will!"

The Highborn were distinguished for never crafting a man-made weapon, as it was against custom and tradition of their kind. Kaelandur had been the exception to this holistic practice. Outside of the occasional walking stick, not many tools of warfare would ever have reason to touch the hand of those blessed by Koldovstvo. Despite such truth, Bran was aware the Highborn would use Koldovstvo to construct armaments in times of distress.

Falmagon Sej, the Highborn Longwalker, mumbled under his breath forcibly, crashing Habërmani against the cavern surface. The foggy mist spiraled and enveloped the man, taking hold as Koldovstvo pulsed through his veins. His brown hair, frayed and unraveled, blurred with his cloak as he shifted from shadow to shadow. With a stab of Habërmani into the nearest rock, two stone staves erupted and were supernaturally flung toward Kinhar and Dorofej.

The three Highborn formed a protective circle, standing back to back, each defensively holding a staff. The Skyrz clamored toward them. The movement in the dim light was difficult to make out as staves twirled and gloomy Skyrz lunged for flesh. Again and again, the Skyrz plunged to taste fresh blood and met a grueling strike. As more Skyrz surfaced from the depths of the underearth, another would fall dead at the feet of the Highborn, honored guardians of men, revered keepers of Koldovstvo, and esteemed wardens of Melkorka.

The continued wailing of howls that rebounded in the dark tunnels grew closer. The sounds went unheard by the frenetic Highborn that battled the Skyrz. It was Branimir's pinpointed ears stretching beyond the top of his hairline that caught the commotion.

Branimir was still crouched in hiding behind Oreg'henite. As the sound of the howls grew near, Branimir fuddled with the pack on his back that he had been holding for Falmagon. It suddenly struck him that where the Highborn had Koldovstvo, he had nothing in which to defend himself.

Compelled by terror instigated by the nightmarish baying, he reached inside the cloth pack and found the kinzhal. Branimir had never held a weapon before and was pleased that the curved dagger was so light in his grasp. He touched the blade carefully and yelped at its sharpness. It sliced through his red skin with ease, causing crimson liquid to drip. He quickly shoved his finger in his mouth, eyeing the blade with care. The dagger would make do.

"Dreka," Kinhar snarled.

At first, Branimir thought that the dark-haired man was shouting a battle cry, but soon realized he was referring to the demon that sprang from a tunnel above to the great hall. The howl was all too familiar, causing Branimir to duck behind the throne once more.

The Dreka was the size of Branimir with an oversized head with goat horns breaking through the grey wrinkles of skin on its forehead. The Dreka had an elongated, thin body that wrapped behind it awkwardly, swaying and hunched over forebodingly. Yellow, molded eyes scanned the great hall as though the Dreka was the protector of Illuard, Eevaltti.

Branimir gaped like a child at the demonic beast that dwelled in the caves of the lost city of Illuard. The thin-lipped mouth of the Dreka was forced open by overlaying rows of sharpened teeth on the upper and lower gums. The Kras had never seen so many teeth on any one living creature. If such demons were common in mountains, Branimir understood clearly why his race was gone from existence.

The Dreka caught sight of the Highborn about the time that several more leaped from the holes in the walls. The first Dreka howled like a deep-throated wolf, springing to action on all four legs. It pounced about the ground with surprising agility, leaping from column to column like it was walking across a flat surface. The other Dreka, too many to count, joined the charge.

Falmagon dropped the cloth that prevented the gushing of blood from his face with a dark sneer. "No safer here than with the Bukavac!"

"Not the time," Kinhar crowed, dropping the stone stave and throwing up his hands defensively.

The Dreka leaped toward the spearhead of the Highborn and was met with a gust of wind that sent it reeling backwards through a pillar of rock. The second and third demons met similar fates with the impact breaking skin and bone.

Falmagon used a similar method, pulling crumbled stone from the ground and flinging it at the enemy with Koldovstvo. Demon upon demon that assailed at Falmagon collided with rock and met their demise.

Dorofej kept his staff in hand, not risking his life in using Koldovstvo, as he had little to spare. The stone stave struck the nearest Dreka that approached him in the mouth, busting skin and shattering teeth. The Dreka spewed blood and attacked again, before Dorofej could bring his weapon down to shield himself. The cutthroat fangs ripped into his lower leg, tearing a chunk from his calf. Dorofej collapsed and the demon was immediately on his chest snapping at the throat behind his white beard.

"Dorofej!" Branimir screamed. In a moment, he found himself leaping from the cleft, fading from visibility, and blending into his surroundings. On light footsteps, he dashed forward with the swiftness of a Kras in its natural habitat. Through the broken columns, past the bitter basin, Branimir dodged the Dreka that bounded about the cavern in heated disarray.

Dorofej held the Dreka a breath away, its saliva saturated in the old man's beard, when Branimir plunged the kinzhal between the horns on the beast's head. Blood churned over the blade and the creature fell limp.

"Branimir," Dorofej said with heavy breath.

"Lord Dorofej," Branimir acknowledged, pulling the blade free.

More Dreka spilled from the tunnels like a sea filling a void. Falmagon sounded above the demonic howls of the ferocious beasts. "There are too many. We cannot hold here!"

"May the Lightbringer help us," Kinhar proclaimed, pulling Falmagon to where Dorofej and Branimir lay in wait.

Tens of hundreds of Dreka seemed to fill the cavern, spilling over each other like rats over rotting meat. Kinhar, holding true to the Highborn way, threw up his arms, calling on Koldovstvo.

As the Dreka bounded to finish the three Highborn and single Kras, an invisible dome of force, created from the air they breathed, was fabricated around the Highborn men. The Dreka slammed into the wall repetitively, yapping and bawling in retaliation against the unseen energy that held them from their prey. Wrinkles immediately lined Kinhar's temples, his hair graying at the tips, age returning where it had previously been restored.

Branimir clung to Dorofej in disbelief as Kinhar lifted the lot of them above the cavern floor within the invulnerable globe. They sat upon nothing with demons hissing and screeching beneath them, leaping and clawing, intent on preventing escape from the forlorn city.

The edges of the protective orb collided with column upon column, destroying the fabric of their creation. Each column crumbled under the impact. Boulders the size of the sarsens at the entrance to Illuard flattened the enemy. The ceiling of the cavern fell away where water rained to the basin below. The Dreka found futility in their attempts and scampered back to the tunnels beneath.

Still, Kinhar lifted the orb through the ceiling. His features continued to change, bringing him closer to the man he had been at Melkorka, as opposed to the young man he had become. The ashen strands in his hair became more significant, wrinkles flooding his skin like fruit dried too long in the heat of the sun.

"Kinhar," Falmagon grabbed the Highborn in fervor, "if you defeat yourself, the war with Nedezhda will be lost."

The light of Dahz, the Lightbringer, had not yet gone astray, as the day had not come to an end, and shined on the group as they rose over the mountaintop from the cavern depths.

"Bless Dahz, the Protector of Men," Kinhar called to the heavens as though he were standing directly before the white castle of the Beyond. The protective orb lowered to the red rock atop the mountain, beyond the tree line and high grasses below. "Through the Lightbringer, I will preserve justice and the legacy of the Highborn. I will find a way."

As the protective orb dissipated from existence, the three humans collapsed on the ridge in exhaustion.

Branimir stood up determinedly, sliding the kinzhal into his belt for safekeeping. He peered to the northwest toward Arkaim. Kalamaar stretched before them, shaded in gold and scarlet rays of the Sun God. There was no booming voice of Dahz the Lightbringer, and yet, Branimir knew that glory was to be had.

Month of Ripening

Fifth of Warmth

124 CE

Chapter IX

Branimir poked at the fire lazily bumping his branch against the charred logs. It sparked atop the fading embers, looking to spread its flame. He understood the danger of allowing the fire to burn freely. As ravenous as power, a fire would devour whatever lay before it. Without proper tending, it would consume the whole world. Such lessons he had learned from Dorofej in the past two months, late in the evenings and early in the mornings, as they made their way through the Crags of Kazimir to Arkaim.

The journey to Arkaim had been more arduous than any would have predicted, laced with perils like poison on a dagger's edge. The mainland of Kalamaar was not well equipped for men to travel across with only a few scattered villages, making the opportunity to gain supplies or adequate rest minimal. Still, the most difficult of situations was what they had experienced at Illuard.

Branimir knew the battle had changed him. For once in his life, he felt brave.

"What do you want, Branimir?" Falmagon snorted, ripping the leg from the cooked hare and stuffing it in his mouth. It had taken nearly a week for Falmagon's face to heal from the Skyrz, leaving him with a nasty scar down the good side of his face. With the permanent imprint and the missing eye, the youngest of the Highborn appeared to be the most threadbare among them. His attitude, if it were conceivable, had taken a further turn for the worse.

Branimir looked away, not realizing he had been staring at the pink blemishes. He quickly clued in to his red skin, seemingly preoccupied with his hand and five diminutive fingers. His skin was flush with the color of the glowing cradle of the fire pit.

He could not help but notice that the one-eyed Highborn had called him Branimir instead of calling him a Kras. It was becoming a more common event in the past few weeks. Branimir was not sure if it was a gesture of respect or simply an attempt to break up the monotony. Being surrounded by one another for the past couple months had not been easy on any of them, especially after being drawn so far from their destination. The path through Illuard had only lengthened their journey to Arkaim.

Falmagon finished eating by throwing a bone into the fire. "Stare at me again before we reach Arkaim, red brood, and I will cut out your eyes to replace my own."

"Yes, my Lord," Branimir said.

Dorofej nudged Branimir with a snicker that may have been the underpinnings of a giggle. "Stare whilst he sleeps, you must. He does not have an eye to spare to keep open when resting, yes?"

Bran covered his lips with both hands to stifle a chortle. A month ago, Branimir would not have dared laugh at such an insult openly, but Dorofej had been somewhat protective of him since their escape of the underground, Kras city. The aged Highborn had not even asked for the moonstone, Ojenek, outside of telling Branimir to keep it safe. Falmagon and Kinhar seemingly had forgotten about it entirely.

Branimir touched the moonstone in his pocket lightly. He found himself slightly curious as to what exactly it was and why Dorofej had wanted it. He was not used to thinking about these types of things, but it did strike him once more that none of the Highborn around the campfire could have reached the moonstone in its hiding place. Branimir was the only one that could have fit behind the throne called Oreg'henite.

Dorofej widened his eyes playfully and sipped from his waterskin. It dribbled down his chin as he tried to hold back his own mirth.

Falmagon grabbed his crooked staff called Habërmani and stood with fury. "I have smashed your head in once, Kras. Do not think it will not happen again. Know your place!"

Dorofej waved indolently at the younger man. "Put your bent stick away, yes? I made the jest. Moreover, proven his worth in our company, Branimir has."

"Killing a single Dreka does not make him an equal to the Highborn, Dorofej."

"I did not suggest it did, Falmagon Sej, Highborn Longwalker." Dorofej pulled up his robe, revealing the mended flesh of his lower leg, far more severe than the damage inflicted on Falmagon's face. "And yet, he measured his life against that of a Highborn, and chose the latter, yes? Deserving of veneration, the gesture is."

Branimir gleamed a bit at the old man's words.

Falmagon pulled at his mustache that hung over the brown scruff of a developing beard. "Are you going to refuse my right to thrash a slave, Dorofej?"

"The fortunes of men linger in the blight, from which alternative paths for your aggression you should consider, yes?" Dorofej dropped his robe.

Scowling, Falmagon sniffed. "I did not ask for your wisdom and you did not answer my question."

Dorofej separated his lips, taking a deep breath and looked long and hard at the one-eyed Highborn. Finally, Dorofej hobbled to his feet, clutching his waterskin in long, tangled fingers. Branimir could hear the old man's knees grind, bone scraping against bone as he shuffled over to Falmagon. The elder hoisted himself as straight as a hanging man's rope, nose touching nose, with his shaggy eyebrows adding extra shadow to his visage.

Branimir cowered back, scooting away so that he would not be caught between the two. He found himself genuinely worried for Dorofej but could not place how he should think or feel about the old Highborn protecting him.

From the angle, Branimir could not make out the expression of the old man, but he easily heard Dorofej's words. "Unblemished words, it is. Rest a finger on Branimir Baran and your blood it will be that I draft from my waterskin!"

With that, Dorofej lifted the sheep's bladder to his lips and sucked out the liquid and spat it out in Falmagon's face.

Falmagon shoved Dorofej with both hands, and the old man toppled to the ground in a heap. Dorofej grunted, landing rather awkwardly on his shoulder.

Dorofej retorted in feverish laughter, holding his stomach and lifting his waterskin off the ground protectively.

"Mad you are!"

"What has gotten into you, Dorofej?" Kinhar frowned from the fire pit. "What did you put in your waterskin?"

Dorofej hiccupped, rolling over onto his haunches, maintaining the waterskin being held in the air. "A bit of plum when we promenaded through Jh'tutar a fortnight ago, yes?"

"Wine? We were barely in the village for a half an hour," Kinhar started.

"All that was needed to taste the nectar of sweet plum," Dorofej tittered from the ground. "Like Falmagon's mother, it is."

He took another swig.

Falmagon's face turned as red as Branimir's skin.

"Leave him be, Falmagon. He is sloshed beyond reason," Kinhar said.

Branimir kept his hand over his mouth, holding back the merriment that welled up inside of him. Dorofej blundered about on the ground in attempt to stand once more, to move closer to the fire pit. After falling onto his buttocks more than once, he finally laid down. He murmured to himself, curling into a ball inside his dark robes.

"He is going to get us killed," Falmagon said to Kinhar, returning to the stone that he had been sitting upon.

"He has his own merits," Kinhar said.

"His capacity to wield Koldovstvo, to mend our wounds, to manipulate the elements, is restrained by his frailty. What use can Dorofej have besides slow our excursion? Already Nedezhda may have reached the Ash Tree while we have been wandering in the Crags."

Branimir licked his lips nervously. They had not discussed their quest of protecting the Ash Tree since Narthwich. For a moment, he had thought that the Highborn had forgotten their self-proclaimed quest.

"Dorofej has familiarity that is from beyond our time," Kinhar said wondrously, hearing the old man hiccup again in the dark. "From beyond my time. And, from where he obtained such knowledge, I must figure out before his death."

"He rambles."

"If you listen closely, Falmagon, there is truth in his words. If the Kadari are to flourish in the centuries to come, his truth must be ours."

Branimir's gaiety fled like shadow from flame as he grasped the intention of the Highborn. The name Kadari had been mentioned by these two back at Melkorka. He was too afraid to ask its meaning and decided to simply listen, while pretending not to listen.

"Once you learn it, I am going to kill the old cur," Falmagon avowed, pulling Kaelandur from his robes wickedly.

Branimir stifled a yelp. He gaped at the copper dagger that had been forged at Melkorka. His jaw quivered at memory of it being forged by Jhar and Dorofej and then being used to slaughter Nedezhda. The weapon filled him with such distress that it was all he could do to stay seated and not flee from the campfire. From that time, it had remained hidden to the point that Branimir had forgotten that Falmagon carried it on his person.

"A fitting death," Falmagon cackled.

"Only if it is Dahz's will," Kinhar said. "The Lightbringer must guide us or we, too, will become misplaced."

Dorofej snuffled in his sleep, flopping sideways on the ground. A low toned gurgle sounded from his thin lips.

Falmagon harrumphed, pointing the weapon at Dorofej. "That pile of sheepdip? I guarantee you that the Lightbringer wills it!"

Kinhar curved his lips with amusement.

Branimir could not believe what he was hearing. These two men were leaps and bounds beyond the footpath of the Highborn. He understood that the Highborn were meant to protect humans, not meddle with life, and definitely not scheme to murder one of their own. He clamped his jaw hard and bit his cheek. This was unbearable.

"What of the red brood?" Falmagon shifted his gaze to Branimir.

He did not meet the Highborn's gaze, fixing his eyes to Kaelandur. Although the world around him was as clear as day, he swore that it glistened against the dimming cinders.

His fingers trailed to the kinzhal tucked in his belt. It was unusual for a Kras to carry a weapon, but none of the Highborn had questioned it after he had killed the Dreka in the cavern. Even after a couple months in his belt, the dagger was still sharp. It hardly helped him feel at ease.

"Leave Branimir be. He has merit as well," Kinhar tossed a stone toward Branimir. It cracked him in the skull lightly. "Regardless of Dorofej's drunk blathering, the Kras knows to keep his mouth sealed. Is that not so?"

"Yes, my Lord," Branimir shuddered, keeping his eyes dropped. His hand fell away from his weapon.

"Kinhar, you have a funny way of measuring merit, finding purpose in a half-dead carcass and a half-pint slave."

Kinhar rubbed his scalp. His grey hair had returned, leaving him rather flustered. He was not as aged as Dorofej, but the youth he had achieved at Melkorka had been lost at Illuard. "Bah! You undertook the Kalamyr Oath, as I did, pledging fealty to Dahz and the Kadari.

Have some sense, Falmagon, and use what Dahz provides you. Dorofej is devoted by common name and the Kras by station. None could ask for better company, despite their lacking."

Falmagon grunted, signifying compliance. "I trust in you the utmost, Kinhar. You have not led me astray thus far." Falmagon returned the copper dagger to its hiding place.

"Trust in Dahz, the Protector of Men, before all else," Kinhar said.

"Even when the ritual failed us…" Falmagon said, squinting at Kinhar for guidance.

"True," Kinhar said, "the outcome was not what was expected, but I cannot say it was a failure. The Lightbringer simply tests our faith. We will defeat Nedezhda."

Falmagon ran his fingers over his mustache, studying Kinhar. As if making up his decision, he scooped up his hare again and used his teeth to pull the meat from the bone. "It'll be good to see Erzebeth."

Kinhar agreed, "Let us hope that she has the freedom to take leave with us. I will need Erzebeth to guide the way."

"Kinhar?" Falmagon paused chewing. His voice had more distress than what Branimir had ever heard in the tenor of the Highborn. "What are you saying?"

There was an unmistakable mist in the crook of Kinhar's eyes as he bore admittance to his companion across the burning residue. "I cannot seem to remember the way to the Ash Tree."

Kinhar stood up and sighed heavily, tears swelling. He swallowed hard.

"You were honest with Dorofej when you told him that you did not know at Narthwich?

Kinhar grumbled in his throat.

"How long has it been?"

Branimir noticed Kinhar take his time in responding. The Highborn blankly looked at nothing. It was like his mind was wandering through a hundred memories of a hundred lifetimes in a single second.

Kinhar gulped. "I wish that I could tell you, Falmagon. I was young in my existence when I found my way, and timeworn when I finally returned to Kalamaar. I only know the Waters of Life and the Ash Tree are beyond Strega's Deep in a land far more dangerous than Kalamaar.

Kinhar continued, pacing about the fire. "Humans think they know the world. They believe they are powerful, and that they have the gift of wisdom unlike any other living creature. The human creature, in all its perfection, designed by the gods or nay, only sees what it wants to see."

Branimir's mind swelled. Not only was he attempting to understand the ramblings of a man who seemingly claimed to live the lifespan of a Kras or longer, but alleged that mankind, the master of the Kras, were ignorant despite their freedom and power.

Branimir had never known Kinhar to know humility in this way. Despite his professed connection with Dahz the Lightbringer, this measure of humbleness was incongruous with the spearhead of the Highborn.

"What do you see, Falmagon?"

Falmagon gnawed on the hare like a vagrant, talking with his mouth full. "I have journeyed all over Kalamaar and the Seven Islands at your direction from the time that you plucked me from Arkaim as a child. I did not ask for this life, but I also did not question what was meant by being Highborn. I have done what was necessary for the world to be saved from itself, even when I did not completely agree with the path set before me. I have seen what some will never know. I have experienced what some will never have. I have more reason than most to lose my faith. Yet, even when my eye was torn from its socket at Jh'tutat, I found myself blessed, measuring godsend against calamity. There is not always goodness but there is justice. And, justice…righteousness…has many forms. Whether it is thought to be right or wrong, it is still necessary. If we forget justice then we forget reason, and then we forget what is meant by being Anshedar."

Branimir breathed deep, touching his head where he had received the beating from Falmagon on the shores of Kalamaar. The soreness was gone, but the memory of the harshness in the man remained. Yet, after Falmagon spoke, Branimir found himself finding appreciation for the Highborn Longwalker. For once, he used the term for all humans—not Highborn or Northmen—but Anshedar. It was surprising that Falmagon found a connection with something greater than himself.

Branimir suddenly felt very isolated. He was not a part of anything larger than himself. He was alone in this world.

Kinhar paused in his movement. "You have the true sight of a leader, Falmagon Sej. You will shepherd the threshold of the Kadari in the upcoming era. I swear it."

Chapter X

Coming from a place where only a handful of people were ever gathered at one time, Arkaim was prodigious. Branimir gawked in fascination while trying to keep in pace with the long-legged Highborn that walked toward the capital.

"How big is this place?" Branimir asked.

Dorofej responded, "The largest city in the civilized world with nearly a thousand Northmen, Arkaim is. It is the home of Merreider Kal, Twelfth King of Kalamaar, Bearer of the *Svehla*, the Golden Scepter of Svarog, yes?"

Falmagon spit. "Fancy titles for a man who is hardly deserving of them. He spends more time traveling around to Jh'tutar, Valishul, and Jh'terin then caring for the people of Arkaim."

Falmagon headed up the party with his crooked staff repeatedly slamming into the ground, a sign of his irritability. Dust layered the lower seams on his brown robe. The attire had been bought with shana provided by Jarl Likshol Avar of Narthwich. In fact, the Jarl's coin had supported their travels tremendously while traipsing across Kalamaar.

Kinhar dipped his head in agreement, smoothing his own robes. He had bought himself a cream-colored cloth several villages back to replace the brittle pale robe he had adorned. The new, stitched robe was hardly worth the cost in Branimir's opinion. By and by, the two Highborn appeared to have an elevated station with the new attire.

It was only Dorofej who refused to change his mangled garb. That is, he and Branimir, who had not been given the option. Dorofej had said the dried blood and sweat gave his clothes character.

"A King has duty to his entire realm, to administer the law, yes? Occurring in more than just large cities, disease, murder, and squabbling does," Dorofej argued.

"He has Jarls in every village on the Seven Islands, across the countryside, and further down the coastline. The Jarls should travel to the King and take his law back to their domain, not the other way around," Falmagon said. He did not bother to look back at Dorofej to see the reaction to the reasonable suggestion, but Branimir did. Dorofej's face tightened in disapproval beneath his beard and mustache.

"Hopes of recompense in the hereafter helps man survive this difficult life, yes? Hope, like faith, is required to endure hardship, but it can be a fleeting." Dorofej took a breath before continuing. "If there is no sign of existing, a god will not have believers. It is the same, yes? An icon for hope and be seen, a King must be, lest the country will crumble."

Falmagon snorted in disapproval but said nothing.

As they neared, Branimir noticed that the construction of Arkaim was like other settlements in Kalamaar. The buildings were variable in size, built square from wooden frames, each layered with a straw roof. Steppingstone walls had just begun to be assembled around Arkaim to replace dug palisades that had probably provided its defense for the past century. Boulders, chiseled from the Crags, were laid about the terrain in heaps in preparation for stacking. The sight was exceptional to the eye; strange devices of harvested timber fastened with pulleys and levers and rope. Portions of the wall were scattered about the perimeter of Arkaim.

"Lucky, you are," Dorofej motioned to the flapping tapestries of the golden scepter, Svehla, the signet of King Ker. "The banners are hung, meaning the King is within the city, yes? How wonderful it is that the Highborn Longwalker can share his remarkable insight on leadership with royalty, yes?"

"Maybe I will." Falmagon shockingly showed considerable restraint.

"Enough already," Kinhar said as they passed through the wooden gates of the Arkaim.

The city was alive. Branimir kept his hand near the back of the black robes of Dorofej, as to not lose sight of the Highborn in the throng of people scattered about the city. If they caught him alone, Branimir feared they may beat him like Falmagon had with his crooked staff.

Branimir surveyed men and women as they muddled down the streets, accompanied by children who ran wildly about. Some children squalled at the sight of Branimir, taking off in the opposite direction. Some of the humans also took special notice of the Kras, and steered clear of the traveling fellowship.

Branimir was not quite accustomed to the reaction, but it was similar to how he had been welcomed within the hamlets of Kalamaar. These people must also believe that he was some sort of a demon.

The Kras had really been forgotten in the world of men.

Branimir pushed away his thoughts of being alone. He had to accept that he was the last of his kind. He did not want to think about what that meant for him.

"What news of the south?" A man shouted, raising his hand at them. "You haven't been to Arkaim since last harvest, Falmagon."

Falmagon stopped immediately and gestured in recognition, as though he had been looking for the yellow-toothed grunt standing at the edge of the street.

Falmagon led the group away from the red dirt road and introduced the man. "Unnvar Grondahl. He drinks at the Kal'bane up the road here."

"Drink at it?" Unnvar hit Falmagon on the shoulder with a meaty hand. The human stood a head taller than the Highborn, with muscle as thick as an ox. "I own the alehouse, you lout."

Falmagon rubbed a hand through his greasy hair, a smile plastered on his face. "You wouldn't know it. Find you thrown in the streets more often than the drunks."

"My father always said if you were going to do something, to do it right!"

Falmagon threw his head back with a laugh that was outside of the man's regular character. He slapped Unnvar on the back in embrace. "Missed you, ole' chump. Good to see that you aren't settled in an urn."

Branimir kept quiet but found himself surprised that Falmagon could be jolly with anyone.

"I'm fortunate of that. I hear those in the south aren't as lucky." Unnvar wiped slime from his nose to his pant leg, snot caught in a thick mustache. "Who travels in your company? Friends or chumps?"

"A mixture of both, I'm afraid," Falmagon said. "Kinhar Sayan, you have met before, though some time ago."

"Kinhar," Unnvar bellowed in near disbelief, "you don't look to have aged a day since we last met. How, under Dahz's light, have you done it?"

Kinhar nodded light-heartedly in relative familiarity to the burly innkeeper. "Abstinence from worldly pleasures?"

Unnvar scoffed. "I know abstinence from pleasure, but not from self-restraint like you insane Highborn. I'll tell you that. I've been wedded for fifteen years. Hasn't done a lick of good for my body?" Unnvar slapped his stomach that protruded slightly over the line of his trousers.

"That it has not," Falmagon agreed with a hoot, his smile stretching the scar along his cheekbone. "The other is Dorofej, and the Kras is Branimir Baran."

"Not a demon, then? Haven't seen your kind before, although Falmagon has talked about it, I suppose, more than once. I say, you fit the fireside story, though most would say the Kras are myth. A walking testimony you are, eh?"

Branimir dipped his head, unsure how to respond.

Unnvar coughed with another snort, quickly blowing his nose into his hand and wiping it on his clothing. "Well, enough of this. Come to the Kal'bane to fill your bellies and get a good rest. We can talk over some brew about the rumors of Netherworld demons raiding villages upon the Seven Islands and along the coasts. Gossip is that they come this way bringing mayhem and war. Arkaim is in all sorts of a fuss about the nonsense. Part of me thinks they are trying to construct that wall in defense, as if that won't take half their lives to do. Royals are as dumb as slaves sometimes."

Kinhar interrupted, "We have already lost much time, Unnvar. Your invitation is welcomed, but we *must* speak to Erzebeth."

"Erzebeth? Erzebeth Navenka?"

Kinhar nodded his head. "That is the one. It is important that we speak to her. Do you know her location?"

"That I do, regrettably. The woman has been imprisoned for the better part of two months for thieving," Unnvar's face scrunched up. "Not a trade she will be practicing again, I am sure, if she is ever released."

"Ever released?" Branimir said in a higher pitch than he intended.

Unnvar shook his head. "Indeed. King Kar is under no compulsion to hold trial, especially after the punishment has already been inflicted. Erzebeth is chained in the jails, paraded about as a token and reminder to other thieves of Arkaim justice."

Kinhar's eyes narrowed, his voice was dangerously dark, "Justice? What did Merreider Kar do to her?"

Unnvar looked about the street, but the people paid no heed to their conversation. "Severed her hand and hung it from her neck as a bloody token of her deed. It is a ghastly thing, rotten and beset with maggots."

Branimir's stomach churned. "What?"

"The Lightbringer have mercy…" Falmagon began.

"And, I'd be sure to address the King with his title when speaking his name, Kinhar. I have no personal qualm, and no disrespect, but as stealing takes the hand so does blasphemy steal the tongue. The King's blades are always sharpened and swift to deliver punishment."

Kinhar sneered. "I'll speak as I wish how I wish."

Unnvar contorted his face, clearly meaning to stay on good terms with the Highborn. "Be wary of your audience is all I am saying."

"Quite alright, Unnvar," Falmagon calmly whispered.

Kinhar dipped his head, apologetically. "Forgive my harshness. I forget myself as it has been a tiresome journey from Folkmar. All in all, Erzebeth must be retrieved at once, if we must level Arkaim, so be it. King Kar *will* take an audience with the Highborn."

Unnvar shook his head. "Luck is not so much in your favor, friend. You come to Arkaim during the Festival of Dahz."

"Great." Kinhar's scowl deepened. Falmagon looked equally distraught.

"The King does not see anyone this week," Unnvar said. "He is organizing the events in preparation for the Season of Frost, while we make wolf feasts to protect the herds."

"Wolf feasts?" Branimir pulled at his hooked nose with confusion.

His question was ignored, and instead the focus fell to Dorofej, who spoke with a smile. "After months of hearty travel, what is a week of rest, yes? By all means, lead the way to the alehouse and bring the plum whilst we wait."

Falmagon pulled at his mustache and mumbled under his breath. Even to Branimir's sensitive ears, the words were inaudible.

Chapter XI

Dorofej sipped the wine from the copper cup casually, his frosty eyes fixated on the clay hearth in the central of the one main room of Kal'bane. As with most housing units, the hearth served as a furnace for heat and a kiln to prepare meals.

Branimir did not have any alcohol, nearly afraid to have it touch his lips. He sat relaxed and cross-legged on one of the many beds that protruded into the main living area of the alehouse. The bed was made of straw and covered with blankets of sheep skin. The bedsteads at Melkorka had been naught but stone, meant to teach the value of simplicity to those who resided there, Highborn and Kras alike. This was, by far, the noblest bed Branimir had ever had the pleasure to rest upon.

Kinhar and Falmagon were not as concerned about having the malt. They each held a tankard in hand, enjoying the cheap drink served at the alehouse. Hours ago, supper of porridge and roasted lamb had been consumed. It had been a hearty meal, far better than anything that had touched their stomachs on the road or within the walls of Melkorka.

None of the Highborn paid much attention to Unnvar, who escorted the last of the townsfolk outside into the night before closing the wooden door over the fitted stone slab. The wooden bar was soon secured within the fitted holes of the door jambs.

The innkeeper then took his time closing the wooden shutters that covered the two windows at the forefront of the building.

All in all, the alehouse was cozy, warmed by the inner fire, the smoke taking leave through a hole in the thatched roof. The structure had been built above the ground on midden, giving it more insulation and stability. In the winter months, it surely would fare well against the nipping winds of the North.

Unnvar moved idly past his family and children who filled several of the beds in the room, lifting his own tankard of ale. "Finally, we are alone. Again, I ask what news of the south? Of Melkorka?"

Falmagon, being most familiar with the man, spoke, a rueful look on his scarred face. "Melkorka has fallen, the Highborn nearly doused along with it."

Unnvar lowered his head. "I was fearful that it was true. Rumor rarely holds so much detail as to what had been shared…villagers flooding northbound with stories too similar…and when I saw you this day…I am thankful you did not share that lot, Falmagon."

Falmagon raised his drink. "It'll take more than the rise of demons to steal the charge I must see through."

"You were always the dour sort, even as a child, so grandfather had said. It is good that you have become Highborn. It suits you better than being a Northman."

Branimir rocked forward, hearing that Falmagon was not born Highborn. He had become it! What was it that made a human a Highborn opposed to a Northman? How had he not understood this earlier? The Kras piped up from the cot, speaking without thinking, "You are brothers, Lord Falmagon?"

Falmagon, for once, did not retort at the Kras. It was likely that the alcohol had calmed his tensions. "No, but kin still. His mother was my father's sister from what I know, each long dead and resting in tranquility in the Beyond."

"So, we pray," Unnvar said.

Kinhar, also impacted by the strong liquor that amassed in his belly, spoke in slur, "Just a boy child when our paths crossed. You were nearly an infant, barely able to walk. As an orphan being raised by a man who was too old to care for himself, I had little difficulty convincing your grandfather to let me take you to Melkorka. The craft of Koldovstvo was imprinted on your soul, marking you as a prodigy, to achieve greatness, even at such a young age. A gift bestowed on you by the gods as payment for stealing your parents away to the hereafter."

"Prodigy, indeed," Dorofej muttered with derision, heard only by Branimir. Dorofej gulped the rest of the wine in his clay cup. Branimir was not sure how the man could even taste the drink as fast as he was swallowing it. The wrinkled Highborn hurriedly filled it and gulped it down again before filling it once more.

Falmagon shrugged. "To be stolen to the Beyond is a boon I would wish upon any man, as opposed to living this life."

Unnvar slapped his knee. "Hear, hear! Frailty, disease, death. What was Perom thinking when he created man into existence? What was Svarog thinking when he commended man to be created? What was Dahz thinking when he shielded man from annihilation? The will of the gods I will never understand. I suppose that is why they are divine, and I am a Northman."

Dorofej again spoke in tones that only the Branimir could hear, sipping on his plum wine. "The only reason understanding evades you, it's not."

Branimir scratched his black hair. Dorofej was abnormally bitter as of late. But it was the mention of the handful of gods that caused Branimir's confusion. Overall, there were more gods than he would ever be aware. The Kras generally only heard of Dahz from the Highborn, particularly from Kinhar and Falmagon. Though, as Nedezhda had clearly indicated before her execution, the Highborn were meant to hold allegiance to no specific deity. Branimir had a diminutive understanding of human law, but his family had served the Highborn over many lifetimes. The Kras had a basic interpretation of their beliefs, even when he did not understand their mannerisms. His father had told him of a time when Dahz's sigil had not hung on the walls of Melkorka.

A pounding on the wooden door interrupted Branimir's thoughts and the conversation of the men.

"Coming," Unnvar hollered, quickly glancing at his family that lay sound asleep before making his way to the door.

"Late hour for visitors," Kinhar commented, slumping back in his chair.

Falmagon took the interruption as an opportunity to refill his tankard. He offered the same to Kinhar.

Unnvar unfastened the door, cracking it slightly to peer out before opening it fully. An older gentleman dressed fairer than a peasant but not at the class of nobility, near Kinhar's age, stepped into the Kal'bane. At first, his face appeared relieved to see the Highborn but as he scanned the room, his face fell in dismay.

"Lubos, what can I do you for at this hour?"

"My daughter," the man was nearly weeping. "Where is she?"

"Your daughter?"

"That man," Lubos pointed at Falmagon accusingly, "he took her to Melkorka! It was his tongue that swayed her to become Highborn!"

Kinhar began, "I—"

Lubos didn't hear him. "I have heard the stories. I know Melkorka has been deserted and that the Highborn have run away to Arkaim. I have heard it as I have passed through every village this side of the cursed Crags. Where is my daughter, Highborn scum?"

Unnvar raised his hand, "My family sleeps, Lubos—"

"Where is she? Where is Katerina?"

Branimir scurried off the animal skin to the far corner, away from the enraged Northman, the merchant father of Katerina Gajic. The answer was already as obvious as it could be. There could be no painless way to say that which had no need to be said.

"Split legs from torso by the demonic Bukavac, she was. Her blood showered down like a mid-spring rain." Dorofej sniffed, his eyes remaining on the kiln.

Branimir gulped. The white-haired Highborn had chosen a method far less than accommodating.

Lubos's jaw fell, tears crashing to planks at his feet before words could be formed, "What—"

"I know," Dorofej inhaled again, licking the wine from his mustache, "a good pair of breasts is hard to come by, yes?"

Branimir could have sworn Dorofej nodded in agreement with himself.

"Dorofej!" Kinhar roared, suddenly very sober.

"Cursed Highborn!" Lubos lunged for Dorofej with outstretched hands.

Unnvar caught Lubos before he had taken two steps. He clenched him in his grizzly arms holding the man firmly against his massive chest and broad shoulders. If it were possible, it was likely that the merchant would have chewed through his flesh to free himself from Unnvar, living only to murder Dorofej.

Dorofej did not budge.

Lubos kicked wildly toward the tables and beds, off the walls, fighting as though he were an animal in a snare. It did not take long for Unnvar's wife and children to be awakened. The children, barely bigger than Branimir, cried out in panic. The wife hurried to crowd them into a corner protectively. Branimir listened to the woman's voice, squawking at Lubos and her husband to end their folly.

Lubos, try as he might, could not gain leverage against the massive innkeeper as he continued the endless struggle. Unnvar would have made an impressive blacksmith.

"Calm yourself, Lubos!"

Lubos's wails should have made his throat bleed. His tears could have flooded the caverns of Illuard. His wrath could have reached the far ends of the unmapped world. Branimir cried out in unison with the sound, covering his sensitive ears.

In short time, two sentries, with padded armor and copper swords pushed into Kal'bane, drawn by the lamenting shouts of the merchant.

"Unnvar! Labos!" the first sentry lifted his voice over the din. "What madness is this?"

Branimir moved his hands from his ears to his eyes, peeking in panic through spread fingertips.

"Die, Highborn!" Labos finally pulled an arm free, elbowing Unnvar in the side.

The innkeeper held his ground, "Take him away from here."

The guardsmen did not hesitate, determined to keep the peace. There was no oddity in removing a belligerent man, kicking and screaming, hard-set on fighting, from the alehouse.

They each took an arm of Lubos and pulled him from Kal'bane. The merchant, overcome with lunacy, continued to wrangle about. His expletives were heard as he was dragged down the dirt streets of Arkaim.

"It is a marvel that merchant would have any success in his trade with such manners, yes?"

Unnvar slammed the door shut. The house rattled.

"Do you desire death, Dorofej?" Falmagon heaved with clenched fists. "Look at the mark you leave on the Highborn! Have you no honor? Integrity? Decency? I thought you were Highborn!"

Branimir could not tell if Dorofej's face reddened from wine or temper. The clay cup dropped from his hand, shattering on the floor near his feet as he sprung from his chair and turned on Falmagon. "I am Highborn!" Dorofej's voice boomed grander than a thousand trumpets at war, the room darkening. It was as if some unmarked spell had been cast.

"My hand, you forced, in crafting Kaelandur to spill Highborn blood. Imposing your own justice outside of the King's law, naive or uncaring of the harm inflicted! Binding me to the fate of this warped tale, you do, endangering all Northmen and beyond! A timeless war, you have incited, while wearing a mask of purity with the divergence of a virgin harlot!"

"Nedezhda's blood is on your hands, as heavy as any Highborn, if not more." Falmagon squinted his single eye, revealing Kaelandur from his brown robes. "Chance you'd like to taste its edge, too, Dorofej?"

Branimir whimpered. "No."

No one heard him.

The white-haired man was riled, hands shaking as he spoke, dark robes blending with the darkness that enveloped the room. "An impertinent, impenitent dupe, you are, Falmagon Sej. You are no more a prodigy than any other swine pulled from a sow's hind legs! I can only presume that your vast ignorance is caused by your ill-fit mother breeding out of season. You give sight to the dead!"

Falmagon charged with Kaelandur toward the black-robed Highborn but was quickly caught by an invisible strand of rope. The air wrapped around him, holding him steadily in place.

"Dorofej!" Kinhar barked, stepping between them. His hovering hand signaled he held the Highborn Longwalker in place with Koldovstvo. "What do you mean he gives 'sight to the dead'?"

"There is good cause why Highborn do not craft man-made weapons," Dorofej's voice quivered, icy eyes locked on the copper dagger stretched toward him. He spoke as though his words were the last lungful of air in his body, chock full with nightmarish foreboding.

"The Highborn are bound to Koldovstvo, through spirit and blood by the blessings of the divine, for Highborn, we are. With creation, we infect that which is touched, as we are all touched by the divine at our creation, and so, infected by their breath. With such contagion within us, the living are not easily destroyed, even after death, passing to the Beyond or the Netherworld, another life, another providence. So, it is the fate of the weapons that the Highborn create.

"Kaelandur cannot be damaged by any worldly means, and as it consumes life, the weapon will grow in strength, and the victims grow in resilience, tempted to use the weapon with unmeasured enticement. Falmagon's display of Kaelandur has beaconed Nedezhda to Arkaim's gate!"

"Dahz save us." Unnvar dropped to his knees, any vehemence toward Dorofej was seemingly drained.

Kinhar cried out, "Why have you said nothing?"

"Carve our own fates, we must, and you are the spearhead of the Highborn, who should know these things, yes?" Dorofej answered. "And how could I know that you had Kaelandur among you? Highborn only by name, it is, and torn asunder through secrecy, yes? Tell me what else you hide from me?"

Branimir wanted to scream out the word *Kindari*. He wanted to tell the secrets of Kinhar and the Ash Tree. But, more than anything, all Branimir could think was that Falmagon planned to kill Dorofej. His chest tightened as he restrained himself from speaking the truth.

Falmagon's deep voice croaked, realizing his fault, "Nedezhda's life has been appropriated twice by this blade, once in life and once in death."

Dorofej collapsed to the ground, the gloom flooding from the room as though it had never been. "Abandon hope, for thieved by halfwits, it has been."

As tears swelled in Dorofej's eyes, it was the weeping of Branimir that was heard. It was not the words he wanted to hear, but it spoke of the vainness of the Highborn's quest. In killing Nedezhda again, she had become more powerful.

Branimir saw Kinhar release Falmagon from the clutches of Koldovstvo and then join Dorofej on the floor in a heap. Only a few seconds elapsed before Kinhar spoke with intent to restore lost hope, to continue the tale. A single name was all that could be considered that might give way to the glory coveted. "Erzebeth. Erzebeth will know a way to make this right."

Chapter XII

The morning was filled with gloom. An overhang of clouds obstructed the sun from view. The world was so full of grey that it seemed the cold months were already upon Kalamaar.

"Bad omen," Unnvar said looking at the dark clouds that shadowed the crowd gathered in the town square. "By no means will the Season of Frost be mild this year."

Branimir trembled in the zephyr that blew southeast off the western coastline. The scent of saltwater and fish was stout this morning. Indeed, winter was already on the wind's breath.

"How long is this going to take? Do we really have to do this every day?" One of Unnvar's children pulled at their mother's long, layered skirts.

Branimir watched in amazement. He had seen many children in the past month as he journeyed through villages, but never in the context of parent to child. If only Mojmir were here now to see that the Highborn did not come from lightning bolts.

Dorofej whistled between his teeth, setting his old hand on Branimir's shoulder tenderly, as if reading his mind and giving comfort, like a grandfather over his grandchild. The two of them walked down the road still in the company of the other Highborn and Unnvar's family. The horde gathered from their homes around them, falling in step with other townsfolk who funneled to the center of Arkaim.

Branimir tried his best to ignore the idle chitchat among the commoners.

"I'll be done soon enough," Unnvar responded over the stirring hum. "The sacrifice has to be made each day during the Festival, or we will not receive Dahz's blessing."

The center of the town was marked by the front of the courtyard that led to King Kar's manor house. The King's living quarters were multiple stories tall, which was unheard of anywhere outside of Arkaim. To see a building with multiple rooms that was not a castle, not Melkorka, Branimir was flabbergasted. King Kar had outdone himself when having it built.

Cheers and applause replaced the chatter among the crowd as a string of guards in layered armor, made of leather upon stitched cloth, made their way from the manor house into the King's Courtyard.

Unnvar cheered in a booming tone, forming no words, along with the deafening crowd. He lifted one of his small children on his shoulders to see more clearly. Branimir looked at the small child in envy. All he could see was the back of Falmagon and Kinhar. They were fifty yards from the guards, at minimum, with people shoulder to shoulder every step of the way.

"Do not fret, Branimir." Dorofej shouted above the roar of the masses. "Missing much, you are not."

Branimir raised his head at Dorofej. "I do not even know what I am not missing."

As he finished his sentence, the townsfolk quieted down. Several looked toward him, stepping away. He knew how odd he may appear to them with his pale eyes, hooked nose, and blood skin.

Branimir stuck his tongue out at them in response. He was accustomed to being treated unfairly, but the response of the Northmen was wearing on him.

"Branimir, mind yourself, yes?" Dorofej rustled through his fuzzy whiskers.

He turned his head away and frowned at the buttocks of the other Highborn, frustrated. "Yes, my Lord."

A voice at the front boomed, addressing the people of Arkaim with authority, "On this day, we offer the sacrifice to Dahz, the Lightbringer, Protector of Men, the White-Clad, who convinced Perom, the Creator, to make man in the image of the gods. Dahz carries Mulafell, the Hammer of Righteousness, steadfast while guiding his chariot, Mioengi, over the expanse, carrying the sun from our world to the Beyond."

Branimir pulled on Dorofej's black robes, feeling braver in raising questions with his curious mind. "Who is speaking, my Lord? What is he talking about?"

"The Viceroy, possibly," Dorofej said. "He speaks for the King when the King is not here and apparently when he is, yes? A reiteration of custom, and nothing more, the speech is."

An animal bleating rang from the King's Courtyard. Branimir heard it as clearly as Dorofej's words. He looked at the withered Highborn for explanation. "They are killing something, aren't they, my Lord?"

"Yes. I say, a red stag is being brought to the chopping block by rope. Large, beautiful, and magnificent, the beast is. Its blood will be drained from its neck, yes? An offering to Dahz, it is. Before the day is out, the stag will be dragged outside the palisades for the wolves to feast upon, yes?"

Branimir was dumbfounded. "They will waste the meat, my Lord?"

"This is the practice, the primordial custom, of the Northmen, yes? Passed down through word of mouth from father to son since the birth of man on Kalamaar, it has been. All things have been done this way among humans. Tradition demands lavishness without question, even with the Kras, yes?"

The stag bellowed in the distance.

"My Lord, I would not know." Bran was growing tired of this feeling of emptiness but could not seem to rid himself of it. At every turn was another reminder of his lonesomeness.

Dorofej grunted, and looked off in the distance, murmuring to himself as if being reminded of some faint thought or dream. Then, with frightening certainty, he said, "You may never know, yes?"

Falmagon turned his head. "Quiet yourselves, will you? This is not the time."

For once, Dorofej had no response for the one-eyed Highborn and sealed his lips with respect to the ceremony of the Festival of Dahz.

Branimir turned back to face the Highborn that stood before him. Kinhar had barely seemed to take notice of the Viceroy speaking and looked through the people standing about.

The Viceroy continued his rhetoric. "Dahz the White-Clad, praise be sung for the life you gave, the sacrifice you undertook. The sustenance you provide in your holy light nourishes life, laying waste to our suffering. This stag is offered as sacrifice to cool your fury. Come, come quick to release us from the Frost."

The stag wheezed and bleated, grunted and bellowed in defiance to the sacred practice of the Northmen, as though it knew what was to come. Its hooves beat against the dusty ground, stamping and pawing for release, the rope tightened around its neck. A growl reverberated in the animal's throat, but the sentries held fast.

Branimir nearly had to cover his pointed ears as the dirges of the beast rose over the speech of the Viceroy. It was painful to hear, even after what he had witnessed at Melkorka and at Illuard.

Kinhar, apparently giving up in his search, turned to watch the ceremony.

A drum sounded in the King's courtyard, and those in the town square spoke in unison, a song repeated generation upon generation. Branimir was not sure why, but he was absolutely astonished to watch Kinhar, Falmagon, and even Dorofej, merge their own voices to recite the tale, told from grandfather to father to child for all of time.

White-Clad said unto Perom,
Before the Grandfather of Gods,
"The expanse above and under,
Beyond Thrice Nine Lands,
None is worthy of sacrifice,
Nor of praise to covenant.
Construct that which is worthy,
That will sheen in utmost glory."

Thunder-Bearer said unto Svarog,
Before the Lightbringer with Mulafell,
"O how unworthy must we be,
Without welcome, without veneration,
Across the expanse of neither here nor there,
All creation unworthy of covenant.
Bless me to make the worthy,
That will sheen in utmost glory."

Keeper of Kowin the Deathless,
Lord of Lords, said unto Perom and Dahz,
"Craft the Northmen, called Anshedar,
Craft the Highborn, called Anshedar,
Beyond the expanse of here nor there,
Impart unto them the covenant,
Give them charge; pray they are worthy,
To fulfill for all time, for glory."

We are worthy, O Dahz the Lightbringer.
For utmost glory, O Dahz the White-Clad.

Branimir heard the knife plunge into the thick skin of the stag. He did not have to see it. The bawling cries of the deer were silenced, its throat cut in this fruitless moment.

The townsfolk of Arkaim raised their hands, roaring in approval of the sacrifice, praying to Dahz the Lightbringer that it would be enough to lessen their struggles in the winter months to come. As was the circumstance every year, the Northmen yearned for a short winter.

"A vain deed," Kinhar said, turning to face the rest of them. His eyes scanned the clouded skies above. "Dahz has turned his eyes away from us this day. It is unlikely that the Lightbringer will be welcoming of this sacrifice."

Falmagon nodded. "I feel it, too. Our worthiness is to be tested. We are on our own in this quest."

Unnvar shooed his family back toward the alehouse and huffed up at the three men in their robes. "Not completely. I have given it thought since our conversation last night, Highborn. I will accompany you, at your will, until this evil has been forced from Kalamaar and back into the trenches of the Netherworld where it belongs."

Dorofej watched the innkeeper's family depart. "Obligations here in Arkaim, you have, yes? What does your wife say?"

"I do not need my wife's approval, Dorofej. I choose my own path."

Branimir's jaw dropped. The innkeeper clearly had just sent his wife away before announcing his decision. The scowl beneath Dorofej's beard suggested he had come to the same conclusion.

"You know not what you ask, Unnvar," Kinhar replied.

"I know well enough what tales I have heard of Highborn and what peril follows your number. Though, death in battle brings more glory to my family name than my throat being slit by demons while I sleep."

Dorofej said, "Chance of either fate is not altered by the road we travel, yes? Your throat still may find itself split open and your family name without honor, yes?"

Unnvar insisted, "Your numbers are lacking. I can offer more than what this Kras can provide, that much is for certain. Will you have me?"

"Fleeting, certainty is."

Falmagon ignored Dorofej's clashing comment. "I welcome you gladly among us, Unnvar, as kin and friend."

Kinhar nodded. "I do not contend with your words, Unnvar. If you wish to come along, I will not hold you from it. Though, our priority in this instance is to reach Erzebeth. You had said she would be here this morning?"

"I did." Unnvar nodded at the King's Courtyard at Kinhar's back.

The five of them, Branimir included, looked onward at the Courtyard expectantly. The town's people had meandered out of the square, back to their shops, to their homes, and to their daily obligations, leaving full view of King Kar's manor house and courtyard.

The red stag lay bleeding, dead at the feet of the several guardsmen who had led it by rope to the slaughter. They worked idly to clean the yard, preparing the stag to be dragged to the wolves, and for another slaughter tomorrow morning.

The doors to the manor house opened, and out stepped four guards, suited in their padded armor and equipped with copper swords. The woman, known as Erzebeth Navenka, trailed behind them into the King's Courtyard.

Even at a hundred yards, Branimir could see the prominent woman that Kinhar continuously spoke of as though she were a deliverer of their salvation, destined to pull them from the clutches of their own folly.

Erzebeth was a tall, slender woman with dark disheveled hair that hung to her shoulders, as unkempt as Falmagon's. Her eyes were blue like that of all the Highborn and Northmen, marking her among their kind. Her skin was exceptionally pale, more so than most of the humans upon Kalamaar. Though this may have been from residing in a cell for the past month. It was hard for Branimir to say.

The most distinguishing feature on Erzebeth was the decomposing hand that hung from her neck, missing from her right arm. Under her dilapidated white cloak, more rags than cloak, the severed hand hung loosely. The stub had been cared for with relatively decent precision, considering it being a penalty for a crime of thievery. Bone and flesh had been sewn shut and cauterized, seemingly healed as well as it could be.

"In the mornings she walks about the courtyard," Unnvar said. "As I said, a constant reminder to those that may employ thievery here in Arkaim."

"Why was her wrist mended? Why did they not let her die, my Lords?" Branimir asked.

"It is a greater punishment to live in dishonor and humiliation than to be allowed to die," Kinhar puffed, clearly upset after seeing Erzebeth in her deprived state.

"How long has she been put on display?" Falmagon shuddered.

"Since the hand was cut off," Unnvar answered.

"Bah! Enough of this." Kinhar scowled. "We have wasted enough time. The King will have counsel with the Highborn this very moment."

Kinhar stuffed his hands to his sides in fists and entered the King's Courtyard without hesitation. Falmagon and Unnvar quickly jumped in step with Kinhar, warily watching the four guards and Erzebeth walking about the courtyard.

"This is unwise," Dorofej said from behind Branimir, "and yet, naught else can be done. Here we go, yes?"

Dorofej pushed Branimir forward to catch up with the other three men, and Dorofej hobbled along, covering the rear.

They had only taken three steps into the King's courtyard when Branimir noticed from the corner of his eye that Erzebeth had raised her head. The woman held her gaze longingly toward the men that approached the manor house. Her eyes gave away her recognition of the men, and although not one of them returned the gaze, a glimmer of hope surfaced on her trodden face.

"Hold there," a guard jumped up from the slain deer. He ran forward and stepped in front of Kinhar.

The Highborn did not slow his pace and walked right around the man as though he had said nothing. In moments, the group was nearly halfway across the courtyard.

"I said 'hold' or you will be cut down!"

Branimir was the first to see the archers on either side of the manor house. A quick count told him that there were nine, already with the arrows nocked on the luks, or shortbows.

Kinhar stopped. "I wish to see King Merreider Kar. He necessitates my counsel."

The guard moved his body in front of the grey-haired Highborn, taking a deep breath, seemingly outmatched with Falmagon and Unnvar on either side, but well protected by the archers at his rear. "King Kar does not receive *counsel* from anyone during the Festival, and when he does receive any *counsel*, he decides when it is necessary. Now, return the way you have come, or you will be cut down where you stand."

Kinhar's eyes were cold, staring into the guard's eyes for what felt to Bran like the entire harvest past. "You will take me to the King. I am Highborn, and I will give him *counsel* as I choose when I choose. If you refuse, I *will* cut you down!"

The man's eyes quaked in hesitation, the word 'Highborn' shaped his mouth, likely determining whether he should believe the threat or consider it rubbish.

The guards approached them as the door to the manor house opened again. The Viceroy stepped forward, with a copper sword in one hand and a rod in the other, marking his position.

"I am Viceroy Stepan Komarov, the voice of King Kar. What is going on here? Who are you?" he demanded.

Kinhar put his hand on the guard and shoved him to the side, taking two bold steps toward the Viceroy, who lifted his sword in response. "Kinhar Sayan, Highborn from Melkorka upon the Seven Islands, and I will speak with the King, lest he wishes the destruction of all Arkaim and the end of whatever legacy he plans to bestow on his children, Viceroy Komarov."

Stepan kept his sword at the ready. "We were informed that Melkorka had fallen and that the Highborn were dead. I'd say you are a bit late to attempt such a ploy here."

"We are not all dead," Kinhar declared, taking another step toward the Viceroy. Falmagon stepped forward as well, leading with his crooked staff, Habërmani, holding his typical iron visage.

"Leave this place," the Viceroy said with poise, "and do not return."

"I will speak to Merreider Kar."

"What is this? You outwardly refuse to address the King by his title, and in front of the law at that!" the Viceroy exclaimed. "Sacrilege! Penalty by death!"

"Wha—"

Unnvar did not have a chance to finish his protest before archers released their sharpened projectiles. The arrows flew with precision from their luks toward the lot of them.

For once, Branimir was not surprised when the stone wall flung up, stopping the arrows and snapping them in half. As the wall fell away, as quickly as it had formed, the archers immediately reached for another round from their quiver. Kinhar swept his hand toward them, tearing the luks from their grasp one by one and flinging them back toward the town square. The guard that had stood nearest reached for his sword but was struck across the jaw by Habërmani. He slumped to the ground in a heap.

Kinhar flew across the ground to the Viceroy's side, though his feet never moved, the wind carrying him a hundred paces in a heartbeat. His tone was as full of authority as it had ever been. "Do not speak to me of sacrilege. I am Highborn! I know what is sacred better than any Northmen. Now, show me to your King."

Stepan did not muddle over the demand. The archers had been disarmed and the guards would prove equally useless against such power.

He cleared his throat. "Follow this way, Highborn."

Kinhar pointed to Erzebeth with commanding authority. "The woman comes with us."

"I—"

It did not take more than a look from the spearhead of the Highborn to cut the Viceroy from any dispute.

"Very well. Bring her along," the Viceroy yielded.

"Dorofej and Unnvar remain here at the door," Kinhar ordered as they stepped toward the manor house. "If any one of these men attempts to enter these doors before we have exited, Dorofej will use Koldovstvo to rip out the man's intestines."

Dorofej's bushy eyebrows could not have lifted any further off his forehead. "Kinhar, hardly do I—"

Kinhar kept his chin suspended, a sudden reminder of who held sway over the Highborn. "Will you not, Dorofej?"

Dorofej blinked several times before painting a wide grin on his face. His tone raised with unmatched giddiness as though ripping intestines from men was his favorite pastime. "Like gutting a fish, yes?"

Color completely drained from the Viceroy's face. He gave further direction to the archers and sentries. "Yes, well, each of you stay out here, and wait for our return."

In a matter of moments, Branimir found himself being led into the manor house. The Viceroy's footsteps were quickened as they made their way into the two-story building, hurrying to end this madness once and for all.

Kinhar and Falmagon walked ahead of Branimir. The Kras looked uneasily behind him at Erzebeth, her skin as white as frost.

The tall woman followed behind with her head lowered, her eyes averted from Branimir, and locked on the hand hanging from her neck. There was no mistake. The woman was actually smiling, a gleam in her eye.

Branimir winced.

They were led into a large room where the King's chair sat against the backdrop of violet tapestries. The signet of the King, the

Svehla, was sewn with gold thread upon the fabric. It was the same as the banners outside the gates of Arkaim.

The chair itself was made from wood, possibly elm from the nearby forests, inscribed with circlets of an alloy in which Branimir was not familiar. It had a hint of the orange found in copper but with a darker brown color to it. Branimir was intrigued, as each circlet held a small diamond. He barely noticed King Kar sitting on his throne.

"King Merreider Kal, Twelfth King of Kalamaar, Bearer of the Svehla, the Golden Scepter of Svarog, I present Kinhar Sayan, Highborn of Melkorka from Folkmar, upon the Seven Islands of Forghar."

Branimir did as the Viceroy did, kneeling on one knee in respect of the nobility before him. As for Kinhar and Falmagon, their necks were as stiff as stale bread. Branimir could only guess that Erzebeth held a similar stature as the Highborn men, snickering under her breath behind him.

King Kar sat with elbow on knee, a piercing gaze behind a flat nose and beneath a balding scalp. "What is the meaning of this, Stepan?" He waved off two servants that were near the throne. They bowed and made their way out of the room. "It is the Festival of Dahz."

Viceroy Stepan Komarov stood. "I am aware, my King. These men—"

Kinhar interjected, "We must set aside custom for what comes, King Kar. Have you not heard of the battle at Melkorka? The Bukavac who march on Kalamaar? The hell that comes to claim the lives of Arkaim? Why do you not prepare for battle? Why do you waste hours slaying stags and feeding wolves?"

The King stood up from his throne with a clenched jaw. Irritation immediately lined the wrinkles in his forehead. His voice was unmatched. The King surely was accustomed to speaking to those lesser who flooded his courtroom. Smoothing the fur cloak, he rumbled, "What right do you have to speak to royalty in this way? The Highborn have an oath to protect the King and the law of men. Your twisted tongue does not mark you as Highborn. Such brashness in Arkaim will only end with your head on a wooden spike, Highborn or not."

Falmagon hit his crooked staff against the ground but was stopped by Kinhar's hand.

Kinhar said, "Find forgiveness, King Kar. I know my place and my duty. I also know what evil comes, and that is why I speak with sureness, not to be confused with arrogance. My allegiance is to virtue and justice, as is yours, but war is coming."

King Kar plopped back down, his face softening considerably as though he may have accepted the quick apology. His beady eyes, sinking into his skull beneath the layers of age and fat, skimmed over the Highborn. He forced a grin with his gapped teeth. "Rumors of war and demons have haunted Kalamaar for as long as I can remember, even when my father reigned. Northmen are uneducated and full of superstition. For a month, the blathering of fools has been brought to my manor house and Arkaim still stands."

"Now," the King pressed on without breath, "tell me who this other shabby peasant is, the imp kneeling behind you, and why you have my prisoner in your possession when she should be plodding in my courtyard, inhaling the stench of her own filth. Make haste before I have you all gutted upon the palisades."

Kinhar's ears reddened. Curling his upper lip and holding clenched fists, he said, "Falmagon Sej, Highborn of Melkorka, and Branimir Baran, a Kras slave, also from Melkorka. We have traveled to Arkaim to—"

The King stood again from his throne, making his way toward Branimir. His spoke with amusement, "A Kras, you say? Well, that is something. No one has seen a Kras in two-hundred years, so they say. How can you be sure it is not a demon?"

Kinhar threw his head back and exhaled. "Branimir is not a demon. The Kras have served the Highborn for a long time and have resided at Melkorka without interruption throughout that time.

I am quite aware of what a Kras is, whether Northmen, nobility, or otherwise has seen one. Now—"

"I will keep him!" King Kar proclaimed. "He is already trained as a slave, you say? Most excellent."

"You cannot keep him. He is my property and must stay in my company."

The King did not appear to hear Kinhar. After a few more steps, he reached out and touched Branimir's red, pointed ear. The Kras kept his head stooped and shuddered again.

Bran was relieved that Kinhar was not planning on trading him off. He no longer was afraid of being killed by the Highborn, especially with Dorofej among them. But, he had the sense Kinhar might risk anything to acquire Erzebeth. At first, Branimir thought Kinhar had dragged him into the manor house for the sole purpose of trading him. Though, he now guessed it was to keep him from being alone with Dorofej.

"You cannot deny me what I want. I am the King."

"And, I am Highborn," Kinhar said.

King Kar raised his hand to strike Kinhar, but it was quickly held by a strand of air woven from Koldovstvo.

Branimir found himself sneaking a glance at the woman. She stood with exceptional composure, her lips sealed.

"Careful, my King." The Viceroy warned meekly, taking a step backward. "The Highborn's power was displayed in your courtyard. And more wait outside."

"More of them?" King Kar said nervously, struggling against the unseen hand that grasped his wrist.

Kinhar let him loose with an untamed scowl.

The King stepped back, lowering his hand in bewilderment, as though he were seeing daylight for the first time. "You are Highborn, truly?"

Falmagon and Kinhar had such fury in their eyes that they could have instigated the sun to fall across the sky backwards.

Kinhar spoke as level as he could. "I am. We are all who remain from Melkorka. We have come a long way to receive returned service, from the royal family that we have, for so many millennia, protected, King Merreider Kal, Twelfth King of Kalamaar."

"What returned service? What is it that you require?"

"The release of Erzebeth Navenka into my custody."

The King frowned. "Why do you want her? She is a thief and as unrighteous as any Northmen can be."

"She has skills that we require, skills that will ensure the protection of this kingdom and future kingdoms of men. That is all that you need to know, King Kar."

The tides had quickly turned between the Highborn and the King of Kalamaar. Branimir did not understand how the craft of Koldovstvo held sway over men, even Kings, for that matter. The Kras had never known any other way, but to the Northmen, it seemed Koldovstvo was feared beyond any nightmare they could muster.

The King looked about his manor house, considering the words of the Highborn. "I will trade her for the Kras."

Kinhar was quick in his response. "I said you could not have him. This is not a negotiation, King Kar. We are not bartering. If it were, I have already paid my dues in the deaths of the Highborn who fought against the Bukavac."

Curiosity touched the King's tongue. "What talents does this Kras have? Why would a slave be so important to you?"

Kinhar spoke carefully. "He is the last of his kind and must remain in my protection. If there were others, I would freely give him to you."

King Kar licked his lips again and rubbed a hand over his smooth scalp as though it were flooded with hair. He finally conceded, and said, "Tell me of Dorofej then. What is the fate of the old man?"

Branimir could not stop himself from gaping like a fool. Was it true that Dorofej had left Melkorka and had known the King of Arkaim? He nearly fell over from where he kneeled.

Kinhar pursed his lips, eyes widening, nearly as speechless as Branimir. "He is outside your manor house… in the courtyard."

"I will permit for you to take, Erzebeth. I have grown tired of her presence in my dungeon. But, I wish to speak with Dorofej before you leave. I want to hear of the Bukavac from him, a man who I can trust, a Highborn with whom I am familiar."

Kinhar dipped his head. "As you wish, my King." The title was spoken with a hint of mockery, barely discernible, but caught easily by the ear of the Kras, who knew the spearhead of the Highborn too well. "Branimir, fetch Dorofej and make it swift."

Branimir had no qualms in following the simple order of the Highborn, as he had for the last half century.

Chapter XIII

Unnvar had shut down the Kal'bane upon their return. He then had sent his family outside of the home to make room for Kinhar, Falmagon, Erzebeth, and Branimir. The man worked quickly to close the shutters and door as the fellowship made their way into the alehouse.

Erzebeth stumbled into the large room and slowly removed the severed hand from her neck. As though she were seeing it for the first time, she laid it down on one of the crafted tables in the room. The decomposing appendage, grey, shriveled and wilted, had maggots tearing through it. Her eyes were glued to the hand that had once been attached to her wrist.

Branimir, second behind Erzebeth, crunched up his face in disgust, feeling his stomach churn. The hand alone was worse off than any corpse he had ever seen.

"Erzebeth," Kinhar said, his feet echoing on the baseboards. She said nothing. The grey-haired man approached her from behind, embracing the woman.

Branimir watched as Erzebeth shuddered.

She lifted her good hand and placed it on his before turning around and hugging the Highborn somewhat clumsily.

Her voice quivered, holding an accent that was beyond anything Branimir had ever heard, stranger than Dorofej's. "I knew not what my fate was, but the gods have looked after me. Never would I have thought you would come to liberate me in such a dark hour."

"If I had known, I would have come all the quicker."

Falmagon dipped his head from the door. "We both would have, Erzebeth. By Mulafell, we would have!"

Branimir raised an eye at Falmagon's use of the name of Dahz's hammer. It must be a form of Highborn swearing that he was not familiar with. He had never heard a Highborn curse before.

Erzebeth forced a smile at Falmagon, taking a deep breath between clenched teeth, and still clinging to the robes of Kinhar. Her teeth were yellow against pale lips, black strands of tattered hair, strung about her face as though she had been on a battlefield for months. In this moment, she appeared to be a savage, a stranger to civilization.

That strained smile only lasted a matter of seconds, before the tears burst and her mouth opened in lamentation. She buried her face into Kinhar's shoulder.

Branimir did not want to be rude, but he had to cover his ears from the overwhelming sound of her weeping. The wailing for her suffering, the mourning for her lost hand, the grieving for her lost time was strewn together in a pitfall of misery. In all Branimir's time, he had never seen a human so vulnerable, so forsaken, as Erzebeth was in the arms of Kinhar.

After several minutes, the bear of a man, Unnvar, became noticeably uncomfortable. He shifted about the room and started to pace before muttering something about checking on his family. With that, he made his way out the door, shutting it quickly behind him.

Kinhar hushed the woman softly, rubbing her head in comfort, like a mother would with a child. Never had Branimir seen the man display such compassion.

As Erzebeth's sobbing visibly subsided, Branimir removed his hands. He could not blame her, considering she may have been withholding such pain for a month or more.

Falmagon found a seat and held Habërmani in his lap, having less feeling in his voice than Kinhar. "How did this come to be?"

Branimir was not sure what the one-eyed Highborn was referencing, but assumed he meant the missing hand from the woman's arm.

She lifted her head, eyes drained. The shallow lighting in the room caused her eyes to appear brown, and then turned blue once again. Branimir seemed to be the only one who noticed.

"I was with…I was with Ragnarok…"

"Who is Ragnarok?"

Erzebeth paused before replying. "It is no matter now. He is dead. It is well enough to know I was with…him. It was the day before harvest and Pal'ka was taking place as custom."

Falmagon lowered his eyes, taking full meaning of what it meant to be *with* Ragnarok. Pal'ka was branded as a festival of fornication among the Northmen. It was a time when lovers intermingled for the pleasures of the flesh for blessing before the harvest.

"You always looked to Myestera for guidance." Kinhar spoke in reference to the festival that worshiped the Mother of the Stars, the Moon Goddess.

"And that day was no different, though I still do not understand what she aims to tell me."

"How so?"

"I'm trying to explain. Arkaim was enjoying the bonfires, filling their evening with drinking and dancing. The girls had made their wreaths of ferns, to learn how they might marry. Ragnarok had asked me to make a wreath too. He had given me his signet ring as a gift if I would only make a wreath. I had never made a wreath before, but I wanted to please him, so I accepted the ring. Never had I wanted to please any man, the way that I wanted to please Ragnarok. Not for years…not since Meimer…"

She paused to cover her mouth in remembrance. When she raised her stub to her face, tears formed once more in her eyes.

"Branimir," Kinhar said. His hand was still placed upon Erzebeth as she spoke. "Some wine."

"I'm sorry," she apologized.

"It is quite alright. Continue when you are ready." Kinhar led Erzebeth to a table nearby, where they sat across from one another.

Branimir rushed to grab the jug of wine in the corner and fill their clay cups. They paused as he poured their drink, serving the pale woman first. Again, he thought he saw remnants of brown in her blue eyes.

Erzebeth ignored the Kras, seemingly unsurprised by the Kras and his loyalty to the Highborn. She continued, "I made the wreath and tossed it into Strega's Deep. He had been with me and we watched it float out into the waters. We thought that we would watch it until the sun was gone, as was custom, but … but…"

"What?" Falmagon insisted, suddenly appearing annoyed by the woman's emotional reaction to her memories.

Erzebeth breathed deep. "A beast, a serpent, lifted from the ocean and swallowed it whole."

"What are you speaking of?" Kinhar huffed. "A true serpent in Strega's Deep."

Erzebeth dropped her head into her hands, while Falmagon looked at her in amazement. His expression indicated that he thought Erzebeth had gone mad.

"Yes," Erzebeth said shrilly. "I know what it sounds like, but it is the truth. It was black and scaled unlike any beast I have ever have seen, its mouth cone-shaped and full of razor teeth. From the water depths, it rose, and down it plunged again, in a moment quicker than breath. But, not so quick that I could not see it, nor Ragnarok."

Falmagon shook his head. "Did any other see it?"

"No," Erzebeth said, "otherwise, I might still have my hand."

"I do not understand, my Lady," Branimir said. He could not help but be fascinated by the tale.

Erzebeth twisted sharply at Branimir, taken aback that he had spoken to her at all. Branimir nearly apologized for the question. Though, the look on Falmagon's face suggested Branimir was not the only one completely confused by the jumbled story.

Erzebeth explained further, "Ragnarok dived into the waters to fight the beast and to return my wreath, as he thought it was a bad omen. I screamed for him to stop, but the wool-headed man would not listen to me. He was slain by the beast, though I did not see it.

"My screams for Ragnarok were eventually heard by the guard when I stood on the shore. The curs thought my screaming was due to a quarrel between us. When his bloody limbs washed ashore the next day, they thought I had killed him for the worth of his signet ring I wore on my hand. They could not prove the murder, so the King chose to take my hand, labeling me thief."

Kinhar shook his head in bewilderment. "I am so sorry that this has happened to you, Erzebeth."

"I have seen men live and die. I grieve for Ragnarok, but I will heal in time. What I need is to understand what Myestera is trying to tell me."

"Clear, it is," Dorofej smacked his lips from the doorway with a half-witted smile. The door was already fastened behind him. None, not even Branimir, had seemed to hear him come into the alehouse, as though he had come through like smoke through the cracks. "The wreath, a symbol of forthcoming bethrothment, was on the water and then it was not, swallowed whole by a beast unsought, yes? Clear, it is, that you are *not* to be married."

Falmagon jumped up at the Highborn's face, whipping Habërmani defensively toward Dorofej. Yet when he saw it was Dorofej, he slammed the crooked staff down. "Your wisdom was not requested, old man."

Dorofej dipped his head half-heartedly. His words were crisp. "Freely, I offer it."

Kinhar moved from his table, and approached Dorofej, almost falling over his own feet. "Why did Merreider Kar want to speak with you? Why did you not say that you knew him, Dorofej?"

Dorofej's eyebrows reflected their own language, lifting and falling in deliberation. "Ah, I did not know I knew him, and I am still not sure how I do. Awkward when someone says they know you, and talks to you and you just cannot seem to place them, yes?" Dorofej shrugged his shoulders. "By and by, the King wished to speak of the weather at Melkorka."

Kinhar scowled. "I do not have patience for your riddles or your games. What did the King want?"

Dorofej grunted, stumbling past Kinhar and finding a seat at the nearest table. "If you must know, he wanted to know what happened with Lubos Gajic last night."

"What did you tell him?"

"Told him the Jarl of Narthwich would need help against the Bukavac as we had promised, I did. We did promise to tell King Kar of their plight and send aid, did we not? Keep our word, the Highborn must, yes?"

"What did you tell him about Lubos?"

"Ah, the simple truth. Exceedingly distraught by the death of his daughter, the merchant was."

"That is not the full of it, Dorofej."

"Perhaps, no, but my mind is a bit foggy on the issue, yes? Full as my belly with plum, my head was. Regardless, I'm afraid that it matters very little, yes?"

Branimir asked the question. "Why is that?"

"Given freedom this morning to go find his daughter's remains, Lubos was."

"There will be nothing worthwhile to find at Melkorka, if he even makes it there." Falmagon said in shock. "It has been too long."

"Comforted in knowing Katerina had a fitting death, the man can be. Much more proper than being left alive with a missing appendage, yes?" Dorofej smoothed out his robes, shrugging his shoulders with feigned innocence.

Bran was awestruck by the old Highborn's hateful words.

Erzebeth stood from her chair with a sneer. "Excuse me? Who is this old man?"

"Bah!" Kinhar threw his hands in the air. "He only aims to rile you up, Erzebeth. Ignore him! We all must."

The woman fumed across the room, her steps heavy, and stood over the long-bearded Highborn. Dorofej looked up at her, crossing one leg over the other. She growled at him. "Do not push me. I will tear you limb from limb."

Dorofej cleared his throat, leaning over his knees toward Erzebeth. "With just the one hand or should I expect gnashing of teeth?"

Erzebeth screamed, her eyes flashing blue to brown and back again. She raised her foot and slammed the heel into Dorofej's chest. The old Highborn busted through the back of his chair, toppling over twice before landing sprawled out near Branimir.

Dorofej wheezed, rolling over on his knees with what little strength he had. His icy gaze locked onto Erzebeth as she approached him.

"Anshedar… you are not, yes?" He used the old term for human before they were separated between Highborn and Northmen.

If there was any response from the woman, Branimir did not hear it. Erzebeth lifted another chair and slammed it down upon his head.

Bran squealed, rushing to Dorofej's side. His eyes fluttered and he fell into darkness in Branimir's arms.

Chapter XIV

Branimir sat among the shards of wood that were scattered across the floor. He lightly placed the damp wool cloth on Dorofej's head. The old man moaned and exhaled heavily but remained unconscious. The old Highborn was lucky he was not dead. The kick alone should have crushed his brittle chest, or at least, caused his heart to stop beating.

The swelling over his right eyelid was already turning purple. Blood had been wiped away from his temple and cheek. Bran had gotten the wound to stop bleeding, forming a dried barrier of blood for the time being. As for Falmagon, Kinhar, and Erzebeth, they had ignored him and Dorofej for the past half hour.

Branimir could only glare at the two men who were meant to be Dorofej's Highborn brethren.

Falmagon's voice echoed in the room from near the kiln. "What is this land called again?"

"Maharia," Erzebeth said.

"Maharia?" Branimir repeated beneath his breath as an echo. It had a strange sound to it.

"It is a month journey on the boat, but that is where we must go if you want to find the Ash Tree."

"I have never heard of Maharia. The Ash Tree must be on Kalamaar or the Seven Islands. This is where man was created. If there were land beyond the ocean, the Northmen surely would have found it. We all know the sea is endless, pouring off into nothingness, into the mouth of Strega himself," Unnvar claimed before gulping the rest of his drink.

"Maharia is very real, and so are the many lands beyond it," Erzebeth assured the innkeeper. "Maharia is a land much different from this one with beasts that are unlike anything you have seen. The road to the Ash Tree is well guarded and dangerous. Making it there alive will not be an easy task."

Unnvar gulped, squinting his eyes. "How do you know so much about Maharia, Erzebeth?"

Erzebeth did not respond.

But Kinhar did. "Erzebeth has been there before and can lead us there. She is the reason we have come to Arkaim."

"And I am thankful you did, Kinhar Sayan," Erzebeth picked something from her teeth roughly with her fingernail. "You risk much by sharing my name and my life with men hardly known to me. Knowledge of the Ash Tree is sought by every man living, seeking eternal life and the secrets of the gods. Men would easily kill to gain my knowledge!"

"These are trusted men, Erzebeth," Kinhar assured her with gentle eyes.

Erzebeth turned to look at Branimir, who continued to care for Dorofej on the floor. She may very well have been taking a glance at the old man, but Bran felt her eyes in his direction regardless.

"I hope you are right, Kinhar. Too much is at risk if they are not." She stared into the fire, the wild strands of her hair hanging over her eyes. "Let us hope they are."

Falmagon pulled at his mustache. "Will you come along as a guide?"

Erzebeth looked at her forearm that had been stitched shut, skin wrapped on top of skin. "I have good reason to travel there once again. You will be coming along with me and not the other way around, Falmagon."

Branimir wrinkled his nose, suddenly noticing that her severed hand was sweltering in the kiln. The burning flesh smelled acrid. He had not seen her throw it into the flames, but she must have.

Erzebeth added, "Though, I would be surprised if you all survive beyond the voyage." Her eyes glanced to Dorofej's body again. "It is a grueling journey and not suitable for most."

Branimir spoke up, feeling it necessary, "Dorofej is stronger than he looks, my Lady. He will keep up just fine."

"That is twice you have spoken to me without being spoken to," Erzebeth scolded. "Who keeps the reins on this Kras? I know enough of the Highborn and their kind to understand what is and what is not acceptable."

Branimir turned his face away.

Kinhar put his hand to his head. "Branimir has been allowed more autonomy in recent days, as he continues to prove his loyalty to the Highborn and serve us. His insights are worthwhile. Even now, he speaks truth. Dorofej has surprising fortitude despite his appearance and lack of manners. The question is who will take this journey to Maharia?"

Falmagon lifted his hand. "It is no question that I am with you in this tale until the end, Kinhar. Through blessing and misfortune, I will see this through."

"I gave my word that I would travel with the Highborn to save my family from a terrible fate," Unnvar spoke deeply, "but I fail to understand what need there is to go to Maharia and find the Ash Tree?"

Kinhar explained, "Nedezhda has said she will destroy the Ash Tree to destroy all life. We must find a way to stop her. We must protect the Ash Tree for all we are worth."

"I don't understand. Just go find her and kill her again. Strike the Eretik down," Unnvar said.

"Not that simple, Unnvar. Nedezhda cannot be killed without returning from the Netherworld again. We must find a way to destroy her soul and not simply the undead body she maintains. Not to mention, Nedezhda has unlimited access to Koldovstvo in battle. Even the Highborn are unmatched against her."

Unnvar scratched his head and grunted. "You think to have a better chance at the Ash Tree?"

"The Ash Tree is surrounded by the Waters of Life. If we Highborn can stand within that pool during battle, we, too, can use Koldovstvo without the effects of aging or death."

Branimir promptly spoke again. "My Lords, you cannot battle Nedezhda for eternity within the Waters of Life, forever protecting the Ash Tree."

"We will if we must," Kinhar said sullenly.

Dorofej stirred on the ground.

Erzebeth thoughtfully shook her head. "That will not be necessary, I would not think. Though, the alternative brings more danger than any deed done by any man."

Branimir stared at Erzebeth in waiting for her explanation.

"The world has many exits to the Netherworld, but none of those openings provide passage both ways. The Crags of Kazimir near Melkorka, for instance, are only one of the exits from the frozen wasteland. The entrance to the Netherworld is at the Ash Tree, although you cannot exit the Netherworld from there."

"What are you suggesting?" Falmagon looked horrified.

Kinhar bellowed with equal confusion, "Why would we want to enter the Netherworld, Erzebeth?"

Erzebeth stared hard into the fire, as though she were reading from a scroll smothered in ink stains. "The soul can be eternally killed if it is taken in this life and the next. You could stop Nedezhda's ascent from the Netherworld if you can send her back to the Netherworld, follow her over, and defeat her in the frozen wasteland."

"In the realm of the gods?" Unnvar nearly fell back in his chair, the shutters shaking with his booming voice.

The sound jarred Dorofej into consciousness. He sputtered in surprise, trying to look around with little success. Dorofej had likely not been in this much pain since the Dreka nearly tore his leg off at Illuard.

"I thought you were dead, my Lord," Branimir whispered.

Dorofej's frosty eyes peered back through half-open eyelids. He lay his head back against the floor. "Not quite."

None of the others noticed Dorofej stirring. They were much too caught up in their musing.

"I did not say it was easy. I do not know what lies on the other side, nor would I know the way to return."

"By Mulafell," Falmagon gripped Habërmani until his knuckles were white.

Dorofej cleared his throat, forcing himself to sit up off the floor. It was a slow ascension. "What…what madness is being shared whilst I rest my eyes?"

Falmagon and Unnvar snickered and stared at the Highborn who had been matched by the woman only hours before.

Kinhar spoke with the leadership that gave him the title of spearhead. "We are going to Maharia, Dorofej, to protect the Ash Tree from Nedezhda. Erzebeth knows the way."

Dorofej snorted, the bristles of his mustache rippling, giving no suggestion of being shocked. "Indeed, she does."

Dorofej struggled to make it to his feet, clambering about, causing a rumpus as he scraped chair and table against the floorboards. The rest of the gathering, including Kinhar, raised their eyes in his direction. He waited until he was fully standing before he opened his thin lips again.

His words were blunt, in the way that was no less expected from him. "You are not Anshedar, nor from this age, yes?"

Erzebeth stood up, the blue eyes completely faded, leaving brown in their stead. Every other feature was remarkably the same, skin as pale as the first snowfall.

Unnvar and Branimir were the only two who moved backwards. Unnvar was taken aback enough to stand from his chair and skip backwards across the room nearly toppling over. Branimir simply stepped backwards and moved behind Dorofej. Branimir had known Erzebeth withheld something strange.

"I am Vucari of Anaerfell, beyond the shores of Maharia, Dorofej. You would not know my kind unless you had been to Rhian. I am a Warden of the Ash Tree."

Dorofej stood, shoulders broad, and faced the Vucari with a scowl. "Skin-switchers still walk on Maharia, yes?"

"I have not been to Maharia for half a century, but I imagine the Vucari remain among the forests, keeping a watchful eye on the Ash Tree."

Unnvar's voice did not quiver, but it did crack. "How have you remained alive so long, and still remain so young?"

"The same as I have," Kinhar said evenly, his eyes meeting each around the room. "The Ash Tree restores life and youth. Erzebeth has been a friend longer than any of you have been alive, including Branimir here. She and I have traveled the lengths of the world, and seen many things, including the Ash Tree."

Dorofej's eyebrows raised as the confession left the lips of the Highborn. "So, you have been to the Ash Tree, Kinhar."

"That I have, Dorofej, but it was a very long time ago. I do not remember the way any longer. I had brought its fruits, in the form of ash branches, with me back to Kalamaar and have used them with the power of Koldovstvo to sustain my life for years. The ash branch that was used in the battle at Melkorka against the Eretik was the last of its sustenance."

Dorofej goaded. "You seek the Ash Tree and the Waters of Life to replenish your life, yes? To share it with your prodigy, the Highborn Longwalker, yes?"

Kinhar spoke carefully. "I seek the Ash Tree to stop Nedezhda from claiming the lives of the innocent. I seek the Ash Tree to bring exaltation to the gods that give us life. I seek the Ash Tree for the Highborn. I seek the Ash Tree for the Northmen. And, I look to share the reaping of such a holy treasure with any who accompany me to righteousness and glory!"

Branimir could not help but wonder if that included him, the lowly Kras, as well.

Falmagon and Kinhar were quaking, their secrets seeping through to Dorofej's ears. There was no other way. The old man would eventually be able to put the pieces together, if he had not already. Branimir only hoped Dorofej would share what he was learning. In the meantime, Branimir gawked at Falmagon and Kinhar, who looked like children caught taking a pie off the shutter ledge.

"Will you accompany us to Maharia, Dorofej?" Kinhar asked.

Dorofej looked around the room, as though he were a blind man weighing silver pieces against cowries, before finally relaxing his face. "Not much of a choice, yes?"

Kinhar let loose a sigh of relief. "Then, it is settled. We will need to acquire a boat."

Dorofej scratched his white beard with care, tassels swaying. "By chance, have one, I do."

Falmagon stomped at the wooden baseboard, with an unexpected laugh, escalating to a hearty chuckle. "Of course, you do, old man. Of course, you do."

Chapter XV

Within the hour, Branimir and the rest of the fellowship left the alehouse. Their quest had been defined.

Kinhar stepped lightly, leading the small group, with Falmagon and Erzebeth at his heels. The three were the most determined of the bunch, walking into the dirt streets of Arkaim. Their focus was purely on the docks where Dorofej said his boat, gifted by King Kar, awaited them.

Unnvar followed carrying two doloire, long-handled single-edged axes, on either side of his belt. His large frame filled the doorway, swallowing the light of the kiln, where his family huddled and prayed to the gods for their protection. His wife and children promised to tend to the alehouse and pray for Unnvar's return. Branimir did not believe Unnvar would return from Maharia. The demons were too many for a simple man to contend. But Unnvar insisted he had a duty to stand against evil, no matter the strength, to protect what life he had brought into the world. Come war and blood, Unnvar swore he would fight for his children to live and to see children of their own.

Dorofej and Branimir traipsed out of the wooden door behind Unnvar, as though they were being dragged by a noose around the neck. Bran's head hung low and his fingers trembled, realizing that he may not be the only slave in this tale. Dorofej was equally bound to the fate of the Highborn.

"Sound the alarm! We are under attack!" Sentries screamed near the gate of Arkaim. The sounds of clanging weapons and shrill cries echoed into the night.

"Nedezhda!" Kinhar hissed under his breath. "She has made it to Arkaim."

Branimir gasped, stepping back, eyes peering through the moonless night with ease. "I can see the Bukavac, my Lords. They come by the hundreds, maybe more."

"This is not our fight. Not here, Kinhar," Falmagon shook his shaggy head. "Let Arkaim fall as Melkorka did. We must flee to the boat to fight another day and protect the Ash Tree."

"Falmagon speaks truth," Erzebeth said.

A group of sentries ran by the alehouse, shouting for the citizens to take cover. One stared at the Highborn as he passed. His face held the features of a young man, barely knowing his first love, if any love at all. His death was nigh. His copper sword would be useless against the thick skin and the strong metal blades of the Netherworld monsters.

Unnvar grunted in surprise. "I pledge my life to your cause, and you would leave my family and my people to die? The Northmen cannot fight against these demons. We are not Highborn."

Dorofej pulled a dark hood up over his head, completely shrouded in murky robes. "Unnvar, contend against this evil, we cannot either. Maybe it was Kaelandur, maybe it was our sin in killing the Eretik, or maybe it is our very existence on Aenar. No matter the reason for our suffering, Nedezhda is far stronger than any could have thought possible, yes? Fight here and all mankind is lost, or to the Ash Tree we flee."

"We haven't the time to discuss, my Lords," Branimir squealed.

The Bukavac tore down the streets of Arkaim. Like a stampede of cattle, their blue skin blended in the night, lighted by torchlight. Their hands gripped weapons of the deep, forged by demon and devil, designed by the Mistress of Nightmares, Marheena, the Frozen Goddess.

The first carried a large spiked ball at the end of a long leather cord. The weapon circled over the Bukavac's head, sweeping through the air like an extension of its strapping arm. It roared with its charge, leading the many at its rear.

As Unnvar stepped backwards, Falmagon stepped forward. Wielding the crooked staff, which gave him power beyond the other Highborn, Falmagon slammed his weapon against the ground with ire. Dust surfaced and fluttered around his brown robes in half speed.

Branimir could have counted every speck.

The dust turned to boulders. One after another, the Highborn Longwalker launched the stones at the frozen demons from the Netherworld. The common maneuver from Falmagon was worthwhile. Chunks of earth crashed into the Bukavac, smashing in their heads before they reached him. Yet, a few Bukavac smashed through the solid rock and charged.

In desperation, Falmagon furiously continued to wield Koldovstvo. Boulders were shattered, stone walls were torn down, and rock was fragmented. In short time, the young man's hair began to show signs of recession, his face wrinkled at the cheekbone. Habërmani could not contain Koldovstvo flowing through his veins.

"We must go," Branimir shouted over the din.

Falmagon's throat reverberated louder with cries of battle. It was the sheer robustness of a man meant to lead armies and destroy wickedness that caused Branimir to shudder and back away slowly. Falmagon's single eye was feral, holding the might of a thousand men behind its gaze, the sway of the gods.

Branimir slipped into the shadows, disappearing. He scooted back to the alehouse in hiding. This was how his people had survived as long as they had. Battling demons was for those who manipulated Koldovstvo. Their chance to escape without a battle was gone.

Another spiked ball on the end of a cord split the air toward Falmagon. At the last moment, he fell to his back with a thud, barely dodging the deadly blow aimed for his chest. Another Bukavac stormed toward him while the first spun the strange weapon to deliver a second attack.

The Bukavac who came next wielded a one-handed weapon with thick metal spikes on the opposite side of a mallet. Branimir cringed at the sight. The armament could batter the insides of an enemy to mush. The mallet came down toward Falmagon but was deflected mid-swing by Unnvar who grabbed the handle with a single hand.

The beast of a man stood a head shorter than the massive demon who growled ferociously at the unshaken Northman. The innkeeper roared back with equal ferocity, bringing his doloire from his side and slicing the demon across the neck with the blade.

Where the bluish-white blood of the demon should have gushed Branimir was surprised to find that Unnvar's handaxe snapped against the harsh skin of the demon. It was like frozen rock, unbreakable against the soft copper.

The devastating surprise only lasted momentarily as Unnvar dropped the handle and pushed with all his strength against the Bukavac. The demon slid inches, wrestling against Unnvar for control of the mace. Branimir had never seen such strength in a man.

"For Dahz the Lightbringer and glory!" Kinhar bawled. The spearhead raised his hands to the sky. As the Bukavac brought the flail down to strike Falmagon, a bolt of lightning tore from the heavens and ripped through its skull and chest. The weapon fell to the earth among the remains of the scorched carcass of the demon.

More Bukavac filled the streets.

Branimir, in fear, peeked through his fingers, knowing nothing but panic. He was motionless in his hiding spot.

"Victory here we will not find," Dorofej said, pulling Falmagon to his feet.

Falmagon ignored the old man. "Unnvar!"

The Bukavac and Unnvar continued to push back and forth on either side of the mace. From the road, another Bukavac charged with the intent of crushing Unnvar where he stood.

Erzebeth pushed past Falmagon to intercept the attack. In a moment, her body shredded away, and a bestial form rose from the remains. Where skin and blood fell, fur and muscle erupted into a creature similar to a great bear. The brute animal rose to the height of the Bukavac with strength of equal measure. Brown eyes of the Vucari remained, as well as a missing limb from the right arm, but it was no matter. Erzebeth, in the form of the beast, was powerful, unstoppable.

The bear collided with the Bukavac and its weapon fell to the ground. Erzebeth tore her teeth into the Bukavac's shoulder, breaking through with ease. The light liquid flowed across her gums as the demon roared, grabbing the Vucari in rage. It tried to tear apart the jaw of the bear, but her grip was locked.

Kinhar threw fire at the Bukavac. The blaze ruptured the gut of the demon struggling with Erzebeth. She crashed to the ground with the beast and tore out its throat, silencing its roar.

To her left, Unnvar finally yanked the mace from the hands of the other Bukavac and smashed in its head with a final blow.

Fire and stone, sea and sky flowed together through the darkness of the night. The Bukavac laid waste to Arkaim from palisade to seashore with ease, striking down sentries and civilians with little resistance. The sounds of blood gurgling in the throats of children, and women shrieking as their stomachs were torn from breast to belly, filled Branimir's sensitive ears.

At Melkorka there had been a battle. At Arkaim, it was a massacre. Branimir had no time to process the horror.

"Branimir," Dorofej cried, searching the streets, "let us flee."

At command, Branimir reappeared and rushed to the head of the group. Through the smoke-filled streets, the Highborn, innkeeper, and the Vucari, still in her bestial form, sped through Arkaim behind Branimir. He was exceptionally quicker than the lot of them, dodging obstacles in the road with ease. The docks were near but the enemy was closing.

"Falmagon, there," Kinhar directed. "And there!"

The one-eyed Highborn responded by throwing up a series of rock walls in front of the Bukavac that tore through the streets. Using Habërmani, he did his best to funnel the enemy away from them, to keep them safe. The endless casting of Koldovstvo was becoming costly to him though, his hair turning grey.

Though, Falmagon had little choice if they were to survive this night. He was the only one who had the power to see them through to the docks. He was the only one who could withstand the constant flow of Koldovstvo and pave their path to Maharia.

Another Bukavac approached and was torn down by Erzebeth. The claws ripped through its face, its brains spilling out from the shredded, frozen flesh.

"You are hurt," Falmagon cried to the Vucari after the demon had fallen. She rumbled in response, stumbling at the speed of Dorofej. She had a gash across her belly and another across her right arm.

"No time to bandage her. We must hurry," Unnvar growled, the mace heavily swaying in his hands.

Dorofej hopped over broken timber. "We cannot get on a boat for Maharia without provisions, yes? Starve to death, we will."

"We have not the time to find supplies," Kinhar muttered. "We will have to make do."

Dorofej grunted in condemnation.

Falmagon scowled. "Come, Dorofej! Hurry before Nedezhda—"

The lightning striking in front of Falmagon cut him off. He reeled backwards, clinging to Habërmani tightly in his hand.

The Eretik, Nedezhda, stood with an army of Bukavac between them and the docks. Branimir could see every stitch connecting her head to her neck. Her thin lips curled. "Where is Kaelandur? Give it to me, Highborn!"

Branimir hissed the thought haunting his mind, "You should have never killed her."

Erzebeth let loose a guttural roar from her throat, drowning out his words. She dropped to all fours, baring her teeth at the undead Eretik.

Kinhar growled. "Bah! What do you want the weapon for, Nedezhda?"

"Found your wrinkles so soon, Kinhar?" she cackled hatefully. "Give me Kaelandur."

"Why do you want it?" Kinhar repeated.

"Marheena desires it. Kaelandur was crafted for a destiny beyond what any of you can foresee. It will rip through the fabric of this world, laying waste to man, and preparing the way for the Likhyi."

"The Likhyi," Dorofej gasped from the rear. "The gods desire nothing, yes? I say, even the Frozen Goddess wants nothing from men," Dorofej said, pulling Branimir behind him. "Destiny is an untruth of men and demons alike to give life purpose outside of their charge."

"You know little, Dorofej, and even less of men. Most of all, you know nothing of those who reside in your company," Nedezhda said.

Dorofej's could not keep the smirk from his face. His voice was nearly as mocking, "Do I not?"

"Stop this, Nedezhda," Kinhar bellowed.

Nedezhda folded her arms. "Are you afraid of your secrets being revealed, Kinhar? You could not silence me in life. What madness would give you reason to try now?"

"I will cut off your pretty head a thousand times over to keep your mouth shut," Kinhar rushed at the undead woman, his fists glowing with a bluish glint of light.

Nedezhda met him with the Bukavac at her back.

Branimir vanished.

Kinhar flung blue flame from his fists at the demonic woman. Nedezhda dodged the fire, her bright blue eyes seemingly seeing Koldovstvo before it was cast. Her discolored hair, like moss against the tree's edge, clung to her face as she raised stone and fell water from the sea upon the Highborn.

Erzebeth and Unnvar were caught in the first wave that crashed down. Erzebeth was swept away and thrown through the side of a wooden structure. The impact knocked her unconscious returning her to human form. Unnvar, on the other hand, was able to withstand the impact, preventing himself from a similar fate.

Falmagon focused on the Bukavac, using his crooked staff to mold stone as though it were clay. Weapons slashed and crashed against his flesh, his face aged, and his skin tore. The man was being ripped to shreds, skin falling from bone, and yet he stood with all the poise of a Highborn.

Despite holding hate against those he called master, Branimir wept from the shadows. The salty tears burned his eyes.

Kinhar aged rapidly, rarely able to attack against Nedezhda. The undead woman was not affected by Koldovstvo, having the ability to mend the elements together with ease. Stone walls blocked fire. Protective orbs of air defended against frozen daggers of ice. Rocks rained from the heavens to collide with earth raised from Kinhar's feet.

The Highborn weakened in moments, collapsing to his knees as his bones grew brittle. He continued to craft Koldovstvo, even after his eyes sunk into his skull, even after his breath had grown weak.

The end was nigh for all of them.

"Kinhar!" Dorofej screeched, helpless as the Bukavac descended upon him. The old man had found a makeshift stave from a broken branch that he swung wildly at the menacing demons.

Kinhar faced Nedezhda on his knees. The saltwater from Strega's Deep crashed around him, muddying the streets of Arkaim. Branimir's heart hurt in his chest as he watched a Bukavac advanced behind Kinhar, sinking a blade through the back of his head.

Branimir stared with blurred vision.

Life fled from Kinhar's blue eyes, blood pouring from his mouth and head. His body hung limp, held in place only by the metallic blade of the demon at his back. When the Bukavac yanked the sword clean, Kinhar's body fell for the last time.

The corner of Nedezhda's lips twisted into a smile.

"No!" Falmagon wailed. He raced to Kinhar's body, his wrinkled hands clinging to the bloodied, cream-colored cloth. The robe darkened further in a pool of Kinhar's blood.

Unnvar stumbled back to the battle, falling to Falmagon's side. He lifted the demon's mace he had carried and buried it into the Bukavac's skull behind Kinhar.

No more had the demon crumpled that Branimir helplessly watched another Bukavac slam a maul against the innkeeper's head. Blood gushed.

Unnvar joined Kinhar in the mud.

Falmagon, in his overwhelming misery, barely saw his kin collapse. Through the haze of tear upon tear, Falmagon did not see the hammer collide into his head either. He dropped over Kinhar's body.

Branimir's stomach churned, but he stayed hidden. He ignored the urgency to run to Dorofej. At one time, he may have felt pity for the Nedezhda, but she was no better than the men who had first killed her.

Nedezhda raised her hand and the Bukavac stopped their assault. The woman approached Dorofej, who sunk to his knees in defeat.

"Where is Kaelandur?" she said. "Tell me, and I will let you live."

Dorofej hid his emotion, gazing into the eyes of Nedezhda. "You make me an offer you have no intent of holding to, yes?"

"I will keep my word, Dorofej." Nedezhda kneeled, returning the emotionless façade. "It is more than what Kinhar and Falmagon would have done."

"What do you speak of, Nedezhda?" he asked.

"You really do not know?" the pale woman laughed at the old man. "You are Highborn and yet know nothing of their scheme? You crafted the weapon that killed me, and know not why I was killed?"

Dorofej licked his thin lips patiently.

Nedezhda looked amused. "I will let you live and tell you of their secrets, if you give me Kaelandur. Give me the weapon that delivered my death."

Dorofej stared across the bare streets and the burning city as he weighed the offer. His voice was silent but heavy on Branimir's ears as he gave up the copper dagger to the hand of Marheena. "Falmagon carries it."

Nedezhda rose to her feet. She gracefully walked through the mud, and then searched the body of the one-eyed Highborn. In a matter of moments, she held the copper dagger. With a satisfied grin, she held the weapon high in the air as though it were a rod that controlled all living creatures.

The Bukavac, her army, roared in approval. The sound of the demons echoed throughout the city of Arkaim.

Dorofej lowered his head.

Nedezhda tucked Kaelandur into her belt and glided back over to the old man. Her eyes narrowed. "Kinhar and Falmagon intended to fortify the Kadari. Both have recited the Kalamyr Oath. My death was their needed sacrifice, cloaked as righteousness, labeling me Eretik, and Kaelandur their talisman. They mean to destroy the name of the Highborn and bring one religion to the world. They want every living creature to worship the Lightbringer."

Dorofej could not silence his gasp.

"But it is no longer important. You are the only Highborn left in this world, and the world will decay at my hand. The Ash Tree will be destroyed through the taint of Kaelandur, and the Likhyi will be released."

"What dark magic do you wield that could destroy the Ash Tree with a copper weapon, Nedezhda?" Dorofej shuddered, masking his thoughts with a simple misdirection.

"Don't insult me, Dorofej. You know as well as I that this weapon is touched with Koldovstvo. I could not have returned to this world without magic being melded into this blade. The Bukavac will find the Ash Tree and I will do Marheena's bidding."

"This cannot be the will of Marheena." Dorofej's blue eyes twinkled as he dropped his gaze.

Branimir's mind riddled. Jhar was responsible for the Eretik's return. He had used magic to make Kaelandur.

Nedezhda signaled the demons to follow and soon Dorofej was left alone, kneeling in the ruins of Arkaim.

The old Highborn's voice could be heard reciting prophecy.

The Lightbringer will wed,
The Countess of the deep,
The Kadari reigns.
A Defender will be slain,
The Harbinger will ascend,
The Kadari reigns.
The Serpent of the Empress returns,
The dark Prophet will emerge,
The Kadari reigns.
A time of plenty will end,
Come war, come famine, come death,
The Kadari reigns.

The last word slid off of Dorofej's tongue like the last rain drop of spring falling before summer's heat. He buried his head in his hands, looking more defeated than any man, dead or alive.

Branimir approached slowly, revealing himself from the darkness. "What does it mean, Dorofej? What does all of this mean?"

Dorofej looked upon him, his eyes weeping for all of humanity, all living creatures. "It means our suffering has only begun, Branimir Baran. Darkness swells in demon and man alike, yes?" The old Highborn pulled at the braided tassels on his chin. "Yet we may have the advantage if Nedezhda does not know the location of the Ash Tree, yes? Swift, we must be!"

Branimir looked to the Highborn Longwalker. Falmagon's hand twitched.

Chapter XVI

Smoke from Arkaim rose with the morning light of the sunrise. Fires still burned the city to ashes with very few alive in its wake. The world looked to be in ashes, without hope, without direction.

Only a handful of buildings still stood throughout the expanse of the city. The palisades were torn down, the gates broken open, and the streets littered with the bodies of its many citizens. Nothing seemed to stir, a thousand dead, fallen where they had stood.

Branimir stood at a distance, reflecting on Kinhar's body that lay upon a stack of charred wood near the water's edge. His grey hair had turned white. His furrowed skin, pale and bruised, already showed signs of decay. The body had little to no blood left, drained through the gaping hole in his skull. The spearhead of the Highborn was truly gone from the world of men.

Falmagon was close. His brown hair had turned to grey. He limped forward using Habërmani as a walking stick. He swayed with dizziness and slight confusion as he approached the corpse of his friend. The wound on his head was clotted in blood and gave indication that he was lucky to be standing at all. If that were not enough, his right leg was in shambles, torn from the blades of the demons, wrapped in bloodied cloth. His left leg was not in much better condition.

Falmagon lowered his single eye, sunken behind swollen, purple flesh. "By Mulafell…"

Falmagon's hand shook as he reached to touch the man, balancing himself with the crooked staff. Branimir could feel the man's suffering. He could barely believe Kinhar could be dead? The man had lived lifetimes upon lifetimes and now his spirit had fled to the Beyond? It was unthinkable.

Falmagon's fingers hovered over Kinhar's blood-stained lips as though he hoped for breath to stir. For a moment, the Highborn Longwalker could only stare at him with tears in his eyes. His teeth bared, and nostrils flared as he tried to fight those tears back. He choked with a strangled throat.

Branimir folded his arms and gulped. Watching Falmagon in anguish did not make him feel good. He almost felt like he was watching Kinhar die all over again.

With a cry of frustration, Falmagon pulled away and gripped his tangled hair. He screamed at the sun, at Dahz, at the Lightbringer who was the Protector of Men. There were no words in his roar.

At the end of his breath, the weakened man lowered his head, shaking in rage and fear.

"We will make this right, Falmagon," Erzebeth said, approaching him and placing her hand on his trembling shoulder. She stood slumped, holding him for support. Her other forearm clung to her midsection, seemingly holding her guts in her body even without her hand. The cloth that wrapped around her repeatedly covered the thick stitches that had been sewn to bind the deep wound. She, surprisingly, showed no signs of aging from using whatever magic had turned her into a bear.

Falmagon shook his head despairingly, "We have lost. Kaelandur has been taken. Kinhar is gone. What more is there to do?"

Dorofej held a torch in his hand, the flame searing, "Plenty, there is. Travel to Maharia and defend the Ash Tree, we will. Take back hope for the Northmen, we will. We are Highborn, and glory is to be had, yes?"

"Yes," Erzebeth agreed, her eyes locked onto the body of Kinhar.

Falmagon bobbed his head, his voice shaky. "You are right, Dorofej. It is what must be done. Even with Kinhar dea—dead, we must press forward."

Branimir felt his heart flutter, rocking back on his heels. Dorofej rallied those who stood against him for a purpose greater than himself. The man held more goodness in him than any Highborn.

"I will not accompany you," Unnvar said from the far rear where he sat slouched in the dirt, holding his dented head. Blood still oozed from the broken skin. He had said nothing for most of the morning, except a grunt when asked if he would live. "My family is dead. My King is dead. My people are dead. There is no reason for me to go to Maharia. There is nothing left to save."

Falmagon did not look at his kin. "There are plenty of Northmen left in Kalamaar worth protecting, Unnvar."

The innkeeper twisted the heavy mace in his hand, a weapon never seen by man. The metal was solid, stronger than anything crafted by a Northman in the history of the world.

Dorofej hummed in agreement. "Speaks the truth, Falmagon does. Yet Unnvar must remain here in Arkaim and rebuild and tell what he has seen. Convinced to join our cause, he should not be."

Unnvar scowled with hatred, looking around at the dead flooding the deserted streets. "I will not stay behind to do the work of the Highborn. I stay behind to die in peace. Why would I ever do as you ask, Highborn?"

"Because," Dorofej said, "you will take the title of King of Kalamaar, Unnvar Grondahl, yes? Others worthy of the cause, there are not. And there is none other to walk away from this defeat, yes?"

Branimir was equally confused.

Unnvar balked, staring at the ashes of the city. "What are you talking about, old man? I am not nobility. I am not a King! I am a simple innkeeper."

"You are a warrior, yes?"

"I—"

"You will find the King's body, take the crown and you will place it on your head, yes? You will rebuild Arkaim and you will give hope to the Northmen on Kalamaar. The Jarls will follow you just as they did the King throughout Kalamaar to the Seven Islands. This day is not your day to die."

Dorofej spoke with the authority of a thousand kings, looking down upon the over-sized man that piddled in the dirt.

"Kings are not made in this way, Dorofej," Falmagon said flatly, finding little strength to argue his point.

"Are they not?" Dorofej asked.

Erzebeth coughed, holding her stomach. She finally swallowed her pain long enough to speak. "Kings come about in many ways, Falmagon. Unnvar will do as well as any other and someone must lead. He has seen and survived the demons. That is bold enough to give people reason to follow him."

Branimir tilted his head at the notion, repeating the thought in his head. Kings come about in many ways. If he was the only Kras left in the world, maybe he could also be King.

Falmagon snorted. "The Highborn should guide the way for the Northmen."

Unnvar pulled himself to his feet. "The Highborn, Falmagon? Bah! I would have thought you would be raised better, but your mind was fouled at Melkorka! Can you not see? The Highborn have only brought death upon the people they swore to protect. If I lead it will be without the wisdom of the Highborn! Such men should be banished from Kalamaar."

Falmagon raged. "The Highborn uphold justice!"

The innkeeper sneered, his voice menacing, "You uphold nothing. Nothing!"

Branimir jaw quivered, frightened by the larger man who screamed at them. "I don't understand. Why are you so angry, Unnvar? Men have always known war."

The large man turned on him. "Are you so different that you cannot see the truth of it? The Highborn have led the world to ruin. They killed these people! This is greater than any war. This is eternal death."

"We did not," Falmagon said. His voice fell to a whisper. "We will fix this."

"You brought the demons to Arkaim," Unnvar said.

"It was a mistake," Branimir said. "This has all just been a terrible mistake."

Unnvar pointed the mace at Branimir. "If you believe that, Kras, then you are a fool."

Branimir's lip trembled, not knowing what to say.

Dorofej tried to ease the tension. "So be it."

Falmagon huffed, gripping his staff until his knuckles turned white. "What do you mean by that?"

"So be it." Dorofej repeated in a softer tone. "Go, Unnvar, and give your family name the glory you seek, yes?"

Unnvar turned as red as Branimir. He looked at each of them as he made his first decree as King of Kalamaar, "Yes, well. Get what supplies you can muster and leave this land. Go to your precious Ash Tree and do what you must do."

Dorofej dipped his head in acknowledgment. "As you wish, King Grondahl."

Unnvar gripped the mace, his weapon and scepter, and left them where they stood without another word.

Falmagon stared in bewilderment, "Are you out of your mind, old— Dorofej?"

Dorofej waited for no ceremony, throwing the torch down on the body of Kinhar. "I think not, Falmagon Sej. You and I are all that left of those who wield Koldovstvo. The Highborn will die along with us. Return to Kalamaar or Melkorka, we likely will not."

Falmagon watched Kinhar's skin cling to bone under the heat of the fire that spread over the timber. "No, Dorofej, you are wrong."

Dorofej's jaw fell, realizing that the man spoke beyond rashness. "What do you know, Falmagon?"

"Kinhar…" Falmagon hesitated. "Kinhar spoke of more Highborn at a place called Shayol Domier."

Dorofej's breath fled from his lungs. "Impossible."

Kinhar's body burned, finalizing his passage into the Beyond. The stench of his seared flesh lingered on the wind.

Branimir chocked on the smell.

"Falmagon speaks the truth," Erzebeth said, ignoring the reeking of death. "I have been there with Kinhar, though it was many, many years ago. The stronghold is located on Maharia, deep in the southern forests known as the Dyndaer. Kinhar helped build the city with a man named Moreth several hundred years ago."

Branimir's hands shook. "If there are more Highborn…are there more Kras? Did Kinhar take the Kras to Shayol Domier?"

He was not alone!

Dorofej's repetition of the name outweighed the questions of the slave. "Moreth?"

"Moreth Eanbald," Erzebeth clarified, "he is the Vicar of the… of…"

"Are there more Kras?" Branimir tried again. He had to know.

He was ignored.

"The Kadari," Dorofej finished with a snarl, curved beneath his white mustache.

"Y-yes," Erzebeth admitted.

Branimir gaped, his mind riddled with more questions. Was the Vucari a member of this religious sect, too? He wanted desperately to know more about this Kadari and why Dorofej held such bitterness toward them.

Dorofej's eyes turned to Falmagon, who met the gaze with equal caution. "Asked once, I have, of what secrets were being kept. I fear that it would be pointless to repeat the question, yes?"

Branimir bit his tongue.

The two old men clearly loathed one another but were bound by their duty as Highborn. They had little choice but to work together to stop Nedezhda's schemes.

They should have never killed her.

Falmagon responded to Dorofej, ignoring the indictment. His words implied that he was taking charge as the new spearhead of the Highborn. "We sail to Maharia."

Month of Wine Flowing
First of Frost
124 CE

Chapter XVII

Branimir's small, crimson knees sunk into the cool sand of the shoreline that led into the unexplored lands called Maharia. He lay on the wet, dark earth that seemed to stretch for eternity. He had never been so thankful to have solid ground under his feet.

The clouds were thick overhead, blocking any attempt that the sun may have to warm him, but he barely noticed. Even though the breeze off the water was shrill, tearing through his red skin like ice, Branimir clung to the sea-stained sand.

The ground was hardening, close to freezing, giving sign to how much time had passed since the four of them had sailed from Arkaim. They had spent nearly two months on the boat through sunshine, rain, and storm. Branimir never wanted to touch foot on a faering again. He may very well have to make his home in Maharia.

"I nearly thought I would never see land again," Falmagon wheezed with a half-smile plastered on his face. He pulled the faering onto the beach with a rope, while clinging to his crooked staff. Once it was secure, the aging man collapsed onto the dirt and rolled over onto his back.

It was amazing that none of them had died on the long voyage in the small faering, especially when considering the wounds of Falmagon and Erzebeth before leaving Arkaim. Fortunately, the Vucari had found enough herbs in Arkaim that she could tend to

154

their injuries. Her knowledge of the medicinal properties should have given her the title of herbal healer. Alas, most of their suffering had to be withstood, as supplies ran low and food became scarce. Branimir only knew that somehow they had managed to overcome the impossible.

Dorofej joined Falmagon on the sands of Maharia, "Much too long of a journey, yes? I fear, forgotten how to walk, I have. I say, a decent meal would be warmly welcomed." Any disdain for Falmagon was gone from the old man's voice for the time being. The Highborn, although confined on the boat together, had barely spoken. Time had been the remedy for their anger.

The two Highborn had little choice but to get along with one another. Dorofej and Falmagon had a similar quest with similar limitations. The Highborn Longwalker's age was not as great as Dorofej's, but it was beyond anything he had ever known. Falmagon's hope was the same as Dorofej's, to reach the Waters of Life to restore his youth.

"Rabbit stew," Branimir said, rubbing his hands together at the thought.

"Anything but fish," Erzebeth muttered, joining Falmagon in the sand with her arms folded to stay warm in the cool breeze.

Falmagon laughed.

Branimir chuckled to himself, realizing it had been a very long time since any of them had even broken a smile.

Kinhar's death had not been forgotten, but it was not talked about among the fellowship. Branimir had tried once and was shushed by Dorofej before Falmagon lectured Branimir on manners and respect. None had said a word about the death of the spearhead again. Branimir assumed none of them ever would.

"We are going to need to find shelter, yes?" Dorofej interrupted the mirth before it could fully begin.

Branimir nodded, standing fully to take a good look at Maharia in the dimming light. He assumed the comment was a request for him to find something suitable.

To the east and north were grasslands, rising and falling over high hills that blocked his vision of the land beyond. A few trees dotted the hills, but not anything significant. To the south, nearly half a day's travel, were the remnants of a small mountain range that stretched along the coastline. He heard birds and small critters making movement in the grasses.

"There is no sign of a settlement," Branimir said, somewhat relieved. "Actually, I do not see any sign of movement. It seems safe enough."

Erzebeth pulled herself to her feet, pushing her hair behind her ears, brown eyes scanning the land as though it were a home she had long forgotten. Branimir nearly took offense as though the Vucari did not trust his judgment, but kept his lips sealed.

Her eyes locked onto the mountain range, and she shook her head upsettingly. "We are leagues away from the Ash Tree. It is to the south beyond those mountains. It'll be weeks before we reach it."

"Traveling through the mountains does not sound appealing," Falmagon added.

"No," Dorofej scowled, "it does not. Maybe we should take the boat along the shore, yes?"

Erzebeth nodded. "I would advise not to travel inland too far. Taking the faering along the coast is probably the quickest way to travel, but there are likely jagged rocks among the waters. It will not be safe either."

Branimir gripped his chin with both hands. He was lucky to not have drowned in the last two voyages. He did not want to push his luck.

"I am not sure getting back on a boat is any more appealing than the mountains," Falmagon groaned, placing his head in his hands.

"I agree," Branimir said.

"I don't see many other options for us," Erzebeth said. "Maharia is a hundred times larger than Kalamaar. Traveling to the Ash Tree is not going to be a quick venture. We are lucky Falmagan and Dorofej have made it this far at their age."

Falmagon snapped, "You would not have made it this far without me, Erzebeth. I risked much to keep you alive at Arkaim."

The Vucari lifted her hands. "I am not your enemy. I am just telling you what you should already know."

Falmagon snorted.

Dorofej interjected, seemingly having no desire to pay attention to Falmagon's cantankerous behavior. "Decide, we must. Land or water?"

Branimir raised his hand as though they were taking a vote. "Land. We may take more time, my Lord, but I prefer the shelter of the mountains against the nipping wind. The gale will only grow colder with the Season of Frost."

Erzebeth flared her nostrils. Clearly, she was still not sympathetic to him speaking his mind. "The red brood makes sense. We may all catch sickness on the sea if this cold increases, which will leave us nowhere. Besides, I have been relatively relieved that the serpent was not seen in the weeks at sea. I would prefer not to test my luck on the water. It may still be lingering in the depths."

"Glad we agree," Branimir murmured.

She glared at him, and he hurried to turn his eyes to Falmagon.

The Highborn Longwalker wrapped his brown robes tightly around himself and snorted again. "Dahz knows I have no interest in being on that boat. But, Dorofej, hear me when I say that I equally have no desire to go trudging about in underground caverns."

Dorofej dipped his head. "I hear you well and clear, Falmagon. It is decided then, yes? Let us make for the mountains before we lose the light, yes?"

Branimir said, "We will not make it before dark."

Dorofej started toward the peaks. "Make it as far as we can, we will."

Erzebeth pulled herself to her feet to follow. Branimir watched her head south for a moment, waiting for Falmagon. The Highborn grumbled, but eventually started after them, and Branimir trailed behind.

The four of them traveled over the grasslands and toward the mountains for several hours without anyone saying much. The land seemed to be completely barren, as though it were a man without a tongue. Erzebeth kept them close to the water's edge, maintaining that they must stay away from the inland.

Falmagon gripped Habërmani firmly in his right hand, using it as a walking stick as he scanned the horizon around them. The waters of the ocean were an eerie sight, hazed and dark as far as the eye could see. The terrain appeared as though it had not been touched by any man or beast in a thousand years.

"Maharia truly is barren," Falmagon growled in a harsh voice.

"I would not be so sure," Erzebeth said. "This land is never what it seems to be. It is best to remain vigilant."

Falmagon did not argue with the Vucari, who had more experience upon Maharia than any of them. The gale that lifted from the north made the world of the west seem even more ominous. Without doubt, Bran thought, Maharia was cursed.

The screeching howl that erupted from the ocean water lifted with a gust of wind. Each of them sprang backwards, but none as quickly as Branimir.

"What was that?" he hissed.

The sound rumbled again. It was shrill, riding the wind like the deafening cries of battle.

"Stay behind me." Falmagon said, pulling Erzebeth to his rear. He raised Habërmani defensively, scanning the surface of the ocean for the monster that could have made the sound.

"It must be the beast," Erzebeth said hastily, swatting Falmagon's hand away.

Dorofej squinted at the water.

Branimir squeaked again, "If so, where is it?"

Nothing stirred.

Erzebeth stood with composure, finally pointing out to the clashing waves. There was no light from the sky, the clouds still fully blocking the sun's rays. But beneath a ripple of a wave there was a vision of the creature. It glistened against the water's edge, a dark blue hint to the scales that lined its massive body.

A monstrous creature was nearly concealed within the waters. It was serpent-like, swaying like a snake on the surface of a pond. The bluish color of its skin was veiled to near perfection against the shade looming over Strega's Deep. A red, fiery tongue lashed against the waters as it took scent of the wind. The beast was larger than the manor house in Arkaim.

"Our position, it has not found," Dorofej said.

"If it were to find us, we would be dead within an instant," Erzebeth said. "It is best that we move forward."

Falmagon nodded. "You will get no argument from me."

Branimir stepped further back from the ocean, feeling his hands shake slightly at the sight of the beast. "Move forward and inland."

Falmagon agreed, "The Kras may be right, Erzebeth. I would rather not contend with the creature if it can be helped. It would tear us to shreds with little effort."

Erzebeth frowned, looking back toward the hills to the west. "Very well, but there are equally dangerous creatures inland."

Dorofej said, "There is no other way, yes? I say, I fear we will find good reason why humans do not traverse these lands."

Erzebeth wrinkled her nose, rubbing the nub of her severed hand. "No place is truly safe from wickedness, Dorofej. But, you are correct. Whatever hardship you may have experienced before in Maharia will seem little in comparison to what lies ahead."

As they moved away from the ocean, Branimir secretly wished they would stop condemning their journey with a foretelling of suffering.

Chapter XVIII

Branimir's fingers traced over the bluish-white stone that he retrieved at Illuard. Ojenek was smooth, with the interior reflecting a dark blue as though it were filled with an inner fire. Branimir has spent much of the past month looking at the stone as they traveled on the faering. Before that time, he had nearly forgotten he had kept it in his pocket.

Dorofej seemed to notice his movement by the small fire they had built along the coastline. "It is safe, Branimir, yes?"

He looked to the mountains, still a quarter day away in travel, and then back to the old Highborn. "Yes, Dorofej, but what is it for?"

Dorofej scrunched his nose. "Let us hope that need of it, we will not have."

Branimir nodded, figuring that the man's wisdom was far greater than his own, especially in the matter of shiny stones from abandoned, underground cities. Bran immediately thought of Oreg'henite within the Kras city of Illuard. If he were ever to be a King, he would want a similar throne made of shiny stones.

"What are you two whispering about?" Falmagon asked from across the fire.

"Nothing of interest," Dorofej said offhandedly, looking to the stars, and then to face the fire.

Falmagon grunted.

Branimir believed Falmagon had completely forgotten about the Ojenek.

Erzebeth approached the fire and sat between Falmagon and Branimir. "Nothing for supper. Maybe I can find something in the morning."

"We should have stopped sooner for hunting," Falmagon said. "We are not going to be able to stay on foot through the mountains on empty stomachs. Food will be scarcer once we reach them."

The woman sighed. "The weather is growing cold, Falmagon. Animals are not going to stay this far north regardless during this time of the year. We must find the strength to make it to the Dyndaer."

"The forest?" Branimir clarified, doing his best to become familiar with the names of things in Maharia. He found it interesting that anything had a name in an unexplored land, but Erzebeth suggested the Vucari had traveled over this land nearly as long as humans had lived on Kalamaar.

"Yes, Kras. The Dyndaer is a dark forest that most would avoid if given the chance, but the Ash Tree lies within."

"Do you know where exactly it is?" Branimir asked.

Erzebeth glowered at the Kras. "We would not be here if I did not."

Branimir lowered his head.

A couple minutes passed and Erezbeth spoke once more, "We have gained enough warmth for the night. It is time to douse the fire."

"Are you kidding me? We will freeze out here without a fire." Falmagon parted his mouth as though he were swallowing a river.

Branimir could not help but agree with the Highborn Longwalker, feeling the chill of the frost on his skin even though he sat by the flame. The Season of Frost had begun, and it would only become colder as the days carried forward. The days may be tolerable for a few months, but the nights would already be dropping below the level of comfort.

The Vucari attempted to keep the sneer from crossing her lips. "You must make do with your bedroll. It is not safe to have fires burning at night. You will draw unwanted attention."

Branimir twisted his head around, peering across Maharia. It may have been darkness for his companions, but he could see the land clearly. The sound of waves crashed in the far distance. The world was as still as a sculptor's muse.

Falmagon spoke Branimir's thoughts. "Attention from what, Erzebeth? There is nothing out here but us and the moon."

Branimir looked up at the pale moon, barely giving off enough light to consider it worthwhile. It might as well be hidden from sight all together.

"Maharia is much different than Kalamaar and the Seven Islands, Falmagon. Much of the land is ruled by Czern, the God of Darkness. The Grey-Clad, as he is called, wanders the night stirring evil with his breath. The Light that fights against his breath will draw him and bring evil with it."

"I know of Czern," Dorofej nodded. "The brother of Dahz, yes? He wears the stone crown of sacrifice called Maelifell, it is."

"By Mulafell," Falmagon muttered, using the name of Dahz's hammer to curse once more. It was becoming a habit for the one-eyed Highborn.

Branimir shivered in the cold.

"Myestera," Erzebeth pointed to the moon, "does what she can to watch after Czern, to place restraint on his mischief. But, she has little power in Maharia. She grows weakest in the Season of Frost."

Falmagon breathed heavily. "The Lightbringer needs to keep his brother inhibited, lest we freeze to death before reaching our mark. It seems that even the gods are working against our quest."

Dorofej pulled at the tassels of hair that hung from his chin. "Interest in our quest, the gods have not, I assure you, Falmagon. They continue on in existence regardless of the existence of man."

"Blasphemous words, Dorofej." Falmagon scoffed.

"Hardly, I think. Words that speak against your reasoning do not evoke blasphemy any more than a boy with a sword makes him a man, yes?"

"And yet, you made Unnvar a King."

Dorofej laughed out loud at the comment, rephrasing the statement with what appeared to be a cheer. "And yet, Unnvar is a King. Ha!"

Falmagon shook his head, likely reminding himself that arguing with Dorofej rarely rendered an efficacious ending.

"He will be lucky if a Jarl does not run him through after he makes such a claim," Falmagon said in finality.

The Vucari stood, holding her severed limb against her body and quickly kicked dirt over the embers. The flames died in the covering of dust.

Branimir pulled his cloak and blanket around his small body, eyes unaffected by the impending darkness. He watched as Falmagon and Dorofej adjusted themselves awkwardly, trying to find comfort in the dim light.

The Vucari did not seem to be affected by the loss of light. She shifted easily back to her place of rest, pulling her own blanket around her shoulders. She licked her lips in the dry air as though she were thinking deeply before turning her eyes to look at Branimir.

The Kras froze realizing she could see him as easily as he could see her in the darkness. Her brown eyes seemed to glow to the Kras, staring intently as though they were looking at the very fabric of his soul. Branimir met the gaze bravely, fearful of maintaining the look and equally scared to turn away. The moment could have lasted the entirety of the night if it were not for Dorofej, who interrupted the awkwardness.

"Erzebeth Navenka, tell me of the Vucari, yes? I would like to learn of your people and their existence here on Maharia. How you came to be, as it were."

Erzebeth turned her head to Dorofej, who lay on his back with his closed eyes facing the moon above. "Okay. I will humor you for the evening, if it is truly your desire."

Dorofej smiled. "What I truly desire is plum wine, but that nectar seems far from accessible this moment. Thus, it must be knowledge, my second favorite mind-altering sap, to intoxicate my senses, if you please."

"So be it." Erzebeth laughed, with a nod of her head.

"You are out of your mind, Dorofej. Make as much sense as a half-witted mule," Falmagon muttered, falling back to the ground, and covering himself with his blanket.

Erzebeth ignored him. "The Vucari were initially said to be born from the breath of the animals, the first creatures to crawl upon the earth and fly through the wind. Our savants would later say Wolos called us into this world."

"Wolos?" Branimir scrunched his nose. He could not keep up with all the gods the humans kept going on about.

Dorofej cleared his throat. "The Horned God, Branimir, with far too many roles to go into right now, yes? Please, Erzebeth, continue with your history."

The Vucari woman sighed. "We were the first with mind and heart, caring for the living and breathing of the world. The Vucari did not originate from Maharia in the time before time, but came from the northern isle that long ago lost its name, but should be remembered as Rhian. I remember the ice-tipped mountains, known as Valarun, stretched across the expanse of the frozen world, beyond any realm that any man or beast has ever seen. Hidden within *Valarun* was the mountain city of Anaerfell, my home."

A moment of silence passed then Erzebeth continued.

"I left Anaerfell when the savants spoke of the Ash Tree hidden deep in the forests to the south. I left with many of my own kind, destined to find this mystical tree of the gods, a tree that gave eternal life to those who tasted its fruit. We were informed that Wolos, the Protector of the Eternal Spring, had charged the Vucari to become the enduring Wardens of the Ash Tree, to protect it from any evil. We had not known that evil was among our own ranks. We could not have known what destiny would wrought—"

Dorofej jolted upright, "What do you mean, Erzebeth?"

"I mean what I say, Highborn. The Vucari whom I traveled with became twisted in thought, their minds torn from a path of virtue. The Vucari were hungry for absolute power and found it through the consumption of the Ash Tree. With eternity in their hands, the Vucari quickly learned the craft of Koldovstvo, but differently than what the Highborn typically master." She paused, staring at Branimir for a moment, as if expecting something from him. Yet he had the impression she was purposefully leaving out the full history.

"That is how you turn into animals?" Branimir wondered, filling the void of silence. "All Vucari change shapes then?"

"I suppose so, yes," Erzebeth continued "though not all use it for the same purpose. Those who were meant to protect the Ash Tree from evil used it to bring hardship and pain upon those who lived in this world. Though, not even the Vucari were the first to be corrupted by their duty. Yet they scattered across Maharia, never again to return to Anaerfell. The home I once knew has long been in ruins."

"In light of their evil, what did you do, Erzebeth?" Branimir asked.

"I had no choice but to follow the example of my people, if anything, to maintain a sense of what it meant to be Vucari. I took the fruit of the Ash Tree and consumed it. I found my youth again through the lake that surrounds the mystical tree. And then, I set out to find those of goodness to help me maintain the balance of the world. It was in that search that I found Kinhar."

"What happened to the other Vucari over the decades, Erzebeth? Are they here in Maharia?" Branimir asked. He secretly wondered again if the Kras could also be here in Maharia.

"I could not know. It has been half a century since I have come to these lands. Last I knew, they were still the Wardens of the Ash Tree, or at least, viewed themselves as such. They will kill any living creature before they reach the tree, keeping the secrets for themselves. They are cruel, unkind creatures. I assure you the Vucari are far more ruthless than any human I have come across…"

Erzebeth again paused. "Though humans are not the foulest of living beings."

Branimir scratched his thin, black hair, missing her suggestion. "How is it that you and Kinhar reached the tree and took branches back to Kalamaar?"

Erzebeth pulled at her hair nervously. She seemed to be caught up in the moment, not recognizing that he was asking the question. "I am Vucari. At the time, there was very little that prevented me from being accepted with my own kind. I fear times have changed."

Falmagon responded, "Let us hope it is not the case."

Dorofej grunted in what may have been agreement.

"How about you, Dorofej?" Falmagon said.

Dorofej smacked his lips. "What do you mean?"

The Highborn Longwalker clarified, "How did you become a Highborn? I have never heard the story of your coming to Melkorka. Kinhar never spoke of it."

Branimir noticed the hint of sadness in Falmagon when saying the dead Highborn's name.

"I imagine he would not have, yes? To share the story, he would need to have known it," Dorofej replied.

"How would he have not? Was he not the first Highborn?" Branimir asked foolishly.

"Ha!" Dorofej laughed out loud. "Is that what you believe? There have been those who have known the craft of Koldovstvo long before Kinhar Sayan."

"Alright, Dorofej," Falmagon licked his lips. Branimir realized he was trying to pry the secrets from Dorofej that Kinhar had long wanted to know. "How did you become Highborn?"

Dorofej put his finger to his nose with a chuckle. "To tell that story, I would have to know."

"You mean you do not know?" Branimir wrinkled his nose.

The old Highborn shrugged beneath his heavy, black robes. "I do not remember."

Falmagon snorted in frustration. "That is ridiculous."

Branimir watched the one-eyed Highborn fumble about awkwardly near his bedroll, clearly frustrated at Dorofej's insistent mystery about himself.

Erzebeth said, "You must know something, Dorofej."

"I could tell a story, yes? I know many stories," answered Dorofej.

"Would you?" Branimir smiled widely, clapping his hands together.

Dorofej began with a boom, his voice full of strength and vigor, like a minstrel speaking outside of song. "A straw house, there once was, which none visited due to the lingering of a she-wolf. To escape the squall and downpour one night, a brave warrior went into the straw house and made a fire. He also slept beneath a pile of rubble. From his place beneath the rubble, he could watch the door and innards of the straw house without being seen, you see? By and by, the she-wolf came and warmed near the fire, not knowing that the warrior was hiding within."

"You are trying to impart your wisdom on us again, Dorofej, aren't you?" Falmagon asked distastefully.

The old Highborn ignored him. "The she-wolf stood like a woman and her skin fell away, yes? The wolf skin was hung on a peg and she was no longer a wolf, but a damsel, full of beauty never before seen by the warrior. Fell asleep in short time by the fire, the damsel did. The warrior was overwhelmed with wanting, he was. Leaving the rubble, he stole the skin and hid it away from the damsel."

"A terrible thing to do!" Erzebeth said with a knowing look.

"Isn't it though?" Dorofej lifted his bushy eyebrows, "When morning came, the damsel screamed at the sight of the warrior, and searched for her skin, but to no avail. After time, the pair married, and had some children, you see."

"That does not make any sense, Dorofej. Why would the damsel marry the warrior that stole her skin and her identity?"

Dorofej raised his finger as if Falmagon understood the point of the fable, but he continued the story. "That his mother was a she-wolf, the oldest child soon learned. The knowledge ate away at the child for some time, yes? While out in the field with his father, finally asked about his mother's skin, he did. The father shared the hiding place with the child and the child with his mother."

"Then what?" Branimir said when Dorofej had paused for more than a second.

"Then the she-wolf took her skin, went away, and was never heard of again. The warrior was filled with grief for the rest of his days."

Branimir wrinkled his forehead, along with Falmagon. "I don't get it."

Falmagon reiterated, "If there is a lesson in all that rubbish, it is truly lost."

Erzebeth tried to interpret. "It is an old story with similar versions among the Vucari. The she-wolf was not the one who was caught, but instead, the warrior. We are blinded by desire, sometimes not knowing the control it can possess. Whether it is good or evil, we crave what we should not have. The gods, as represented by the child, will intervene to save us, but we still choose our own response. In this case, the warrior chose grief."

"One of many interpretations," Dorofej indicated with a dip of his head. "Also, it has been said before that the she-wolf is our soul and the gods are the warrior, stealing away our true identity in this life. Fate, chance, or luck, it is, as signified by the child that sets us free from the sway of deities, yes?"

"Freedom by death," Erzebeth concluded.

"Nothing but a bunch of drivel," Falmagon said. "Enough already. We need rest. I imagine tomorrow will be trying."

As they lay down, a resounding howl echoed in the night. Branimir nearly sprang out of his bedroll. The image of the she-wolf was fixated in his mind. The Highborn and Vucari ignored the sound, turning under their own blankets. A shiver struck his spine that was beyond the cold. Branimir could not help but think that Falmagon's words had just sealed their fate.

Chapter XIX

Erzebeth had been unsuccessful in finding them food again. After taking less than an hour to grab their things, they set off toward the mountains with empty stomachs. Branimir's stomach growled several times before the sun peaked over the landscape, but he knew that he was not alone. The Kras could easily hear the bellies of his companions making similar noises of irritation.

A cold mist sat upon the shriveled grass in the early morning hours. The mountains to the south were still barely visible above the fog, but they were fading from sight. Branimir glanced about feeling a cold emptiness inside. At first, he thought it was from the poor night's rest that he had received, but he was uncertain. All he knew was that something did not feel right.

By and by, the morning hours escaped them and he forgot about his uneasiness. The group walked in silence, lost in their own thoughts. After two months on the faering, none had much to say to any one of the other. Whether there was more to be asked, or shared, was beside the point. To Branimir, it seemed that each had said all they wanted to say to any other, except for him.

Branimir always had a question. He found enjoyment in expanding his mind with knowledge.

"Erzebeth, what is the name of these mountains?" he asked.

"I do not know that they have ever been named," she replied with a sigh.

"That is funny. I would think something as apparent as mountains would be quick to be called something."

"I am afraid they are nameless."

Branimir hummed to himself, pulling at his hooked nose in thought.

Falmagon addressed him. "What is wrong with you?"

Branimir shrugged his little shoulders. "Homesick, I guess, my Lord. We have been gone from Melkorka for a very long time."

The Highborn Longwalker tilted his head with a strange sense of understanding. "You get used to it after a while. Before long, no place is home."

Branimir shivered at the thought. Not having a home had to be a terrible feeling. Though, he supposed that he never had a home outside of Melkorka. The castle was never really *his*, but the Highborn's.

"I have an idea. We should name them," he said with a bounce. His mind immediately went to the memory of his father. "Let's call them the Hrani Highlands."

"The mountains?" Dorofej questioned.

"Yes!" Branimir exclaimed with excitement.

"You cannot just name mountains," Falmagon said.

"I believe he just did," Erzebeth hooted.

Branimir smiled widely, nearly causing his cracked lips to bleed. The idea that the mountains were named after his family, his father, gave him a sense of security.

Dorofej chuckled at the sight for what seemed to be hours, his laugh echoing throughout the newly named Hrani Highlands.

The day pressed on.

Branimir had barely noticed they had gone into the mountains before they were deep within the shadowed peaks. The Hrani Highlands were marked with frequent ups and downs as though they were oversized hills. The rise of the mounds behind them blended into the green-laced mountains so perfectly that there was barely distinction between the two.

At the high points, the Kras looked back over his shoulder toward the way that they had come. He quickly found that he was looking over the expanse of Maharia for miles upon miles. Hills stretched as far as he could see to the north and the west. Branimir could easily see the ocean to the east as the fog lifted near midday. The waters stretched for what seemed like an eternity. Branimir almost thought that he would be able to see Kalamaar from the heights of the mountains. It was a foolish notion.

It was around the third uprising that Branimir turned to glance back the way they had come when something caught his eye in the distance. In fact, it was a lot of somethings, and they were moving across the hills at an exceptional pace. By the time he noticed the creatures, they were already nearing the mountains.

Branimir was not afraid at first, but his voice still squeaked. "What are those?"

Falmagon twisted around, peering at the hundreds of creatures galloping across the hills toward them. "Horses?"

Dorofej's face turned paler than death.

"Those…those aren't horses, Falmagon." Erzebeth started to back up. "Those are Svet! Run! Run for all you are worth!"

Erzebeth took off through the mountains to the south with exceptional speed. Dorofej followed, clearly aged since the last time they had to run from an enemy. His movements were slow, and his pace was excessively unproductive.

"What are Svet?" Falmagon screamed as the Vucari pulled away from them. The one-eyed Highborn pushed past Dorofej, trying his best to catch up with the woman who was becoming smaller in the distance.

Branimir kicked his feet up pushing past both Highborn. The Kras were known for their ability to run fast, especially when afraid. He had the impulse to catch up with the Vucari but felt he could not leave the Highborn behind.

"We must move faster, my Lords," Branimir urged. "I—"

He stopped, seeing the Vucari woman leap over a hill in front of them. In mid-air, she transformed her skin from human to wolf. The clothing and flesh fled from her body like the skin from a snake. Grey fur laced over her features. He could not see for certain, but he was sure her brown eyes had changed to yellow.

Branimir had thought only he could see her at the distance, finding himself more than puzzled when Falmagon spoke up. "By Mulafell, did you see that? She just left us! We saved her just to be left behind like the scraps from supper."

Dorofej lagged. "She is a survivor, yes? You'd likely do the same if you knew what we know."

Falmagon replied fiercely, "What is it that you know?"

Dorofej amended himself hastily, "What she knows, I mean."

The younger Highborn harrumphed and pushed forward, following Branimir who led the way with a wave of his hand.

"Come on," he said.

The three of them ran through the green mountains, not having any idea where they were going but always heading south. The Highlands were extensive, extending and broadening across Maharia down the coastline of the large land mass. If there was an end to this world, Branimir figured the three of them were not going to reach it any time soon.

It did not take long for Dorofej, and then Falmagon, to lose their breath, walking and stopping to regain some energy. They ordered Branimir ahead many times to find Erzebeth, or at least a cave for hiding. For the next hour or more, Bran found nothing. He and the Highborn men pressed onward. After time, the sounds of hooves upon the rock reached Branimir's ears.

"They are growing closer, my Lords," he said.

Falmagon gripped his crooked staff. "We must make a stand, Dorofej."

The old man shook his head, clinging to the rocky wall. "Too many, Falmagon, there are. It would be a futile attempt, yes? Besides, you and I are far too weak to wield Koldovstvo without inviting our deaths, yes?"

"These Svet may kill us regardless," Falmagon argued.

"No, I think not. At least, not immediately, I am sure of it."

"You speak outside of your knowing, Dorofej. These Svet are as unknown to you as they are to me. Do not act as though you have wisdom where there is none to be had!" Falmagon heaved. "Habërmani will give me enough strength to lay waste to these Svet, and still we will make it to the Ash Tree."

Dorofej scowled. "I say, will you then defend against the Vucari who Erzebeth claims guards it or powerless, will you be?"

Falmagon cried out in frustration, his hands spread open to the heavens. Branimir had never been one to know power. He could only imagine what it meant to hold so much power and be able to do nothing with it.

Dorofej moved forward with a bound and slapped the one-eyed man across the cheek. "Screaming like a lunatic will only give away our position, you fool!"

Falmagon growled, raising Habërmani. "Keep your hands to yourself."

"Bah!" Dorofej turned on his heel, his black robes consuming what heat there was to gather, sweat glistening on his brow. "Branimir!"

"Yes, my Lord," Branimir said automatically.

"You must remain in service to us in this moment, yes? Require it desperately, we do."

"Of course, my Lord," Branimir looked with uncertainty at the Highborn. "What is it you need from me?"

"You still have Ojenek, yes?" Dorofej asked.

"Of course." Branimir pulled the moonstone from his pocket. The blue stone shined as though it were freshly polished.

"The gem from Illuard?" Falmagon said with confusion lacing his brow. "What good does that do us?"

"Quiet your tongue, Falmagon Sej, or I would cut it out," Dorofej screeched with a mad gleam in his eye.

Falmagon did not test the old man, holding his lips fast together.

Dorofej turned his attention back to Branimir. "Hold to it and follow wherever the Svet take us, you will. You must find a way to free us before—"

Branimir interrupted, "I do not understand, my Lord! How am I to free you?"

"There is no time. Go!" Dorofej pushed Branimir away from him.

Branimir rocked backwards, hearing the stamping of hooves, like an army of horsemen coming down upon them. They were closing quicker than a pack of wolves on their prey.

"Hide, Branimir," Dorofej said. "Hide yourself!"

Branimir vanished, heartbeats before the first Svet rose over the hill to the north.

The Svet stood over a foot taller than any man, and likely weighed six times as much. The head, arms, and chest of the Svet were that of a human with the rest of the body, including four legs, hindquarters, and a tail like that of a horse. Hair grew down the neck and back like the crest of a horse. The mane was as black as the dark skin and penetrating eyes of the creature, more beast than man. Erupting from the forehead were massive horns that jutted forward made for ramming or impaling an enemy.

Branimir was terrified.

The beast barely wore anything but the skin on its back. Due to the long hair, Branimir was unsure if it was man or woman. That is, until a female galloped up beside the first, her bare chest like that of a female human. Her mane was brownish in color, distinguishing her from the male. There was no sense of modesty, exposing all that there was to be exposed.

"Centaurs?" Falmagon said disbelievingly. "The monsters of fairytales?"

Dorofej stayed quiet, lifting his arms and exposing his hands, showing he was harmless.

Both Svet, male and female, raised bows that resembled the luks made by Northmen, their arrows pointed with stone and aimed at the Highborn. Extra arrows were held in a quiver hanging on the right side of a makeshift leather belt.

"Die, Vucari," the male snarled between fanged teeth, his ears were like that of a horse, twisted backwards behind his horns.

Branimir gasped realizing that every single tooth was sharpened, made to the tear flesh.

Falmagon and Dorofej said nothing. Branimir noticed Falmagon's face was twisted in confusion, whereas Dorofej held a façade carved in stone.

"We should take them back, Asgrim, for the herd," the female Svet said.

"Not alive," the Svet called Asgrim responded. "They are in our lands and deserve death. They threaten what is sacred."

"You know the meat would spoil if we kill them now."

Asgrim turned toward the female and bared his fangs. She responded with equal ferocity, a growl reverberating in her throat.

Several more Svet approached from behind the first two. Each creature was equally dark of skin with coarse hair that thickened near the hoof. Each Svet had different colored crests down their human backs and clutched the weapon of an archer.

The next over the ridge stopped at the sight of the Highborn and said, "Do not leave them standing there. They will use their magic, Asgrim."

Asgrim responded to the other male, "Felitch insists we keep them alive and return to Sorod."

"Gah! So be it. But if it must be that way, do not leave them awake," the centaur responded.

Asgrim growled, rushing forward toward Dorofej and Falmagon, stomping his feet, throwing up dust. He towered over both old men with a fierce gaze.

Falmagon stared in astonishment at Asgrim.

The male Svet moved forward cautiously toward the one-eyed Highborn, licking his lips. "I do not like the way this one looks at me. It is as though it thinks it were my equal."

Falmagon kept his gaze steady as if trying to understand what the Svet was saying.

More centaurs lined the hills behind the others. There seemed to be hundreds of the horse-like creatures. Their faces etched in brutality and hate. Dorofej and Falmagon were heavily outnumbered.

Branimir gripped the moonstone, hoping for a miracle to happen.

"Careful, Asgrim," Felitch warned. "He may be preparing to change."

Asgrim roared, slamming his luk against Falmagon's head, and then did the same to Dorofej. Both old men fell to the dirt unconscious.

Satisfied, Felitch dipped her head and snorted through hollowed nostrils, larger than that of any human. "The High Priest can bless the meat when we return to Sorod."

Asgrim grabbed Dorofej's body and slung it onto Felitch's back. Falmagon was then picked up by Asgrim and placed on his own back.

Asgrim stamped its feet again, seemingly in agreement with Felitch. His voice was deep. "For glory! For Rujan! We ride!"

As the many Svet rode back north, Branimir sprinted after them. He would not abandon the Highborn. He was Kras and they were his Lords.

Chapter XX

The day had come and gone. The night rose with Myestera, the Moon Goddess, shining dimly overhead. Out of the Hrani Highlands and over the adjacent, unnamed hills, Branimir ran northwest after the mass of centaur archers. He sped as fast as he was able, chasing after the Highborn like he had been ordered to do. In his heart, he gravely feared failure. To be trapped in this strange land without a master, to live anywhere without a master, would leave him without purpose.

As the Svet pulled leagues away, Branimir found himself blubbering, tears blurring his vision as he ran. The cold wind stung his eyes, the tall grasses whipped against his red skin. It was no matter. Branimir quickly found that the centaurs were far superior in speed compared to the Kras.

Still, he was not completely hopeless. The centaurs left clear marks of their path, tearing down the terrain like a sickle against the crop. The heavy hooves of the creatures pummeled the grasses back into the earth, giving Branimir direction to run, even after the sight of the Svet was long lost.

Branimir could not have guessed how many hours he ran. His legs continued to fall in rhythm against the ground long after he lost feeling in his feet. His arms had grown weak, the muscles in his shoulders and back aching as though he had spent a lifetime lifting rocks. His head ached, ears frozen against the coolness of the northern wind. Whatever gods the humans prayed to did not look down positively on him in this moment. He fought against negative thoughts. He fought against fate. Branimir took every feeling within his being—hate, love, sadness, fear—and pushed himself beyond his limitations.

Branimir refused to abandon Dorofej.

The moon had passed through the sky, nearly indicating the next dawn, with light barely illuminating the far horizon. Delusional with exhaustion, Branimir stumbled in the grass, and fell to his knees. His pale eyes scanned the world around him seeing nothing different than he had for the hours prior. Hill upon hill stretched in every direction. The mountains, the Hrani Highlands, were but a shadow in the distance.

The sounds of war cries reached his delicate, pointed ears. Branimir heard the noise like a whisper in a dream. He barely believed it to be real, but it gave him the strength to return to his feet.

He pushed onward, faltering over hill and hill again. The sounds of battle, high-pitched howling, and fierce cries of warring beasts echoed through the hills. Soon, he learned the battle he heard was real, and not just in his head.

Branimir's chest heaved with heavy breaths, his small hand clutching the kinzhal tucked in his belt. He again became invisible to the world around him for protection, and advanced. The crumpled grasses crunched under his light footsteps with every step as he moved over another hill.

The sight in the hazy pastels of the waking world filled him with untamed horror.

The Svet, monstrous creatures beyond anything that Branimir could have ever imagined, were an intimidating force alone. The many archers circled, bare chests and fanged teeth exposed, thundering with the ferociousness of a thousand demons. A hundred stood in defense with half more lying dead in the grasses, their shredded bodies a token of their bravery. Crimson colored the grass more than the green that should have painted each blade of the earth.

The arrows of the Svet were fired with the precision of skilled combatants toward monstrous wolf-men that attacked relentlessly. The wolves, layered in shaggy grey hair from snout to paw, walked upright on their hind legs with strength comparable to the mighty centaurs. The creatures leapt about the battle scene with impressive quickness, claws slashing and teeth gnashing. Their fangs buried into the dark flesh of the Svet over and over again. The roars and howls of the beasts were more ferocious than the wolves of Kalamaar.

Though, the Svet barely seemed intimidated. Branimir awed at the centaurs, who stood their ground against the enemy. If it were him, he would have fled from the wolf-like creatures. Yet as one Svet fell, the next would take its place. They were a single unit battling against the multiple foes. Stone arrow after stone arrow tore through the wolf-men, tearing down their ranks in equal measure.

He found comfort that he was hidden and searched for Dorofej and Falmagon. He hoped that neither had been caught by a loose arrow or worse. It only took a few minutes before Branimir decided neither Highborn was on the battlefield. If either man was among the ranks, he had fallen permanently or was unconscious under the bodies of those who were dead. Then again, it was quite possible that the two men were laying within the ranks of the Svet behind the massive bodies, hidden from the sight.

He had to be certain.

Ever slowly, Branimir walked through the battlefield, creeping toward the raging onslaught like an insect on a spider's web.

"Come! We feast on Vulkodlak tonight!" a Svet cried from the ranks, dark hair flailing off his back, firing a series of arrows from the quiver at his side.

A female Svet near him laughed, catching a wolf-man by the neck as it jumped at her. She crushed the larynx in her hand before pulling it close and ripping a chunk of flesh from the side of its neck with her teeth.

Branimir turned his eyes away before the bile in his stomach emitted from his mouth.

Branimir scurried over the many dead bodies and frayed limbs. Death cries echoed. Branimir could not help but think back to the battle of Melkorka, the battle of Illuard, and the battle of Arkaim. His life had been haunted by death.

Branimir ran under the crushing hooves of another large Svet who wrestled with a Vulkodlak. The wolf-man held the arms of the Svet at bay. Each gnashed teeth at the other, before the Vulkodlak thrust forward and locked jaws on the bicep of the Svet. The arm was torn from socket by the massive fangs and the Svet screamed. The Vulkodlak had drool drip from its blackened lips, mixing with the blood drawn from its enemy.

The Svet male responded with head-butt to the beast, causing it to drop the hunk of meat from its mouth. The Vulkodlak was barely fazed, leaping onto the upper body of the Svet and burying its teeth into the centaur's face.

As the two crumbled to the ground, Branimir rushed forward to avoid being crushed. Either of these monsters would make quick work of him if he were captured.

Unseen, he kept moving to and fro through the battle, avoiding collision with either warring party.

Svets flung arrows from their luks as their circle grew smaller and smaller. Bran noticed that even in the face of defeat, not one Svet backed down from the battle. As apparent friend or even loved one met their death, the Svet fought onward with the vicious, relentless retaliation.

"War and glory!" a male shouted from the ranks.

"For Rujan!" cried a female with a voice as deep as the man.

"For Rujan!" the rest echoed. The bawling of the Svet resounded repeatedly as they matched brawn against brawn.

Branimir squirreled through the front legs and haunches of the Svet, eventually making it to the inner circle of the holding.

He gasped in surprise. The Highborn were not in the inner circle of the Svet. They were nowhere to be found.

Branimir wanted to cover his eyes, but instead covered his ears as the din of victory sounded among the many centaurs. The remaining Vulkodlak retreated across the hills to the south.

Branimir was overwhelmed with emotion and utterly exhausted. He had told Dorofej that he would remain loyal and free them. His stomach gurgled. He felt feverish.

Hope was lost.

A female voice, deep and sturdy rose behind. Branimir felt something grip his shirt tightly, lifting him directly off the ground. "Hold on! What is this?"

Branimir squealed. He twisted and fought as he flew off the ground in the grasp of one of the mighty Svet. He had forgotten to concentrate and had become visible.

He was lifted past the Svet's firm, small breasts, marked with dark nipples before catching sight of her face. Her black eyes peered at him under two curved horns, smaller than the male Svet, but threatening still. "Is this a polevik?"

He furrowed his eyebrows in confusion. He had never heard of this thing called a polevik.

"No. Its color is too wrong to be one of those broods," said a male harshly, fangs clicking together as it spoke.

"I just want to know if I can eat it. What is it?" she snorted through her nostrils and twitched her ears.

Branimir frantically jerked against the grip of the beast. He squeaked, kicking his legs. "You cannot eat me! I am a Kras!"

"Gah!" she screamed, nearly throwing him. "It understands me. And, it speaks our language."

"What sorcery is this?" the male Svet gasped, rearing back, lifting his forelegs in the air like a horse throwing a rider from its back.

Several Svet gathered to look at the sight. Grumbles, growls, and snarls resounded through the ranks.

Branimir stopped twisting, his hands flying to the fingers of the Svet, fearful of being thrown from such a great height. "Of course, I can understand you. Why would I not be able to?"

The Svet glared and spoke more from surprise than purpose. "Our language is our own, small beast. Nothing but a Svet speaks Svet!"

Branimir looked as staggered as the Svet who surrounded him, completely speechless. He understood them as well as any other.

The male who spoke next. "Take him to the High Priest for blessing and be told if you can eat him."

"You cannot eat me," Branimir cried.

The woman nodded with a dangerous smile of sharpened teeth, her angled ears twitched again. "Gather what of our dead you can muster. There will be a great feast. Praise Rujan!"

The other centaur replied, "He truly smiles on us this day!"

"Don't eat me!" Branimir wept in frustration. He struggled against the overpowering creature; yet he was no match for the strong grasp of the Svet. "Don't eat me," Bran repeated fervently.

The centaur frowned and hit him over the head.

As the world darkened, Branimir had made up his mind. He wanted to return to Melkorka. He did not like this place called Maharia.

Chapter XXI

Branimir awoke with his hands bound behind his back, bouncing slightly on the back of the female Svet who had captured him. He was slung over the hide awkwardly on his side. His first thoughts were to remain still. He feared to move a muscle, thinking that the Svet may whack him over the head again to keep him unconscious.

His head throbbed, swollen and tender from being struck by the centaur. A boulder may have well had been dropped on his head. His vision was blurred momentarily, but the world eventually came into sight.

He found himself in a meadow a score of miles west of the battlefield where Vulkodlak and Svet had fallen. He found himself being taken into what appeared to be a centaur city. There were more Svet here than there had been humans at Arkaim. Their numbers stretched for miles. This Svet settlement was larger than Branimir could have ever guessed, stretching across the hills with man-horses and woman-horses scattered across the terrain like sand upon the water's edge.

The structures built for the Svet were odd compared to the structures built for men. Each building towered as though towering trees had been cut in half, shaved clean of their bark, and then a wooden flat roof leveled, stacked, and placed overhead. There were no walls on any of the buildings, but simply four corners that were spread at length from each other, fastened by the stilted roof. Each makeshift home gave enough room for many Svet to lie under at one time. In the center of each wooden structure was a fire pit that roared. It was surprising that the fire did not burn down the building. If anything, the homes appeared to be half-constructed stables without stalls.

The streets in between each housing unit were worn and hardened from constant movement upon its surface. Even now, Svet after Svet traipsed down the streets with heavy hooves, plodding the dirt deeper into the earth. The grasses within the settlement, if there ever had been any, were nonexistent compared to the tall grasses in the hills.

Branimir struggled to keep his eyes open as they passed by a massive bonfire. Many of the centaurs gathered around the flames, pulling their dead near. Branimir watched, mortified, as the Svet would approach the dead and nod as though identifying the deceased, and then cut off the head of their own with a massive curved axe.

The blade reflected off the fire, showing that it was not copper, but something different. The color very much resembled the metal seen at King Ker's manor house, a mixture of copper and a stronger element.

Human head after human head fell away from the bodies of the half-horses. And then, the bodies were thrown on the fire to be thoroughly roasted.

Branimir wanted to shake his head, or turn away from the sight, but remained fixated. Still, he feared to budge. He had great sight of the Svet gathering their own from the fire and tearing into the meat. They were feasting on their own dead.

"A great victory this day!" A Svet cried, riding up to the female who carried him across the city.

"Many died, giving us nourishment, bringing glory to the clan," the female said assuredly with a dip of her head in return. She continued to push forward barely looking at the male that had approached.

He pursued. "Melyena, you were battle hardened against the Vulkodlak, so I hear."

The female snorted with what may have been a giggle, turning her eyes to the male, her fawn-shaped ears wiggling excitedly. "Wish I could say the same for you, Asgrim. Running with your tail between your haunches is not the Svet way."

"Bah!" Asgrim pushed her lightly, throwing his head back at the jest, "You know what I was after. The Vucari had to be brought to the temple. Their kind have not been seen this far north for decades. Questions need answered before we skin them!"

Melyena sighed with a smile, her ears calming, "Make your excuses. You missed battle, hardly honorable!"

Branimir dared not move his head but peeked at the male Svet that had approached. It was definitely the beast that had taken Kinhar and Dorofej. His strapping chest was as solid as stone, as were the gigantic, muscular arms. The Svet could break him with threat.

He could not believe his luck that he had come to the same place as the Highborn. He found himself thinking that they were still alive.

Asgrim ignored her. "What is this *thing* on your back? It is too red to be a polevik, though it is about the same size."

Branimir shut his eyes quickly, playing as though he were still unconscious.

"It called itself a Kras."

Asgrim poked Branimir. "Must be lying. I have never heard of such a thing."

"It is a strange creature," she admitted.

Asgrim leaned forward and inhaled deeply as though he were sniffing the skin right off Branimir. The brown, coarse hair on Melyena's back waved slightly in the heavy snort. Asgrim then blew out disgusted, snot spewing onto Branimir.

Branimir held his body still but could not stop from scrunching his face in disgust.

Asgrim did not seem to notice. "It definitely doesn't smell like a polevik. But, you smell nice."

"I will rip out both of your hearts, Asgrim. Keep your hands to yourself," she said with crude humor. Branimir wondered what she meant by both hearts.

Asgrim laughed, shoving her again with a wink. "You stole my hearts a long time ago, Melyena." He suggestively raised his eyebrows.

She snorted, turning her head with embarrassment.

"In all truth, I wonder what this thing tastes like. I bet it tastes no different than a polevik."

Melyena shrugged her shoulders, the luk on her back shifting, the string taut between her naked breasts, "I'll tell you after the High Priest blesses my capture. I found it. I get to eat it. You get to watch."

Asgrim growled. "What if the High Priest doesn't let you eat it?"

"It is my right, Asgrim."

"Not if the Oracle says otherwise."

Melyena twitched her ears with aggravation. "Why would he consult the Oracle?"

"The two Vucari captured and this … thing … all in one day," Asgrim shrugged. "I am no High Priest, but it seems like something one would consult the Oracle about."

Melyena shook her head. "No. No. I will receive my blessing and be roasting this little red creature by nightfall. You will see. I bet it is made of the most delicate meat."

It took everything in Branimir's power to keep himself from leaping from the Svet's back and scampering away as fast as he could.

"Ha! Doesn't appear to have much meat worth mentioning," Asgrim said. "But Melyena always gets her way, doesn't she?"

The female Svet raised her dark eyes, her nose uplifted making the large nostrils swell. "Yes, Asgrim. I do."

The two Svet trotted along for some time in silence through the city. The centaurs who passed by stared at Branimir on Melyena's back, sometimes asking questions, sometimes saying nothing at all. There was not a single centaur who did not take at least one look at Branimir.

Bran could not say he was shocked by the interest, considering the men of Kalamaar and the Seven Islands, a place that he called home, knew of his people and had reacted in a very similar way. He could not expect the Svet to not be curious about him. Their confusion told him what he had dreaded all along. He really was the last living Kras.

Melyena and Asgrim stopped near a large structure with significantly more poles upholding the roof than the other makeshift buildings. It was about four times the size of most of the structures they had passed. Several centaurs walked underneath the shelter, with more surrounding the edges, peering past one another, as though they were eager to get inside. Most held weapons. A constant growl like a pack of wolves feasting on their prey, flowed through the spectators outside the place.

A stone table sat in the center, lit by torchlight. The dirt floor was compiled of piles of skulls, with a lone pile of decaying Svet heads. Branimir could not keep himself from shuddering at the hollowed eyes, gaping mouths, and the pool of blood collecting underneath.

"These Vucari smell strange," a dark-haired male said with a throaty rumble. The Svet had a light-colored mane down his crest and matching tail, a tan color to him that offset him from most of the centaurs who Branimir had seen. "I wonder if they are Vucari at all, or something else."

"What else could they be, Saint Isaak?" a female shouted from the side.

The Svet male shook his head, responding off-handedly, "If I knew that, I would tell you."

"Isaak, where is the High Priest," Melyena said. "I want his blessing on my capture." She trotted into the holding, displaying Branimir on her back.

Branimir squeezed his eyes closed.

Isaak gawked. "What demon have you brought into the temple, Melyena? Your father will have your hide!"

"It is not a demon, Isaak," she said willfully.

"Saint Isaak," he corrected. "You will address me with reverence, Melyena Rogov."

"Saint Isaak," Melyena smiled. "Where is my father?"

"The High Priest visits the Oracle to find meaning of the Vucari advancing into our lands before the Season of Frost. They may be planning to use the cold against us, believing they are superior in the frigid weather. War may be coming!"

Growls erupted around the temple from Svet that watched the exchange. Branimir peeked to see the female centaur from the Highlands step out of the midst.

"Asgrim and I captured these two with ease after one of their own shapeshifted into a wolf and fled. It is clear what they are, Saint Isaak."

"Is that so, Felitch?" the Saint asked. "Then why did they not also change and outrun you in the mountains?"

"Our numbers were too great. They were filled with fear!" Asgrim bellowed, stepping behind Melyena.

"Don't be foolish," Isaak said with a pointed finger.

Asgrim sprang forward, grabbing the hand with a meaty fist. "Foolish, is it? I can smell the fear off your holy skin. If given the chance, you are the one who would bolt; or perhaps, you would stand and fight me to the death?"

Isaak tried to pull away. "Your hand should not touch me. I am of the temple, Asgrim," Isaak cried out.

Asgrim snarled, baring his sharpened fangs. "I will do as I wish. I will not have any Svet question my honor."

"What honor can be found in injuring a temple priest?" Isaak asked.

"Injure? I would kill you, Saint Isaak. What honor is there in keeping a priest who dribbles hateful words from his tongue against his own kind?"

"Let him be, Asgrim!" a voice barked.

Branimir slowly turned his head to keep from drawing attention. He saw the massive Svet who stepped into the temple. It stood a head taller than Asgrim, horns twice as large, with a white cloth draped over its back. Dark colored hair fell from the top of its head past the barrel of its body, shrouding the animal ears that perched with authority. The beast was magnificent.

"High Priest," Asgrim bowed his head, releasing the Saint immediately.

"Father," Melyena dipped her head in respect.

"What is that *thing* you carry, Melyena? Does it come with these—these creatures?" The High Priest waved his hand at the two Highborn men who were heaped on the ground. They were stripped naked, dropped near the skulls and the stone table.

Branimir jerked at the sight of Dorofej and Falmagon, searching for any sign of breath in their chest.

"I think not," Melyena said, grabbing Branimir by his leg and twisting him about to display him to the High Priest. He struggled slightly, but remembering the throbbing in his head, stopped abruptly. "I caught it after the battle with the Vulkodlak in the meadows, sneaking among our ranks."

"Quite a distance from the mountains then."

"Yes, Father."

Branimir swayed upside down by the ankle, considering the dark eyes of the High Priest, seemingly in charge of the settlement. The male Svet held sway over the strong warrior, Asgrim, who remained silent.

Branimir had no idea how he was going to save Dorofej and Falmagon. He had to do something.

"As is my right, Father, I wish to eat him with your blessing," Melyena said.

The High Priest leaned forward, sharp teeth spread slightly in consideration at the request. "I am not certain it is safe to stomach the creature. It may make you ill, daughter."

There were murmurs within the tent.

"I do not want to be eaten!" Branimir finally shouted louder than expected. His shrill voice silenced the Svet throughout the tent.

The High Priest stumbled backwards, his rear colliding with the stone table, knocking it over and causing it to split down the middle.

He spun around anxiously, his hand reaching for a weapon he did not carry. When he found that he was without arms, he roared, ears lifting from the bulk of hair.

There was a similar response from those who watched, suddenly searching for their weapons. When the stone table broke, gasps of astonishment echoed, followed by gruff growls that gave hint to an army ready to go to war at first suggestion.

Branimir froze, lips pressed, hands clinging to his shirttail as they stayed bound behind his back.

Melyena did not budge, dropping her head as though someone had revealed a great secret.

"It speaks. It speaks Svet." The High Priest squinted his eyes at Branimir.

"Yes, Father," Melyena said, "and seemingly understands us as well."

"Of course, I understand you," Branimir muttered, struggling against the female Svet's hold.

The Svet High Priest ignored Branimir, easing forward. "You knew this, Melyena, and chose to keep it from me after all that has happened this day."

"This is not related," she said.

"Bah! Do not lie to your father." The large Svet stomped forward, clacking his hooves against the hardened dirt. He lifted a hand as though he might strike his daughter. Almost colliding with Branimir, the High Priest invaded the space of his daughter with Branimir hanging inches from his chest.

Branimir gagged, turning his head. The smell of horse and manure overwhelmed his senses.

"Can I eat him or not?" Melyena hissed.

"No!" Branimir shouted.

The High Priest looked down at Branimir, "You understand us? You speak our language? How is this possible?"

Branimir trembled, but he kept his voice steady. If anything, he had plenty of practice in serving the Highborn and speaking when he was afraid. "I am not sure what you speak of, honestly, my Lord. I hear no difference in your dialect than my own, and I hear myself speaking in my own language."

"He attempts to deceive us," Saint Isaak said. "He dishonors Rujan with his demon lies in our temple."

The High Priest lifted his hand. "Quiet, Saint Isaak, or I will have Asgrim finish what he had started."

Asgrim grinned, tilting his head toward the Saint. "Say another word. I beg you."

The High Priest shot a look of disdain at the strong warrior, silencing him as well, before turning back to Branimir. "What are you? Where do you come from?"

"I am Branimir Baran, a Kras, from Melkorka, upon the Seven Islands of Forghar, on the island of Folkmar, near the island of Kalamaar. It is a small place compared to Maharia, my Lord," Branimir rattled as quickly as he could spit out the words.

Wrinkles formed around the High Priest's eyes as he tried to make sense of the new words and places. "Is that so? Are there more of your kind at Melkorka?"

Branimir shook his head. "No, my Lord. I am afraid I am the last of my kind."

The High Priest twisted his head to see the broken stone table and growled fiercely. "Leave us. All of you, leave us!"

Melyena protested. "Father! He is mine by law!"

"And bound to him, you may be, my daughter! For now, you leave us, so we may speak in private. Am I understood?" he replied with a darkened gaze.

Melyena rumbled, showing her fangs. Asgrim placed a hand across her chest with an unheard whisper, and Melyena took a breath. Reluctantly, she handed Branimir to the High Priest, who gripped the other leg as though he were grabbing a burning branch.

Branimir blinked his eyes several times as he was passed off from one beast to the other. He had no chance of leaving the camp alive.

Melyena, Asgrim, Felitch, and even Saint Isaak removed themselves from the temple with the several dozen Svet who had crowded on the sides. Objections and criticisms, and even whispers of conspiracy were shared among the large man-horses and woman-horses. Branimir did not know what to make of all of it.

The High Priest did not loosen Branimir's bindings, but he did put him down carefully on the ground. Branimir, seated, barely reached the Svet's knee, and would probably stand just under the foreleg if he was standing at full height.

"Do not run. We will run you down if you do, Kras."

Branimir nodded. "I know." He did not have to be threatened by the Svet. After running across the countryside, he was easily convinced at the speed of the Svet. Besides, with his throbbing head, he was sure that he could not concentrate long enough to stay invisible to escape Sorod. Even if he could, he would have no idea where to go without the Highborn.

"Are you familiar with the Svet, Kras?" the High Priest asked.

"No, my Lord," Branimir said, continuing to give title the Svet as he was accustomed. "Your kind is not found on Kalamaar or the Seven Islands."

The High Priest nodded, deep in thought. "Then you are not familiar with our prophecies?"

Branimir shook his head, black hair clinging to his crimson forehead.

"We have many, but one," the High Priest's hoof scraped against the broken stone table.

When the last speaks in tongue
The breaking of rock has rung
The talisman of treasures gifted
The era of eras will be lifted
Come strange and wyrd
The enemy has reared
Come blood and death
Come era of shared breath

Branimir wrinkled his nose. "What does it mean, my Lord?"

"I do not know, Kras, but you speak in the tongue of my people. You have also instigated the breaking of the *Solheimasandi*. This sacred stone table has been among the Svet for age upon age, crafted and carried from the dark mountains of the west before my grandfather came to the Hyaendi Hills."

Branimir rocked backwards, utterly confused by the High Priest. "I did not break the table, my Lord. You ran into it."

The High Priest's throat rumbled and softened, "Things happen for a reason, Kras. Do those where you come from not believe in fate."

"I suppose some do, my Lord."

The High Priest dipped his head, ears lying flat behind his massive horns. He tilted his head as if listening to the wind, in deep thought. After several moments, he shook his head. It was either in response to an unheard voice, or perhaps not hearing anything at all. Regardless, his face was clearly painted in frustration.

Seeing the ferocious, barbaric nature of the Svet, Branimir decided it was wise to remain silent. He peered at Dorofej and Falmagon again. Each had a significant bruising on their face where they had been struck by the heavy hand of Asgrim yesterday. It was likely they had been hit several more times to keep them unconscious. If that were the case, they were lucky their faces were not complete mush.

Branimir noticed each of them had a steady rise and fall to their chest. He sighed in relief.

"What are you doing in the Hyaendi Hills, Kras? Why have you come to Maharia from Melkorka?"

Branimir compressed his cracked lips and wrinkled his nose. The question was more complex and difficult than any question he had ever been asked.

Several minutes may have passed before the High Priest growled impatiently. "What is your answer, Kras?"

"These two," Branimir pointed at Falmagon and Dorofej, "journey with me. I need them to complete my quest."

Branimir cringed, wondering if he had just incriminated himself permanently to whatever fate befell the two Highborn lying amongst the decaying skulls.

The High Priest kept his jaw locked, but his eyes were full of bewilderment. It was evident he had expected an answer that would lead him to deep deliberation, but nothing linking Branimir with the bodies at his hooves.

The patience and understanding of the High Priest was unlike any other who fell among the ranks of the Svet civilizations. "These are Vucari from the Dyndaer, and not from the place you call Melkorka?"

Branimir said, "They are not Vucari, my Lord."

"What are they then?" he replied.

Branimir was not sure why he answered with the ancient name of humans instead of referring to them as Highborn or Northmen. It was likely a question he would reflect on for the years to come. "They are Anshedar, my Lord."

"Anshedar…" the word slid off the pointed tongue of the High Priest as though it were a word that could move mountains, carve oceans, and even change the arrangement of seasons. He said it again. "Anshedar."

"Yes, my Lord."

Dorofej stirred. Branimir heard him snort as he twisted slightly on the ground.

"What is your quest, Kras?" The interest of the High Priest was exceptional. Branimir had a sense of calmness rush over him, hearing the soft tone of the great Svet that stood before him.

Branimir swallowed, finding honesty to be the best course to follow. "We seek the Ash Tree within the Dyndaer to—"

"What?" the High Priest roared, clamoring forward, nearly squashing the Kras where he sat. "What did you say?"

The rage that filled the Svet came without warning, sending Branimir reeling backwards into a pile of skulls. They collapsed down on his little body, hitting him in the head over and over again.

"What did you say?" The High Priest grabbed him by his throat and lifted him off the ground, nearly killing him from the mere grip.

The voice boomed with the ferocity of a thousand beasts followed by a thousand demons, carrying through Sorod like war drums. Branimir's ears hummed.

He wriggled, choking against the grip.

The High Priest cried out again, not noticing he was strangling Branimir, "Answer me!"

"The Ash Tree," Branimir croaked. "We … protect it … demons …"

The Svet let loose Branimir, falling back on his haunches in a daze.

Branimir had no ability to even wave his arms with them tied behind his back and fell four times his height to the ground with a thud. His body cracked against the solid earth. The air was stolen from his lungs, a sharp pain tearing through him from chest to spine.

The High Priest spoke to himself. "I stand at an impasse, to follow tradition and eradicate those who tread on my lands or welcome blood and death by the beasts of the Netherworld. If the Kras speaks truth, I will welcome the destruction at my doorstep. Or, I can let this Kras and the Anshedar complete their quest, holy or not, futile or not, and forsake my people. I will lose any authority as High Priest, and worse yet, the admiration of my daughter. What choice will bring glory to Rujan? What choice will bring glory to the Svet?"

Branimir rattled for air, trying to understand the Svet through his panting. He crawled up to his knees and fell over with his cheek against the dirt.

Dorofej moved again, followed by a groan from Falmagon.

The High Priest raised his horse body and stepped toward the two Highborn with a shake of his head. He looked at Branimir with an empty gaze. Then, with a quick stamp of his front foreleg, he connected hoof to human forehead, sending each Highborn spiraling back into sleep.

Branimir dropped his head in defeat, jaw quivering. He heard the High Priest approach him slowly, halfheartedly.

Branimir did not even feel the hoof strike him. In seconds, he joined his masters in the shadow of dreamless dreams.

Chapter XXII

The Kras did not know how long he had been unconscious. His head was flooded with aches and twinges, his own blood caked to his black hair. The dirt room, although massive, had little to no ventilation, like an underground tomb. There was no sign of the outside world, no view of the sun, stars or otherwise. He gasped for fresh air.

Night swept through Sorod, the centaur city, like locusts on the summer crop. Loud banter, singing, dancing, and feasting could be heard among the Svet throughout the city. The ground above Branimir shook under their falling hooves. The Hyaendi Hills, as they were called, reverberated with sound of the countless Svet. It seemed their voices and songs and praise would be heard for time without end.

"Oh," Branimir groaned, grabbing his stomach with both hands. To his recollection, he had gone nearly three days without food or drink, and his stomach had finally decided to remind him of it. It growled and tore at his insides as though it were intent on eating his guts. In the half decade he had been enslaved to the Highborn, Branimir had never known such treatment, nor had he been in such pain, even when Falmagon had beaten him with Habërmani.

With sudden awareness, Branimir jumped up and looked at his hands. He was not bound. He was free.

The moment only lasted a moment before his knees gave way and he weakly collapsed again to the ground.

"Branimir, come eat," Dorofej's voice echoed off the solid dirt walls.

He looked to Dorofej, who stood at a wooden table at the opposite side of the room. Falmagon stood next to him, stuffing his face with meat. He was relatively pleased to see that each of them had reunited with their robes, covering their aged nakedness. Though, Bran nearly fell backwards upon seeing the High Priest standing across from them, an enthralled look on his flattened face.

"What is happening, Lord Dorofej? What is with all the noise?" Branimir murmured, moving toward the table, the only object in the square room. On all fours, he crawled, barely finding any strength to stand. Besides the table, the room was completely bare, one door on one wall made of wood, large enough for the Svet to pass through.

"Celebrating victory and worshipping Rujan, the Four-Faced God of War, the Svet are," Dorofej explained. "Expect peace and quiet, I would not."

The High Priest spoke after listening to Branimir's speech and Dorofej's answer. The old Highborn lifted his hand as though he were about to provide solution to a grave concern.

Branimir stopped moving in astonishment. The words of the Svet were completely garbled nonsense, full of grunts and harsh consonants. It was absolute gibberish.

Dorofej must have used Koldovstvo to make the High Priest a babbling idiot. He and Falmagon must be holding him captive in this hole in the ground.

Branimir screeched in fear. "Where are we, my Lords? What have you done?" The stomping of hooves, thousands of them, echoed from above. The Svet were likely going to come crashing through the wooden doors in the room at any moment and slaughter them all.

He noticed the swollen faces of the Highborn, regardless of the dim torchlight eating at the air of the room. Each Highborn had a large lump with a hoof imprint upon the wrinkles of their foreheads. Branimir could not believe they were not as distressed as he was from the massive blow. If they were even close to being distraught, Falmagon and Dorofej hid it well.

Dorofej held up his hand teasingly and opened it slowly, revealing the moonstone, the Ojenek, in his palm.

Branimir instinctively checked his pocket and sure enough, Dorofej had swiped it from him while he was unconscious.

Dorofej handed it to the High Priest, placing the small stone in his massive hand delicately. The stone continued to flicker as though an inner fire were deep within its core. The towering, Svet male looked at the stone in amazement.

"You say this stone allows me to understand the language of any creature, as though I am speaking in their tongue and them in mine?" the High Priest asked.

"Is it not so?" Dorofej said simply.

Branimir's jaw dropped. He now understood why he could speak Svet. He had been carrying Ojenek.

Falmagon shoved the meat into his mouth again without manners. "It is about time I can understand you two. Been cackling and coughing for a half an hour back and forth, leaving me in the dark, hearing nothing but rubbish! Why did you not just give it to him to begin with?"

"It was not the way that things could be done, yes?"

Falmagon harrumphed and took another bite, "Dorofej, why did you just not talk to the brute who brought us here in the first place? We could have explained ourselves and been on our way!"

"My apologies, High Priest," Dorofej started, as he explained his reasoning to Falmagon, "but the Svet are not accustomed to hearing explanations, especially from those who resemble the Vucari, yes? Explained what we could not, Branimir did. The Kras paved the way, yes?"

The High Priest nodded. "That he did, Dorofej. I fear if you would have spoken directly to Asgrim, he would have killed you on the spot. Such a thing would have been greatly feared. Besides, the Svet are not generally aware of the prophecy of our people. They are not gifted with the knowledge of the Oracle. Moreover, Rujan does not speak directly to them."

Branimir wondered at Dorofej. It was like he knew what was going to happen before it happened.

"Prophecy? Oracle? Rujan?" Falmagon muttered. "You speak outside of our knowing, High Priest. We are not from these lands."

He finally made it to the table, looking at Ojenek. Branimir repeated what the High Priest had told him earlier. "The 'talisman of treasures gifted'.

The High Priest nodded. "Yes, Kras. That is exactly what this is, and I accept the gift graciously as it should be done."

Branimir almost wanted to scream. The shiny stone was supposed to be his!

A warning look from Dorofej held him at bay. "High Priest, yours to keep, it is."

Branimir watched Falmagon rip another bite from the bone he gripped in his fist. "Do you know what you are eating, Lord Falmagon?"

Falmagon arched his eyebrows at the Kras in exasperation. "Meat."

Branimir winced but found himself quickly devouring his own hunk of meat attached to bone. Some type of rib, he guessed, maybe from the fallen Svet or Vulkodlak. He did not want to think about it. He was too hungry to have to think about it.

"I imagine you exchange the stone for your freedom, so that you may continue your journey," the Svet said to the old Highborn.

Dorofej did not flinch. "Give nothing to the Svet, do I, for they take what they want. It is my hope the Oracle and Rujan see to it that we may continue our journey. We have traveled a great distance for a cause affecting the entire world, Kalamaar and Maharia alike."

Branimir took another bite from the red meat, feeling his strength begin to return to him. It was startling as to what energy could be gained through a few simple bites.

"You are wise beyond your years, Anshedar. You speak as though you are familiar with the Svet."

Dorofej dipped his head. "I am familiar enough to know the bounds of my choice, yes?"

"Hmm," the High Priest moved away from the table. "I must consult with Oracle to decide the best course of action. I cannot decide, and should not decide, on my own. Remain here."

The High Priest galloped full speed toward the southern wall of dirt, solid in appearance. The wall waved like an ocean, and the Svet disappeared into its depths.

"By Mulafell," Falmagon said, watching in astonishment. "Even in all my years with Koldovstvo, there are still things that I cannot believe."

"Quite a sight, yes?" Dorofej agreed.

"Where did he go?" Branimir questioned.

Dorofej explained, while chewing on the red meat lay before them. "The Svet worship the god called Rujan, a god who is quite similar to Svathevit, who is worshiped by the Highborn and Northmen, yes? Rujan is a God of War and Glory, said to have a face on each side of his head to be watchful and vigilant in battle, he is."

Falmagon pulled at his grey beard. "Just like Svathevit. That must be more than a coincidence, a god having the same characteristics of another god from across the world. What can that mean?"

"More common than we might think, yes? Our level of understanding can be most frustrating at times, I would think." Dorofej continued, "Rujan is everything to the Svet. I say, they worship him with all of their being and communicate with him through the High Priest, who is given secrets to accessing the Oracle."

"Through that wall?" Branimir scrunched his face. "Is it a person? A thing?"

Dorofej shrugged with a chuckle, causing the tassels of his beard to bounce. "That is for the Svet to know, I suppose. Some say the High Priest travels directly to the Beyond or perhaps the Golden

City, *Iriy*, to converse with Rujan about matters related to their fate, or so they say."

Falmagon suddenly dropped his hand holding the meat, and stepped back, his single eye peering at Dorofej, as though he were looking at him for the first time. "Who says, Dorofej? My education was the same as yours at Melkorka and none knew of the Svet. Even Kinhar, living a thousand years, who shared more with me than any other, never told me of the Svet."

Dorofej did not blink, scratching his beard in consideration. "The only Highborn to have been to the Ash Tree, Kinhar was not. Nor, living lifetime beyond lifetime, he has not been."

Falmagon spewed the meat from his cheek onto the table, a wild look filled his visage like a rabbit who had just stepped into a snare. "But—"

Branimir could not believe it, though he might have guessed it, if he had spent the time to consider the possibility. There was more to Dorofej than an old man.

Dorofej raised his hands ruefully. "It was not, and likely still is not, for you to know, Falmagon Sej. Young and rambunctious, you are, without understanding, I am afraid."

Falmagon did not hear him, slamming his fist down on the table. "How old are you exactly, Dorofej? You ridicule men of their secrets while holding your own."

The old Highborn lifted his shoulders, seemingly without a reasonable response. "I lost track centuries ago—"

"Centuries?" Falmagon stammered. "By Mulafell and all that is righteous. Centuries!"

Dorofej took another bite of the food on the table.

Branimir awed at Dorofej while trying to keep from giggling at the one-eyed Highborn. Falmagon could not make a coherent thought, let alone a sentence.

Without warning, the High Priest burst back through the wall. He stamped his feet against the ground and shook his head as if shaking a ringing from his ears. It was likely he had just escaped the eternal cries of suffering souls in the hereafter.

Falmagon did not even look up, staring at Dorofej with his mustache separated from beard, as though they may never reconnect. Branimir nearly laughed out loud at the exasperated facial expression. He covered his face with his hands.

Dorofej remained unaltered, facing the High Priest, speaking before swallowing, "I say, what word does the Oracle give, High Priest?"

"What did I miss?" the overbearing Svet asked after looking at Falmagon's gawking face and Branimir's half grin, barely hidden by small, cupped hands.

"Imagine they have finally ate their fill is all, yes?"

The High Priest licked his lips. "Good! The Vucari are delicious when tenderized correctly. I was hoping you found it tasteful."

Branimir's smile had never fled from his face so quickly. "Vucari? What do you mean Vucari?"

The High Priest grinned. "Yes, we caught a female Vucari shortly after finding you. She was without a hand, but there was no sign of disease."

Dorofej's composure broke as he gripped the table, face pale as a winter sky. He spit the meat out of his mouth as though it were poisoned.

Falmagon immediately fell to his knees, gagging and vomiting. His fingers dug into the dirt with every convulsion.

Branimir dropped the meat that he held in his hand immediately, his eyes tearing up. Never had there been a fouler trick!

They had eaten Erzebeth!

The High Priest twitched his ears, gawking at them with confusion. "What has happened?"

It was Dorofej who finally found the strength to speak. "What of the Oracle?"

The High Priest winced, but answered, "You are free to continue to your quest on one condition."

"Please, tell me, what is that?" Dorofej said.

"Rujan desires a Svet to accompany you to add our lineage to this tale. The Svet will share in the glory."

Chapter XXIII

It was mid-morning when the High Priest gathered the elders to the temple to make the announcement. Dorofej and Falmagon stood boldly among the Svet with Branimir meekly standing in front of them. It was not a ceremonious occasion, but it was one worth mentioning.

"Brethren of Rujan, we have been tasked to send one of our own to journey with the Anshedar and the Kras, last of his kind, for the glory of the Svet. The Oracle has spoken!" The High Priest shouted to all those who were gathered.

An elder cried from the crowd, speaking in a tongue that Bran could not understand without the Ojenek.

The High Priest raised his hand. "These are not simple trespassers deserving of death, Augastaoir. These are warriors who come to battle against demons that delve in the Deep."

Another elder interrupted with laughter, making comments in the Svet tongue pointing at the Highborn and then the city. He lifted his hands up, indicating the Svet were stronger and more powerful than the 'warriors' who stood before them.

Branimir could not blame them for doubting the two old men and a half-man, without weapon or army at their backs. The Svet had every right to laugh. Even Branimir wondered how they were going to accomplish something that the Svet could not rightly do on their own.

"No Svet will touch the Anshedar," the High Priest boomed.

The garbled argument came again from the Svet called Augastaoir.

The High Priest interrupted the objection. "This quest has been sanctioned by the Oracle. Listen, I questioned the decision of aiding these strangers too, but I do not disregard the wisdom of Rujan! Do you? If so, speak so that we may call you blasphemer and give you the death that you seek. Then, you can face Rujan in the hereafter!"

The roar of the crowd fell silent.

Branimir could only wonder what death a blasphemer would receive in this barbaric culture.

The High Priest continued, his ears flicking irritably at the many Svet that questioned his judgment and that of their god. "I will not ask any of you to accompany them on this journey. The Vulkodlak still threaten our lands and we must protect them. The beasts grow stronger with each passing moment, more daring, threatening our lives and our way of life.

"There has already been word that Fenna and Kilmuir called for reinforcements. Belgorad has had none to send and so we must rely on our own to defend against the wolf-men. I would not risk the livelihood of our own."

There were shouts across the crowd, but there was no indication to Branimir as to whether they were positive or negative based on the dialect. The language was so harsh, and the body language so foreign, he could not make sense of the guttural sounds that erupted from the throats of the Svet.

"It is for that reason that I will send my daughter, Melyena Rogov, to accompany them into the Dyndaer to see their task through," the High Priest said. "My own blood will be put at risk at the command of the Oracle."

As shouts erupted, the color in Branimir's face drained. It was just his luck that the one centaur that wanted to eat him would join them.

Asgrim pushed through the crowd, screaming at the High Priest. His voice was like thunder, bellowing through the temple and beyond.

"I will not stop you, Asgrim Garoar. You are a strong warrior and would fight alongside her well. However, you would be desperately missed in the war against the Vulkodlak. Your luk and labrys is greatly needed against the wolf-men."

Melyena stepped into the temple as well, placing a hand gently on Asgrim's shoulder. She spoke softly.

Branimir tried to make sense of the conversation between the two centaurs. The large male Svet snarled harshly at her with a whip of his head, his dark hair flipping around his face fiercely. She reared up slightly and hissed between her sharpened fangs before turning away. Asgrim slammed his hoof against the ground, and then grunted at the High Priest once more.

The High Priest responded with a dip of his head. "It is settled. Asgrim and Melyena will accompany the Anshedar and Kras. Let it be sung for ages to come."

Another roar sounded from among the crowd. It was strange that it erupted from the rear of the group instead of the front where the High Priest spoke. Branimir tried to peer through the centaurs to make sense of the noise. He could not see anything.

The High Priest cried out, spinning around to address all the Svet. "To arms. We are under attack!"

"What?" Falmagon cried, obviously as confused by the back and forth as much as Branimir. The words from the High Priest were unexpected.

The High Priest turned toward the Highborn. "The Vulkodlak have come into the city. You must go! You must flee!"

Falmagon shouted with the intensity of a thousand men at the High Priest. "Where is my staff? We cannot leave without it!"

"What staff?"

"It has a crook that bends at the top. It was with me when Asgrim brought me to Sorod," Falmagon explained in desperation. "Where is it?"

"Asgrim, this Anshedar is looking for the staff he carried. Where has it gone?" the High Priest said as Melyena and Asgrim trotted toward them.

The sounds of battle echoed in the distance. The Svet's fingers twitched, looking toward the beginnings of the battle.

Asgrim responded hastily, loosening a glimmering two-sided axe from his belt. His voice was deep and hurried, making no sense to Branimir.

Melyena retrieved the luk from her back and nocked an arrow. Her eyes scanned her quiver to make count of the rest.

"What did he say?" Falmagon demanded, folding his fingers into a fist.

The High Priest turned back to Falmagon with hesitation. "He said that they burnt it. He also said if you want a real weapon instead of a stick, we have bronze weapons at the armory."

Bronze. The metal was called bronze, not copper.

Falmagon's cry was like a madman watching his own child dismembered. He launched himself at Asgrim with outstretched hands. "Burnt it!"

Asgrim bared his teeth at Falmagon.

Dorofej grabbed the Highborn Longwalker before he could get his hands on the Svet. "Tear you apart, Falmagon, he will. Keep your head."

"He burnt it, Dorofej. He burnt Habërmani!"

The High Priest stepped in between them, speaking to his daughter. Quickly, he opened her hand and gave her the Ojenek, their hands both cupping the moonstone.

"Take this, my daughter, and keep it safe," he said. "It will allow you to speak to these strangers from Melkorka."

Melyena closed her eyes, accepting the gift. "Thank you, father. I will bring glory to our family and to the Svet."

The High Priest smiled. "I knew you would understand. Make haste! For glory! For Rujan!"

"For glory! For Rujan!" Melyena repeated.

Inhuman roars and howls of the Vulkodlak packed the streets of Sorod. Melyena turned her head with a snarl and bolted toward the west. The rest shadowed her as best as they were able with Asgrim at the front.

The wolf-men were smaller than Bukavac, but massive to Branimir as they bounded through the streets, clawing and tearing at the centaurs. No Svet, whether it be man, woman or child, backed away from the attacking Vulkodlak.

Branimir pedaled his feet, staying in front of Falmagon and Dorofej with ease. His eyes locked on the monsters that tore across the town like a sweeping river. The place was booming with the brutal growls and roars of beasts. Without doubt, the dead would litter the streets of Sorod this day.

"Move faster," Meleyena bellowed from the front at the humans behind her. She did not even bother turning her head. It was as though she could smell them falling behind. Branimir would believe it; none of them had bathed in months.

A Vulkodlak sprang into the streets in front of them, but was dropped by Melyena. Her arrow penetrated the wolf-man's eye socket as soon as its paws touched the dirt road.

Making such a shot while running had to be the best form of luck, Branimir decided.

Another beast approached the side of the party as they ran. Asgrim caught the Vulkodlak midair with the shaft of his two-sided axe. A guttural sound trembled Asgrim's throat as he flung the monster to the opposite side like he was tossing a hay, using the wolf-man's momentum against him. However, Asgrim did not stop with the deflection. He trampled forward and stamped the beast as it slid on its back. Hoof met skull several times, followed by the blade in his hands.

The hunger for blood surprised Branimir. The death delivered was not quick or merciless.

"We cannot run forever," Falmagon shouted, already tripping over his feet, chasing the hurried Svet.

Melyena twisted her head and raised her eyebrows at the two men who had fallen even further behind in just a few moments. It was as though she had just realized that they were not Svet.

"The stables are beyond the gate," she said. "Come!"

Asgrim mumbled something in the Svet language to the High Priest's daughter before glaring back at the Highborn.

Branimir ignored the two centaurs. He was bothered that the situation mirrored the events in Arkaim, which had ended in terrible bloodshed. Now, once again, the group was running from imminent death. He did the only thing that had kept him alive before and clung to hope.

Chapter XXIV

They fled beyond Sorod, into the Hyaendi Hills, with Vulkodlak in pursuit. The sound of battle echoed in the wind. The sounds of beasts battling beasts resounded in their ears as the Svet of Sorod defended their home and the lands they considered holier than any other. While the Vulkodlak hit the city by the hundreds from the west, the fellowship followed the direction appointed by the High Priest and rushed to the east.

Branimir rode bareback upon Melyena, with his small hands holding tightly to her leather belt strap. She galloped at full speed, luk in her hands as she ran. The long black hair flowing down her back and head hit him in the face, catching awkwardly in between his lips. He spit out the hair, tucking his head against her back, and attempted to use his arm to shield his face. She ran with all the speed of a faering at sea.

Ahead of her was Asgrim, pushing forward, with a luk across his back and his own quiver of arrows attached to his belt. His strong arm carried a labrys, swaying heavily with every bound. The large Svet was full of force, dashing back and forth across Hyaendi Hills.

Lastly, covering the rear of the two Svet, sprinted a painted horse and a black mare, carrying Falmagon and Dorofej. The Highborn, riding bareback as well, clung to the necks of the beasts that pushed forward to keep pace with the Svet. It was said that the horse was a sacred animal to the Svet and to their god, Rujan. These animals were frequent visitors among the Svet, not held by any means, but seemingly at the command of the man-horse and woman-horse of the hills. It was as though they were kin, only separated by culture and civilization.

The Highborn had been fortunate that the High Priest had allowed for the two horses to be taken in order to keep pace with the quick Svet.

"Where to?" Melyena shouted over the clopping of her hooves.

"To the Dyndaer to the far east and south," Dorofej said loudly, his old frame clinging to the mare.

Melyena nodded and shouted instruction to Asgrim. The black-skinned beast at the head of the fellowship changed direction.

They had only traveled for about an hour when Asgrim slowed them to a stop. He turned to look back the way they had come.

"What is it?" Falmagon said. "Why are we stopping?"

"Vulkodlak have been giving pursuit since we left Sorod," Melyena said, pulling Branimir from her back with a single hand and setting him down into the grasses.

Falmagon tilted his head. "I don't see any reason why we should stop moving then. If anything, let us pick up the pace."

"No!" Melyena said. "The Vulkodlak do not tire like the horses. Besides, the Svet do not run from battle, Anshedar. Stay back with the Kras and keep the horses calm.

Asgrim and Melyena trotted forward to the top of a hill, their bows held in hand, stone arrows nocked.

Falmagon and Dorofej slid from the back of their horses, their hands grasping onto the mane of the animals. The Highborn intentionally turned the horses to face away from the Svet.

Falmagon complained, "How will we hold the beast still without a harness?"

"Maharian horses, these are," Dorofej said. "I say, they will not stir as easily as those found on Kalamaar. Let the Svet do what they must, and hope that no Vulkodlak make it past them, yes?"

Branimir held his head, still aching. If the wolf-men made it past the Svet, they would surely die or the Highborn would die using Koldovstvo. Dorofej was far too old to even touch the craft, and Falmagon was close to it.

Branimir used his far-sight to watch the Svet. Already they were firing arrows at enemies beyond the hill.

Melyena fired arrows at twice the speed of Asgrim, but Asgrim's shots seemed to deliver more impact, the string stretching further back. The quivers emptied quickly as they pulled arrow after arrow from the holding bag on their right sides.

As Melyena fired her last arrow, she backed up, waiting for impact. The first Vulkodlak Branimir sighted over the hill came with the speed of a northern gale, the grey fur whipped back. It snarled and hurled itself at the female Svet.

Melyena swung her luk as she would a sword, striking the Vulkodlak across the jawbone. Branimir heard the beast yelp like a pup struck by its master, before gnashing its elongated teeth at Melyena again. It struck at her forelegs, and she reared up, kicking both legs downward, striking the wolf-man's head over and over again. As each hoof hit the monstrous creature in the head, its body jolted and eventually went limp. Melyena continue to stamp upon the Vulkodlak to be assured that it did not stand up again.

"We must help them," Branimir finally said. "It is the right thing to do."

Asgrim had already thrown down his luk and held the labrys in both hands. He had two Vulkodlaks advancing on him, one with a mangled eye and the other with blood already dripping from its chest.

The Vulkodlak was hungry for blood, hungry for death. It lunged, claws striking at the Svet as a man would in a fist fight. The second moved to the rear to sink its teeth into Asgrim's hide.

Asgrim was quick, using the butt of his labrys to strike the first in the forehead, making it stumble backwards. The centaur than twisted his upper body and flipped the double-sided axe, catching the blade in the chest of the second. The Vulkodlak was suspended, its rib cage caught on the blade. Asgrim tried to rip the blade free but it was caught.

The first Vulkodlak dove again, side stepping and biting at Asgrim's human body. The Svet roared, spinning his body and rearing. His hind feet struck the Vulkodlak in the chest, sending the beast sprawling onto its back.

With a snarl, Asgrim's muscles bulged, lifting the Vulkodlak on his labrys in the air. The wolf-man howled menacingly as the bronze blade dug deeper into his midsection. With perfect timing, Asgrim rotated around again, slamming the Vulkodlak on his labrys into the one standing with the missing eye. The impact tore his weapon loose and he charged to finish the first.

More Vulkodlak stormed.

"We must help them, my Lords," Branimir said, looking at the Highborn on either side of him. "They will die."

"What can we do?" Falmagon asked. "They have gotten us this far and are truly not needed to reach the Ash Tree. Dorofej knows the way. I say we ride onward and leave them to their fate."

"You are a coward." Branimir puffed up to the Highborn Longwalker. "You have the power to help others and you do nothing! How can you call yourself, Highborn?"

Falmagon gaped at Branimir, shock lining his face.

In the distance, Melyena swept up Asgrim's bow, and held it in her opposite hand, swatting at the advancing beasts that charged at her. As one locked its teeth onto her shoulder, she screamed.

Asgrim ripped the beast from his companion, crushing the skull beneath his massive fist.

"Branimir speaks the truth." Dorofej scowled. "We do not leave the Svet behind, unless you wish the entirety of their armies to come after us, yes? A race to be reckoned with, Falmagon, they are."

"I am not a coward," Falmagon struggled. "There is nothing we can do. We have no weapons and I am without Habërmani. Must I remind you that we still have Nedezhda to contend with at the Ash Tree? The Eretik may be there already!"

"Finish this, Falmagon," Dorofej said. "Strength, you still have, even without Habërmani."

Falmagon frowned. "I could kill myself, Dorofej."

"You are Highborn!" the old man screamed, his face shaking with absolute rage. "You are Anshedar! I say, does Branimir have better sense of those titles than you? How long has it been that you have diluted Koldovstvo through that crooked staff, Falmagon Sej? Forfeit glory for greed, you should not. If truly faithful to the Lightbringer, you are, then fight you must."

The grey-haired man, called the Highborn Longwalker, tore off the patch that had long covered the gaping hole in his skull where an eye should have been.

His lip curled, shaking with fury, as he turned to face Dorofej. "You know nothing of my sacrifice. You have lived a thousand years or more, so you say, and still you send other men to their death. You ask me to readily throw away what you have long coveted." Falmagon visibly was shaking. "Sit back and idly watch, Dorofej. So be it!"

Before Dorofej could say a word in protest, Falmagon tightened the grip on his horse and galloped full speed toward the battle on the hill.

As the ground lifted and rocks fell, as stone melded into flesh, and Koldovstvo seared through the veins of Falmagon, Branimir trembled in absolute horror.

The man, once younger than Dorofej, aged beyond reason. Hair whitening and skin wrinkling until there was barely hair or muscle left on the man. He slumped on the horse, clinging to the mane of the painted creature as he continued to wield the craft of the Highborn.

The Vulkodlak howled as they fell in their own blood.

Falmagon moved beyond Branimir's sight.

Bran trembled when realizing the power of his words toward Falmagon. In months past, he would have said the Highborn had never taught him anything. He was wrong. He, too, had learned how to lead others to their death.

Branimir did not think he would ever see the Highborn Longwalker again.

Month of Falling Leaves
Third of Frost
124 CE

Chapter XXV

Another two months had passed, and the Season of Frost was heavily upon them. The first snow had blanketed the world, melted, and another layer of the white fluff had fallen again. The winds nipped at Bran's skin, chilled with the breath of the Seamstress of Nightmares, known as Marheena. She seemed to bless Nedezhda and the demons with every passing day, making it more difficult for the fellowship to find their way to the Ash Tree. Czern, the Grey-Clad, was seemingly allied with her. The days grew darker as the God of Darkness lengthened his gaze on the world. Together, Marheena and Czern prepared Maharia for death and decay.

The Hyaendi Hills had long ago faded, the Hrani Highlands had blended into the Dyndaer, and two weeks ago the mountainous region had completely disappeared. While at the peaks of the Hrani Highlands, Branimir had witnessed the sight of the massive, enigmatic forest. It stretched further than any forest he had ever seen. Tree towered next to tree, higher than any man-made structure, wrapping around each other like a bandage that could never be uncoiled.

Somewhere within this forest was the Ash Tree. Dorofej claimed he knew the way. They had no choice but to trust the old man, who claimed to have lived longer than Kinhar and Erzebeth together.

Branimir shivered, pulling the deerskin around his body, lips nearly frozen together. The deer that now served as his cloak had been eaten for their supper two weeks ago. At the time, when Melyena shot it down, Branimir had crossed his fingers, hoping it was not a Vucari transformed. He had to push the thought from his head to keep his belly full, and his skin warm. Now, all he could think about was how odd the spotted fur looked against his red skin.

"Be'er learns to like da cold, Kras," Asgrim rumbled in the broken language of the Anshedar. Dorofej had finally taught him some words after passing the Ojenek back and forth between him and the Svet had become tiresome, but the language was still considerably choppy. Branimir had wished they had continued to pass Ojenek between them to help in the communication. "Dis is mild to what wills come."

Branimir stared at the black-skinned centaur that towered above him, pulling the skin tighter. It smelled terrible but did the trick in blocking the cold. "I will cope, my Lord."

Branimir's feet sunk into the icy slush as he stepped over another fallen branch. The leaves had fallen from many of the trees and were weighed down by the dampness of the snow. He found himself somewhat grateful. A couple of weeks ago the leaves had fallen across the ground so thickly that he nearly had to swim through them to keep up with the rest of the party.

Even with the leaves fallen from the trees, Branimir could barely make out the sky above. The branches were so thick that there was barely any room for light to make its way through. The entire forest was murky, laden with fog and shadow.

The Dyndaer was as mystical and petrifying as anything Branimir had ever come across. The trees were black and grew in such a way that Branimir could not see far into the forest. This made it difficult to track location, especially when there was no set path to follow. There was foliage upon foliage, trees, and warped vines from the moment they had stepped into the wooded forest. If they were lost, they would not even have the insight to know it.

"How much further to the Ash Tree?" Melyena said, lifting her voice so that Dorofej could hear her at the front.

Branimir shivered again at the sight of Melyena. The Svet remained without clothing across her chest, like her counterpart, Asgrim. Her flesh alone gave indication of how cold it truly was in the frost. Branimir decided the Svet were mad.

"I say, it lies at the third bend of the most eastern river," Dorofej said, licking his thin lips. He walked by foot through the woods, pulling his black robe around him tighter. He stood out like a sore thumb in the whitish landscape. "Pray that it is still there, we must."

Branimir was the first to stop in his footsteps, hearing the last of Dorofej's words. "What did you say?"

"Hold on," the voice of Falmagon boomed from the painted horse at the rear. Branimir had to agree with the man's shock. Falmagon was barely a skeleton beneath his aged skin. He was blessed to have breath in his body. He had no hair left on his scalp, and his fingers shook, gripping the brown mane of his horse as he tried to keep himself alive in the brutal weather. "Did I hear you correctly? What are you rambling about, Dorofej?"

The old Highborn turned, fingering his white beard in contemplation. "Did you not know the Ash Tree does not always remain in the same place, yes? Moves about the world from time to time, it does. Makes it quite hard for anyone to find it twice or three times for that matter, yes?"

Dorofej winked.

"This sounds like something we should have heard before leaving Kalamaar," Branimir claimed. He was actually becoming angry. "You play with our lives when you keep your secrets, Dorofej."

Falmagon started, "But Kinhar and Erzebeth—"

"Fortunate, they were, to find the Ash Tree where I had last found it. But limited, their knowledge was, making them quite poor leaders, I would say. Found myself reluctant to follow their advice, but another place to look for the Ash Tree, I do not know."

Falmagon curled his lip. "Speak up, Dorofej, I cannot hear you." The man held tightly to the horse, turning his head so that his flattened ears, drooping and wrinkled, could pick up the sound. He had said that the world was more muffled since the battle with the Vulkodlak.

"What are we talking about? Who are Kinhar and Erzebeth? Have we spent the past two months pursuing hearsay?" Melyena said in confusion, her fingers brushing against the arrows in her quiver that she had crafted at their evening campfires.

Falmagon lifted his voice, increasing the volume after each question. "Are you saying that we could have come all this way for nothing? That the Ash Tree could be anywhere? Even back at Kalamaar? The Seven Islands?"

Dorofej placed his finger to his chin. "That would be unfortunate, yes? Though unlikely, the entry to the Netherworld is rarely near an exit. The exits do not move about so sporadically, I think."

"Rarely? You think?" Falmagon fumed.

Dorofej replied, "Calm yourself, Falmagon, before you faint from exhaustion, yes? You are much too old for such heated rhetoric, yes?"

"This is ridiculous," Branimir howled, barely believing he sided with Falmagon.

"It is what it is." Dorofej concluded.

Branimir exhaled. "I don't think it is."

Falmagon grunted and coughed, giving clear indication of how old he had become. His single eye was barely noticeable. It made it seem as if both of his eyes were missing from their sockets. From what Branimir could tell, Falmagon was blind or nearly so in his good eye anyway.

Branimir still felt somewhat responsible for the Highborn Longwalker's deterioration, but the loss of hearing and sight had not humbled the man. His nonstop, brash behavior made it easier for Branimir to stomach his guilt, especially when knowing how

Falmagon had treated him in the past. Besides, he knew that once they reached the Ash Tree, Falmagon could regain his youth.

Falmagon placed his hand on his cheek, completely distraught. "We must hurry. I cannot take much more of this place."

Asgrim responded, "Da horse ca'ot take much in dis forest or it will die likes da ot'er Anshedar's did."

"By Mulafell! What?" Falmagon said, "Bad enough I cannot hear, but my reply has to come in fragmented drivel."

Asgrim roared, bounding toward the Highborn Longwalker. The Svet's hand already reached for the labrys at his belt.

"Asgrim!" Melyena howled, stepping between him and the Anshedar. Falmagon nearly toppled off his horse at the sound, though the horse remained unmoving.

Asgrim stopped at sight of the High Priest's daughter.

The male Svet bellowed in his language at the other in guttural sounds that Bran thought would make the trees of the Dyndaer wither.

"We are here to bring glory to Rujan and to the Svet, Asgrim," Melyena said. "We will not blemish our kind in this tale."

"Den when da tale is done, I will kills him."

Melyena, who seemed to have a bit more sense about her, attempted to change the conversation. "How long have you been away from your Melkorka?"

Branimir responded quickly, "Nearly six months."

If any Svet could have been merciful or compassionate, the look on Melyena's face may have marked the moment in history.

Dorofej called out, "Come. The light of the day is wasting, yes?"

For hours, the five of them slipped between the trees, keeping their trail as south and east, as best as they could tell. Dorofej had clearly made their situation seem direr than previously thought, but none had any choice but to continue to follow the old Highborn. Despite his frustration, Branimir had come to the same conclusion as the rest. This was the only path that lay before them.

Wildlife was scarce in the Dyndaer, primarily due to the cold. Branimir spotted a couple of rabbits near midday, and pointed them out to Melyena, who cut them down. They were cooked immediately and then they continued forward, unwilling to waste any time.

An hour later, Dorofej cried out from the front, "Whoa! We have reached a river." He hit his foot against the ice that sat on the surface. It broke straight through.

"Perfect," Melyena snorted through her enlarged nostrils. "If it doesn't hold you, it definitely will not hold us!"

"How wide is the river?" Falmagon asked, blind to the world around him.

"Doesn't matter," the female Svet said. "Anyone wades in that freezing water in this weather, and they will catch sickness and die soon after."

"Then we go around."

Dorofej shook his head. "Back north we would have to go, yes? I say, it would be another month before we reach the end. And many more rivers to cross, there are."

"There must be something we can do," Branimir said.

Dorofej fell to the glazed ground, covered in his murky robes. "The weather will grow colder at night, yes? A better chance of crossing, we will have."

"You want us to walk ov'r a frozen river in da dark?" Asgrim questioned. "Dat is madness, Anshedar! We are barely making it in da li'le light dat we have!"

Melyena twitched her ears. "I do not hear a better idea, Asgrim. We cannot wait here until the Season of Warmth, can we?"

Asgrim grunted, twitching his ears. "Der is no honor in drowning, Melyena."

Falmagon huffed. "I have to agree with Asgrim on this one. I cannot see the way that it is, and I must rely on you four with eyes. How is this going to work if none of you can see in the dark? We should be spread out on the ice so that it does not give way, if we make it beyond the bank of the river. We could easily become separated, lost, or worse."

Melyena started, "We could connect ourselves together—"

Dorofej interrupted. "A rope, we do not have, and even if we had it, straight to the bottom, you or Asgrim would drag us."

"I can see in the dark," Branimir offered. "I could give direction and lead you each across."

"That could work," Melyena agreed. "It at least assures that we will know the fate of one another."

"That is real assuring," Falmagon nearly fell from his painted horse as Dorofej and Asgrim bobbed their heads.

They made camp for the remainder of the day and into the evening. Each took a turn sleeping on and off to gain some extra rest. Branimir, try as he might, had a hard time finding sleep in the cold.

Branimir felt enthused in the forest, every sight and sound overwhelming him in its elegance. He could not help but pinpoint each sound of the forest. The creatures, such as the dormouse, hedgehog, and many birds seen a month ago, were no longer active in the woods. Bran assumed that they prepared for hibernation. Yet there were still many others that continued to make the forest their home.

Shortly after huddling in the deer skin, Branimir sighted a fox close to their camp. It had scurried off before he could mention it, which was fine by him. He was still plenty full from the rabbits eaten that afternoon. He had also seen deer on the opposite side of the river, but they were well outside of the range of the luk.

"You said that you were the last of your kind, Kras," Melyena stated to Branimir. The sentence may have been a question, but it was said so matter-of-factly, that Branimir was uncertain.

He looked at Dorofej and Falmagon who slept soundly against the black trees, and then Asgrim, who treaded near the frozen river. "Yes, my Lady. To my knowledge, I am the last surviving Kras."

"How strange that must be for you."

"I suppose. I have tried not to give it much thought, my Lady. My duty has always been to the Anshedar and not myself."

"So you are a slave? I had thought that you were but could not be certain. You speak so freely among the Anshedar."

"At one time, at Melkorka, I would have said that I was a slave. Anymore, I could not say what I am, but my priorities are the same," Branimir said. "My purpose is their purpose; my will is their will, as it has been for my father and his father before him. This is what it has always meant to be Kras."

Melyena raised an eyebrow, her ears lifting from beneath her dark strands. "Always?"

Branimir thought back to Illuard, to what the history of his people might have been. "Always for me, my Lady."

"You have surely known of other Kras," she said.

"I—I did, my Lady," Branimir stammered. "There were few of us who remained at Melkorka before…there was Mojmir…" Bran hesitated, realizing this may have been the first time he had said his friend's name since his death. "Poor Mojmir."

Melyena's face etched with concern. "What happened to him?"

Branimir's eyes glazed, the memory of Kinhar snapping Mojmir's neck flashed across his memory. "He didn't make it, my Lady. He did not survive the battle."

"You are brave," Melyena dipped her head, her dark skin crisped over with cold. "I hope you bring your people glory."

Branimir was not sure what to say. "You are brave too, Melyena."

"What do you mean?"

His face split into a crooked grin. He pulled at his nose nervously. "Bounding about without a shirt in these frigid temperatures. I do not envy you!"

Melyena laughed heartily, in a way he had never heard from either Svet. "Does it really bother you so?"

Branimir shrugged. "I've grown accustomed to it, I suppose. Just not natural for a lady to be showing off her…um..."

Melyena chortled. "They are called breasts."

If Branimir could have turned red, he would have in that moment.

Asgrim bolted toward the two. The ground shook as he stamped forward. His face etched in absolute fury.

Branimir quickly scooted backwards, frightened under the gaze of the massive male Svet.

Asgrim spoke in Svet to Melyena as he reached his hand toward his weapon. It was clear Branimir had done something to threaten Melyena or her honor.

He cowered.

Clear laughter followed from Melyena, who playfully kicked snow toward Asgrim. "I assure you Asgrim, the Kras and I will not be mating."

Asgrim looked at Branimir for a moment and then chortled as if he were measuring the Kras's worth, or maybe his diminutive size in comparison to Melyena.

Branimir's eyes were wide with disbelief, a grin splitting his own face at the thought. "Ha. I assure you that we will not."

The two centaurs chuckled again, pointing at Branimir with amusement. Then, without rhyme or reason, Melyena slid her fingers along Asgrim's chest before trotting off into the Dyndaer beyond Branimir's gaze.

Asgrim twitched his ears with delight and followed.

Branimir smiled.

Chapter XXVI

The ice was solid but likely not solid enough. Branimir could hear it cracking under the weight of the Svet.

"Hold!" he cried, from the opposite bank of the wide river. Getting across for him was as easy as running along solid ground. It was not quite as simple for his companions.

Asgrim took another step, and Branimir heard the ice shift beneath the surface.

"I said stop," he cried sharply, bouncing on the edge of the river, waving his hands as though any of them could see him.

"Listen to Branimir," Dorofej shouted with equal panic in his voice. "Lest we all meet a watery grave, yes? Come now!" The old man stood awkwardly balanced on one foot. His arms were stretched out as though he were attempting to fly, swaying back and forth at the far end of the line. The old Highborn was clearly fearful of taking any step in the pitch darkness without Branimir's direction.

Asgrim, twenty feet to the right, seemed less concerned. It could be he was having difficulty understanding the language, or maybe he did not care enough to consider Branimir, but he still did stop easing forward, even with Dorofej's warning.

Beyond him were Falmagon and then Melyena. Falmagon was crawling on all fours in his brown robes, bald head forward like a battering ram. The painted horse followed slowly behind him, moving at his command. Melyena was as cautionary as Dorofej and kept a large distance between her and the other three. It was only by chance she could hear anything Branimir was shouting.

"What do we do, Kras?" Falmagon yelled loud enough to wake the entire forest. Branimir guessed the man was minutes away from uncontrollably weeping.

Branimir's anxiety increased, doing his best to ignore the fact that he had never overseen anything before. If this were a less serious situation, he might have been laughing at how ridiculous the lot of them looked. Instead, he was nearly shaking out of his own skin. "Dorofej, put your foot down!"

The old Highborn did as he was told and heaved a sigh of relief as he regained his balance on the slippery ice.

"Now, Melyena move forward…slowly…and everyone else stop moving," Branimir said.

The female Svet did as she was instructed, her hooves clopping along the ice. The centaur was around twelve hundred pounds and stepping on ice that was barely hardened. If they made it through this, Branimir may believe a god was looking after them.

The ice popped and cracked again. She was only halfway across, just past the center of the river crossing.

"What is dat?" Asgrim yelled, holding firm with his front leg extended.

Branimir heard the ice loosen and fracture, with the shift in weight. "Get across, Melyena, and make it quick!"

The female Svet threw her weight to her rear and bounded forward, the ice shattering and breaking about her, while the other three remained unmoving, their faces stricken in terror.

"No one else move!" Branimir shouted frantically.

Melyena reached the tree line on the opposite side.

"I'm across!" she shouted.

"Good for you," Falmagon said. "The rest of us have nearly pissed ourselves!" Falmagon turned his head to the side to yell at Asgrim. "By Mulafell, do you know how to keep your hooves steady, or do you have sheepdip for brains?"

"What is dat?" Asgrim hollered, touching his labrys, but remaining still. Then, as if giving up on the meaning of Falmagon's words, the Svet said, "Gah! I will kills you, Anshedar!"

Falmagon shook his fist in the brute's direction from where he sat hunched on the ice, "Learn my language first!"

"Learn mine!"

"Shut up!" Branimir shrieked, scanning the cracking ice. "My Lords. I must think."

"That'll be new," Falmagon said under his breath, inching toward Branimir, directing the horse to follow behind him.

Bran disregarded the insult but considered letting Falmagon stay out on the ice a bit longer.

The ice groaned from the pressure as Falmagon's horse scooted closer to Asgrim's spot on the ice.

Branimir yelled. "Falmagon, you will kill everyone. "Hold steady. Hold your horse steady. Do not move!"

The blind Highborn flattened himself to the shelf atop the river. "I don't want to be out here all night, Kras."

The horse halted as well.

"Dorofej, you can come across."

As Dorofej walked carefully to the shoreline, Branimir slipped down to line himself up with Asgrim and Falmagon.

"Asgrim, you must move to your left and put more distance between you and Falmagon. The ice will give if you draw too close to his horse."

"I've made it," Dorofej said. "Nicely done, Branimir."

Bran called back to the Svet. "That is it, Asgrim. Just a little bit more." The male centaur stepped sideways over and over, putting distance between himself and Falmagon.

Ice crashed from where Melyena had been, water washing over the top of the ice shelf.

"Good," Branimir said. "Now, come forward, both of you, at your own pace."

Falmagon uttered curses as he wriggled along the frozen river. Asgrim moved with less subtlety, eager to get off the deathtrap.

The water from the broken ice shelf trickled down toward Falmagon and Asgrim. As it struck Falmagon's hands, he cried out.

"Ignore it, Lord Falmagon," Branimir ordered. "Just come this way."

The horse behind him whinnied and reared, the water sloshing past its hooves. Falmagon twisted onto his back and screamed at the horse, sensing its movement. "No!"

The ice shattered beneath the horse. Its legs breaking through the solid surface.

"Leave the animal, my Lord! Move!" Branimir yelled.

Falmagon, blind as could be, crawled on all fours. The ice broke away around him, the back of his feet sinking into the lake. He cried out.

"Falmagon!" Branimir screamed.

The old man's fingers dug into the ice, clawing desperately against the slick surface. Branimir dived onto the ice, grabbing a hold of the old man's clothing, pulling for all he was worth.

Branimir was not strong, but he helped provide enough resistance and leverage from the rushing waters so Falmagon could secure his grip. Slowly, the Highborn Longwalker pulled himself back to the surface.

With all his strength, Falmagon scuttled forward as fast as he could. Branimir clung to the man's hand and pulled him, led him, to the bank of the river.

"Thank you," he mumbled, "thank you." He shivered, crumbling to the snow.

"My lord…" Branimir gasped, more from fright than exhaustion.

Dorofej pulled at his beard. "I say, might have been better to go across one at a time, yes?"

Branimir shook his head at the comment. He should have thought of that. He was too dumbstruck to even respond to the old Highborn.

"Gonna need da fire," Asgrim said.

The Svet had barely let loose the words before Melyena cried out in pain. Branimir spun around to where the female centaur had been standing.

"Melyena?" Asgrim nearly toppled over Falmagon and Branimir in attempts to reach her.

Branimir jerked around to see three white-furred foxes approach Melyena, snarling. She bled from one arm.

As he made out the animals' brown eyes, Branimir said their name. "Vucari."

Asgrim cried out. "We ca'ot fight dem in da dark! Dey have eyes like da Kras."

The first and second lunged, easily taking chunks out of Melyena's forelegs and springing back before she could respond.

She cried out again, swinging her luk wildly at her attackers, having no idea where they were. She sniffed the air and swung a second time. Nothing.

"Dorofej," Falmagon groaned.

Branimir watched as the Highborn in the black robes stood, wrinkling his nose.

"Be quick, you must! My power is limited greatly," Dorofej counseled. Branimir barely believed it as the old Highborn wielded Koldovstvo. He had not touched the craft since Melkorka, since he had attempted to give life to Andrik Hjlavok and failed.

Blue and gold glowed in a swirling ball about the old man's hands, glowing heavily, and emitting light like the sun at autumn's twilight. Branimir stared through the immediate brightness, his sight adjusting with ease.

"I see the radiance of the light. Bring glory to the Lightbringer, Dorofej!" Falmagon breathed.

The Dyndaer shown with more brightness than it may have ever witnessed as the light illuminated the expanse of the area. The dark trees became clear and the snow in the immediate area began to melt. The power was impressive to Branimir.

Each fox, white in color, stepped back, squinting its eyes as though they were staring directly into the sun. The animal on the far left had an arrow through its skull before it could react to the magic that circulated from the Highborn.

Melyena reached for another arrow after killing the white fox. Asgrim charged.

Another fox retaliated with a bark, springing forward. It leaped through the centaur's legs with striking dexterity.

Branimir could not believe what he was witnessing as the fox changed shape from beneath Asgrim. The white fur shed in a moment and the creature sprouted into a bear much like Erzebeth had done at Arkaim. Claws from large paws cut through the underbelly of the Svet.

The centaur snarled, leaping off the ground, before the claws could dig to his vital organs. Blood dripped. The first layers of his flesh fell away, blood staining the frozen ground.

The bear twisted full circle, back to its four legs, and barreled at Dorofej with exceptional swiftness.

The other fox leapt at Melyena again, but quickly met the blade of the labrys as Asgrim crashed down for his landing. The creature was split in half, falling to the ground. Upon impact, the dead body shaped back into the human form of a naked Vucari.

Branimir marveled at Asgrim. He was truly a warrior at heart, ignoring pain and focusing on victory.

Dorofej rotated the ball of light in his hand and flung it forward at the bear bolting at him. The light, like fire in the kiln, seared into a cylinder and tore through the chest of the bear. The innards of the animal exploded through the back, near the spine, and the light went dim. The Vucari joined the other attackers in immediate death.

The battle had lasted mere seconds. Dorofej fell to his knees, coughing heavily.

"Dorofej, my Lord," Branimir squealed. "Dorofej, are you okay?"

The old Highborn lifted his blue eyes to Bran sputtering, "I still have my sight if that is what you mean."

"Oh, Dorofej," Branimir clutched the human. "I could not go on without you."

The old Highborn returned the embrace.

Falmagon said nothing, still shaking, his feet frozen from the river water.

"Asgrim!" Melyena stumbled to the centaur. "You are hurt."

"Eh, and you," Asgrim exhaled loudly, looking at the wounds of Melyena, "but we wills live to see tomo'ow! Dis journey is not yet done for us, Melyena."

Melyena nodded, placing her hand on Asgrim's shoulder. Her eyes drifted to the Vucari with the smoldering, fiery hole in its chest that gave minimal light to the area. Burnt flesh seared.

"The power of the Anshedar is great, Dorofej. If all Anshedar hold the potential of you and Falmagon with this magic, demons will not stand a chance in destroying this world. What can compete with such power in combat?"

Dorofej spoke softly, "If all Anshedar could do what we do, demons would not have need to threaten the purity of the world, yes? Already have stolen pureness, the Anshedar would have."

Melyena could not help but take a step back, weighing the implication of the old man's words.

Chapter XXVII

The Vucari were as thick as the trees in the early light. Branimir had no time to count their number as they swarmed around the makeshift camp near the riverbank.

Branimir plunged the kinzhal into the back of the bear's leg as it clawed and snapped at Asgrim in the midst of the Dyndaer. The animal roared, twisting to swing at him. Branimir ducked, the long claws narrowly missing his ears. Asgrim took advantage of the distraction and slammed the labrys into the side of the creature, ripping it open and spilling its guts out onto the snow.

Branimir disappeared again and raced to Melyena who fought against a wolf. With the Highborn limited, he was doing all that he could to aid the centaurs in the battle.

He sped past Dorofej and Falmagon. The white-haired man had a makeshift club that he held defensively over the Highborn Longwalker, who remained completely helpless. Dorofej swung the branch at the animals as they ran by him, doing all that he could to keep Falmagon from being killed. Asgrim stood on one side and Melyena on the other, circling as they attempted to keep the Anshedar safe.

Branimir reached Melyena as she slaughtered the grey wolf before her with a point blank shot through the skull.

Melyena shot true, cutting down the enemy. Her quiver was filled with arrows. Fox and owl and wolf crumbled under the stone-tipped arrows that impaled them through their flesh. As each animal exhaled their last breath, their body shifted and waned back to the human form of the Vucari, naked and bleeding in the snow.

It seemed that no creature who burst through the forest was safe.

Crouching, Branimir watched the snow owls that flew overhead. The large birds spiraled toward the centaurs with fierceness in their large, brown eyes. As they neared the ground, they transformed into grey wolves and snow leopards and large bears.

Asgrim swung his labrys wildly, striking bear and leopard. The white frost turned as crimson as Branimir's skin. Centaur and Vucari each bled, and it seemed that none would survive the day. Still, Bran had hope. After seeing the many Svet at Sorod, he knew that the centaurs were battle-trained and fought with the precision of any known warrior.

Melyena caught the first grey wolf that landed at her feet. She grabbed the beast by the back of the neck with her hand and threw it toward the frozen river. It howled as it crashed through the melting ice in the morning warmth. The current beneath the ice pulled the wolf down and under, out of sight of the Kras.

A leopard with thick grey fur vaulted at the female Svet immediately after, catching its powerful jaws around her neck. Blood spurted from her vein. She stood for only a moment before the large cat twisted its body and took her to the ground.

"No!" Dorofej cried.

"What is happening?" Falmagon shouted looking around unsuccessfully, hearing the constant ferociousness of the beasts that assailed them.

Melyena convulsed on the ground, clawing at the beast on her neck. Her hands reached for the cat's eyes, its neck, anything to pry it loose before her life slipped away.

"They will kill us," Branimir said to himself. "They will kill me." His body shook with emotion. He could not believe what he was doing. There was blood on his hands.

Branimir sprang over her midsection and slammed the kinzhal deep into the neck of the snow leopard. It scrambled frantically as it released and pulled away, its sharp claws nearly catching Branimir in their grip as it fell over into the snow. It took Bran's weapon with it, lodged in the thick flesh.

Branimir forgot his weapon and covered the puncture wounds on Melyena. He urgently tried to hold back the flow of blood. It gushed and pulsed through his small fingers.

"I cannot stop the bleeding—"

She gurgled, her luk fallen from her hands, her chest heaving. Scratch marks lined her torso and several pieces of flesh gaped across her body. Her hooves twitched as her life fled.

"I cannot stop the bleeding, my Lady!" Branimir wept, pushing with all his might on the wounds.

Branimir watched her eyes flutter, her ears lying flat against her head.

"You cannot die!"

"Branimir!" Dorofej swung his branch, connecting with the snout of a wolf that snapped at him.

He had not even heard it come at him in the chaos.

Branimir squealed, dipping his head down on the woman Svet. He could nearly hear her heartbeat slow.

Dorofej stood between the grey beast and Branimir, swinging the branch as though it were a stave, keeping the animal at bay as best as he was able.

Falmagon crawled behind Dorofej, following the old man's footsteps, not having enough strength to stand.

"It is over," he said.

The wolf clutched a hold of the branch by its teeth and ripped it out of the old Highborn's hands. Dorofej gasped in surprise at his own weakness. His muscles shook and shuddered. He could not be frailer than what he was without being in the same state as Falmagon.

Dorofej did have a chance to respond before Asgrim barreled through and struck the wolf with his labrys.

"Stay behind me!" he boomed.

The Vucari circled them. There were several dozen with their brown eyes pinpointed on the enemy against the riverbank.

The Svet roared, his sharpened teeth bared at the beasts who threatened them.

Branimir looked into the Dyndaer. Something stirred beyond the trees that he could not quite make out. There were footsteps, lightly falling on the snow.

"Something else is coming," he said. "Be ready, my Lords."

"What more?" Dorofej said under his breath, more to himself than any other. He stood in front of Branimir and Falmagon with his arms spread protectively. Asgrim stood beyond him.

Half a dozen men and women burst through the brush. Bright blue eyes and light hair was quickly masked by light blue orbs springing up around them as they prepared for battle.

The Vucari changed focus and attacked these other humans. Branimir noticed they greatly resembled the Highborn and Northmen of Kalamaar.

"By Mulafell, what's happening?" Falmagon asked.

The roar of a windstorm emanated from the heavens, mixed with falling shards of stone and fire and ice. The humans manipulated the elements as the Highborn would with considerable power. Air picked up animals flinging them from the riverbank, fire tore through others, and ice and stone pounded them into pulp.

Few Vucari made it past the display of the craft of Koldovstvo. Those that did bound around the elements hit the blue orbs only to be thrown back by an unseen force. Lightning was flung from the orbs, tearing through the creatures, taking their lives.

Branimir was somewhat pleased to see the young faces of the men and women that wielded Koldovstvo show signs of aging as it would be with the Highborn of Melkorka. Branimir could not imagine holding such power without having a cost.

Faces had added wrinkles, hair color changed, and skin drooped, depending on the spell that was cast. The men and women worked together to blend their magic, and to destroy the Vucari.

As the battle ended, a few Vucari scattered off into the forest, still in their animal shapes. The men and women released the orbs and approached the group huddled around Melyena's fallen body. Asgrim stood defensively with a sense of fear in his features, the labyrs raised. He was prepared to die.

Falmagon begged, "Someone please tell me what is happening?"

"Believe it, you would not," Dorofej smacked his lips and dropped his hands, where they had remained suspended the entire time.

Branimir kept his hands fastened on Melyena's neck, although she had surely already passed to the Beyond. He could no longer feel her breathing.

"I am Valya Shelagin of Shayol Domier. These are my companions," a man said flatly, stepping in front of the rest. The individuals on either side of him did not budge. "Identify yourself. You clearly are not the Vucari."

"Shayol Domier…" Falmagon said hastily, looking around at the voice that spoke. He tried to pull himself up and failed miserably, falling back to his knees. "Falmagon Sej from Melkorka upon Folkmar from the Seven Islands of Forghar. I am friend to Kinhar Sayan. I need to speak to Moreth Eanbald."

"Kinhar, you say?" Valya said. "I have heard of the name more than once. If you know of him, where is he?"

"Passed from this world, he has some time ago, Valya," Dorofej responded, taking measure of what was being said before him.

Branimir easily took hint that the old Highborn did not want to be where he was in this moment.

"And, who are you?" Valya asked.

"I am from Melkorka, called Dorofej, a name you should remember well, I imagine. Here is also Branimir Baran who has come with us from Melkorka, yes?"

Valya raised an eyebrow. "A Kras?"

Dorofej lifted his bushy eyebrow in return. "Yes, he is. Asgrim Garoar and Melyena Rogov of Sorod are the Svet before you, and aid to Melyena we would value before our yammering outlives her life."

Her warm blood still flowed through Branimir's fingers. "She is gone, my Lords. She is already dead."

"Brought back she can be, if not too far gone," Dorofej said. "Koldovstvo can still save her. Do any of you have the sacred blood? Make haste!"

One of the women lifted her voice. "We are familiar with the savage Svet of the north. We will not give aid to their kind. Let her die."

"It is quite questionable you even travel in their company, Highborn," Valya spoke steadily, squinting his eye suspiciously.

Branimir gasped, "You cannot be serious."

Asgrim howled, throwing his labrys down and pushing past Dorofej. He spoke heavily, screaming in the language of the Svet. Branimir barely moved out of the way before the large Svet fell to Melyena's side.

The beast roared in sorrow as the crimson liquid flooded from Melyena's neck, the skin already pale. He lifted the human half of her body and hugged it closely to his chest.

Branimir noticed the nod from Valya about the time Dorofej shouted in defiance.

A male behind Valya wielded Koldovstvo lifting three stones from the ground. The stones were flung through the air with enough force to crush Asgrim's skull before he knew what had struck him. The Svet did not have a chance to cry out before his breath fled from his lungs. Asgrim fell dead atop of the High Priest's daughter.

Branimir scurried in shock back to the two Svet, touching them lightly. Only yesterday, he had shared conversation and joy with the two centaurs, and now they were dead. They had found their way back among evil men.

With a heavy heart, his fingers traipsed along Melyena's skin. Soon, he found Ojenek held in her fingers, and returned it to his pocket.

He would keep it safe.

"Why?" Dorofej cried out, helpless against the many who faced them.

Valya grinded his teeth, clearly not used to being questioned. "We are Anshedar and Highborn. They are Svet. Svet cannot be trusted, being both reckless and inherently stupid. The beast would have turned on us sooner or later."

"The way of the Highborn, this is not. The way of the Anshedar, this is not," Dorofej said, clenching his fists at his sides.

Falmagon opened his mouth once more, curving slightly in a smile, mocking Dorofej. "But, the way of the Kadari, it is. The old ways will come to pass, and the Lightbringer will lift up the chosen. We will rule over this world and all the lesser creatures!"

Valya nodded in respect to the blind Highborn. "You must be familiar with Kinhar. You speak of the wisdom that he taught many years ago before the Vucari lost their way."

Dorofej's thin lips quivered. "What of us? I say, will stones be thrust into our skulls as well?"

Valya shrugged in disinterest. "You will come to Shayol Domier. Patrician Moreth will decide your fate."

Chapter XXVIII

The cold chilled Branimir to the bone throughout the half day that it took to travel to Shayol Domier. He desperately hoped it was closer, but it seemed luck had left the fellowship some time ago. Despite the bitter weather, drops of sweat still slid down the back of his neck, causing his black strands of hair to stick to him like a wet cloth. The walk had not been strenuous, but he still had uncalled-for perspiration. Without a doubt, the Kadari, as they were called, made him nervous.

Gripping the fur around him, the frosty wind sputtered against his flesh. The makeshift cloak flapped wildly around him. He shivered and kept his eyes on Dorofej in front of him. The cold was the worst.

Branimir's eyes burned in the stinging, dry air. His pupils wanted to water, but the tears would not come, and so he was simply left with the sensation of pinpricks on the whites of his eyes. He wanted to cry for Melyena and Asgrim, or even Kinhar and Erzebeth, but no tears came.

The far-reaching sky was hidden beyond the branches, giving little light and giving a pure bleakness over their path. Bran took in the group who held them captive, not bothering to look for an escape. Branimir have been many things, but a hero was not one of them.

Valya stopped the group of them as they approached the gates of Shayol Domier. The home of the Kadari was not anything Branimir would have expected it to be. The wooden gate was massive. It was made up of two, inward-swinging doors and looked sturdier than Melkorka. The gate was three times the height of any man, giving reason to believe it was crafted from the trees of the Dyndaer. From the wear on the wood, the place had to have been built over half a century ago.

Matching banners flapped at the top of stone towers. They were marked with the image of the sun, the same sign found at Melkorka. The golden, dancing swirls was the symbol of Dahz, the ruler of the golden sun and Protector of Men. It was no surprise to Bran that it was found here as well.

Palisades lined the outside walls in hand-dug trenches, preventing any beast from charging Shayol Domier down without impaling themselves first. Men and women walked along the top of the walls, their heads peering over the top watchfully for any enemy that may approach their holding. The fence stretched thirty feet in either direction before twisting at rock towers that were made up of flat stones. The rock towers were accessible from the walkway around the fencing. Branimir gawked at the structure.

"Looks like we made it back," one of the Kadari men said with a smile, slapping a female next to him on the back.

She grimaced from being jostled, eyeing the lithe man while rubbing her mouth as though she were scraping off dried saliva. Branimir noticed she barely turned her head toward him.

The man continued in his talk, paying no mind that she had not responded to him. "We are returning to camp like snow in summer or rain in harvest. Moreth will be pleased. Though, it is awkward being here after being gone for so many weeks," he said seriously. "You know, the world makes sense in its telling of how things should be. We do not use a whip on a horse, nor do we place bridles on donkeys," he shook his head despondently, "and yet, here we come, shaped by the gods, living our lives as though we should be equivalent with the idols of children's dreams. Not sure we all can be what we want to be, you know?"

"Good that you recognize your plainness, Artemiy," a thin smile twisted on the lips of the woman. "And to think, I had always thought you to be more conceited."

Lowering his eyebrows, Artemiy responded as though reciting a verse from an ancient text. "In the end, Alyona, the arrogant are always caught in the schemes they devise. If I were prideful I would never prosper."

Suddenly, Branimir noticed Alyona was looking at him with her purplish eyes. The young woman inclined her head slightly, not even looking at the man as she talked, a hint of satisfaction in her smile. "It is still to be determined if we are presently," she nodded her head toward Shayol Domier, "thriving in life or heading to our demise."

A larger man behind the two of them dropped his jaw slightly, turning his head to match the cold eyes of the woman. "What is meant by that?"

Artemiy seemed equally shocked. "This is a blessed prospect for each of us, sister. Be sure your words are not wicked; it will only bring despair upon us. The Lightbringer shines down upon us this day! Do not hex us!"

Branimir was sure he heard Dorofej harrumph under his breath.

Alyona swallowed, appearing less robust than she had a moment ago, retracting her statement. "I do not know what I mean."

"Ah," Artemiy lifted his voice as though he were addressing all of them. "Do not fret. Alyona speaks outside of her knowing. It has long been a common occurrence." The crooked grin on his half-haired face returned.

Branimir turned back to Valya, who had signaled to a handful of sentries at the opening.

It was probably just a bit past midday, and already there were lanterns hanging around the area, adding to the pale light. As they moved forward, barely making it twenty paces, a man approached dressed in a bulky, black, wool cloak. His shoulders were broadened, and his triangular features were steadfast. He did not appear to be a man that was easily manipulated, having odd strands of crystal white hair despite his middle-aged face. He scanned the group, particularly Branimir, so it seemed, before fixating his eyes on Valya. He dipped his head with reverence.

"We come from the depths of the Dyndaer with prisoners and wish to speak with the Patrician," Valya directed.

"Naught worthwhile, Valya," the man muttered as though he despised the chore of giving details. He offhandedly brushed the cold off his outer cloak. "There is no place for prisoners. If your intent is to hold them captive here, may I suggest you kill them instead? Last night, Aravdur reported he seen a human figure westward of the palisades. Said the woman walked like death, never touching the ground. Delkarv was with him and said he saw nothing. Mayhap, it was just in Aravdur's head, but it has the Patrician jumping at ghosts and not in the mood for audience."

Valya scowled.

"Nedezhda." Branimir whispered, clenching his teeth.

They did not come all this way to be cut down. Why was death always the answer, no matter the question?

"Fie!" The guard paused, his eyes squinting at Dorofej, Falmagon, and Branimir. His eyes lingered over Branimir a few extra seconds before continuing. "Then again, they may provide the men something more to do besides freeze. A tournament, perhaps? Seems suitable for the Kras, at least. Teach a lesson, I would think. Besides, some entertainment would be welcomed before we are all neck high in frost."

"There will be no tournament, Orgath, and this Kras is not one of our own," Valya's mouth tightened as though he were upset that the man's tongue was flapping so loosely, but he said nothing of it. "These men claim to be from the Seven Islands and Highborn. Patrician Moreth will see them."

The guard raised his eyes in surprise, but kept his mouth shut. Without a word, he turned and steered the lot of them through the wide angled doors into Shayol Domier. No other humans at the gates or within the palisades said a word as they passed through Shayol Domier.

The inside of the stronghold stretched beyond what Branimir could see, primarily due to the many Highborn who were scattered throughout the area. There had to be hundreds of men and women. Many fires were burning brightly with the Anshedar gathered around them for warmth.

In the center of the structure was a keep that sat below the walls. There were several small buildings constructed of the same stone as the tower, possibly a guardhouse or armory of sorts. There were cottages and workshops scattered along the fences on the inside that stretched beyond the keep with the long wall that marked the boundary of Shayol Domier. In addition, there was a large garden that ran on either side of the keep, wrapping around the building out of sight.

Even with all Shayol Domier's splendor, this was not the reason Branimir stopped walking.

"Kras…" he whispered to himself. Among the Anshedar, the Kadari, there were many Kras, possibly half the number of men and women. The red creatures scampered across the area at the beckoning of their masters. He had never seen so many. "Kras!"

He nearly jumped, turning to Dorofej. The old man had a half smile under his beard, sharing the joy with Branimir. He was not alone after all.

"Move, Kras," Alyona said behind him, pushing him forward to keep pace with Dorofej.

"Don't touch me," he muttered. He turned to face the woman.

Alyona lifted her hand to strike Branimir but showed surprise when he did not lower his gaze and did not back away.

"Lay a hand on him, my Lady, and my wrath you will experience a hundred times over," Dorofej intervened.

The woman halted her movement, unsure of how to respond to the threat.

"Come, Branimir," Dorofej directed.

None of the Kras who worked in Shayol Domier seemed to notice the scene. They did as the Anshedar told them. They were as much slaves upon Maharia as they would have been on the Seven Islands.

Bran followed reluctantly. He asked Valya, "Why is the keep so small, my Lord,"

"It is not small, Kras. You are awfully brave to speak to me as an equal. I have not seen the like from your kind. Perhaps, the Highborn were not strict enough with you at Melkorka."

Dorofej interrupted. "Mine to discipline as I see fit, this Kras is."

Valya snickered. "We will see what the Patrician says."

"This way," Orgath instructed. The guard nodded to a full-bearded, bulky man sitting on a bucket near the keep doors. "We need to speak with Patrician Moreth."

"Not sure if he will see the likes of you, but you can try," the man laughed, his ale-shaped belly shaking softly with his chuckles.

Branimir hitched his cloak around himself again as they stepped inside the keep. He wished he were better at ignoring the cold. Perhaps, if it were simply cold, he could ignore, but not with the wind that sprung through his bones like a wraith.

The keep doors opened. At the top of the stairs stood a giant stone statue holding a massive hammer. Based on the constant reference of Dahz's hammer, Branimir could only guess that it was supposed to be the sun god. The craftsmanship on the statue was perfect, even down to the single hairs of the pointed beard.

Three light brown stone pillars lined either side of a substantial staircase that led downward to the thick wooden doors of the underground keep. In between each of the pillars hung imposing tapestries of Dahz, like those that hung at the gates.

"The White-Clad," Artemiy explained.

"Familiar with Dahz, we all are," Dorofej said.

Falmagon made a face. Branimir was certain that the man was frustrated by his lack of sight. He was likely the only one of them that would truly appreciate the glamour of the entrance hall.

Valya moved to open the second set of doors ahead of them and the ground changed from dirt to red brick. Red bricks had been stacked against the dirt walls, but it seemed that they had run out of the material mid-development. Still, Branimir could only guess that the ceiling above was over seven feet thick with the downward slope of the stairs into the room.

This place was grander than Melkorka.

As soon as they stepped through the doors, two sentries stepped out of the shadows. Each of the Anshedar, apart from Dorofej and Falmagon, fell to both knees and bowed their heads with their palms firmly set on the red stone. The guards patted down Branimir and the two Highborn men, ignoring the members of the Kadari.

Falmagon cried out in surprise as the hands started touching him, but did not draw back. Branimir smiled to himself, enjoying the spectacle, nearly laughing out loud as their hands scanned his smaller body. He found himself lucky that he no longer carried the kinzhal.

"Welcome back, Valya," the nearest guard clamped a hand on the man's shoulder. "You were gone longer than expected. I assume that this is the one they have been waiting for." The blue-eyed man eyeballed Dorofej.

Valya rose to his feet with a snort. "Forgive us. We do not have time for idle talk."

"Think nothing of it," he chortled. "Be on your way. I am sure that the Patrician will be eager to hear of Kinhar's adventures."

Moving past the guards, Branimir could see the large square room. It was about the size of a small hut. There were five doors evenly spaced on the south, east, and west walls and torches along the walls. Branimir could see well in the dim light. He noticed thin red lines forming paths just thick enough to walk on in a single file line across the dark brown floor. The lines connected at the center of the room at a blue-painted circle. In following each of the red lines, Branimir found they all led to one of the doors on the walls.

"Do not stray from the lines," Valya muttered under his breath.

"What lines?" Falmagon asked.

Branimir took the bait. "What happens if you step off the path, my Lord?"

Valya did not miss a beat. "Take a step and you will find out, Kras."

"What lines?" Falmagon said louder, waving his hands.

"Hold onto me, Falmagon, yes? Lead you along the path, I will." Dorofej offered.

Valya grunted. "This way." The man turned down the fourth path heading to the north. When he reached the solid wooden door, he paused for a moment, and then knocked four times before pushing it open.

The other Kadari followed without hesitation as though they had walked the path a hundred times over. Branimir followed behind Dorofej and Falmagon, who took their time reaching the end. Falmagon held onto Dorofej's dark robes with both hands, following his instruction.

"Put your feet heel to toe, yes? Slowly. That is it!"

The room they were led into was no smaller than the previous one, and it held just as many doorways, these immediately led into open hallways instead of being blocked by a typical wooden door. Six red brick pillars stretched up to the ceiling, surrounded by limestone walls. Between these pillars was a large crimson rug covering the red brick floor. Candles and torches lighted the walls. The room was decorated heavily in interwoven tapestries of Dahz comparable to the ones Branimir had seen outside.

"How large is this place?" Branimir said to himself in wonder. It made Illuard look like nothing but a hole in the ground.

Dorofej whistled, as though that were answer enough.

At the end of the woven rug sat a single throne, more decorated than that of the King of Kalamaar. Facing the throne stood a tall man in a blue, shimmering cloak.

The Anshedar of the Kadari bowed again with palms firmly on the ground in the same manner as they had outside the door.

The guard from the front gates spoke first. "Valya returns with his scouts from the Dyndaer. They have come with prisoners from across Strega's Deep, Patrician."

He turned around giving full view to his scarred face. "This is not Kinhar or Erzebeth. I was told Kinhar had come. Who are they?" The man's voice was deep with a slight rasp, as though he were getting over a recent sickness. However, it did not keep it from echoing in the sizeable room.

"They say they are Highborn from Melkorka." Valya answered. "They said they know Kinhar, Patrician. They have insisted that they speak with you."

"Speak with me, huh? If this is true then tell me where is Kinhar," Moreth said with a curled lip, turning and sitting on his throne. "Moreover, tell me why demons lurk on my doorstep."

Falmagon did not move, the torchlight reflecting off his bald features. His voice lifted at equal level with Moreth. "I am Falmagon Sej of Melkorka, and I speak as the new spearhead of the Highborn, by commendation of the former."

"Kinhar put his trust in you?" the Patrician asked, outwardly startled by the news.

"Without question," Falmagon said boldly.

Dorofej said nothing against the brash proclamation.

"I am Patrician here, Falmagon, and it is best that you not forget it. It was decided that I would rule here and Kinhar at Melkorka. Now, where is he?"

Falmagon paused. His unseen eyes looked in the direction of Moreth as though they were two beasts ready to kill for the fresh meat that lay between them.

The Highborn Longwalker continued with a half sneer on his face. "Kinhar Sayan is dead. He was murdered by Nedezhda Mager, an Eretik, who has risen beyond the dead after receiving her sentence at Melkorka."

Moreth clicked his tongue on the roof of his mouth. His knuckles grasped the sleeves of the throne, nearly turning white. "You mean to tell me that the Highborn killed one of their own?"

"Yes," Dorofej whispered before Falmagon could respond. "Exactly what he means to tell you, it is."

Moreth nodded. "With what did you take the head of the Eretik?"

Branimir could not believe Moreth was so calm. Moreover, he was surprised at the familiarity the Patrician had with the ways of the Highborn and the Anshedar, especially when so far separated.

Falmagon spoke dully as though he were tired of repeating himself. "Her life was taken with a copper dagger called Kaelandur. Kinhar said that you would know all of this, Moreth. He said that all of you had taken the Kalamyr Oath at Shayol Domier. Were we mistaken to have come here? Thus far, we have only been identified as enemies and guarded like rabid hounds."

"We could not know who you were for certain," Valya interrupted, defending his actions.

Branimir gulped.

"Of course, I took the oath. We all have," Moreth said, ignoring Valya's attempt to give any excuse to Falmagon. "But, I did not think the old fool was rash enough to actually attempt what he has done. He talked about this years ago but showed no sign of making the sacrifice. In truth, I had thought he had either given up or died. Alas, there is no turning back now."

Falmagon heaved a sigh of relief while Dorofej smacked his lips.

"Using Kaelandur was a delicate task, which Kinhar obviously botched if the victim, this Nedezhda, still walks upon Aenar," Moreth said. "Nothing in the task should have brought her back from the dead."

Branimir scrunched his nose. He rarely heard anyone speak of the world, Aenar. People rarely had seen much beyond their own homes. For Moreth to use the name freely suggested the Patrician may have been as old as Kinhar or even Dorofej.

Though, it was the thought of Nedezhda's death being a deliberate act that chilled his spine. This ritual somehow was meant to give power to the Kadari. What more power could the Highborn be after? They already had found a way to escape death with the Ash Tree.

"The ritual plainly was not done correctly when Nedezhda was slain." Moreth scratched his head in thought, spewing questions. "She was kneeled facing east of Dahz's last light? Her hair was burnt outside of any Anshedar's sight before her beheading? The cut was clean through her neck?"

Falmagon faltered, "The first and third were completed beyond doubt, but Branimir had lit fire to her hair outside of the sight of Highborn. I could not guess at the exact timing."

Branimir's knees nearly gave out as he heard the Highborn speak. Their words indicated that it was he and Mojmir who had caused Nedezhda to come back to the world for her revenge. His mind raced back to those moments when he returned from Melkorka. Kinhar had been insistent that he had tarried in his task.

Branimir's mind swirled! Was he guilty of all this atrocity? All this death? It could not be the full of it. Nedezhda had said at Arkaim that magic had been used to create Kaelandur. That had to be the true cause.

Branimir opened his mouth to object but stopped as Moreth continued.

Falmagon cleared his throat. "Kinhar wanted Branimir to stand before you so he may be judged for his mistake. If the Kadari are going to rule this world, we must have justice on all living creatures."

"I will not pass judgment on this Kras," Moreth said, not bothering to even look at Branimir. "There is little that we can do about what has already come to pass. The Kadari must listen fervently to the Lightbringer to lead this world. Our feet have been set in motion."

Kinhar had planned to have Branimir executed for completing the ritual incorrectly. His stomach churned at the realization.

Falmagon opened his mouth to protest, but Branimir cut him off, taking the attention off him. "What is the Kadari? I don't understand."

Moreth entertained his question. "The Kadari are Dahz's chosen that will rule over this world. We have the wisdom to give guidance.

Those that know the Kadari way understand that it is our purpose to help all living creatures accept the will of Dahz, without question, so that they may find themselves in the Thrice Ten Kingdom in the Beyond. The Kadari will keep the races of Aenar out of the Netherworld forever, weakening Marheena and her demon armies."

Branimir had heard the Highborn speak of Thrice Ten Kingdom a long time ago. It was said that traveling through the Thrice Nine Lands and beyond the Netherworld would lead to a paradise, to the Beyond, to Thrice Ten Kingdom.

Bran reasoned, suddenly realizing why Dorofej held such rage toward the sect. Even now, Branimir noticed the dissatisfied look on the old Highborn's face. "You will take away people's choice of gods…their free will to worship?"

Falmagon answered, "If that is what it takes."

It was Artemiy who spoke up next. Branimir had nearly forgotten that so many of the Kadari were in the room with them. "Where is Kaelandur?"

"Nedezhda has it," Falmagon spoke.

Alyona nearly screamed. "How did she get the weapon? We are doomed if she holds the weapon from the ritual."

"What? Why?" Branimir screeched.

"Destroy the Ash Tree with the blade, she believes she can," Dorofej said.

Moreth answered. "If Nedezhda believes this to be true, we must as well. If the Ash Tree is destroyed, it would kill us all."

Dorofej asked, "It was said that there is a woman, possibly undead, that walks beyond your walls this past night, yes? Nedezhda, it is, yes?"

"Yes," Moreth said. "From what you tell me, I am afraid that Nedezhda is already within the Dyndaer.

Dorofej smacked his lips. "To rid Aenar of the Ash Tree and bring demon hordes from the Netherworld, she comes. She wishes to kill us all."

"She must be stopped!" Valya bellowed. His scouting crew raised their voices in support.

"We will cut her down again," the Patrician said, "but first, I imagine these two men would like to have their strength returned to join in the battle."

Falmagon's eyes lit up at the suggestion.

"What do you speak of, Moreth," Dorofej said, intentionally leaving the title of Patrician to the wind.

Moreth paused and then decided not to correct the old Highborn. "We keep barrels holding the Water of Life here at Shayol Domier for the Kadari to replenish their strength. You take a drink and you will be returned to your youth but maintain your knowledge. You see, the Waters of Life are not far from here, giving us unlimited power and strength against those who would stand against the Lightbringer. The Kadari have long been blessed by the Lightbringer."

"Is that so? Take a drink, I might." Dorofej spoke as though it were the first time he had ever done such a thing.

Moreth signaled to a couple Kadari who hurried to fetch drinks for the Highborn. They returned a moment later, each holding a clay cup brimming with a watery liquid.

"Please, drink," Moreth said.

Falmagon wrenched his hands together hungrily for the taste of immortality.

Chapter XXIX

"I do not understand, my Lord. Why cannot I stay with Dorofej and Falmagon? Will they be okay?" Branimir asked as Valya led him back toward the courtyard of Shayol Domier.

"Your loyalty to your masters is commendable, Kras," Valya said. "But you speak far too much. Some conversations are not meant for your ears."

Branimir rubbed his cracked lips, trying to understand. He had overheard nearly every conversation that the Highborn had ever had, whether it was important or not. Branimir frequently stood in the shadows, almost like a keeper of history, taking in the accounts of the Anshedar whom he served. To not be a part of that history was almost painful.

"I understand, my Lord," Branimir lied.

"Good," Valya said. The two of them stepped into the courtyard from the keep.

"Run along but do not venture too far. The Patrician may change his mind about your judgment," Valya muttered, adjusting his cloak. "You may stay with your own kind until you are called upon."

"When might that be, my Lord?" Branimir asked.

"Soon or never," Valya said with ice on his breath. "It does not matter. Your time is not your own to be measured, Kras."

Branimir dipped his head, watching Valya speed back into the keep and shutting the door behind him. Branimir stood alone.

"Where did you come from?" a Kras asked, who formed in front of his eyes. The creature was as red as Branimir with similar dark hair and black, oval eyes. Outside of the male's flattened nose and high cheek bones, he looked very similar to Branimir. They were even the same height.

"I am Branimir Baran from Melkorka," Branimir introduced himself. "I am from the Seven Islands of Forghar."

"Where's that?" the creature scrunched up his nose.

Branimir took a deep breath, somewhat surprised that the Kras did not know about Melkorka. "It is…a long way from here. It is where the Kras come from."

"What? You know where we come from?" the Kras smiled wide, showing his own crooked teeth.

Branimir nodded solemnly. "Yes. Do you not?"

The Kras shook his head, scooting closer. "We were told that we were created by the Highborn, but we did not believe it. Not really."

"That you were what—No, the Highborn did not create the Kras," Branimir scoffed.

"Oh, you must come with me. You must tell the others what you know. They will be so thrilled." He snatched Branimir's hand and pulled him through the courtyard.

Branimir could hardly protest as the Kras firmly yanked him to and fro past the Highborn who walked through the open space. In just a few moments, the Kras brought him to a small door that angled downwards, encased in stacked stones.

Branimir was dragged down a stone staircase to a dirt path in dark tunnels. He noticed that no lights were lined in the damp hole, which, of course, mattered very little to any Kras. His escort pulled him past several tunnels and rooms carved out of the earth. He saw a few Kras roaming about the enclave, staring at them as they flew by.

Within seconds, they stepped through a doorway leading to what appeared to be a common area. There were so many Kras that it was hard to make out much more in the room than small red heads bobbing. At the far end, Bran found small wooden plates and bowls filled with goo resembling food. The dishes were being passed around to the several hundred Kras. The commotion was deafening to Bran. They had come right during mealtime.

"Shanna! Lona! Come here!" The Kras shouted at two female Kras who passed by them. "He says our kind came from a place called Melkorka."

Branimir licked his cracked lips. Women of his own kind walked toward him. Real women! What would Mojmir think if he were standing here?

Branimir started to clarify, stammering as the females approached him with half-crooked smiles. "Well—"

"You know where we come from?" one of them said happily, clapping her hands. "We knew the Highborn could not have created us?"

His escort chimed in. "I know, right? We have never seen them create anything. They only destroy."

"Oh Shanna, isn't it exciting?" said the other female. "Who would have thought there were other Kras in the world?"

"I am actually the only one left," Branimir said. "At least, as far as I can tell. I thought I was the only one until I came here."

"Oh, there are lots of us here," the male said, bouncing from foot to foot, full of excitement.

"What happened to all your people?" Shanna placed her hands on her cheek.

Branimir felt overwhelmed, "There were many battles that we died in, and…well, how many of you are there exactly?"

"Around five hundred," the male answered.

Shanna leaned into Branimir, touching his arm. "Died! Oh, my! You are a warrior?"

He flinched at her touch. "I—"

"Oh, he is a brave warrior from a distant land. Killed hundreds, even thousands. It is likely there were even more. It is hard to count once you start getting so high, you know?" the male said with a firm shake of his head.

"How do you know, Potap?" Lona tapped her foot at the red male.

He raised his hands in the air definitively. "Because we were talking before you two came over. Tell them, um…what did you say your name was…Branimir."

Branimir's pale eyes swelled. "Yeah. I wouldn't say, I mean, I have killed—"

"See! See! He is a warrior that has come to lead our people to freedom," Potap claimed.

"Are you sure?" Lona pursed her lips, "He is awfully unsure of himself."

"I am not!" Branimir claimed.

"You don't want to anger the warrior," Potap warned with a raised finger.

"Shut up, Potap!" Lona raised her hand as though she were going to slap him.

"Put your hand down!" Branimir demanded, stepping between them. "Our people are not violent toward others, unless, well— unless we have no other choice!"

Potap and Shanna sighed in admiration.

Lona faced Branimir boldly, her voice suddenly full of spunk. "Who are you to command me, Branimir? You are not a Highborn. You are not Anshedar."

Branimir looked around the courtyard, wild-eyed. More of the Kras in the area had begun to gather around. His people circled around Branimir, males and females by the hundreds. They scattered from the hallways, shouting at others in their rooms.

Branimir took a deep breath. He had never seen so many Kras in all his life. It was likely his father and grandfather had never seen the like either.

"Well?" Lona stamped her foot.

"Tell her, Branimir," Shana urged, her large black eyes looking up at him.

Branimir reached in his pocket. He felt something smooth.

It was his shiny stone!

"I hold the stone of our people, the Ojenek, from Eevaltti, the distant city of our people, called Illuard," Branimir cried out into the room. "This stone gives me the right to command the Kras, the ancient Ojenan; the Red from Beneath the Mountain!"

The crowd of Kras gulped and awed and cooed at the grandeur of the moonstone. The light from within flashed brighter than the dim light of the Dyndaer.

"Ojenek" was whispered among the Kras. Many of them stared helplessly at the shiny gem, their hands reaching toward it as though they would give their lives just to touch it once. The power of the moonstone was incomprehensible.

Potap shrilly hollered. "Bring him a plate of food!"

In a moment, slop on a plate was thrust toward Bran.

He took it awkwardly, looking at the zealous faces of his people. He had never felt empowered before. He was a god among these Kras who had been sheltered from the history and knowledge of the world, and of his beloved people. He was overwhelmed with a pity that he had never experienced before.

Lona was the first to kneel on one knee, eyes raised to the shiny stone that Branimir held in his free hand. The rest followed quickly.

Branimir looked around nervously, thankful that there were no Highborn. From the size of the Kras's quarters, it was likely none could fit without crawling.

"What are we to do, Warrior?" Potap raised his head.

Branimir gulped, looking at the many eyes of the Kras who watched him. There was only one thing that he could offer them. It was what every living creature wanted, whether they were aware of it or not. It was what the Kadari planned to steal away.

Branimir licked his lips, his squeaky voice holding the authority of a King, saying words that he had never thought he would hear, especially from his own lips. "We are going to be free. All of us! We are going to make our new home, deep in the Dyndaer, and without the Anshedar."

Whispers flooded the courtyard of Shayol Domier as his words spread among the ranks of the Kras.

"Is that possible?" Shanna said, as baffled as the rest that gave sight to Branimir.

Branimir manipulated the words he had heard Dorofej say in the past. "Every living being has the right to carve their own path. The Kras are no different!"

Voices of approval were heard among the crowd and Branimir could see heads nodding. He smiled, feeling the power of leadership.

"How, Warrior?" Potap wondered.

"This night, when they are asleep in their beds, you will disappear from sight. Each of you will run and hide in the forests, the Kras way! The Anshedar will not be able to find you if you do not want them to. You will head north to the Hrani Highlands, and we will make our home in the mountains."

"You will come with us, Branimir?" Shanna asked in a worried voice.

Branimir assured her, resting his hand on her shoulder softly. "I will come for you when I am done with my quest. I have a commitment that I must see through to the end, for the sake of the Kras and for the world,"

"Why don't you come with us?" several cried out in argument.

Branimir took a moment to look around at the many Kras. "Because, I am a warrior."

Chapter XXX

"Stop it, you daring man," a woman leered in a drunken slur, slapping Dorofej's hand away from her layered skirt.

Branimir watched in amazement.

Dorofej was draped in his insidious robes as black as storm clouds, ragged as any robes from the long journey he had taken. He raised his head to the young girl, the tufts of his dark red hair bulged from his hulking hood. His face was young, shaven, and all features of age had left him entirely.

"Not only was my body rejuvenated, but so were my boyish desires, yes?" Dorofej laughed. "Come now, this man may die tomorrow in glorious battle. Give him a raucous night to remind him why he is fighting, yes?"

Laughter erupted around the table in the small wooden cottage near the eastern wall of Shayol Domier.

A handful sat about in the room drinking from the barrels of ale and wine that were sitting in the cottage. Branimir noticed most of the individuals, including Artemiy and Alyona.

A strongman, who had identified himself as Dobromil, cackled, "This man has a way with women, does he not? I would not have believed the old man had such spunk in him."

"If he even looks at Alyona wrongly, I'll knock him upside the head," Artemiy threatened, not amused by the redheaded man, sipping on his tankard.

"Meh. Leave him be," Alyona chortled. "I can take care of myself. Besides, he is cuter than any other man at this forsaken place."

"It's not forsaken, sister," Artemiy wallowed in his chair, slapping the table.

Branimir noticed Falmagon holding his stomach, giving sign that he had been doubled over for some time to the point that his abdomen was beginning to hurt. Both of his perfect blue eyes watered, watching Dorofej with absolute amusement. "You do have quite the charm on the ladies, Dorofej. I would have never guessed that you had it in you."

"A charmer I am, yes, with women both in and out of the cloth?" Dorofej chuckled.

Branimir wrinkled his nose with disgust. "What do you mean, my Lord?"

Trying to understand Dorofej was like meeting a stranger for the first time. He was nothing like he was in his frailty. Then again, Branimir did not recognize either of the men in their fledgling bodies. Falmagon had two eyes that actually worked.

By and by, he ignored the two of them for the most part, sipping on his own drink. The hope he had given the Kras that afternoon would soon be known. In due time, they would be escaping into the Dyndaer away from the clutches of the Highborn. Forever.

"Suggestion is determined by the amount of plum in the veins, Branimir. Full of it, I am." Dorofej's laughter continued to ring.

The cottage roared in laughter with the man. Wooden flutes and a string instrument played in the background as more alcohol was passed around to those that united together in the establishment. It was not an alehouse, nothing like the Kal'bane, but it suited the purpose for the evening.

"Never has this man spoken more truth," Falmagon garbled, slapping Dorofej on the back heartily.

The unnamed woman winked at Dorofej. "Just keep your hands to yourself, and we will see where the night leads, eh?"

Dorofej puckered his lips and whistled, ending with a satisfied smile on his young face. The man had likely not experienced this type of frolic in nearly a century. He danced in his chair, twisting his head back and forth, whistling with the tune of the pipes.

Branimir could not blame Dorofej for enjoying himself, but he felt that the man had forgotten a piece of himself in the change. The Waters of Life had transformed the old man into his younger body nearly instantly. It was not long before Dorofej was bouncing around Shayol Domier, shouting and carrying on like he had just found a priceless treasure.

Branimir did not recognize him in face or spirit. The wise man's concerns of all that had befallen them had seemingly fled his mind.

"Dorofej," Branimir nudged him, "you may want to hold back on the plum."

Dorofej scrunched his face at Branimir as if trying to remember him. His hand ran through his red locks several times, his eyes spacy and jaw drooping halfway open. Slowly, he set down his tankard of wine. "You are more than right, Branimir! There is evil afoot, yes?"

Branimir nodded.

Falmagon raised his voice, "Let Nedezhda come! I have never felt so alive. A lifetime of Koldovstvo flows through my veins. I will cut her down and take back Kaelandur to be used for the glory of Dahz and the Kadari!"

The men and women in the tavern shouted approval at the Highborn Longwalker.

Falmagon raised his hands. The flutes and strings continued to play as the dark-haired man began speaking the Kalamyr Oath passionately. The crowd of Anshedar men and women that gathered around him smiled in recognition of the words.

Held fore'er by a simple word,
To defend against the impious,
Ne'er to kneel nor fall or lured,
Lest blood and death descend.
Beyond wealth and a princely home,
Trust held for'ever unto the Sun,
We war, we worship, we roam,
Lest blood and death descend.

The Kadari within the cottage raised their voices alongside that of Falmagon with the second verse. Dorofej and Branimir watched in absolute trepidation.

Rise above the frail and weak,
Fore'er standing beyond frailty,
Let all men hear us speak,
Till blood and death descend.
Feel the warmth of the White-Clad,
Blessing the Highborn in eternal glory,
Let none meander or fall gad,
Till blood and death descend.

As the last word boomed from the voices in unison, the music silenced. The Highborn clapped and hooted in recognition of their unified faith.

All except Dorofej, who seemed suddenly sober, staring at those who held the power of Koldovstvo. Branimir saw the flicker of reason flutter across the man's vision. Dorofej's blue eyes darted about the room like an animal caught in a snare. Whatever effect the Waters of Life had on his mind was slipping.

Falmagon shouted into the cottage at the many that whooped in admiration. "Bah! Are we not Highborn? Are we not Anshedar? Why do we stay hidden in this stick castle when evil sifts through the Dyndaer? Who said they had seen Nedezhda the Eretik during the night outside the gates? Let us find her and her hordes of demons and cut down the lot of them!"

"Aravdur was the one that had seen the woman. Said she was like a wraith, a ghostly demon, and as pale as death," Dobromil shared.

"Where is this Aravdur?" Falmagon asked.

Marina answered, filled with vigor, "He is a little red brood. A Kras. Likely, he is back on watch outside on the wall. We can find him easily enough."

More shouts of encouragement sounded with clinks of tankards as they downed more of the alcoholic liquid.

Branimir tried to hide his look of fear. If the Highborn went looking for the Kras now, they may find that there were none left in Shayol Domier.

Valya, who sat near the back, stood, lifting his tankard high. "Falmagon Sej, you speak like the Patrician himself, like a true spearhead. You say that Kinhar had chosen you to take his stead, to lead the Kadari on Melkorka. I cannot dispute from what I have seen and heard. You take action with enough force to cut the path to glory. In truth, your words hold the truth that each of us have longed to hear."

The Kadari clapped in response, agreeing with the bold man who spoke for them like they were mindless children.

The idea of seeking Aravdur fled from their mouths and their minds. Branimir sighed relief.

The man continued, "Why hold this power if we cannot shape this world? What can stand between the Kadari and the rule of the kingdoms of men, especially when such strength is at the forefront?"

"There is nothing!" Falmagon cried out, rising from his chair. "I am your spearhead and will be your Patrician as Kinhar desired, if you would have me. What say you?"

The roar of approval that sounded from those in the cabin was silenced as quickly as it had begun. The door creaked open from the rear before slamming shut behind Falmagon.

Moreth, the Patrician of the Kadari, walked forward. He scanned the room nervously, before eyeing Falmagon with a quivering lip. His hands shook as though he had been chopping wood for half his life without rest.

The silence was as still as the grave. The Highborn Longwalker glared at Moreth with the fury of a thousand warriors.

Moreth showed no sign of violence, speaking with a quaking voice, taking a deep breath between each sentence as though it could be his last. "I give you hospitality. I share the secrets of immortality with you, because you are Highborn and therefore, my brother. I gave you back your life like it had never been taken. I welcome you with open arms and your repayment is treason against me! For a thousand years, I have walked this earth and given direction to men where none could be found. To each of these, even in this room, I have given everything. Never have I given to a man as treacherous as you, Falmagon Sej."

Falmagon raised his hand, as though he were about to lift stone through the floor, to obliterate Moreth where he stood.

"Hold!" Moreth commanded, his voice having the authority of the gods. "Do not strike down your own, lest you curse the Kadari for eternity. You have already witnessed firsthand what happens when you lay waste to those of your own house, Falmagon. I had given warning to Kinhar before he made his schemes and he would not heed it. Be the wiser."

Falmagon swallowed, saying nothing.

"It is clear to me that my leadership has come to an end. My ... my brothers and sisters have accepted you as their leader and wish me discarded from my position."

"Patrician Moreth—"

"Silence, Valya! I have already heard you speak, and you have been bound by your words under the Lightbringer," Moreth said. "I will leave you to your fates under the direction of Falmagon Sej, and I pray he can offer the Kadari what you think I obviously could not."

Falmagon stood all the taller, physically accepting ownership of the hundreds of Highborn at his back, "I will lead you to glory. I will give rise to Melkorka beyond anything the world has ever seen. I will bring Dahz, the Protector of Men, more honor and glory than he has ever received. We will have his full blessing from our sacrifice, from our offering, and from the blood of evil that we spill, in His name. You can hold me to that! Tomorrow we go to the Ash Tree. Tomorrow we put an end to Nedezhda and this madness!"

"Hear, hear!" the Kadari raised their tankards.

"That is a story I will have no part in." Moreth opened the door and stepped into the darkness.

Chapter XXXI

The following morning was as frigid as the day before while the Highborn prepared in the courtyard. The world was grey and bleak like a shadow on a grave. If ever a curse had seemingly befallen the world, now was the time.

"Where are those little red broods?" Valya said with a flick of his tongue. "How do five hundred Kras just disappear?"

Falmagon snorted. His raggedy hair was wilder this morning than usual. His eyes locked onto Branimir, who stood close to Dorofej's dark robes.

Branimir turned his eyes away, his hands stuffed in his pockets. The Highborn Longwalker had to know what had taken place. Branimir trembled, fearing the punishment to come.

"You tell me, Valya," Falmagon said. "Why does the single Kras of Melkorka stand ready to fight at our side and those of Shayol Domier flee in fright? Have they no wits about them?"

Valya turned his gaze away from the Patrician. "Maybe so. They are not accustomed to having demons at their gates."

Falmagon snorted. "It would serve them well to be cut down by the Bukavac while they tried to route like scared children! Let us hope that we find their mutilated bodies along our path."

"May very well be that they are already dead, yes?" Dorofej smoothed his robes and rubbed his temples in a circular motion.

"Slaughtered them whilst we slept off a drunken stupor, the Eretik may have, even within these walls."

"Dorofej, don't be a fool! Where would the bodies have gone? And why would they not have done away with us as well." Falmagon said.

"Don't shout, yes? Aching terribly, my head is."

"It is no matter whether the Kras are here or not. There are plenty of Highborn at our backs and with the Waters of Life, we will win this battle with ease." Valya reasoned.

Branimir hoped that the Kras were well beyond the reaches of the Eretik and the Kadari. They were the last hope for his people's survival.

Falmagon shook his head. "You know nothing of the Bukavac or Nedezhda."

"I have fought the Vucari for two decades, Patrician. I have some understanding of difficulty."

"Not like this, Valya," Falmagon muttered.

Dorofej clenched his red hair. "Shouting, you are."

"Maybe you should not have drunk so much wine," Valya said, peering at Dorofej and shaking his head.

"It would not have improved his thinking," Falmagon said, his hand moving as though he were wanting to slam a staff against the ground to finish the insult. He did not seem to notice that Habërmani had been lost.

Dorofej's eyes glanced toward the woman from the night before, wearing her split skirts, walking nearby among the Anshedar. "Worth it, a hundred times over, it was."

"By Mulafell," Falmagon turned toward the gate. "Get us to the Ash Tree, Valya, before my mind is branded with images I cannot erase."

"Of course, Patrician Falmagon. It is not far," he replied.

Several hundred Highborn moved through the Dyndaer Forest. With no organization, they moved through the dark trees, through the underbrush, toward the Ash Tree. The sound of their feet on the earth was like drums to Branimir, who walked up front with

Falmagon, Dorofej, and the scouting party of Valya. The rest, none known to Branimir, trailed behind their new Patrician.

Dorofej seemed to sober as they moved through the trees of the Dyndaer, or at least his complaints of noise lessened considerably. As the distance to their location shortened, Valya instructed them to be at the ready.

It did not take more than an hour to reach their destination. The thick, tall trees of the Dyndaer did not sway or change in any way as they moved through the forest. There was no clearing. The Ash Tree suddenly just became visible through the haze of the forest as if it was where it was meant to be among the trees.

The over-sized Ash Tree melded in a dismal pool of dark water that was unlike any pond Branimir had ever seen. The tree sprung toward the heavens, brimming with leaves as large as Branimir, and plush fruits, and flowers more decorated than any ever seen. Its base was wide, and the expanse of the branches were wider yet. The roots of the tree spiraled in and out of the waters that simmered like they were hovering over a furnace beneath.

Surrounding the edge of the pool, the door to the Netherworld, were the Bukavac, their bluish flesh melding with the fog of the forest. Their crafted blades of death were clenched in their hands, hacking at the many roots of the tree, tearing it asunder from the world of the living. Their numbers were equal to, if not greater than, those of the Highborn.

Close to their number, stood the Eretik with Kaelandur seized in her hand. Nedezhda barked orders at the demons beneath her, demanding that they work quicker. Half of the Ash Tree was already dismembered, lopsided in the Waters of Life.

"For Dahz," Falmagon mumbled.

"For the Lightbringer," Valya reiterated.

"For the Lightbringer," many more echoed.

At the sound of their murmured voices across the two-hundred-yard expanse, Nedezhda flung her head up from where she stood. Her lips curved in disgust.

Her mouth formed words that were unheard, her greenish, mucky hair clinging to her cheekbones as they rose and fell. Branimir still could not take his eyes off the black stitches circling her neck.

The moment of demons facing the living could have lasted an eternity. The Highborn stretched out among the trees, a low hum of whispers of encouragement. The Bukavac turned and stepped away from the waters, their roars reactive to the enemy. Any sounds of the forest in the cold months were deafened.

As the Bukavac sprang forward on their clawed feet, Falmagon's hands moved quickly, rending the dust of the ground into the air. A storm of sand erupted from the floor of the forest to slow the charging demons.

"Attack!" He screamed at the legion of Kadari.

While the Anshedar wielded Koldovstvo, Branimir took a step back, feeling as though he was not meant to be here in this moment. He suddenly wished he was among his own kind in the Dyndaer, hiding from the bloodshed that would soon follow.

This battle was beyond him. The Bukavac charged, tearing through the trees, their blades were deadly shadows in their hands, cold and menacing in the layered snow and ice. The Highborn screamed and bawled glories to the Lightbringer as they heaved stone and wove vine, laid fire and felled ice. This was a war for the divine or those close to it, not the meek Kras.

Branimir did as the Kras do, and faded from sight, clinging to the nearest tree within the Dyndaer. He was a warrior, perhaps, but he was not a hero. He definitely was not a fool.

Branimir cried out as the first Bukavac reached the Highborn ranks. It swung a labrys, wildly missing Dorofej who had pulled ahead of the other Anshedar. The redheaded Highborn twisted his body, embracing his renewed agility, lost for so long in the years that had passed. Dorofej laughed wildly as though battle was his voice and death were his song, reaching out to embrace Koldovstvo.

Branimir was nearly frozen, watching Dorofej wield magic beyond the skill of any other Highborn. The black mage grasped onto something deeper than the physical world, tearing through dimensions unknown to the living, touching the sacred world beyond anything known to any Highborn. The Bukavac froze in response to the unseen magic. It was as though the beast were living within a dream, a nightmare, deep within its mind.

Dorofej jumped, the air around him suspended him, and flung his body toward the beast that stood twice his height. In his hands, two swords purely made of fire formed, lashing and blazing, hungrily reaching for the icy skin of the Bukavac. Dorofej fed his weapons, plunging them into stone-like flesh of the Netherworld demon. In its daze, the demon did not utter a sound, but simply collapsed, absent of life.

Branimir bit his tongue as he watched Dorofej free the flame swords and rush into the masses of demons that assailed with a glimmer of madness in his eye. Koldovstvo flowed through him with minimal aging effects as though his body were accustomed to the current of the craft, like a river bed to the flow of water. It gave him far more strength than any of the other Highborn. Branimir was almost certain that Dorofej could lay waste to the entire army with his power, if he so chose.

Dorofej was not alone though. Falmagon flung his rocks and raised his strong-walls, controlling the movement of demons toward his army, giving example as to why Kinhar had once called him prodigy. Valya used similar magic, maintaining walls of air, constructing unseen barriers to protect the Anshedar as they manipulated Koldovstvo.

The Kadari stood close to those they were familiar with, bringing on their own wrath through Koldovstvo. They cried out to one another as more Bukavac raided their fortifications, overcoming their own barricades, made of the air and the twisted trees of the Dyndaer.

"Dobromil!" One Kadari man screamed before a demon fist collided with his skull. His head caved inward.

"No!" Artemiy shouted.

Dobromil, the strongman from the tavern the previous night, charged at the demon. He crafted a mystical sword from stone out of the earth while he sprinted. In a fluid movement, he stabbed it through the gut of the demon. Bluish white blood spewed over his hand as the demon roared.

A second Bukavac came from behind, quickly grabbing Dobromil's leg. He pulled him from the ground and sunk his teeth into the man's calf. Dobromil howled in agony, the massive man feeling the fangs scrape against his bone. He lost consciousness mid-scream.

Artemiy was on the demon as quick as maggots on decaying flesh. Artemiy did not hesitate. His hand clasped over the demon's face and a fireball released upon impact. The demon's head was hurled backwards from the impact, singed and blackened beyond recognition. The demon would not roar again.

"Artemiy, watch out!" A Kadari woman screamed, forming the earth into a shield to take the impact of a sword swinging at the young man's head from another Bukavac that entered the area. The shield shattered from the blow, but Artemiy was saved. He reared back in time for Alyona to lift the beast with wind and fling it back the way it had come.

Falmagon smashed another advancing demon to mush with a solid stone from some distance away. The pasty guts of the beast splattered across the foliage. There were so many battles ensuing within battles that it was difficult to keep track of them all.

Highborn and Bukavac circled one another, cutting down one another as though they were ancient enemies destined to wage war with the other.

Branimir struggled to watch every action of the battle as Highborn and demon clashed. At any moment that it seemed the humans gained the upper hand, several more Highborn would fall to waste on the battlefield, from either a deathblow or from crippling themselves with Koldovstvo.

Falmagon stepped beside Valya and Dorofej, beginning to resemble his older self. "We must reach the Waters of Life to replenish our energy. We must kill Nedezhda."

"Push forward!" Valya ordered.

The Bukavac slowed in their advancement as the Highborn collided with the beasts. The area was falling to pieces, trees laying over trees, grasses burning, snow melting, and corpses well within its mix.

"Nedezhda!" Falmagon shouted.

The pale woman sneered, firing a shard of ice through the skull of a Highborn who advanced toward the Ash Tree. Blood splashed from the back of the skull of the long-haired woman. Ice shard after ice shard was loosened from Nedezhda's hand and the Highborn fell.

"I should have killed you when I had the chance, Falmagon," she shouted. "A mistake I will not make twice!" The ice shard meant for the Highborn Longwalker skimmed by his head.

Falmagon, Dorofej, and Valya rushed through the trees dodging the projectiles, crimson blood and pale blood painted the ground beneath them as they struggled to reach Nedezhda. They flung fire and stone, only to be met with more ice and water from the Eretik. No blow seemed to land, but the sounds of battle forever echoed.

As they neared, two women rose from the waters on either side of Nedezhda. Their hair was a blue wave, laced over their bare skin. Their eyes resembled the iris of a flower, shimmering like crystal.

Dorofej stopped immediately, throwing himself to the ground in a curled mess.

"Dorofej!" Falmagon slowed.

Valya pushed forward, flinging currents of air at the strange creatures.

"Stop!" Dorofej raised his hand toward Valya and Falmagon.

Dorofej was too late with his caveat as one of the females raised her hand at Valya and a cylinder of light pulsed into the man's flesh.

In an instant, he was swallowed by nothingness, gone from sight, gone from existence.

Falmagon hit the dirt, giving no sign of caring for the slain Valya. "What are they, Dorofej? Speak to me!"

"Vila!" he hissed.

"The maidens of Marheena," Falmagon gasped, pulling himself behind a tree before another cylinder of light volleyed through the Dyndaer. "They exist!"

The Highborn around them screamed as their companions vaporized from existence through the magic of the Vila. Nedezhda only fed their fear by dropping balls of ice from the sky that caused the ground to quake. Along with the ice storm came a cloud of shadow sifting through the forest eating away at the flesh of the living. Flesh melted and tore from bone. Men and women screamed in agony.

"We cannot lose, Dorofej!" Falmagon said hastily.

"We are losing!" Dorofej shouted back.

"You must take her into the Netherworld and kill her eternally!"

Dorofej, in his new-found youth, looked at Falmagon as though he were mad. "Why me?"

"You have lived beyond your time, old man, and it is time for a new order to rule over this world."

"You mean the Kadari, yes? Stand for it, I would not!"

Falmagon grabbed a hold of Dorofej's dark robes, pulling him so that their noses touched, "This is the way that it must be. Have I not suffered enough? You must do this in the name of glory!"

Dorofej glowered, his red hair burning as bright as his eyes were cold. "Your glory is not the glory I seek, Falmagon Sej! Asking me to sacrifice myself, you are!"

"Have you not asked the same of me?" The Patrician roared over the screams of the dying that began to flee from the Dyndaer. Men and women crawled and weaved through the trees in absolute terror of the Vila and the Eretik.

"Your sacrifice—"

"Do not waste your fancy words on me, Dorofej the Highborn! You claim to care for this world and the people within it, but what have you sacrificed? What greater thing could you give than your life? End this! I have seen you wield Koldovstvo. Only you have the power to end this madness!"

"Bah!" Dorofej had tears in the corner of his eyes. Even in a lifetime of living, he wanted death no more than the next man. "So be it!"

Darkness enveloped Dorofej, as dark as Czern's breath, expanding around his body, hiding the murkiness of his cloak and placing him within the deepest shadow.

Branimir screamed, overhearing their words.

Dorofej was going to die!

The Highborn stepped away from Falmagon with a sneer. "If you bring blight to this world, Falmagon Sej, every drop of blood that has dripped by your words or at your hands, I will come back and see to it that you taste it!"

"So be it!"

Focusing on Koldovstvo with all his strength, Dorofej charged toward the water of life in the shroud of pitch, like dragon fire. Reddish yellow light dimmed over his body as his skin began to mend itself with every aging affect that impacted his flesh. The Vila screeched at the haunting visage, releasing ray after ray of imminent death at the ancient Highborn. As every ray approached, time appeared to stand at a still, as Dorofej twisted, leaped, and rolled out of harm's away.

"Dorofej!" Branimir shouted. "Don't do this!"

The Kras ran toward the redheaded Highborn with every intention of saving the man that had kept him safe. He twisted in and out of the Bukavac, avoiding the massive weapons that swung about, cutting down the fleeing Highborn. Battle cries of man and beast echoed in the cavern surrounding the Ash Tree. The echoes would sound for eternity.

"Dorofej! Stop this!" Branimir screamed.

Branimir was answered by the gnashing teeth of a Bukavac that swiped him off the ground. The beast squeezed his delicate body. Branimir could feel his bones crack.

A stone sword plummeted through the Bukavac's neck cavity. Blood gushed. Branimir's bones had not yet completely snapped.

Branimir fell to the ground with the demon crumbling next to him. Branimir crawled along the dirt, unable to climb to his feet. He paid no heed to Falmagon who had saved him.

Branimir pushed forward toward the Waters of Life after Dorofej.

Dorofej hit the waters like a tidal wave. The sound that escaped between his thin lips was a war cry from the depths of his stomach. It may have very well been the sound of death itself.

The blackness around Dorofej was extinguished as he pulled himself onto the roots of the Ash Tree. He swallowed a mouthful of water, replenishing his strength and any youth he may have lost. The Vila screeched as he flung himself through the air toward the Eretik. In a moment, he stood next to Nedezhda.

His icy eyes matched hers. "Time for this to end, yes?"

Nedezhda leered. "With pleasure, Dorofej."

She plunged Kaelandur into the roots of the Ash Tree.

Dorofej bellowed in horror as the tree began to wilt. It smelted and crumpled into the boiling black waters. "No!"

He leaped at Nedezhda, tackling her into the Waters of Life. The dagger was loosened by the impact, still clasped in Nedezhda's hand.

Branimir dived after him.

Kaelandur fell into the waters, out of reach of any outside of the pool. Falmagon ran to the edge yelling and cursing for what may have been for Dorofej, but what was more likely for the copper dagger.

Nedezhda screamed and flailed her arms as they sunk deep into the black void. Dorofej held fast to the demon woman as she clawed at him.

Branimir caught grip of Dorofej's robe. He would not let go. He could not let go!

The roots of the Ash Tree mapped their descent to eternal death, to the Netherworld.

Chapter XXXII

Branimir Baran grunted, his body aching from head to toe. His face was freezing against the solid ground beneath him. It was as though he were lying on solid ice. His body felt like he had been buried in the snow for hours, although he was certain that he could not have been unconscious for more than a few minutes.

Branimir had experienced the cold from Kalamaar to the Hyaendi Hills, but never had he known this type of relentless cold.

"What have I done?" Dorofej's voice echoed nearby.

Branimir turned over on his back, his eyes fluttering open slowly. The world was a daze, blurry and bleak. His eyes fluttered several times before he gained focus.

Above him was a pool of water, suspended in the air, with massive roots stretching like columns down to the world around him. Not one root touched the ground, and yet, it seemed to have no end. The pool of water was beyond his reach, an eternity upwards, but as clear as the clearest lake on the brightest morning.

The world around Branimir was covered in ice, over hill, plain, and mountain. The frozen water was shaped into miraculous glaciers, sharp and menacing to the eye. The distance was filled with darkness, and although he would usually be able to see, his vision was blocked with a frozen mist. With the smell of rotting flesh pulling at his nostrils, he had to consider his limited sight a blessing.

"Arrgghh," Bran moaned, attempting to spring to his feet, only to fall back to the ice. His body was broken and bleeding. The wounds were deep, hidden beneath his flesh. He could feel it as readily as it were on the surface.

"I am not dead," Dorofej realized out loud. "The dead do not know pain, yes?"

Branimir turned to see the man cradling himself, knees clutched to his chest. He pulled at his red strands at his scalp, rocking slightly. Branimir was not sure if Dorofej was expecting an answer from him or not.

"No, I imagine they do not," Branimir said. He wheezed for air as though he were sucking it through a blade of grass.

For a moment, he thought that Dorofej had not heard him. It was possible that the old man had suddenly gone mad. It was possible that his voice was too weak. Branimir hoped that it was neither. The thought of living for an eternity with a madman in the Netherworld was beyond frightful, nearly as chilling as death.

The redheaded man spun his head around on the ground, looking at Branimir. He was only a few feet away from Dorofej. His blue eyes stared into the pale ovals of Branimir, and quickly he crawled across the frost.

The time that it took Dorofej to reach Branimir seemed to be an eternity within an eternity. When he finally did reach him, Branimir could have sworn another lifetime had passed by him.

With a grunt, Dorofej pulled at him, falling on the small body of the slave of Melkorka. He put his head to Branimir's body. In a moment, outside of time, Dorofej sobbed over him.

"Why did you follow me through, Branimir Baran?" Dorofej blubbered over the body. "Why did you follow me? This was my fate!"

"I could not leave you, my Lord," Branimir said, cringing at the weight of the man.

Dorofej lifted himself and ran his hand through Branimir's wet, stringy hair. "Served the Highborn for so long, the Kras have, sacrificing so much. None have ever done so as gallantly as you, Branimir Baran."

Branimir could barely look into the blue, gentle eyes of the Highborn.

"You are hurt, yes?"

Branimir nodded, suddenly realizing the measure of his injuries. He would not be able to continue.

Dorofej raised his hands to bring healing to the Kras's body.

"No!" Branimir commanded. "You will need your strength, Dorofej. You will need to find your way out of the Netherworld and back to the land of the living."

"If I do not mend you, you will die," Dorofej said.

A tear touched Branimir's eyes, "I…I know. It's okay." Branimir coughed, blood spilling over his lips.

It was worse than he had thought.

"Death comes for most—"

Dorofej tried again to touch Koldovstvo.

"Please! You must let me go. I…need to find…my wolf skin."

Branimir smiled as he referred to Dorofej's fable that had seemed to have been told so long ago. Branimir was finally going to be released of his duty.

"A warrior you truly are, Branimir," Dorofej said before turning his head away in anguish. "I would not have done this had I known."

Branimir coughed. "You have done nothing, Dorofej."

The man was speechless. Branimir followed his gaze to Nedezhda who also was lying on the ground. Branimir's eyes focused on her pale skin against the ice several feet away. Her dark hair flattened against the ice, like moss against bark. Not an eyelash even flinched on the woman. She was motionless as though she had died again.

"This cannot…"

Dorofej cut himself off, not finishing the thought. Branimir lifted his head slightly, watching the Highborn move to the body of the undead woman carefully. As though brimming with rage, collective of the thousands of battles the man had fought, he screamed. It may have been for what Nedezhda had done to the Ash Tree, Aenar, or even how her actions had led Dorofej and Branimir to their fates.

Branimir was certain that Dorofej's wrath stretched beyond Nedezhda. Kinhar had lied. Falmagon had betrayed. The Highborn were lost! The Kadari would take control of Aenar and Dorofej was trapped for eternity in the Netherworld with the dead and the demonic.

No matter what the reason for igniting the fury, it was clear. Dorofej needed release for his ire.

The ancient Highborn lifted himself up over the undead Eretik, not bothering to check for breath. With a sneer, he made a fist and struck the woman in the cheek. She did not respond. He struck her again in the stitched neck. Bones broke. Flesh bruised.

"Dorofej! Stop!"

Dorofej ignored Branimir. He hit Nedezhda repeatedly until his knuckles were bloodied and his skin was torn. Lastly, without any hint of where he found it, Dorofej pulled Kaelandur from his robe and plunged it through the chest of the Eretik. The demon never stirred, never fought.

"Dorofej," Branimir sputtered blood over his lips once more. He tried to wipe away the liquid that dribbled down his cheek. It was pointless. He could not even raise his arm.

When Dorofej had finished, Branimir could no longer recognize the woman that had been killed with Kaelandur, executed at Melkorka. The face was sunk in and broken, the stitches around the neck loosened, and the white pale liquid spread across the ice.

Dorofej spread his arms toward the waters above him and screamed again.

Branimir wanted to cry, but even that would take strength that he did not have. Hearing the man's laments, the ultimate defeat of the heart, shredded Branimir's hope. Dorofej knew there was no escaping through the Waters of Life.

From where Branimir lay, he could still see the Ash Tree and the fragmented roots. He had no understanding of it. He had seen the Ash Tree destroyed before sinking into the frozen Netherworld. Even if the Ash Tree had survived through some miracle, the entrance was never the exit and the exit was never the entrance. It was in the darkness of the frozen Netherworld that Dorofej would have to find his path back to Aenar.

"You … must find … a way." Branimir struggled to keep life in him.

Dorofej stood to his feet slowly and moved away from the corpse of Nedezhda. The Waters of Life swelled and bubbled outside of his reach, taunting him with every gurgle.

"You must…save…your strength." Branimir said.

Dorofej wept, stumbling to the red creature. "Understand, you do not, Branimir Baran."

"Tell me."

The Highborn gripped Kaelandur forcing a smile through the tears. "Your concern, it is not. Maybe in another time, another place."

"No matter how long it takes, you must find your way out of the Netherworld. Do not lay down. Do not rest. No matter the pain or the regret, you must cling to hope." Branimir gasped for air.

"Do not cry for the lost. You will find me in the world after this. For you, there is still glory to be had."

As the words slipped with Branimir's last breath, he saw a glowing light.

DYNDAER

BOOK 2
The Kaelandur Series

THRICE NINE LEGENDS

Joshua Robertson

There once was a time when the gods were gods without question. When men were men without example. When heroes were only the frivolous dreams of lurid mortality. It was a time when truths and untruths were indistinguishable, hatred and love were equally excusable, and life and death regaled all of humanity in the same breath. Myths of old were realized and legends were born from the very dust man was formed of, to be told and retold until the grace of time altered them beyond knowing or forgot them completely. Still, some tales were preserved deep within the hearts of mankind, for reasons that could not be fathomed. Perhaps bearing the fruit of some profound truth or kept alive merely by the strength of the men who lived them. Some tales would never be forgotten.

Month of Wine Flowing

First of Frost

1348 CE

Prologue

Age-old promises kept Dorofej alive. At the outset, he could not say how many years had passed. Time and space were distorted in the realm of the dead, but the stint had not caused him to stumble in his walk. Upon returning to Aenar, even after a thousand years, the Highborn found the world had not changed. Men were still enthused by power and gain, leaving sagacity to those who retained ideals but had nothing to show for it. Still, he had his promises.

"Another storm is coming. We should find shelter." Sulanna Maelthirren spoke in the tone of a true diplomat. Her voice was terse, yet gentle. At one time, she might have been found within the fastened bodice of a noble. Now, she wore the strapping armor of a soldier.

In the preceding months, Dorofej found Sulanna had the knack for speaking her mind, whether one wanted to hear it or not. Even now, her words served as a fair warning when considering the dimming light that gave shadow to the Hyaendi Hills.

The middle-aged man who led them responded. "Nowhere to go out here but forward."

Thunder rumbled overhead.

Dorofej disregarded the imminent storm. His companions were far more interesting. Sulanna and Alden had inadvertently educated him about what he had missed during the past millennia when he had been traversing the Netherworld.

Sulanna tightened her cloak, her brown hair falling against her cheek. "There is no chance of reaching Eldhaft this eve, Alden. We are over a hundred leagues out. Be sensible."

Alden gazed over his shoulder, letting the horse guide him. "Sensible? The only cover you will find out here is your horse's ass. Look around you. There is nothing but dirt and grass, woman."

Sulanna glowered at the warrior.

He pressed, "Besides, we have nearly reached the outer bounds of the Svet territory. I'd rather not spend another night risking our necks sleeping in the lands of the centaurs."

The belly of the sky was gutted, adding weight to his words. Rain pattered down into small puddles around the clopping hooves of their horses. Their stamping reminded Dorofej of the centaurs. He had learned the Svet were nearly slaughtered to extinction by the Northmen in past years. The thought still made his stomach upset. The centaurs may have been fierce, but it did not discount their goodness.

Sulanna centered herself on her mare. "These are their Holy Lands, Alden. You cannot hate them for protecting what is rightfully theirs."

"I can hate what I wish. The savages should have been cut down years ago. Maharia was given to the Anshedar."

"Given? Men took Maharia by force, slaughtering thousands."

"With the blessing of Svarog."

The woman tilted her head, squinting at the man ahead of her. The spear on his back bounced in rhythm with his horse's clopping feet. "Do not bring your god into this."

"You cannot ignore Svarog forever."

"I'll acknowledge the gods when they do something worth acknowledging." She shot back with irritation.

"Svarog will see to His children, my sweetness." Alden spit harshly and then licked the driblets of saliva from his lip. "Listen, I will not be sleeping on the ground tonight. My frame is too old and my ass cheeks too wrinkled. Riding this gelding for weeks has likely caused what little hair I have left to fall from my head."

To make his point, the warrior threw back the olive-colored hood of his cloak. His receding hair sparsely covered his scalp, covering just the tips of his thin ears.

A chilled wind advanced from the rear.

Dorofej held his black robes and watched Alden. The warrior had no less hair than when they had left Tamarri, but even in the failing light, Dorofej could see the scabbed cuts along Alden's arms. The blemishes joined many scars, which staggered his wrinkled skin; some were fresher and deeper than others.

Sulanna did not stumble over her words. "I do not see any gods helping us, Alden."

The man swiftly pulled his hood over his head, seemingly frustrated for not getting the hoped for reaction from the woman. Alden spoke again, but this time his words were directed at Dorofej. "What do you have to say about this?"

Dorofej adjusted his hood, to keep his tufts of red hair dry. He could not agree with Sulanna, who had no belief in the gods. Nor, could he side with Alden, who had a misconstrued understanding of them. "I say, there is more than one god by far."

"That isn't the question, Dorofej." Alden spat again.

"It wasn't? Oh, I do apologize. I must have been distracted by the rain, yes?"

"You are kidding me?"

Sulanna scoffed. "Leave the boy alone."

Dorofej grew silent again, taking advantage of his dark robes to slink back into the darkness.

"Fine. I'll let it be, but he is not a boy. He is a young man and should learn to speak his mind once in a while. He cannot spend all of his time with his nose in a book," Alden muttered. A few seconds later he added, "We will press forward until the storm lets up or we find shelter."

The lightning flanked them, snagging the sky, as they meandered west. The jagged earth was layered in small patches of greenery through the muddied soil with tall grasses stretching in every direction across the swells in the land. With each step forward, the rain only thickened.

In the many leagues that passed, as the hours of darkness further set, there was no disrupting the melodic tune of raindrops, besides that of the horses' hooves stamping through the mire. Hill and hill again, they traveled over, rising and falling in their saddles.

"For honor, for glory," Alden uttered in a whispered prayer. Dorofej barely heard the words against the metallic sound of Alden's belt knife sliding from its scabbard. Even in the dark, Dorofej saw the loosened bracer hanging from Alden's forearm, and the sharpened blade slicing through his sensitive flesh.

He had to turn his eyes away.

Dorofej had learned the warrior cut himself as penance and would not stop until he felt he had brought glory to Svarog. Dorofej had attempted to explain to Alden the nature of the gods, of Svarog, but the attempts were futile. In time, he discovered Sulanna had spent the better half of a decade attempting to convince Alden of his irrationality. It did not do any good. The man was beyond help. Of course, this was not Svarog's way. Nor was this the way of the Anshedar. This was Alden's way.

The Highborn did not look again until he heard the blade return to its holding. Alden's blood washed away with the downpour, dripping from his fingertips.

Sulanna interrupted Alden's continued prayers, which had given undertone to the falling rain for the past mile. "I do not understand why anyone would hide this relic here in the North. Maybe the old Anshedar who Ivarr speaks about buried it, during the War of Shayol Domier."

"The War of Shayol Domier, Third of Frost, Month of Falling Leaves, 124 CE, it was, when demons last walked upon Aenar," Dorofej whistled from the rear, welcoming the conversation. He was eager to take his mind off of Alden's life-threatening pastime. "That battle was leagues to the south. Further than either of you have traveled, yes?"

"The mysterious, all-knowing Dorofej," Sulanna mocked. "There surely is some use to those books but I was not asking for a history lesson."

"Sweet Sulanna, through history we find the road to our destiny, yes?"

Sulanna turned to him sharply. "Either of you men call me sweet again, or any variation of, I will run you through personally."

Dorofej tittered with amusement.

Sulanna bit her bottom lip and tried again. "Seriously, what of the relic? Any ideas as to what we are looking for exactly?"

"We are searching for what is called Kaelandur, yes?" Dorofej said. "The power to bring the demons back to Aenar, it possesses."

Sulanna raised her eyebrow. "And what exactly is this Kaelandur?"

Alden coughed, finally joining the conversation. "No one knows."

"Then why were we sent after it?"

"Would you like to ride back to Tamarri and ask, my swee—"

"Alden means to say we do not know, yes?" Dorofej flashed his white teeth in a smile with the break of lightning, interrupting the balding warrior.

Sulanna glared at Alden, nearly reaching for her belt knife to follow through with her threat. She grimaced. "I certainly cannot imagine what would be buried in these hills."

Silence ensued.

At the bottom of yet another hill, a small, wooden farmhouse seemed to rise magically from the earth. The dark clouds lightened, though the rain continued, giving enough light to roughly see the terrain. A faint glow of a lantern's light radiated from a second-story window on the eastward side of the building, barely casting an outline of the diminutive home. A tattered fence of thin branches shaped the land around the place. Strangely enough, the structure stood alone with no outbuildings for livestock or farming equipment.

Oddities such as these briefly slipped through Dorofej's mind, but was forgotten in anticipation of a warm fireplace.

The barking of dogs erupted into the night air, announcing their arrival. A small smile lifted on Sulanna's face. "I stand corrected. It seems your god has finally decided to do something worthwhile."

Alden ignored the sarcasm. "Something does not feel right."

Sulanna heatedly pushed back the soaked strands of hair from her eyes, attempting to regain a bit of composure. "Are you suggesting we refuse the mercy of your god?"

"Svarog does not simply give mercy to those who ask. We may be fools to seek sanctuary at this farmhouse."

"We are fools to sit here in a downpour discussing this nonsense," Sulanna barked with frustration. "We have been traveling in the rain for hours."

Alden met her unblinking eyes in complete wonderment. "There is something amiss, Sulanna."

"You are amiss, Alden," Sulanna retorted.

Alden frowned in defeat. "You are going to get us killed."

Dorofej followed them down the hill, watching the noble woman sitting high on her horse as though the edge of any sword was too dull to leave a mark on her throat.

Dark shapes distinguished to be the barking dogs ran towards them. There was a mutter from Sulanna indicating there were two in number. In a matter of seconds, the animals sprung over the fence and were next to them.

Even in the heavy rain, it was easy to tell these were nothing but ordinary dogs. The three riders ignored the mutts snapping around their heels and at the legs of their trained mounts. A couple measly dogs were not threatening.

Drawing near, Dorofej could see shadows through the window bouncing off the walls from a lantern's light. The shaggy animals jumping about his feet continued to snarl and yap, creating a great ruckus. Though, the booming voice of a man caught his attention as the narrow door at the front of the home opened.

"Jorwarg! Worlack! In the name of Marheena, stop…!"

The silver-haired man who stepped out into the rain appeared at least twenty years older than Alden. His face was wrinkled and unkempt with coarse patched hair that could not rightly be called a beard. He wore a white shirt with the collar untied and short brown trousers. Once seeing the riders, he froze barefooted in a mucky puddle of rainwater, holding his bulky body up with a fat branch in one hand. In his other hand, a lantern hung from his fingers swaying as his staff settled itself in the loose sludge.

In a moment of silence, Alden and Sulanna stared wide-eyed at the older man as he did back at them, his mouth crooked with his jaw dropped. He could have very well been the oldest man in the world.

Dorofej tugged back the hood of his robes. He was uncertain whether the man's words regarding Marheena had been a curse or a prayer. As if understanding the unknown, the yipping dogs became eerily quiet, and trotted off around the back of the house.

Sulanna introduced them. "I am Sulanna Maelthirren and these are my companions, Alden Forgaaf and Dorofej Creighton. If you would be so kind, we seek shelter from the storm."

Dorofej nodded at the made-up surname he had given himself upon returning to Aenar. Fortunately, it had been accepted by strangers with little question about its origin.

The stranger's brow wrinkled as though he were seriously distressed by Sulanna's words. His expression hardened, lips curling into a sneer. "Bohumir is my boy! You cannot take him from me."

Sulanna loosened her long knife from her belt. "I do not know any boy named Bohumir. We simply need a place to rest for a few hours."

"Bohumir Mager? You know Bohumir Mager!" The man spouted in laughter, tilting his head backwards.

Alden turned his head sideways to speak into Sulanna's ear. He was loud enough that all could hear him. "He is mad."

"Maybe not," Dorofej muttered.

She ignored them both, nudging her horse a step closer. "These rains do not show signs of stopping anytime soon…"

"Curse you!" The man croaked, his laughter abruptly ceasing with a sinister gaze resting on Sulanna. "Curse you and the foul rain!" Then, under his breath as if asking a question, the man spat, and whispered feverishly.

Dorofej leaned forward to try to grasp the words. They sounded ancient, familiar.

The lantern flying towards Sulanna's chest stole away his concentration. He watched as she dived from her horse, avoided the object, and landed in a grimy puddle.

The man reacted before Dorofej or Alden had a chance. He bolted to Sulanna's side with his staff raised over his head. In no way did the movement appear to offset the older man's balance. Sulanna, who acted more on impulse than anything else, rolled out of the away to avoid certain death. Then, with a quick sweep of her leg, the she took the aggressor off his feet.

He landed with a thud, the staff bouncing far from his grasp. His white shirt was dirtied, covered in both rain and mud. With a bestial snarl, he spun onto all fours like a rabid animal and rushed the noble woman again.

Sulanna cried out. She scurried backwards to regain her footing, fighting to pull her dagger from her belt.

From the side, Alden had dismounted from his gelding. With expert timing, he stepped forward and kicked the charging man sending him sprawling backwards once more. The old man clamored in the mud. Alden did not waste any more time, lifting his spear and pointing the tip at the fallen foe.

"Find salvation in this life or the next, it is your choice," Alden sneered. Sulanna pulled herself to her feet, finally yanking her dagger from her belt.

The man rolled over in the mud, gasping and wheezing. The white shirt was barely hanging on his body, torn down the front, staying in place with caked mud. He glowered, trying to stand, only to slip to his knees again. Alden kept his gaze on the man, allowing the stranger to stand erect.

He shifted his full attention to Alden and his spear. He spoke in huffs, "Marheena will smolder the lot of you!"

None of them had a chance to respond.

The stranger spun around the spear with inhuman dexterity. He had not taken more than three steps before Sulanna flung her dagger, the blade sinking into his neck.

Blood spurted to the sound of his horrific, gurgled scream. With a jolt, he staggered, crawling back toward the entrance of his home. His blood mixed with the moist earth.

"No," Dorofej inhaled. He raised his gaze from the dying body to see a small boy in his sleeping garments standing in the doorway. The boy did not return the look, but instead stared in shock at the dying man who had fallen near the doorstep.

"Father...." the boy was barely audible through tears.

The man struggled, raising his arm towards the boy, who rushed to him. The son fell to his father's embrace, weeping uncontrollably. The father cupped his hand on the young boy's cheek, and in a curdled moan stammered, "Bohumir, my son. Come with me."

With his remaining strength, the old man pulled a dagger from the back of his belt. In a moment too quick to respond, the father sunk the blade into his son's chest. The father crumpled in a heap, lifeless. The son spurted blood from his mouth, his face aghast in bewilderment.

"Dorofej!" Sulanna cried, running to the boy's side.

He threw himself off the horse and ran to the doorstep, his eyes locking on the copper blade within the boy. He knew it well. "Take the dagger and quick, you must be." Dorofej kneeled, peeling back the eyelids of the boy called Bohumir.

Sulanna jerked the dagger from the cavity of Bohumir's chest. Dark red blood spewed from the wound. "Save him!"

"His spirit has not fled from the body. Time there may be." Dorofej was delicate in his movements.

Dorofej caught sight of Alden, who was kneeling in the mud a few yards away with his bracer dislodged. His belt knife was clutched in his left hand as he cut another gash into his forearm. It may have been a third cut, possibly fourth. He could not tell from the overwhelming amount of blood streaming down his arm. The old man's prayers to Svarog for forgiveness were choked and difficult to understand. His words were suffocated through gasps for breath, through tears and mucus. The warrior was lament with grief.

He spoke to Sulanna, "Go to Alden."

The Highborn's hands touched Bohumir, covering the wound. Blood flowed freely over his steadied hands. A glow of red and yellow glowed beneath the boy's skin as Dorofej manipulated his craft, the Koldovstvo, ever ancient and powerful.

From the corner of his eye, Dorofej saw Sulanna rush to Alden. She grabbed him, screaming, all noble equanimity was lost. "Stop this, Alden! No god is worth this!"

Alden shouted back. "Let me go, Sulanna! I must save him with my sacrifice!"

"No, Alden," she pleaded. "Think for yourself."

"You must let me go. I must do this."

Sulanna clutched the powerful man's arms in defiance.

From the depths of his gut, Alden bellowed. With merciless strength, he picked Sulanna off the ground and flung her to the side. She spiraled into a roll, slamming her face hard against the wet ground. Mud splattered into her eyes and covered her hair.

Determined. Gasping for air. She rolled against the sludge.

Dorofej winced, knowing he could not help. His task was too important.

Alden cut himself with more intensity. His prayers were screams. Pleas. He was going to kill himself.

The boy suddenly twitched beneath Dorofej's trembling hands. The black mage cried out, "He will live!"

Alden dropped the knife, his arm, shreds of flesh hanging from bone. "Praise Svarog! For the Kingdom and glory."

Dorofej joined Sulanna in the mud, knowing not else to do, and wept.

Month of Falling Leaves
Third of Frost
1350 CE

Chapter I

"Stone the crows! Is your name really Branimir?" Drak Ghas clicked his tongue. The Kras clenched his red fingers around the handful of twigs inside the leather pouch. The smooth, shortened sticks poked upward over the lip of the leather giving view of the strange carvings on the end. He continued with a wide grin. "Did you know we were freed by a Kras named Branimir Baran?"

"I did hear something about that," Branimir said from the opposite side of the table. He wrung his hands together to calm his nerves. He could not tell this stranger, here in Ojenir, the truth. Instead, he played dumb. "What had this *Branimir* done?"

Drak pulled the twigs from their pouch. His voice was jarring, giddy with glee. "Branimir saved our kind from the Kadari. Those evil mages once kept the Kras as slaves—in the Dyndaer—at Shayol Domier, a thousand years ago and more."

The Kadari had seemingly destroyed any record of the Highborn after their victory at Shayol Domier. Bran doubted if anyone knew the mages had once been called Highborn.

Drak shuffled the many sticks in his hands.

Branimir realized Drak was gawking at him, possibly looking for a reaction. He forced his lips to part. "That *is* something."

"It is," Drak agreed. "My grandfather was among those freed; the same is true for most Kras who live here within Ojenir. You are

295

lucky to have come from another place and born free. Where did you say you were from?"

Branimir hesitated, scanning the underground cavern called Ojenir. The Kras city bore no natural light. Without torches or lanterns, the cavern was but a chasm of blackness for all living creatures, save the Kras. "Across the ocean."

"You traveled across Strega's Deep? I have never known a Kras to go far from their home. Though, I admit I have always thought about going on an adventure." Drak dipped his head and pressed on with his story. "Did you know these mountains, the Hrani Highlands, are said to be named after Branimir's father?"

"That," Branimir moved his hands to rest against the leggings of his trousers, concealing his grin, "that is *really* something." He found himself amused that he had been remembered over the course of a millennia. He would have never thought a slave from Melkorka would be considered a celebrated hero in the modern age. He had been written into history and was not yet dead.

He felt Drak's eyes on him again and had to look away to keep from beaming. The cavernous chamber, beneath the Hrani Highlands, had little movement from its inhabitants on the other levels. Night had settled beyond the rocky walls about an hour before he had arrived. Somehow, Drak had taken it on himself to give him a warm meal and welcome.

In many ways, Ojenir reminded him of the Kras city of Illuard, within the Crags of Kazimir, where he had traveled a lifetime ago. That is, with the exception, Ojenir was not in ruins.

The hollow of the cave was a wide-open space with an area in the center for mining, and small workbenches to cut sediment from any stones found by the diggers. There were a few burrowed holes in the rock or makeshift mudhouses lining the walls, suitable as sleeping quarters. The place was anything but civilized compared to the outside world.

Tunnels lined the expanse of the circular, rocky dome, leading deeper into the Highlands. Branimir almost expected demons to rush from the burrows as they had at Illuard.

He shivered, but nothing ominous emerged from the depths.

"Will you be staying long?" Drak asked. "I know you have only gotten here, but it would not be hard to find an extra den. I have an extra bed inside, if needed." Drak pointed to the mudhouse behind the stone table they occupied. "We have never had another Kras visit before. I would be glad to hear about your home across the sea."

"No thank you, Drak, is it?" Before the other Kras could answer, Branimir added, "It was only by chance I came to Ojenir. I might stay for the night, but no longer."

"Where are you heading? Winter in Maharia is wicked. It is hardly the time to be traveling on the road."

Branimir shifted his gaze to his small hands. "The cold does not bother me much." For a moment, his mind wandered to the many centuries he had spent in the Netherworld. The experience had hardened him, but time did not flow the same in the realm of the dead. Where his mind had grown wiser, his body had remained ever young-looking. Of course, there was no way he could tell this stranger, or anyone else, what could not be explained.

"Are you alright, Branimir?" Drak asked.

He scraped his teeth against his cracked lips, giving Drak his attention. Branimir knew he would never again taste the acidic breath of the Netherworld. Yet, scarily enough, he found some days he longed to return to the place he had traversed for a thousand years. For three years, he had drifted aimlessly across Maharia without any particular place to go. The frozen wastelands of the dead were still more familiar to him than Maharia or the Hrani Highlands.

"Yes. I will be just fine." Branimir said. "Were you not going to tell me my future?"

"Ah." Drak shifted on the stone rock, widening his eyes at the twigs in his hand. "Stone the crows! I nearly forgot about the rune staves. I suppose you have finished your supper." Drak fiddled with the twigs, eyeing Branimir's empty bowl on the table. The Kras said, "These were passed down from my father, who taught me the secrets of *div-i-nation*."

Branimir smiled as the friendly Kras struggled to say the word. "And, where did your father learn it?"

Drak knit his brow.

Branimir did his best to not grin. "I am sorry, but I have never before heard of this talent."

"My father never told me," Drak said.

"Okay," Branimir straightened himself on top of his own rock, "what do I need to do?

"Nothing," Drak said. "I just throw them in the dirt and then I tell you what the sticks say."

"The sticks talk to you?"

Drak angled his eyebrows over his black-filled eyes, looking seriously at Branimir. "They are called rune staves, not sticks—and yes. Do you always ask this many questions?"

Branimir smiled. "I have been told I do."

Drak clicked his tongue, rubbing the twigs between his red hands with fervor.

"Alack!" Drak squealed hurling the twigs to the cavern floor.

Branimir jumped at the sudden exclamation while Drak hurriedly stooped over to examine the rune staves.

After steadying his heartbeat, Branimir crooked his own neck in trying to make some meaning of the weird black scratches on the wood. Most of the staves were faced down, hiding the markings, but there were a few that were exposed.

"Oh, my," Drak whistled. "Yes…oh my, my, my."

Branimir tightened his lips to keep himself from making a comment on the usefulness of Drak's mumblings. He did not want to offend the stranger, who clearly took this rune-reading business very seriously.

"You will never find love, or peace, or riches in your lifetime," Drak started. His finger was on the edge of his pointed nose, tapping it while concentrating.

"Ha!" Branimir slumped on his rock. "Perfect."

"Hold on," Drak narrowed his eyes, glimmers of black flashing, like jasper. "You will soon be traveling into the frigid cold with a man. No something more than a man—he is coming for you."

Branimir felt his eyes widen. "Are you talking about the future or the past?"

Drak was off his stone and on his knees, drawing closer to the scattered twigs. His pointed ears twitched like the staves were actually making a sound, which only Drak could hear. "The rune staves only tell the future."

Branimir shoved his hands into his pockets to keep them from trembling. He bumped into something buried in his pocket. With recognition, his fingers skimmed the soft surface of the bluish moonstone, the Ojenek.

He had found it at Illuard within the Hall of Gravels, the Eevaltti, when he was still a slave to the Highborn. Now, he always kept the precious relic close. The gem allowed the holder to speak and understand any tongue; Ojenek was as much a part of him as his own hand. It had always given him an unexplainable comfort.

He took a deep breath, calming his nerves.

"There is more," Drak jerked his head to stare at Branimir. "I have never seen this…"

Branimir turned his head, reaching for his pack of extra food and his cowl. "I must be going." Despite being comforted by the moonstone, he did not want to stick around at Ojenir any longer. He did not want to know what else these rune staves said.

Drak reached out and clutched Branimir's arm, holding tight. "Stone the crows! Your life, and your death, is somehow connected with the gods, Branimir. I know it sounds *ominous*, but the death rune is leaning against the rune of the gods."

Naturally, Drak would know the word ominous but could not say *divination*.

Branimir stood, throwing his cowl over his head. "I don't know what you are talking about, but I don't plan to die anytime soon."

Even Branimir was surprised at the smooth tone of his voice.

"You must be Master Branimir," a shrill voice acknowledged from the rear. "There is a man waiting outside the gate. He specifically asked for you—by name."

He turned around to face another small, crimson creature. "Who?"

The Kras shrugged. "He did not give his name."

Drak tried to gather all his sticks. "A man has come to take you on an adventure."

"I don't think so," Branimir trailed off. His mind riddled with confusion. He did not know anybody.

"If you would please come with me," the messenger said. "We would prefer the man not tarry outside of Ojenir."

"Wait for me," Drak said. "I must go with you on this adventure. I want to know more about the meaning behind the rune staves."

"I think it would be best if you stayed," Branimir frowned. Recalling his manners, he bowed his head. "Thank you for the meal, Drak. It was nice meeting you."

Without waiting for a response, he turned to follow the messenger. He was led away from his stone seat and through a tunnel to the outside. As he walked away, he heard Drak yelp for him to wait, scrambling to put the rune staves in the pouch.

The breeze rolling through the Hrani Highlands hit Branimir before he reached the exit. The coldness reminded him of the Netherworld's frosty ether. He tightened the red cowl around his shoulders to keep himself from shivering and exhaled. The misty vapor fled his lips, dissipating into nothingness.

The moment he could see the frozen dirt of the Hrani Highlands, the Kras messenger said his farewells and turned to go back to Ojenir.

Bran bobbed his head and followed the clatter of a horse's hooves against the ground. He no more had stepped outside the tunnel before a familiar voice called out with a heavy accent.

"Branimir Baran, yes? Too long, it has been."

Branimir halted. He gaped at the red-haired man atop the dark horse near a ridge. The two had not been affected by the passing of time while in the Netherworld together, but since returning to Aenar, Branimir had felt the impact of age on his body. He swore his knees creaked whenever he stood. He noticed little change in the black mage though.

"Dorofej?" Branimir nearly cried, his eyes watering in the breeze. "You have come back for me?" The Highborn looked almost as youthful as he had at Shayol Domier a millennium ago. His hair was a bit longer, and there were a couple of extra lines around his eyes, but he was still a young man. It could not be possible unless… unless, he had found the Ash Tree, again.

"My dear friend," Dorofej beamed, his brow unruffled with reassurance. "Over, our adventure is not. I must call on your service once more, yes?"

Branimir's chest tightened in a mixture of fear and excitement, no longer worried about the foretelling of the twigs.

"It has been three years. What has happened? Did you find what we sought?"

Dorofej did not hesitate, revealing a copper dagger from his cloak. He held it outright over his horse's head with a firm grip. "Something worse, I am afraid."

"Kaelandur!" Branimir gasped in recognition. "It's not possible. I watched you cast it from the Tower of Eresh. The dagger was left behind, forever lost in the Netherworld!"

Dorofej flared his nostrils. "As it should have been, yes? Yet recovered somehow and carried back to Maharia, Kaelandur has been. We can speak on the road, but time is fleeting. Come with me, you must."

"What a pigsticker," Drak piped up next to Branimir, appearing from the tunnel behind him. The Kras's eyes were glued to Kaelandur.

Branimir jumped, frowning at Drak. "What are you doing out here? I said not to come."

"And, I said I am coming with you."

Branimir grunted. "No, you most definitely are not."

"Yes, I am. The rune staves say you will have the greatest of adventures. Alack! Your name is already marked for greatness, *Branimir*. If anything, I must come with you to tell your story."

Dorofej spoke with amusement, "Let him come, Branimir. I say, we could use a guide, and the Kras would know Maharia well, or at least have a greater knowledge of its history. Besides, an extra hand may be helpful, yes?"

"Anything you need to know, I could tell," Drak agreed.

Branimir gave a side-long, scrutinizing glance at Drak, and spoke to Dorofej. "What is happening?".

Dorofej answered, "You have seen it too, yes? Rumors of the dead spilling over from the Netherworld, there are; a place for them to find rest, there is not. Rumor, there is, that Wolos, the Horned God, has been slain. I say, if true, the Likhyi will come."

"Huzzah. I said you walked in the footpath of the gods. *Div-i-nation.*" Drak slapped his hands together and flashed his crooked teeth. "I will fetch us ponies."

Chapter II

Branimir did not own a weapon, armor, or really anything useful when considering the dead were *spilling over*, as Dorofej indicated. His pack had a few pieces of dried meat and unleavened bread atop an extra set of clothes. From the looks of it, Drak had brought even less.

"What are the Kras doing with ponies?" Branimir murmured, fearful of startling his tan mare. He gripped onto the yellowish mane, his fingers warmed by the thick strands of hair. He sat only a few feet above the ground with his body slanted in the small saddle. He was certain he had never ridden an animal before in all his life.

Drak, who rode next to him, bounced on his pony like it was an extension of his bottom. "What do you mean?"

"I mean, Kras are quicker on their feet and do not tire easily. Why would you own a pony for riding?" Branimir asked.

"Oh," Drak shrugged, keeping his dark eyes on the path ahead, "we do not ride them often, unless the snows are too thick, or the road is too long. And the snows will be deep soon enough."

Branimir scrunched his nose. "But where did you get them? How did you train them?"

Drak laughed out loud, patting the neck of his black pony. "We did not train them. We traded stones for them last year with men from Hleduk. These are Dukeson ponies from the far north. Trained, short, and sturdy." Drak clicked his tongue, and continued,

"We mostly use them to pull our wagons to Halderon when we go trade at the market. I don't like trading stones, but these ponies were worth it. We have to make a living. Don't you have ponies across the ocean?"

Branimir had not yet traveled to the coastal city of Halderon, which he knew to be located on the other side of the Hrani Highlands. In the past few years, he had mostly circled through the inland villages and cities. Branimir responded to Drak, keeping to his lie. "No, we have no ponies across the ocean."

Wanting to avoid a discussion about his origins with Drak, Branimir slowed his mount. Allowing himself to fall behind several paces, he focused on trying to learn how to maneuver the animal. Straightening his back, he clung to the pony with his knees, and pulled at the reins softly to redirect when needed.

To help ease his tension, Bran spent many miles focusing on his breath, watching the patterned air mist in front of the edge of his pointed nose. Soon, he found it was not as difficult to ride as he might have imagined. Relaxing, he watched the terrain around him, knowing he could see better than Dorofej in the dark. The Highlands had a thin layer of frost in some areas, but mainly, Bran saw hardened red rock and discolored foliage.

The first real snowfall would be coming soon.

Half the day had passed and Ojenir was well behind them when Drak whistled through his teeth. He wiggled his pointed nose against the cold wind. "I should formally introduce myself since we will be spending time together. I am called Drak Ghas, son of Figkor, son of Callux."

Dorofej dipped his chin. "Dorofej Creighton."

Branimir was speechless, not remembering Dorofej to ever have had a surname. Either he finally remembered it, or he had made it up altogether.

He was not sure Drak would be sticking around for the entirety of the journey, especially if he had anything to say of it, but he followed Dorofej's example. "My name is Branimir Bar—" He stopped, remembering Drak's familiarity with history and the Kras. "Branimir Barthor." He lied.

Dorofej glanced over his shoulder with equal surprise.

Drak did not seem to notice. Scratching his hair, black and frayed, from beneath the gray linings of his hood, he said, "Pray tell, where are we going, Anshedar?"

"An Anshedar, I should not be considered," Dorofej said. "I am Highborn. And to Cavell, within the Dyndaer, we are riding."

Drak gasped. "You are Kadari?"

"No," Dorofej said. "I say, considered among the Kadari, I will never be."

"Then, what do you mean by Highborn?" Drak whispered, trying to make sense of the word. "And why do you talk with that silly accent? I have never heard anyone talk like you before."

Dorofej's forehead crumpled.

Branimir answered, reiterating what he had come to learn in the past few years. "Highborn is an old word once used to describe the Kadari. The mages used to be respected, but long ago, there were men…" Branimir thought of Kinhar Sayan and Falmagon Sej, the Highborn Longwalker, "…who craved power and—" Branimir, suddenly serious, turned to Dorofej for help.

Dorefej picked up on the pause and continued the thought, "And the blessing of Dahz the Lightbringer, these men sought, to acquire said power. These men destroyed what the Highborn were meant to be, they did."

"You know the Kadari then?" Drak responded, lifting his nose to look at Dorofej.

"From Maharia to Kalamaar, I have heard mentioning of the Kadari, yes? In the past thousand years, gifted the world with vast death, the Kadari have. I say, I know them well, better than most. The first to seek power and immortality, they are not; and the last to pay with their lives, they will not be."

Drak's mouth was wide open. His feet bobbed on either side of the pony. "Alack! Aren't the Kadari keeping demons at bay on the other side of the world?"

Dorofej rubbed his chin. "I say, heard such rumors, I have. Whether true or not, time will tell."

"Did the Kadari make the pigsticker you are carrying about?" Drak asked.

Dorofej hummed in response.

Branimir gulped, his throat dry. He struggled not to blab the tale of him and Dorofej right then and there. A thousand years had passed since Kaelandur had been removed from the world of Aenar and taken to the Netherworld. Branimir wanted to know why it had been returned to the north, to Maharia, and who was responsible.

"Dorofej, what have you learned since we parted at Strahil?" Branimir probed, again, fiddling with the reins of his pony. His red fingers were already chilled, but it was nothing he could not withstand. He had spent a lifetime and more in the frozen Netherworld. The winter in Maharia did not compare.

Dorofej peered at Branimir from beneath his black hood. He considered Drak before answering, "Little, I am afraid. I say, the past years have been spent with the Crimson Sun at Tamarri in attempts to learn what the world has become."

"Crimson Sun?" Drak repeated under his breath.

"And what has the world become?" Branimir turned from Drak, disregarding his widened eyes and twitching ears.

"You heard the tales, as much as I, or any other who listens, yes?" Dorofej said. "Dragon-men and skin-switchers continue to clash in the north, the Kadari spreads their reign here and in the east, and warring races in the southern deserts expand toward Maharia, yes?"

"I have," Branimir agreed. "But I also heard whispers of the Crimson Sun and what they do; though, I did not know you were with them. Aren't they sellswords who mostly do business for the Kadari?"

Dorofej laughed, cheeks red from the cold. "I say, I have forgotten what you have become. A servant no longer and again, you never will be."

"You were a slave? I thought you were born free." Drak intruded leaning over on his pony. "Were the Kadari your masters?" Drak ogled and then hissed, "Or Dorofej?"

Branimir avoided the question.

Drak may get caught up in Dorofej's rhetoric, but Bran knew better. He had spent enough time with the Highborn to know when he was being sent on a wild goose chase. Praises and poppycock was Dorofej's way of swaying a conversation.

"That is not an answer, Dorofej," Bran said.

The black mage smiled. "Keep the enemy close, I thought I would."

Branimir pressed, "And, in doing so, what did you learn about Kaelandur?"

Dorofej grew stone-faced, glancing sideways at Branimir and exhaled. Dorofej acquiesced, "In 1348 CE, Ivarr Gauthus, the now standing master of the Crimson Sun, directed myself and two others to find Kaelandur for the Kadari."

Branimir gasped, gripping the saddle. "This man, Ivarr, knew Kaelandur by name?"

Dorofej dipped his head. "Indeed, but tell him of its discovery, we did not. Alden Forgaff and Sulanna Maelthirren, my companions, had the same opinion as myself to withhold Kaelandur until the truth of its wanting was learnt. Luckily, motivated merely by money, not all sellswords are."

Branimir recognized the riddlesome words of his friend, and demanded, "How did you convince them to keep the secret? How could you trust them?" He could only think that Dorofej had revealed all to this man and woman: his age; the Ash Tree; the Netherworld; and the history of Kaelandur.

Dorofej rocked in his saddle. "Oh, dear Branimir. I am a man of erudition, yes? I say, I am known to have an uncanny and unhealthy fascination for knowledge."

Branimir snorted, catching sight of Drak, whom was gawking at them as though they were from another world.

Branimir smiled, knowing they were.

The Kras must have taken the gesture as an invitation to join the conversation. "Did you find out why Ivarr wanted the pigsticker?"

Dorofej, again, hesitated before replying. "As I said, the Kadari commissioned him to find it, yes? Know why the Kadari wanted the dagger, the Crimson Sun does not."

"Is Falmagon still alive?" Branimir screeched louder than he intended. He had to pull on the reins to keep the pony from jutting forth through the mountainous terrain. When he finally gained control of the animal, he considered kicking himself for uttering the Highborn Longwalker's name in the same vicinity as Drak.

"We cannot be certain, yes?" Dorofej said simply, but the Highborn could not hide his grimace. "Yet regained Melkorka as a stronghold, the Kadari have, so time we may still possess, if we are quick. Cling to hope, dear Kras; hope the Kadari know less than we know and remain at Melkorka, yes?"

"Time for what?" Drak squinted like he was trying to see through Dorofej. "What do we know? What does all of this have to do with the gods and Branimir?"

Drak clearly attempted to match his understanding of his rune staves with the information he was being told.

Dorofej dropped his head in defeat. "Correct, you may have been, Branimir, to leave this Kras at Ojenir. He is as tireless in his questioning as you once were, yes?" Dorofej exhaled noisily.

Branimir smiled, mocking Dorofej's speaking pattern, "*I say,* fair questions, are they not?"

"Some, yes? Though, unaware of the significance of the inquiry, you are," Dorofej frowned, seemingly unaware of the joke Branimir aimed to make. The black mage tapped his fingers on the saddle, and finally making up his mind, he resumed, "Time to recover a boy, we have. A boy, who I have hidden away, called Bohumir…Mager."

Branimir stopped his pony on the path with a jolt, comprehending the importance, and history, of the name. Mager was the last name of the Eretik, a dark magus, whom the Highborn had executed at Melkorka.

Snowfall began to descend down from the heavens, settling atop his pony and the rocky terrain around them. He scarcely noticed. "Dorofej, could it really be?"

"Afraid, it is true," Dorofej said, laying out the measure of their journey. "Bound by the same bloodline as Nedezhda, our quarry is, and through death affixed to Kaelandur, he might be. I say, the Kadari will want him as desperately as the copper dagger."

Half the night had passed when Dorofej stopped them to rest. The red rock of the Highlands rose on either side of them with only a few scattered trees. Branimir hoped there would be enough timber to make a fire.

He slid sideways from his saddle, missed his stirrup, and clumsily bounced on a single foot away from his pony. His animal stood, unaffected, nuzzling against the snow for something to eat.

If Dorofej or Drak had noticed his near collision with the lightly powdered ground, neither said a word.

Branimir cleared his throat and tightened his cloak while steadying his feet against the slick ground. "Do you have any grain for the ponies, Drak?"

The other Kras, already down from his mount, gritted his teeth and looked at Branimir with pause. He blew air between his teeth, giving the clear answer, and said, "Marry! I forgot."

"No matter," Dorofej said. "Plenty of grain, I have, until we reach Cavell."

"Oh, good," Drak said.

The Kras from Ojenir started to loosen and unfasten the straps across his pony. Branimir attempted to mirror the action with hopes to remove the saddle from his own mare. His cold fingers had difficulty trying to manipulate the hardened leather.

Drak talked while he worked. "Cavell is a dangerous place to be traveling this time of year. There are only two towns with Northmen in the Dyndaer: Ariadne and Cavell. Folks in Halderon say the men who live in either place are a bunch of boobs."

"What?" Branimir faltered. "A bunch of what?"

Drak casually looked over his shoulder. "Boobs. You know—chumps, fools, dupes."

"Um…" Branimir looked to Dorofej, who he could see broadly grinning while ducking behind his horse. Bran hesitated before replying. "Why would they say that?"

Drak did not miss a beat. "Because of the number of cities that have turned to ruins over the years. There is *Shayol Domier*, of course, and *End'augh*, and *Undril*. The last Ariadnean city before they built Ariadne was Garain'l. There is some question as to whether the Northmen really lived there. No matter, the place is now home to the dead and who knows what else."

Low murmurings came from Dorofej, but Branimir could not make out the words. He watched the Highborn pull his saddle free from the back of his dark horse.

Branimir racked his memory. He knew of Shayol Domier, but the other cities were a mystery. They must have risen and fallen while he was in the Netherworld with Dorofej. "Why were so many cities lost? War?" asked Branimir.

Drak scratched his head. "That is right. You are from across the ocean and do not know these things like I would think you would." Drak removed the saddle from his pony, laying it on the ground. "War has had its place, but more so, the Dyndaer is a cursed place with many sorts of creepy crawlies. I hear they are as thick as the trees, but I know little of what they're called. I guess it would be hard to keep a city if there were always beasts running through the streets."

Branimir swallowed. Once more, he expected Dorofej to respond or give some sense of comfort. The black mage retrieved a grain bag for his mount, and no longer appeared to be listening to Drak.

Drak continued, "I have heard folks in Halderon say the ruins are grand, maybe even built with magic. We know Shayol Domier was built with Kadari magic, but who would have built the other ruins? No one really has ever said."

Thinking of the Kadari at Shayol Domier halted Branimir from trying to loosen the straps. The mages, who once would have been called Highborn, had built a suitable stronghold in the Dyndaer. Branimir remembered Shayol Domier to be far more impressive than Melkorka. Knowing as much, he wondered why the Kadari would have withdrawn back to the Seven Islands, to Melkorka.

Drak approached Branimir with a smile, stepping between him and the horse.

"Here," he offered, "let me get the saddle for you. It can be tricky if you haven't done it before."

"Thanks," Branimir said.

Drak slackened the leather strips when Dorofej absently said, "Branimir, firewood needs to be gathered, yes? Freezing through the night, we should try to avoid."

"I will see what I can find," Branimir said.

Drak pulled the saddle to the ground with a grunt. "Let me go with you, Branimir. I would like to help."

Branimir led them to the few scattered trees. The two had only gone around thirty paces when Bran found several dampened sticks beneath the slush. He knocked each broken branch against his foot to loosen the wet snowfall, and then placed them under his arm. Drak circled around him to discover more buried wood.

"I'm curious," Drak whispered so quiet Branimir had to strain to listen to him, "why did you come looking for wood as soon as Dorofej said? Why didn't you tell him to get it himself?"

Branimir turned his chin in surprise, clamping his jaw shut to keep from huffing. The question was bizarre. He shifted his gaze from Drak to Dorofej, who moved to feed the ponies with the extra grain.

"That is an odd thing to ask," he replied, tightening his grip on the timber under his arm. Considering his thoughts, Branimir glanced around the Highlands. Then, as if realizing the truth of it, he said, "It is nighttime. Dorofej cannot see in the darkness like you or me. I can find the wood in half the time."

"That may be true," Drak nodded. "But earlier, Dorofej had said you were no longer a slave. What did he mean by that? I tried to ask before…"

"I know you did," Branimir said, stopping to nibble on the end of his lip. He could feel himself fidgeting while he stared back at Drak. "I am not a slave, Drak. He and I have been through a great deal together. I doubt there are any in the world who could say as much."

Drak slid another branch under his small arm. "Like what?"

"Like what?" Branimir echoed. The words were faint under his breath. "We haven't the time for me to tell all our tales."

The doubtful tone Drak responded with put Branimir on the edge of his heels. The Kras spoke hesitantly, "No time? It will take several weeks to journey to Cavell. We have all the time in the world to tell stories."

Branimir shook his head and tried to respond how Dorofej might. He answered the original question with a question. "Why do you want to know?"

The other Kras continued to scoop up sticks, not realizing Branimir had stopped to watch him. Drak spoke at length. "Marry! I don't know. I am curious, I guess. You are marked with greatness, according to the rune staves. I could have a better idea of where you are heading if I knew where you had been."

Branimir's mind raced to change the subject. He had no interest of telling Drak about his adventures in the Netherworld. He interjected, "I had a friend who was curious like you."

"What was his name?"

"Mojmir," Branimir answered. Although he brought up the subject, he did not want to see Mojmir's red skin and single black bulb staring back at him. He pushed away the image of his one-eyed friend from Melkorka. The Kras had died as a result of his loud mouth the same night in which Branimir's real adventure had started.

Drak balanced the wood in his hands, suddenly turning about. "What happened to him?"

"He had his neck snapped," Branimir said, "for talking too much." He saw Drak's noticeable gulp before turning his back. Branimir kept all emotion out of his words, ending the conversation. "Now, let's go get the fire started."

Chapter III

Twelve more days had come and gone since Ojenir with little excitement. Drak had slowed in his persistent questioning, while Dorofej and Branimir had conceded to staying hushed about the road ahead. The urgency of their quest remained, but Branimir found himself with more questions than answers about the nature of their charge. He could only wait until he had an opportunity to speak with Dorofej alone.

The Hrani Highlands to the north had greyed once Dorofej had guided them into the dark woods of the Dyndaer. The trees were five times thicker than their ponies, towering around them with the space in-between filled with corroded, wilting hedges and speckled undergrowth. Vines snaked between the boughs above, the ends hanging inches above the ground or buried under snow. If ever there had been a path through the Dyndaer to Cavell, the road was hidden in the wintery weather.

Branimir lay on his back within the Dyndaer wilds. The layered snow beneath his blanket was hardened against his back, unaffected by the radiant heat from the fire. He half-listened to Drak throw his rune staves against the forest flooring. The other Kras mumbled under his breath while the sticks clacked and smacked together.

He did his best to ignore the sound with his head resting against his pack. He watched white flakes spin down from the crown of branches above him. Besides the small fire flickering, almost failing near his feet, the forest remained as dark as Ojenir. Though, for Branimir, being a Kras, his eyes gave him clear sight.

A thousand years ago, Branimir had walked through the Dyndaer in the heart of winter, the same as now. Bran would have never thought the Dyndaer could have become so much darker in the elapsed time. Where the forest had been enigmatic then, the ambiance had become more fear-provoking than ever.

Dorofej rustled from under his hood, raising his voice in the darkness. "Another stick I hear clattering and snap the twig in two, I will."

"The gurgling mire makes it too difficult to sleep," Drak said, turning around from the other side of the fire. "And, they are called rune staves, not sticks."

Dorofej raised his head, propping himself up on an elbow near Branimir. He blinked irritably at the Kras. "Keep at it and called firewood, they will be."

Drak grumbled, clutching his twigs to his chest. "It's too noisy here to rest."

"Do stop your sniveling, yes? I say, if you are upset by the noise then go and tell the swamp to shush."

"Marry! I was simply saying," Drak faced the Highborn with a scowl. "You do not have to be bad-tempered about it."

Dorofej snorted. "You wanted to come on an adventure, yes? Be glad the bog is only blubbering and there are no beasts dragging you beneath, you should." The Highborn pulled his hood over the back of his ears and laid back down.

"What beasts?" Branimir shivered, watching Dorofej with sudden interest. Drak had mentioned creatures roaming the Dyndaer when they left Ojenir, but Dorofej had not said a word. The Highborn always had his secrets.

Drak stood. "I told you this forest is full of monsters."

Branimir looked toward the mire on one side, and the half-frozen river they had been following on the other. "I cannot think of any monsters I know in the Dyndaer, save the Vucari."

"Spoilt since our last coming, this place has been. The Vucari abandoned the Dyndaer for good reason, yes? A wisdom unknown by men, it is." He paused to sink further into his wrappings. "In the Dyndaer, vili and bagiennik; bluds and mylings; you will find." Dorofej reshuffled, again, against the ground, twisting over onto his side.

Branimir could make out the tufts of red hair sticking out from his hood. How could he lay so calmly after saying such things?

Drak seemed to have a similar mind, no longer giving any sign of resting. He scanned the trees around him. "Stone the crows! Mylings are the worst," he shook his head, "but what are those other *things*?"

Dorofej murmured, near napping, again, "Nymphs and fays. Imps… and wights. The fire keeps them away… yes?"

Branimir shuddered, scooting closer to the flames.

Drak stood. He turned his neck, inspecting the trees and twitching his ears at the nearby mire. With droplets of sweat swelling on his forehead, he looked to Branimir and pursed his cracked lips.

"Suppose, I can gather more wood for the fire."

Branimir could only nod.

Drak scuttled off.

The ponies nickered, followed by a whinny from Dorofej's horse several feet away.

Branimir realized he could not sleep either. "Dorofej?"

The Highborn grumbled.

"Being back in this place is unreal, like I am dreaming, or in a story." Branimir picked at his fingernails, staring into the burning logs. The Highborn had not moved, or even given a sign of listening, but Branimir needed to talk.

"Do you ever think of Melyena and—" Bran tried to recall the centaur's name, who had come with them to protect the Ash Tree so long ago; the mighty Svet, who had been slain by the ruthless Kadari. "Asgrim." He finally said. "I hate that I cannot remember names like I think I should. Though, how much can a mind hold before it begins to forget? We have lived more lives than most, even since Nedezhda. I had thought the tale of the Eretik had been finished, especially after seeing you cast Kaelandur from the Tower of Eresh." Branimir bit his cheek. "I almost want to go back to see the tower. I want to know the place is as I remember it. The Netherworld really was something, wasn't it?"

He continued to ramble, paying no mind to anything else. "Mm. But tossing the dagger into the abyss should have been the end. And now, the tale has begun all over. Are we meant to live this story again? Maybe…maybe this story will not be quite the same."

Branimir shook his head, his chest tightening, overwhelmed with emotion. He tried to think of something else. Snowflakes skidded down from the treetops, catching his attention. "Do you remember when we last came here? It was the same time of the year; the first snow had just fallen. By what chance would we enter the Dyndaer during the course of winter, again? Maybe we are actually dead, and caught in some vortex of time and space, reliving a nightmare."

Branimir laughed at the thought. The flames flickered against the wood, pressing heat against his cheeks. "I keep thinking about the cold here in Aenar compared to the Netherworld. I guess nothing will ever compare. Even more, I cannot help but think this place, Maharia, feels deader than the realm of the dead. Is that strange?"

"It is not," Dorofej said.

Branimir lifted his head, seeing Dorofej sitting upright, listening intently. His hood was pulled back, revealing his full features, including his flaming hair and wide nose.

"A longing for lost memories, I, too, have found." Dorofej averted his eyes. "The fascination for what cannot be attained guides us toward our charge in life, yes?"

Branimir scrunched his face. "What do you mean?"

"Most measure the worth of something based on constructs of good or evil, justice or corruption, and beauty or defilement, yes?" Dorofej rubbed his hands together, warming them near the fire. "Each paradigm is a puzzle, and the definition of each differ from era to era, yes? A riddle for the living, it is. But an infatuation with puzzles, the dead and the gods, have not."

Branimir said, "Because, they have the answers?"

Dorofej shook his head. "Because, answers to these questions, there are not. I say, there is no gamut to be measured. These questions were created by men; not gods. Hard to understand, I know, for the living have not the scope of immortality. Bound by time and our flesh, we are, yes?"

"Why, then, did you bring me back to life in the Netherworld? Why did you not let me die as I should have?"

"Should you have?" Dorofej elevated his eyes, cheekbones lifting in a warm smile. "Time does not make me any more of a god than you, Branimir. Value in healing the ailments of others, I have found, yes? Whether false or otherwise, my talent with Koldovstvo may grant me admittance into Thrice Ten Kingdom, yes?"

Branimir matched Dorofej's smile. He could not remember when the Highborn had ever spoken of life beyond death, in a thousand years, and specifically never had talked of reaching Thrice Ten Kingdom. Bran had grown accustomed to thinking Dorofej would never die and live forever.

Dorofej must have picked up on his unspoken thoughts, "We must all die eventually, yes?"

From the brush, Branimir saw Drak rushing towards them. The Kras shimmered against the backdrop, telling Branimir that Drak was invisible, blending in with his surroundings. The skill was only known to the Kras, to disappear when needing to stay safe, but a Kras was unable to hide from the perceptive eyes of another Kras.

Still, Dorofej's attention was caught in a similar way. He watched the patterned footprints appearing in the snow, nearing the illuminated area of the fire.

Drak skittered towards them, talking before materializing next to Dorofej. "Alack! Something is coming through the brush behind me."

Branimir barely made it to his feet before a bellowing voice boomed, "The pint-sized bastard went yonder."

With Drak at his side, Bran retreated. At the same time, a hulkish giant smashed through the scrublands, cracking the base of a tree in his wake.

Branimir first thought the huge man was a Bukavac, a frozen behemoth from the Netherworld. His mind hastily painted sporadic memories of battles at Melkorka, and Kalamaar, and the Netherworld before dissolving into nothingness. He quickly discovered this giant was not a demon.

The tyrant appeared more humanoid, with tannish skin, dark hair shaggily hanging over his ears, and piercing blue eyes. More than anything, the giant seemed to be an oversized Anshedar.

The oversized man looked directly at Dorofej and the two Kras standing in the firelight. The giant stopped, steadying his uncovered feet in the snow, and yanked a large two-sided axe from the strapping of his back. He gripped the handle in the meaty grasp of his two six-fingered hands.

"He is not wearing shoes," Branimir whispered in surprise. The giant should have been freezing but seemed unaffected by the cold.

"Bah! I found two foul half pints and a Stuhia, by the looks of it. You know him, Eisliev?"

Stuhia? Branimir had no way to place the word but could only think the giant was speaking of Dorofej, who clearly was *not* a half pint. The Highborn, who had found his way to his feet, pulled the black hood over his head to better conceal his reddened hair.

"What in the Nine Lands, Tyr," a heightened voice snickered, with undertones like Dorofej. A flash of red robes surfaced through the brush while an unseen man attempted to push his way around the giant. "You are going to alert every living thing in the Dyndaer with your ruckus. The Stuhia do not travel this far east, and if they did, we do not inherently know one another. I have never met such a boorish swine."

The man, called Eisliev, barreled around the growling Tyr, who kept his eyes on Dorofej and the Kras. Eisliev carried a torch, wearing robes as red as Dorofej's were black. He shoved on Tyr unsuccessfully with irritation, standing just beneath his chest, and lastly smacked the giant in the forearm with the back of his hand.

The bare-chested brute shoved him back, without looking, sending the robed man sprawling to the ground. "Ah! If you are looking for a fight then jump upon my blade and your death thereafter, Eisliev. I have no interest in hearing your blabbering squall."

Eisliev grunted, somehow keeping his torch from being doused. He flung himself back up from the ground and approached Tyr with a sneer. His own hood had fallen back giving full sight to his long, reddened hair and light eyes.

Branimir raised his eyes to Dorofej for direction, but the black mage acted equally surprised by these mens' sudden appearance.

A third voice, unhurried and balanced, redirected them, "Enough, the both of you. What have you found, Tyr?" An Anshedar, covered in an array of greens and grays, who carried his own torch, stepped from the tree line on the opposite side of Tyr.

Branimir noticed the impression of the head of a horse imprinted on the iron breastplate glinting beneath the flaps of his cloak. The swordsman had a long piece of sharp iron hanging from his belt within a decorated scabbard.

"Teodor Bacheva," Dorofej finally acknowledged, sounding comforted. "A long way from Tamarri, you are?"

Teodor gazed at them, and then rushed to dip his chin to the black mage. He dropped his resting hand from hilt of the long sword at his belt. "Dorofej Creighton, whatever are you doing here in the Dyndaer? Ivarr has been asking of you for many months now." Dorofej clicked his tongue. Before he could answer, Teodor said to Tyr, "Put your weapon away. He is with the Crimson Sun."

Bran bit his tongue, recognizing the name of Ivarr, who Dorofej had said was the master of the Crimson Sun. According to the

Highborn, Ivarr also had been responsible for sending Dorofej to find Kaelandur.

Tyr relaxed, easing the weapon back into its holding.

Eisliev, however, tightened his hands into fists and took a step toward them. On impulse, Branimir reached for a dagger from his belt. When his hand swiped at nothing, he gritted his teeth in frustration. He had traded them for food and supplies weeks before reaching Ojenir.

Dorofej answered Teodor, "I may ask you the same question, yes? I say, did Ivarr send you to the Dyndaer to find me?"

The Anshedar dawdled, "Not hardly. Ivarr sent me to complete another assignment for the Kadari. It is a simple task of retrieving a young lad who has eluded them. Nothing too difficult." Teodor shrugged.

Branimir straightened his back, seeing Dorofej's jaw drop at the mention of their intentions. These three were also seeking Bohumir Mager.

Teodor said, "I would have liked for Ivarr to have given the task to you, or even Alden and Sulanna, but you all have been gone from Tamarri for many months."

"My sincerest apologies, Teodor. Still been seeking the relic the Kadari sought, I have, and distracted by other matters, I have been."

"Weren't you sent for that relic several years ago? You and I had returned from signing a treaty at Mabek when Ivarr gave you the job, right?" Teodor asked.

"A few years, it has been," Dorofej agreed.

Eisliev took another stepped forward, practically glaring at Dorofej. Branimir could not ignore the look of contention from the red-haired man.

Teodor replied casually, "Indeed. Your service to the Crimson Sun has been remarkable. Ivarr talks about you like you are some legend from the stories."

Branimir thought he heard the undertones of jealousy in the Teodor's voice.

Dorofej cocked his head and scoffed. "Trust in you equally, Ivarr must, to send you after a helpless child, yes?"

"Is that sarcasm?" Teodor laughed and went on. "If I recall, the relic you were meant to find was not in the Dyndaer. The Kadari reported it was buried in the Hyaendi Hills."

"An impressive memory you have." Dorofej flashed his teeth, lying, "After several months, other options, I thought I might consider."

"I am certain Ivarr will be glad to know of your reconsideration," Teodor replied with a sly smile.

Dorofej matched the expression.

Eisliev, suddenly interjected, as though he had finally gained the courage to speak, "Time seems to have treated you well, Dorofej, is it?" Eisliev curled his lip. "How long have you been away from Lairhein? It is rare to find a Stuhia this far from home."

Branimir noticed Dorofej swallow air. "Long enough," he answered.

"What did you say your surname was?" Eisliev pressed.

When Dorofej did not immediately answer, Teodor answered, "Creighton."

"Creighton?" Eisliev repeated with doubt, and then accused, "I am not familiar with the name among the Stuhia bloodlines."

"And, you are?" Dorofej asked, suddenly full of fire.

"Ah," Teodor elevated his voice, "Eisliev Kluk and Tyr Og have recently joined the Crimson Sun."

Eisliev glared at Teodor for a moment, and then turned his gaze back to Dorofej

"How pleasant," Dorofej murmured with less enthusiasm. He smoothed his robes, focused on Teodor. He changed the subject. "Listen, since I am here, I would be glad to fetch the lad, yes? You can be on your way back to Tamarri."

"No," Eisliev nearly shouted, his voice echoing through the trees behind Branimir. "We will be taking the boy to Melkorka."

Drak sprang back at the outcry.

"Eisliev," Teodor cautioned, lifting his hand.

The red mage curled his lip, but said nothing more.

"A bit late on the offer, Dorofej. We hope to arrive at Cavell by morning." Teodor said casually

"If you don't get us lost again," Tyr added with a smirk.

Teodor frowned, ignoring the giant. "Perhaps, you—" The man dipped his eyebrows at Branimir and Drak, peering in the dim light, though he were trying to identify what they were exactly.

Drak filled the blank, "Kras."

"Of course," Teodor said with a nervous laugh. "Send them back to their home and return to Ivarr. He will be eager for you to explain your absence."

"Heading another way, we are," Dorofej replied, forcing a smile at the opposing group.

"I see." Teodor tensed. "Should I report to Ivarr for you, then, when I return?"

Dorofej pushed his teeth outward, doing his best to maintain the phony smile. He looked like a half-brained horse. "I say, do whatever you must, Teodor. Best of fortune on your journey, yes?"

Chapter IV

The next few minutes were a blur. In one moment, Branimir was watching Teodor, Tyr, and Eisliev tramp off into the Dyndaer, and then Dorofej was kicking snow over the fire, shouting orders.

"Follow the river to Cavell, they will," Dorofej said. "Make haste. Ready your ponies, you must. I say, we will reach Cavell and find Bohumir first, yes?"

"How do you plan to get to Cavell without following the river?" Drak squealed. The Kras dashed by the fire to start placing his bridle on the animal. "Alack! We will get lost."

"Hope we do not," Dorofej said.

A few moments later, Branimir's tan mare scrambled behind the other mounts. He clung to the pony, bouncing inches off the saddle, barely staying atop. Ahead of him, the black mage led them through the thick trees. The bog bubbled wickedly alongside them.

Branimir almost considered forsaking the ponies, knowing he and Drak could likely run faster than the creatures. Though, with foresight, Bran was also aware he would exhaust himself long before the mount would lose wind. So, he held to the reins and mane of his animal and bolted after Dorofej into the Dyndaer.

"Gah!" Dorofej shouted, hunkering down on his horse, slapping its hind quarters with the reins in one hand while holding a torch outright with the other.

"Can you see?" Branimir called out. He hoped Dorofej did not lead them straight into a swamp. Branimir was certain the Highborn could see no more than a haze of shapes and shadows rushing on either side of them.

"Well enough," Dorofej cried.

Drak squealed from either fear or amusement, galloping right in front of Branimir. After a short time, any sign of the river leading directly to Cavell disappeared entirely behind them.

For almost an hour, they were hard-pressed, making their way through the Dyndaer without saying more than a few words. At last, thinking they had made up enough time moving west and south to get past the other group, Dorofej slowed.

Branimir's pony huffed and snorted.

"Climb off of her, Branimir," Dorofej instructed, breathing heavily himself. He dismounted from his black horse. "Breathe for a moment, we all must."

"We will be lucky if we are not totally lost," Drak said, gasping for air. "Hard to keep any sense of direction in the Dyndaer. We could be near the ruins of Shayol Domier at the rate we were going. I bet we looked like a bunch of boobs speeding in between the trees."

Branimir shook his head at Drak's choice language.

Dorofej whipped his torch around. "Similar to anything boobish, we are not." He cleared this throat. "Shayol Domier is further to the east and south, yes? Overshot our mark, we have not."

"How do you know?" Branimir asked, while Drak twisted his face at Dorofej.

"I say, look at the trees, Branimir," Dorofej said. "Many have been cut, leaving stumps between those fully grown, yes? Harvested for the buildings, and homes, and palisades, they have been."

Dorofej was right. If Branimir had taken the time to look around, he would have noticed the mangled remains of many chopped trees. Though, the crown of limbs that thatched the ceiling of the forest was as concentrated, if not moreso.

Drak's pony whinnied. He did not bother to shush it, but instead counseled Dorofej and Branimir. "You should know people in the Dyndaer do not think well of the Kadari. Saying anything about them or—"

"Told you, Kadari, I am not," Dorofej interrupted.

"I know," Drak said, "but any talk of Dahz the Lightbringer should be kept to yourself. The Dyndaer is different than the rest of Maharia. The folk here worship Czern, the Gray-Clad."

"So, they hate the Lightbringer?" Branimir clarified.

"Mostly yes," Drak replied, "and anything to do with the Kadari."

"As dark as the Dyndaer is," Branimir pondered. "I can see why the people would respect the God of Darkness. Yet I wonder…"

Dorofej tilted his head with interest.

Branimir continued, "Why don't the Kadari take the Dyndaer as they have the rest of the north? Their stronghold had once been here—the Ash Tree, too. From what I have heard, the Kadari have forced people to worship Dahz all across Maharia. Why not do the same here?"

Dorofej raised his eyebrows with matched curiosity.

"Well, most would tell you the Kadari are locked in a battle at Melkorka against demons," Drak explained. "The storytellers say the monsters came after Wolos was killed. I heard the Netherworld has no more room for the dead."

"Isn't that only a rumor?" Branimir asked, looking to Dorofej uneasily. He had seen the numerous dead scouring the frozen wasteland of the Netherworld. At the time, he had thought it normal.

"It is," Dorofej said, wrinkles forming at the edges of the Highborn's eyes.

Drak rubbed his chin, looking southward. "Ariadne is another possible reason. The city is said to be greater than Gaetana." Branimir recognized the name of the capitol city, home of the nearest King. Drak went on, "In Halderon, folks say Ariadne is time-honored, for over five-hundred years now, birthing Aenar's greatest hero-warriors. Not only were the soldiers from Ariadne critical in the final wars with the centaurs, but they are still called on again and again to fight battles for the Northmen."

"*Hero-warriors*," Branimir wondered for a moment. He then added, "How do they keep the Kadari out of the Dyndaer?"

"They don't. Not really," Drak said. "The Kadari need the Ariadneans for them, especially now, against the desert people."

"In other words, the Kadari don't oppose Czern because the Ariadneans fight their wars," Branimir finished. "Do the kings and queens of Maharia have no say?"

Drak scrunched his shoulders. "From what I know, the Kadari controls them. What can simple Northmen, or even Kings, do against magic?

"Plenty," spouted Dorofej.

"I wonder what the Kadari would do if the Ash Tree were in the Dyndaer," Branimir said.

"Oh, they would attempt to convert Ariadne, for sure," Drak agreed. "Some Kras at Ojenir repeat the stories of their old kin. Of course, there are none left who remember the Ash Tree being in the Dyndaer, but I have heard of how the Kadari once fought the Vucari over their difference in belief. All that is left are the stories."

Branimir thought to mention how it all was more than a simple story but decided against saying anything.

Drak said, "War springs the quickest from those who have faith in gods, even the peaceful ones. It is likely why our people worship nothing."

The words left Branimir speechless. He had never considered why he did not worship like most. In hindsight, he figured there was little difference, whether forcibly enslaved to men or blindly following the gods. In either case, he would have no freedom. The thought mortified him.

Drak gradually added, "You know, there is another reason why the Kadari might leave the Dyndaer be." Drak's voice was almost wistful while sharing his knowledge. "I forgot about the Lilitu. They have built seafaring, trade cities all along the edge of the Dyndaer.

Any destruction within the forest would surely upset their market on the coast and spur them to war, too."

Branimir's mind raced to place the name. "Who are the Lilitu?"

"Alack! I know you come from across the ocean, but how could you not hear of the Lilitu?" Drak crooked his neck. "The Lilitu have been in Maharia since the beginning of the Third Age. They come from the south, from Haemus Mons. Our people trade gems with them often in Halderon."

Branimir asked, "Why would the Kadari be afraid of the Lilitu?"

"Their sheer size," Drak said. "Even when counting the Kadari, the Lilitu exceed the Northmen fifty to one."

Dorofej said, "Expanded greatly, the world has."

"When compared to what?" Drak raised his eyebrows in confusion. Before either Dorofej or Branimir could respond, Drak threw up his hand to stop them. "Wait. Something is moving in the clearing ahead."

Dorofej swiftly flipped his torch upside down and pressed it to the earth to squelch it. "Branimir," he whispered, "see what stirs, yes?"

Branimir reacted, becoming invisible to all who might be able to see him, save Drak, who directed the ponies back.

He had become familiar with the scout and report routine when traveling with Dorofej in the frozen wasteland of the dead. The tactic had kept them from many skirmishes which might have left them bloodied or worse.

Branimir zipped ahead, his feet lightly crunching against the snow. The sound was hardly audible, even to his ears; however, the footprints he left in his wake were unavoidable. The surrounding swamp bubbled and gurgled nearby, swollen against the blackened earth. He considered the bizarre swamp babbling in the Season of Frost while he advanced.

The moment slowed.

Branimir took two steps into the clearing and stopped dead in his tracks. He goggled at a young, dark-haired boy, likely ten-years-old, who held a torch to inspect a woman dangling from rope by the neck. The corpse hung from a straight branch, swaying to and fro. The limb which she was attached to creaked. Her face was grayish-blue, barely observable through her mangled, golden hair.

Branimir had seen many dead bodies in his lifetime. He guessed she had been dead for the better part of the afternoon.

The boy climbed carefully up an adjacent tree for a better look. His torch flickered from the ground below, crackling against the snow. He took his time, unhurried, without worry.

A brown horse whinnied from behind the boy, burying its nose into the snow, searching for fresh grass. The animal's reins sagged against the ground.

"Bohumir Mager!" An aged man in a fancy jacket shouted from the opposite side of the clearing. The boy sprang from the tree, falling to the mush below. "Czern's breath! What are you doing?"

The child recoiled from the dead body, bright blue eyes wide with horror in the faint light of his torchlight, but clear to Branimir. His leather boots slipped in the snowfall that covered the ground, but he steadied his feet. The boy gawked at the older man hesitantly, lifting his hands innocently.

"I didn't kill her, Lamont. I found her like this," Bohumir's voice trembled. "Please, you must believe me."

Lamont eyed the child, angling his thick brow, as if appraising his worth.

The boy shouted, "Lamont, please! There's no need for your sword."

Branimir jerked toward the man in the fancy coat. True enough, he held a short, heavy sword in his hand. The single-edged blade curved slightly at the end, looking more like a farmer's tool for harvesting the crop than a warrior's weapon.

"I am not going to kill you, you looby," Lamont snorted. The gray-haired man stepped closer, shaking his head with disbelief. "You really think anyone would believe you'd have the strength to hang a grown woman, boy?"

"Well..." the boy stammered.

"Climb back up there and cut her down," Lamont ordered. He tossed his sword at the boy's feet.

"I say, what has happened here?" Dorofej's voice rumbled across the space of the clearing.

The man, likely a noble, jolted at the sound. He observed the black mage and then the weapon he had thrown. When Bran materialized in front of Dorofej, the boy and man both took a noticeable step backwards.

"Who are you? What are you doing here?" Lamont asked, stepping nearer to the boy. Bohumir shifted his own gaze toward the sword.

"Lamont Dthais," Dorofej eased, "leave the sword alone, yes? Familiar with me, you are. It is I, Dorofej Creighton."

"Dorofej," Lamont crooned with a relieved sigh, pushing his chin forward and squinting his eyes, "Is that really you? I hardly recognized you in this terrible light. Why have you come back?"

Bohumir stared at the black mage.

Dorofej hummed, ignoring the older man. "The girl hung herself, yes?"

Lamont answered, measuring Dorofej with his eyes. "I truly do not know. Lady Nitalia went missing and now, here she is."

"Lady Nitalia?" Dorofej's eyes slightly widened.

Branimir shifted his feet with discomfort.

"Yes," Lamont whispered. "The Count's daughter disappeared this morning. The whole village has been searching for her."

Her golden hair and bluish-gray nose caught Branimir's eye again. He had to turn away.

Lamont continued, "Czern's breath has been exceedingly dark these past months. The people of Cavell are on edge, plagued with superstition."

Dorofej said, "I say, darker times are coming, lest I can take Bohumir with me. This is the boy I had left in your care, yes?"

Lamont adjusted his jacket, frowning. "It is."

"You are one of the men who came to my father's house," Bohumir glared at the Highborn. "Where is the woman who killed him?"

"I am, yes," Dorofej said. The black mage side-stepped the second question. "Saved you once, I have, Bohumir, and again, I must. I say, you need to come with me."

Lamont tightened his jaw. "An explanation would be welcomed, Dorofej. When you left Bohumir, I did not expect to see you again. The boy has just begun to settle here. What is the meaning of all this? I had meant for him to take over my business someday and provide care for my daughters."

Drak suddenly piped up, joining them, "They have a pigsticker—"

Dorofej hushed him. "I say, the less you are aware, the better, it is. Best for Bohumir gather his things and we be gone at once, yes?"

"No," Bohumir said. He reached down gripping the handle of the falchion in his fist. It was off-balanced in his hand. He barely could lift the blade from the ground. "I am not going anywhere with you. This is my home now, and my family."

"Here, you have lived," Dorofej said, "but your home, it is not. And I imagine neither was the Hyaendi Hills, yes?"

The boy jerked his head toward Lamont uneasily.

Dorofej shifted in his robes, saying, "Saved you after your father stabbed you, I did, and not for you to ignore reason when it is plainly given to you, nor raise a sword against me when I aim to help. Come with me, you must, or die, you will."

"That is hardly a thing to say to a boy," Lamont protested.

"The truth, it is," Dorofej replied.

Drak's eyes widened. "Alack! Put the sword down."

The boy shuffled toward Dorofej, dragging the sword behind him.

"Enough." Dorofej used Koldovstvo, the ancient magic, pulling the sword through space and time from Bohumir's hand and into his own.

Bohumir cried out as the weapon was yanked from his hand.

"Marry!" Drak bawled. "Pray tell, how did you do that? I thought you were not Kadari."

"Kadari?" Lamont wondered, scanning Dorofej with wide eyes. "You worship the Lightbringer?"

"No, and no, again," Dorofej said.

Lamont grunted, second guessing himself. "I don't want to know what this is about, Dorofej. Let's cut down the Princess and return her body to the Count. Afterwards, you can do as you wish with Bohumir."

The Highborn tossed the falchion back to the ground in the boy's direction.

"As you say, Lamont." Bohumir said, retrieving the sword with less fervor. Bohumir began to climb back up the tree.

Branimir watched uncomfortably. The hanged face of the girl was twisted, either from the strain of lack of breath, shock of what she had done mid-drop, or the sudden snap of her body lurching towards the ground. Her lifeless blue eyes matched the tenor of the expression.

"Hurry up with it," Lamont said crossly, "I said to cut her down."

Bohumir hoisted the sword against the rope and sawed through the hemp with a few quick movements, causing the threads to split. The body clamored to the ground.

Branimir held his breath. The Princess reeked of urine and feces.

Lamont, who seemed unaffected by the stench, heaved the Princess over the saddle of the horse. Bruises and rope marks lined the neck. The head fell awkwardly.

"Her spine is broken," Drak said, making a face.

"Commonplace in hangings, it is," Dorofej said, clearing his throat. "Drak, gather our horse and ponies, yes?"

When Drak returned, Lamont handed the reins of their horse to Bohumir. "You can lead the horse back to town."

Supper had passed by the time the five of them reached the dirt path outside of Cavell. The small hamlet was nestled within the Dyndaer, awkwardly wedged between the river and the woods.

Branimir first noticed the looming towers of the stone castle on a small rise.

A single sentry at the open gate approached Lamont, an unusual hammer strung across his back in leather fastenings. The path beyond the gate was lit with torchlight.

Lamont stopped several feet from the guard. "Good evening, Ignac."

The guard called Ignac tilted his head. "And to you, Lamont. Who have you brought with you?"

"Dorofej Creighton of Tamarri. Branimir Barthor and Drak Ghas of Ojenir," Dorofej answered for him, luckily remembering Branimir's false surname.

Drak shifted his weight when realizing Branimir had been included in being from Ojenir. Branimir caught his eye with his own and shook his head to indicate to keep his mouth closed. Drak looked down at his feet nervously.

Ignac tilted his head. "I did not realize the Kras ventured from Ojenir, unless trading in Halderon with the Lilitu."

"Much is unknown of the Kras, yes?" Dorofej thinned his lips.

"I suppose," Ignac said. "Lamont, what news of Lady Nitalia? Count Frantisek has been waiting eagerly in the Great Chamber for hours. He has barely moved since sending out sentries this morning."

Lamont nodded towards the horse. There was no way to hide the body from any who took a simple glance. The girl was easily identified with her blonde locks hanging toward the dirt. "Lady Nitalia Frantisek is dead."

Ignac's jaw dropped, seeing the woman slung over the horse. He likely was cursing himself for not noticing when they had approached. "We should not waste any more time. I will lead you to the keep, Lamont. Right this way."

The guard led them through the gates where several armed men dwelled in the shadows. The men stepped from their post momentarily to stare at the dead girl as the horse carried her by them. Her name was whispered.

Ignac led them through the dusty streets, past open taverns and closed shops. Home fires burned in the village of Cavell, the odor of stewed pork and breaded stew creeping out of the chimneys with gray smoke. Branimir's stomach rumbled at the smell despite him eating only hours ago.

Few men hastily moved through the streets and lighted a few torches to accompany candlelit windows. Though, they halted their chore when they noticed the Princess slung over the back of the brown mare. Without doubt, rumor would flood the streets before reaching the castle wall.

Lamont broke the silence. "I am surprised to see folks still meandering about this late. Why have the taverns not closed down?"

"The village has been on edge with the disappearance of the Princess, Lamont," Ignac said. "Keldron decided to keep his place open a bit later. Seems half the town has gone there to drink and who knows what else. We have increased the number of sentries."

"Are you expecting trouble?" Lamont asked.

"Not especially," Ignac said, looking back at Nitalia's body, "but once they hear the Princess is dead…" he glanced around the streets, "… or see it. Who knows what will come?"

Dorofej interjected, changing the subject, "I say, have any others passed through tonight?"

Branimir winced, knowing Dorofej was asking about the three from the Crimson Sun. He, too, had wondered if Teodor, Tyr, and Eisliev had arrived in Cavell yet.

"None," Ignac replied with caution. "Are you expecting more companions? You should know Cavell is not used to many travelers, especially during the winter."

Dorofej shook his head. He slipped back into their walking formation without another word.

The road was practically desolate from the main gate to the opening to the keep. The walls were elevated only a few feet above the city wall. The arch leading into the keep was simple with the wooden portcullis strung up. Two more guards stood idly at the entrance, barely noticing the line of men before they had passed.

Branimir stepped closer to Dorofej, recognizing how unaware the guardsmen acted. He guessed the edifice of the hamlet had been built more for display than defense. Perhaps, the people did not fear battle or war with other nations—not in the Dyndaer—but what of the beasties Dorofej had mentioned earlier?

At the steps leading up to the wooden, double doors of the keep, Lamont left the girl's dead body for Ignac to tend. He walked up the stone steps with Bohumir and Dorofej at his heels.

Branimir and Drak followed.

The Great Chamber had a fire pit in the center of the stone floor. Branimir noticed he did not feel much heat from the pit. The temperature in the chamber was only a hair warmer than outside. There were no windows in the room. Only a hole in the ceiling allowed the smoke to escape from the room.

The lord and lady's chairs had been situated on a small rise beyond two long tables on either side of the fire pit accompanied by wooden benches. There was another smaller fire pit near the throne chairs. Sconces lining the stone walls held torches on both sides, separated by embroidered cloths of purple, red, and black hinting at the history and lore of the royal family and Cavell.

A man dressed much like Lamont entered the room and announced the noble family, "Count Vlaskhorn Frantisek and Countess Maja Frantisek."

The Count and Countess entered the chamber from a stone staircase near the rear of the room and approached their thrones. The husband and wife appeared exhausted, slouching in their step, stricken with concern. Maja's eyes were especially puffy and bloodshot, telling Branimir she had been crying. Her blonde strands were halfway pushed into a bun atop her head with loose ends hanging. The mother of Lady Nitalia did her best to remain poised and placid.

Branimir did like the others and bowed his head. He did not lift it again until the couple had taken their place at the head of the Chamber.

Count Frantisek loosened the pin that held his purplish cloak across his shoulder, letting it fall to the throne behind him. Leaning forward over his plump stomach, he eyed the three men and Kras. He blinked several times with his oversized blue eyes, finding confusion in the presence of the strangers. "Lamont, I was told you had news regarding my daughter. Has she been found?"

Lamont nodded, contorting his face. "She has been found, Count."

"Where is she?" Countess Maja's lip quivered.

"I apologize to tell you, but Bohumir found her hanging dead in the forest," Lamont swallowed. "These travelers, and myself, came upon the scene shortly after he had discovered her."

The Count did not move.

"Nitalia!" The Countess covered her mouth in horror. She looked at Bohumir. "Poor boy." As if not knowing where to direct her sadness, she dropped her face to her hands. She held the position, heaving, choking on her own breath.

The fire crackled as the members of the Great Chamber stared empathetically at the Countess. None, including her husband, had the words to comfort her.

Finally, Maja stood from her chair, unable to regain her composure. She stumbled to the room from which she had come.

Count Frantisek attempted to speak, but had to stop, suddenly coughing into his fist. Bran thought it was possible he was holding back tears of his own. Clearing his throat, the Count sat up in his chair, and said, "Lad, what were you doing in the Dyndaer? I do not recall giving instruction to go beyond the wall, even to find my daughter."

Bohumir sniffled. "I thought, when she was not found here, I should check the forest. I am sorry for not asking to go."

Vlaskhorn clenched his fists, his voice winding into a growl. "If only you would have gone sooner..." He took a deep breath.

"Still, you were wiser than any other. Tell me what you know." He shifted his gaze over his shoulder to where his wife had retreated. "Anything that may bring some comfort to my wife."

Bohumir stiffened, keeping his hands firmly pressed to his sides. His boyish hands shook against his pant legs. "I went to find Princess Nitalia after lunch. There were tracks in the snow not far from the gate, and I followed them to a clearing. I found the Princess hanging from a tree. She was… already dead when I got there. The others," Bohumir lifted his hand at Dorofej, Branimir, and Drak, "arrived soon after."

"What else? Were there any other footprints in the snow?" The Count rumbled, "This does not sound like suicide."

"There were no footprints besides her own," Bohumir said. "Count, there is nothing else to tell."

"I see," Vlaskhorn swallowed, "then, can someone explain to me, why strangers appear at the same time of her death? It is the Season of Frost. It is strange to see visitors this time of the year."

Dorofej pulled his hood back. "Business for the Crimson Sun, we have, Count. I say, their work is not bound by the weather, yes? By happenstance, passing through Cavell in these dark times, we are."

Lamont nodded in agreement. "Count, I am afraid it looked as though she had taken her own life. I understand this does not provide much comfort."

"It does not provide anything. Czern's breath! There is no reason why Nitalia would hang herself." The Count's anger came without warning, any calmness in his tone disappeared. "You may be a member of this court, Lamont, but I will not accept your ineptitude. You will investigate this crime, and you will be thorough."

Branimir instinctively stepped back from the throne. He had not realized Lamont was a noble among the court.

The Count continued in his rage, "Someone must have murdered my daughter. I want them found!"

Lamont whispered, "As you wish, Count."

Chapter V

The sound of flutes and cellos drifted through the street from the main tavern in Cavell. Branimir half-listened while leading the mounts behind him. The entire populace of the village might as well have been relishing in the hubbub of debauchery, storytelling, and dancing.

Drak skipped and pirouetted in the streets in step with the melody, humming to himself. His red, pointed ears twitched while flapping his brown cloak about with more jollity than the rest of them combined. If Drak had been affected by the conversation with the Count, he did not show it.

"What are we going to do?" Lamont groaned, leading the company away from the Count's home. He looked over his shoulder nervously, his wrinkled face hanging in despair.

"Do nothing, we will," Dorofej muttered. "I say, there is no time to deal with the witlessness of Counts, especially those who wish to seek a murderer when there is none to be had. A charge of folly is given to senseless men; the burden we carry is of greater consequence, it is."

"I don't know it was really suicide," Branimir said. "The Princess would have a hard time hanging herself from the tree alone. And why go to all the trouble? She could have just as easily hung herself in her own chambers."

"Bah! Matter, it does not," Dorofej argued.

Lamont's jaw dropped. "You are suggesting one man's charge is greater than another? Who are you to gauge the tasks given to men? My station demands I investigate this death, Dorofej."

"Go and investigate, if you must," Dorofej said. "I say, the Princess's death has nothing to do with us. The time, we have not."

Something cold struck Branimir's cheek. He lifted his head upward, feeling another bit of wetness against his shoulder. He stopped Dorofej from engaging with the man. "This is not the time to argue theology. We need to be away from Cavell."

Gentle rumbles of thunder echoed in the distance, stopping all but Drak's gambol. The other Kras continued to listen to the harmony from the nearby tavern, tapping his feet against the hardened, dirt road.

"Thunder in the winter," Lamont peered at the overhanging trees, a mixture of sleet and rain dribbled quicker from above. He whispered, sticking to his accusation, "You have upset Czern with your words, Dorofej."

"Ha!" Dorofej laughed, scratching his head. "Find meaning in things which have none, men always will." Dorofej turned to Bohumir. "Time, it is, for you to come with us."

Bohumir shivered, lifting his hands to touch the cold pellets of ice that fell. "Can't we wait until morning?"

"Best, we do not," Dorofej replied.

"I agree we need to leave," Branimir said, "but the boy is right. We won't make it far in the slush. We will be looking for shelter in an hour. Let's get food in our bellies and rest and leave before first light."

Drak nodded, orienting toward the tavern. "A piping hot bowl of soup would be nice."

The sleet increased, almost to the frequency of rain. Dorofej frowned. "Very well. Drak, take the horse and ponies to the stable boy, yes? Then go with Bohumir to gather his things. Return when finished, you must. In the commons of this tavern, Branimir and I will wait."

Drak's head sagged, dancing subsided. "Stone the crows! The Kras aren't slaves any longer. I am sure Bohumir can find his way back. I am hungry."

"A matter of slavery, this is not," Dorofej said. "I say, talk to Branimir alone, I will, and without your pestering questions."

Drak's face twisted into a pout, hurt by Dorofej's candor. Reluctantly, he took the reins from Branimir.

The boy, however, continued to argue. "I can sleep in my own home and meet you in the morning. Give me time to say goodbye to my sisters and Lamont."

"No. Return at once, you must," Dorofej waggled his head. "Lamont, see it is done, yes? Under our watch, Bohumir must remain."

"Whatever you say, Dorofej. Clearly, you are going to do what you want." The old man jerked his head in accord. His face was etched in a permanent scowl.

Dorofej nodded idly, his hand resting on Branimir's shoulder. Branimir watched Drak saunter off to take the animals to the stable around back of the tavern, covering his head with one hand. Lamont and Bohumir, recognizing the conversation was at an end, followed after him.

Dorofej leaned forward and whispered hastily under his breath. "Keep an eye open for the Crimson Sun, we must. A great risk to stay here overnight, we take."

Branimir nodded, allowing Dorofej to lead him toward the oak door of the Stone Crown. Stepping inside, they were welcomed by roaring laughter and hearty songs playing from the stage. Tankards of ale clashed together as drunkards and tavern wenches danced about between cramped tables. The Stone Crown embodied nothing of the alehouses from when he traveled across Kalamaar during the Second Age.

He looked for Teodor, Eisliev, or Tyr, but no sooner had they stepped through the door of the place then a greasy haired man in his midyears approached with a crooked grin on his thick lips. His black hair was cut short and receding above his forehead. "Humph.

Strangers—and a Kras, too? Well, I'll be," he forced himself, as if trying to find the proper words. "Name is Keldron Luben, what can I do you for?"

"Some plum and something to eat with it, yes?" replied Dorofej. "Also, welcoming of a room for rest, we would be."

"Plenty of space upstairs. Most these folks are from these parts, and I'd be wary of those who weren't, if I were you."

"We have also animals sheltering in the stables," Branimir chimed.

"I figured you did, Master Kras," Keldron flashed his teeth. "Wouldn't imagine you would have walked here from anywhere, considering the weather. A few silver should cover your meal and a bit of wine."

Dorofej revealed coins from a leather pouch and dropped them into Keldron's hand. His bag still had plenty of jingle in it when he was done.

Branimir put his hand in his own pocket, recognizing he did not have any silver coins of his own. All he had was his moonstone, the Ojenek.

The owner of the Stone Crown must have also noticed the hefty size of Dorofej's bag, because he added, "Anything else I can do you for?"

The black mage shook his head, already looking beyond the Anshedar. "Only tell me when the room is ready, you will. Leave us be, otherwise, you should."

Keldron shifted his weight at the direct tone, placing his hand on his belly, muttering something about *strangers*.

Dorofej did not notice. He squeezed through the crowd in search of empty chairs. Branimir hurried to follow, remaining cautious not get trampled by the other patrons.

The Highborn steered them to a small, round table near the back corner buried in the throng of townsfolk. He signaled the barmaid for drinks before speaking in a low undertone with Branimir. The Highborn jumped straight into matters of strictest importance, realizing their time alone was short. "Remember the pact before parting from Strahil, we made, yes? Know what you have discovered, I must, while Drak and Bohumir are away."

Branimir locked onto Dorofej's blue eyes, his red tufts falling from his hood once more. After exiting the Netherworld and learning the Ash Tree was no longer in the Dyndaer, he and Dorofej had agreed to separate in order to determine its location. Dorofej had once said the Ash Tree would vanish and reappear to new regions across Aenar, but Branimir had not truly believed it until their return to Maharia. It had been three years since they had last seen one another at Strahil, far northwest from where they currently roamed.

Unfortunately, Branimir had not paid much mind to the pact. He had not found the agreement between them to be of great importance, particularly when Kaelandur had supposedly been abandoned in the land of the dead. Who would have thought it would have been found? More importantly, *who brought it back?*

The Kras cleared his throat, keeping his voice small by the same token. "Hard to say anything of true worth. The *tree* could be anywhere from the Shade Fells to the Dyndaer, within Maharia, or even this place called Haemus Mons."

Dorofej could not hide the disappointment from his face.

"Though," Branimir shared, leaning closer, "after our conversation on the road...I wonder of Kalamaar."

"Kalamaar?"

He wobbled his head. "I find it odd the Kadari took Melkorka back as their home when the greater number of people are here, in Maharia. After listening to you and Drak thus far, I find myself questioning the Kadari's motive. Why abandon Shayol Domier, the Dyndaer, and leave Maharia unless..."

Dorofej brightened, "Ah, yes? What ruler, who craves power, rules from a distance? Best to be in the mix of things, it is. The Ash Tree must be back on Kalamaar, or even at Melkorka."

Branimir shrugged, "As strange as it sounds, it is what I keep thinking. There are folks all over Maharia. You would think if it was here, someone would have said something."

"I say, rumors of demons would keep any from looking for it at Melkorka," Dorofej added. "Leaving the power of the Ash Tree for the Kadari and the Kadari alone, yes?"

"Exactly," Branimir said.

"Given us the advantage once more, your meddlesome mind has," Dorofej hit the table with a cheer. "Glad to have scooped you from Ojenir, I am."

"And, I am glad to be back with you, Dorofej," Bran said, "but I am curious as to how you knew where to find me. We have not spoken in years."

"Old tricks," Dorofej touched his nose, "of which I have told you not to pry, yes?"

Branimir interlaced his red fingers, settling on the chair, feet hanging above the wooden flooring. He thought of the red mage from the Dyndaer called Eisliev, and said, "Did you learn said trick, locating people—or perhaps even objects lost—from the Stuhia?"

Any manner of mirth Dorofej held departed from his eyes.

"We have known one another for a very long time, old friend," Branimir said. He no longer struggled to meet Dorofej's eye as he might have in his youth. He spoke boldly, "I wonder who or what you really are, and where you have come from. Not truly a Highborn, as you have claimed to be, and plainly not an Anshedar."

"Someday," Dorofej said, removing all emotion from his words, "tell you who I am, I will."

Feeling content, knowing he had gained something, Branimir chuckled, "Do not let the riddle die with you."

A serving girl eventually reached Dorofej and Branimir bringing stew, biscuits, and wine. Whenever their drinks went empty, the girl fought through the throng with her small frame to fill their clay mugs, over and over again.

The evening dragged on, and as expected, the storm outside intensified.

After about an hour, the clamor in the Stone Crown elevated as the musicians changed their tune from a small stage on the opposite side of the room. Branimir had heard the song, The Gal from Garain'l, sung on the streets in other cities, telling the story of a woman who was said to haunt the ruins of the lost city of Garain'l in the southern Dyndaer.

He bobbled his head, mouthing the first couple of verses while sipping on his wine.

'Though the gal from Garain'l did not chide; she had lied, about the silver strung,

When evening comes in Garain'l, hear men mull, pay the toll, from her neck she hung,

Alas, a comely gal comes, who lost her head; she is dead; O' poor Garain'l.'

The pangs on the windowpanes and patters on the roof accompanied the instrumentals resounding off the walls. Folks continued to play from song to song with little intermission. After a time, none in the tavern seemed to care enough to make requests— their bellies were too full of alcohol.

Branimir felt tipsy, but not so much he would forget his list of questions he had reserved for the black mage. "At Melkorka," Branimir started, "Nedezhda had told Kinhar she had been dead for years but only moments had passed. But when we were in the Netherworld, time stayed the same for us. Why?"

Dorofej rocked forward, pressing his finger to his lips, having the sense to not blather to a room full of strangers all that was known, but still he said, "The passage of time flows differently for the deceased than for the living, yes? *Here* and *now* is assembled so the living can have meaning, it does. In death, find *before* or *after*, you will not."

Branimir put his hands to his ears, cupping them to hear Dorofej better, thinking the action would help him understand what he heard. "How do you mean?"

"Deviate from the narrow path, time does not, for the living. We live and die, yes? Straight line." Dorofej jutted his hand forward, his arm straight. "But for the dead, *everywhere* and *nowhere*, time is, at once. A jumbled mess for them to make sense of, it is."

Branimir scrunched his nose.

Dorofej waved his hand. "An example, I will provide." He lifted his tankard. "Time for you and I is like the plum contained, *unwavering*, in this mug, yes? For those not living—" He paused, swooping up the drink; and then, after swigging a mouthful—to make his point—spewed it out at Branimir.

The alcohol splattered and sprinkled Bran's face, his clothes, and the table.

Branimir blinked, gawping at Dorofej's exposed violet-stained teeth. The effects of his own wine fled his senses.

Dumbstruck, he wiped the purple liquor from his face with a fixed stare. Whatever other questions he may have had were forgotten.

"I get it."

The black mage erupted into laughter, throwing his head back and pointing at the Kras, while wine driveled down his lip and pointed chin.

Chapter VI

The night deepened. Another hour may have passed, and Drak and Bohumir still had not returned. Many patrons had left the tavern, calling it a night, but overall, the place had maintained its elevated din.

Branimir had found his mirth again and chortled alongside Dorofej, who amalgamated with the rest of the Stone Crown in rancorous laughter.

"Remember the time we were sneaking through the halls of Heshayol," Branimir said, holding a hand halfway over his mouth, "and I heard the hissing you could not."

"Stop it." Dorofej rocked forward in his chair, his face growing pale. His hands slapped down on the table. "Time after time, you bring this up. If I could forget about Osiscica for the rest of my life, soon enough, it would not be. And likely, I would forget, if you would stop talking about it."

"Never have I seen such a big snake," Branimir wiggled his eyebrows, continuing, "nor have I ever heard you shriek so much like a woman."

"Branimir, snakes are serious business," the black mage warned, tightening his cheekbones to hold back his own smile. "Killed us both, *Osiscica* would have."

"Should I imitate the scream?" Branimir chortled, hardly hearing Dorofej. "I am not certain my voice can get as high, but I will try."

"Nine Lands, Branimir," Dorofej said with a shake of his head, "in real danger, we were."

Branimir pointed at Dorofej, keeping his grin. "The danger was tenfold after your display of girlish tenor. How long did we have to run from the demons you drew our attention to?"

Dorofej puckered his brow, running his hand through his red hair. "I say, more than a day, it was."

"More like a week." Branimir opened his mouth to silently imitate Dorofej's scream, bobbling his head back and forth for an added touch.

Dorofej good-humoredly swatted his hand toward Branimir before leaning back and gulping another mouthful of plum.

"Evening, mind if me and my friend take these seats at your table?" a bulky, black-bearded man said throatily, tapping on the table near Dorofej. "Seems they are the only chairs left in this place."

The man took Branimir off guard, stifling his chuckle from his and Dorofej's conversation. The man who spoke had more muscle on him than a centaur, with arms thicker than Branimir's body.

Of course, the comparison was an exaggeration, but the Anshedar was robust, nonetheless.

The Kras swallowed, eyeing the thick, polished breastplate, made of something other than iron, bronze, or copper. Branimir had never seen a metal so shiny. The material used to forge the protective covering also had been used to create the oval shield and the half-moon, bladed axe hanging at his waist.

Dorofej leaned back, less impressed. "Expecting two more, we are. I say, reason for the additional chairs, it is."

The man plucked a chair away from the table and plopped down. "Too easy. We will only stay until they arrive. I have been on the road far too long and my belly is aching for some ale." As if he were making his point known, he saluted them with his mug. "The name is Adamus Ebordon from Ariadne." He unexpectedly roared out to the tavern almost knocking Branimir from his chair in surprise. "All you remember that name! Tis not the last time you will hear it!"

Branimir found his smile again when none in the Stone Crown so much as turned in their direction. Though, he could not help but wonder if this was one of the *hero-warriors* Drak had talked about from Ariadne.

A woman, unlike any Branimir had ever seen, emerged from the crowd and occupied the remaining chair. The bow slung over her shoulder, and the quiver on her back were the last things Branimir noticed. She was shorter than most Anshedar with an oversized head, a scrawny neck, and a sickly, thin frame. Yet her skin, smooth and colored a reddish brown darker than Branimir, caused him to lean toward her. A sash, red as blood, hung across her shoulder, angled over her small chest.

She sat with her back stiffened and chin jutted forward. Pushing long black strands behind her ears, she introduced herself, "Hanna Bretka, daughter of Briv, from Danduher in Haemus Mons." She sloshed her mug onto the table after taking a gulp.

"Branimir and Dorofej," Bran said, "And, excuse my asking, but what are you?"

Her eyes swelled like an owl, a circular black center and the rest filled with a cerulean orb. The colored ring twinkled like the Ojenek in his pocket. "What do you mean *what* am I?"

Adamus and Dorofej merged in laughter.

"Kras," she said. "I am a Lilitu. How would you not know my kind? The Kras frequent trade with the Lilitu in Halderon."

Branimir rubbed the back of his neck with a crooked smile, and meekly shrugged. He could not take his eyes off of her.

"*What are you?*" Adamus repeated, wiping a tear from the corner of his eye. "Best thing I have heard in two months. Having you travel with me never tires, Hanna."

"Glad to please you, Adamus," Hanna muttered, rolling his name off her tongue. "Is this why we detoured to Cavell? I thought we were aiming for debauchery, not expanding on our alleged *friendship*."

Adamus waved his hand. "Do not be sour. We are going home. I will see my sister, and you will rejoin with your *nest*. Our part in the war is over."

"We do not have nests," she scowled. "They are called colonies."

"War?" Branimir perched from his mug. "What war?"

"Must you blab our history to every passerby who shares a table with you?" She spoke in a monotone, without emotion.

The bearded man gulped down his drink and raised it toward the passing serving girl to fill it once more. After she filled the mug to the brim, he said, "You were paid, as was I, to fight at Raybin, lest we would not have gone. We did our part and received our papers. The battle was lost; but the people are safe. There is no shame in going home."

"I did not say there was shame, but the war is not over," Hanna said. "I am a Rudhira, a warrior. The war is never over."

Dorofej interjected, "You are speaking of the war with the desert people, yes? Among their ranks, you were?"

"Mm," Adamus grunted. His hand touched the top of his axe, grinning wider when he realized it was intact. "We fought for the Gaetanaen Kingdom for two years and dismissed after the Uvil took the field."

"And, you call that winning," Hanna said.

"I am not dead, am I?" He lifted an eye to Hanna. "If you are so bent, then go back."

"When the coffers are refilled, I might," Hanna took another drink and Adamus received another from the barmaid. "Fighting without payment is a fool's task. Most true when fighting for the Anshedar, who fight without any sense."

"You rely too much on the fellow soldier," he said. "Your people will never know glory."

"Glory is a concept for the poor," She scoffed, sipping at her drink. "Consider the fact your people will never know victory."

Adamus glared at her under bushy eyebrows and downed his mug in a single swoop. He signaled for the wench once more.

"Dorofej," Branimir tapped his fingers on the table, changing topic, "we need to go, and leave these two to their drinking. Drak and Bohumir have been gone too long."

"Right, you are, and well said," Dorofej agreed, guzzling the rest of his drink, before adding, "but the way is blocked, if noticed, you have not?"

"What?" Branimir hissed, turning in his chair, his leg smacking the edge of the table. "

At the opening of the Stone Crown, Branimir saw the red mage, Eisliev, and then a second later, the Anshedar from the Crimson Sun, Teodor. If the two men were inside the tavern, it could only mean the giant guarded the road outside.

"That must be what has kept them," Branimir said out loud, "but whether Drak and Bohumir have been found remains to be seen. Come, Dorofej," Bran whispered, almost forgetting about Hanna and Adamus, "what do we do?"

"Hidden here for a short time, we are," Dorofej settled lower in his chair. The Kras caught sight of Eisliev's light eyes skimming by them. "But leave at any time, you are able, Branimir."

"I am not going to leave you," Branimir said. "I am not a coward."

Adamus, who had found his mug refilled, stayed attuned to their conversation. He leaned inward. "Hanna and I can create a bit of a distraction, if tis required for you to duck out."

Dorofej raised his eyebrows, contemplating the offer, "I say, how many silver to divert the two near the tavern door?"

"What is your *price*, Hanna?" Adamus said, pressing his lips together as though his teeth would burst through.

"Ten silver," she said, finishing up her drink, and pulling free her bow. The offer was so quickly given Branimir almost wondered if she had prepared a number before sitting down.

"You shared your table freely. Besides, I like to receive my payments in loyalty and friendship," Adamus downed his drink once more, most of it dripping down his beard.

"Whether too generous or too drunk, you are, I cannot say," Dorofej slapped the table, sliding ten silver to Hanna, "but in our debt, you will be; loyalty and friendship abound."

Adamus said, "Heh, generous or drunk? I imagine I am a bit of both."

"You speak only to the Anshedar," Hanna clinked the coins together. "Our deal is satisfactory, unless I die, and then I'll expect double." The Lilitu, who had called herself a Rudhira, did not so much as crack a smile.

Branimir had to admit he was shocked by the emotionless attitude of the woman, who seemed motivated solely by the pursuit of coin. More surprising was how solemn she was about wanting the silver.

The Ariadnean narrowed his beady, gray eyes. He stood from the table, wobbling slightly from the alcohol. Bran watched him while burying his own drink. It was thick and burned his throat.

"Hanna," Adamus said. "Keep an eye on my back, will ya?"

"I have been paid, haven't I?"

Adamus murmured in agreement.

Branimir stooped down as Adamus stumbled by him toward Teodor. Hanna shifted around the table to where Adamus had been sitting.

Teodor talked to Keldron, unaware of Adamus approaching fast. Teodor's hand rested on the sword hilt. The horse head inscribed on his breastplate stayed partially hidden among the greens and grays.

Adamus stormed forward, pushing Teodor to the side and getting in Eisliev's face. He garbled, breathing fumes, "If you grew a beard half as long as mine, you would still look like a wench. Never disfigured a woman before but suppose I gotta rip a belly open."

"Stand back," Keldron said, stepping between Adamus and Eisliev, arms crossed over his chest. "Do not have me call the guards."

Adamus did not hesitate. He planted his right fist across Keldron's jaw. The man fell flat to the floor, unconscious.

Gasps of surprise and nervous laughter echoed.

Eisliev glared, his light eyes smoldering beneath his red bangs. "Find somewhere else to meddle."

Adamus struggled to stand. Branimir was sure the poor man was inebriated, namely because it took him three wild swings to reach the axe at his side and shield on his back.

Branimir tugged at Dorofej's dark robes "Better make haste while we are able." Dorofej thanked Hanna, who waved him off and nocked an arrow.

The two of them twisted and turned, ducking behind the people who circled to watch the commotion.

Somewhere, outside of Branimir's sight, Adamus let out a roar. The sound of clashing weapons echoed, giving the suggestion Teodor had pulled his sword.

An arrow zinged.

Branimir and Dorofej sprung into the streets of Cavell.

Chapter VII

Within the Stone Crown, Branimir could hear the clamouring of screeching voices, tables crashing, and chairs being thrown. He stumbled away from the tavern with Dorofej muttering offhandedly at his heels.

The outside cold tore into his bones, worse than it had before, whirling down the main street of Cavell from the north to south. Faint lights of lanterns, hanging on either side of the snow-covered road, were blurred to Branimir with his Kras vision. He teetered forward to take a gander between the closed shops. The plum had taken its toll. The world spun around him.

Branimir sucked the icy air into his lungs. When he exhaled, his breath erupted as a misty vapor. "We should not have drunk so much."

"Fortunate, we are," Dorofej said, joining Branimir in looking either way. "The Ispolini is nowhere to be found, yes?"

"The what?" Branimir finally mumbled when realizing Dorofej's words had no connection with his own.

Dorofej hiccupped. "The giant, Branimir. Also known as an Ispolini, from the far west, beyond the desert and the Shade, he is."

"Ah," Branimir sighed, rubbing his temples and recalling the oversized mercenary with the Crimson Sun. The giant had been called Tyr Og. The name sounded like a guttural grunt. "Is there anything you do not know, Dorofej?"

"Certain, there is," Dorofej laughed. "And, tell you, I will, when I recall what it is."

"Dorofej. Branimir." Drak shouted, making his way to them from down the road. The Kras clutched his cowl, running with a weird waddle, while slipping on the frozen ground.

Bohumir, who faltered several paces behind, tried to keep pace with the faster Kras. The boy gripped his own pack in his hand.

Dorofej raised his fist at them, shaking it with force. "Waiting for hours, we have been. I say, where have you been?"

"Alack! If I were any bigger, I would have dragged the boy back sooner. He took his sweet time gathering his things." Drak looked pleadingly at Branimir. "Are they still serving food?"

In response, the door of the tavern banged open, and several patrons flooded into the streets. Drak looked past Branimir, horrified, as the men and women began screaming for the guard. Their cries were coupled with a piece of wood, which may have been a stool leg, busting through a window and into the streets. Several tankards— some still holding ale—followed. Then, without warning, a man was tossed through the open space. He howled in shock and slammed into the frozen ground with a hollowed grunt. Inhibited by alcohol, he shakily rose to his feet and stumbled away from the place as quick as he was able.

Branimir froze, ogling with the others, dumbstruck, while the man, too, screamed for the sentry.

"What did you two do?" Drak asked in exasperation.

"We didn't do anything, but I don't think you'll be eating here," Branimir said, "Teodor and Eisliev are in there."

"Here already," Drak blew out his cheeks and whined. "Stone the crows!"

"I say, fetch the horses," Dorofej said, "and one for Bohumir too. Make haste, you must."

Branimir spun around for the stables when the door to the Stone Crown burst open again. Any hint of intoxication Branimir may have felt moments ago fled from him like shadow from flame.

More townsfolk ran from the tavern, springing into the streets. Nevertheless, to his dismay, calmly stepping through the hoard of men and women, emerged Teodor, sword in hand, his iron breastplate gleaming. Teodor yanked an arrow from his left arm and tossed it on the ground. Ignoring the dark blood coloring his shirt, he cast an eye over the scattering people. His nostrils flared, and eyes narrowed, taking only seconds to pinpoint Dorofej and Branimir on the road.

Following directly behind him, strode Eisliev drenched in his red cloak, the hood pulled over his long fiery hair. His face was completely hidden beneath, but the wind carried the growl that escaped his lips. "I have waited too long for my revenge. I will not be stopped now."

The racket from within the tavern grew louder. The brawl inside continued, accompanied with whooping and hollering. From the sound of it, the place was being torn apart.

"Allow them to have Kaelandur, we must not," Dorofej instructed at a whisper, "nor slay Bohumir!"

"What? Kill me?" The boy's gaped. "Czern's breath!" He grabbed at Dorofej. "Why would you say that? Who are they?"

"Bohumir Mager, is it?" Teodor guessed. "You will be coming with us, lad. And Dorofej," he sneered, "do you think yourself clever? You can consider your contract, and all future contracts with the Crimson Sun, expired."

Bohumir clenched his jaw, using the black mage to shield him from the assailants. Dorofej pushed Bohumir behind him protectively with his hand.

"Saddened by the revelation, I truly am," Dorofej said, "but part our separate ways, we must." He bowed his head, placing his other hand on Bohumir's chest to guide him backwards with him. "The boy, you cannot have. Consider the earnings from the *Kadari* forfeit, yes? Understand the impact of his deliverance, you do not."

"No," Eisliev shouted over the noise in the streets, "you do not understand. Give me the boy! I will have my revenge on Dagmar Kaligula."

Branimir twisted to Dorofej, his mind muddled. "Who is that?"

Dorofej took a step back from Eisliev. Branimir thought he saw fear in the black mage's eyes. His mumbled words were quiet. "A name long forgotten, that is."

"Who is it?" Branimir earnestly repeated. Dorofej could not have responded if he had wanted. The main road became even more chaotic.

"Tyr," Teodor hollered, disregarding Dorofej's speech, while suspiciously looking at Eisliev from the corner of his eye, "bring me the lad."

Bohumir cried out, likely shaking more from fear than the cold, "What is going on?"

Tyr lumbered into the street from the shadows adjacent to the tavern. Those making their escape cried out when seeing the towering frame of the giant. Likely, none in the Dyndaer had seen an Ispolini before. Tyr was a stone tower, etched with muscle from foot to forehead. His flesh seemed unaffected by the cold from his bare chest to his bare feet. His only attire were his dark trousers and the angled, leather belting which held the battle axe on his back.

His towering frame caused many of the patrons to screech and run in the opposite direction. Tyr removed his weapon from the latching on his back, holding it at the ready in his massive six-fingered hands.

The boy's face fell at the sight of the giant. "Nine Lands."

Branimir lunged in front of Tyr as the Ispolini started across the road to grab the boy. "Stop. You don't know what you are doing."

Tyr paused for a moment, considering the words. He looked back to Teodor.

However, Eisliev gave the order. "The boy, Tyr."

With a growl, Tyr moved forward again, lifting his battle axe threateningly toward Bran. "Step aside, or I will cut through you, half pint."

Branimir braced himself for the giant's death stroke.

A gust of wind blew past Branimir spiralling his cloak around him. The blast struck Tyr in the chest, sending him reeling backwards. Branimir nearly fell to his knees as the ground shook under the weight of the massive Ispolini.

"Tyr," Teodor shouted as the brawn of his party fell. He spun on Dorofej, who had delivered the simple display of Koldovstvo.

"I say, I do not wish to fight, but a choice, you leave me not," Dorofej pleaded. "Let us be, Teodor. Take these men from here."

Teodor scowled, speaking to Eisliev, "Take the quarry."

"Branimir, fall back," Dorofej shouted, eyeing the red mage.

Branimir had not the chance to move before a woozy feeling washed over him. He felt as though something had struck him, an unseen energy, but he could not place it. The thought slipped away.

His stomach churned, pain surfacing in the pit of his belly, and creeping up his chest and throat. Another thought rebounded against his skull, forced into his thinking, *too much plum*. He could not believe the lie; it came to him like a voice across a great distance. Inside his head, he heard his own scream in defiance. No sound came from his lips.

The street dimmed temporarily. His hands moved like spiders through the air to grip his head with aim to clear the clouded feeling swelling into his ears and mind. From somewhere, he could hear battle echoing, but he was blind to the world around him.

"Branimir!" a voice cried, aloof and far away. He thought he knew the voice, but he could not place it.

Memories of the Netherworld danced in his mind. Flying, demonic Skyrz flew from nothingness toward him with their sharpened claws and fanged teeth. They had not only been at Illuard but also across the frozen wasteland, where Marheena ruled over the dead. The little beasts were the size of bats with horned skulls and spindly forelimbs. He could not let them suck his blood.

From somewhere, a dagger had found its way into his hand. He did not think he had his weapons any longer, but here they were. He could not deny it. He could not think about it fully. The Skyrz were coming. He swung madly.

For a moment, the scene disappeared, and he was back in the streets of Cavell. A stone the size of Branimir's head flew over him. White dust powdered the air.

Drak grabbed Branimir's arm, pulling him back from wherever he had been. "Stone the crows! Stop this, Branimir! What are you doing?"

"*Mojmir*," Bran believed, before remembering Drak's face. He held his head, stumbling to stay on his feet. He felt faint. Something hard was held against his head, clasped in his hand. He lowered his arm and jerked back when seeing a dagger between his fingers, dripping with blood. It did not look familiar. This was not a dagger he had ever owned.

He lifted his eyes to Drak. The Kras clutched his arm where his flesh had been cut. Red seeped through his fingers.

"I cut you..." Branimir gaped. "How did I get this weapon?"

"From him," Drak winced, pointing behind Branimir. "You stole it from his boot after he saved you from the giant's axe. You stabbed him in the leg, and then I pulled you back. That is when you cut me."

"No..." Branimir twisted to see Adamus battling against Tyr. The Ariadnean had his smaller axe lodged against the battle axe of the Ispolini. Even at a distance, the stench of ale wafted off the man's long, black beard like manure from a horse's ass.

Adamus bellowed from his gut, throwing Tyr back, an inner rage unleashed. Branimir gawked at the blood oozing from the man's thigh. Tyr slid back on his bare feet, surprised at the strength of the human. The giant released his own primitive roar. The battle axe crashed down toward Adamus again and again, deflected and met with equal ferocity.

Scooting back, Branimir looked to Dorofej for an explanation. The black mage could give none. Dorofej stumbled, intoxicated, doing what he might to avoid Eisliev's magic. Stone and fire was flung through the air at his friend.

Bohumir, the poor boy, crouched fearfully behind Dorofej.

Branimir gripped the curved dagger in his hand, still feeling sick. Ahead of him, Eisliev snarled. The red mage peered over his shoulder at Teodor, who had fallen. Branimir counted two arrows in his chest and one in his skull.

"The haze in your eyes went away when he fell," Drak said, answering the unspoken question. "I think it distracted the Stuhia."

Hanna, the Lilitu, a ghost in the shadows, had turned to fire arrows at Eisliev, the Stuhia, who Drak referred. She crouched near the tavern wall, releasing arrow after arrow like a true warrior. Yet the Stuhia from the Crimson Sun swatted away her arrows with Koldovstvo, while continuing to attack the drunken Dorofej.

"Come on, Tyr," Eisliev shouted. "Finish this."

The giant slammed a fist into Adamus, reeling the Ariadnean backwards. And still, Adamus advanced at the Ispolini.

"Get the boy to safety," Branimir said, feeling the weight of the dagger in his hand, as though it were the first time. He made eye contact with Eisliev and glowered.

"But are you alright?" Drak asked.

Branimir tried to say he was fine, but he could not form the words. Eisliev's light eyes caught his own and burned into him, again, striking him with some unseen magic. Bran sputtered, vomit burning with ire in his throat. Sourness filled his nostrils.

His feet carried him across the dark, frozen battlefield, but soon, he no longer recognized Cavell. The demons of the Netherworld chased him. Four-legged, wolf-like creatures, known as Dreka, rammed their goat horns at Branimir. The grey, wrinkled skin clung to their gaunt frames. Thin lips stretched back displaying rows of teeth on the tops and bottoms of their bloodied gums.

Branimir tumbled, swinging his weapon and feeling it tear through flesh as easily as a hot blade through frost. For a moment, he may have heard Dorofej's riddlesome voice—no, his cry—but Branimir had not the time to listen. He had to scramble, and sneak, and stab.

And stab. And stab. And stab.

The urgency of the battle and the demons thumped inside of his head.

"Stop!" A familiar voice, again, cried in desperation.

Crimson splattered his vision as his dagger cut through skin once more. Blood dripped from his blade.

Pain stung his leg, but it was quickly forgotten as demon after demon lunged for him. The Dreka were ever persistent in their attack. He spun, and twisted, and disappeared to avoid every demonic beast soaring through the air, vicious teeth aimed for his throat. They would not reach him. For a moment, he thought he saw a flash of Hanna's wide eyes, but they looked unfamiliar. Treacherous. Evil. Besides, his dagger was already cocked behind his ear and he felt incapable of restraining himself.

With a growl, Branimir let the dagger fly, the blade slamming into his target. Blood spurted from the gash in the chest…of the Lilitu.

Cavell rushed back to him as Hanna fell to her knees, clutching the hilt of the weapon protruding from her torso. Branimir collapsed, his hand hurriedly finding two sharp arrows lodged in his leg.

Drak shrieked.

Branimir turned in time to see Tyr smack the Kras from his path. Adamus, only feet away, bled from his side and his leg, twisting in pain against the ground, near dead. The fighter fought to stand.

"Hanna." Branimir could hear Adamus's strained whisper.

Dorofej also writhed on the ground. Blood oozed from his black robes where a dagger—Branimir's weapon—had pierced him multiple times.

"Glad your mind magic does not affect me, Eisliev," Tyr grunted, picking up the whimpering Bohumir in his oversized hand.

"The guard are coming," Eisliev said. "Grab Teodor's body and let's go."

"What about them?" Tyr asked.

"Let them bleed out," Eisliev said, touching his face tenderly. His skin had aged considerably through his use of Koldovstvo. "We have what we came for. This boy is the key to Melkorka. Patrician Sej can have him as long as I can have Dagmar Kaligula."

Falmagon!

Chapter VIII

The Great Chamber had been eerily quiet for several minutes while they waited for Count Vlaskhorn Frantisek to come into the room. The mood within the keep had changed little since the previous night. If anything, the gloom feeling had intensified following the battle outside of the Stone Crown.

Branimir stood erect with his knees locked, unwilling to look at any of his companions. He ignored the purple, red, and black tapestries hanging around the room, shadowed by the failing light of the fire pits. He could not focus on the throne, where the purplish cloak remained from the previous night. Instead, he felt trapped in his own mind, doubting what he had seen, and doubting what had happened.

He wanted to go back and save Bohumir. He wanted to be able to fight against Eisliev's magic, and battle alongside his allies instead of against them. He wanted too much, all at once. He fought hard against his emotions. He did not want to cry.

An oak door creaked open from the corner. Count Frantisek walked to his throne, as he had done the night before. Sitting forward, the noble man stared at them for several minutes, tapping his pudgy fingers on his round belly.

"They worship Czern, remember? He is going to hang us all," Drak said, slanting over to murmur in Branimir's ear. The Kras may have been talking to Bran since they entered the chamber. He could not be for certain.

Branimir tensed his shoulders, trying to recall what Dorofej had taught him about the gods. Something about the living making gods seem more good or evil than they were. "I don't think so, Drak."

"What if they learn you are not from Ojenir? Why did Dorofej say you were? Why can't they know where you really came from, across the ocean?" Drak, who stood next to him, quivered where he stood, stealing frightful glances at the Count. His fingers fiddled with his brown cloak, pulling at the fabric.

"Calm down," Branimir said between clenched teeth.

Bran lifted his eyes to Dorofej, who watched the Count with intensity. The black mage stood proper with back straight and chin up. Branimir could see the dried blood caked across his robes from the many wounds he had received from the dagger in Branimir's hand.

Dorofej had not wasted much energy in fighting Eisliev, but he had used Koldovstvo excessively while healing himself, Adamus, Hanna, and lastly, Branimir. He had been wise in healing only what was fatal for each of them, leaving the minor bumps and bruises.

The Highborn, if he was really a Highborn, had absolved Branimir's actions, saying there was no fault when considering Eisliev's wicked magic. Dorofej said he did not know the source of the Stuhia's mind magic but was certain Bran had not been at fault. Adamus and Hanna, who now stood with them, had also exonerated him after given an explanation.

Branimir could not forgive himself.

As if reading his mind, Drak said under his breath, "Let it go. It is done."

Branimir exhaled. His gaze shifted momentarily to the dagger returned to Adamus's boot. He never wanted to touch the dagger again.

Ignac, the guard from the gate, shooed away those who had helped escort Branimir and the others into the Great Chamber. He stepped around the center firepit and the Count acknowledged him.

"What is the meaning of this, Ignac?"

Ignac dipped his head, "I received a report of a *scuffle* in the streets. Those here were found at the scene. Presented are Dorofej Creighton of Tamarri, Branimir Barthor and Drak Ghas of Ojenir, Adamus Ebordon of Ariadne, and Hanna Bretka of Danduher."

"A peculiar group of travellers." The Count pulled at his black beard, eyes still swollen from crying over his dead daughter. His eyes rested on Dorofej. "He and the Kras were here last night. When did the others arrive?"

"The guard at the gate reported they also arrived yesterday evening, Count," Ignac answered.

The Count continued, speaking to Dorofej, "You said you were here on business for the Crimson Sun, right? Was this event associated with that business?"

"Yes, it was, Count," Dorofej said, "but Adamus and Hanna were there only by happenstance."

"I see," the Count tilted forward until he was stopped by his round stomach pressing against his knees. "You claim you do not know them?"

"Beyond name, I do not, Count Frantisek," Dorofej said.

"How many dead bodies were there, Ignac?" the Count questioned, resting back in his chair. He seemed to believe what Dorofej shared.

Ignac answered, "None, Count. There were traces of blood outside of the Stone Crown, but no bodies were found."

"Hmm. Tell me, were these men responsible for the hanging of my daughter?" Vlaskhorn turned his attention fully on the guard.

"No, Count."

"Did they kill anyone?"

The guard fidgeted. "I am not aware—"

"Have you lost your sense?" He hissed. "My wife and I are in mourning, planning a funeral instead of a betrothal, as we should have been," Vlaskhorn wheezed. "I am beginning to wonder why you have disrupted this chamber, Ignac. You are testing my patience."

"According to witnesses, Lamont Dthais's boy, Bohumir, was abducted as a direct result of the conflict," Ignac explained.

"The boy who found Nitalia?"

Adamus cleared his throat. "That *is* interesting."

Branimir saw Hanna elbow him in the side before the warrior could say anything more.

"A citizen of Cavell has been captured, which requires a report to the King in Gaetana. These five have the details," finished Ignac.

"I am aware of my duties," the Count breathed. "Next time, try starting with the pertinent details."

Ignac found his composure again, responding at the same time, "Yes, Count."

"Of interest, there is nothing, Count," Dorofej interjected, but the Count silenced him.

"I do not want to hear from you, Dorofej. Your riddlesome accent hurts my ears. Let me hear from one of the Kras. Their reputation for honesty supersedes that of the Kadari."

"Kadari, I am not," Dorofej snapped.

"You work for the Crimson Sun," Vlaskhorn accused, spit flying from his lips, demonstrating anger at having his direction ignored, "who offer service to the Kadari more than any other. Dorofej, you are an associate, whether you claim to be or not. Let it be known those who follow Dahz, and their associates, have no voice in Cavell."

Branimir tightened his jaw, remembering Drak's warning about the people in the Dyndaer and their hate for the Kadari. The Kras from Ojenir had been accurate in his assumption.

"A weak argument, you have, when your brother, the King of Gaetana, also holds allegiances to the Kadari and the Lightbringer, yes?" Dorofej said, his eyes icy.

The Count's face darkened, "I said I will hear from the Kras. Don't open your mouth again, Dorofej."

The black mage grumbled.

Drak scooted further behind Dorofej and Adamus making himself hidden from the pungent eyes of the Count.

Branimir sighed and stepped forward to speak with the Count. He would prefer to speak than allow Drak to talk at any length. "What do you want to know, Count Vlaskhorn?"

"Plainly, I want to know why you have come to Cavell and what happened outside the Stone Crown," the Count said.

"We came here to protect Bohumir. Last night, we failed to save him from those who took him," said Branimir. The truth seemed simple enough to share.

"See, the Kras is able to tell me exactly what I can report to the King. Simple. Eloquent. Now, why did the boy need protected," asked the Count, "and, why was he taken?"

Branimir grinded his teeth but did his best to keep his eyes locked onto Vlaskhorn. Dorofej had told him they were working for the Crimson Sun, so Branimir could not imply Teodor, Eisliev, and Tyr were with the same organization. At the same time, Bran could not speak of the Kadari, the Ash Tree, and he surely could not say anything about Kaelandur.

He reached for a less noble response. "My apologies, Count. We never did ask. The silver promised in finishing the job satisfied our curiosity."

The Count did not directly scorn Branimir, but stated, "I would not think any greater of the Crimson Sun or the foul Kadari. They make claims to the Lightbringer but hold corruption in their hearts as well as any other." Vlaskhorn shifted in his seat, waving his hand out toward the Chamber, but speaking of the Dyndaer and Cavell, "Here, the God of Darkness, the God of Sacrifice, appreciates and understands who we are as living creatures. We are imperfect, flawed; and we are loved and accepted as such."

"Glory to the Grey-Clad," Adamus hear-heared, marking him as the only true follower, coming from Ariadne.

"Yes, glory to the Grey-Clad," Vlaskhorn repeated, nodding with respect to the so-called hero-warrior. "I welcome your openness,

Branimir, is it?" He waved at Ignac. "They have committed no crime in Cavell; no more than any drunkard who brawls nightly at the Stone Crown."

"Keldron was beat unconscious by Adamus," Ignac tried. "There must be more to the story."

"The man was hardly beat," Hanna said, plain-faced. "It was a single punch." She said her words so matter-of-factly Branimir almost laughed, nearly forgetting his misery.

"You probably did him a favor," Vlaskhorn smiled for the first time since Branimir had met the noble lord. "Still, I think it is best none of you tarry here any longer. Ignac, you have their horses readied and waiting at the edge of town. I want all of you gone within the hour."

"Thank you. We will, Count," said Branimir. The others echoed his sentiment and assurances of following his word.

Ignac lifted his hand. "One more thing." He pulled coiled piece of paper from his pocket. "A letter arrived for Dorofej a fortnight ago. I admit, I do not know that the message was fully transcribed by the courier. It is about as puzzling as your tongue."

Dorofej lifted his eyebrows with interest.

"Since when do you withhold mail, Ignac," the Count said. "Give it to him."

"The letter is signed by Sulanna Maelthirren, a noble name from Eldhaft," Ignac said, "and it reads: '*We have the artifact. We wait in Ariadne.*"

"Maelthirren?" the Count raised an eyebrow. "You have strange friends, Dorofej. Be warned, there are no roads to Ariadne from Cavell. The safest pathway is the river, and it is frozen solid this time of year."

"What does it mean?" Branimir looked to Dorofej, whistling between his teeth.

Dorofej turned his head toward the north, as though contemplating giving chase to Bohumir. His head fell to the floor, speaking softly, "Safe or not, a way to Ariadne, we must find."

Month of Slaughter
Fourth of Frost
1351 CE

Chapter IX

The ice from the forked river creaked and shifted under the dimming rays of sunlight. Branimir listened to the sound absently, focusing on the golden orb shimmering through the thinning canopy of branches. He could not remember the last time the sky had been clear of clouds. In the two weeks since leaving Cavell, he had seen little more than a dark grey and milky white haze through the limbs above.

Though, now, as long as they kept to the river's edge, the sky stayed in open view. He took delight in the beams warming against his face, smiling for what felt like the first time in forever.

Dorofej's horse plodded alongside his pony with the rest of the group meandering in the front. Branimir shifted his gaze from the sun to the black mage, pondering their situation. He stared for some time before finally saying in a hushed tone, "You know, I suddenly realize you never asked me where I have been the past few years."

Dorofej kept his eyes forward, fixated on the backs of Adamus, Hanna, and Drak. Branimir saw the wrinkles around his eyes deepen before he responded. "Searching for the Ash Tree, as we said we would at Strahil, I assumed you were."

"True. I did for a while," Branimir admitted. "Though, being a Kras is not any easier in this world than it was in the last. I drifted from place to place, having to rely on the kindness of others to survive."

"Stones and gems from the Netherworld, you had collected, and sell them, you could have," Dorofej said with a sigh. "Elected to hold onto them and hide them, you did."

"How did you know that?" Branimir asked. "Or, are there more secrets to be kept from me."

Dorofej half-heartedly grinned, giving Branimir the sense it was not genuine. "Held onto Ojenek, you always have. Selling your stones, even for food, would be against your nature, yes? I say, you found a way to survive, yes?"

"I did find work in Gavlok for a time," Bran replied. He rubbed his fingers together nervously, wondering if he had just given away the location of his buried treasure.

Dorofej hummed, "I say, what did you do there?" His tone gave the indication Branimir had told this to him before and was simply entertaining the story.

Branimir shivered. Of course, Dorofej was not interested in his shiny stones. No, something else likely perturbed the man. The thought unexpectedly crossed Branimir's mind that Dorofej might be angry about what had happened in Cavell, despite him saying Branimir was forgiven.

Suddenly, he remembered something of importance from the night in Cavell. He remembered what the red mage, Eisliev, had said. "Who is Dagmar Kaligula?"

Dorofej turned his head away, eyebrows angling with annoyance. "I say, that is not a topic I wish to discuss with you, Branimir," he objected, flaring his nostrils. Branimir thought it may have been the most direct Dorofej had ever been with him. The tone gave him chills. The black mage relaxed his voice, likely realizing his harshness. "Tell me, at Gavlok, what did you do?"

"Very well," Branimir anxiously said, and then continued at length, "I worked as a serving hand at a tavern called The Oaken Bard. At times, I would perform for the folk by throwing knives. After half a year or so, the owner told me people talked about my dagger tossing all the way in Eldhaft. He said someone would likely come and talk to me. I got scared and left before anyone had the chance."

"A good thing, you did," Dorofej said idly. "I say, it may have been someone from the league of thieves. And, being a thief rarely ends well, yes?"

Branimir shook his head in agreement. He would be ashamed to admit he had stolen, more than a handful of times, when his stomach would not quit growling.

Afraid to continue the conversation, or admit to anything he may have done, Bran turned from Dorofej.

Ahead of him, Adamus and Hanna steered them toward Ariadne with Drak bouncing on his pony at the center. Branimir had been surprised the Ariadnean and Lilitu had joined them, particularly after he had nearly killed them both while under Eisliev's control. Luckily, Adamus continued to talk about friendship and loyalty, and Hanna had been more fascinated by his fighting style than vindictive. In addition, Branimir had sworn not to touch any of their weapons, especially Adamus's dagger. The last bit had been Bran's decision.

For a good many hours, the lot of them carried on along the river. They swapped riding and walking to allow the horses to rest when needed. The river winded and bent, heading south, with ice chunks mashing into one another or with the surface frozen altogether. Hoarfrost covered the ground. Nothing melted.

In time, Drak complained of hunger and they stopped to eat meat and unleavened bread. The supper shushed his mouth and his stomach; and then, they rode onward again.

The day passed and dusk came. The sun eventually dipped below the trees, taking its warmth with it. The cold wind that followed from the north not only chilled Branimir through his cloak, but also his skin. The strong breeze pitched along the surface of the adjacent frozen river, adding to its bite. He did his best to ignore the frigidness.

Inhaling the cold air through his nostrils, Branimir expanded his lungs. Mile after mile, frustration poked at his gut. He admitted the feeling had been with him since riding out from Cavell. He could no longer contain his worry and turned to speak to Dorofej again. "Are we going to leave Bohumir be? I did tell you what Eisliev said. He is bringing the boy to Falmagon?"

Dorofej, who had been leaning over his horse, stroking the mane and whispering in contemplation, pulled himself upright and looked down to Branimir. "Yes, you told me what Eisliev said, and forsake the boy, we will not. I say, what would make you think we would abandon what we had set out to do?"

Branimir heaved a sigh of relief before continuing. He had been beating himself up for days and had chosen to say nothing. "Because, we ride to Ariadne at the direction of your letter when Bohumir has been taken the other way?"

"To Melkorka, yes, Bohumir is being taken," Dorofej agreed. "Though you must think why Falmagon wants the boy, yes?"

Branimir turned his head back toward the way they had come. He had not thought of asking what Falmagon—or the Kadari— would want with the bloodline of Nedezhda Mager.

The black mage hummed in his throat, rubbing the neck of his mount. "A fair question, is it not?"

"It is," Branimir said, moving his eyes back to the Highborn, who he certainly did not believe could be called a Highborn any longer. No, the man had been called something else at some time in history. Branimir wondered if Dorofej was a Stuhia like the man named Eisliev. "Why does Falmagon want the boy?"

A moment of silence passed before Dorofej finally rubbed his prickling red beard. "Uncertain, I am. But I can only guess they try sacrificing the boy to gain more power, yes? I say, old rituals requiring magical weapons, there are."

"That is terrible!"

Dorofej smiled. "Except, Kaelandur, they would require to see it done, which we hold. So, time, we have, yes?"

Branimir felt a knot in his throat. "I hope you are right."

"I say, the Kadari are likely scheming more than a simple sacrifice, yes?" Dorofej said. "So simple, nothing ever is."

Drak clearly eavesdropping, leaned back in his saddle to be heard. "I could use my rune staves and attempt to find more answers."

Dorofej's eyes flashed, glancing at Drak over his shoulder. "Helpful, it might be, when we make camp."

Drak beamed, bouncing excitedly in his saddle.

Dorofej leaned toward Branimir, saying in a quieter tone, "To Melkorka, we will travel after Ariadne. Until then, be comforted, yes?"

"I will try. But what are we after in Ariadne? The letter from Sulanna mentioned an artifact. You said she and Alden were with you but also the Crimson Sun. What did she find for you?" Branimir questioned.

Dorofej looked to Drak ahead of them, and then placed a finger to his lips. "The time for questions, it is not." He adjusted his black hood, and again, faced the road.

Branimir writhed with the response. He and Dorofej had wandered the Netherworld for a thousand years, and still the black mage kept his secrets. He hoped the reaction was due to Dorofej realizing Drak could hear them.

The Kras were known for their excellent hearing.

Night had set when they stopped to build a fire. Among the five, setting camp did not take long.

After they had eaten, and fed the mounts, Drak assembled them all around the fire. He waved his hands with encouragement. "Gather around, gather around," He pulled the rune staves from his pack and out of their leather holding. "Dorofej, let us get started and find what answers we can about the Kadari. Now, to use *div-i-nation*, I need to know what question I am asking."

Dorofej did not have an opportunity to respond.

Hanna stopped him. "Hold on, Drak. Where did you learn to read rune staves?" Hanna scooted away from the Kras, her oversized eyes wider than ever. The Rudhira adjusted the crimson sash over her shoulder.

Adamus raised his eyes from his burly eyebrows and grunted. "Let him be, Hanna."

"The only people I know who use runes to tell the future is the Uvil. Their fortune-telling is wicked," she said.

"The desert people?" Branimir clarified, placing the name of the Uvil.

"Yes," Hanna said. "The future should stay where it belongs. Trying to predict what will happen is unwise."

"Ha!" Drak laughed. "My father taught me, and I have been telling futures for years. There is nothing evil about this."

Hanna winced. "The Dyndaer is enigmatic enough without playing with dark magic."

Branimir peered through the flames. "I don't understand. What are you scared of?"

"I am not scared; I am vigilant. Looking into the future suggests we should have no concern of our actions," she explained. "To think we know what will happen may cause us to worry unneedingly or to have false hope. Or, worse yet, you may indirectly create this prophesized future because you think you should."

"You are overthinking, Hanna," Adamus defended Drak, again. "Czern oversees the Dyndaer. He will not frown on fortune-telling or lead any astray. He is likely the only god who understands the nature of men."

The Lilitu shook her head. "Your God of Darkness is not as longstanding as the Dyndaer. No matter what Czern values, this wood holds greater evils, more powerful than him."

"Like what?" Drak asked, shaking under his skin.

"We cannot know everything," she responded. "There is a time and an order to all things. There are rules, and one of those is not to consider the future. The Dyndaer is an aged place, and we cannot say what all has happened here over the past millenniums."

Branimir swallowed. He knew some of what had happened in this forest. Though, he asked the question anyway. "What do you think has happened here?"

"Who can say," Hanna said. Her vagueness was paired hastily with her next statement. "But my people know the Uvil once meandered through the Dyndaer, even before the Northmen, long, long ago."

"I don't know anything about desert people in the Dyndaer," Drak said. His trembling had not subsided. "Why did they leave?"

Hanna leaned closer to the flames. "The desert people go from place to place based on their divinations. I would guess something drew them away from this place, and if that is true, I would say it is worth heeding."

Adamus grunted. A stick had found its way into his hand and he poked it into the fire. "Even I am surprised by the weakness of your argument, Hanna. If fortune-telling led the Uvil from the Dyndaer, there seems to be all the more reason to use their magic and see what they may have seen."

"Unless their magic elicited unwanted attention from the evils already here," Hanna argued. "Such curiosity may lead you to your grave."

Adamus snorted. "I am going to die anyway. I might as well do it on my own terms."

Branimir squirmed with uneasiness. He looked to Dorofej, who added nothing to the conversation.

"You are just trying to scare me," reasoned Drak. His sticks clinked together in his hands, while he stared wide-eyed at Hanna.

Hanna's large eyes remained emotionless, looking at the Kras across the fire. She waited.

Drak licked his cracked lips, rolling the rune staves in his hands. The twigs clacked and clicked between his fingers. Then, after making a final decision, he shoved them back into the pouch. "Another time, eh?"

Branimir did not miss the glare which arose from Adamus. The Ariadnean only took a moment before tearing into Hanna. "For years we have stood by one another, Hanna, and still, you shame yourself by shaming other cultures and their practice. Do you have no honor? What would your god think of this?"

"My god is a goddess, Adamus," Hanna said with absolution, "and the Mother would bless me for sharing wisdom with the world. Informing lesser beings of the danger of their actions is not shaming.

You forget—the Lilitu were not created like the Anshedar or the Kras. We were born from the union of gods, not their imagination."

"No honor," Adamus repeated.

"Your definition of honor is echoed in the vain applause of men," Hanna said, slowly clapping her hands together three times, mockingly. The dryness of her tone made the fire feel wet. She dropped her hands back to her lap. "I have no need for mortal praises. Honor comes to me from the Mother."

"Who is the Mother?" Branimir asked, steering Adamus's wrath from unfolding. He admitted he was intrigued by the Lilitu and their peculiar culture. He had never heard of a place in the world who shared this strange belief. He wondered if all races in Haemus Mons worshipped this Mother.

Drak, who had stuffed his sticks away, answered, "The Mother is also called Lillith. The Lilitu lore says Lillith lay with the great spirit, Anu, and bore the Lilitu."

"It is not lore, Drak," Hanna said. "It is the truth of our people. We are the children of Lillith and Anu."

Branimir's mind swarmed with questions about Lillith and Anu. How were they created? Where did they come from? How did they align with the pantheon of gods in Maharia? To his memory, he had never heard of either in the history of the old world or the new.

Before Branimir could ask anything, Dorofej piped up, changing the topic, "I say, how much longer until we reach Ariadne?"

"Tis a bit more than a week on horseback. Just have to stay along the river," Adamus said with aggravation, keeping his eyes from Hanna. "The road has been quiet, surprisingly, but tis not natural. I had expected a few more snags."

Hanna lay her small bow on the ground. "There will not be any snags, Adamus. Don't start your naysaying already."

The mood around the fire turned for the worse as Hanna's voice trailed off. Several minutes passed before the Lilitu slanted her head toward Adamus, and said, "No reason in waiting until tomorrow to say something."

Adamus snorted with discomfort. He glared at her from beneath his bushy brow.

"What needs to be said?" Branimir asked. Dorofej and Drak, equally bewildered, stooped forward.

"Tis the time of *Koricern*," Adamus pronounced, "the celebration of the longest night of the year, a tribute to Czern. Tis a blessing to pay homage to our ancestors during Koricern and my own are buried at the ruins of Garain'l."

"Why would you bury your dead at a ruins?" Branimir wrinkled his nose.

"Tis sacred ground, Branimir," Adamus said. "This is a tradition of my family for generations."

Branimir, realizing he may have struck a chord, retracted his statement. "Your family?"

Drak added, "I have never heard of any Anshedar, or even any Ariadnean, doing this."

"I said, it is a custom for *my* family," Adamus boomed, a threatening tone on the edge of his voice. "Garain'l is only a few days ride from here." Adamus reached to touch his axe and then the shield on his back. "I am not asking any of you to come."

Dorofej dipped his chin. "Trekking into the Dyndaer wilds would cost us more than time, I am afraid. Wish you the best, we will. I say, to Ariadne, we must hurry, yes?"

"It is settled then," Adamus said. "Hanna and I will part paths with you in the morning."

"As long as you pay me what is owed, Adamus. Do not forget our agreement." Hanna narrowed her large eyes.

"I would not dream of forgetting," Adamus forced a smile under his black beard. "You will be paid when we reach my sister's in Ariadne."

Hanna turned her head to the rest, satisfied by the answer. "Ariadne is built directly on this river. Keep following it south and you will have no trouble finding it."

Branimir hoped she was right.

Chapter X

Branimir woke to the sound of rummaging. He tried to fully awaken, humming softly in his chest. He yawned wide, and then sputtered uncomfortably. He heard Drak stir next to him with a half-snort and whimper.

Branimir kept his eyes closed and reached out to find his bedroll and found nothing. Irritated, he cleared his dry throat. An itch coursed beyond his tongue, subdued from breathing the cold air throughout the night. He coughed and hacked while rubbing his eyelids. They felt frozen to his upper cheeks.

The noise he had heard lingered and then carried on with more intensity. With some work, he struggled to open his eyes and realized morning had not yet come. Dark greys still painted the sky.

The bedroll he had been searching for lay several feet away beyond his feet. Branimir grunted with a weak voice, reaching for the blankets. He was answered by a guttural uttering.

The scuffling and shuffling halted.

He wrenched his head around the campsite to discover the source of the sound. Dorofej, Adamus, and Hanna slept, bundled beneath their blankets, and Drak snored all the louder. And then, there was something else.

Branimir froze.

Lingering over the top of Hanna lurked a hideous thing comparable to Branimir in size and breadth. It crouched with glowing, bulbous, yellow eyes locked onto Bran across the short distance. Its corroded skin had mold growing at the bloodied edges, globbed up in rolled spurts from neck to knee. The extra flab of skin did not make the creature look so much fat as it did malformed.

The thing gurgled in its chest, demonic eyes lustrous between its oversized round ears.

Branimir's scream came as a silent bawl, his throat too dry to alert the others.

The beastie, the thing Branimir could not name, leaned toward him, taking a delicate step, soundless against the sleet-covered moss. Its fingers scraped, clacking together, advancing footfall after footfall in a hunched ball. With its back curved, the monster lifted one arm ending in clawed fingers—more claw than finger—and pointed at Branimir with deep interest.

"Eats it."

Branimir choked, forcing the wail to finally escape. He sprung to his feet, reeling backward from the thing.

He was too late. The imp pounced, soaring through the air with its claws extended. The hooked fingers dug into Branimir's back, legs wrapping around his chest. He shrieked in pain; the knife-like nails tore into the muscle beneath his shoulders.

Tears swelled.

Yellow eyes, round and filled with animosity, clouded his vision. The beast's teeth gnashed, using its hold to direct Branimir backward. He stumbled, unable to direct his feet or even fall to his knees. His feet etched backwards where he knew the frozen river awaited. Horror filling the cavity of his chest. He jerked his head away from the gnashing teeth. Putrid breath, like death, opposite side of yellow-caked gums flooded his senses.

"Eats it."

The imp grew heavier against his torso with the claws seeming to tear deeper into his muscle. He staggered, toppling nearer the ice.

"Help!" he managed to cry, again.

A meek war cry resounded, followed by something striking the creature. Branimir hobbled back several steps from the impact, his foot crunching against the edge of the riverbed.

"Get off," Drak squawked, raising a stick to hit the imp another time.

"Stand aside," Adamus grunted, grabbing the Kras and lifting his axe. Drak moved hastily before Adamus sliced his blade into the fat rolls of the monstrous beastie. Blood spewed. More blood than what one creature should have within it.

Branimir's legs weakened.

The imp howled, rocking headfirst, screeching in Branimir's face.

"*Eats it!*"

Branimir felt warm blood trickling down his back against the bottom seam of his britches. The beast clung onto him all the more, claws cutting through muscle from back to chest, causing him to wobble onto the ice.

Adamus fell his axe, again. This time, he chopped the weapon directly into the imp's skullcap. The creature's brains splattered, eyes dimmed, and it dropped from Branimir.

He wheezed with a snivel, falling sideways onto the solid ice. He tried to roll to solid ground but could not budge, his back muscles torn to shreds.

"Branimir!" cried Dorofej, dashing to him.

Adamus reached Branimir first, throwing his weapon to the ground. He scooped Branimir from the river and rushed him to the hardened ground. "A myling. The imp would have killed him for sure if we had not woken."

Hanna spoke little by little, "His injuries will take weeks to mend. Any herbs for healing will be impossible to find in the hoarfrost. Dorofej can you use your magic as you did at Cavell?"

"He would die long before reaching Ariadne," Adamus agreed, holding his head gently.

Bran's back itched and prickled, throbbed and stung. He felt light headed, sleep pulling at his senses. He tried to focus on something, anything. At the angle he lay, he could see the myling, as Adamus called it, swollen against the ice. It had grown twice the size it had been with the fat rolls now bulging and filled, instead of folding over one another. There were several arrows sticking out of the imp from where Hanna must have struck it while it had attacked him.

Blood oozed from the punctured wounds.

"The thing sucked his blood through its claws?" Drak asked.

"Fed on his blood, it did," confirmed Dorofej. His voice sounded a lifetime away. "And, unquestionably heal him, I will. Now, step back, and give me room to work, you must."

"A nasty creature," said Adamus.

"Indeed," Hanna stated, "but where is the Branimir we saw at Cavell, who nearly butchered us all? He came at us like a warrior then, but here, he showed no more prowess than a sheep."

"Leave him be," Adamus boomed. "This could have happened to any one of us."

"You should have left him your knife," she concluded.

Hanna's words stung Branimir's ears as Dorofej loomed over him. A familiar red and yellow glow flooded Dorofej's hands as he reached for Branimir's body.

Branimir convulsed before Dorofej's hands touched him, feeling his insides stitching themselves back together, skin weaving together. Like bristles against his back, he itched and shivered, feeling Koldovstvo creep through his body. He whimpered and jerked again, sensing an itching from the back of his spine to his skull. Dorofej was mending him; it was the same as when Branimir had fallen to the Netherworld ages ago.

Once more, the black mage had kept him from certain death.

After an hour, Branimir had fully recovered and Dorofej's healing talent with Koldovstvo had been acknowledged, again, by the others of the party. By first light, the campsite was packed and they were prepared to ride off.

"It has been quite an eventful morning." Adamus circled his horse around to face Dorofej, Branimir, and Drak. "I suppose this is where we say our goodbyes."

"Ah," Dorofej hummed, "actually, with the tumult this morning, forget to request to join you, I have."

Drak almost fell from his saddle. "You want to go to Garain'l? What about Ariadne?

"Ariadne, we will go," Dorofej assured, "but something in Garain'l, there is to be seen. By happenstance, crossed paths with Adamus, I do not think we have, yes?"

"Are we speaking again of fortune and fate?" Hanna gleaned from the top of her mare.

"Call it whatever you wish, Hanna," Dorofej said, adjusting his hood. "I say, accompany you, we would like, if you would have us. The road is difficult, yes?"

Branimir cowered. He had partially been looking forward to parting from the two, particularly Hanna.

Adamus pulled his beard, staring into the wilds of the Dyndaer. "I would not turn you away. There are worse things than mylings at Garain'l."

"Yes," Dorofej gritted his teeth. "Aware of the dangers, I am, Adamus."

The first several miles were uneventful. Branimir rocked in the saddle on his pony's back. He stayed in the hindmost position behind the other four with Hanna and Adamus leading the way to the ruins of Garain'l.

The company journeyed southeast, away from the river, and back into the deep of the Dyndaer. The path had become pitch-black within an hour with Branimir and Drak scanning the trees for movement. Hanna, no more hindered by the dark than the Kras, rode at the front. Adamus and Dorofej carried torches in the middle.

Branimir's mood had turned increasingly sour since the campsite. He wanted to bury himself in his cloak and hide from embarrassment. Not only had he nearly killed the lot of them at Cavell, but now, he had been helpless against the myling.

"Branimir," Drak said, drawing out his name while, at the same time, slowing the pace of his pony. He spoke to him in a child-like way, chock-full of concerned innocence, "Are you going to be okay?"

"I will," he fibbed, turning to stare at anything else. Bran had fought demon after demon in the Netherworld. He should have been able to face the myling with little dispute. If only he had a weapon, he could have proven himself. Instead, Hanna's comment about him hung on his mind. *Sheep*.

Branimir tightened his jaw. Maybe he should have kept Adamus's dagger.

"You are brave," Drak awed, "like the *Branimir* from the old tales." He did not detect Branimir's discomfort. "If I had a myling jab its claws into my backside, I would forever be scarred. I would be afraid to carry on living, and you have climbed back on your pony and strode back into the Dyndaer."

He cringed, feeling the myling's claws ripping through his flesh. "Have I?"

"Oh, yes," Drak said. "You have made it look easy. If it were not for the dried blood on your back…and clothes, I would never guess you had almost walked the Nine Lands."

"Thanks," sighed Branimir.

"If Dorofej had not been there to save you with his magic, you would be dead," Drak scratched the edge of his hooked nose, black eyes widening for emphasis.

The statement stung Branimir. He suspected he would have died many times over if it were not for the black mage. Maybe, he was not a hero after all.

"Drak," said Branimir, turning his tone cold, "can we ride in silence for a while?"

"Marry!" Drak grinded his teeth to his cracked lips. "Did I say something to sadden you, Branimir?"

"I will—"

"Simargl!" Hanna shushed, sliding off her mare and whipping her bow from her shoulder. "Keep your mouths shut."

"What?" Drak asked, raking the Dyndaer with his black orbs. "I thought they were myths."

"There is very little that is myth," Branimir said, elevating his head. He heard the low rumble ahead, which he would have picked up on earlier had Drak had not been talking. He searched the thick trees.

"Whoa," Adamus pulled on his horse's reins. Dorofej did the same, and both men climbed down from their mounts, retreating from the way they had been heading.

"Just our luck," Adamus mumbled, pulling his shield from his back and the axe from his belt. His torch dropped to the ground. "First the myling, and now these curs."

Drak hissed between clenched teeth. "Alack! Why are we getting off the horses? You plan to outrun the beasts on foot." He rocked on his pony as though he were debating whether to join the others on the ground.

Branimir tensed his throat, holding his breath, finally noticing the three giant, black wolves called simargl. He followed suit and climbed down from his pony. The wolves ambled lazily in the direction they had been riding.

He gaped at their size, which were comparable to the frozen Bukavac of the Netherworld. The monstrous beasts had leathered wings etching from their longhaired backs, and stood taller than the horses. The simargl's head was bulkier than Branimir and Drak combined.

Drak squealed, falling off his mount and landing with a thud to the ground.

The three simargl abruptly lifted their heads, cream-colored eyes focusing in their direction.

"Nobody die," Hanna said in her no-nonsense tone.

Branimir could have sworn she looked in his direction.

"Reassuring, you are," Dorofej snorted, throwing down his torch, and casting a light above them with Koldovstvo. The action hastened the next moments.

The simargl sauntered between the trees, large paws marring the layered snow. The oversized beasts kept their webbed wings tucked, while pacing wide to encircle their prey.

Branimir shuddered. Again, he found himself at the mercy of the fighters around him to protect him—to save him. He was incapable of fighting against these beasts.

A loud bark signaled the wolves to advance. The first leapt forward through the trees while the other two dashed to either side. Hanna loosened arrow after arrow, striking the wolves in the cheek, neck, and head. The animals whimpered, and slowed, stumbling in their attack, but still, they came.

Adamus moved in front of the rest to face the lead simargl. He held his shield upright to prepare for the impact of the charging animal. As the beast neared, Dorofej touched Koldovstvo and loosened fire to the simargl's fur. Flames erupted, and the beast howled, stumbling with a snarl. All the same, the beast propelled itself into the much smaller Anshedar. Adamus rocked backwards, shield—shining silver—vibrating from the impact, sending him tumbling back across the ground, head over heels. Any lesser substance would have cracked under the impact. Again, Branimir questioned its crafting.

The thought was brief as Branimir found himself face to face with a snapping row of sharp teeth. The wolf-like creature lurched forward to take a bite, and Branimir dodged the attack. He quickly rolled forward under the beast, and then, realizing the danger, jerked sideways between the front and back paw to avoid being squashed.

Bran bounded to his feet and ran past the second simargl, who leaped at Dorofej.

"Alack!" Drak twisted away from his pony which the third simargl tackled, wings spread with fangs sinking into its neck.

Adamus shouted something unintelligible and charged past Hanna again, his shield thrown to the side. The fighter hurdled by Dorofej, who used Koldovstvo to jump through space and time to avoid certain death. Adamus reared his axe with immense potency. The blade caught the edge of the simargl's cheek, tearing through the thin membrane and splattering blood.

A yap of anguish hummed, and the black beast whipped its head from the impact. At the same time, a roar from the second softened; Hanna rapidly unleashed several more arrows into its skull. It crumpled to the snow, eyes blackening.

The first, injured from Adamus's axe, drowned out the dying animal with a bark, and snapped at the Anshedar once more. Adamus stepped back, defending his unprotected arm.

"Over here!" Branimir screamed, rushing forward and peddling backwards again.

The simargl turned toward the Kras, snarling. It had barely taken a step when Adamus raged forward, swinging the axe upward and cutting into the throat of the beast. The wolf gurgled, juttering to snap at the man, before falling over and bleeding out.

Adamus roared with victory. The shaggy black hair and beard nearly covering his triumphant expression.

Hanna turned her attention on the remaining simargl. It howled as she buried an arrow under its eye.

"One more," Dorofej cried. "Adamus!" The black mage flashed white light into the eyes of the dark-furred wolf, blinding it. With a haughty thrust, the Anshedar hastened forward and crushed his axe into the temple of the simargl. The silver blade slashed through the flesh like fire through frost. It dropped without much more than a whimper.

Adamus ripped his blade free, brought the axe down again at a downward angle into the neck.

Branimir panted for air, whirling to face Dorofej. The black mage had a patch of gray in his red hair.

"What is your axe made from?" Drak cried.

"Steel." Adamus answered, cleaning it on the hide of the beast. "Glorious steel from the south."

Branimir gawked at the size of the simargl. "How much further until we reach Garain'l?"

Hanna smiled. "Oh, Branimir, we have only begun."

Chapter XI

Two days passed and the forest had become more subdued. Branimir spent most of the time in his own head, captivated by the events at Cavell and with the myling. He tried to forget his failings, but the thought would not escape him. Even if he wanted to forget, Drak would not let him.

Even last night, Drak had challenged his wits while they had been keeping watch.

"Do you think there are mylings at Garain'l?" Drak had asked. Branimir had noted Drak spent more time frightening himself to tears than doing anything else, whether or not they could hear the bawls of beasts in the surrounding wild.

"Whatever comes will come," Bran said. Through talking to Drak, he had realized he was angrier at himself than afraid. "We must trust Dorofej knows what he is doing."

In truth, Drak's constant worrying reminded Branimir of how he had once been. He had changed in the Netherworld, long before returning to Maharia. Now, the eerie sounds here had no more effect than the grating dead there.

"Stone the crows! Why put so much trust into him, Branimir? He hasn't told us why we are going to the ruins, or even Ariadne for that matter. We left the boy we were meant to save, and now, he is going to be sacrificed" Drak debated.

"Not without Kaelandur," Branimir argued.

Drak retorted, "We hope."

"Dorofej has his secrets," Branimir had finally responded, assuring himself more than Drak. "He will tell us more when it is time."

"You said you were not his slave."

"And, I am not," Branimir said.

"You do his will, follow him wherever he goes, and ask little to no questions. That sounds like slavery to me," Drak contended.

"It can also sound like faith," Branimir had argued.

Drak whistled between his teeth. "You talk as though we are all slaves."

"Maybe we are," Branimir had concluded. "It could be there is only freedom in death."

"Not if Wolos is really dead," Drak said. "If that is true, then we will all be slaves to Marheena, trapped in the Netherworld."

Bran ended the conversation, saying, "Maybe freedom doesn't exist."

Morning had come, and Branimir could not shake his and Drak's conversation. He did not want to be a slave, and he did not want to die. The thoughts lingered with him throughout the day.

As of now, they had skipped the midday meal, and quickened their pace for Garain'l. Adamus promised they would reach the ruins before long.

Bran walked alongside Dorofej's horse, keeping his gaze fixed to the snowfall that patterned the landscape. Even with the thick awning of trees, stopping the white fluff from collecting on the forest floor was impossible. Branimir's leather shoes sunk into the slush, freezing his feet and toes. He told himself he had been through worse, and still he suffered.

"Do you want your turn?" Drak asked, bouncing atop the pony. The Kras swayed with a tune in his head, one which he always seemed to have. He had more giddiness in him than what any creature should carry about.

Branimir scowled, keeping his head down. For the past couple days, he and Drak had taken turns on the single pony after the other had been lost in the skirmish with the simargl. In truth, the two could ride the pony together, but Branimir did not want to share the small saddle.

He finally said, "I would prefer to walk a bit longer."

When Branimir had traveled with the Highborn from Melkorka to the Ash Tree, he had found purpose in being among them. He had led them to Illuard, saved them from the clutches of the centaurs, and led them across the frozen river near Shayol Domier. He had given the Kras the courage to find freedom. He had been a hero.

But why was he here? He was supposed to be a warrior and a hero, not a liability.

Through the shadows, without any noticeable landmark except tree next to another tree, the company continued to create their own path. Adamus, who led them, would share songs of Ariadne, and from distant battlefields. His words often enchanted Branimir, rescuing him momentarily from his self-doubt. Adamus sung with a deep baritone, at a slow pace, which seemed to bring peace to the shadows of the Dyndaer.

Lost is the large mountain,
Beside the river swift,
Within a joyless wood,
O death has come for me.

To grind the iron blade,
Kneel to the crown of stone,
Fell hero; warrior,
O death has come for me.

Hatred and sacrifice,
In faith kept me hither,
Wherefore morrow n'er comes,
O death has come for me.

Anon! ere you fade,
O death has come for me.

The words gave Branimir chills. He could only guess the words were an ode to Czern, speaking of the crown of stone and sacrifice.

Branimir settled his hand in his pocket to touch the Ojenek. Feeling the smooth surface of the stone comforted him.

Ages had passed since he had relied on the magic of the moonstone. Then again, in a world where trade connected kingdoms and culture, folks were persuaded to learn new languages. Even now, he journeyed with an Anshedar, Highborn, Lilitu, and Kras; and they could all speak to one another without constraint. Bran wondered if he would ever need the gifts of the Ojenek again.

"Branimir, my friend, you have not been yourself for many days, yes?" probed Dorofej, dipping down from his black mare. "In your mind something is disturbed, yes?"

"It is nothing," Branimir said, distancing himself from Dorofej's horse, but only slightly.

"I say, *nothing* is temporary, yes?"

Branimir frowned. "I don't know what that means, Dorofej."

"Fades quickly, *nothing* does, and soon, what is *nothing* becomes *something*," Dorofej expounded, rubbing at his half-grey, half-red beard. The stubble had grown out to a full beard with his casting of Koldovstvo. At this rate, the black mage would kill himself before they rescued Bohumir. Bran wondered at Drak's suggestion as to whether they should have joined Adamus and Hanna on the trip to Garain'l. It may have been wiser, instead, to pursue the lad, or at least gather whatever Dorofej wanted in Ariadne.

"What is your point?" Branimir griped.

Dorofej whistled between his teeth, giving an air of annoyance. He breathed slowly and enunciated each word to make sure he was well heard. "I say, my point is pouting, you are, and no one pouts about *nothing*."

Branimir turned his head further away. He fought against the urge to make claim that he was not pouting, even when the truth was he most definitely had been. After a time, he turned back, and the truth came forward, "I do not want to die, Dorofej."

"Ah, brave you are to admit what most would fear, yes?"

Branimir sniffed, his nose numb. "I do not feel brave."

"I say, none of us truly want to die, even with the promise of something greater. Clear to me, it is," said Dorofej, "broken, one must be, to want to abort the blessing of life."

Hanna turned her enlarged head to join the conversation. "You claim every life is a blessing. Since when are all of us created to find joy? What of those who suffer from their birthing til their passing, finding no time for reprieve? The message you are presenting is false."

"There is no joy in war," Drak agreed. "Those who survive it leave with less of themselves than when they started."

"What do you know of war, Drak?" Adamus snorted. "Most men don't truly find what they are made of until they go to war."

"Not only war," Hanna insisted, "whatever point Adamus aims to make. But what of the starving or sick? The unloved and misused? The dull-minded and broken? I would think it better to end their suffering than expect them to find joy when there is none to be had."

Dorofej grunted. "Speak as though sorrow is pressed on you by another, you do."

"Tis true," said Adamus, his voice flattened after being disregarded by Hanna. "Misery and blessing comes from the gods. It guides men to complete their charge so they may find rest in the Thrice Ten Kingdom."

"The common belief, it is," said Dorofej, responding to Adamus. He tugged at the scruff on his chin, as though he had forgotten the feel of facial hair and had missed its absence. He said, "Have the gods come from Iriy, or the heavens, or some other place, and came to you with an unexpected windfall or woe? I say, I think not. Despair does not come from anything outside of the self, but from within, yes?"

Dorofej's suggestion that the gods might swoop down to speak with the living caused Branimir to laugh. He had once told Branimir that Iriy was the city of the gods found within the Shade Fells in the far west; though Dorofej claimed he had never been to this mystical place.

"I don't understand what this has to do with Branimir talking about dying, but," Drak said seriously, "the gods would not speak to us. They might have folks close to us cause pain or happiness—to teach us what we should learn."

"I would have never thought to hear such wisdom from a Kras," supplied Hanna in her even tone. "Yet the way to the Beyond is not easy, and its blessings are withheld only for the strong. If you want to have eternal life, toss aside the weak and persevere with the blessed."

Branimir gaped. "You mean kill those weaker than yourself."

"Not necessarily kill," Hanna narrowed her eyes. "But can the weak really live? Truly not. Best to give them a better chance in their next life. You would not fear death if you were strong."

"What madness! There is nothing that guarantees another life." Branimir shook, from either fear or fury. "And who here is weak, Hanna?"

"It has yet to be determined," she answered.

Drak, who must have felt similarly snubbed, said, "You are the one fighting with a teeny bow. You are no stronger than me."

Branimir covered his mouth with both hands, taking notice of the weapon, half the size of what a normal archer would carry.

Hanna stayed serene, saying, "I will let my actions speak for my strength. Can you say the same, Drak?" Her red sash caught Branimir's eye as Drak looked away. Hanna's point could not be missed. She had proven herself in the battle at Cavell, against the myling, and the simargl. Drak had done nothing of consequence in any battle. Hanna continued her lecture, "I am a warrior of the Lilitu. I am a Rudhira. I was born to fight. I succeed or I die, and I am not dead."

Drak gulped, lowering his own offset, blackened eyes to the back of Dorofej.

"There are other gifts besides fighting," Branimir said, attempting to convince himself more than the others. "Do you not think of that when measuring a person's worth?"

Hanna kept her eyes on the road. "Your argument is an old one, and I will tell you what I tell Adamus. Worth is calculated by many things: knowledge, influence, and utility."

"She is speaking in riddles," Drak mused.

"I am not," Hanna said. "Let us consider the value of your people. The Kras are one of the longest living races in the north, and hold historic knowledge, but they do not use it to their advantage. What the Kras know is not used to govern or manage battles or control trade but is squandered on their pursuit for gemstones or to craft trinkets."

Drak sniffed, and squeaked, "What do you have against shiny stones?"

"Nothing," Hanna said, "when it lands a hefty profit and rises my people to greater prosperity."

Branimir felt Ojenek in his pocket. He could not imagine giving away the moonstone for something as meaningless as silver. The same was true of his gems buried back at Gavlok. Ridiculous. "What of influence?"

"Influence?" Hanna awed with amusement. "The Kras have no influence on any civilization. The people are not motivated by politics, war, religion, or any other thing that motivates the world. The Kras may very well engage in trade but only to endure, and not to thrive. They only give away the jewels they must part with to make enough to survive, do they not?"

Again, Drak fidgeted on his saddle. "And why should we hand over the stones we discover in the soil? They are ours." Branimir smiled at Drak's argument, similar to what he had thought himself.

"I would be ignorant to encourage you to change," Hanna said, "but your lack of influence speaks to your lack of utility and your ultimate annihilation. The Kras serve to add flavor to the marketplace with their ornaments, but their role otherwise is undefined. In fact, I would argue the Kras could disappear entirely from Aenar and very little would change in the course of the world."

Not having the words to dispute Hanna's allegations, Drak said with a snivel. "You're a boob."

Adamus nearly slipped sideways from his saddle. "Don't be cross, Drak."

"You're saying we are useless," Branimir concluded quietly, "because we do not force others to bend to our will?"

Hanna replied, paying no attention to Drak, "You do not have a will for others to bend toward."

"Seems to me," Branimir considered, "the world has enough pokers in the fire."

"A common viewpoint for the weak. They minimize the value of power because they cannot obtain it." Hanna settled with satisfaction. "Also, why the Kras will never thrive. The race would better serve another as slave than to be left to their own devices. The Kras have talents wasted because they are too ignorant to know how best to apply them."

Branimir scowled. "You think the Kras would better be slaves again than have their freedom?"

"Ah, I remember they were slaves once, were they not?" Hanna must have realized she struck a chord, but went on, "I saw how you were used by the Stuhia at Cavell. You fought better under his mind control with his magic than I have seen from you at any other time."

"I say, that is enough, Hanna." Dorofej choked.

Hanna stayed stoic, though she were reading from the most boring of stories. "Do not fret, Branimir. Most of the northern races are equally useless. Freedom is a gift for those worthy, and truth is, most are not."

Adamus growled. "Hanna, you need to be more careful with your words,"

"Indeed," Dorofej said louder.

"You separate the north from Haemus Mons, even suggesting the desert people are superior," Adamus disputed in his deep baritone. "Tis they who have been advancing into Maharia and slaughtering my people. I hardly see how that is commendable."

"The mark of a person's virtue does not match his or her greatness. The path of power is not decorated with honor; and decency does not win wars. Nor is value found in integrity or morality. The question of utility lies in whether or not what one can offer is greater than another."

"You misjudge the Anshedar. May I remind you that you have fought for us in the war against the desert people," Adamus said.

"I fought for the Anshedar because the desert people do not pay sellswords," Hanna said plainly. "Do not misjudge my actions as allegiance."

"So, you believe the Uvil are the greater race?" Adamus challenged, his grimace hidden beneath his black beard.

"Don't you?" Hanna shifted her bulbous head toward the hero-warrior, and almost grinned, for what would have been the first time. "Our greatest fighters in Lilitu cities carry their weapons, which we won in battle. Even you are carrying their shield and steel on your back."

While Adamus bit his tongue, Branimir combed the trees for movement, and ignored Hanna. He knew he would feel better about the journey if she were no longer with them.

Chapter XII

Garain'l materialized, shrouded in shades only a hair lighter than the rest of the forest. The stone archways were corroded and laced in creepers, coiling and curling around the molded grey edifices. The few towers, constructed from ancient wood, had collapsed into dilapidated piles of mush or sunk into the expanding marsh snaking through the ruins.

The vinegary odor poked at Branimir's senses. He pulled his cowl over his nose, scanning the white flakes that painted parts of the ruins.

"Stone the crows! Are there treasures buried here?" Drak straightened on the pony, smacking his lips. The Kras scanned the shapes of broken statues and half-raised buildings emerging from the puddled muck.

Branimir shivered, seeing the besmirched edges of snowfall. "I do not think I would want to go searching for silver or stones here, Drak. You would find yourself falling into hidden bits of swamp and drown before you could find solid ground again."

"Which is why tis best to leave the horses here. We can't have them bolting into the bog." Adamus dismounted, directing his horse to the nearest tree, and tying him off. "Follow me on the old footpath until we reach the burial ground. Fiends, likely mylings, lurk among the swamp and the buildings from time to time."

"Then, why did you come here?" Branimir shivered.

"Tradition," Adamus said. "Tis custom to pay respects during the Koricern. You came of your own accord."

"If it is a tradition, where is everyone else?" Drak asked.

"I told you," Adamus explained, "tis tradition of my family, passed down through our bloodline only."

"How long will we be here?" Drak shivered, looking across the ruins.

"I would not risk staying more than a night," Adamus said. "We will complete the sacrifice and make headway toward Ariadne in the morning."

"Sacrifice?" Branimir whispered in confusion. He thought of Bohumir.

"Best not to tarry too long, yes?" Dorofej slipped from his mount. The black mage's calmness caused Branimir to grow in concern.

"What is it, Dorofej?" he urged.

"As I feared, lingering among these stones, something ancient does," Dorofej forewarned. "Not quite a part of this world, it is not. I say, I fear it—"

"Come out with it, Stuhia," Hanna demanded, her feet crunching against the snow. "Demon, devil, or something more?"

Dorofej raised his eyebrows and angled them over the bridge of his nose. His brow had become noticeably bushier since the simargl. In short time, Branimir thought he may be speaking with the old man he had known at Melkorka. "Too dangerous to fully know, it would be, but a Likhyi, methinks. Though, the power of the spectre is weakened, still held at bay by the Ash Tree, it should be."

"A Likhyi?" Drak scratched the thinning hair on top of his head. "You mentioned the name back at Ojenir, but I have never thought to ask of its nature."

"I have not heard of this *thing*, though many dangers creep within Garain'l," Adamus responded.

Branimir realized he, too, could not answer the question of the Likhyi. Beyond what Dorofej had recently said, Bran had only heard it mentioned by Nedezhda at Melkorka, years ago, when she vowed to release the Likhyi.

"Clear, it is not," Dorofej tried to explain, "but ancient, it is. I say, there are some who claim the Likhyi are older than gods or may even be gods themselves from a time before time."

Hanna cleared her throat. "You are talking about an epoch when the world was still being formed. It is when the first magics, called the Runista, were made, in a time prior to our creation. We tell stories—tales known well by the desert people—of primordial wraiths who warped this world, who had been trapped by the current gods in a place between this world and the next. Our people have often thought the Mother wants to free them again."

Branimir scratched his head. "You are talking of your goddess, Lillith? How does the Lilitu god fit with the gods of the Anshedar?"

Drak said, "Did I not say before? Lillith is the same as Marheena for the Northman, or close enough."

Branimir's jaw hung. "The Frozen Goddess of the Netherworld! No, you did not tell me. You mean the Mother is the Seamstress of Nightmares."

Drak, who did not seem to understand the implication, mashed his lips together and sluggishly nodded.

Adamus had a similar expression, eyeing Branimir with caution.

Branimir wailed, turning to Dorofej for help. "Say something to her. We cannot stand here and support a follower of Marheena when the aim is to let loose wraiths into Aenar. This is why Nedezhda came for the Ash Tree a thousand years ago! There must be reason why these old gods, the Likhyi, were trapped."

The forest fell quiet for many seconds after Branimir's lamenting. Dorofej said nothing. The black mage simply looked around at the company in contemplation.

Adamus spoke first, like he was joking, "The Kras do know their history, don't they? We have heard of the Ash Tree in Ariadne, but it is more myth than history. Some say, it is somewhere within the Dyndaer. But Nedezhda? I know nothing of that name."

The Lilitu woman's eyes were exceptionally round, her tone also elevated with a hint of humor. "Maybe this Kras is different from the rest. Motivated by something, indeed; though, poking at me would be ill-advised, Branimir."

Branimir puffed his chest, finding his strength returning. He would not be threatened. "I am nothing that you think I am."

"The old gods," Drak paused, rubbing his chin in deep thought, offsetting the tension, "were entombed to give us life. All of us. The Kras have told the stories for centuries, even before Shayol Domier. I had heard the stories from my grandfather growing up about how the essence of the old gods were encapsulated into the Ash Tree to give birth to the living. I have never heard them called Likhyi before, but to free these… these Likhyi… you would have to have something strong enough to destroy the Ash Tree."

Kaelandur, Branimir thought.

At least Drak was beginning to understand the seriousness of the situation. Branimir moved to clasp his hand on Drak's shoulder, almost screaming, "And you," he pointed his finger at Hanna accusingly, "want this to happen. You want Marheena to kill us, don't you?"

Adamus moved to intercept. "I do not see why you are attacking Hanna. Tis the gods who have a better understanding of the cycle of things than the living. Czern teaches us that we are imperfect. We cannot hope to fight against the gods. If our time on Aenar is done, tis done. If the Likhyi must come, then let them come. If the gods wish the Ash Tree to be destroyed, let it be destroyed."

"Life is about the perseverance of the mightiest," Hanna echoed a similar sentiment as the hero-warrior from Ariadne, holding her ground. "Lillith, or Marheena, as you would say, will see to her will. The Mother will do what must be done."

Branimir's body shook with fury. He felt Drak wince under his grip, but he could not believe what he was hearing. "Dorofej, say something to this. The world will crumble around these two and they will watch it happen without even lifting a finger. Dorofej! Why have you said nothing?"

The black mage grumbled, adjusting his robes, nodding his head at Branimir.

"Each of us have our own reasons for doing what must be done, yes?" Dorofej staggered his words, having less poise than Branimir generally found in the ageless Highborn. "Difficult to believe, it is, Marheena, or any deity, acts with accordance, or interest, of the nature of men, yes? Men have motivations. Demons have motivations. Even my horse finds motivation." Dorofej patted the animal softly against the cheek. "But not the gods. Reverence in the gods is found—not for what they have given or what they have taken—but because of whom they are, yes? I say, reason for their being and their doing is not for me to consider."

"So, you will do nothing, too?" Branimir asked in shock.

"Say that, I did not," Dorofej whistled. "I say, as I have said before, Branimir Baran. I am but a man—"

"Branimir Baran!" Drak yelled. "Dorofej, why would you say that when his surname is Barthor?"

Branimir cowered at the lapse.

"Yes, yes, yes," Dorofej waved off Drak, finishing his thought. "I am but a man and I have no interest in dying. Bohumir must be rescued, the Ash Tree must be protected, and the Likhyi must be withheld, but first Adamus has a grave to consecrate, yes?"

Adamus adjusted his weapon and shield, nodding with respect to Dorofej. The black-bearded man turned and led the way into Garain'l. Hanna followed behind him, averting her eyes from Branimir as she passed by, and Drak pulled from his hand to take his place in the solitary line.

"Go on, Branimir," Dorofej said. "We can speak more of this later."

Bran sighed and headed into the ruins. Dorofej trailed behind him.

Garain'l gave the impression of being trivial at the front arch where the horses remained, but the girth of the place was greater than anticipated. The shallow light from Adamus and Dorofej's torches gave them minimal sight while Hanna, Branimir, and Drak peered through the trees and structures for any sign suggesting the fiends of which Adamus had spoken skulked. Several times, Adamus asked Dorofej to cast light into the darkness of the Dyndaer and had been refused. The black mage spoke of the importance of saving his power.

Nothing stirred.

The pathway twisted from time to time, covered with debris of broken limbs and cracked stone. Vines and branches lay half-buried in the snow like snakes on the surface of water. In some areas, the bog ran alongside the makeshift trail, overwhelming their senses with the stench. Adamus moved slower in these areas to assure his footing was never misplaced. Slipping into the muck would have left any of them damp, and likely would have played negatively toward their already sour tempers.

At one point, the company reached a shattered stone building of sorts across the footpath. Instead of going over or through, Adamus elected to double back and take another path to the burial ground. He welcomed the Anshedar's sense of caution. Bran could not ignore the intolerable sense of distress that stayed with him as they moved through Garain'l.

They had passed by another curve in the path when Drak broke the silence.

"Look there," the Kras rustled, stopping suddenly in front of Branimir. He pointed across the mire through the trees toward one of the many structures.

Adamus halted the group, lifting his hand, "Tis too far to see, Drak. What moves?"

Branimir looked in the direction Drak pointed and saw nothing. The building bowed near the flattened top, stones jutting from their holdings in several places. The opening in the front was hollow without a door without any movement inside.

"Simargl?" Adamus asked.

"No," Drak replied, "something strange, green and ghost-like. It was there and wasn't there, floating when it moved. The thing drifted into the hole on the side of the building. It was a woman, I think."

Branimir shuddered at the bizarre description. Dorofej shook his head unknowingly.

"You think it was the gal of Garain'l, like from the song?" Drak cringed, tightening his pointed nose.

Hanna said, "Whatever it was, if it was anything, is gone."

"Something was there," Drak declared, rising on his tiptoes.

"Doubts you, no one does, Drak," Dorofej said. "Best we move with haste but silently, yes?"

Adamus grunted in acknowledgement and drifted forward again, almost crouched. Those behind him maintained a similar station and tiptoed across the wet snow. Branimir watched the doorway of the building until he could not see it anymore.

At length they came to a sharp bend and turned left to a series of stone steps leading down beneath three archways. They were adjacent and parallel to one another, and amazingly, each were still intact. Adamus took the lead beneath the archways. The snow swirled around their feet from piled drifts on either side of the discolored stairs.

When the stairway ended, a building, a shrine, set in between two trees loomed. Green gunk painted the greying rock which formed its bulky structure. Branimir halted behind those in front of him, mesmerized by the magnificence of the building's height and thickness. A statue, marked by a man with a crown and scythe, stood, as though keeping guard, on either side of the shrine.

"An image of Czern, it is," Dorofej identified with a rise of his hand, and a pull at his beard.

Adamus turned to face them, and said, "I will enter alone and pay respects to my fallen kin. Please, make camp here and I will return by morning."

None protested, but Branimir noticed Drak shift uneasily at the request.

As the dark-bearded warrior disappeared into the shrine, Branimir could not help but want to know what was inside.

403

Chapter XIII

The deep, singsong voice of Adamus rumbled from the deeps of the shrine behind the campfire. The words were indistinguishable, but the hum of song teased Branimir's ears. The tune was lovely and cavernous, profound and arcane, and he pined to know the words.

Instead of tiptoeing into the place he had been asked not to go, he leaned toward the fire. His body had numbed to the point he had forgotten the biting cold. Now, with the fire cackling, warming him, Branimir was reminded how chilled he must have been before making camp. He enjoyed the moment.

Drak spent the last hour standing in the far corner by two stones, throwing his rune staves against the ground and mumbling under his breath. Hanna had disappeared somewhere nearby to keep watch, saying something about scouting the area. Dorofej had disappeared shortly after without a word. Branimir could only guess he was off looking for whatever he had come here to find.

Before long, Drak kicked at the ground with frustration and joined Branimir at the fire. His sticks were gathered in his hands. "I cannot seem to make anything of what the rune staves are trying to tell me."

"What do you mean?" Branimir said, wringing his hands over the flames.

"My mind is mush," Drak said. "I throw the rune staves down, but I cannot hear anything."

Branimir smiled. "I forgot they could talk to you."

Drak scowled at the remark. The red-skinned Kras plopped down on his bedroll, dropping his hands and sticks into his lap. His dark eyes blazed in the flickering light. "I might be too tired."

"You can try again tomorrow," Branimir encouraged, still not certain whether there was anything to the rune staves. "Drak, did you really come with us simply because of the sticks?"

"Marry! I keep saying they aren't sticks." Drak scrunched his nose at the question. "And, yes. The rune staves said you would do something great, and along the path of the gods, remember? I haven't forgotten."

"Well, we are beside a shrine of the gods," Branimir mused.

Drak looked up at the statues of Czern. "I had thought it might be something a bit more than listening to an Anshedar sing in a tomb."

Bran pointed at the sticks. "Do you really think those *things* tell the future?"

"I do. Why are you asking me this?" Drak wondered.

Branimir shrugged. "When we first met, and you read my *fortune*, you had said something that troubled me. I have not been able to get it out of my head."

Drak blinked with confusion.

"You told me that I would never find joy," Branimir went on. "I can't help but think the rune staves might be right, mainly when I think of these past several weeks."

"Oh." Dorofej shuffled out from the shadows, rejoining them near the fire. He appeared disgruntled, despite his words. "We have shared pleasant times together, yes? I say, do not sum up all arduous times to be grievous."

"I was only telling you what I was seeing," Drak explained. "I did not mean anything by it."

"All the same, your words have stayed with me," said Branimir, scooting over to make room for Dorofej.

"I say, Hanna did warn us that we may create our own future by thinking that we know what to expect, yes? Emotions can create your reality if you are not careful," Dorofej softened his gaze.

Drak sniffed through his nose. "The rune staves tell what will happen. Branimir cannot change it, no matter how he feels about it."

Dorofej furrowed his brow. "Know that for certain, we do not. Regardless, whether our paths are fixed or not, we choose how we walk them. Dangerous, it is, to find comfort in sadness. Leads only to more sadness, it does."

"I like that thought," Drak granted, and then grinned wide. "Feelings are unseen and untouched by anyone or anything. Fate cannot tell you how to feel."

Branimir held his face, pondering the wisdom of the two. "Telling yourself how to feel seems easier to think about than to do."

"Such is the task of the living, yes? I say, our minds are riddled with grand ideas and limited enthusiasm to see it done. Driven towards the things we wish to avoid, men are. Drink, does the drunkard; fight, does the warrior; and on and on, it goes."

"Is it not what they want?" Branimir asked.

Dorofej lifted his eyebrows. "What do you want, Branimir?"

"I want…" Branimir may have never thought about the question before. He had always been entertained with trying to survive, the question of *what to live for* was beyond his knowing. Yet when taking a moment to think, the answer was not hard to come by. "I want happiness, Dorofej."

"What we all want, it is, and also the drunk, the warrior, and any other, yes?"

Drak, who had still been holding his rune staves, slid them back into their pouch. "I wonder what you are driven to do, though."

"Flee!" Hanna's voice thundered over the sound of anything Branimir might have said. The flash of her reddish-brown skin rushed between the trees fifty feet away. "Get Adamus! Flee for your lives!"

Branimir stared in bafflement, hearing barking resounding in the distance. The sound was too familiar. Drak sprung to his feet.

Dorofej's eyebrows came together arcing over his wide nose. He shouted back. "What is it?"

The Lilitu woman skidded into the camp, covering the distance. "Has the chill stolen your senses? I have seen Drak's green ghost. And simargl have picked up our scent!"

"I told you I was telling the truth," Drak hollered.

"What was the ghost?" Branimir asked.

Hanna lifted her bow as though she might smack them all, including Dorofej, who stood dumbfounded. "This is not the time for questions. For all I know, it is the Likhyi. Now, come! We cannot win a battle here."

Dorofej halfway nodded, the sounds of the simargl echoing through the ruins. Battle was going to be upon them in moments.

"Branimir, fetch Adamus, you must," Dorofej directed, rubbing his head. "Found what I needed to find, I have not." He looked around the ruins expectantly. "Something hidden here, there is. Douse the fire, we will, with hope they stay clear from us. Make haste."

Hanna could be heard arguing with Dorofej as he skidded toward the steps, nearly falling. Steading himself, Branimir rattled down the slick, stone stairs. With every step, Adamus's song intensified, but he did not have the time to enjoy the words.

"Adamus," he screamed.

A putrid smell touched Branimir's sensitive nose. He gagged and pressed forward, reaching the bottom. The disheveled crypt had skeletons and half-rotten corpses flung about the underpasses, running in either direction. It appeared whomever brought the bodies had thrown them down the steps or had simply piled them in several disorganized mounds. Despite the smell, the bodies looked as though they had been sitting for some time.

Branimir's stomach roiled. In the Netherworld, he had witnessed many *dead* things, but they did not carry the smell like the corpses here. He could ignore the lifeless eyes and decayed flesh collecting in piles. He could even overlook the rodents—despite the cold—who tore skin from bone and gnashed. But the smell was unbearable.

The barking from above ground had turned into growls and roars. He had to hurry.

A torchlight flickered in one of the many directions, and Branimir rushed toward the soft, orange glow. He stepped over mangled arms and shriveled stomachs, keeping his eyes focused on the light as much as he could without tripping over the pile of dead Anshedar.

As Branimir neared the door, he heard Adamus continue to sing in soothing, muffled rumbles. But there were other voices too. He barely had time to consider what it meant before he burst into the chamber.

"Adamus," Branimir shouted.

The Anshedar did not respond.

"Oh, son, you have grown strong. I have missed the light in your eyes," said a motherly voice.

Branimir stood, uncertain, in the entry way with Adamus facing a table, his back to him. He stepped forward carefully.

"The *way* is shut. *The way is shut.* The way is shut," cried another.

"More wine," a third begged. "Never have I been so parched."

Laughter.

And, still, Adamus sung.

"Adamus!" Branimir called out, tugging on the back of the man's cloak.

The black-bearded hero-warrior spun from the stone tablet, his eyes rolled back into his head, whites showing, and blood oozing off his lip. He spat, coughing blood into Branimir's face.

Bran swiped his hands in front of him in attempt to block the blood. "Adamus."

"It cannot be," something cried.

Branimir tottered into the table, raising his chin to find three severed heads, one skull with a green light blazing within its empty orbs. The others were half decomposed, looking back at him, with an undead gaze. They circled a pool of blood which had seemingly come from Adamus's cut tongue.

Branimir screamed flailing, away from them, and back into the wall.

One by one the heads shrieked, mouths gaping and blackness flooding the room from their opened orifices. As the gloom flooded the room, the energy in the lifeless heads drained and they each returned to death.

"Wha—What?" Branimir tried.

Adamus roared from his chest, convulsing, jerking his head like an upset mule. His light eyes rolled back into their place and he hurriedly wiped the crimson liquid from his lips.

"Branimir," he retched, spitting blood. "Why have you interrupted this time with my family?"

"I—I'm sorry, Adamus. We are under attack," Branimir stammered, staring at what must have been the man's relatives lined on the table. Small bulbs of fire burned in containers between each skull, but the fresh blood is what kept his eye. "Dorofej said to…"

"Czern's breath!" Adamus choked, checking his armaments and staggering toward the door. "Come on."

Bran backed out of the chamber to follow Adamus, unsure about the dark magic he had witnessed, and hastily tried to push it from his mind. He did not want to think Adamus to be as wicked as Hanna. Though, perhaps this god called Czern was as terrible as Marheena, no matter what Dorofej claimed the will of the gods were.

Branimir climbed up the steps from the shrine, hearing the grating snarls of simargl. When he reached the smothered fire, he saw the winged wolves flooding in columns from the trees in packs of three and five. There were dozens.

Drak cowered near the steps with their items gathered, cheering at Adamus's emergence from the catacombs. Hanna stood several feet in front of him, her quiver nearly emptied, entombing her arrows deep into the skulls of the beasts. Simargl after simargl fell, crashing and skidding across the hoarfrost.

Dorofej stood beyond them all, protecting the path, casting Koldovstvo without restraint. The black mage flung ice shards and spheres of fire, exploding the earth, and pulling trees down atop the backs of the beasts.

Adamus had his axe at the ready, sprinting to Dorofej's side. Soon, his axe was rising and falling, hacking through skin, fur, and bones as if it were snowfall.

The dark-haired man called out to Dorofej. "We cannot win this. Move back." He plunged his blade into another razor-toothed simargl with a growl of savagery. Another beast slammed into his steel shield, knocking him back. The Anshedar skidded and twisted, ramming back into the creature. He worked his axe methodically, slashing at every opening, giving no notice to the blood that spurted.

"Leave Garain'l, we mustn't," Dorofej said. "I say, something stirs here, yes?"

"Mm," Adamus huffed. "The simargl."

Branimir could hear Dorofej's dissatisfied groan.

"We cannot stay here," Drak shrieked from Branimir's side. "They cannot kill them all."

Branimir knew the other Kras was right. The black mage had already aged considerably. Adamus and Dorofej had already begun to inch backwards towards the shrine, overwhelmed by the packs of wolves. Hanna screamed out to them as more appeared further back in the trees.

Dorofej and Adamus hardly heard her warning, shouting back and forth to each other, cutting down as many of the beasts as they could. The craft of Koldovstvo lighting up the Dyndaer almost matched the rhythm of the falling axe. Ice and fire surged through the shadowed forest at every shape that stirred.

"I am out," Hanna said, hooking her bow back onto her shoulder.

"Hanna!" Drak screamed, cowering back.

From the side of the shrine, a simargl crashed into the Lilitu, sinking its teeth into her arm and side in a massive bite. Branimir scooted backwards while the simargl picked Hanna off the ground and flung her about. Her body twisted and heaved in between its jaws, from her chest to her midsection; she screeched in agony. With desperation, she struggled pulling on either side of the creature's curled lips. Blood slopped down the side of her body; her innards exposed through the gaping hole of her split skin. With a final rumble, the simargl pitched Hanna to the snow.

Branimir vanished from sight, shouting at Drak to do the same. The beast sniffed at the air, considered the shrine, and then raced toward Adamus and Dorofej with its wings stretched behind its back.

He did not care to watch the fate of the beast, his eyes locked on Hanna who wriggled about on the ground in pain. He crept toward her, hidden by his invisibility.

"Help…me," she choked. He knew she did not speak to him. He was not where she could see him. "Adamus…"

If Dorofej caught sight of Hanna, he would spend his years healing her. Branimir was not certain if he could allow it. Hanna worshiped Marheena and Dorofej could not die!

Branimir glanced at Dorofej across the field, hair already whitening, using Koldovstvo to protect them all. Indeed, Dorofej would kill himself to save her.

"What do we do?" Drak whispered over his shoulder, eyes tearing while he watched Hanna with his beady black eyes.

Branimir could not look away from Hanna. Her owl eyes were searching for something, anything, and yet, Branimir and Drak were unseen.

"We need to get her away from here," Branimir said.

Gritting his teeth, he scrambled forward and clamped his hands under her arms. Surprised at his own strength, he began to pull her back across the stone into the catacombs with ease. She flailed her good arm in the air trying to help. She had little strength, floundering hopelessly.

"It is no use," Drak cried.

Branimir ignored the Kras, holding fast until Hanna's stifled cries finally ceased and she lost consciousness. Even though her body went limp, he continued to pull her until she was safe within the shrine at the top of the steps.

Pulsating, he pulled himself away from her body and stepped back.

"She's dead." Drak said.

"No," he blanched. "she is still alive." Branimir stepped away from Drak, shouting. "Retreat, Dorofej. Adamus. Retreat!"

He heard Adamus in the distance. "I told you we had to run. Back to the catacombs."

Dorofej yelled in defeat and fled with Adamus. The black mage caught sight of Hanna as he neared. "Lost, she is." Dorofej said stepping by Hanna. "No time for sadness, there is. Run!"

"Not quite!" Adamus cried. The burly Anshedar scooped up the woman and sprang into the depths. Branimir and Drak kept to his heels.

Chapter XIV

He tried to find the strength to tear himself away from the stone wall within the chamber. His hands quaked beyond his control. He had placed his hands between his knees to stop them from trembling, and still it did nothing. Dorofej and Adamus hovered over Hanna, the Rudhira, gawking at her insides spilling out across the stone table. Her crimson sash was stained with her blood.

"Are we safe?" Drak mouthed softly, sitting next to Branimir. The Kras eyed the dead bodies in the room and the severed heads on the stone table, seemingly distracting himself from Hanna.

"Should be," Adamus said, gritting his teeth. "The simargl are too big to squeeze down here. You could have come down here to begin with and avoided them altogether instead of attempting a stand-off. I told you we should have fled."

"Hanna is dead," Dorofej whispered, stepping away from the body and leaving Adamus alone. Dorofej moved to the doorway and peered into the catacomb. "Other dangers, there were said to be. Hanna alleged she saw the green ghost and thought it to be the Likhyi, yes?"

"She did," Drak nodded. "And we thought to run away. I wonder if the thing will come for us down here."

Adamus turned his head from Hanna's lifeless corpse and sniffed. "We can leave in short time, if that is what must be done.

The simargl are mindless brutes. They attack for play more than anything, and soon something more will grab at their attention."

As if on cue, growling resounded from above.

Dorofej ignored the simargls and said, "First, find what lingers here in Garain'l, I must."

Drak shook next to Bran, clenching his jaw between his words. "Is this what adventures are like?"

Branimir frowned, looking at Hanna's corpse. "More or less. Most stories you hear would tell the better parts and ignore the rest."

"I can see why folks would rather hear a story than live it. I will get a fire going," Drak said, tearing up at the corner of his eyes. He moved away to dig about the room to find something to kindle.

Adamus hit the table, and then placed his face into his hands. "Hanna faced legions, steel swords and worse, and only to be slaughtered by beasts. She saved my neck more times than I can count. I should have been there for her."

Branimir looked away. He was glad Adamus could hold himself back. He nearly expected the man to rush back atop for vengeance.

Time slowly passed in the catacombs while they listened to the simargl snarling amongst each other. Drak started a small fire in short time, and soon began wheezing next to the flames, falling asleep in a curled ball. Branimir kept his ears covered, doing his best to clear his thoughts. He wanted to join Drak in sleep, but each time his eyes closed, he could only see Hanna's strained expression, gasping for breath.

Adamus remained in a half-kneeled position leaning against the stone table next to her body and the severed heads of his kin. From time to time, he would splutter or sob only to grumble and groan back into a mumbled prayer.

Dorofej, hair greyed and wrinkles thickened around the eyes, remained at the opening of the chamber. He sat cross-legged in his robes, head resting with eyes open, against the doorway. Branimir did not think the black mage kept watch, but instead wandered among his own inner thoughts. His eyes were glossed over, and he hummed to himself.

If Branimir did not know any better, he may have claimed the black mage was dead, or at least, his spirit had fled from his own skin. His body appeared as lifeless as the dead tossed around the catacombs.

The ruckus of the wolves eventually subsided, and the tomb quieted.

Sleep overtook Branimir. He slumped his head back, feeling dizzy with exhaustion. Soon, a dream begun to form, twisted and accursed. The din of battle echoed in his ears. Branimir stood over Hanna. She struggled against him while he suffocated her breath over and over again. Blood spewed, and her breath speckled with dark flakes like ashes around his fingertips. All the while, Drak whispered in his ear.

Even in his half-sleep state, he could feel his chest tighten and his feet kick, fighting against what he was doing. He could hear her wails under his hands, begging him not to take her life.

Without warning, the reverie changed. Hanna disappeared, and he was back in the catacombs. Near him hovered the green apparition Drak had described, gripping him and shrieking. His ears reverberated with the cries of a thousand dead souls. He fought, contorting his body, trying to see the ghostly face of the undead female. It cried out to him, words jumbled. He strained, crumpling helplessly against the phantasmal spirit.

Branimir lurched, waking from the horrendous nightmares. His scream caught in his throat. He stifled a cough and swallowed. The dryness in his throat burned, but the coldness of his nose caught his attention. The chamber had grown icy since he had fallen asleep, and he realized the fire had been snuffed.

The time that passed while he slept could not be measured. Adamus slept soundly, hunched over, near the smoking residue of the fire, and Dorofej remained unmoved near the hollow that led into the catacombs, his blue eyes open, but unmoving though he were sleeping.

Feeling as though something were not quite right, he turned toward Drak.

"Drak!" Branimir yelped, scrambling to his feet. He searched the room for any sign of the red Kras, and nothing was found. Drak had gone. "Hurry and wake yourselves. Drak is missing."

Adamus rolled over, rubbing his eyes. His shield grated against the stone. What are you going on about?" The Anshedar hesitated while Branimir skittered towards the doorway, peering into the hallway.

"Drak?" Dorofej yawned, moving out of Branimir's way. He, too, twisted his neck to look out the doorway. "Gone, he must've, but how did he slink by?"

"He would not be so foolish as to go above ground to face the simargl by himself," Adamus said. "It would be suicide. He must be in the catacombs somewhere."

Branimir agreed.

"I say, why would he run off?" Dorofej pulled himself to his feet. His movements were slow, telling of his lacking nimbleness.

"I don't know," Branimir said. "But he could be in danger. We have to find him."

"Indeed. Leave him in the catacombs alone, we cannot."

Adamus ripped the bottom cloth from his cloak to make a torch, kindling it from the ash while he talked. "Tis a maze in these tunnels. Even if he wandered off for no reason but to explore, he may not find his way back here anytime soon."

Branimir exhaled. "Do you know the pathways down here, Adamus? I would not want to become lost among the dead."

"Of course," Adamus said. He stepped into the passageway and started off with determination. Branimir followed with Dorofej drifting behind him. "As a child, I spent more time here at Garain'l with my family than at my own home in Ariadne. I could walk these tunnels blind if necessary."

"Necessary, it is not, Adamus," Dorofej said.

Branimir thought not to say anything about Adamus roaming around the ruins as a child. Instead, he looked over his shoulder to see Dorofej clench his jaw, his face altering from confusion to an expression of unease.

"What is wrong, Dorofej?"

"Struck me, it suddenly has, a *dream* I had before awakening. Fear, I do, a boding evil is at work."

"I also had a dream that woke me," Branimir said. "I saw the green ghost. It seemed there was something familiar about it, but I could not place it."

Dorofej hummed, the greying beard bobbing over his chest. "Careful, we must be. I say, its evil essence still lingers in the air, foul and malevolent."

"The Likhyi?" Branimir asked, facing Adamus once more.

Dorofej responded. "For certain, I cannot be."

"Is there a difference in sensing this ghost and the dead, or even the Likhyi?" Adamus muttered, looking at Hanna one last time. "Do not cause alarm among us when the situation is already dire, eh? Let us find Drak and be gone from Garain'l. I could not bear another among us dying."

Branimir and Dorofej grunted in agreement, and the hero-warrior led them out.

Adamus turned left beyond the staircase that led out from the shrine. Branimir looked toward the path out, and was glad to not see a single, loitering simargl.

As they walked, Dorofej said, "Adamus, hear me when I say, whatever the final outcome of our adventure here at Garain'l, it is greater than you and your intention in coming here. Nothing here, did you cause. If you remember, Branimir and I came of our own accord."

Branimir bit his cheek. Dorofej's words were not entirely true. He had brought Drak and Bran here, and with little explanation.

The hero-warrior spun the torch back and forth, illuminating the corpses piled up on either side of the path. "I hear you. Yet the outcome thus far is already more than I wish to bear. Hanna's death will haunt me for the rest of life, no matter how long or short it may be."

"Her death is no more your fault than any other in our company, yes? Tell him, Branimir. The death of friends and more, you have known well," Dorofej said.

"Who do you think you are speaking to?" Adamus barked, not bothering to look back. "Her death is completely your fault, Dorofej. How dare you ask Branimir to support your shallow words."

Dorofej tilted his chin with confusion. "Shallow?"

"Yes," Adamus said. "You demanded we fight a battle we could not win. You would not listen. I have fought many wars for many reasons. I know war, and I know death. I also know glib, and you're full of it."

Dorofej tensed.

"The past is done with," Branimir uttered before Dorofej could retort. "When we are finished we can assign blame, but in this moment, we must find Drak."

Branimir heard Dorofej scrape his foot against the ground behind him, likely stumbling in the dark, or from shock.

Adamus fixed his gaze on the tomb ahead. "Branimir is right. We will talk of this later, if it is even worth talking about."

The three walked in silence for almost half an hour. The tunnels beneath the shrine proved to be a maze. Burial chamber after burial chamber were passed over without any sign of Drak.

"I am not seeing even a scuff mark among the dust," Branimir finally said. "Maybe he did not come this way after all."

Adamus stopped the trek. "Tis likely. Though, the Kras has light feet. I hate to come so far and then turn back when he may be around the next bend."

"True, Kras are light-footed, but not so light as to walk on air," Branimir said. "If he came this way, he would have had to sprouted wings and flown."

A strained bellow, high-pitched and full of torment, abruptly sounded from the path ahead. It may have screamed for help, or it may have shouted nothing at all. Yet the tender lamenting was so heart-wrenching the noise caused Branimir's knees to weaken.

"Drak," he supposed, keeping himself from sprinting ahead. He looked to Adamus apologetically. "Well, either he is ahead, or there is an echo."

"Or, duped by something direr, may befall us," the black mage warned. "Proceed, we must, but with care."

Adamus held the torch outright again. "Your endless foreboding is trying, Dorofej." Despite the words, Branimir took note Adamus freed his axe from its holding before shuffling further down the hallway.

The bewailing of the shrill cry penetrated their ears several more times as Adamus led them through the tunnels. The torturous noise made Branimir cringe in agony. Whether limbs were being severed or flesh was being burnt, he could not tell, but the resounding racket gave him the impression of torture. Branimir felt sickened.

The time spent wading between the skeletons triggered a sensation of nausea, but Branimir pressed on after Adamus. The blubbering wails intensified in duration and length, and though there were no true signs indicating their closing on something tangible, besides sound, Branimir ascertained they were near.

The chamber ahead was dark, and if anything, appeared darker than the veiled hallways of the shrine. The doorway was hollowed like the other burial chambers, but the blackness within was unfamiliar to the Kras. It deepened in pitch unlike anything Branimir had ever seen.

A scream ricocheted. *Drak.*

Dorofej gripped Branimir's shoulder, nearly causing him to scream in response. "What is seen within, you must tell us?"

He juddered, instinctively stepping back, fear crawling up his spine. He did not know how to explain the visage before his eyes, and could only think of what Adamus and Dorofej, and other living things, underwent whenever the sun fell from beyond the horizon. Branimir had never known darkness until now.

"I...I cannot see anything. It is *dark*."

Chapter XV

Branimir gawped shakily into the abysmal black, overwhelmed with feelings of despair. He had never looked into nothingness before. Though, the stabbing in his gut came from the overwhelming sensation that the nothingness was looking back.

Not in a thousand years had he ever felt this sense of dread. He shuddered from the tip of his crooked nose to his bent toes. His thin dark hairs on the base of his neck prickled. His words flooded from his lips, caught in the breath he had been holding. "I feel scared, Dorofej." He managed to say, turning to the black mage for help. "I can't go in there, even for Drak."

The words brought vomit to the edge of his throat. He had been unable to save Mojmir at Melkorka, and now, Drak would die too.

"I feel it." Adamus forestalled his gaze from the chamber. The beastly man's voice cracked as he retreated a couple steps, trembling. "I have fought hundreds, and now, there is this thought…" The hero-warrior dropped his axe to his feet. His hands balled into fists. "…it is useless."

"I say, pick up your axe, Adamus," Dorofej insisted.

While Dorofej's words were sensible, Branimir knew the tone of the black mage. The broken tenor reminded him of when he and Dorofej had faced Osiscica, the giant white snake, who lingered in the halls of Heshayol, in the Netherworld. They had lived long enough to laugh at Dorofej's rampant, girlish screaming.

Here and now, Branimir could not laugh.

Adamus bumped into Branimir, stepping backwards again, oblivious to Dorofej. "Tis hard to admit my dread, but whatever lies in there is neither human or inhuman." His torchlight wavered, the light rescinding away from the darkness, and meandering back toward the passageway from which they had come.

"Please," Branimir whined, "say the word and we will flee. What else could we possibly do?" Words filled his mind and he repeated them, no matter how strange they sounded to him. "A single life cannot be worth our three."

"Hold fast to your wit, you must, or you will be bound to this darkness," Dorofej commanded, stopping Adamus with his hand. "Neither of you are yourselves. Leave Drak to his fate here, we must not. No more than leave Bohumir on the dastardly road to Melkorka, yes? Stand fast!"

Drak's screamed filled with the gurgle from inside the chamber.

Adamus clutched his fist around the torch. For a moment, the Ariadnean hesitated under Dorofej's gaze. He finally spoke between clenched teeth. "What must we do?"

"Grab your weapon and be ready for whatever comes, you must," Dorofej inched closer toward the blackness.

"And, what about me?" Branimir asked, thankful that Adamus swiftly scooped his weapon back from the ground.

"If the darkness wanes, you find Drak and pull him free," Dorofej gulped. "And then we flee."

Branimir steadied his breath. His rib cage rattled with every gasp of air, bracing himself against the stone wall. The stench from the bodies at his feet strangely intensified, suffocating him. He did not know if he could grab Drak from the shadows. It may swallow him whole, too. "And, what if it does not?"

Dorofej did not answer, casting light within the tunnel, illuminating all but the gloom within the chamber. His light pulsated in the passageway. "Ancient devil, your name, tell me," Dorofej commanded at the impermeable shadow.

A hissing wind swirled from inside the chamber, shade forming upon shade. The gust blustered against Dorofej, causing his beard and robes to whirl against his body. No shape formed but a crowing voice cackled, primordial and crashing against them. It sounded more like a god than a devil.

> *'One of the eight who dwell within,*
> *Named the Old-dark akin to men,*
> *From nothingness, from earth and sky,*
> *From the Deep returned, called Likhyi.'*

"Likhyi," Branimir gasped, rattled by the eerie voice. His fear could have stopped his heart cold. He felt the sudden urge to kneel to the blackness, but somehow kept his feet beneath him. This spiritual essence held more strength than anything he had ever known.

"I say, the Ash Tree has not been destroyed, and still births life to this land. You have no power here, yes?" Dorofej cried. "Return to your casting. Depart from this place."

> *'Too weak the Ash Tree has become,*
> *When death returned wherever from,*
> *New gods die; Old-dark born anew,*
> *What men made, the eight will undo.'*

"Underestimate, you do, the power of the gods, Likhyi. Too great for you to overcome, they are," Dorofej glowered. "As done in days before our birthing, Marheena, Czern, Dahz, Svarog, Perom—"

> *'The time for salvation has passed,*
> *The frost falls and fades by fire vast,*
> *The age of the Likhyi returns,*
> *The dark within endlessly churns.'*

Drak's whimpering could be heard, but Branimir could not see the Kras beyond the bleakness. Even if he could, it would not matter. He was immobilized by the haunting words, struggling to make sense of their full meaning. The damaged Ash Tree had given the Likhyi enough strength to have some power, but it spoke as though there were a total of eight old gods to be released from the Ash Tree. Branimir could not imagine being in the presence of such powerful beings.

Where the concealed fiend seemed to respond in riddles, or perhaps prophecy, the next few words changed tone, addressing Dorofej directly. The shadows shifted from the depths of the chamber.

O' Dorofej Kaligula,
Ye accursed bloodline cursed Aenar,
Freeing the Old-dark from afar.
Embrace sorrow and ever weep,
Now comes the Tree's eternal sleep.

Branimir perked his ears upon hearing the true surname of Dorofej, spoken by the Old-dark deity, who knew what had long been kept unknown. *Kaligula.* Could Dorofej be a relation to this mysterious Dagmar Kaligula? Unmistakably, Dorofej had kept it secret for a reason, what did the Likhyi mean, saying Dorofej's bloodline had freed them?

The implications haunted Branimir.

"Enough! Unswayed by trickery, we are. Be away, I command you!" Dorofej shouted, using Koldovstvo to further irradiate the light against the black essence of the ancient god. The Likhyi screeched in pain, dipping back into the chamber. Branimir felt strengthened by black mage's display of power while the darkness diminished.

Branimir squealed, inching forward. The black mage held great power to withhold the might of a god.

The thought had barely been had when a howl suddenly absconded from the chamber and the Likhyi struck in full force, a haze emanating from the opening and shrouding Dorofej's magic. The colorless gloom flooded the hallway, mightier than before.

Branimir screamed at Dorofej, urging him to fight. The black mage thundered in defiance. His hair whitened and the old Highborn Branimir had once known at Melkorka materialized before him. Branimir's howl did not lessen when he realized his friend would keep to his principles, killing himself to save all else. Yet though his magic flickered and waned, the light stayed against the devastating power of the Likhyi, and Dorofej still stood in defiance.

"Branimir!" Adamus's howl echoed from stone wall to stone wall as the Anshedar crashed down next to him, the blade of his axe cutting down, scraping and clanging, near his feet.

Branimir gasped, flinging himself sideways. There, from beyond the grave, lay a drooping corpse with its head split from Adamus's blow. Brains, grey and slimy, spilled across the stone. An exasperated moan escaped the carcass.

Before he could utter a word, the dead rose on either side of him, staggering to their feet. Skin sagging, eyes gaping, and insides spilling outright denoted the undead creatures. Unearthly yowls tremored against Branimir's ears. Chaos filled the catacombs.

Again, he found himself without a weapon in the battle. He could not fight the dead with his bare hands.

Adamus wasted no time. Finding his vigor, he flung the torch behind him into the masses of walking dead, and yanked his shield to his arm.

Dorofej roared with intensity against the strength of the Likhyi. The blackness bellowed from the chamber in waves like fog.

"Destroy them all, Adamus, you must," Dorofej groused, his arms shaking, fixated in place to maintain the energy of the delicate light. "Aid you, I cannot."

Branimir scuttled back, watching the Ariadnean slam his shield into the nearest moaning corpse, smashing it into the stone wall before driving the blade through its skull. The undead fell lifeless once more, and Adamus hurled his bulking frame into another without pause. His axe twisted and fell, carved and plunged, over and over into the army of undead that paraded through the catacombs.

The roars of the hero-warrior resounded. He sprung back and forth on either side of Dorofej with the strength and power that gave him the name of hero-warrior, tireless and true.

Branimir dipped from the reaching arms of another undead and crouched behind Dorofej. He thought to scream for Adamus's dagger when he fastened his gaze to the leather belt of a fallen body. Four daggers rested in proper clasps near the buckle.

Luck had finally come to him.

He scrambled for the familiar weapons. Yanking them free, he did not look too closely at the bloodied carcass. Instead, he kept a wary eye on Adamus and Dorofej, who cried out mercilessly against their foes. With haste, he shoved two daggers in his own belt for safekeeping. Then, he gripped the two remaining and rose to his full height, hardly reaching Dorofej's waistline.

The mistakes of Cavell and the myling fled his mind.

The tempest from the Likhyi bayed in the midst, with winds reeling the span of the underground tunnels, igniting life into all the dead inside. From beyond the immediate hall, the undead screeched and stumbled toward them, tripping over the dead collapsing under Adamus's onslaught. The comatose creatures gnashed their teeth, bony hands flailing, with eyes hollowed from rot and rats.

Branimir launched himself into battle, comfortable with the dead while holding the daggers; he might as well have traveled back to the Netherworld. He stuck the nearest dagger into a nearby undead's leg, above the knee, and yanked it free. Ducking his shoulder, he avoided the monster's counter, and plowed the second dagger into the creature's gut, emptying its insides. Branimir stooped two steps back and leapt forward again before the corpse could react. He had to get nearer to kill the creature. His foot found the corpse's thigh, giving him enough momentum to drive both daggers into the undead's chest. The corpse fell helplessly backward, slamming to the ground with a final twitch.

Pulling his daggers free, Bran flipped one to balance the blade between his fingers, and then hurled it into the eye socket of another corpse. He side-stepped, and tumbled, through the dead, slicing and stabbing, until he retrieved his blade from the gory skull.

"Help," Drak's voice rebounded through the bedlam. "Please…"

"Weaker, the Likhyi is becoming," Dorofej faltered the power of Koldovstvo dwindling, and the light shaking against the dark. "Claim Drak, you must, Branimir. Hurry."

Dorofej's cry had never been more desperate.

Branimir vanished, starting toward the chamber where the black fog swelled. Still, he could see nothing within, but at least Drak was conscious.

A corpse swayed in front of him, unaware that Branimir had approached him. He moved quick, cutting his daggers through the tendons on the back of the leg of the undead. The monster crumbled and Branimir pierced his blade through the temple.

"Keep talking, Drak," Branimir yelled, staying invisible. "And I will find you."

"I don't know where I am," Drak snivelled. "I cannot see. I think my eyes have been taken from me."

"It is a dark magic," Branimir said, cutting down another walking corpse with the same method. Ashen blood colored the daggers from the disgusting monsters.

Drak cried out in pain. "Alack! Something has bitten me. Oh, it hurts."

Branimir could only think there was an undead monster within the chamber. He cried out from the doorway of the chamber. "Hold on."

He faced the shadow. And then, with grit, he stepped into the chamber.

No more had Branimir stepped beyond the opening, completely blind, than a green light emitted amongst the magical darkness. A female figure shaped within the burning light.

"The ghost…" Drak cried, curled beneath the apparition with his hands hovering over his leg. Blood oozed from a wound, but Branimir had no time to inspect the injury.

Inches away, crawled one of the undead. The neck looked broken, limply hanging against the shoulder with every vigorous lunge at Drak. The skinned fingers stretched, clawing for its quarry.

Branimir glided across the ground, ignoring the ghost and plunging the daggers into the skull, felling it in a quick swoop. Drak yelled again, for although he likely had seen Branimir within the jaded light of the ghost, he had missed the monster coming for him.

"Be gone," the ghost screeched, ear-piercing, masking the room in her off-colored light.

At first, Branimir thought the spirit screamed at him, but realized her undead gaze was fixated on the shadow. She spoke to the Likhyi.

Drak whimpered next to him while he stared at the woman, empowered with some power in a realm beyond their own, battling against the ancient god. The power of her essence tore through the Likhyi. An unearthly sound rocked the shrine, and the remaining dead collapsed back to the ground wherever they stood. The blackness vanished and the Likhyi was gone.

Dorofej's white light vented from the doorway, connecting with the spirit's magic.

Dorofej lurched through the doorway, gasping, and barely able to stand. Adamus sprung to his side to give him a hand, stabilizing him against his oversized frame. Yet Branimir still found himself gawking at the woman who floated inches above him and Drak.

What seemed like a lifetime passed and Branimir's memory finally gave him the name he had forgotten.

Erzebeth.

Chapter XVI

Erzebeth Navenka, the skin-switching Vucari, who had once claimed she was from the northern ruins of Anaerfell, hovered serenely in the chamber in her ghastly form. She gazed indolently at them, eyes glossed over, lacking any sense of recognition. The brown eyes and dark hair had been replaced with shimmering greens, like emeralds embedded with pale light.

However, despite the difference, the woman was undoubtedly Erzebeth Navenka, who had joined them at Arkaim and traveled to Maharia to protect the Ash Tree, a thousand years ago. She had been missing her hand when she had come with them, punished as a thief by King Merreider Kar—before King Unnvar Grondahl took the throne. Branimir noticed both of her hands were intact in her current form, and as strange as this was, he could only focus on the ultimate fate which had befallen Erzebeth.

Branimir's stomach churned at the thought of her untimely death. She had been captured by the centaurs of the Hyaendi Hills, the Svet, before he and the others had been tricked into… eating her remains. He had done his best to push the memory far from his mind, but upon seeing her, it flooded back in waves.

"I am sorry," he murmured.

Drak kept his hands clasped on his wound and tried to scoot away from the spectral figure. She made no move to stop him.

"Is this the Likhyi?" Adamus doubted, still clinging to his weapon while trying to hold the black mage upright.

"No," Dorofej said, mustache pressed against beard in contemplation. He also recognized her, his blue eyes widening. "I say, how is it you have come to be here, Erzebeth?"

Again, her eyes stared at nothingness, but something moved her to speak. "I have not been called that name for a very long time, but how much time has passed I cannot say. For too long, I have been called the gal of Garain'l."

"They have written songs about you," said Branimir.

Motionless, she remained. "Do I know you? From what age have you come?"

"You *know* us," Branimir furrowed his brow in confusion. "But you died. Why have you not gone on to the Netherworld?"

Erzebeth drifted downward, her emotionless gaze resting on Branimir. "Ah, I remember now; though, it was so very, very long ago. The Kras from Melkorka, and the Highborn, who is not an Anshedar." She faced Dorofej and tilted her chin. "I refused to cross the Kalinov Bridge into the Nine Lands after my soul fled my body. I am not quite dead; I do not think. Though I am not living either. It was a fate I could not embrace, knowing what I knew."

"You kept yourself from death, even after you were killed?" Branimir choked. "How is that possible?"

"I am a Warden of the Ash Tree. I found the means to anchor myself to this world for time beyond time. In life, I thought I had known about the magic of this world, but in death, there has been new truth. I once believed Koldovstvo came from Wolos, and it was the source of my magic. I was wrong. Only the Stuhia and the Highborn use Koldovstvo. The magic of the Vucari is not the same."

Branimir interrupted her rambling. "But how did you stay here with your magic."

She hummed. "A tale for another time, perhaps."

Dorofej scrunched his face. "What is it you know?"

Her answer came without pause. "I told you I had lived for many years, traveling across Maharia and beyond. I may have said something when I had known you before about my adventures and what I had seen. I knew the Carian Council in Lairhein, and also the savants at Anaerfell. Did I not tell you why I had returned to Kalamaar?"

"Say nothing, you did," Dorofej said, trying desperately to stay on his feet with Adamus's help.

Drak groaned, holding his leg. Branimir noticed the Kras tried to stifle the pain to hear the conversation. Branimir listened while tearing a strip from Drak's cloak and tying it around his thigh. The bleeding had slowed.

Erzebeth twinkled, fading slightly before radiating once more. She spoke as though she had a story, which she had waited a thousand years and more to tell. "The Second of Frost, 45 CE, I returned to Anaerfell after receiving a vision from Wolos. The Horned God had implied the Ash Tree was in danger. He called for the Wardens to return to Anaerfell."

"To speak to him?" Branimir asked. "Since when do the gods come to Aenar?"

"He did frequently," Erzebeth said. "Each and every winter. He came to give blessing to the Vucari and to battle Marheena in the north until Strega would ultimately send her back to the Netherworld. But Wolos was slaughtered at Anaerfell. I was there; I saw it."

"You saw the God of the Dead die?" Drak wheezed. "How?"

"I saw two Stuhia fight him in the snows against the mountain," she explained. "I think they killed Wolos, but I cannot say for certain. I don't know if they knew their actions would cause demons to come back from the Netherworld or the Ash Tree would be threatened, or...," she glanced around the chamber. "The Likhyi would eventually return. I am not even certain either of them knew who the Likhyi were. They had said the intent was to defeat death. I can only think they wanted immortality."

"Why did you not stop them?" Branimir howled.

Erzebeth replied without feeling. "You expect me to destroy those who can defeat gods. I am not great. I was Vucari. I did not hold the power of the dragon-slayers."

"What happened to these two men?" questioned Drak.

"They were imprisoned at Anaerfell under the guard of Lahmia. Likely, they are still alive, but weak. The Stuhia's blood allows them to be forever living as long as they do not cast Koldovstvo," Erzebeth explained. "Unlike the Vucari who change our shape at will but age as the Anshedar would."

Dorofej shifted in his robes. Adamus must have noticed because he finally let loose of the black mage, letting him stand on his own.

Drak held a curled fist again against the ground, swallowing a moan from the pain in his leg.

"I have answered your questions," Erzebeth said. "Now, answer mine before I go. Why have you come here? When we were last together, you were meant to protect the Ash Tree from Nedezhda, but the Old-dark—the Likhyi—had come here to Garain'l. Did you fail?"

"Not entirely," Branimir responded when Dorofej said nothing. He had turned his gaze away from Erzebeth as though he were in deep thought.

"What does that mean? The Likhyi could not be here if their essence was not released from the Ash Tree," she said. "The gods had trapped the eight Likhyi in the Ash Tree to give life to Aenar."

"Part of it withered after it was struck by Kaelandur but most of it remained intact." Branimir lost sense of who was in the room with him. He was mesmerized by Erzebeth's knowledge, wishing she had shared more with him when they had first met one another. "Though, the last Dorofej or I saw the Ash Tree, it was a thousand years ago at the battle of Shayol Domier."

"What?" Adamus bellowed. "What trickery is this?"

"Huh, you are talking about the pigsticker? And," Drak squawked, "stone the crows! Are you really Branimir Baran, from times long past? How is that possible? How could you have lived so very long?"

Branimir hung his head, realizing his error. The Kras spitballed question after question. There was no hiding who he was anymore. He used Erzebeth's words. "A story for another time."

"What is this thing you call Kaelandur?" she asked.

Branimir raised his eyes to the green haze, hardly believing the question he was hearing. Though, when he thought hard enough, he remembered Erzebeth had most likely never seen the dagger or heard of it in her time with them.

Adamus and Drak eagerly awaited the response, watching Branimir.

"It is a copper dagger, created by the Highborn to behead Nedezhda Mager back at Melkorka," Branimir finally said.

Adamus said, "The knowledge of the Kras is ever amazing."

"A weapon?" Erzebeth lifted her voice for the first time, in shock. "A weapon was created by the Highborn?"

"Yes," Branimir said. He noticed Dorofej became more uneasy in his dark robes. He stared at the bodies littering the ground of the chamber.

"It must have been crafted with Koldovstvo then," she claimed, "or it would not have the power to cut through the Ash Tree. Only magic, gifted by the gods, could destroy it."

Branimir jarred his memory, nodding. "Nedezhda said Jhar, another Highborn, had created the dagger at Melkorka. I remember her claiming he had crafted it with magic when we were at Arkaim."

"Where is Jhar now?"

Bran lifted his head, troubled that he had to answer the questions. "He died in the first battle at Melkorka. I watched him fall."

"You are certain he is dead?" Erzebeth asked.

"Yes."

Erzebeth now focused her gaze on Dorofej. "Then, he did not create the weapon."

"Alack! I do not understand what you two are going on about," Drak mumbled, ridding himself of whatever fear had ailed him before. "How can you be certain?"

"The Highborn are not a natural race of men," Erzebeth said. "They are born from the union of the Anshedar and Stuhia. The Stuhia, or dragon-men, is where they claim their power; it is where the power of Koldovstvo comes from."

Adamus finally interrupted. "Tis interesting but what does it have to do with this *kae…kae…*this copper dagger?"

"The Stuhia culture forbids any of their kind to create weapons for this very reason. It has been as such since the First Age. Their magic embedded in armaments makes the blade unbreakable with one exception." Erzebeth kept her eyes locked on the black mage. "It becomes destroyed when the maker is destroyed."

"*What?*" Branimir shouted. "You mean to say if the Highborn who created Kaelandur dies, the copper dagger will cease to exist."

"Yes," Erzebeth said.

Branimir's mind riddled. There could only be one other who could have made the dagger. His eyes locked onto the black mage.

Dorofej. It made no sense. There had to be another explanation. Branimir had thought Dorofej to be furious at the creation of Kaelandur. He had once even ridiculed Falmagon and Kinhar for its making.

There had to be something more to be said.

Dorofej at long last rumbled. "I say, Erzebeth, our quest here on Aenar is not yet done. The Ash Tree can still be saved and the Likhyi will be trapped again, yes? Something worthwhile, you should tell us."

The ghastly figure distended, rising toward the ceiling of the catacombs. Branimir could only guess Erzebeth spurned Dorofej's words. He suggested the information she shared had been worthless to them.

"You are ever wise," Erzebeth said in a mocking tone. "I trust you will find and protect the Ash Tree before further harm will be done. But the Ash Tree is weakening each day and the Likhyi are growing stronger."

"In what way is it becoming weaker?" Branimir wanted to know. "What is causing it?"

She had become emotionless again. "I do not know. I can only feel it."

The Vucari woman had begun to fade.

Drak tried to stand and fell back down on his injured leg. "Where are you going?"

"To see whether Wolos is dead, and if so, that he is reborn. If you fail, the God of the Dead may be our only chance to defeat the Likhyi, and restore balance," she answered, and then she was gone.

"Impossible," Dorofej grunted, shaking his head at the ceiling where Erzebeth had disappeared.

"Tis indeed," Adamus said, looking around the room at his companions as if seeing them for the first time. "The conversations had in the past few days have truly come to light. Czern's breath. The two of you are setting out for dark times."

Drak snivelled still, his hands wrapped around his leg.

Branimir ignored the Kras, looking to Adamus, hoping against hope the hero-warrior would join them in their fight.

He was disheartened by the Anshedar's words. "I will lead you to Ariadne, but there we must part ways. My past years have seen too much death, and now with Hanna…" he sighed, shuddering. "I cannot stomach it any longer."

"I say, you are required to do nothing, Adamus Ebordon," Dorofej dipped his head. "Already, learned much at Garain'l, we have; and survived, we would not have, without you."

Adamus stroked his beard. "Tis true, I suppose. Many dark things I have seen, especially when fighting against the desert people, but nothing like this. I have to ask, what was said when you and the Likhyi were speaking to each other?"

Dorofej started to open his mouth, but Branimir interrupted.

"I don't understand. What are you asking, Adamus?" Branimir scrunched his nose at the hero-warrior. "Could you not hear them?"

"Hear them?" Adamus lifted his hand. "The two were speaking in some abysmal tongue I have never heard before. Did you not hear it, Branimir? It sounded like a drowning demon, grating as constant thunder. Czern's breath! What was said?"

Branimir fingered Ojenek in his pocket, realizing the stone had allowed him to understand the conversation between the black mage and the Likhyi. It did have a purpose after all.

Dorofej returned with a smile. "I would prefer not to repeat such swearwords, yes? I say, let us rest and then leave at once for Ariadne. My artifact awaits, it does."

Chapter XVII

Branimir blew his breath into his cupped hands, and then tucked them into his red cloak. For three weeks, they had been trudging through the Dyndaer without any sign of Ariadne.

Adamus had guessed the trek to Ariadne would have taken a week or less from Garain'l. Though, this would have only been true if they had been traveling by horseback. Sadly, to their dismay, their mounts were found half-eaten by simargl just outside the stone archway. After regarding the gory scene, glazed with guts, they departed from Garain'l on foot.

The days and nights soon swam together, giving Branimir a sense of discomfort and disillusion. He could not remember how long they had been walking, or how long ago they had built a fire. He heard Adamus grumble ahead of him, likely having similar thoughts.

Again, he wrapped his hands inside his cloak to warm them, catching sight of Drak limply lying across the Ariadnean's arms like an infant. Two days ago, Branimir had woken to find Drak feverish and unconscious. Adamus had carried him ever since.

Bran checked on him when he could. Every so often, Drak would wake—long enough to swallow a few snowberries or water—and then he would mumble incomprehensibly and fall asleep again. The last time, Drak's skin had felt hot to the touch, and his heart had beaten so faintly, Branimir had struggled to find it. Dorofej, who had been completely exhausted from his battle with the Likhyi, did not have the magical energy to heal the poor Kras. If they did not reach Ariadne in the next few days, he feared Drak would die from his fever.

Branimir dropped his eyes to Adamus's feet, failing to see any city through the trees.

"Not much further," Adamus mumbled from under his beard. "A bit more."

Outside of his grousing, Adamus had murmured similar sentiments each day while they walked. Branimir gritted his chattering teeth. "We will make it."

Another three hours passed before the towering walls, as large as the trees of Dyndaer, caught Branimir's attention. Torches marked the tops and lanterns were situated around the base of the fortifications. The wall stretched as far as Branimir could see in either direction.

"At last, Ariadne," Adamus said, taking a breath. Drak still lay unconscious in his arms, curled up against his chest and ruffled, black beard. "Been three years since I have seen my sister. I had not thought the war campaign would have lasted so long." The Anshedar swelled his chest and exhaled again. He looked back at Branimir and Dorofej. "I suppose tis nothing compared to what you have lost. I cannot imagine what it would be like, knowing how long it has been since you have been with old friends or family, eh?"

Branimir forced a smile. His face was too frozen to attempt a suitable response. Instead, he said, "What time is it?"

"Tis well past supper time," Adamus guessed. "Likely closer to midnight."

Branimir's stomach rumbled. They had not stopped to eat since…he could not remember when they ate last.

Dorofej sludged forward, the snow crunching beneath his feet, urging them along. For once, he did not appear interested in lengthy dialogue. "Let us find a place to rest and then part ways, yes? I say, you need to reunite with your family, Adamus."

The Anshedar nodded, keeping his eyes fixated on the walls in front of him.

"I say, at least the trees have thinned," the black mage said, leading them toward the lofty gates. "Beginning to wonder if we would ever make it out of the darkness, I was. If it were not for the trees, I would think I was walking through the Netherworld again, yes?"

Branimir half-listened to Dorofej, finding it difficult to keep his eyes off the place stretching along the river. No buildings were raised higher than the walls, but with the gates opened, he could already make out the shops and houses.

Each building had been constructed from the same timber, without any hint of stone, built directly against one another.

"How far are we from Strega's Deep?" Branimir asked, turning his head to the south. He could almost smell the saltwater.

Adamus cleared his throat, uncomfortably shuffling Drak in his arms. "Tis a day, maybe a day and a half, from here on horseback. If you need a boat, there is an Ariadnean port at the mouth of the river, or you can travel further up the coast to a Lilitu city. That is, given nothing has changed while I have been away."

A cold chill swept Branimir's back. Hanna's dimming eyes stared back at him from nothingness. He did not want to face another Lilitu for as long as he lived. "I thought the Lilitu lived on another continent, in Haemus Mons."

"The bulk of them live in Haemus Mons, but the Lilitu have cities all along the coast of Maharia. Our two lands are connected, if you did not know. You will see as much if you plan to sail anywhere. Talastein is the largest Lilitu city to the east, and the largest port city in Maharia. Every boat passes through Talastein before venturing any further."

"What for?" Branimir asked.

"Inspection," Adamus said, repositioning Drak in his arms and following Dorofej through the gates. The handful of guards barely stopped the conversation they were having when they passed by.

Branimir could only guess that visitors frequented Ariadne more often than a place like Cavell. The Anshedar continued, "The Lilitu have complete control on trade down here. If they think you are smuggling anything by them, they will take your head and feed it to the fishes."

Branimir gulped a mouthful of air.

"Worry about it, we will not," Dorofej said.

Branimir's feet crunched against the snow. The paths were perfectly squared between what appeared to be blocks of adjacent shops and houses. He noticed the shops were closed, and there were few people on the street.

Dorofej peered around the streets, possibly recognizing how late it was. "I say, we will take a boat north for Melkorka as soon as I have located Alden and Sulanna."

"Tis my hope they are still waiting for you, Dorofej. Ariadne is not the worst of places to hole up, but tis quite bleak in the winter," Adamus replied.

Bran had gotten the impression that the artifact Dorofej sought was important, but the black mage had still given him no indication as to its identity or purpose. He reminded himself to press for the details later, and instead, he asked, "What about Drak? Should we seek out someone to help him?"

"Look for Alden and Sulanna, first, we should," Dorofej said. "Besides, too late to find a human healer, yes? Look for one in the morning, we may."

Adamus grunted. "I agree. You won't find a healer at this hour."

Dorofej added, "But wait for Drak to recover, we must not. We should hurry for Melkorka and find the boy, yes?"

Branimir twitched his nose. He had been saying to pursue Bohumir since Cavell and had argued against bringing Drak since Ojenir. He hoped Dorofej's rationality had not come too late. Bohumir had been gone for over a month now. Anything could have happened to the boy.

"Here," Adamus stopped in front of a wide inn, Greywood, pointed towards the sturdy door. "Tis Hoda's place, and she'll do right by you. If your friends are not here, they might be over at the Scythe and Chalice, but I would not count on it. Her stewed mutton is worth the silver. Better than Gorg's oat biscuits."

"There are only two taverns in Ariadne?" Branimir asked. He twisted to look at the oversized keep towering above the buildings several streets away.

"No, no. There are dozens, but only two worth mentioning," Adamus grinned.

Branimir suddenly realized he did not want to part from Adamus. He rather enjoyed the Anshedar's company.

His stomach growled. "Well, I am ready to eat something. I am tired of boiling snow and chasing rabbits."

"Come on," Adamus stepped toward the door. "I will help you get settled."

The door closed behind them and the innkeeper waved them to the countertop. The place only had a few late-night patrons left, sipping at their mugs.

As they approached, the woman eyeballed Drak warily in Adamus's thick arms. "Welcome to Greywood. Name is Helda and…" she paused, raising her blue eyes. "Adamus Ebordon, is that you?" She pushed her long dark hair behind her ears, staring wistfully at the man.

"Helda," Adamus half-grinned, "tis good to see you. Is Hoda in the back? A bit late to still be cooking, eh?"

The young woman skimmed the tavern for a moment before returning her attention to Adamus. "Died from a sickness last year. I have been keeping up the place."

"Oh! I am sorry," Adamus said, his brow knitting.

Helda ignored the sentiment. "It is good to see you home, at last. Are these friends of yours? Need a room?"

Adamus nodded. "Friends, indeed. It has been a long road and they could use good food and a rest." He looked to Drak in his arms. "And, this one needs a healing touch."

Branimir listened, gladdened to be called a friend by Adamus. He felt pleased, too, that Dorofej had been included. After Garain'l,

Adamus had said little to Dorofej about Hanna's death, who he had given blame. Something about the urgency of protecting the Ash Tree, and their encounter with the Likhyi, had resolved his accusations.

"I see," Helda grimaced at Drak. "Best keep him from my customers. Take him up to one of the rooms and I will call for Mira, the herbal healer, in the morning."

"Thank you," Branimir blurted. "Thank you for your kindness."

The innkeeper smoothed her apron, and then shooed them toward the stairs. "Tis not a problem. I'll have a meal waiting when you come back down."

Adamus and Dorofej led the way up the stairs to the room, where they found two beds. After lying Drak down, Adamus left the room and returned with an extra bedroll from Helda. It only took a few moments to situate the room with Drak occupying the bedroll in the corner.

Afterward, Adamus excused himself, eager to find his sister. The farewell was quick with awkward waves. Adamus finally backed out of the room, wishing the best, and skittered away into the city of Ariadne.

Once Branimir checked on Drak again, the two eventually returned to the commons to eat. As promised, Helda had a meal ready as soon as they stepped off the bottom rung of stairs.

Song and storytelling had ended hours ago. Sitting alone in the Greywood, Dorofej and Branimir were served intermittently by Helda while she cleaned off tables and stools. Bran hardly noticed. The meal tasted better than anything he had eaten since Cavell, and soon, he had gulped down his stewed mutton and pecan bread. The wine he savoured was stale, but still more flavorful than melted snow. Dorofej ate with equal intensity, drinking three glasses of plum before suggesting they head back to the room to rest.

Branimir knew night would be turning to morning in a few hours. As tired as he was, he needed answers from Dorofej before resting.

He waited until they had reached the room and closed the door. While trying to formulate his question, Branimir checked on Drak, who looked sickly thin. His soft snores were muffled, speaking to what little energy Drak had left. His forehead felt warm, but not nearly as hot as it had earlier that morning. After several days, Branimir hoped the fever might break soon.

The bite on his leg from the corpse had scabbed over. It continued to seep yellowish fluid from the cracks in the hardened shell, but even it looked better. The skin around the mark had darkened against his red skin, but no longer had any tint of blue or green like it had a week ago.

"He will be okay," Branimir said, standing back to his feet and shuffling toward his bed.

Dorofej had not bothered to remove any garments, or even his boots. He simply threw himself down on the bed, bones creaking with the boards beneath. "Hoped they would have had feathered pillows, I did. Suppose there are no chickens to pluck in the Dyndaer, yes?"

Branimir shrugged, clasping his hands together in his lap and sitting down.

"What is the artifact, Dorofej?" Branimir garbled nervously. The alcohol had not jumbled his words, but his wits wavered when bringing up the question again.

Dorofej sat up, eyes bright beneath his bushy, white eyebrows. "Oh, Branimir," he smiled, teeth wide and cheekbones high, "the skull of Moreth, it is."

For what had seemed so secretive on the road from Cavell suddenly was expressed in the most jovial of moods.

Branimir winced.

The answer did not help him understand more. He sat there and blankly looked at Dorofej, who grinned back at him with purple, plum-stained teeth. The black mage clearly was sloshed on wine.

The name sounded familiar but Branimir could not place it. "What are you talking about? Who is Moreth?"

He chortled, "I say, Branimir, your memory is slipping from you. The Patrician of the Kadari when we were at Shayol Domier, Moreth was. Fled into the night when Falmagon assumed control, he did, and ventured south into the realms of the desert people, yes? There he learned the ancient, dark arts of Runista and acclaimed a power to restore youth without the Ash Tree, and soon after," Dorofej paused for emphasis, wiggling his eyebrows, "lost his head."

"How do you know all of this? We were trapped in the Netherworld for a thousand years."

"Klukas." Dorofej said plainly. "An eye on him, I had, and Falmagon. Ha!"

The black mage tittered, throwing himself back against the bed and almost smacking his head against the wall.

Branimir barely remembered the man who Dorofej spoke of, but did remember there being a leader at Shayol Domier so many years ago. It was a fleeting thought and hardly been important to him at the time.

"What is Klukas?" At every bend, Dorofej had another secret.

"A place which only the Stuhia can travel, it is," Dorofej said, finally admitting to his true birthing. "A place between this world and the next where the spirit can travel, yes? I say, we, Stuhia, use Klukas to scout ahead mostly, but long ago, I discovered the know-how to locate people."

"You can find anyone?"

"Hmm," Dorofej lifted his eyebrows, "unless they know how to hide themselves from the power of Koldovstvo."

Branimir gaped. "That is how you found me at Ojenir then?"

Dorofej nodded. "Worried of losing you, I never was, Branimir."

"And what about objects," Branimir urged, "can you find them too? The Ash Tree?"

The black mage shook his head. "Impossible, it is."

Branimir slumped his shoulders. "I don't understand why you hide your secrets from me, Dorofej. You could have said something even before we parted at Strahil. I was worried I'd never see you again." Branimir frowned, shaking his head. He watched his old friend lose himself in drunken laughter "Have you seen Falmagon?"

"For short while, I could," Dorofej said, holding back his snort, "but hidden from me, he has been."

"Why?" Branimir asked. The black mage quickly lost his laugh and scowled, leading Branimir to guess, "Dagmar Kaligula? Is that why? You are a Kaligula, too, are you not?"

"I said," Dorofej blinked. "Talk about Dagmar, I will not."

Bran clenched his fists. "Then, tell me, what are you going to do with the skull of a dead man?"

"Restore my life, I will," Dorofej said, sitting upright again with newfound youth. He admitted. "Of the Kaligula bloodline, I am, gifted with Koldovstvo, and more so, the crux to touch the void and the essence of living things. Reach through space and time to steal what Moreth gained in Haemus Mons, I will. His gift of youth I will take on myself, being young again, and then, venture to the Ash Tree, we will."

Branimir's jaw dropped. If he had trouble speaking before, the struggle was now tenfold. "I—I mean, you—the power is…" he took a breath. "You would kill yourself doing something like that, would you not?"

"Close to it, I may," Dorofej shook his head, "but know how to use Koldovstvo, I do."

"I thought you were a healer."

"Yes, yes," Dorofej nodded, "and lucky, I am, to have the gift of healing, too, but manipulating the void is in my blood."

He was shaking uncontrollably, pulling the pieces together. "So, at Garain'l, you…you knew you would not die? You knew there was a way to be young again once coming to Ariadne?"

"Never does one know whether death will come, but at Cavell, I had hope," Dorofej grinned, "when the Count told me of the letter from Sulanna. In Klukas, something at Garain'l, I saw. Either Erzebeth or the Likhyi, I think. I say, the time spent there was worth it, yes?"

Branimir instinctively looked to Drak, heaving in the corner, sweating. He wailed with words forming through the high-pitched scream, reiterating his question, "Why do you hide your secrets, Dorofej? Why could you not tell me?"

His smile dispersed. He took a moment, teeth clacking and lips parting. "I say, what has happened?"

"For a thousand years, there has only been you and me, and no one else." Dorofej paled instantly, and Branimir struggled to find his words. "I don't have anyone, Dorofej. I told you I don't want to die, but seeing you die is worse."

"Death has never been welcomed, Branimir, but come eventually, it will," Dorofej drew back, "even for me."

"No," Branimir flinched. "You have saved me time and time again. It is not fair that you can save me, and I cannot save you."

"I say, loss is something we all must learn, yes?"

"No," Branimir squealed. "You don't feel it. You keep me alive. Why? Why do you keep saving me?"

Dorofej swallowed, standing from the bed.

Branimir realized he had answered his own question. He leaned back. "You are afraid, too."

"Go find Alden and Sulanna, I must," he spurted out, lip quivering. He swayed slightly from the alcohol, keeping his eyes away from Branimir.

"Dorofej," Branimir pleaded.

The black mage staggered out the door and slammed it behind him.

Chapter XVIII

Branimir suspected he had not slept more than a couple hours. He had hoped the inn's bed would bring him some comfort, but after talking with Dorofej, he only tossed and turned. Groggily, he sat up on the bed. His eyes burned, and his muscles ached. He swung his feet over the edge and faced Dorofej's featherless bed.

Branimir gritted his teeth. The other bed was empty, and from the looks of the unwrinkled sheets, Branimir doubted Dorofej had returned last night.

Drak mumbled in the corner of the room, trying to sit from his bedroll.

"Drak," Branimir said, nearly falling over in attempt to get to the Kras's side, "you are awake."

There was no response.

"How are you feeling?"

The Kras groaned, mumbling again. His hand fell on his head as he collapsed back down to his blankets. Branimir scrunched his nose, smelling what may have been sweat mixed with urine.

"Drak?"

As he approached, he noticed the Kras's hair stuck to scalp, soaked in perspiration. The moisture had seeped into the bedroll, and had also dampened the edges of Drak's clothes. His fever had definitely worsened.

Branimir removed the heavy blankets that lay over Drak's legs. "You are going to be okay. You are going to be okay." Branimir patted him, feeling his forehead. "I will get you some water."

> *'One of the eight who dwell within,*
> *Named the Old-dark akin to men,'*

Branimir paused his frantic hands, hovering over Drak in fear. "What did you say?"

Drak's eyelids popped open, eyes wide and blacker than usual, muscles tightening. His mouth popped open and closed like a fish, a strange sound emitting, like the undead moaning in the catacombs of Garain'l.

Drak's real voice sounded weak against the raspy wailing. "Please…no."

Branimir could not understand how two voices came from the single mouth.

"Hang on, Drak," Branimir cried. The Kras writhed on the ground, curling into a ball and clutching the bedroll against his chest. Again, his voice rasped.

> *'From nothingness, from earth and sky,*
> *From the Deep returned, called Likhyi.'*

Bran scooted back on his haunches, the words bellowing out of the small creature like some massive beast. "No, no, no." Branimir whispered to himself. The Likhyi had gotten *inside* of Drak.

Drak breathed heavily, cradling himself by the knees. He rocked back and forth, mumbling while squeezing his eyes shut. Branimir bumped into the bed.

"I am going to get help," he said, afraid to touch the Kras. "I will find Dorofej."

Branimir was up and out the door without bothering to grab his cloak or shoes. He pushed into the hallway, emptied, and rushed toward the stairwell that led into the common room. His feet were like thunder, no matter how small they were, slamming down the staircase and bursting into the wide-open setting where locals and travellers were eating their breakfast.

If the time were not as urgent, he might have enjoyed the scents of porridge, coffee, and fresh biscuits.

Several humans peered at him as he flung himself into the common room but turned back to their meals without a second glance.

"Master Branimir," Helda, the innkeeper, acknowledged with her hands on her hips, chin cocked with her dark hair pulled up into a bun on top of her head. "There is no need to cave the house in with your stomping about. Breakfast is available whenever you want."

Branimir shook his head. "Where is Dorofej?"

"The bearded gent?" she motioned to the door. "Left hours ago. Spent most the night talking with a couple patrons and headed out before first light."

"Alden and Sulanna?" Branimir remembered.

"Those are the ones," she grinned. "You know them, too. Well, I imagine you should, but tis not my business to go around handing out names freely."

"Where did they go?" His voice had elevated and several in the Greywood turned to look at him and Helda. "Did Dorofej leave me a message?"

"No, no message," she tensed her jaw. "Is something the matter? How is your sick friend doing?"

Branimir grimaced. "Not well. He could use some water, and…" Branimir looked about the room, almost wishing Dorofej would suddenly appear. "Did you send for the herbal healer?"

"I did." Helda widened her eyes, a dark blue like pending storm clouds. "Your friend does not have something catching, does he?"

"Nothing of the sort," he said, hoping he sounded believable. "Drak is not going to make anyone else sick, but I think it would be helpful for him to see someone very soon."

"I am certain Mira will be here as soon as she can. You can always go find her, but tis awfully nippy this morning."

He considered the idea, looking to the door. Drak might be fine in the room, unless someone heard him. Branimir was not sure if he should leave him or not.

Helda turned to return to her customers, grabbing his attention. "I will send her up when she arrives. Again, breakfast is ready when you want it."

He nodded, spinning on his heel. Branimir's stomach rumbled at the suggestion of food, but he could not think of eating right now. He scrambled back up the stairs, but with a lighter step, and pushed through the door to his room.

Drak had not moved from his fetal position in the corner and seemed to be snoring softly. Branimir cursed at himself for forgetting a mug of water for Drak.

After a few minutes, he thought he should go find this Mira after all. He put on his cloak and boots and checked his daggers.

He felt Ojenek press against his leg. He paused with his foot halfway in his boot. He had forgotten it was in his pocket. The realization rocked him. Drak may have been speaking in the abysmal speech and not regular language. Branimir could not be for certain, but it would confirm the Likhyi had embodied Drak.

Branimir reached for the door handle when it suddenly swung inwards towards him. He stepped back quickly to be met by the black mage, shrouded in his cowl and cloak. Dorofej wasted no time throwing back the black hood hiding his face. The old, wrinkled Dorofej with the white, tasselled beard had vanished, and the young, vibrant Dorofej had returned.

"Branimir, my friend," he cooed, pushing his red strands aside, "Moreth's skull restored me, it has. And now, pursue Bohumir, we must."

"Dorofej!" Branimir balled up his fists, snorting from his nostrils with irritation. "What has gotten into you? You left me alone all night with Drak."

He raised his eyebrows. "I say, gone to find Alden and Sulanna, I had, and found them, I did." He gestured to the hallway behind him. He looked Branimir over. "Going somewhere, you are?"

Before Branimir could answer, a middle-aged man stepped into the room from behind Dorofej. The man's white eyebrows came together arched over the thick arc of his pointed nose. His head was bald, and his beard was as flimsy as the flurries of mountain snow.

His light eyes pierced into Branimir. "So, this is the Kras. Peculiar creatures with their mountains and their stones. You have many secrets, Dorofej, and even stranger friends." He crossed his arms, studying Branimir.

Bran returned the gaze, seeing the falchion hooked to his belt and the long spear fastened on his back. The Anshedar stood a head taller than Dorofej, and although aged, was almost as burly as Adamus.

"Leave the Kras alone, Alden," a woman, who clearly was Sulanna, piped up from the back before stepping into the room. She glanced at Branimir for only a moment, disinterested, and scanned the room. "What is wrong with that one?" She gestured with her pointed chin, cupped by brown hair.

"Sick," Dorofej said, "since Garain'l, he has been. Bitten by an undead fiend, he was."

"It is worse than that," Branimir said, staring up at the three who crammed into the doorway. "He has a Likhyi inside of him. I heard it speaking only this morning."

"A Likhyi?" Alden huffed through his hooked nose, cringing his neck toward Dorofej. "An *Old-dark*? What is going on here, Dorofej?"

Dorofej paused, staring with intensity at Drak in the corner. The Kras breathed heavily. The sweat dripping from his face glistened, even in the low-lit room.

"Yes, tell us, what tale are we stepping into?" Sulanna questioned in her singsong voice. "For the past two years, Alden and I have risked our necks gathering your relics, betraying the Crimson

Sun, and from what you shared last night, we have likely marked ourselves as enemies to the Kadari. It is near time your secrets are no longer secret."

"Correct, you are," Dorofej cleared his throat, "but if what Branimir says is true, we must make haste for Melkorka. We can speak on the road, yes?"

Alden argued with the Stuhia. "You have shown us a great many things in the past couple years, Dorofej. And, I admit, more times than not, your wisdom has kept us safe. Though if you want our swords on this quest, Sulanna and I need more than faith to ride on." Alden tilted his chin, taking only a moment to swallow. "Now, you told us last night we would need to go to Melkorka but failed to tell us why. We should not have to wait any longer."

Sulanna elevated her tone. "For once, I agree with Alden. I do not answer to blind faith, Dorofej." She paused, raising an eyebrow at the black mage. "You have traveled with me long enough to know as much."

Dorofej groaned in defeat, looking away from his two companions. "Please do not take my silence over the years for faithlessness, but know you well, I did not. Honest with you, I have not been. The Ash Tree is dying, yes? A long while Branimir and I have spent trying to preserve it, and still, it falters. The only explanation for the Likhyi being freed, it is," Dorofej explained. "I say, Branimir and I have come to believe it is at Melkorka. The fight to save it from annihilation will continue there, yes?"

"Why would you think it is at Melkorka?" Sulanna asked. "No one in this age has heard of the Ash Tree beyond the legend. In truth, you have spoken of it more than any other in the known world."

"Most know too little of the Tree of Life to speak of it," Dorofej said, "but exist, it does. Proof of its existence, I am. Drank from its waters and restored my youth many times, I have."

"It is true," Branimir said. "I have seen it."

Alden turned his gaze to Sulanna, grumbling, "We saw what he did with the skull, Sulanna. There is no reason not to believe him.

When we met, I thought him to be just a boy, but he would have had to live several millennia to know what he knows."

Sulanna folded her hands. "I am not questioning his knowledge or his claim, Alden, even if it sounds farfetched. I want to know fighting the Kadari is worthwhile. It will be the end of us, you know?"

"Svarog will bless us, Sulanna," Alden said. "If our deeds are righteous, Svarog will bless us."

The woman scowled in response. "Keep your god out of this, Alden. There are no pearly gates waiting for me. If I am going to die for something, I need to know why."

"Listen," Dorofej interrupted, redirecting with a sense of urgency, "Tell me, who is the Patrician of the Kadari?"

"Patrician Sej," Alden answered, taking the bait. "It has always been a Sej in my lifetime, and the lifetime of my father."

Dorofej nodded with enthusiasm. "And lifetimes before his, yes? His name is Falmagon Sej, and he has been the only Patrician of the Kadari."

"The same man?" Sulanna asked.

"Yes. I say, how else do you think he and the other Kadari have maintained their power of Koldovstvo—and their youth? The answer is clear, yes? Power over the people of this world, the Kadari hold, because their access to the Ash Tree. Freedom the Likhyi found because of Falmagon's greed."

Branimir cringed at hearing the Highborn Longwalker's name. He could not believe Falmagon had found the means to stay alive for a thousand years.

"Very well," Sulanna finally said, "but what does that all mean?"

"I say, the world will perish indefinitely if the Kadari continue to destroy the tree," Dorofej said plainly. "Stop them, we must."

Sulanna swallowed, lowering her chin for the first time since entering the room.

Alden straightened his back. "Do you need further reason, Sulanna."

Sulanna's face paled indicating the weight of Dorofej's words. She shook her head.

"What about Drak?" Branimir asked, pushing Falmagon from his thoughts. "There is an herbal healer in town. I was going out to find her before you came back."

"If Drak is as you say, help him, she cannot," Dorofej said. "Best to leave him here, yes? Too dangerous for him to accompany us, it will be."

Branimir stammered. "From the start, I said he should not have come, but we cannot leave him without anyone to care for him. He will die."

Dorofej glanced behind him, already speaking, "Death would be a blessing to what he will undergo with a Likhyi under his skin, yes? I say, we must do what must be done, Branimir." Dorofej reached into his robes and displayed Kaelandur. "Remember what is at stake, we must."

He slammed Kaelandur down on the table next to the bed. Branimir stared at the copper blade.

"The dagger from the Hyaendi Hills," Sulanna acknowledged, raising her chin once more. "Have you learned of its purpose?"

"Mm," Dorofej nodded. "Always known, I have."

"You lied to us," Alden rumbled, eyebrows rising.

"Forgive me, you must," Dorofej responded. "Created with the purpose to slaughter an evil magus, it was, but has since been tied to ancient prophecies. The talisman for the Kadari, and an object capable of destroying the Ash Tree, Kaelandur is."

"The gods are at play?" Alden mused. "If the Kadari held the weapon, Dahz might be able to keep Marheena and the Old-dark trapped. The dead would pile up in the Netherworld for eternity. But if the Ash Tree is pierced by its blade, the dead will find reprieve in the world of the living."

Branimir scrunched his nose. "I don't understand. If the Old-dark are released from the Ash Tree, won't they kill the other gods anyway?"

"Marheena would have no choice if the Netherworld is flooded with the dead," Alden explained. "If the God of the Dead is really dead, as people say, there is none to take the souls to Thrice Ten Kingdom. Marheena is inundated with the dead."

"I cannot believe I am even listening to this," Sulanna hung her head. "Even if I were to pretend gods cared about this world, the argument does not make sense. Why would Marheena release the Likhyi if their intent is to kill her? Do the gods not have any sense of self-preservation?"

"Misunderstand the gods, you do," Dorofej swallowed, before reiterating what Branimir had heard many times. "Correct, Alden might be. If unbalance is found, a new balance is sought by the gods. The Frozen Goddess has her part to play in the cycle of our existence. Broken, the sequence is, and fixed, it must be."

"So, we are to die by the hand of the Likhyi?" Branimir huffed. "Is that what you are saying? We should go to Melkorka and destroy the Ash Tree ourselves?"

"No, no." Dorofej pulled at his robe.

"Then, we destroy the dagger?" Alden asked.

Branimir covered his face at the thought. He knew they could only destroy the dagger by destroying the creator, considering what Erzebeth had claimed.

"No, destroy the dagger, we cannot," Dorofej said. "We will stop Falmagon from destroying the Ash Tree, yes? And keep the dagger hidden from the world forever, we must."

Sulanna clenched her jaw, clearly disbelieving the entirety of the story. "I am finding this all difficult to stomach, but I will play along. You are suggesting an eternal deadlock? It seems far easier to find the maker, as the Kras suggested, and slit his throat."

Dorofej gulped. "A month ago, Branimir and I ran into an old friend, yes? Suggested a way to bring Wolos back from the dead, she did. Do our part, we must, and hope against hope she does hers. Balance will be reclaimed, yes?"

Erzebeth.

Branimir lifted his head, having no understanding how the Vucari ghost would accomplish such a feat. Though, if Dorofej truly was the creator of Kaelandur, it was the only scheme that left him alive. Branimir did not want to see Dorofej dead.

"Very well," Alden consented, while Sulanna grunted nearby, "but it makes little sense to flee to Melkorka while holding onto the very *thing* the Kadari are seeking. Should we not be fleeing to the south with the dagger, far from their reach?"

Before the black mage could respond, Branimir interjected, looking to the table, "Where is Kaelandur?"

Dorofej spun around frantically, while Sulanna timidly asked, "Where is the other Kras?"

"Drak..." Dorofej looked to the door, still standing open. "Invisible, he must be. Branimir, find him!"

Branimir bolted from the room, racing down the steps into the commons of Greywood. He saw the front door slam shut as he hit the bottom rung of stairs. Helda's shouts to slow down echoed behind him.

Flinging himself into the wintery streets, Branimir peddled onto the snow-layered cobblestone. People ambled up and down the road in all directions, including the patron who had just left the inn.

The walls around the city blocked the wind, but the cold could not be ignored. Branimir's fingers quickly went numb and gooseflesh pimpled his legs even beneath his trousers. He ran willy-nilly through the streets, past the Scythe and Chalice and several shops of trinkets. Desperately, he looked for small footsteps in the snow.

It was hopeless. Drak, possessed by the ancient devil, had taken Kaelandur.

Chapter XIX

Dorofej sat against the wall within the small bedroom of the Greywood. His eyes were glazed over, as though he may have been sleeping, breathing softly through his nose. Alden and Sulanna stood near him like two sentries guarding a chest of silver.

Bran paced the room nervously, glancing at Dorofej as often as he dared. He had returned to the tavern and had told the three of Drak's desertion. Dorofej had wasted little time in falling into this trance-like state. The black mage had said something about locating the missing Kras with Klukas.

Dorofej had talked of Klukas just last night. He had said it was a place between the fabric of this world and the next, somewhere only accessible by the Stuhia people. Dorofej had not only used Klukas to find Branimir at Ojenir but had also used it to keep an eye on Falmagon.

Branimir's head hurt from thinking too hard. When had Dorofej lost sight of Falmagon? When they were in the Netherworld? The black mage never did say. If the Ash Tree were at Melkorka, would Dorofej had seen it when he saw Falmagon?

"How long must this go on?" Sulanna said, sitting up from the bed. "He has been like this for hours."

"So sorry the timing is not appeasing you, my sweetness," Alden mocked, leaning against the wall. "Would you like me to send for a fresh pot of tea, or perhaps, a flutist to help pass the time?"

"Oh, please, would you?" Sulanna swooned with sarcasm, raising her voice. She curled her upper lip losing all sense of being ladylike. Her words were iced over, "I don't understand why you continue to mock me. I have not been in my father's house for the better part of a decade."

Alden grunted. "Once a noble, always a noble."

"For all your blathering about the gods and forgiveness, you truly are merciless, Alden," Sulanna said. "And, may I add, you are making a great impression on the Kras, you crabby, old man."

"I am not a god," Alden said, like it gave him permission to be unforgiving He shifted his blue eyes to Branimir and harrumphed, settling back in his chair. He pulled his own belt knife from its scabbard. "Besides, the Kras doesn't have the mind to be impressed or otherwise by what men do. It is not in their nature. The red broods find fascination that men do anything at all."

The claim caused Sulanna to lift her eyes to Branimir as if expecting a rebuttal.

Branimir lifted his shoulders to his cheeks. "It's true." It had been quite some time since he had heard anyone call him a *red brood*.

Suddenly, Branimir caught sight of Alden's left forearm. The deformed arm was laden with scars. The older man did not seem to favour the arm, but the disfigurement was beyond evident. Branimir wondered how he had missed it earlier.

The coarse skin could only be described as ugly from the elbow to the wrist with indentions and blotches of white daubing his pinkish skin.

Alden took his knife, held it against his forearm, and sliced the blade through the film of flesh. Blood trickled and dropped to the floor.

"What are you doing?" Branimir exclaimed, stepping back nauseously.

Sulanna exhaled noisily and said, "Pay no attention to Alden and his nonsense. Those pockmarks are more from himself than from his enemies. He claims it to be a reminder of mistakes he has made toward his make-believe morals."

Branimir retorted with bewilderment. "But why now? I did not see any mistake."

Alden remained stone-faced, carving another bleeding wound into his arm.

She rolled her eyes, apathetic to Alden's behavior. "He probably didn't say his prayers this morning."

"Not funny, Sulanna. The laws of the gods are not pretend," Alden barked. "You will learn soon enough. Wait until you are judged in the Beyond. Your eyes will be opened to the signs you have chosen to ignore."

Sulanna shook her head. "I don't question there being order to the way things are, Alden, but it's not your way. Even if the gods did create our bodies, they did not do so for us to mutilate them in repentance."

"The body is a simple vessel," Alden said, putting his blade away. Branimir had to look away from the blood. "The real work is done within our spirit. What I do lifts my spirit to greater heights, giving me sanction to enter Thrice Ten Kingdom. Why can you not understand this?"

"Do you not have any duty to lift others up?" Bran asked, almost afraid to enter the conversation.

"Whether other souls make it to the Beyond or not is not my problem," Alden replied.

Sulanna blinked, glancing at Alden's arm before lifting her eyes to the old man. "There are many things I want to understand. But I have no interest in torturing myself."

"You are selfish," Alden said.

"Selfish? You just said you only worried about your own soul," Sulanna mocked.

"You are selfish when it comes to your relationship to the gods. That is the only relationship which matters in the end," he retorted.

"Our relationship doesn't matter?" she challenged.

"Yes, of course," he said, "but it is nothing compared to my allegiance to my faith."

"So much for being humane," Sulanna said.

His throat rumbled. "This is sacrifice, Sulanna."

"It's stupid."

Branimir watched the back and forth in shock. He regrettably brought attention to himself by covering his mouth with abhorrence.

Alden turned his frustration on the Kras. "And, what of you, Branimir? How do you see the gods? What does life mean to you?"

Branimir's mouth dried at the sudden question. He barely thought of these things. He spent most his days trying to survive to the next, not contemplating over the meaning of his existence.

Dorofej stirred, gasping for air and clinging onto his darkened robes. His abruptness interrupted the need for Branimir to respond to the old Anshedar.

"Dorofej." Branimir sprang to his side, putting a hand on the black cloak of his friend. "Are you okay?"

Through heaved breathes, Dorofej said, "Fleeing north by pony, Drak is, making his way for Melkorka. I say, the Likhyi has taken full control of the poor Kras. Little, if anything, remains of the Drak we knew."

"No," Branimir mouthed. "The Likhyi goes to destroy the Ash Tree and gain full freedom."

"I will gather the horses and we will set the pace to intercept him," Alden pushed off from the wall. "The Old-dark can be stopped. It has little power in the Kras."

"You did not see its power at Garain'l," Branimir muttered under his breath.

"No," Dorofej shook his head, speaking over Branimir while catching his breath. "Catch him, we cannot."

"In the middle of winter? In the snow?" Alden fired the questions in disbelief.

"Quite." Dorofej nodded. "Possibly powered by the Likhyi, he is. Make our way south to the shoreline, we must. Find a ship, yes?"

"You want to sail around the bulk of Maharia for the shores of Melkorka," Sulanna reasoned. "You hope to beat the Kras by sea?"

"Another choice, we do not have," Dorofej said.

Sulanna scoffed.

"Come," Dorofej said, pulling himself to his feet, light and agile in his youthful appearance. "With haste, we must move, if we are to outdo Drak."

Alden set out to ready the horses while Sulanna packed his and her belongings. Dorofej sent Branimir to the commons to speak with Helda, since the black mage was unrecognizable in his boyish state. Branimir used Dorofej's silver to purchase rations from the innkeeper.

Within the hour, the four of them were riding out of the wooden gates of Ariadne.

Branimir was nestled on the saddle with Dorofej on a brown horse. Alden took the lead on his darker brown gelding, and Sulanna kept at the rear atop her black mare. They had only made it fifty paces up the snowy path before shouting erupted behind them.

"Dorofej, Branimir. Wait!"

Branimir twisted in the saddle, recognizing the voice of the hero-warrior from Ariadne. "Adamus."

"I am coming with you," he cried, galloping forth on his own black steed. His dark cloak bounced around his strong frame while he quickly gained on their small caravan. He directed his horse in step among their own. Adamus almost fell from his saddle seeing the black mage. "Dorofej, how have you become young again?"

Dorofej smiled, "The artifact I sought has given me the strength for what is to come, yes?"

Adamus bounced his head, his beard waggling. "I had spoken too hastily at Garain'l. You must forgive me."

"What of your sister?" Branimir questioned, paying little mind to the inquiring looks of Alden and Sulanna.

"My sister is well, and she knows my nature." Adamus avowed, "War is what I know, and knowing your quest, I can't abandon you."

Branimir said, "There is no guarantee of coming back, Adamus. You may never see your family again."

Dorofej nodded. "I say, it is much to ask."

"Please," Adamus held out his hand.

"I have no qualms in having another among our numbers," Sulanna interjected.

"The man seems certain in his conviction," Alden said. "Every blade we can gain is worthwhile, especially one who hails from Ariadne. But does he know the full of what he is asking?"

"Mostly. Share the rest with him along the way, we will." Dorofej clasped Adamus's outstretched hand.

Chapter XX

Branimir inhaled the strong scent of ocean water on the frigid breeze. The horse beneath him and Dorofej stamped through the snow with the other mounts, clamoring toward Strega's Deep. From where he sat, he watched the road along the river. The path was clear from any sign of life, and the snow and trees seemed to stretch for miles.

Dorofej provided Adamus the details regarding Drak and Kaelandur. After what had transpired at Garain'l, Adamus hardly seemed surprised by the information. He had only tugged at his beard and grunted when Dorofej paused in his telling.

After a long day's ride in the cold, and with the promise of reaching the Ariadnean port in the morning, they settled for camp late that evening.

While in camp, the warmth of Greywood was a fleeting memory. Winter's chill pierced through Branimir's flesh and touched his bones as if he were without skin. He could only guess the single night of warm fires and hot foods had made the cold seem worse. Yet drops of sweat still slid down the back of his neck, causing his hair to stick to him like a wet cloth. He could not identify the reason for the unwarranted perspiration but found a certain familiarity while sitting near the riverside.

His mind flooded to the myling south of Cavell. The last thing he wanted was another scenario with the impish beasties.

The frozen river bed and the darkened forest were quiet, save the clopping of horse's hooves. Alden had just fed the mounts and made his way back to the small campfire.

Adamus sat near Branimir with his silvery axe across his lap. He must have had similar thoughts as the Kras. "We should stay awake and watch the camp. I'll take the first watch with Branimir."

"I will take second watch with Dorofej," Alden said, removing the spear from his back and laying it behind him on the hardened ground. "We will let sweet Sulanna get her precious sleep."

Adamus, who had picked up on the temperament of the two's relationship, remarked, "Careful, Alden. She is likely to cut off your bits if you keep at it."

Sulanna situated herself with her back against a tree, settling against the hardened ground. "Not like he has ever used them anyway. He'd be more motivated if I threatened to take his sword."

Adamus cackled deep in his chest. "A difficult tossup, to be sure."

A frosty wind sputtered through Branimir's cloak, flapping it around him. He readjusted the hood over his head with a shiver and scooted nearer to the fire.

Dorofej sat on the other side of him, unmoved by the humor and the cold, looking intently into the fire.

Branimir ignored the Stuhia. The black mage had been quiet for the better part of the day. "If it is this cold on the coast, I can only think how cold it will be on the ship," Branimir said.

Sulanna assented. "It will be miserable."

Branimir leaned back to gaze at the far-reaching sky through the few overshadowing branches above. The trees had thinned considerably through the day, looking less and less like the Dyndaer. The trees had likely been cut, not only to build Ariadne, but also to add to the ships at the promised port ahead. The stars were visible again, distant sparkles. Unlike the others, the world was still visible for his eyes.

His mind wandered. He considered his companions were anything but heroes, and yet, they sought out to claim the title. They had ignored the Count's request to find his daughter's *killer*, lost Bohumir to the Crimson Sun, and had, most certainly, failed Drak. He had seen Adamus meddling in dark magic. He believed Dorofej to have created the very dagger which threatened all of creation. And, according to Alden and Sulanna, the Kadari, the most accepted and most powerful leaders in the world, were their enemies. Yet they still ventured forward with the sense that they would do something great, something memorable.

A mild push on his shoulder snapped Branimir from his thoughts, "Don't fall asleep on me," Adamus whispered.

Branimir sprang back to the moment, glancing around the campsite. Dorofej, Alden, and Sulanna had already nestled down for the night. The two men were snoring.

"Sorry," Branimir said. "I was thinking about what makes a person a hero."

Adamus pulled at his beard. "How so?"

Branimir sat up, realizing the hero-warrior from Ariadne, likely had the answers he sought. "I guess I am unsure how to measure heroics. Is it about triumph or defeat?"

"Both and neither," Adamus said, relaxing his hands in his lap. "You do not have to be victorious to be heroic. In the same way, having victory doesn't always earn the name hero. You do what you think is best and leave judgment for the gods."

"What do you mean?"

Adamus answered, "Take the war with Uvil, for instance. When we abandoned the battlefield at Raybin, it had been taken by the Uvil. They had sacked the city, and we had to flee back to Draha."

"The Uvil were victorious," Branimir chimed.

"Sure, they had won the battle; and they continue to win *this* war," Adamus admitted, "but they are not heroes, not to me."

"They must be heroes to their own people," Branimir replied.

"Indeed. That is my point. Tis the same in how we Ariadneans are called hero-warriors by the Anshedar for fighting the Svet in the early wars," Adamus said. "Do you think the Svet call us heroes? No, they call us murderers, rogues, and worse."

Branimir held his head, recalling all he had heard from Adamus over the past month. "So, what does make a man a hero?"

"Being a hero is in here," Adamus touched his chest, "and here." He touched his forehead. "Being a hero is doing what you know needs done, even when standing alone; and when facing defeat, you stay standing."

Branimir thought of his sleeping companions around the fire. "I think we are doing that."

Adamus chuckled. "I would not be here if I did not think so. Now…" he settled back, again. "Tell me about Melkorka."

"That was a very long time ago," Branimir said, surprised by the sudden question.

"But you are the Branimir who Drak thought you to be," Adamus said. "I do not know the history of the Kras, but Drak seemed to think it was important. Besides, tis a tale I would like to hear, and I can think of no better way to spend the next few hours."

The coals of the fire crackled. The snow had melted, skirting the charred wood.

Branimir stood and stepped lightly to gather another log from the pile collected earlier. He took his time, considering Adamus's question. Dropping the wood onto the embers, he watched the sparks dance.

"What do you want to know?" he asked, after sitting cross-legged near the flames. The smoke spiraled toward the tree tops.

Adamus hummed in his throat. "Tis hard to ask anything specific when I know nothing. Tell me about Melkorka."

"Melkorka," Branimir reminisced, "is a castle built near the Crags of Kazimir on the island of Folkmar, one of the Seven Islands. At one time, I thought it was the grandest place in all the world, but the world has grown. Now I think about it, Ariadne's keep is larger than Melkorka. I have not been there since coming back to Aenar."

"Where were you?" Adamus insisted.

Branimir raised his eyes to the bulky man. "I thought you knew. Dorofej and I were stuck…in the Netherworld." Adamus's jaw fell open, staring hard at Branimir. "We were there for over a thousand years."

Adamus narrowed his gaze. "I am unsure whether to believe you, but it would be a strange thing to lie about. A thousand years is a long time to keep alive… Then again, Dorofej looks nothing like he did at Cavell or Garain'l, and I could not guess at your age."

Branimir smiled. "The Kras usually live a long time, sometimes five hundred years; and the Stuhia, it seems, live even longer if they can keep themselves from touching Koldovstvo, which is the source of their aging. But time passes differently in the Netherworld altogether. I am not sure Dorofej or I aged a day in the time we were there, even when he cast his magic. We did not really know how much time had passed until we returned here."

"Did you fight demons?" Adamus said incredulously.

Branimir held his smile, looking at the Anshedar's expression. "It would have been hard to escape the dead without killing a few."

"I imagine so," Adamus flashed his teeth, "and even harder to kill what had already been killed. Though, I cannot imagine what it would be like to see the frozen wasteland, and then to return to Aenar. Did you see Marheena?"

"Thankfully, no," Branimir answered, twisting back to the fire. "But the place was scary all the same. Still," he paused, almost afraid to admit what he had thought many times before. "I miss it sometimes. It was surreal being there amongst the demons in the cold. And the Tower of Eresh was huge, even greater than Melkorka."

Adamus scratched his beard, a look of puzzlement painted on his face. "I do not know what the Tower of Eresh is, but I believe you. I imagine I would be overwhelmed by a place ruled by the gods, even if it were Marheena's abode. I wonder at how much grander the Thrice Ten Kingdom would be."

"I had never thought of that," Branimir pondered, sucking air in through his cracked teeth. "That *is* something to think about. It is scary to think that none will ever see it again."

"I was thinking the same thing after Dorofej told me the full of what was happening. If Wolos is dead, there is no one to lead the dead to the afterlife. We all will become the pawns of Marheena." Adamus swallowed.

Branimir said, "Were you not speaking to your dead family members at Garain'l?"

"Yes," Adamus disclosed, "but I did not know to ask questions of Wolos, and even if I did, the dead don't necessarily know everything because they are dead."

Leaning closer to the fire, Bran warmed his hands. He remembered how confused Nedezhda had been when she returned from the Netherworld. She surely did not know everything.

Adamus added, "Tis sad to think Hanna might be in the Netherworld now, already being warped by Marheena's magic."

Branimir could only shake his head. The thought was something he had not considered at all. "Didn't she worship Marheena—or Lilith—as she called her?"

"In a way, yes," Adamus admitted, "but it did not make her evil, nor did it suggest she should be chained to the Netherworld in death. She respected Marheena for the role the goddess has in the cycle of life and death. Many also find Czern to be evil in nature, who I pay homage to, but does that mean I am evil or should suffer indefinitely?"

"Mm," Branimir wondered. "I suppose not."

"I would hope not." Adamus chuckled. "Many think one god to be greater than another god, instead of recognizing each god has its purpose. If one were to not exist, the entirety of the system would fall apart. All would lose their purpose."

"Like Wolos," Branimir said at the simple realization. "I think Dorofej would agree with you."

Adamus glanced offhandedly at the Stuhia. "Tis the same way we teach men to fight in battle. Stand together or crumble."

Branimir knew not what to say, and Adamus quickly continued as though he had another question he had been meaning to ask.

"Were you always at Melkorka, Branimir? I mean, did you have another place you called home?" He watched Branimir with admiration, intently.

Branimir squirmed a bit under the gaze but found himself excited by forming a real friendship with the Ariadnean. He had never talked to another about these things besides Dorofej. He was glad Adamus had decided to come with them.

"For a long while, I was a slave to the Highborn and Melkorka was the only home I had known. My people had come from cities within the mountain. I eventually had the chance to visit one of them. It was not what I had expected it to be—to be honest." Branimir rubbed his pointed nose, thinking of Illuard. "Melkorka is probably the closest thing to home I have known, but really no place in this world has ever felt like home. Maybe—maybe that is what Thrice Ten Kingdom will be. Do the Kras go there, too?"

A thin smile twisted the lips of Adamus. "I would think so, Bran. Thrice Ten Kingdom is reserved for all living creatures. That is, if we can find a way to restore this imbalance."

Branimir smiled. "Good. I wish the way of things was clearer for us to understand. It is awfully hard trying to figure it out on our own."

"Tis why we have friendship, methinks." The flames finally melted the frost on the wood and wrapped around the log. Smoke rose from the campfire. Adamus continued, "How else can simple men," he glanced to Sulanna with a raised eyebrow, "and women, aim to be heroes. There is nothing which suggests we will be successful, and in the same breath, how can we not be?"

"I think," Branimir gulped, reflecting on Adamus's question, "I think, if history teaches us anything, our success or failure will depend on what we are willing to sacrifice."

Adamus nodded to the Kras, the blazes of the fire reflecting against his blue eyes. "Tis likely it cannot be any other way. But is it important whether we win? Every race looks for meaning in life, discovering their charge. Tis the hardest thing for any to do. But at the same time, tis a struggle we all share. I am saying the real fight is finding friendships, and then, despite it all, holding fast to them."

Chapter XXI

Sulanna's small frame silhouetted against the morning sunbeams. She tenderly nudged Bran's shoulder waking him from sleep. "Come, Branimir. A short road this morning to the Ariadnean port, and then onward to Melkorka."

Branimir blinked several times, taking in the warm sun rays penetrating through the tree line. The light was nearly blinding to Branimir. He shielded his eyes, faintly hearing the drops of melted ice pattering around him.

"Spring comes early this year," Adamus said, scooping up his bedroll from near Branimir's bedside and carrying it to his horse. "This is the warmest morning I remember in months."

"Could not have come at a better time either." Alden grunted in agreement, gathering his own items from where he had kept watch for the remainder of the night. "The warmer the weather, the smoother the sailing will be in the north."

"I, too, had wondered about sailing through ice chunks," Sulanna added, eyeing the frozen river. "I know there is a joke about Alden's god in all of this, but I am too tired to think of anything."

Alden grumbled. "I don't want to hear it. You have slept more than the rest of us."

Dorofej overlooked them, with his hood thrown back, already settled into his saddle. He motioned for Branimir to hurry while

Sulanna climbed onto her horse. He looked back the way they had traveled and then toward the riverbank. "I say, Drak rested little during the night. Pushing him, the Likhyi does. We must hurry, yes?"

"Does anyone else find it strange that Dorofej roams the countryside watching people when we think he is sleeping, or is it just me?" Sulanna smirked.

Branimir stifled a chuckle.

Alden picked up his pace, fastening his own pack to the gelding. He swung himself over the animal, pulling at the reins. "Let's not waste time with Sulanna's blathering. We will not sit by while the Old-dark undoes what the gods have done. This world was created for men, not demons."

Sulanna waved a less than inviting hand gesture at her long-time companion, while gripping the reins with the other.

Branimir gathered his belongings and raced to the brown mare. Dorofej snagged his pack and tied it off. Then, he hoisted Branimir up onto the saddle with ease.

Adamus made his way to the front of the fellowship, guiding his horse with equal eagerness. "Onward then. Let's hope there is a boat awaiting at the docks."

Branimir groaned. He had not realized they might arrive at the dock and find nothing to sail on.

The next hour felt like a year to Branimir as they raced towards the shoreline. The sun seemed to shine all the brighter as the morning lengthened. By the time the wooden buildings appeared ahead of them, Branimir was nearly ready to take off his cloak.

The group of them paused at the edge of the tree line to gawk at the Ariadnean port. A handful of single story wooden homes were built in the open, away from the trees, and fifty yards from the water's edge. Snow drifts were piled against the buildings, plagued by footprints across the terrain.

Branimir noticed a centralized building, slightly larger than the others, but looked beyond it when catching sight of the blue ocean.

Strega's Deep was eternal, stretching beyond the horizon. To the south, Branimir could see more land against the skyline where Saudis Dar, the landmass that included Maharia, extended into the notorious Haemus Mons. Dark trees lined the landmass, even across the waters, where the massive Dyndaer continued to grow. Truly, the forest was immense, extending hundreds of miles.

"It goes on forever," he whispered to himself.

"The gods may bless us yet," Adamus said, not hearing the Kras. He pointed ahead to the docks. "Indeed, there is a knarr in port."

"A single boat," Sulanna said dryly. "It is hardly anything to get excited about. I doubt it could make it to Melkorka without capsizing."

"It'll do," Adamus said.

Branimir lifted his chin above the horse's head in front of him to see the small wooden ship. It sat opposite of the larger wooden structure. The faering he had traveled on from Melkorka to Kalamaar a lifetime ago had barely fit a handful of men. The knarr, as Adamus called it, was wide and deep, and over a hundred and fifty hands long. It looked to be four times greater than the faerings built a millennium ago.

"Let us just hope their sail is not torn, and the sailors have already loaded their supplies," Adamus added.

Branimir asked. "Loaded supplies?"

"Of course. All boats from these ports are cargo ships," Adamus answered. "The Lilitu in Talastein all but eliminated the trees nearer to the coastline, and they often send for more wood from Ariadne."

"It is going to be difficult to convince a shipmaster to allow five strangers with horses on a cargo ship," Sulanna said. "A knarr usually has enough room to carry the crew and supplies, not passengers. We likely will not be welcomed. We should ride up the coast. Riding to Talastein will take less than a week, and the Lilitu ships are more impressive."

"Still, taking this boat saves time, it does, even if we find another up the coast," Dorofej cleared his throat. "I say, the horses we can leave. Time is of the essence, yes?"

Sulanna did not turn back toward Dorofej, so Branimir could not catch her expression, but her tone was flat. "The pintsize boat, it is."

"Wait," Branimir whispered, twisting to see around the neck of the horse. "What is that?"

He pointed amid the buildings at what appeared to be a water well with a horizontal post fixed on top of two vertical poles. Ropes were suspended on from the center, hanging toward the well. One of the ropes surely held a bucket deep within the enclave, but on the other ropes were...bodies.

"Someone has been hanged," Alden pulled his horse back a couple of steps. "We should have been more cautious approaching this place."

"Ariadneans don't hang their own," Adamus growled, leaning forward to scan up the coast.

"But most Northmen would," Sulanna started.

"The bodies are human," Branimir confirmed, squinting against the bright sun, "but I don't see any movement down there."

Alden patted his horse's neck. "Me either."

He had no more than said the words when the twang of a bow sounded.

"There," Sulanna pointed while the arrow wavered through the air toward them, "from behind the building."

Dorofej reached out his hand, and using Koldovstvo, yanked the arrow through the air and straight to his hand, catching it by the shaft. The arrow moved so quickly by Branimir, he barely had time to flinch in his saddle. Dorofej threw the projectile to the ground behind him.

Adamus offered an explanation, pointing at the red-hooded figure Sulanna had noticed. The individual ducked behind a wooden beam. "Lilitu pirates."

"Cut them down," Dorofej commanded plainly, "and take the ship. We haven't the time for this, yes?"

Branimir twisted in the saddle to object, but before he could say a word, the three Anshedar roared by, storming the hamlet.

Dorofej wrenched the horse's reins and shouted, causing it to take off behind the Anshedar. Bran clung onto the mane of the mare as it crashed toward the shoreline.

They had only made it about halfway when the Lilitu started coming out of the woodwork. A single, brown-cloaked bowman, wearing a red sash, sprung from the side of a building. He fired arrows at them, which Dorofej easily swatted away with Koldovstvo. Adamus broke away to run down the bowman. Branimir lost sight of the Ariadnean about the time he had pulled his axe loose.

Alden flung his spear into the gut of a second bowman, who had barely pulled back on the sinew of his bow. The Lilitu fell on his back, clutching his stomach. Alden pulled free his sword, the falchion, and pulled his horse to a stop near the water well, dismounting. Another attacker was cut down by the warrior.

Sulanna was more dexterous than Branimir would have guessed. She guided her mare, balancing in a single stirrup on one side while the horse galloped. The move helped her avoid several arrows aimed for her chest. As she rounded one of the buildings, she dove from the mount into another pirate, tackling him to the ground. Her knife sunk into the chest cavity of the Lilitu before it could make a sound.

Branimir watched Sulanna sprint to retrieve Alden's spear while Dorofej sped his mare around the larger building. He directed them back toward the wellspring.

A sound caught Branimir's sensitive ears.

"Let me down, Dorofej," Branimir squirmed. "There is someone inside calling for help."

Unwilling to stop their momentum, Dorofej slowed time with Koldovstvo, while guiding the horse. With his free hand, he jerked Branimir from the saddle and released him just inches above the ground. Time wavered.

Branimir's thoughts moved at a regular pace, but his physical body froze, dangling above the ground. The world around him blurred—distorted—with Dorofej shimmering like a wraith.

The moment passed and Branimir fell half an inch to his feet in the snow. Dorofej sprung away, galloping away at full speed as though nothing irregular had happened.

Branimir turned invisible and raced toward the large wooden building. Several voices could be heard crying out with desperation. His hand grabbed the wooden knob and he pushed his way through the door.

An arrow punched through the air above his head. If he had been at a human's height, it would have instantly killed him. Luckily, he held his tongue and pushed forward. His momentum caused him to stumble ahead several more feet and then he slunk to the side, remaining unseen.

He noticed the Lilitu woman with her oversized head, slim neck, and scrawny frame. She lowered the bow that had loosened the arrow, yanking another arrow from the quiver on her back. Her skin was reddish brown—like Hanna. Though, her clothing was colored in blues, including a knotted blue cord that hung next to her cheek.

A male Lilitu, also decorated in blues, spoke in a granular voice. "The wind pushed it open."

She said, "I think not. You saw the men on the hill. You heard the horses. Something opened the door and fled away."

"It could have been the wind," he argued.

Muffled cries behind them distracted them. Three humans, two men and a woman, struggled against their bindings.

The male Lilitu kicked at one of the men. "How hard is it to stay quiet?"

The woman's eyes, wide like an owl, skimmed the room, glancing past Branimir several times. "You telling them to be quiet is not going to make them any quieter. I say, let's slit their throats and be done with it."

"We are not Rudhira," The male shrugged, "but if that is what you want, Margya, then just give the word and it will be done. This is your expedition. Though, you will have to answer to the Arjuna when we return. You shouldn't even be holding the bow."

The bluish orbs in the center of her eyes glimmered. She dipped her head.

Branimir pulled two daggers free from his belt and eyed the Lilitu cautiously. He did not know what they were talking about, but he could not let them kill the human captives.

His experiences in the Netherworld suddenly pinpricked his mind, whether he was climbing the Tower of Eresh, scouring the halls of Heshayol, or tiptoeing within the shadows of Breyntor Gate. Branimir generally did not like to think of the warrior he had been forced to become in the Netherworld, but admittedly, the weight and balance of knives were more than familiar to him.

He already knew what he must do. Otherwise, he would not have lifted the daggers to his hands.

The female reached for another arrow and took a step toward the tied humans. The male captive with his grizzly black hair and a round belly struggled to scoot back.

Branimir did not hesitate. He flicked the dagger from his fingers. The blade had no more impaled the Lilitu's skull before Branimir threw a second into the male's chest. The female crumpled. The male stifled a surprised moan, joining his comrade on the ground. Branimir scrambled to him, ignoring his round eyes, and ripped the knife from his chest. He could not fight him when he could not see him.

He slit the thin throat. His hand grazed the blue cord next to the Lilitu's cheek.

Inaudible whimpers came from those bound on the ground. Branimir appeared before them, pressing his finger over his lips. The single story building did not seem to have anyone else within its quarters. He glanced quickly towards the windows, boarded up for the winter. No sign of movement through the cracks.

Branimir used his knife to cut the rope that gagged the round bellied man and set to work on the bindings on the arms and legs. "Who are you?"

The man sputtered, falling over his own words, "Sefton Jegger. I am the captain of the *Winds Rising* on the dock. We arrived this morning to collect our batch of wood for…uh, Talastein…when these pirates attacked us."

"What about the people of the hamlet?" Branimir asked.

Sefton replied, "The pirates had already killed everyone."

"And, the men of your ship?"

"Killed, too," Sefton swallowed, glancing uneasily at his two companions. "They were good friends, Master Kras."

"Is that so?" Branimir said steely. He sounded fouler than he intended, but after being forced to kill the two Lilitu, he found it appropriate. He sawed at the binds on the other two, the gaunt, bearded man and the light-haired woman, who was nearly as skeletal as a Lilitu. "And, these two? They are from your crew?"

"Yes, Gaewl Farlin and Jelena Moosc. They are both shiphands. Good people… Listen, we owe you our thanks, Kras. If you had not come, we would be food for the fishes."

Branimir grinded his teeth, sighing, "I'm sorry, Master Jegger, if I am upset." He looked to the bodies of the two Lilitu bleeding out. "Taking a life is not something I take lightly."

"And thankful for that, too," Sefton muttered, rubbing his wrists once the rope fell away. "We, ourselves, are simple merchants. We are not warmongers or death dealers."

Branimir retrieved his dagger from the skull of the pirate. He hurriedly cleaned both his weapons on the clothes of the dead.

"Are the rest dead?" Jelena asked. A flicker of fear danced across the woman's eyes.

He nodded solemnly, ignoring the nauseating feeling springing up in his stomach. "If they are not, they will be soon enough"

Sefton heaved a sigh, not missing a beat, "There must be some way we can repay you."

"You can." Branimir locked his black eyes onto Sefton's blue irises. He knew too well what Dorofej would bargain. "We need passage to the north, to Melkorka."

Gaewl was the first to jerk his head toward Branimir at the blunt request.

The shipmaster eyed the daggers as Branimir placed them back on his belt, befuddled by the response. He opened his mouth like he had something further to say but stopped.

"Sefton," Jelena protested.

The portly fellow silenced her with his raised hand. "No, it is quite alright, Jelena." He bowed his head. "For my life, it is a fair trade, Master Kras. A fair trade. We will take you to Melkorka."

Chapter XXII

"Ahoy, Lady Sulanna!" The corpulent man, named Sefton, shouted from the stern of *Winds Rising*. "We will set sail at once." Sefton gave a wave before disappearing into the bowl of the craft.

Sulanna shouted something inaudible back and made her way down the dock and onto the knarr.

Branimir watched Sulanna step on board the ship. On her heels, the black mage nearly ran down the wooden planks, fumbling with his belongings, skittering about in his robes.

An hour had passed since they had taken the hamlet and rescued Sefton and the others. After formal introductions, they cut down the dead from the water well, and laid them out with the slain Lilitu on the frozen ground. There was little more they could do for the bodies without wasting more time. Branimir had been surprised at how little Sefton cared for the dead, assuming some had been crew among the ship.

Sulanna had convinced Sefton to forego his shipment of timber for silver, saving them from loading wood onto the knarr. The woman had pulled several coins from her pouch and placed them in the shipmaster's hand. Sefton had all but agreed to the deal at the mention of silver. Branimir knew little of commodities and their worth, but from the smile on Sefton's face, Branimir guessed Sulanna had paid more than the shipment would have been worth.

Alden had watched the exchange, mumbling something about nobles.

The group of them searched the hamlet and found additional provisions among the houses. With so many hands, the ship was loaded in short time.

Branimir could hear Sulanna, Dorofej, and Sefton talking within the knarr.

"What are you going to Melkorka for?"

"We have business there," Sulanna replied. "Do not worry about it."

Sefton asked, "Do you know the quickest way to reach the place?"

"Follow the coast east and north, you must," Dorofej answered.

Jelena interjected, also from within the boat. Her voice was crisp, accented, "What about the Kadari?"

Sefton laughed. "I do miss me some Kadari. You mix it up with some soy oil and rice from Haemus Mons. Best raw fish—"

"The Kadari are not a type of fish, you fool," Jelena scorned.

"Oh, yes," Sefton chuckled. "You mean the dreaded fish women, who lure sailors into the water to eat them."

"Those are rusalki. You have no idea what you have agreed to do, do you?" Her words were followed by the clamor of wood hitting wood, as though she might have thrown something.

Branimir stood a distance away with Alden and Adamus at the edge of the dock. He had not heard of the rumored rusalki since living on Melkorka.

Alden shifted his pack from one shoulder to the other, glancing at the horse he was leaving on shore. "Something about this shipmaster rubs me the wrong way. Do me a favor and keep an eye on him, Kras."

Adamus grunted in agreement. "I get the feeling he might've been a mule in a previous life. Working his way up, it seems." Adamus looked east. "We still have time to turn back for the coast. Tis safer to swim to Kalamaar than to sail with him. He doesn't even know where we are going."

Branimir said, "Sulanna has already paid him the silver."

Alden lowered his head. "Let us have faith Svarog has guided us wisely. We cannot turn back now. The quickest route is forward."

"As long as you know, forward may result with my axe in that man's skull," Adamus flashed his teeth.

"Master Kras, are we ready to set off? Master Dorofej says to hurry." Sefton raised an eyebrow, peeking over the edge of the knarr again. "I hope the *Winds Rising* is to your liking? I presumed it would be. Ha! I have never had an unsatisfied traveler on my ship. I assure you that this will be a most splendid voyage."

"Czern's breath! He talks a lot," Adamus muttered,

Bran yelled back, "We are coming."

The hull was wider, deeper, and shorter than what Branimir would have imagined from the shore. Surprisingly, they fit more comfortably in the ship than what he would have thought.

Branimir was the only one who could not help row them out to deeper waters. He did not have the strength to manipulate the long oars. The rest grunted and heaved, taking the knarr out to the ocean. In short time, Sefton sprung the woolen sail, colored blue and gold, and the knarr practically sailed itself for the rest of the afternoon.

Sefton steered the boat with a mechanism near the back, and Gaewl and Jelena managed the sail when needed. The rest of them used the space to meander comfortably among each other.

Evening was beginning to set when Branimir caught up with Dorofej alone at the front of the boat. Adamus and Sulanna had joined in a game of dice with Gaewl, and Alden had fallen asleep across one of the plank boards. Sefton and Jelena tended to the boat, or were caught up in their own daydreams.

Branimir sat for some time without saying anything, listening to Gaewl tell stories while they played dice.

"Gebereht, was once a hero of Ariadne," Gaewl said with a hint of excitement. "Had an old friend who use to tell the tale often."

Adamus said, "There is not a fighter alive who has not heard of the legends of Gebereht. He brought more glory to the God of War than any other ever born."

"But did you know he was said to be reborn?" Gaewl challenged. "People say he came back from Thrice Ten Kingdom at the request of Svathevit the Red."

"Why would the God of War call him back?" the Ariadnean asked.

Gaewl threw the dice. "Someone needs to save this world from itself."

Sulanna sighed heavily, muttering something about *god rubbish*. Branimir stifled a smile.

"Something you want to ask me, yes?" Dorofej said, diverting Branimir from the conversation, and pulling his black hood over his red tuft of hair. The breeze had cooled in the last hour, reminding them they were not entirely out of the Season of Frost.

A great time had passed since Branimir had felt this powerless around Dorofej. In many ways, the two of them had worked together as equals to survive the Netherworld, but here, back on Aenar, Dorofej seemed to be the wiser once more, full of his secrets.

"I want answers," Branimir said. There was a short moment of silence while he waited for the black mage to respond. When Dorofej said nothing, Branimir blurted out what had been most on his mind. "Did you make Kaelandur?"

"Mm. No longer can I say I did not," Dorofej gazed across the water. "Crafted it with Koldovstvo, I did."

Branimir caught his breath, trying to endure the truth which Dorofej said so matter-of-factly. Dorofej had more chances than Branimir could count to admit to creating the copper dagger. And he had never said a word. "Why? Do not tell me, you do not remember."

Dorofej dropped his bushy eyebrows, touching his smooth chin. "Requested to, I was. Though I did not fully know what I was being asked, yes? I say, I did not know demons would come, nor did I know the Ash Tree would be endangered."

His words made Branimir feel a bit better. It was something to know Dorofej was not intentionally trying to destroy the world. "Who asked you to do such a thing? I mean, you had to know it was forbidden for you—a Stuhia—to make a weapon with Koldovstvo, like Erzebeth said?" Branimir hissed under his breath, intent to keep attention off their conversation. He peeked over his shoulder at the other shipmates.

None bothered to look in their direction.

Dorofej dropped his hands into his lap, half-smiling at Branimir as though a great joke were being told. "In Klukas, a long time ago, I was visited by a woman, yes? Make it, she told me, and it will be called Kaelandur. Maybe, it was my charge to do such a thing."

"Who was she?"

The black mage's light eyes seemed to glow in the lowering sun, and then he said in a hushed tone, "Why *Marheena*, of course."

Branimir almost screamed, barely catching himself, "Marheena! Why would you listen to the Frozen Witch?"

"Much you do not understand, I know," Dorofej concurred, tilting his head toward Branimir, "despite what I try to teach, yes? Verily, know if it was her or not, I can never truly say, but I believe it to be. And listen to Marheena, I always have. See the power I have—the Koldovstvo—she bestows upon me."

"Were you not the one who laughed at the gods coming to speak with men?" Branimir asked in confusion.

"Typical, it is not. But long ago, more frequent, it was," Dorofej said, "as Erzebeth plainly said."

Branimir held his head, slumping over. "But that is where Koldovstvo comes from? From Marheena? Do the Kadari know? Did any of the Highborn?" Branimir already knew the answer, especially when remembering how Falmagon, and his predecessor, like Kinhar, spoke of Dahz the Lightbringer.

Dorofej shaking his head only confirmed what Branimir knew.

"But… you worship Marheena!" Branimir cried again. He had to let go of his leg, realizing how tightly he was pinching himself. This could not be real.

"Branimir, my friend," Dorofej soothed him, reaching for his shoulder. "She has no more evil in her than you or me, yes?"

He pulled away from the Stuhia, hearing commotion on the boat behind him. With a quick glance, he found his companions, as well as the *Winds Rising* crew were looking at him. Bran had a hundred emotions flowing throughout his body like drops of rain.

He glared at the black mage. "You are wrong. How can the whole world say she is bad, and you argue against it?"

"Because many think a thing does not make it the right thing, dear Branimir," Dorofej said.

"Why compare us to her?" He lowered his eyes to the floor, listening to the creaking boards of the ship. He felt the boat rocking against the water. His voice was barely a whisper, nearly a plea. "Are we the heroes in this tale? Please, tell me, we are the heroes."

Dorofej looked longingly toward the horizon. "That, my friend, is yet to be learned."

Chapter XXIII

Branimir could not sleep. At one time, the rocking of the boat would have caused his stomach to churn, but now, he hardly noticed. The smell of the sea and salt stung his nostrils, and the cold chilled his nose. Though, neither were the reason he stayed awake. Despite his burning eyes, his mind was peppered.

Hanna haunted his thoughts. He had been captivated when he first met her, and then he learned of her worship of Lilith, or Marheena. He almost found himself hating her for worshipping such a despicable god.

Then, to learn Dorofej had followed Marheena all these years, and had said nothing. More than that, Dorofej had created the very weapon which was meant to destroy the Ash Tree and release the Likhyi.

Branimir buried his head in his hands, trying to make sense of it all. Dorofej was his friend. Dorofej had saved him from death more times than he could count. Yet Dorofej revered the most hated goddess in Aenar, and led them to fight the Kadari, who spread the teachings of the Sun God, the most loved of all the deities.

Branimir feared he was fighting on the wrong side, but how could that be? They were defending the Ash Tree. They were stopping the Old-dark from returning to the world and killing the living. Falmagon was the evil one. He was.

Branimir trembled, glancing at Gaewl, who guided the boat on the opposite end of the ship. The man sluggishly gestured for Branimir to join him. He then glanced out across the deep waters, rubbing his beard.

Branimir carefully crept along the boat, passing Dorofej, Alden, and Adamus, over Sulanna, and beyond Sefton and Jelena. Each of them was curled up or sprawled out across the planks of the knarr, breathing steadily. He found himself glad he could see them as clearly as he could with his Kras vision. He hated to think what it would be like to be challenged by darkness like he had faced at Garain'l.

"Evening, Branimir, is it?" Gaewl said. "I thought you would be sleeping. Always best to get rest when you can and it sounds like you have a long journey ahead."

"Too much on my mind," Branimir said. He changed the subject. "Where are you from, Gaewl?"

Gaewl pulled at his facial hair again, steering the boat with his free hand. "Born in Mecka, east of Gaetana, up north. It is a decent sized village, but many have not heard of it. My father ran the ferry across the lake."

Branimir felt good hearing about the normalcy of the man's life. He found it pleasant that not every man had to be on epic quest to find purpose in their life. He pressed to continue the conversation. "I see how you might have become a sailor then," he said. "How long have you been doing this?"

"Oh," Gaewl hesitated, "only a few years. Still getting my feet wet, you might say. The pay is decent, and it gives me a way to see the world without having to fight with armies. I had heard of the wars with the desert people in the south. I have no interest in that sort of thing."

Branimir bit his cheek. Gaewl was talking about the war with the Uvil. "Adamus fought in the war."

Gaewl looked to the sleeping Ariadnean. "Did he now?"

Branimir nodded. He scanned the sky, speckled with faint stars behind thick, scattered clouds.

The small waves crashed against the side of the knarr harmlessly. "Can this boat really carry us all the way to Melkorka?" Branimir asked.

"Not rightly sure," Gaewl said. "If we keep out of the deeper waters, it might. Though, I hear there are some big fish out here, and even larger ones in the far north. I suppose one could easily topple us over. To make matters worse, we'd freeze to death in the water before we could swim to shore."

Branimir spread his thin lips, showing off his crooked teeth. With sarcasm, he said, "You like to keep things light, don't you?"

Gaewl chuckled, holding a wry grin. "I like to tell it like it is."

Branimir turned from the glimmer in the man's eye. He glanced past the blue and gold sails of the *Winds Rising*. He could see lights far off in the distance. "What is that?"

"Akothiya, I think." Gaewl squinted. "One of the Lilitu cities along the shore. I am surprised you can see it from here. I can barely make out the lantern lights of the village."

"You have probably sailed this passage a hundred times." Branimir eyed the man, rocking on his haunches. "Is it close?"

Gaewl licked his lips, and then shook his head. "No, no. It likely looks much closer than it is. It is surprising how far a small amount of light can travel when surrounded by darkness."

Branimir considered the words when, suddenly, a shadow passed overhead. Gaewl must have noticed it too, because he glanced at the sky.

"Gaewl," Branimir's voice dropped, standing up from the plank. He clearly could see the stark white beast swoop overhead. Its three crescent-shaped heads twisted every which way to look at them. Bright blue eyes shined on each head, observing the knarr and its occupants.

It was a monster from legends.

An unearthly screech arose from the center head chilling Branimir's skin, stealing away his cry and anything Gaewl may have said. The creature spun in the air, flapping its fibrous wings. The gusts of wind blew Branimir's hood back, and water sprayed across his face. The freezing water felt like icicles piercing his crimson skin.

He gathered his courage. "A dragon."

The scaled monster was enormous. He could fit inside one mouth and not even need to stoop.

The creature swayed and coiled keeping above the craft with its two thin, yet sizeable, wings. The lower half of the beast was slim for the most part, until it erupted into two overly large feet and a massive tail, tucked up against its body.

The monster twisted another head towards the sky, emitting another screech that was hundred times worse than the first one, causing the entire boat to shake and creak under the sound. Branimir clutched his ears instinctively.

The knarr had come alive with movement. Branimir bent his body, hesitant to take his eyes off the beast, to see Sefton standing in the soft glow of a lantern. He held it up into the night to get a better look at the leviathan.

"This drake will eat us alive."

Branimir stared up at the shipmaster blankly.

Directly behind him, the rest of the crew had found their weapons. If any of them had been initially surprised at the dragon hovering above their vessel, there was no sign of it now.

Jelena followed Sulanna to the opposite end of the knarr. "Watch for its firebreath. Better to drown and freeze to death than be burnt alive."

"Wrong sort, yes?" Dorofej educated them, peering at the dragon. "*Lahmia*, the name of this dragon is, and an icebreath, it has. I say, she has a fondness for the blood of children and must think Branimir to be one."

Branimir glared at Dorofej. "I am not a child!"

"Convince me, you do not, Branimir," Dorofej cried. "Convince her, yes?"

Sefton ducked away from the beast. "Why has it come this far south? We are leagues away from the Shade Fells and Lairhein."

"Even further north, she normally resides," Dorofej said, ducking his head.

"And, how do you know all this?" Gaewl asked, cowering behind the steering mechanism.

"The Stuhia are known for their knowledge on dragons," Alden offered.

Lahmia swooped down, slamming her clawed feet onto the edge of the boat and pushing back off into the air. Adamus swung wildly with his axe, missing the dragon entirely. Lahmia circled the boat, pounding her wings.

"She is playing with us," Alden said, pulling his spear from his back.

Sulanna eyed the dragon warily. "I am not certain the dragon is here to eat any of us, even the Kras. Dragons are not stupid creatures."

"Not known to be generous either," Sefton said.

"Be ready," Gaewl shouted, holding onto the side of the boat. His warning was only in time as Lahmia clawed the mast that held the sail, causing the boat to sway and nearly topple over.

Branimir rolled across the bottom, holding tightly to one of the planks. The others frantically shouted, floundering about the knarr. As the boat heaved to and fro, the fellowship crashed into one another, desperately clinging onto anything and anyone.

The creature swooped downward, again, but only for show. Its claws, black and curled, stayed tucked under its body, though it could have snatched any of them from the boat.

The rocking slowed, and Branimir pulled himself to his feet. "Tell us what do you want, Lahmia? I am not a child to be eaten." He was not sure what being child-like had to do with anything, but Dorofej said to convince the three-headed dragon as of much.

Adamus stumbled across the boat to stand in front of Branimir protectively.

"Wolos must be freed from the Netherworld," she rustled back. The voice had a hint of sweetness under the gurgled tone, like a myriad of voices uttering the same words at the same time.

Branimir looked to see his companions on the boat gripping their heads, covering their ears, as though pained by a sound he could not hear.

Branimir looked intently at the white dragon. With Ojenek in his pocket, he quickly solved the riddle of understanding the dragon's tongue. "Then, it is not a rumor; Wolos was killed. What does freeing the God of the Dead have to do with us?"

"Erzebeth sends for the stone you carry, Branimir," Lahmia hissed. "Give it to me so I may deliver it to those who venture forth. It will aid them in completing their charge."

"Ojenek," Branimir whispered, gripping the moonstone in his pocket. He had never thought he would be asked to part with his trinket.

He pulled it out and looked at the glowing stone within the palm of his hand. For a thousand years, the gem had been in his possession, found at Illuard within the Hall of Gravels, the Eevaltti. If he gave away his stone, he may never be able to talk to dragons, or centaurs, or the Old-dark.

"How did you know I had it?" Branimir asked. "How did you find me?"

Each dragon head snapped its cone-shaped mouth, revealing the sharpened teeth. The nonverbal threat could not be missed. "Give it to me!"

He was certain the dragon would take it by force if necessary. Half-heartedly, he pulled his arm back and flung the moonstone into the air toward dragon.

"Branimir!" Dorofej cried.

Lahmia snatched Ojenek with her center mouth, and spun northwest instantly. Her white, leathery wings spread wide, and she soared through the sky at an unmatched speed.

"What has happened?" Jelena demanded, holding herself against the side of the knarr. "Those beasts don't belong here."

"What did you give the beast, Master Branimir?" Sefton interrogated, his voice booming in the night air. "First, you speak of following Marheena, and now, we watch you aid the Frozen Witch's servants."

"A bad omen for our voyage," Jelena curled her lip, "to aid Marheena."

"The creation of Wolos, dragons are, and not Marheena," Dorofej corrected, looking at Branimir with bewilderment, "but I say, why did you give Lahmia the Ojenek?

"Wolos is dead—" Alden started.

"Your argument makes no sense, Master Dorofej," Sefton sustained. "It is well known Zyem safeguards the Kalinov Bridge leading into the Netherworld. The monstrous Lord of the Dragons is controlled by Marheena, not Wolos."

"Understand the gods, you do not. Tired of trying to explain it, I am," Dorofej attested with a curt snort. He emphasized his question. "I say, Branimir, why?"

"Did you not hear Lahmia? Of course, you would not have when I held Ojenek." Branimir gazed off into the distance. "Erzebeth sent for Ojenek to free Wolos. If we fail, perhaps her plan will help balance what has been unbalanced."

"You mean the *Gal of Garain'l*?" Adamus pulled at his beard. "What in the Nine Lands is going on?"

"But—" Dorofej started.

"And, if I had not," Branimir faced Dorofej with fortitude, "Lahmia would have frozen us solid with her icebreath. Better to live another day than not live at all."

Dorofej folded his hands. "Your wisdom, I do not question, Branimir. A way to save us from ourselves, I pray Erzebeth has found. Save us yet, she might."

Chapter XXIV

The Lilitu metropolis, Talastein, was incredible, sitting on the southeastern coast of Maharia. The city was positioned south of the Dyndaer, on the mouth of a river, which Branimir did not know the name. The longships lined in the harbor were twenty times larger than the knarr with white sails reaching toward the heavens. But the stunning city beyond, built layer upon layer, surrounded by red brick, took Branimir's breath away.

Towers and edifices, which Branimir could not identify, stretched well above the walls, overlooking the tops of the trees of the nearby Dyndaer. Reddish-brown Lilitu scaled and scrambled across all areas of the city. Even from the knarr, Branimir could see them marching along the walls, conducting business within the harbor, and walking atop the towers. Though, everything about their movements appeared ordered and systematic.

The Lilitu walked with their chins elevated and backs straight—each and every one—wearing different colored clothes and sashes. Branimir's mind raced back to Hanna with her red sash, then the Lilitu at the Ariadnean port with the blue clothes. The Lilitu at Talastein primarily wore blues and yellows. He noticed a few wearing a red sash like Hanna, and a couple fully dressed in white. It had to mean something.

No matter what they wore, each Lilitu spoke with precision, dipping their heads when beginning and ending their orations, paying mind only to their task. At simple glance, from the harbor, Branimir guessed the numbers of Lilitu within Talastein to be in the thousands. He remembered Drak talking about the Lilitu having cities all along the coast and Haemus Mons. The possibility of a population so large was unfathomable.

"The city is so big," Branimir said, gazing up at the fixtures.

"Ho," Jelena laughed. "Wait until you see that the depth runs as deep as the elevation. The Lilitu do not waste any space, scurrying like beetles beneath the surface and spreading like ants above."

"You mean to say this city is twice as large as what I can see," Branimir said, eyes widening.

"If not more," Jelena granted.

"We can talk about the Lilitu all day if need be, but someone tell me why we are towing into the harbor?" Alden asked. "We have enough supplies to continue for Melkorka."

"Inspection," Sefton said, shifting his eyes back and forth across the bay. He dropped the sails, and signaled Gaewl to line the knarr up with the docking. "No one passes through Talastein without inspection unless they wish to be run down by the Sirens. I promise we will be drifting toward Melkorka shortly enough."

"Sirens?" Branimir asked.

"An elite, Lilitu warrior class of women," Gaewl stated, guiding the boat as instructed. "They say their blades can cut through any blade made by Northmen, taken from the Uvil in the south."

Branimir scratched his head. The world had grown.

Gaewl must have noticed the confusion because he clarified, "Their weapons were collected from the desert people through trade. Surprisingly enough, at one time the Lilitu and Uvil had warred against each other in Haemus Mons. But the day after the war was done, the Lilitu were in the Uvil cities trading again. The buggers never miss the opportune chance to make coin."

"And, their best fighters are women?" Branimir asked with disbelief.

"Not all fighters are men, Kras," Sulanna huffed.

"Oh," Branimir said sheepishly, as the boat slowed in the harbor. "I am not saying they are, or should be, but I have never seen a place send their women to war."

"Might be what is wrong with the world, considering the Lilitu win nearly every war they have been a part of," Gaewl winked. "Truth be told, the Rudhira are not just women. The Lilitu have fighters that are male and female. It is just the Sirens who are women. I must say I am surprised you have not heard of them, Master Branimir. The Lilitu society is governed by females; it only makes sense their best swordsmen are also women. I have seen them fight. I'd put my money on a Lilitu Siren against any man, any day."

Branimir dropped his jaw. The Rudhira was the name of the warrior class in the Lilitu society. He was starting to put the pieces together and understanding why Hanna had worn the red sash. The colors must indicate what part of the society each citizen belonged.

"What of the inspection?" Dorofej redirected the conversation back to Sefton. "The Lilitu are searching for something of value, yes? Looking for what, exactly, are they?"

"Precious wares," Jelena replied for Sefton, pushing her thick hair behind her ears with bony fingers. "Gems, jewels, or trinkets. Anything which might be considered rare, or they can use to elevate their status further with."

"Shouldn't be a problem, then," Sulanna mumbled. "With the moonstone and dagger gone, we are as empty-handed as a beggar."

"Dagger?" Sefton cast an eye over them, while he used an oar to help steer them toward the dock.

"Nothing to worry about anymore," Branimir said.

"Be sure not to mention any of such things, we should be," Dorofej reminded. "The Kadari may have ears, even here in Talastein."

Adamus rumbled his mustache and beard with his breath. "We are not fools, Dorofej."

The Stuhia adjusted his hood. "Better to say I said to say nothing than something be said and we all lose our heads, yes?"

The boat rocked against the wooden deck, settling into the port.

"Indeed," Branimir garbled, watching the two Stuhia clerks, wearing blue sashes, approach the knarr as Gaewl tossed the rope to the dockman to be tied off.

"Welcome, *Winds Rising*," the first clerk said, holding a piece of parchment in hand. "Who here is the Captain of this vessel?"

Sefton, already moving forward, waved his hand, introducing himself, "Sefton Jegger, at your service. We are only passing through, voyaging for northern waters."

"You are the Captain of the *Winds Rising*?" the look of skepticism was plain on the Lilitu's face. The bulbous eyes expanded to the point of popping out entirely.

Sefton shifted, shoulders relaxing. "Certainly."

Before the shipmaster could say more, the second Lilitu extended his hand. "Let me see your manifest, Captain Jegger."

"Gentlemen, I am afraid there is no manifest," Sefton answered. "Our shipment from…er, the Ariadnean port…was voided."

"Surely, you have been through Talastein before, Captain Jegger. Is the *Winds Rising* not a cargo vessel?" The first Lilitu said mockingly, glancing over the several Anshedar, outfitted for war.

Branimir did not blame them for their concern. He could only imagine what they looked like with Adamus with his axe, Sulanna in her breastplate, Dorofej in his darkened robes, and Alden, who looked like he had stepped straight off the battlefield.

"Yes, quite," Sefton smiled, jingling the rings on his wrists. "but the hamlet at the Ariadnean port was overrun by pirates, and so we…turned back, you see?"

"Pirates, you say?" the second said with a flat affect, motioning his hand off to the side. "You are certain about that?"

Sefton gulped, "More than certain." The man put his hands on his extended belly, shifting as though he might turn back toward Dorofej, or even Branimir, to confirm his story with the clerks.

Instead, he simply dipped his chin. He repeated himself, voice quivering, "I am quite certain. See, the Northmen were hanged, and the town raided."

"Let me see your papers," the second clerk demanded.

"I told you, I do not have my manif—"

"Not your manifest, Captain Jegger. Let me see your registration papers for this vessel."

Sefton faltered, conclusively twisting toward Jelena, who gawped back with a dumbfounded expression. She shook her head and finally lowered her eyes from the shipmaster.

From up the docks, a handful of Lilitu briskly walked towards them. The cluster was dressed in red tunics, covering their armor, fitted to their slender frames. Each held two long swords dual sheathed on their left side, one sword strategically placed over the other. Branimir eyed the decorated hilts with the black lace wrapped around each handle. He lifted his eyes to the hooded, crimson cloaks covering their faces, hiding their features.

"Just our luck," Gaewl whispered. "Sirens."

"Let me educate you," the second clerk said. "Your flags have the colors of the *East Point Traders* from Badsehra, *Captain* Jegger, which if you are not aware, is a Lilitu settlement. According to our registrar, the captain of this particular knarr is Margya Corran."

Branimir's chest stiffened with every word, but upon hearing the name, his knees buckled. He fell back onto the planks within the ship. The truth of the matter sunk in.

Sefton, Gaewl, and Jelena were the pirates.

"No," he murmured.

He had cut the throat of the Lilitu named Margya in the longhouse at the port.

"Branimir, get up," Dorofej insisted, grabbing him under the arm.

"He lied to us," Branimir felt tears surfacing. He glared at Sefton, who cautiously peered at Branimir over his shoulder. Branimir snarled at the so-called shipmaster. "He lied to us."

The Sirens arrived next to the clerks, uniformly, facing the troupe on the boat. The first clerk stepped back. "The punishment for piracy in Talastein is death."

In fluid motion, one Siren reached across her body with her right hand and pulled a sword from the top scabbard.

"Wait!" Sefton stepped on the deck toward the clerks, hands raised and bracelets jingling. "Hear us—"

The Lilitu Siren was swift, the slanted, silver blade flashing level through the fat man's neck. It cut clean through flesh and bone. Blood misted. The frame suspended for only a second before the head toppled off, and the body collapsed.

Branimir recoiled. The Lilitu would kill them thinking they were all the pirates.

Adamus wrenched his axe free. "This is madness!"

Sulanna reached to grab Adamus's arm. "Hold on—"

Alden interrupted the noble woman, jerking his spear from his back. "It is not the time for diplomacy! They will not hear it."

The other Sirens unsheathed their swords and advanced.

The old warrior sprang to the edge of the boat, swiping the spear in a wide flowing arc, the bladed edge slanted for the first Siren's head. The Siren was quick, tipping backwards, dodging the attack. Alden, balanced on the knarr's perimeter, did not hesitate. He rocked back, continuing the movement, and thrust the spear. The blade caught the Siren as she sprung back up from the initial attack.

The Lilitu cried out as the spearhead tore through her midsection, the shaft ripping through her back and then yanked back through as Alden retracted the weapon.

He bellowed, "For Svarog, the Kingdom and victory!"

The clerks tumbled away from conflict as the other Sirens advanced. The first broke Alden's guard, knocking the spear sideways with her blade. Another entered his space with her weapon raised.

Adamus rushed into the aggressive Siren with his shoulder, causing her to lurch sideways. With a cry, she was sent sprawling over the edge of the knarr. A splash sounded as she fell head first into the water.

A second, who had deflected the spear, swung her blade down toward the Ariadnean. He speedily met the blow with his weapon hand. The silver against silver reverberated, causing the Siren to stagger; perhaps, surprised her blade did not cut through the Uvil-crafted axe. Adamus took the moment to reach across Alden's weapon and pummel the woman in the face with his closed fist. The wallop knocked her flat on the dock, stock-still.

Branimir sunk against the opposite end of the boat.

"Untie the rope," Dorofej shouted, scanning the city beyond the bay. "Set sail, we must."

Alden shouted at Gaewl and Jelena. "Help us row this thing out of here, and we might let you live."

Jelena's tensed her jaw. "Killed by the Lilitu, by you, or by the Kadari at Melkorka. I'll take my chances." With a shake of her head, she sprang sideways off the boat into the water.

Gaewl clicked his tongue, looking to Alden and then Branimir. His hand inched toward the oars before he finally said, "I'm sorry."

He fell overboard after Jelena.

"Cowards!" Sulanna screamed after them.

Branimir twisted about on the boat, wondering if the water was the better option. He raked his eyes across the choppy water contemplating if he knew how to swim or not. After a short time, Gaewl and Jelena surfaced several yards away, swimming for the shore.

From the look on their pale faces, the water had to be freezing. There was little chance of them surviving, even if the Lilitu did not catch them.

Shouts from the dock brought Branimir back to the fight.

Red-clad Lilitu carrying bows began trotting down the docks in thick branched columns. He could not have guessed how the Lilitu had become so organized so quickly, as though they had an entire army waiting on standby.

Branimir barely caught sight of them before the remaining Sirens rushed the boat. Sulanna joined Alden and Adamus at the threshold of the knarr, struggling against the Sirens. In moments, the other Lilitu were positioned across the docks.

Arrows fired across the gap, dipping toward them with deadly accuracy.

Branimir shrunk back as Dorofej swiped his hand through the air, using Koldovstvo to direct the arrows away from the knarr. The projectiles plunged into the water harmlessly.

Sulanna cried out, oblivious to the archers, and charged past Branimir. She held her long belt knife, her noble features rigid, attacking the Lilitu warriors. Her weapon sliced and stabbed while swords flashed toward her in rhythm. She stepped lightly, dancing back and forth, evading the quick blades. A blade nipped her shoulder, and her thigh, but she held her ground.

Alden's spear turned and rung through the ranks of the Sirens. He kept them back, extending and withdrawing the pole with immeasurable precision. The spear was quick, in the flesh and back before the eye could catch its movement. Yet, he too, was decorated with cuts and nicks on his face and arms.

Adamus held the left of Alden. The stocky man was a brawler, his axe rising and falling, hacking through skin and bones, and ignoring the cuts he attained. He had no fear of death, meeting every Siren with an abysmal growl of savagery.

"The rope," Dorofej shouted, again, over the din, using another blast of Koldovstvo to steer Lilitu arrows from hitting their mark.

Branimir disappeared, hurdling to the rope that fastened them to dock. He wasted little time slicing through the threads, ignoring the Lilitu who could not see him work.

"Dorofej!" Branimir yelled when finished.

The black-mage, who had been withholding his power, unleashed Koldovstvo on the Lilitu.

Ice shards exploded through the dock dismantling the ranks of warriors. Bodies were flung in all directions and screams resounded.

Battle cries echoed in some throats and screams of pain and anguish were found in the throats of others; some throats were no longer intact.

Branimir gripped onto the boat, shutting his eyes. The world was full of chaos; the cacophonous cries were devastating to his ears.

Seawater splashed around them and the *Winds Rising* was swept out of the bay, steered by a massive tidal wave, guided by Dorofej with his magic.

Branimir looked over the hull of the boat again. More Lilitu surged from the depths of the city. They were thick. Many sprang to their ships with the intent to give chase.

"No!" Sulanna's distorted cry sounded over the clashing waves, and commotion from the harbor. "Alden. Alden!" If a heart were ever to be blackened in fervor, this sorrowful sound spoke of such a darkening.

Branimir cringed.

He gripped onto the boat as it rushed away, looking for the holy warrior, who must have fallen over board when the waves jerked them to sea.

"Alden!" Branimir merged his voice with Sulanna, bawling with dissent.

In the distance, the old man was briefly spotted, overwhelmed by the rolling waves, sinking from sight.

Adamus, his eyebrows angled in temper, also caught sight of Alden crumpled under the sprung waves. "He is gone!"

Month of Birch

First of Warmth

1351 CE

Chapter XXV

Branimir carved another notch into the side of the knarr to mark their forty-sixth day on the ocean. They had stayed in the deep waters to avoid the coastal cities of the Lilitu, sparingly using Koldovstvo to outpace those who had given chase from Talastein. Branimir had not seen any ships following them for nearly two weeks. He dared to think they were safe for the remainder of the journey.

The wind blew strongly for most of the journey, carrying them briskly across the choppy waters. Even now, the springtime breeze filled the sails. With only days into the Season of Warmth, Bran was surprised by the tepid feel.

Branimir returned his dagger to his belt, watching the Ariadnean. The boat rocked and creaked under Adamus's weight as he moved to hang the lantern. The glow radiated like a small, bright beacon to Branimir.

"Branimir," Sulanna waved at him from near the mast, gesturing toward his dried meat and cheese, "come get your supper before it gets cold."

He stepped away from the stern, glancing past Adamus to the golden orb falling below the skyline. Its golden rays glistened off the endless waters, sparkling against the dark blues and whipping whites of the distant waves.

"We are lucky to have lost the three pirates," Adamus said while Branimir reached for his supper. "It has given us enough rations to make the journey without looking for another port."

Branimir took his first bite, hesitant to say anything. It was true that without Gaewl, Jelena, or Sefton, there had been more than enough food for them. If anything, Branimir had become plumper over the past month than any other time since he had returned from the Netherworld. Though, the three *pirates* who had previously procured the *Winds Rising* were not all that was lost.

He could not forget Alden.

Adamus found his seat between Sulanna and Dorofej, who already had their supper, and continued, "Sefton had gotten what he deserved after his show at the port. You really think they hung all those men?"

Branimir detected Sulanna drawing away from Adamus, unresponsive. Her hair was disheveled and eyes darkened at the edges. Branimir knew she had not slept well since leaving Talastein. He was certain the woman had been affected by Alden's disappearance more than any other.

"Speculated over this many times, we have," Dorofej said, chewing. "Some of the dead must've been a part of his regular crew, yes? I say, overrun by the Lilitu from the *Winds Rising*, they likely were, before we arrived."

Branimir partially listened. Again and again, the two had deliberated how Sefton and the others had ransacked the port, and then had been captured by the Lilitu.

"The Lilitu should not have attacked us," Adamus replied. He pondered for a moment, and then added, "Just like them to strike first. The Rudhira tend to ask questions after the fact."

"I am sure they thought we were with Sefton," Branimir assumed, looking away from Sulanna. "We might have done the same."

A moment passed, and Adamus continued, unable to let the topic go. "If there had only been *Nili*, we could have talked, but I know the Rudhira. Hanna was Rudhira. If they felt threatened, they would fight. And the Lilitu do not bother with prisoners."

"The *Nili*?" Branimir asked.

"The ones in blue," Adamus clarified. "They are the traders and merchants. They don't fight; they aren't allowed to. I have met a few, but I know more from what Hanna had told me."

Branimir garbled in response, signifying he did not need to know anymore. He remembered the blue worn by the two he had murdered in the longhouse. One of the Lilitu had held a weapon, even when the other had said to forego it.

He did not like this conversation, or any talk about the Lilitu. The banter generally ended with Adamus bringing up Hanna, which reminded Branimir of the Lilitu goddess, the Mother. In turn, this led to recalling Dorofej was faithful to Marheena. The black mage said the Frozen Goddess had given Koldovstvo to the Stuhia, the same magic which had saved Branimir's life more than once.

The correlation made his stomach uneasy and his head spin.

The details were so convoluted. Branimir's only reprieve came from considering what he was doing had to be done, no matter the discomfort. He had to keep Bohumir from being sacrificed and protect the Ash Tree from the Kadari.

"How much closer to Melkorka?" Adamus asked. He scooped up another bite.

Dorofej ran a hand through his red strands, eyeing Adamus. He chewed his food slowly with an aura of stubbornness. The Stuhia seemed bent on using his manners, savoring each bite. As if making his point, he gently placed another piece of meat into his mouth and finished it entirely before responding. "Ask me each and every night, you do."

The Ariadnean chuckled, holding his food between his teeth. "There is little else to talk about."

"Yesterday, passed beyond Salahan, we did. A few hours ago, the Hrani Highlands made their appearance on the western shoreline, yes? I say, shift our heading northeast in the morning, and soon find Melkorka on the horizon, we will."

"And, what of Drak?" Sulanna asked with as much composure as she could achieve. She had scarcely touched her own food. "How much further has he made it today?"

Branimir dug into his bowl while Dorofej received his nightly interrogation.

"Spent time in Klukas today, I did," Dorofej confessed, rubbing his chin. "On a boat north of us, he is. I say, exceptional progress, we have made. With enough luck, we might reach the Seven Islands before him."

"And Alden?" She mumbled, turning her head back to her bowl.

"You need to let him go," Adamus cut in. "I told you, the Lilitu do not keep prisoners."

"He hasn't been killed yet," she snapped back. Then, resting her gaze, turned to Dorofej again, "Has he?"

Dorofej's eyes glinted, as blue as the northern snows. "Comforted, you will be, to know he lives, yes? Still alive at Talastein, he is."

Adamus turned his head. "It makes no sense why they would keep him this long?"

Dorofej looked to Branimir for a moment and back again. "No certainty in anything, there is."

The growl in Sulanna's throat started before she could speak. Her chin quivered, elevating her eyes to meet those of Adamus. "Alden does not die so easily."

Adamus, as if recognizing his error, stared into his bowl for a moment. "I am not questioning his fortitude. By all means, not having him with us at Melkorka makes our road all the more difficult. I am only saying, we must focus on what lies ahead. Not behind."

Sulanna screamed out, throwing her entire meal off the *Winds Rising* and into the water. She stood, glaring at Adamus. "I know my duty. But I will not forget Alden."

Branimir jumped back from the eruption.

"I did not say to forget," Adamus softened his gaze.

"Sulanna," Branimir reached out with his hand to comfort her.

"Quiet," she said through clenched teeth, shaking, "all of you."

Branimir pulled back, while she stared at Adamus for several minutes. The only noise was Dorofej, who continued to chew, twisting his neck back and forth to look at the two deadlocked.

Finally, she half-stumbled, half-crawled to the other side of the boat, near the steering mechanism. She flopped against the side, throwing her hood over her head, staring back toward Talastein.

"Adamus," Branimir uttered.

"I am alright, Bran. She knows I did not mean anything by it." Adamus sighed. "I've seen grief a hundred times on a battlefield."

"She will be alright," Branimir said.

Adamus pushed the last of his supper into his mouth, grunting in agreement.

Branimir turned to face Dorofej. "What else have you found? Have you found Falmagon in this shadowy place you talk about—Klukas?"

"Told you, I did, at Ariadne that I lost track of Falmagon some time ago. While we traveled the Netherworld, he disappeared from my view," Dorofej adjusted his robes, and sighed. "Dead, I think he is not; but instead, hidden, I believe he is. I say, if I could have seen Falmagon, I would know for certain whether the Ash Tree was at Melkorka, yes?"

Branimir rubbed his nose. Admittedly, he did not know enough about Klukas and how it worked to understand what the black mage was trying to explain. "How could he be hidden, Dorofej?"

"Secret ways of manipulating Koldovstvo, there are. I say, such ways were once recorded in an ancient codex called the Varkolak. Many things, a wandering mind would learn within the vellum. See, within its bindings, it shows a Stuhia, not only how to find a person, but also how to conceal oneself from the scrying eye within Klukas." Dorofej rubbed his chin roughly, then threw his hands together in his lap. "To not be able to find the Highborn Longwalker…makes sense to think he has found a Stuhia to hide him, and who has learned the secrets of the Varkolak."

"Could he not have learned the skill and hidden himself?" Branimir guessed.

"No," Dorofej spoke softly. "Like any Highborn—or Kadari—who has mixed blood between Anshedar and Stuhia, does not have the power to manipulate Klukas."

"Then it must be Eisliev?" Branimir suggested unnervingly. His stomach tightened at the thought of the red mage, who had controlled his mind at Cavell. If he never saw the Stuhia again, it would be too soon.

"Maybe," Dorofej replied. The black mage looked off into the distance, seemingly captured by his thoughts.

Adamus, unaware of Dorofej's lost look, asked, "Who else could it be?"

Dorofej tilted his head. "Questions, I have been asking myself. I say, there are more than a handful of Stuhia in the world, yes? Remember, Branimir might, that Falmagon once had a crooked staff, called *Habërmani*, whence had once come from the Stuhia city, Lairhein. Knew of it before he had it, I did. Such peculiarities, I have considered for some time. Yet the Likhyi gave me a greater answer at Garain'l."

Adamus took his turn, asking the clear question. "What did it say? All I heard was gibberish speak within the catacombs."

Branimir's mind raced back to the riddled words of the Old-dark. Faintly, he recalled learning Dorofej's true surname from long ago: Kaligula.

The black mage had the same surname as this mysterious Dagmar Kaligula. Branimir kept himself from mentioning the name, from which Dorofej had insisted on keeping secretive.

Thinking of Garain'l also reminded him of having Ojenek, his moonstone. He turned his hand into a fist almost hoping it would magically appear, or even press against his leg within his pocket. Wishing it to him was useless. The three-headed, white dragon,

Lahmia, took the shiny stone for Erzebeth. Brave, daring Erzebeth, who thought she could bring Wolos back to life.

He wanted to know how Erzebeth would see it done.

Dorofej answered Adamus and confirmed Branimir's assumption. "I say, the Likhyi alleged my bloodline assisted in the destruction of the Ash Tree, yes? Clear, the Old-dark was, that my bloodline, and not myself, it spoke of."

The Ariadnean fit the pieces together. "You are saying someone from your lineage is helping Falmagon destroy the Ash Tree and free the Old-dark. You think he or she is using this Varkolak to hide what they are doing?"

Branimir gazed at Dorofej, who shuddered against the warming ocean breeze. The black mage dipped his chin to his chest.

"Surprised, I would be, if Falmagon or any of the Kadari are aware of what they are doing," Dorofej responded with a grunt. "Pray they act in ignorance and might be swayed to help save the world, we must. For now, too many things are unknown. Who brought Kaelandur back from the Netherworld? Did this person from my lineage only recently act, and what is their motive?"

"What of Bohumir?" Adamus wanted to know. "Have you seen him in Klukas?"

"I did," Dorofej said, "before he, too, disappeared from sight. Studied the Varkolak well, someone has."

"Has he been sacrificed?" Branimir said worriedly.

Dorofej shook his head. "I think not, or turn this vessel around, I already would have."

Branimir gripped his trousers, swaying with the rocking knarr, asking one more final question. "How do you know so much about the Varkolak, and what it teaches?"

"Transcribed it, I did."

Chapter XXVI

Branimir sat next to Sulanna as she guided the knarr eastward through the water. Settled beneath their blankets, Dorofej and Adamus still slept, snoring in harmony.

Rubbing the sleep from his dried eyes, Branimir yawned. Morning had come quicker than he would have liked. Fog hung above the surface of the ocean, hovering in threaded mists, while the *Winds Rising* lobbed toward the distant Seven Islands.

Appearing to be lost in thought, Sulanna gazed into the distance at nothing, and Branimir gazed at her. She held the mechanism for the boat loosely in her hand, piloting in the great body of water. Sulanna's long knife had been in her hand from the time he had woken and found her operating the knarr. Her brown hair whisked against her cheeks, threads striking her in the nose and eyes; and still—as stagnant as a stool—she sat, staring at nothing.

"How are you, Sulanna?" he prodded with a tender tone.

The woman did not answer right away. He almost feared the wind had taken his words, but finally, with a long enough lapse of silence, she lifted her chin and faced him. "Why would you ask me such a thing, Kras?"

"Because," Branimir said, "last night was hard. I know Alden was… *is* your friend, and if you need to talk, I would listen to you."

At first, Sulanna did not change her sullen expression. "I am fine," she murmured. She closed her eyelids for a moment and took a deep breath, swelling her chest. When she opened her eyes, she spoke louder, "I don't think talking will help, but I will say this. I am not angry at Adamus. I know he meant well."

Branimir paused, searching for the words to fill the void between them. He and Sulanna had not spoken much while together, and it was only now he realized how awkward he felt with her. He should have started with small talk.

After bouncing across several waves, she said, "I know Alden and I have had our disagreements, but he is my friend." She fiddled with her dagger, running her fingers along the flat of the blade. "I was born in Eldhaft, a city of liars and thieves. I learned there to not treat friendships daintily," she continued. "Nothing in the world demands we have friends."

"No, there really isn't, is there?" Branimir glanced at the black mage thoughtfully. Branimir weighed on the many disputes he and Dorofej had come across over the years. In the past months, he learned Dorofej worshipped Marheena and created Kaelandur. He added, "We choose who we keep close and who we push away. Finding good friends is difficult. You should hold on to the ones you have. I think they help us see what good there is in the world."

Sulanna twisted to look to where Talastein would be, hundreds of miles away. "An interesting thought, Branimir. I have often debated how *good* of a man Alden is, despite all his sermonizing. Sometimes I wonder why I love him at all."

Sulanna gasped at her own admittance, turning her face from Branimir, reddening. The response had come so fast, Bran struggled to find an appropriate reply.

Instead, he fought the smile from forming on his face as they bounded through the fog. He was uncertain what she meant by *love*—whether friendly or more—but the sentiment softened him. When Sulanna slipped her long knife back in its scabbard, he said,

"I have come to find I can control how I feel pain, hate, or even fear—but not love. It is the one feeling that reminds me I am alive."

Sulanna looked back to Branimir, visibly moved by his words. At the same time, his mind wandered to all he had seen in Aenar and the Netherworld.

He added, keeping his grin, "Even living among the dead for a little bit will show you they can't know love or friendship."

Sulanna mirrored his expression. It was the first time he had seen her smile since leaving Maharia. She said with amusement, "Tell me, how did you come to be alongside Dorofej and his scheming?"

Branimir scratched his head. "A long time ago, he was my Master at Melkorka."

"So, you are as old as him?" Sulanna reasoned. "Is that where your wisdom comes from?"

"No, not quite," Branimir eyed the Stuhia, who still snored, wrapped up in his robes. "I really do not know how old Dorofej is; I do not think he knows either. At one time, I thought he was a crazed, old man, but he has shown there is more sense in his head than most would dream to have. Sometimes, tidbits of what he knows trickles out, but it is hard to find in all his hubbub."

Sulanna laughed out loud, throwing her head back with a snort. "When I first met him, I thought he was a smart boy, who had read too many books. I would have never thought his knowledge came from somewhere else." Her tone shifted, becoming more serious. "It makes me question a lot of what I had known."

Branimir scratched his head.

Sulanna exhaled, recognizing his confusion. "There has to be some reason why you and Dorofej came back to Aenar. Why now?"

"You think it was fate?" Branimir asked.

"No, I don't believe in fate," she said, "but I admit this quest is more telling than anything I have experienced. All this talk about the Ash Tree and the gods sounds like something out of legends."

"I thought you did not believe in the gods," Branimir said, scrunching his face.

"I never said that," Sulanna said. "I just don't have a need to kneel to them as others might." Sulanna lifted her finger to her lips, thinking. "The Kras were subjugated at one time. Wouldn't you prefer to be free than be a slave?"

Branimir parted his lips with amazement. The ridiculous question had but one obvious answer. "Of course. No living being wants to be caged, even if it is the only thing known."

Sulanna said, "That is what keeps me from bowing to any god, or at least any god which men teach other men about. The simplest of creatures know freedom is righteous, and superior. I would think a grander being—a god—would uphold such a thing for all living creatures. Gods should be nobler, more honorable, and full of humility. If they cannot be virtuous, they are not worthy of my reverence."

He admired her. "Most would not dare to question the gods."

"From what I can tell, there is little to lose in thinking for myself. If the God of the Dead has been killed, as we believe, I will suffer the same fate as countless others in the Netherworld." Sulanna turned the mechanism to the knarr to keep it on course.

Branimir asked the same question Dorofej had presented to him months ago. "At the end of the day, what do you want out of life?"

"The same thing anyone wants, I imagine," she raised an eyebrow, blue eyes widening. "I want to be happy."

"How do you do that?"

"I think if the answer to happiness were easy, we would all easily find it. Though," she looked south toward Talastein. "I would not be surprised if the answer is found in friendship."

Chapter XXVII

Adamus called from the rear of the knarr. "Land." He gestured to the north, where a dark sliver contrasted against the light surroundings.

Branimir joined Sulanna in covering his eyes to see into the distance. The brilliant light of the sun reflected against the sleek, blue waters.

"Change course, we should not," Dorofej said, sweating beneath the heavy wool. "The cape of Kalamaar, you see there. I say, upon the Seven Islands, we will be, within the hour."

"I cannot believe we will see the Islands of Forghar again," Branimir said, feeling his chest tighten with excitement. "If I recall, the first island is called Cyreus. The boldest Anshedar were said to live there. What was the main hamlet? Mjovadalsa?"

"An unparalleled memory, you have, Branimir," Dorofej agreed. "Brave, the men from Mjovadalsa must've been, lest death they would have found, yes? Hordes of rusalki once gathered near the reefs, yes?"

Sulanna, who had been tugging at her hair, folded her hands and addressed Dorofej. "Rusalki? You mean to say the tales of the half-fish women are real?"

"Quite," Dorofej whistled between his teeth. He tensed his jaw, rubbing the stubble of his red beard. "I say, it could be the rusalki were slayed over the years. Heard of them much since returning to Aenar, I have not."

Branimir nodded half-heartedly.

"You have been around the wrong type of folk then. Tis something talked about often enough," Adamus spoke in his deep baritone. "Tales of fish people are spoken of frequently at any seafaring town, and even in Ariadne. Cannot say I have ever crossed one, but," Adamus winced, "even Hanna spoke of them. She said they were real."

Branimir slanted his eyes from the hero-warrior. He did not want to get wrapped up in another conversation about Hanna or the Lilitu. He veered the conversation. "Let's not risk getting too close to the reefs."

"I agree," Adamus said. "I hear the rusalki first kiss you, and then eat you. Though the first sounds pleasing, especially after bouncing about on a boat, I have no interest in being fish food."

"Impossible to avoid the reefs, it will be," said Dorofej with a shake of his head. "Covers the entire area, it does."

Sulanna snickered, blocking the sun from her eyes and scanning ahead. "Let's just stay in the boat then and keep an eye out for any watery tarts."

Dorofej leaned back against the mast, and said, "Until then, let's get what rest we can, yes?"

A bit more than an hour had passed and the sun had barely moved above them. Kalamaar had grown in its breadth to the north. Green trees outlined the bank and the mountainous Crags of Kazimir swelled in the far distance. Branimir guessed he may have seen an animal or two along the coastline but could not say for certain for they sailed miles away from the shore. His eyesight was superb, but still, it had its limitations.

When the toothed cliffs of Cyreus crested from the waves ahead, Adamus marveled and called to Sulanna to look upon the isle.

The red rock that colored Cyreus was the same as the Crags of Kazimir. The sight pulled at Branimir's heartstrings, reminding him he was nearly back to the place he might call home. Trees, olive-colored and far-reaching, darkened the tops of the cliffs and sides of the mountains, scaling five-hundred feet above the surface of the water.

"I do not see anything, not even a hamlet," Sulanna said, "but the sight of solid ground reminds me how much I dislike the look of water."

"I, too, am ready to be back on land. Though, I can only imagine what this is like for Branimir," Adamus responded, gawking at the bluffs.

Bran turned to him with a questioning gaze.

Adamus acknowledged him with a nod. "You had once said Melkorka was the one place you might call home. What is it like to almost be back?"

"Unbelievable," Branimir replied. "I feel excited and scared at the same time. When I left, I had looked back for what I thought was the last time. Coming back again is unnatural… I almost feel like I shouldn't be here."

Adamus shifted in his seat, manipulating the steering mechanism to sail between the mainland of Kalamaar and the island. He gave Branimir a knowing look. "Tis the same anytime I have gone to war. I leave and think I'll never see my home again, and I return with mixed feelings."

Branimir looked at the cliffs. He thought of those he had traveled among, who were stronger, wiser, or gifted in ways he was not. He said faintly, "I wonder why I lived and others could not."

"The answer is not difficult really," Sulanna said, "and, it has nothing to do with the gods, or skill, or luck."

"Why then?" Branimir asked.

Sulanna said, "Men spend all their years trying to figure out why they are here. They explore the world, wage wars, and write laws as though it may give them a grander sense of themselves, or help them conquer their charge. But there is a truth buried within each of us, and it is meant to be shared with those whom we cross paths."

"You pay no reverence to the gods but give a lecture on fate. You are a strange mystic," Adamus laughed with astonishment.

"I am not speaking of fate," Sulanna frowned. "I am talking about balance."

"How can you say there is balance when there is clearly so much evil?" Branimir scrunched his nose.

"There is not more evil, Bran," Sulanna explained, tucking her hair behind her ears. "We simply notice the wrongs in the world without seeing the good. See, there is no value in *knowing* what good looks like, but when you *know* evil, you can recognize what dangers to avoid. Those who have some sense about them *know* evil because they have no interest in dying."

"I don't know how this relates to why I survived when others have failed," Branimir said.

Sulanna shrugged. "Maybe you have something the others did not."

Branimir paused. He did not think himself to be special.

"Tis something to think about." Adamus cleared the smile from his face, but still joked. "Though, our skulls must all be cracked to be here. There can be nothing more waiting for us at Melkorka than death, and yet, here we are sailing toward it. No matter what Dorofej says, the four of us cannot hope to defeat the Kadari."

Branimir practically fell over. "If you think that, why did you come, Adamus? Do you want to die?"

Adamus laughed. "Of course not. I am here for loyalty and friendship, Branimir, or have you forgotten?"

He returned the smile. "No," he said, pressing his hands together, "but facing death...." He trailed off.

The Ariadnean picked up where Bran stopped. "I face death every day whether I am fighting on the battlefield or sleeping in a bed. I would rather have a choice in how I depart from this world."

"I agree with Adamus," Sulanna answered, dipping her chin at the other Anshedar, "and to die for something meaningful holds value to me. Not for the sake of glory, or riches, but because I believed in what I fought for, and I believed it would make a difference." Sulanna's blue eyes twinkled. "We may die at Melkorka. It is true, the odds are not in our favor, but if we succeed in the task, our lives will not be wasted."

"Our death would not be in vain to protect something as sacred as the Ash Tree," Adamus nodded back at Sulanna. "Perhaps, Sulanna is right. Maybe there are no gods, and no fate, but it is hard to believe our crossing of paths in Cavell was simple happenstance. No, I am meant to be here with you, Branimir."

Branimir glanced back and forth at Adamus and Sulanna, hearing his inner voice secretly hoping neither would die in the days ahead.

"I just hope we can save Bohumir from whatever evil Falmagon has planned for him," he said.

Suddenly gray webbed hands sprung over the shoulders of Sulanna, yanking her backwards over the knarr and into the water. She cried in alarm, flailing her hands as she went.

"No, no!" Branimir screamed, rousing Dorofej from his sleep. The black mage bumbled, sitting up from his plank, crying out questions among the uproar.

Adamus's bawl joined chorus with Branimir, ignoring Dorofej's shouting. The hero-warrior lunged forward, letting loose of the steering tool and reaching for where Sulanna had been.

His hands grasped at air.

The knarr whipped forward, still pushed over the waves by the sail. Dorofej and Adamus sprung to the back of the boat to look where they had come from, while Branimir leapt to where Sulanna had been.

"Sulanna!" Adamus roared. His muscles tensed. He reached over and loosened the sail to slow their speed.

"What has happened?" Dorofej asked, grabbing his arm.

"She was taken by something," Branimir said swiftly.

"Taken by what?"

"Cannot say," Adamus answered, pulling away and slackening the cloth, "but we cannot leave her."

"Where is she?" Branimir cried.

Dorofej's blue eyes looked back across the expanse of the water hopelessly.

The knarr slowed, bouncing along in the water, drifting away from the place where Sulanna had disappeared. Time inched along, but only after a moment, Branimir heard a weak voice whimper from the side of the knarr. It was soft beneath the colliding waves.

Branimir leaned forward, raking the side of the boat, when his eyes caught sight of Sulanna. She moaned, eyes closed, with blood oozing from her neck. Miraculously, her fingers clung to rope moored to the side of the boat. She drooped in the water, the waves washing over her shoulder as she bumped against the knarr, half-conscious.

The Kras opened his mouth to yell for the others when he saw a golden-haired woman bob up from the surface of the sea. His mouth was dry.

Her two round, golden eyes sparkled beneath the yellowish strands of hair, locking onto his own with a mesmerizing intensity. Her thin lips were pressed closed, spreading wide to the edges of her jawbone, beneath a small, flat nose. She almost looked human with her pale, pink flesh, but her features were just bizarre enough to distinguish her apart from the Anshedar.

In a weird way, Branimir thought she was rather sweet-looking. His heart pulsated in his chest. He felt light and had to grip the edge of the boat to steady himself, or likely would have tumbled overboard.

The melody that touched Branimir's ears weaved through the wisps of air. The song sounded both distant and against his eardrum, rocking his senses, unbalancing him. He tilted frontward while the girl swam nearer to him. The rusalki did not spread her lips, but Branimir swore the music came from her.

'Come here to me, in the sea,
Crawl on the ocean floor,
I'll show you shining, splendid things,

You've never seen before.'

'Swim here with me, in the sea,
Forget about your lore,
Fill your pockets with shiny things,
You've never had before.'

Bran gawked at the golden hair, his eyes catching sight of sparkling scales beneath the surface of the water. The gal swayed, drifting closer to the knarr, water dripping from her drenched skin. He reached out to touch her. His small, red fingers wavered over the edge, past Sulanna, toward the rusalki.

He could almost touch her. A little more.

Her webbed fingers lifted from the water, and between her long-nailed fingers, she held a glowing moonstone. The Ojenek!

'Fill your pockets with shiny things,
You forever had before.'

Without thinking, he sprung forward for his shiny stone.

"Branimir!" Adamus's voice sounded a lifetime away.

He lurched, suddenly hindered by the Ariadnean's quick hand. Immobilized, Branimir hung, for the briefest of moments, suspended in the air. The moonstone in the rusalki's hand— an illusion—dispersed into nothingness. Her pink skin turned a steely gray, spreading her wide lips and exposing sharpened fangs.

The rusalki suddenly sprung from the water, clawed hands extending for him.

Branimir shrieked as Adamus jerked him backward into the belly of the boat. The hero-warrior kept his eyes on the rusalki, arcing his axe at the beast. His silver blade sliced her up the gut and ripped through her leathery chest. Blood splattered. The rusalki spluttered mid-air, gasping, and splashed back into the seawater.

"Sulanna." Branimir wheezed, pointing to the side of the knarr. "Sulanna."

Adamus guardedly followed Branimir's finger. With a lifted eyebrow, he peered over the edge of the *Winds Rising*. He cried out with surprise, "She lives, Dorofej!"

"Be quick, Adamus, and bring her aboard," Dorofej stood over Branimir, surveying the ocean. "Done with the rusalki, we are not."

Branimir pulled himself to his feet, scrambling behind Dorofej. The water swirled and churned as hundreds of half-fish, half-women, circled beneath them. Colored scales glided across the surface and vanished over and over again.

Branimir said, "Lift the sail and let us flee."

Dorofej did not respond. He seemed lost in thought, staring at the waters and the rusalki beneath.

"There are too many, Dorofej," Branimir reasoned, holding onto the mast to support himself. Something about the rusalki's singing had left him feeling lightheaded.

"Branimir is right. Better for us to run than fight these wenches." Adamus heaved Sulanna into the boat. She crumpled into a distorted heap, eyes closed and mouth gaping open.

"Is she dead?" asked Branimir.

Balancing his axe in his grip, Adamus narrowed his eyes at the rusalki who spun beneath them. "She is unconscious is all. The rusalki took a good chunk from the side of her neck. How she managed to grab hold of the side rope is beyond me with the thing chewing at her face. She is lucky her arm was not torn right off."

"Heal her, Dorofej," Branimir said, peering over the edge for more fish women.

The black mage hurried to Sulanna, stretching out his hands to her wound. "Be at the ready, Adamus."

The hero-warrior grunted in response.

The steady glow of Dorofej's healing power swelled against Sulanna's wound. As he had done with Branimir after being attacked by the myling, Sulanna's skin stitched itself back together, mending back together. Adamus had hardly crossed the span of the small knarr before she was sitting upright, gasping for breath.

"Dorofej," she grabbed a hold of his black robe. His features had barely changed, indicating the little Koldovstvo he had used.

The shrieking of a rusalki jumping from the water silenced Sulanna. The golden hair of the beast flowed over its greyed skin, golden eyes bulging, and arms outstretched. Adamus spun and ducked away from the rusalki. The half-fish, half-woman flew over him. Branimir gawked in amazement at the long fishy body, sparkling red and blue, like gems, down its length before splitting off into a filmy tail.

A second rusalki, with a golden and olive-colored tail, leaped for Adamus from the other side of the knarr. Dorofej struck the rusalki with a blast of Koldovstvo. The small whirlwind propelled the screeching creature back into the seawater.

More and more sprouted from the water, grasping for them. Adamus swung wildly at the rusalki, focusing on dodging their hands rather than killing them.

"Get the sail up," Adamus said.

Sulanna, revived with energy, sprung from the depths of the boat. Her clothes were stained with blood, but her skin was vivid with color. She moved with the grace of a warrior fresh to the battlefield.

Branimir sprung to and fro on the boat, tying off the ropes to hold the blue and gold sail in place while Sulanna worked the crank.

As they rushed about, Branimir noticed the rusalki had stopped springing from the waters. A moment later, the white sail raised across the ship's mast.

"Hold," Dorofej whispered. "I say, the water has stilled, yes?"

"I noticed, too. What happened?" Adamus rumbled, balancing himself. The sail caught wind and the knarr grated against the surface of the ocean.

"There." Sulanna pointed to the north. "It is another knarr sailing this direction."

"But why would that stop the rusalki?" Branimir rubbed his pointed hose with the back of his hand, keeping low.

"Wondered, I had, if we would cross paths," Dorofej grunted. "The rusalki must be frightened by the vessel, which can only mean one thing, yes? The Old-dark, it is. I say, set a course to intercept, and make haste, yes?"

"Drak," Branimir gasped. "Are you going to kill him?"

"Drak is no more, and retrieve Kaelandur, we must. At any cost."

Chapter XXVIII

"He will not be able to disappear and flee from the boat," Sulanna said, "not like he did in Ariadne. He has nowhere to go, if we can only reach him before he reaches land."

"We will," Dorofej assured.

The knarr bumped and bashed against the waves, angling to catch the other boat slightly ahead. The blue and gold sail stretched with the wind, slightly pressed to its limit with calculated surges of Koldovstvo from Dorofej.

The red rock cliffs of Cyreus grew next to them as they neared. Drak's vessel loomed ahead, looking to be the same size as the *Winds Rising*, powered by red and black sails. Though, without the power of Koldovstvo, it was only a matter of time before the distance was closed.

Adamus buckled down against the front of the ship, the wind blowing back his beard and long black hair. "Stay between him and Cyreus. We do not want him fleeing to the shore."

"He could still turn north for Kalamaar," Branimir said as they entered the channel between the islands and the mainland.

"Pray, he does not," Dorofej said, sneering at the boat ahead of them. "Sink his boat before letting him reach land, I will."

Branimir gulped. He called out to Dorofej over the wind. "Tell me, why did the rusalki stop attacking us?"

"The Likhyi," Dorofej answered, nodding at the knarr ahead. He closed his mouth, thin lips pressed together as though his answer was satisfactory. Though, he added, smacking his lips, "A blessing and a burden, it is."

Branimir grimaced, refusing to give up. He ignored the anger that swelled in his chest, considering Dorofej insisted on referring to Drak as the Likhyi, or some variation thereof, and no longer seemed to recognize him as a Kras. The Stuhia seemed intent on killing Drak. "But why, Dorofej?"

"Sensitive to the power of the Old-dark¬, some creatures of this world still are," Dorofej shouted back. "Rusalki have been in this world since time before time, yes? Dragons, too, I would say. Know that chaos and death, the Likhyi brings to all living creatures. I say, its presence, the rusalki likely felt, and fled in fear of its supreme power."

Adamus spun around to look at the Stuhia. "What *supreme* power do you speak of? Tis no mystery an Old-dark is within poor Drak, but the Kras is hardly a threat."

Branimir squinted at the Ariadnean. He supposed in comparison the Kras did not rival the hero-warrior from Ariadne, much less an ancient god.

"Indeed," Dorofej said, "but a month has come and gone since Ariadne, yes? With every day, the Ash Tree is further destroyed, the Likhyi grows more powerful and poisonous. Already touched by the mystical and weird, Drak has been. I say, more has come from him being connected with the Likhyi, yes?"

"What are you saying?" Branimir asked, feeling as though he were picking at straws. Trying to find the right question to ask with Dorofej was tiresome. "Speak plainly."

Dorofej bellowed over the din of their sailing, "I say, Drak knew the knowledge of the rune staves, practicing the primordial craft of the Old-dark, called the Runista, the same magic as the desert people, yes? The act of his dark magic left him vulnerable to the Likhyi at Garain'l, yes? Control of his body, the Likhyi then took. A funnel, he is, to the hoary dark magic, the Runista."

"Can you defeat him?" Branimir yelped. "What power would the Likhyi possess?"

"See, we will," Dorofej flared his nostrils, eyes locked on the knarr ahead. "Weak, still, he may be."

"Tis clear that some quests require more prayer and hope than others," Adamus said unnervingly, looking toward Drak's boat.

Once they were a few hundred feet away, Drak's boat start to veer toward Kalamaar. Bran could see the Kras at the back of the boat, watching them with his coal-colored eyes. His crimson-colored head and pointed ears barely poked above the edge of the knarr.

A handful of men, around a dozen humans, moved around the boat, directing its course at the command of the Kras. Who knew what the sailors thought of Branimir and the others? Or, the better question was how did Drak convince them to give him passage to Melkorka?

He supposed it mattered little in the moment.

"They have weapons," Branimir said. He pointed at several who held longbows with arrows. "Likely waiting for us to draw near."

Dorofej curled his lip, "See them, I do."

Two hundred feet.

"Dorofej!" Sulanna yelled with warning as Drak's boat entered shallow waters. The *Winds Rising* heaved forward with another blast of Koldovstvo to the sails.

One hundred feet.

The mainland stretched in either direction, covered with sandy beaches. Branimir could almost smell the pine of the trees amid the salty water of the ocean. The Crags, which held the ancient ruins of long-abandoned Kras cities, reared toward the heavens beyond the trees.

Branimir was only leagues from Melkorka. He had left Kalamaar in the midst of fighting and was returning again on the brink of battle. Drak had said it best back at Ojenir. Bran would never know peace in his lifetime.

Nearing Kalamaar and the other vessel, Dorofej held to his promise of stopping the boat. The Stuhia cast Koldovstvo pulling at the other knarr's sail. The cloth swiftly ripped free from the binding ropes, flailing and flapping into the waters uselessly.

The other boat slowed considerably, drifting towards the beach.

"Overrun them," Dorofej bade as arrows were released from the sailors on the other boat. The black mage huffed, swiping his hand, and ripping the weapons free from hands of the attackers and the arrows off course. The entirety of their arsenal was flung into the ocean.

The sailors shouting warnings of the Kadari echoed across the spread.

Sulanna yelled from the steering mechanism. "Hold onto something!"

Branimir wrapped his arms around the mast, watching Dorofej duck down and cling to the side of the knarr. In an instant, the *Winds Rising* collided into the back of the other vessel. Voices split the air as wood splintered. Branimir grunted, his hold broken from the shock. The world spun as he flew through the air and knocked into the planks on the other boat.

Pain surged through his back. He flinched, lungs burning for air. With his vision blurred, he sat up against the planks on the opposite boat. Several sailors around him ignored him, launching themselves overboard. He watched them swim awkwardly toward the beach.

The impact had sent waves reeling out in all directions, thrusting the swimmers closer to the shore. The *Winds Rising*, surprisingly still intact, bounced backward, bobbing up and down.

Branimir stood, legs wobbling. He looked back at the *Winds Rising*, feeling dazed. Dorofej struggled to his feet, stumbling to reach Bran. Adamus and Sulanna groaned as they, too, tried to regain their footing.

Then, Drak stood in front of Branimir. His black eyes looked lifeless, empty of the joviality Branimir had once known in the Kras.

"Drak," Branimir murmured.

A hoarse, harsh sound emitted from Drak's mouth, speaking in a language Branimir could not understand. He instinctively reached for Ojenek in his pocket and remembered he did not have it any longer. The noise grated inside his head. He reached to cover his pointed ears.

This is what the Old-dark sounded like; this is what Adamus had heard in the catacombs of Garain'l.

Dorofej crashed to the planks next to Drak with a loud thump. His frame shadowed the Kras, causing the Likhyi to stop speaking. Kaelandur flickered in Drak's hand.

"Dorofej, watch out!" Branimir screamed.

Dorofej vaulted backwards as Drak spun, tearing the dagger through the empty space. Drak vanished, toppling over his own feet to get away from Dorofej.

"Stop him, Branimir!" Dorofej shouted back plainly, his icy blue eyes darting around the boat warily, and to the water, looking for a splash.

Branimir, who could see Drak clearly, even though invisible, saw him scooting toward the threshold of the knarr. He hurled himself at Drak, pulling him back by his cloak.

Drak lashed out with Kaelandur again, slashing the top of Branimir's hand. Pulling back with a yowl, Branimir winced, blood trickling from the cut. Branimir turned his scream into a roar, steadying his feet. He pulled free two of the daggers from his belt.

Watching Branimir's movements, Dorofej flung fire in the direction he thought Drak to be standing. The Kras shifted sideways to avoid the flame and turned toward Branimir.

Even concealed, Branimir could see the darkness in Drak's gaze. The Kras lunged with Kaelandur, and Branimir winced as the blade cut the side of his arm. He ignored the sting, and swiped his own blade forward, followed by a second blow with his offhand.

Drak eluded and evaded each strike seconds before Branimir struck. If he did not know any better, he would have guessed Drak could see seconds into the future. Branimir quickened his pace with the daggers, drawing at the skills he had mastered while traversing the Netherworld.

He twisted and plunged, pitching the blades forward over and over again. When the opportunity presented itself, Dorofej continued to fling fire from nothingness. In spite of everything, Drak moved as though he had spent a lifetime on the battlefield, dodging every attack. He ducked the fire and shirked Branimir's blades. Worse yet, Drak hastened his own actions, leaving nicks across Branimir's forearms with every counterattack.

Branimir stumbled back, exhausted, his own blood oozing down his thin arms. Behind him, he could hear Dorofej saying something about torching the entire boat. He also could hear the *Winds Rising* rocking, slapping into Drak's knarr. The boat rocked as Adamus eased onto the ship.

Sulanna shouted at him to come back.

Cackled words escaped Drak's mouth again.

"He is no longer a Kras," Branimir said to himself, his knuckles ached from squeezing his daggers.

Branimir snarled, throwing a dagger from his left hand, quickly followed by the dagger in his right. The Likhyi dodged each as expected, but Branimir kept coming, tugging the two remaining weapons from his belt. He threw another straight downward, striking the Old-dark¬ in the foot, pinning it to the wooden planks.

Drak screamed, falling backward onto his buttocks, and Branimir dove onto him. The other Kras struggled against Bran, swinging his arms, but Branimir had the advantage.

"Please, no," Drak screamed, raising his hands defensively, becoming visible once more. "Alack! Branimir."

"Drak?" Branimir stooped over the Kras, holding him to the ground with one hand. The other was raised with his last dagger, ready to plunge into Drak's skull.

"Stone the crows! What happened? Where am I?" Drak moaned. He quivered in Branimir's hands.

"Finish him, Branimir," Adamus shouted.

"A trick, it is," Dorofej cried.

The warning came too late as darkness percolated from Drak's mouth and eyes, silencing the voice of the Kras. The Likhyi jabbed Kaelandur into Branimir's side without hesitation. Branimir pushed his own dagger downwards, but it was swiped away by the Old-dark. Scoffing, Drak's thin lips spread into a wicked smile beneath him, displaying his crooked teeth.

"No," Branimir choked, overcome with grief. Ripping Kaelandur from his flesh, he slammed it down at Likhyi. Red hands flailed frantically upwards to stop him, but there was no stopping the copper dagger from sinking into Drak's skull.

The next minutes were distorted. Branimir pulled the weapon free, clutched it to his chest and toppled over. The black mage embraced Koldovstvo, touching the ancient healing magic in his blood. Yellow glowed opposite of Branimir's eyelids. All the while, he cringed sensing his body restoring itself.

"Dorofej, stop," he mumbled. "You will need your strength at Melkorka."

"Patch the greater injury, I must," Dorofej replied with kindness. "Wear the scrapes and bruises for a while, you will, yes?"

"Is it over?" Adamus's voice sounded from nearby. "Is the Old-dark defeated? Is it dead?"

"Doubtful," Dorofej answered, "but dead, its host has become. I say, where the darkness has fled, I do not know, yes?" Branimir fluttered his eyes open to look at the black mage, slight grey now lining his beard. He could see wrinkles at the corner of Dorofej's eyes.

"Oh, Dorofej," Branimir shook with emotion at what the black mage gave others at the expense of his own life. He avoided Drak, lying dead only feet from him.

"Here," Dorofej stretched out his hand, "hold Kaelandur, I will, and keep it safe, yes?"

Branimir twitched his hand, surprised he was still holding the copper dagger. Eagerly, he handed it to the Stuhia having no interest in holding the dastardly weapon.

"Ahhh!"

As the hilt was pulled from his hand, Branimir screamed in pain. His entire body burned from the back of his skull to the base of his feet. He writhed and convulsed, throwing his head against the baseboards of the boat with hope it might end the torture. Tears flowed from his eyes, and through his soggy vision, he found the strength to jerk Kaelandur back from the stunned Dorofej's trembling hands.

"What has happened?" Adamus reached for Branimir for a moment, before pulling back. The Ariadnean had fear in his eyes.

Dorofej's face fell to gloom. "The darkness has enveloped Kaelandur, it seems, and bound itself to Branimir, yes?"

Branimir whimpered, the pain subsiding, cradling the copper dagger to his chest in alarm. "What does this mean, Dorofej? Nine Lands, what does it mean?"

"When and if Kaelandur is destroyed," Dorofej shivered, looking toward Melkorka, "it may be, you will be, too."

Chapter XXIX

Adamus and Sulanna had stayed behind to drop the anchor to the knarr. Branimir observed them wading through the water and making their way back to the light brown sands of Folkmar. The four of them had done it. At last, they had reached the island of Melkorka.

Branimir inhaled the stale air and twisted around to gawk at the familiar red rocks. They were named the same as the mountains on Kalamaar, the Crags of Kazimir. Except, these mountains had birthed the demonic Bukavac, along with the undead Eretik, Nedezhda Mager. The monsters had slaughtered nearly every Highborn and Kras who had been at Melkorka. The casualties had been great, including Jhar, Katerina, and Faina. And then, there had been Mojmir, who had died at the hand of Kinhar Sayan.

Poor Mojmir.

This is the place where Kaelandur had been created, within the walls of Melkorka. Branimir knew with certainty that Dorofej had created the copper blade using the magical craft of Koldovstvo. The black mage had endowed it with the ancient power which brought Nedezhda back to life, and ultimately led to the Ash Tree's current state.

Now Branimir had come back to this dreadful place, and the circumstance had worsened. He worried for Bohumir, Nedezhda's kin, who had been kidnapped by the Kadari to be sacrificed. Though having Kaelandur, the cursed dagger, bonded to him concerned Branimir all the more. Dorofej said he would die if the dagger were taken from him or destroyed.

Branimir did not believe he would live to see the end of this tale. He simply hoped he was on the side of good, and would be remembered as a hero.

"Returned, we have," Dorofej said tenderly, standing tall in his robes next to the Kras. "Just beyond the ridge is Melkorka, yes?"

The black mage dipped his head toward the hill ahead of them. Trees sprung from the top of the hill where the sands of the coast ended and patched greenery began. Branimir was not sure he was ready to see Melkorka again.

"I have asked you many times, Dorofej," Branimir said, "and I would still like to know. Why have you kept me alive all this time? At Melkorka? In the Netherworld? In the Dyndaer? Why do you keep saving me from death?"

"Told you, I did," Dorofej said. "The option to give life, I have, and choose to wield it, I do."

Branimir responded with some heat. "I don't believe you. A long time ago, you claimed you told Kinhar to keep me alive."

Dorofej abruptly chuckled. He pulled at his beard, seemingly comforted by the hair hanging from his chin. "After the demons attacked Melkorka, it only stood to reason to have you on the journey, yes? Agreed, Kinhar did, that a Kras's talents could not be overlooked. And proved your worth and your heroism, and your friendship, at each juncture, you did. Yet, wanting to hold you for accountable for Nedezhda's return from the Netherworld, he did."

"But you were the one responsible for her return by creating Kaelandur," Branimir said. He blinked several times and looked away from Dorofej to keep himself from tearing up, knowing the accusation may have cut wounds in his friend. Maybe, they could remain the heroes.

Footsteps interrupted them.

"What are we to do?" Sulanna approached, adjusting her belt knife with Adamus stepping lightly behind her.

Dorofej's eyes sparkled in the dying light of the day. Fog had begun to settle above the sea about an hour ago, and for the first time in days, clouds gathered in the skies.

"Rescue Bohumir, we must," Dorofej said, "and then, flee from Melkorka, we will. I say, an eye for the Ash Tree, we will keep, but a battle with the army of Kadari, we should avoid."

Adamus said, "Are we not here to also save the Ash Tree? If the Kadari are destroying it, we must stop them, Dorofej."

"I agree," Sulanna said. "Alden and I have made sacrifice after sacrifice for the sake of this fabled Ash Tree, and named ourselves enemies to the Kadari as a result. I do not want to spend the rest of my days running when I could end this here and now."

"And the end of all things tonight may bring," Dorofej licked his lips, "but there is much to risk, yes? Besides, changed, the situation has. Bound to Kaelandur, Branimir undoubtedly is, yes? I say, what if he is slain in battle or is captured? The Kadari had also been seeking Kaelandur to use on the boy, yes?"

Sulanna argued, "So, let Branimir stay here, or back on the knarr, while we venture forward to investigate. If we catch Falmagon, we will take his head and watch the Kadari fall to pieces without their fearless spearhead to guide them."

"If opportunity presents itself, I would welcome it," Dorofej granted with a nod of his head. "Though, recommend the opposite, I would. Sneaking and cunning is Branimir's trade, yes?"

"You mean," Branimir paused, "you want me to go tiptoeing around Melkorka while the rest of you stay here?"

Dorofej arched his eyebrows, looking back at Branimir with an unmistakable expectation.

"That's madness!" Adamus shouted.

"No," Sulanna looked at the black mage for a moment, and then turned to the other two. "Dorofej is right. Branimir can vanish from sight and moves lighter than any of us can on our best day. The mages would not even know he had come, and then he could return to tell us the full of it."

Adamus's hand touched the axe at his belt. He grumbled.

"We can hardly make a plan without knowing anything of the place, Adamus." Sulanna perched her nose. "Be reasonable."

"I know what you are saying," Adamus said, twisting back, face reddened, "but tis hardly reasonable to send Branimir into the last place he should be, especially when he cannot be separated from the dagger." With emphasis, he stepped to Branimir's side.

Dorofej folded his arms, grimacing. "I say, what else can be done? Better chance for survival, we will have."

Branimir touched Kaelandur on his belt and shifted his hand to the one remaining dagger he had retrieved from Drak's vessel. If there was ever a time to be brave, he supposed this was the moment.

"Okay," Branimir consented, looking up at Adamus, "but if I am not back by morning, you best be coming for me."

"Ha!" Sulanna grinned, wrinkling her small nose. "You won't tell us to save ourselves?"

Branimir wiggled his eyebrows. "Sulanna, you wouldn't do it, even if I did. None of you would."

"Wouldn't even cross our minds," Adamus said, touching Bran's shoulder.

Gathering his courage, Branimir scampered off toward Melkorka, scanning the environment, while staying hidden in his realm of invisibility. Dorofej, Adamus, and Sulanna remained on the shoreline, hiding from sight with the knarr.

He raced across the terrain. The night fell and the white moon peaked in the heavens. The broken pebbles mingled among the few strands of grass, barely crunching under Branimir's feet. His sensitive ears could scarcely pick up the sound. With each step, he encouraged himself to press forward and ignore his fears about being captured. He reminded himself the Kadari could not see him or hear him.

He was safe.

Melkorka sat on the same tall, flat hill Branimir remembered, but the castle had changed radically over the past millennia. The earliest stone walls had almost doubled in size and the keep towered higher yet. The stone looked fresher, newer, and even sturdier than it had a thousand years ago. The walls had battlements built across the tops with spacing between chiselled stones. Branimir remembered the Bukavac, the frosty demons from the Netherworld, who had attacked Melkorka when he had stayed here. The giants had no trouble assaulting the castle a thousand years ago. He believed it would be much more difficult if it were to ever happen again.

Additional curtain walls had been built beneath the hill and around the original structure, outlining what looked to be a small hamlet of houses and other buildings. Soft glows blended in the Kras's vision, telling him either lanterns or torches had been lit for the evening. From where Branimir walked, the addition looked to stretch almost half a mile around the hill. Falmagon had expanded the size of the stronghold considerably.

He shuddered to think of the numbers of Kadari residing in Melkorka. Finding Bohumir may not be as simple as he had hoped.

Branimir sneaked closer, clinging to the base of the outer curtain wall. He could hear the murmurs of the Kadari pacing back and forth, visible through the embrasures, on the wall walk above him. He could see the mages clearly, leaning forward, scanning the open grassland and scattered trees beyond the castle.

Ahead of him, a brown horse pulled a cart through the main gate. Several mages, dressed in light leather armor and carrying wooden staves, walked on either side. One of the Kadari led the horse by a rope.

"How much longer can we can keep this up?" one uttered. "The Bukavac weren't any weaker in the winter, and now with the Season of Warmth upon us, the numbers have almost tripled."

Branimir's ears tilted at the sound of Bukavac, but only half-listened. He quickened his pace to walk behind the cart in order to get through the gate. Additional Kadari guarding the iron doors stepped wide to let their brethren pass through.

No one detected Branimir slinking invisibly behind them. Though, he regretted the decision to follow the moving cart once the smell of decaying skin filled his nostrils. He shielded his nose with both hands, lifting his eyes to a decomposed arm sagging over the side of the cart. It was chock-full with dead bodies. Dead Kadari.

"Falmagon and Dagmar will think of something," answered a female voice. "You have been going on about this since we left the field. It is exhausting, Beryl."

Dagmar? Branimir's heart quickened. The stranger named Dagmar Kaligula was somewhere within these walls.

"I don't mean to be exhausting, but our friends are dying," Beryl said sheepishly. "Furthermore, the Ash Tree will not last. Someone has to ask these questions. The Bukavac armies have grown stronger and our numbers are dwindling."

The Kadari leading the horse interrupted, "Listen to Kerra. Neither Falmagon nor Dagmar would appreciate your gainsaying. The Ash Tree is not yet gone, and the rest of Aenar is safe because of our sacrifice. What would you do differently?"

Branimir strained to see Beryl's reaction from the back of the cart. He was not surprised to hear the Kadari talk like they were at war with demons. He had heard the rumors throughout Maharia about their battles against the undead.

Beryl pulled at a yellow sash around his belt and drooped his shoulders.

The Kadari leading the horse noticed the gesture and snorted. "If you do not have a solution, I suggest you stop your snivelling."

The flapping of a banner on the opposite side of the gate, above Branimir, stole his attention. He twisted his neck to see a familiar golden emblem with dancing swirls. The markings, the sign of Dahz the Lightbringer, had been sewn on white and blue fabric. As expected and aligned with what he had heard back on Maharia. The Kadari still worshipped the Sun God.

The Kadari continued to discuss the Bukavac and the Ash Tree, but Branimir barely heard their words. Instead, he gawked at the sight within the walls. The spread of stone buildings and wooden houses formed a much different Melkorka than he had remembered, but it was the massive tree in the center of the courtyard that took his breath away.

He mouthed its name, "The Ash Tree."

The tree held many fruits and massive leaves as large as the Kras, but the wide base, roots, and branches had partially wilted in many sections. The blackened limbs gave Branimir clarity as to why the Likhyi were gaining power. The Kadari had more or less sapped the Waters of Life, and thus, the Ash Tree was fading. The prison for the Old-dark had weakened.

Indeed, the Ash Tree was dying.

Even though he had told Dorofej the Ash Tree might be here, he could not believe his eyes. Dorofej had once said the Ash Tree changed its placement in the world from time to time, but what were the chances of appearing at the stronghold of Melkorka.

He pulled away from the cart and wandered nearer to the Ash Tree within the small pool of dark water, the Waters of Life. The tree had lost its full magnificence since the last time he had stood before it, but it still was breathtaking.

The Kras shuddered. He and Dorofej had thought the Kadari had been regularly consuming its resources for selfish reasons. But from what Branimir had gathered, the Kadari used its power to fight demons on the Seven Islands.

Branimir, staying unseen, leaned forward and scooped a handful of water to his mouth. Despite his assumptions, he could not miss the chance to be rejuvenated. The healing process of the Ash Tree coursed through his body, soothing his aching muscles and restoring the slight injuries that Dorofej had been unable to mend. Branimir sensed his youth return to his body. Instantly, he felt lighter on his feet, and filled with a sprightly energy.

With a light bounce, he skedaddled beyond the Ash Tree, contemplating which structure may have Bohumir within. The main keep caught his eye. He could only presume a prisoner would be kept in the old dungeon beneath Melkorka, the place which once held Nedezhda the Eretik.

The wooden doors on the former walls had been replaced with iron doors like those on the outer curtain. The entrance stood open, giving Branimir clear passage to the keep. He passed by more and more Kadari while he roamed nimbly through the dirt streets.

The white moon hung halfway to its apex by the time he skulked up the stone steps adjacent to the keep, and slinked through the unguarded, wooden door.

Melkorka's keep had been completely redone. Dirt flooring and rotting beams had been replaced with chiselled rock and fresh timber. Lanterns lit the great hall, leading to a hearty throne on a dais, with long tables for feasting along the sides. Wooden chairs lined the tables, and behind them were tapestries with the symbol of Dahz.

Branimir started toward the spiralling stone staircase, once leading to Kinhar's quarters, and stopped. It had been reformed, the sleek and smooth red stone cut and stacked to perfection. Branimir could only think the keep had been renewed with the power of Koldovstvo.

He shifted toward another staircase, once an angled dirt pathway to the dungeon. As he started down the narrow stone path, he could not help but wonder if the dungeon were still located at the base of the stronghold. The voices echoing from an open door below robbed him of the thought.

"Falmagon—" a woman pleaded. The sound of skin slapping against skin exploded in Branimir's ears.

"You will call me Patrician Sej," responded Falmagon's memorable timbre, "or, by Mulafell, a hundred times over I will strike you until you bleed."

Branimir quaked, shuffling slowly, down the stairs. The profane reference to Mulafell, Dahz's mystical hammer, was too familiar to Bran; there was only one man Branimir had ever heard speak in such a way. The Highborn Longwalker lived. Despite all he had heard, Bran had not dared to think he would see the infamous man again.

Sobbing resounded from the depths below. "Please, I don't know anymore."

"She lies," grumbled a deep voice. "She knows where her brother hides. The question is how the boy came to be in Cavell without him or Kaelandur?"

"Alyona," Falmagon said, "you served well in retrieving the dagger, but your subversion cannot go unpunished. Tell me where your brother has gone. Tell me where Artemiy has taken Kaelandur!"

Alyona? Artemiy? The names sounded familiar, but Branimir could not place them. He stepped through the widened door into the shimmering lantern light, still hidden to those within the room.

Bran saw the dungeon had been extended. Hanging from the walls were linked chains with metal bindings. Above each set of shackles was the indention of an eye scraped with a moon and cross. He had seen a similar symbol above Nedezhda years ago, preventing her from touching Koldovstvo.

"I do not know," the woman whimpered, hanging weakly, straining against her bindings. Her chin tilted upwards, purplish eyes watering under the piercing gaze of Falmagon and the other redheaded man. Her mouth was bleeding, eyes swollen and black, and red marks streaking each side of her face.

Upon seeing the woman, Branimir had to cover his mouth with recognition. Of course. Alyona had been one of the Kadari at Shayol Domier a millennium ago. She was the only person he had met with purplish eyes. And Artemiy, her brother, had been the so-called Highborn, who had killed Asgrim, the centaur, who had accompanied them from Sorod. How had she survived this long? How could either of them have survived so long?

Falmagon clenched his fist, as if considering whether to strike the woman again. Leisurely, he raised his fingers and pulled at his thick mustache. "Dagmar," he shifted his head, long brown locks of hair shifting against leather armor, "we are wasting our time with her. Let's *speak* with the boy again."

Branimir's old master had plainly used the Waters of Life to maintain his youth. Falmagon looked as young as he had at Shayol Domier before the final battle with Nedezhda.

The redheaded man pursed his lips, scowling hatefully at Alyona. The man called Dagmar looked remarkably like Dorofej with scraggly red hair and bright blue eyes, filled with incomparable knowledge. He made Branimir's skin crawl.

Dagmar said, "The boy is useless. The immature brat thinks Artemiy is his father and knows nothing about Kaelandur."

"The boy told us about the black mage and Kras at Cavell," Falmagon contested. "He might know more."

"He also said the *Kluk* had killed them." At mentioning the last name of Eisliev, the red mage, Dagmar's face contorted with fury. "Yet you talk about Dorofej like he is still alive."

Falmagon frowned.

"Forget the boy," Dagmar said. He dipped his head at Alyona, slumped against the wall. "I know her type. She will tell us everything. I will pick her apart—piece by piece—and we will see how much she knows when her insides are scattered out in front of her."

"Patrician Sej, please," Alyona begged. "I have been a faithful servant...to the Kadari. I tracked Branimir and the mage...like you had asked...I've given so, so much...let me go..."

She heaved against the wall, tears falling down her cheeks.

Branimir squeezed his hand tighter over his mouth. Alyona had followed them through the Netherworld. How had he and Dorofej not known?

Falmagon backhanded her, jostling her body against the fastenings. She cried out in pain as the skin of her wrists cut against the iron. "And, you were supposed to bring me the dagger! Instead, you hid it from me!"

"I have done…what you wanted. I kidnapped the Mager boy when I returned," she said.

Falmagon sneered. "And, left him with your maddened brother on the other side of the world."

"I did not know Artemiy had Kaelandur," she wept. "I did not know he would hide the boy from you."

"Liar!" Falmagon screamed, hammering his hand into the side of head again.

"I—" she tried, "I—"

Dagmar enunciated his words, speaking with a slow cadence. "Where is Artemiy? You risk everything with your secrets."

She struggled to raise her head toward the imposing man, and when she could not hold herself up, she slouched without strength. Still, she spoke clearly, "We are all dead anyway."

With a sigh, Dagmar lifted his hand toward the woman, giving permission to Falmagon, who readily struck her once more. The simple gesture caused Branimir to deliberate whether Falmagon or Dagmar was in charge.

Alyona fell limp in the chains, unconscious.

"Worthless swine," Dagmar muttered. "Ages and ages pass and nothing changes. When she awakens, we will start over."

"It is futile, Dagmar." Falmagon turned away from Alyona, addressing the redheaded man. "We are running out of time. Dorofej must have Kaelandur. You must look for him in Klukas."

Branimir's heart stopped.

Dagmar reached into the pocket of his red robe, pulling out a miniature book. Using Koldovstvo, the book with its leather casing, enlarged in the man's hand. "I cannot simply find anyone I want. I have to personally know who they are," the man said, placing his hand on the book. "I have to know the essence of their spirit."

"Then, teach me," Falmagon demanded. "I know him. We must be certain he is dead."

"You are not a Stuhia," Dagmar barked. "If Dorofej is like me, as you presume—and for some reason knows the mysteries of the

Varkolak—I have kept us from being found in Klukas. No more can be done. If he comes, he comes."

"You do not know him, Dagmar," Falmagon sniffed, pulling at his mustache again. "Dorofej will be difficult to defeat. I saw the way he fought at Shayol Domier. And you have heard Alyona. If he endured the Netherworld, he surely survived Eisliev Kluk."

Dagmar grinded his teeth. He shrunk the book again and placed it in his pocket. "Our focus is to find the dagger and sacrifice the boy. The ritual with his blood will restore the Ash Tree, keeping the Old-dark at bay."

Falmagon snorted. "The Bukavac will continue to bleed from the Crags. The Ash Tree will weaken again. Destroying Kaelandur is the only way, and I am telling you—Dorofej will have it."

Dagmar's face turned red, turning to Falmagon. Though, before he could say anything, footsteps echoed down the stone path leading to the dungeon.

"Lord Kaligula. Patrician Sej." A short girl burst through the doorway, panting. She did not even look in Alyona's direction. "A knarr has landed on the shore."

Falmagon glowered. "Gather a scouting party. Let's see who has come to Melkorka."

Branimir backed out of the dungeon and ran.

Chapter XXX

Branimir slipped through the streets toward the outer gate, the stale air of early summer filling his lungs. He had to return to the coast before the Kadari discovered the others in hiding. Melkorka was only about six hundred paces from the shoreline. If he was quick enough, Branimir might just outrun them. That is, as long as the main gate was open at the outer curtain wall.

He repeatedly looked over his shoulder, at his flank, fearing that Falmagon might bolt from the keep at any moment and give chase. Branimir did not think he had been discovered, but he could not be certain what tricks Falmagon, or Dagmar, would have at their disposal. If Dagmar could enter Klukas like Dorofej, he may have other secrets, too.

His hand touched the copper dagger at his belt. The risk of being caught by the Kadari was too great. He could not forget what was at stake. If Falmagon retrieved Kaelandur, they would kill Bohumir. He wanted the Ash Tree saved, and the Likhyi stopped, but not at the cost of a child. Besides, he could not be certain Falmagon told the truth. Dorofej said Bohumir's sacrifice would give the Kadari more power. Did he mean by giving life back to the Ash Tree?

The unanswered questions pounded against his skull, while he looked back at the towering keep of Melkorka. Why had Alyona and

Artemiy followed him and Dorofej to the Netherworld? Did Alyona hide the dagger and boy from Falmagon? Did Artemiy? What was their fear? And who exactly was this Stuhia named Dagmar Kaligula?

His mind raced while he ran.

With a grunt, Branimir hit something solid and fell back on his haunches. He flickered into sight for a half-second, before gaining control of his invisibility once more.

He lifted his gaze to the figure in front of him, attached to the oversized leg in which he had collided. The tan skin of the giant looming over him was dreadfully familiar. The piercing blue eyes of Tyr Og were cock-eyed, looking down, examining the ground in confusion.

"Bah! What in the Nine Lands was that?" he bellowed.

The Ispolini stood next to Eisliev. The Stuhia's red robes covered him from head to foot, including his red hair. He stopped in his tracks to glare at Tyr. "What in the Nine Lands was what?"

Branimir's heart stopped at the sight of Eisliev. The scene at Cavell replayed in his head. The magic-wielding Stuhia had somehow manipulated his mind, causing him to attack his friends. He could not allow Eisliev to gain control of him again.

Tyr clenched his six-fingered hands into fists, nostrils flaring. "Ah! I've been hit by something right beneath the knee. With all you foul mages running about, who knows which fool cast what."

Eisliev snorted. "No Kadari is going to waste time prodding at the ankles of an oversized pile of sheepdip."

Tyr growled, reaching back slightly as though he might grab the massive battle axe from his back. He stopped, however, and turned to Eisliev. "Then, what do you suppose it was?"

Eisliev taunted the giant. "I think you tripped over your gargantuan, donkey feet. Now, can you stop your drivel so we can get on with this?"

Breathing again, Branimir realized neither had noticed him. He twisted his neck to check the courtyard. The Kadari nearby either ambled about carelessly or huddled near the Ash Tree. None raised an alarm.

Branimir scowled, catching sight of the gates. The iron doors were closed shut.

The giant stressed the visible muscles in his arms and chest. Branimir stood while Tyr responded. "I did not sign up to kill the boy. The Crimson Sun hired us to deliver him and then be gone."

"I don't care two hoots what the Crimson Sun hired us to do. You know I came here with my own agenda. I have spent years finding Dagmar, and now that he is within my reach..." Eisliev clenched his fists, his voice trailing off. He glared towards the keep.

"I don't understand why you hate Dagmar the way you do," Tyr said.

Eisliev said, "You wouldn't. The blood feud between the Kaligulas and the Kluks is old. That covetous swine ruined my family."

Tyr rumbled. "Then use your fancy, little ring on Patrician Sej. Force him to take you to Dagmar."

Eisliev started at Tyr with wide eyes, crossing his arms with irritation. "The Faegrim only lets me control those who cannot touch Koldovstvo. The Patrician may be a half-breed," the Stuhia paused to sneer at the Kadari in the courtyard, "but he can still touch Koldovstvo."

Branimir raked his eyes over Eisliev, searching for the so-called Faegrim. A silver band on the red mage's left hand—the smallest finger—stood out. The Faegrim was the secret to Eisliev's mind-altering magic.

"You can't use it on me either," Tyr said, "and I have nothing to do with your magic."

"That is because the Ispolini are too thick headed."

"Or too smart."

"Don't flatter yourself," Eisliev said, waving his hand for Tyr to follow. "Bottom line, if Patrician Sej won't let me have an audience with Dagmar," Eisliev hissed through clenched teeth, "he will not have the boy."

Tyr growled under his breath. "You speak of doing a dark thing. We don't even know why they wanted the boy."

"I don't care," Eisliev said. "If he wants to thwart my plans, I'll do the same to him."

Branimir clenched his crooked teeth to hold back a scream. They could only be talking about Bohumir. He could not think of a worse situation. The two were heading to murder Bohumir! All the while, the Kadari prepared to scout the shore, where they would find Dorofej and the others. Once Falmagon learned they had arrived at Melkorka, they would be hunted.

He had to hurry, but he could not let poor Bohumir be slaughtered by the red mage. The whole reason they had come to Melkorka had been to rescue the boy. Being here in this moment could not be any more perfect.

Tyr and Eisliev walked down the road.

Without devising much of a plan, Branimir trailed behind the two. They headed for a common house built among the many other wooden homes.

"How are you gonna do it?" Tyr asked, slowing his step so the mage could keep pace.

"Me?" Eisliev shook his head. "I am not doing it. I come from a respectable bloodline. The Kluks do not take innocent lives. You must be mistaking me for a Kaligula."

Branimir flinched as Eisliev continued to say Dorofej's surname with a negative undertone.

Tyr glanced at the home ahead of them. He said, "And, you think since I am a barbarian I will snap the boy's neck and not think twice about it?"

"Thinking is not your strong suit, Tyr. You are the brawn," Eisliev grabbed a hold of the knob to the door of the home. "It is more in your job description than mine."

The giant put a meaty hand over Eisliev's. "You misjudge me and my people. I have no interest in killing the boy, Eisliev. He has done nothing wrong."

"He has outlived his purpose. He was nothing more than a bargaining chip for Dagmar."

Tyr scowled. "Could just as easy set the boy free, you know? He doesn't have to be killed."

Branimir crouched behind them.

"For them to simply capture the boy all over again? I don't think so," Eisliev's voice was grating, derisive. He mocked the Ispolini. "If you want to forever be known as a coward, I will do it."

Tyr tightened his face, unable to make eye contact with the mage. After a moment, he finally nodded. "It's your revenge. Not mine."

He released Eisliev's hand, curling his six fingers back at his side. He looked away while Eisliev gaped at the massive man.

"Fine," Eisliev said. "Stay out here."

Tyr repeated his question, scanning the courtyard. "How are you going to do it?"

"In a way that assures there is nothing left," Eisliev said, twisting the knob. "Whatever they have planned for the boy will not be done."

Chapter XXXI

Eisliev pushed the wooden door open, flooding the street with white light. He pulled his hood back and stepped through the opening.

Branimir, sprang into action, bounding around Tyr and diving through the doorway. He landed behind Eisliev and then scurried into the corner of the room.

Eisliev slammed the door shut behind him.

"What do you want?" Bohumir squeaked from where he sat cross-legged near an open hearth. The flames flickered near his skin, spindly arms folded in his lap. The room held nothing but the three of them, layered with mildew and dust.

Branimir's mouth dried seeing the boy. Bohumir looked as though he had hardly eaten in weeks. He sat scrunched over, almost too weak to raise his head to Eisliev. He coughed into his hand, spraying droplets of spit onto an empty plate and a waterskin by his ankles.

The red mage squinted at the boy, fidgeting with his fingers. Bohumir glared back at Eisliev with round eyes.

Sliding the dagger soundlessly from his belt, Branimir's skin tingled with anticipation. Even if he killed Eisliev, he did not have a clue how he could escape Melkorka with Bohumir. Tyr stood guard outside the door and the main gate was shut.

Branimir squeezed the dagger's hilt, feeling the weight of the weapon in his hand. He was not a stranger to killing, but he did not take it lightly. At one time, he had been called a warrior among the Kras. The defeat at Cavell haunted him as well as his mistake when killing the Lilitu at the Ariadnean port. Though, he had slaughtered many demons in the Netherworld, and defended Dorofej against the undead at Garain'l. And now, he would be forced to protect Bohumir by sinking this dagger into Eisliev's skull.

His chest tightened, glaring at Eisliev, who had brought him so much grief.

Bohumir cringed, saying, "I already had my supper."

The red mage did not pause. The red mage propelled the wooden plate with Koldovstvo from the floor with the potency of an arrow, embedding itself into Bohumir's neck. The cascade of blood showered down the boy's shirt and the floor. Before Bohumir could gurgle, let alone raise his hands to grab the projectile, Eisliev used Koldovstvo to fling the boy's lithe body into the flames.

The murder was quick.

Bran gagged at the sight. Bohumir wriggled and thrashed on the coals, the flames searing through his skin, eating away at his clothes and hair first. The blood waned in the blaze.

The smell of charred meat infused Branimir's nostrils.

The red mage said, "There would be nothing left of the boy to recognize, let alone use for a ritual."

Eisliev shifted his weight to the back of his heel to turn around.

Branimir chucked his extra blade into the back of Eisleiv's head. The pointed weapon—quick as lightning—bore through flesh and bone until nothing remained but the handle.

Eisliev did not so much as flutter an eyelid. The red mage, the Stuhia, tarried in a standing position while the flames crackled and then collapsed face first into the wooden planks of the home.

Branimir bawled. With tear-filled eyes, he pounced on Eisliev Kluk's back, gripping his dagger with the intent to pull it free. He tugged it, heaving with all his strength, but the blade was stuck. His mind reeled.

Branimir should have separated from Dorofej at Cavell and pursued the boy. Instead, he had abandoned him. And now, his reluctance against Eisliev left the boy dead.

The red robes beneath him were as colorful as Eisliev's blood seeping from under his red strands. Branimir could not help but look to the shriveling corpse of Bohumir once more. He balled his hand into a fist in attempts to stop himself from trembling.

Branimir quaked with fury.

He jerked the other dagger from his belt, Kaelandur, and jabbed it into Eisliev's back. He stabbed the red mage over and over again. In his head. His neck. His shoulders. His backbone.

He hated the red mage. He hated himself.

Droplets of blood disgorged from the skin with every repetitive assault. Crimson liquid wetted his face and soaked his trouser legs. He did not care.

He did not hear the door creak open behind him, but he heard the thundering voice of Tyr Og. "No! Foul half pint?"

Branimir coiled his body to meet the blue eyes of the Ispolini, realizing in his rage, he had forgotten to maintain his hiddenness.

The giant barreled through the door, reaching for Branimir.

The Kras crumpled away from Tyr, disappearing once more. Behind him, Bohumir's remains cackled in the flames.

Tyr faltered, stopping in his tracks. Branimir followed Tyr's gaze to the shredded body of Eisliev. Even the Ispolini would second guess fighting an enemy he could not see. Bran thought him wise to hold back. He had fought plenty of Bukavac in the Netherworld. Brute strength did not contend against his stealth.

From the corner of the room, Branimir watched the giant look to the Ash Tree in the courtyard behind him and then back at Eisliev's body. His eyes reflected his deliberation before he scooted backward from the home.

Seeing the Ash Tree gave Branimir an idea. He acted fast, snagging the waterskin from the ground and dumping its contents onto the ground.

"Killer!" Tyr roared from the doorway. "Killer!"

Branimir slinked around the giant and ran for the Waters of Life. From the corner of his eye, he noticed the gates had been opened, and were slowly being closed again. Either someone had recently returned to Melkorka or someone had just left.

Tyr roared from the doorway of the house at any Kadari who would hear him. "Come quick," Tyr continued with intensity. "Hurry! Eisliev has been slain. There is a murderer within the walls."

The nearest Kadari rushed toward Tyr. Branimir dodged them in the road, sliding to the dark pool with the waterskin outstretched. The liquid flooded into the opening.

Kaelandur, secured in the scabbard at his belt, pressed against his side while the skin filled. He ignored the tension in his muscles, the feeling of wanting to curl into a dark corner and weep. The sense of self-loathing had not left him, but he had his sense of duty.

The Kadari behind him shouted questions at Tyr, screaming for someone to fetch the Patrician.

Unwilling to waste any more time, he gathered up the waterskin and peddled his feet toward the closing doors. As it was said, the Kras were quicker than any human, and Branimir made full use of it.

He bolted around the many scattering Kadari, immobilized carts, and random obstacles. In seconds, he had scampered through the gate, and was darting along the stone wall. Behind him, he heard the iron doors cling shut.

The shadow of Melkorka greyed behind Branimir. He fled toward the shoreline, overlooking the thinning grasses, broken pebbles, and glistening moon which had caught his eye before. There was nothing pleasant about being back home.

He wanted to be gone from Melkorka.

Chapter XXXII

The coast came into sight about the time the first raindrop struck Branimir on his hooked nose. Fitting for the rain to come when their deaths were nigh.

Branimir first saw Adamus. The hero-warrior was humming to himself while testing the weight of his silver axe. Sulanna stood near him, watching the hills leading to Melkorka. The black mage lay between them.

Dorofej exploded up from the sand, pointing in Branimir's direction. "Return, he does." Dorofej climbed to his feet, pulling at Adamus. "Flee, we must. I say, the Kadari are coming."

Branimir materialized several feet from them, causing Sulanna to jolt.

"Branimir," Sulanna gasped, "you are covered with blood!"

"What has happened?" Adamus stormed forward scanning the world behind Branimir, looking for an army to follow.

"You were with me, Dorofej?" Branimir asked with confusion, hearing only the black mage.

"Up until leaving the dungeon, I was, yes?" the black mage responded. "Be with you physically, I could not, but in Klukas, watch you, I could."

Branimir could not hold back his sadness any longer, falling to his knees. Tears streamed down his red cheeks. "I killed him, Dorofej. I…I killed him."

"If a man you had to kill, a choice, you did not have."

"I had to kill Eisliev, but I am not speaking of him. I mean Bohumir. The boy is dead because of what I could not do," Branimir cried.

"The boy is dead," Adamus said incredulously. "Our journey has been for nothing then. We have failed!"

Branimir sunk his hands into the sand, dropping his head. He repeated the words solemnly, "We have failed."

Raindrops started to fall more frequently, spattering around him.

"Know whether or not we have failed, we do not," Dorofej said, looking ominously toward the night's sky. "A blessing in disguise, it may be. Without the boy, the Kadari cannot perform their ritual, yes?"

"They only wanted him to strengthen the Ash Tree, Dorofej," Branimir said. "I heard it clear enough. They want more power to fight the demons."

Adamus took a step backwards, his face rigid with confusion. "That hardly sounds like an evil scheme."

Sulanna dipped her chin. "I agree. Did we not come here ourselves to save the Ash Tree? It sounds like the Kadari had found a way."

"I say, sacrificing the boy would have only bought them time, yes? Saved the world from the Likhyi and stopped the demons from coming, it would not." Dorofej raised his finger with a sense of urgency. "Best to focus on escaping, yes? Find a better solution, we will not, if we are captured."

Sulanna, keeping her forehead crinkled, spoke with insight. "Dorofej is right. We cannot worry over the things which have already come to pass, but only what we can now do. If the boy is dead, there is nothing to be done."

Adamus exhaled loudly, seemingly perturbed by the outcome. Considering the hero-warrior's dark magic displayed at Garain'l,

Branimir wondered if the Ariadnean would have sacrificed Bohumir if he thought it was needed.

Branimir gripped his head in his hands. "Falmagon is determined to find Kaelandur."

Sulanna shifted her weight, shooting Adamus a worried glance. "All of us? What good is the dagger if the boy is dead?"

"He may not want it anymore," Adamus said.

"True, Adamus. Though, risk letting them have Kaelandur, we cannot, yes? For now," Dorofej continued, "we must flee before the Kadari come. Coming with the scouting party, Falmagon and Dagmar are."

Sulanna's irritation came across in her tone, demanding a clearer answer. "They are coming *right* here?"

Branimir demanded, at the same time, "Dorofej, who is Dagmar?"

"How do they know we are here?" Sulanna said immediately after.

"They saw the knarr," Bran explained, waving off Sulanna. He repeated his question to Dorofej. "Who is Dagmar?"

"Let them come," Adamus said. "I have been at sea for far too long and would welcome a battle."

"The time to be brave or stupid, it is not, Adamus," the black mage glared. "The Kadari wield immeasurable magic with access to the Ash Tree, yes? I say, Dagmar holds the Varkolak, yes?" Dorofej shuddered, looking west momentarily, and then said, "Won, this battle cannot be."

Branimir scowled, being ignored again.

"Those are gruesome words, Dorofej," Sulanna said, the rain now coming in a downpour. She looked up warily at the visible moon, and then reached out to touch the rain with disbelief. "What is this Varkolak?"

"A book," Dorofej said. "I say, every time I beseech you to make haste, a hundred questions I then receive, yes? The time for questions is not in this moment. Come."

"Who is Dagmar!" Branimir shrieked.

"My grandson!" Dorofej cried, and then mumbled in a softer tone. "He is my grandson."

Branimir gasped. "Your grandson?"

"Yes." The black mage grimaced. "All the same, leave from this place, we must."

"We aren't going to get out of here without a fight," said Adamus, gesturing to the opposite side of Branimir with his head.

Branimir spun on his knees, soaked by the wet sand. Even through the rainfall, the Kras could see a troop of Kadari striding toward them. At the forefront of the group marched Falmagon and Dagmar.

"Dorofej," Branimir howled, pressing the waterskin into the dark mage's hands, "the Waters of Life. Drink."

With a look of wonderment, Dorofej took the pouch from Branimir and restored what he had lost since Ariadne.

Thunder crashed in the heavens. Lightning danced behind the circling dark clouds, and still the moon shined above them.

The next moment hastened. Dorofej screamed for them to gather close to him. Branimir nosedived to the black mage's feet while Sulanna and Adamus hung close to his side. Dorofej's hands flung upward, using Koldovstvo to create a blue shimmering orb. It encompassed them all, forming from nothing, and expanding wide.

On cue, fire and stone hailed from all directions, cast by the Kadari. The magic slammed into the bluish ball of energy, but held every physical element at bay, including the rain.

"Outside this orb is certain death," Adamus said with bewilderment. He pulled free his axe, looking for a moment to move to the offensive. There was none.

Sulanna said, "You cannot hold this forever, Dorofej."

The black mage, aging gradually responded, "For as long as I must, I will."

"I can fight them," Branimir said. "They will not be able to see me, but I only have Kaelandur for a weapon."

"No!" Dorofej took a step back, empowering the orb as magic struck it again and again with more ferocity. "Strike the copper blade against human flesh, dead or alive, you must not. Saw what happened to Nedezhda, you did, yes?"

Branimir's eyes widened. Eisliev. *No!*

Dorofej truly had not been with him when he killed the red mage.

Adamus, missing the significance of the conversation, said, "Tis a fine plan, Branimir, I have my dagger you could carry. Or, perhaps you could carry Sulanna's knife?"

Sulanna pulled her long knife from her belt, and held it out to him. "It will do better in your hands than in mine, if you can hurry."

Branimir, filled with uneasiness, took the weapon from Sulanna. He could not carry Adamus's dagger again. In his hands, he may as well have been carrying a longsword. The heavy weapon felt strange to him.

"Hurry, Branimir," Dorofej said, flinching as more magic struck the orb. "Weaken their numbers, and join the battle, we will."

Vanishing from sight, Branimir stepped out from the protective globe.

Precipitation pelted his body while he sprinted at the Kadari. He held the long knife to his side, gripping the hilt with two hands to manage the mass. Branimir swept wide, avoiding the whirlwind of lightning, wind, stone, and fire. The Kadari in their leather armor were aging, dark strands collecting shimmers of gray. As he circled to the rear of the horde, more than fifty, he could hear Falmagon commanding the troop.

"Hold nothing back," Falmagon bawled. "We are the stronger. Remember, youth awaits you in Melkorka. Leave nothing to question."

Dagmar walked steadily next to Falmagon. The Stuhia had not touched Koldovstvo. His words were faint in the din of battle, but Branimir's ears could hear the words. "The black mage will not last against us, but we should not kill him until we have Kaelandur. We must know whether he created it."

"Don't be foolish, Dagmar," Falmagon said, twisting his head forcefully at the man. "Dorofej must die. Now!" He screamed at the Kadari force. "Destroy him. He cannot hold his shield forever."

The rain slapped against his face, picking up speed over the short spans. Horrid bile, sour and dry, burned Branimir's throat. Ahead, the first Kadari, a girl in light armor hurled fire at his friends. Her eyes, likely once innocent, were filled with wrath, unquestionably following Falmagon's orders.

Branimir loathed killing.

He slowed and repositioned himself behind her and briskly sliced the blade-edge across the back of her knees. She crumbled to the side with a startled scream and he silenced her, stabbing the sword into her chest.

While she choked on the blood in her throat, Branimir could only see Eisliev's dead body. And then, Bohumir. And then, Hanna. The death never ended.

He would never get the images from his head.

Yanking the long knife free, he avoided her dimming eyes. Battle was not a time for thought; he knew that. He had caused enough damage by thinking too much. He did not have time to contemplate what needed to be done.

Another woman, directly ahead of his first target, caught his attention. She turned around and gasped at the dead Kadari.

Rushing the woman head on, Branimir pushed off the ground, holding the weapon at waist level. Sulanna's knife was too heavy to hold over his head. As he fell into the woman, he jabbed it forward, the blade sinking into her midsection. She fell backwards with him landing on top of her, hanging desperately to the weapon.

Her scream echoed as she scrambled to grab her invisible assailant. He stayed nimble ducking away from her flailing hands. He hurriedly hopped away from her while pulling the sword free. Fire from her hands seared the space where he had been. Right away, he rotated around her, thrusting the sword into her neck.

The flames shooting from her hands ceased, but the harm had been done. Cries of alarm cultivated across the Kadari ranks, and attention turned to the two dead women within feet of each other.

"Sara?" one yelled.

Another shouted, "Who did this?"

The rain turned to ice, forming into balls the size of a man's skull, and slammed into several Kadari near Branimir. He dived clear of the ice shards. Many of the Kadari fell, bleeding from the scalp.

Falmagon, several paces away, shouted, throwing stone back toward Dorofej, who had flung the ice boulders. He, again, raised his cerulean shield to block Falmagon's attacks.

Branimir pushed wet strands of hair from his forehead and ran in the sludge of muddied sand. The rain soaked into his tattered cloak, weighing down his movement. He loosened the string at his neck, and let the fabric fall away from him. It was better to be chilled in the rain than to carry the extra weight of wet wool.

He worked his way toward Falmagon, gathering the courage to strike down the spearhead of the Kadari. He noticed the mages regrouping and marching quicker towards Dorofej, Adamus, and Sulanna.

He picked up his pace, using Sulanna's long knife to slice the tendons of another Kadari, a male this time. He cut the throat after the mage had fallen. He repeated the maneuver on another. And another.

While invisible, Branimir could not be touched. He might be able to kill them all, if he remained undetected. He did not think he could hold up against a single magic user, especially Falmagon or Dagmar, unless he stayed out of sight.

A blast of earth behind him sent him spiraling through the air, the long knife sailing from his hand. Branimir squealed, hurtling into the sodden dirt. He heard the crack of his arm as it twisted beneath him awkwardly. He howled in agony over the racket of the battle.

"Branimir!" Adamus clamored, tearing out from the protection of Dorofej's shimmering shield. The Ariadnean's action told Branimir all he needed to know. He was obvious to the world.

He did not have to turn his head far to see Adamus's breastplate gleaning. The hero-warrior barreled into the first mage, sending the man sprawling, and then sliced his axe into the torso of a second. A third raised its hand but moved slower than the Ariadnean. Adamus grabbed the Kadari woman by the scruff of her robe, jerking her forward, and head-butted her. Blood spurted from her face; she staggered backwards, but he had already let loose of the woman, sprinting for Branimir.

Sulanna, on his heels, grabbed the bloodied Kadari with the broken nose, and snapped her neck. She, then, dived into a roll toward another, who hastily flung fire at her. She sprung up beneath the flame, striking the mage in the arms, veering the attack into one of their brethren. Her target wailed in fury. Sulanna did not flinch, snapping his arm and then his neck.

Her hands moved with untold speed in close combat.

Branimir tried to stand but felt too dazed and wobbly from the pinpointed blast. Pain coursed up his arm and into his shoulder. He winced and sunk back the mud.

"So, you are the Kras," Dagmar sneered, leering over him. "Where is this *dagger* called Kaelandur?"

Branimir inched back from the Stuhia's intimidating gaze. Again, the man looked uncannily like Dorofej, except for the hate radiating from his icy eyes.

"Tell me where it is and I may let you live," Dagmar threatened, quailing his hand.

"No," Branimir said meekly, trying to stand on his feet.

A fist, half the size of his face, struck him. Branimir fell hard, spitting a mouthful of blood.

"It will not do you any good," Branimir said, looking at Dorofej's so-called grandson. "Bohumir is dead."

"So, you do know where it is," Dagmar jeered. He pounded Branimir again, hitting him in the temple. A memory of Falmagon beating him grated his memory. The Stuhia whacked him again, shouting at Branimir to give up Kaelandur. "Give me the location and this will stop!"

Dagmar hit him until his jaw swelled and his cheek felt numb. Blood trickled into his eye and slid down the side of his face. Branimir kicked back, but his feet were feathers in comparison to the man's fists.

Kaelandur pressed against his side. His fingers inched toward the dagger.

In the shadows, in the shield of the rain, Adamus pitched himself into Dagmar. The impact sent the Stuhia roiling across the ground. Adamus pursued the man until he stopped rolling, and then stooped over him. Adamus struck the man with a heavy fist. Dagmar grunted against the blow, his head slamming back into the dirt.

Adamus lifted his silver axe when a rock slammed into him, sending him spiraling away from Dagmar. He twisted mid-air and landed with a thud. He sprung to his feet and was pressing forward again before Branimir could say anything.

Falmagon emerged from behind Dagmar, throwing another stone at Adamus. Before the rock struck the bulky hero-warrior, a blue shield shaped in front of him. The boulder shattered and crumbled harmlessly.

Across the expanse, Dorofej had his black hood pulled over his brow. The lengthening gray beard growing from his chin and down his front was unmistakable. Yet his hands worked meticulously through the air. He cast his craft back at the remaining Kadari while protecting Adamus.

"It is time to end this," Dagmar said, stumbling back to his feet. He stampeded forward, but instead of advancing toward Adamus, he aimed for Dorofej.

"Get up, Branimir," Adamus shouted, eyeballing Dagmar as he ran past him. The Stuhia blurred as he slithered through time and space. Dagmar wielded Koldovstvo like Dorofej. Branimir remembered the black mage saying he held the power of the void within Koldovstvo; he said it had been in his blood.

Branimir lost sight of the Stuhia, glancing across the field, and instead, saw Sulanna struggling against another Kadari. The side of her face was bloodied and burned. Another blue shield from Dorofej hovered around her.

"Branimir!" Adamus yelled again.

The Kras whimpered, holding his arm to his chest. He stumbled several steps towards Adamus and crumbled back to a knee. The world gyrated; his stomach churned.

A foot smashed into his back. "You are not going anywhere, Branimir," Falmagon scoffed, kicking him a second time. "You will tell me what I need to know. I will save this world."

Falmagon continued to wield Koldovstvo, casting stone and fire at Adamus. The hero-warrior sneered at the Patrician of the Kadari and marched forward, protected by the blue shield.

Branimir's insides felt broken, blood oozing over his gaping mouth. His chest burned like fire; his focus hazed. He fought against the blackness, keeping his sight on Adamus, who closed the distance. Branimir wriggled and thrashed to break free, but Falmagon pressed down with more weight.

Branimir convulsed against the pain, his broken arm trapped under his body. He tried to lift himself upward. He tried again. Nothing.

A heavy grunt sounded and the pressure on his body disappeared. He barely saw Falmagon fall as Adamus's fist connected across the man's jaw. An arm wrapped around Branimir's waist with more ferocity than intended. Adamus pulled Branimir to him.

"Come on. Dorofej needs us."

Branimir's feet wobbled as he tried to stand on them, searching the ground for Sulanna's long knife. He could not see anything but sand, but he noticed Falmagon writhing against the ground. The Patrician would not stay down for long.

"I am not sure I can, Adamus," Branimir coughed up blood, nearly collapsing again.

The Kadari were closing on them. In the distance, he noticed more mages advancing over the hill from Melkorka.

"You must get away," Branimir begged.

Adamus sheathed his axe, lifting Branimir fully from the ground. "No, I will carry you, my friend."

From the chaos, Sulanna approached them, contorting her face in pain. She was bruised and bleeding, but she stood. Branimir forced himself to look away from her burnt face.

Again, a vision of Bohumir clouded his head.

Sulanna heaved. "Get Branimir to the knarr if you can, or further up the coast. I will help Dorofej."

"Sulanna," Adamus started to contend, but she ran ahead of them without another word.

Dorofej, with his whitened beard, battled Dagmar, his red hair graying. Fire, ice, and stone erupted as the two of them altered through space and time. The movements were so quick, Branimir could hardly follow the two Stuhia. Their battle raged, a personal war of masters of their craft.

When Dorofej could not move quick enough, the blue orb—a substance like honey—would gel around the black mage and absorb the magical energy. From the rear, the rest of the Kadari hurtled unimaginable bright rays and lightning at Dorofej. He maintained another cerulean wall to block their attacks, but the abjuration had begun to fade.

With a boom, Dorofej finally hit Dagmar with a burst of wind. The Stuhia revolved through the air toward the other Kadari.

Adamus, who had ignored Sulanna, approached Dorofej with Branimir in his arms seconds after the noble woman.

"How do we escape, Dorofej?" Adamus asked.

The Stuhia looked to Adamus, Sulanna, and then finally Branimir. His voice sounded ancient and troubled, "Make a way, I will."

Falmagon could be heard behind them, back on his feet, screaming like a madman. The Patrician wielded his own craft against the magical shield. Each strike caused Dorofej to wince as he tried to hold the glistening wall.

"Keep Kaelandur away!" Dorofej cried, leaving one hand to hold the wall and raising another to the side. "Save yourselves!"

"We all will go," Sulanna said.

Behind her, the fabric of reality was ripped away before their eyes. Where shoreline met water, there was suddenly a gaping hole, large enough for a man to slip through. It led to another place. Low rolling hills were faintly lit by a crescent moon. No rain fell opposite of this gateway.

"Flee!" Dorofej screamed, his arms trembling. It took all his strength to craft this wonder. Branimir feared this was beyond his skill.

"Where is this?" Adamus asked.

"Gaetana," Dorofej said. "Now, go!"

Branimir wept, reaching for him. "We need you, Dorofej. You must come with us!"

"I cannot follow. I can…not…"

Adamus dipped his head, too familiar with the casualty of war. He seized Branimir tighter, in spite of his pleas, and carried him through the gateway.

Sulanna gripped Dorofej's shoulder and with a final look. She stumbled away hesitantly.

Branimir cried, gripping Adamus. He struggled to see Dorofej until the pathway shut. The battle of Melkorka was over.

The black mage was lost.

MAHARIA

BOOK 3
The Kaelandur Series

THRICE NINE LEGENDS

Joshua Robertson

There once was a time when the gods were gods without question. When men were men without example. When heroes were only the frivolous dreams of lurid mortality. It was a time when truths and untruths were indistinguishable, hatred and love were equally excusable, and life and death regaled all of humanity in the same breath. Myths of old were realized and legends were born from the very dust man was formed of, to be told and retold until the grace of time altered them beyond knowing or forgot them completely. Still, some tales were preserved deep within the hearts of mankind, for reasons that could not be fathomed. Perhaps bearing the fruit of some profound truth or kept alive merely by the strength of the men who lived them. Some tales would never be forgotten.

Month of Blossoming

Second of Warmth

1351 CE

Prologue

Dorofej Kaligula angled his eyes to gaze at the iron manacles binding his arms to the stone wall in the lower levels of Melkorka. He shuddered at the sight of his pasty, white flesh, prickled with gooseflesh, hanging exposed against the dry air. His thin legs were also fixed to the floor, keeping him rigidly hooked in place. His brittle bones ached; his strength was ever-fleeting.

His chest tightened with despair—not from the arduous position—but from knowing how *Koldovstvo*, the ancient magic, had once again gifted him with old age. Only weeks ago, he had been young and vivacious; but now, his wrinkled skin hung loose from muscle, and his body twinged as though his insides no longer had the resolve to function another day. His organs were likely as frail as the white hairs dangling over his eyes.

The black mage kept his knees locked to prevent the metal above from digging into his wrists. The blood from past captives staining the metal clasps spoke clearly of the antagonizing pain that would come if he allowed himself to simply hang. He questioned how long any man could hold this position before his wits were broken along with the finite body.

Dorofej did not know how long he had been standing in this irregular position. It may have been days, possibly a week. No light entered Melkorka's dungeon, only shadows. The room changed considerably since he had last been within its confines twelve-hundred-years ago. Where dirt paths and rickety cells once stood, rarely used, Dorofej now saw chiseled red stone, fresh timber, and twice as many chains for prisoners.

With a strained breath, he twisted his neck, where he knew a carved symbol of the eye, scraped with the moon and cross, hung over his head. The magical marking prevented him from touching the craft, Koldovstvo. He whispered its ancient name. "*Znaki.*"

He dropped his head in defeat. Even if the symbol were erased, Dorofej was not certain he had enough life in him to wield Koldovstvo. Another trickle of magic through his fingertips may very well end his life.

He had no interest in dying. Not yet.

He suppressed a cough. The odor of urine and feces clung to the air as closely as a hero might cling to honor and glory. Sadly, his own filth was among the filth beneath his feet. Rats and unmarked pests screeched and scraped across the stone floor. Over and over, the creatures neared him to nibble at his wrinkled toes, checking for decay.

With a shudder, shout, or twitch, Dorofej indicated to the vermin he was not dead. But the rodents were patient, accustomed to the unwritten process of the underground, hollowed chamber. No doubt, in short time, there would be no resistance, no shuffling or screaming, and then they could feast on his flesh.

Across the room, the latch clicked and the oak door creaked open. Air from beyond the dungeon circulated into the room. Dorofej could not hold back his cough this time, and hacked harshly, the ashy dust filtering up to his nostrils and into his throat.

The flickering torchlight danced across the dungeon, nearly blinding him. Twisting his neck, his long white hair fell away from his face, providing a faint image of many shadowed figures slinking into the room.

"Careful," said a man in white robes. "Do not loosen the binds until the giant is chained."

The *Kadari* paid no attention to Dorofej. Their attention stayed on the Ispolini, the giant, who was being dragged across the floor with magical strands of Koldovstvo.

Dorofej recognized Tyr Og. The giant had helped kidnap an innocent boy, Bohumir Mager, for the Kadari to sacrifice here at Melkorka. Though, none would have guessed the plan would have been thwarted by the red mage, Eisliev Kluk, who slaughtered the boy first.

Tyr growled, having the ability to do nothing more but speak. "For the hundredth time, I did not kill the boy. Eisliev killed him, and the half pint killed Eisliev with a dagger."

"Hold your tongue," Falmagon Sej spouted, following Tyr and the other Kadari through the door. The Patrician of the Kadari, once known as the Highborn Longwalker, was easily distinguishable. "We will hear your so-called truth when it is time."

"Listen to me. I helped you," Tyr shouted. "There is no reason to hold me here. Please!"

Falmagon responded to the Ispolini, but lifted his blue eyes to Dorofej, mockingly. "I will be most interested to hear more about this dagger in very, very short time."

Dorofej strained to keep his head elevated to maintain eye contact with the Patrician. The muscles in his neck and upper back ached. He tried to focus on breathing through his nose to forget the pain.

It was a mistake. He coughed harshly again at the rotten smell.

Falmagon maintained the smirk on his face. "Yes, the truth will be revealed soon enough. Won't it, Dorofej? Say, why don't you give up your little charade and tell me what I need to know?"

Dorofej wheezed, desperate for a drink. "Oh, tell me—you must—what needs to be known, yes?"

The demeanor of the Patrician changed as soon as Dorofej opened his mouth. "Do not play your games with me. Where is *Kaelandur*? Does Branimir have it?" Falmagon flared his nostrils, blowing air through his thick mustache. He advanced, holding himself inches in front of Dorofej's face.

Dorofej lingered, stone-faced. Indeed, his friend, Branimir Baran held Kaelandur, the copper dagger, the hourglass of Dorofej's life. Though, he would never tell Falmagon such a thing.

"I say, why do you care?" Dorofej said. "Dead, the boy is. Sacrifice him, you cannot."

"Answer the question," a deep voice demanded from behind Falmagon. The man, called Dagmar, ambled forward from the shadows. Dorofej fought the man on the shores of Folkmar before being imprisoned. At the time, Dagmar lost years of his life casting Koldovstvo. But now, the Stuhia regained his youth. He had a head full of red hair and smooth, unmarred skin. Seeing Dagmar reminded Dorofej the Ash Tree and the Waters of Life were just beyond the castle's dungeon. His salvation was less than a hundred feet away.

Dagmar gripped a thick book under his arm, and continued, "Someone has broken the old laws by creating this dagger with Koldovstvo. If you are truly Stuhia, you know the maker must be killed to abolish the dagger."

"Know the law of the Stuhia, I do," Dorofej said, eyeing the leather book. He knew its name: the *Varkolak*. "I say, why are you eager to destroy Kaelandur?"

Falmagon huffed with superiority, seemingly offended by the question. "Because demons have continued to come from the Netherworld and it must be stopped. They are intent on destroying the Ash Tree. This started with the creation of the dagger, and it will end with the dagger's destruction."

"That is why you sent Alyona and Artemiy after the dagger, yes?" Dorofej contemplated. "Want the dagger, you did, to stop the demons?"

"Why else?" Falmagon squinted at Dorofej, likely questioning how he would know of Alyona and Artemiy. Yet he said nothing of the two Kadari. Instead, he defended his reason. "It was not until I met Dagmar that I learned you were a Stuhia, and I had to kill you to destroy Kaelandur. Everything I do is for the saving of this world, Dorofej."

"Misinformed, you are, Falmagon Sej. Proof, you are, there are worse things in this world than demons," Dorofej said, coughing again. He unsuccessfully tried to find saliva in his mouth. "And come, the demons will, whether Kaelandur exists or not."

"Do not insult me with your lies," Falmagon said haughtily. "You are trying to save your own skin."

"My own skin?" Dorofej said, lifting his eyebrows with as much innocence as he could muster.

Dagmar fell into the façade. "Did you not create Kaelandur, Stuhia?"

"Of course, he created it!" Falmagon cried, glaring at Dorofej. "Don't bother entertaining this pile of piss with such a question. He is talking in his riddles to buy his time, hoping someone will come and save him. Listen, it was only him and Jhar who crafted the dagger, and Jhar is dead."

The black mage snorted, looking to Dagmar. "The law of the Stuhia, I know."

Dagmar tilted his chin to Falmagon, and then back to Dorofej. "Humor me."

Dorofej swiftly stated, "Familiar with the Varkolak, I am." He bobbed his head in acknowledgement of the book under Dagmar's arm.

The redheaded man in front of him stepped backwards in sheer shock, mouth gaping and eyes widening. "How do you know the name of this codex? How does he know this, Falmagon?"

"Because passed it to my son, Mihael, I did, after the fall of the Carian Council," Dorofej kept his eyes from Falmagon, who he could hear breathing heavier and heavier. He locked eyes with Dagmar. "Scribed it, I did."

"What!" Dagmar roared, his voice echoing in the dungeon. "Mihael? You gave this codex to my father?"

Dorofej lowered his head.

"You are my grandfather?" Dagmar asked shakily.

"He is deceiving us, Dagmar. Let us kill him and be done with this. His death will save Aenar," Falmagon demanded.

Dagmar hurriedly grabbed Falmagon's arm, pulling him away. His eyes never moved off Dorofej hanging from the chains. "No. If he did not create Kaelandur, killing him will do nothing but have Dahz find disfavor in you."

"One way or another, the world is better without him. I would rather watch him burn than reach Thrice Ten Kingdom," Falmagon proclaimed.

"If he is my grandfather…if he knows the law of the Varkolak…"

Falmagon interrupted. "Wouldn't you know if he was your grandfather? He is lying."

"I never knew my father's father," Dagmar sluggishly said. "You do not understand the significance of what this man is saying. Whether he is lying or not—even to know the name of this codex—speaks of the knowledge he holds. We cannot kill him," Dagmar said while Falmagon stared incredulously back, "yet."

"Your logic is the same as my predecessor, Kinhar Sayan," Falmagon whispered, "and he is dead. The Kadari cannot fight an endless war against Marheena's demons and lead the people of Aenar to redemption. We can kill him now and end this."

Dagmar shook his head. "The only way to destroy Kaelandur is to kill its maker *with* the weapon."

"What?" Falmagon sneered.

"You cannot simply kill him. His life is bound by the life of the dagger," Dagmar explained. "And you need the weapon and creator to complete the deed. Without Kaelandur, you are powerless. You would not be able to kill Dorofej if you tried."

Falmagon bawled in frustration, folding his hands into fists. "Fine, Dagmar. Then we must find Branimir Baran."

Dagmar curled his lip. "I can find him."

"If you won't tell me where Kaelandur is," Falmagon turned back on Dorofej, staring hard into the black mage's icy eyes, "Branimir will. Even if I must tear him limb from limb, he will talk."

Dorofej hung his head in defeat.

Month of Harvest

Fourth of Warmth

1352 CE

Chapter I

"You don't have to watch me," Branimir Baran said, staring blankly across the subtle ripples on the placid lake, absorbing the morning sun's warmth on his back. He overlooked the strands of black, thin hair tickling his eyelids, situated just above his long, crooked nose.

"You keep saying that, and I keep watching," Sulanna Maelthirren replied from a few feet away. He could hear her fingernails scraping against the smooth rock in her hand patiently waiting for him to finish his morning routine. The two had stuck to the same, mundane schedule since the warm months had come. Branimir knew her and Adamus Ebordon rightfully worried about his affliction, but their constant concern only deepened his distress.

The breeze shifted, filling his nostrils with a hint of the pollen from the poppy field north of the lake, the Gnyn Waters. His stomach tightened with every forced breath, sucking the sweet air through his nose and blowing it out from his lips. More than a year passed since fleeing from Falmagon at Melkorka, and he had come no closer to rescuing Dorofej or ridding himself of the cursed copper dagger, Kaelandur. Moreover, Bran scarcely traveled beyond Gaetana's city walls, remaining under the watchful eye of his trusted friends.

His sigh was long and intentional. "Enough time has passed. I would think if Falmagon wanted me, he would have come by now. We have abandoned Dorofej for too long."

"Adamus and I have told you many times, returning to Melkorka would be a mistake," Sulanna said, her faded brown hair swirling against her thin cheeks. The number of grey strands on her head had significantly increased this past year. "You have only recently healed from your injuries. A broken arm is never easy to overcome. Give yourself some time."

Branimir instinctively rested his left hand on his right forearm. He rubbed his red skin softly with a frown. Falmagon snapped the bone at Melkorka during the battle on the shoreline. Occasionally, the bones still tingled or ached but he would not admit as much to Sulanna.

"You cannot keep me here forever," Branimir said.

"You speak as though we are holding you captive against your will, Bran." She pushed her flailing hair behind her ear. "We did not flee from Melkorka only to watch you go back and die."

"I wouldn't die," Branimir said.

"You have many talents, my friend, but seeing the future is not among them." Her voice lacked her usual sing-song tone, reiterating the same speech she had given many mornings before. "Falmagon Sej has the Ash Tree in his grasp, promising immortality. He can afford to be patient."

Branimir maintained the frown, sitting motionless. His mind wandered briefly through memory like a melody trapped between the ears. The images of battles won and lost weighed on his heart, remembering what had come to pass and what may have been done instead. He envied old men with weak minds. For all his years, Branimir could not forget.

He finally said, "The *Old-dark* are escaping into Aenar and demons flood from the Netherworld." Branimir chewed the inside of his cheek. The entity they encountered at the ruins of Garain'l, and now trapped within the copper dagger, still frightened him.

The dark, ancient god called itself a Likhyi, intent on annihilating the Ash Tree and the world with it. And now, the malevolent deity somehow became bound to him through Kaelandur, promising to kill Branimir if the dagger was ever destroyed. He scrunched his face, doom weighing heavy on his heart. "I do not know what *time* Falmagon would think to have."

"True. The Ash Tree withers more and more each day while the Kadari defend against demons. Maybe his mages are too spent to search for a single Kras," she said.

"Not when I hold Kaelandur," Branimir said. "Falmagon would give everything for this dagger."

"He may not know you hold it." Branimir could hear Sulanna's tongue clicking against the roof of her mouth. She did not even believe her own lie. "Whatever the reason," she finished, "he has yet to come for you. He chooses to wait."

Branimir clenched his fists in angst. "But we cannot. We have lingered around this city for fourteen months and have done nothing."

"We have stayed alive."

Branimir punched his fist through the air. "While Dorofej suffers."

"Dorofej is still alive," she returned with softness. The scraping on her rock ceased. He could feel her gaze burning into his back along with the sun's heat. "Whatever he has suffered at the hands of Falmagon would be wasted if you were to return with Kaelandur."

Pulling his red-colored hands to his lap, Branimir danced his thin fingers along the copper hilt nestled between his belt and stomach. Not long ago, Branimir learned Dorofej had crafted Kaelandur; and per the magical law of the Stuhia, the dagger could only be destroyed through its creator's death, meaning Dorofej still breathed. While Kaelandur existed, Dorofej was living.

His eyes glazed, staring at nothingness across the lake. "You and I cannot outlive Falmagon without access to the Ash Tree, and I cannot unbind myself from Kaelandur. We have remained deadlocked for too long."

Sulanna said, "Dorofej opened the gate for us to come to Gaetana. He must have had his reasons for sending us to the capital. We cannot leave here until an opportunity presents itself."

He remained silent, his shoulders falling. Gaetana was half a world away from Melkorka. He suspected Dorofej had simply sent them as far away from danger as he could with his magic. Branimir doubted any hidden meaning lay in the deed.

Sulanna apparently misread his body language, gliding forward and kneeling to place her wrinkled hand on his drooping shoulder. He often forgot Sulanna was middle-aged for a human. "You have not been the only one struggling this past year. Remember, we also abandoned Alden in Talastein, and I have had to fight the compulsion to rush back south to save him. Every morning, the thought is heavy on my mind. I do not have the comfort he is still alive anymore, but I hope."

"I am sorry, Sulanna." Branimir gave a weak nod, knowing the love Sulanna felt for Alden and the pain she experienced when he was captured by the Lilitu. Branimir long ago considered the old warrior dead; he honestly thought Sulanna did the same, especially with Adamus's insistence that the Lilitu did not keep their prisoners alive.

"Hope is not lost, my friend," she said, "not yet."

"I know what you are saying. But whether we stay here or go, I die at the end of this story," Branimir said.

"The same could be said of any who call themselves mortal. Do not be so eager to rush to your end." Sulanna squeezed his shoulder, hurling the smooth rock into the lake, an indication of the storm brewing inside her. "Come now, Adamus approaches. No more talk of death."

Branimir cleared his throat, watching the ripples expand from the impact. His sensitive ears heard Adamus, the hero-warrior from Ariadne, approaching. The gruff man's heavy footfalls were unmistakable, scraping against the dry ground.

"Who is with him? Wit?" Branimir off-handedly asked. His eyes drifted to the cracking earth. The summer had been scorching, leaving the morning dew to imagination.

Sulanna shifted next to him and hummed in response, indicating the persnickety historian, Witigor Sirska, from the Highspire remained attached to Adamus's side, as he had been for the past month. The undernourished man had wedged himself between Adamus and Branimir, openly ridiculing any who were not an Anshedar or male. Branimir considered silencing Wit with a fist in his loud mouth, but Sulanna coached tolerance, reminding him they would be better off not to draw attention in the King's city. King Frantisek was a man closely allied with the Kadari.

"Wit and I crossed a runner at the gate. The Uvil sacked Draha the night before last," Adamus informed them, stopping a few feet behind Branimir's back.

Sulanna replied, "I thought King Frantisek was taking back Raybin."

"He tried," Adamus said, "and failed. They were pushed back two weeks ago."

"Gaven Frantisek has no sense for war. He probably never read *Fate Without Duty* by Anthony Janes. He is not like his father." Witigor whistled through his lips.

Branimir could already visualize the dozen or so blonde strands hanging from Wit's scalp, bouncing as he talked about his books. His hair would be clinging to the side of his cheek, held in place by the ridiculous pointed hat he often wore. Half of the man's head had been scarred from a fire long ago, decorating his face with folded skin and red lines, leaving him quite bald and grotesque. Without judgment, Branimir understood why Wit had taken up copying books in the Highspire; the capital library was a place where he could escape the disparaging looks of his fellow citizens.

Adamus went on, "No doubt, the cities of Tyrewen and Utulock will form a barrier with their armies; the Ariadneans will send what fighting men are left. But when they fall, nothing will stop the Uvil from sieging Gaetana. With supplies, the King could hide behind the walls for years, but we would be trapped inside with everyone else. We will not be able to stay in the capital."

Branimir's heart jumped at the thought of leaving Gaetana. He spun around and rose to his feet. Adamus faced him, beard hanging to his chest, and blue eyes wild with excitement. Witigor, a head taller than the Ariadnean, joggled his head in agreement, the overhanging flap of his ridiculous brown hat bouncing over his brow.

Sulanna stilled them with her hand. "What about Dorofej? The Stuhia has not survived this long simply to stay captive in a dungeon. Are we to continue to trust that he will find a way to escape?"

"Tis a thought I hope to be true, Sulanna," Adamus said, "though the odds are not favorable. I am not proposing we attempt to free Dorofej. We simply cannot stay here much longer. Besides, if Dorofej does escape, he can always find us with that *thing* he does."

"*Klukas*," Branimir said. "Yes. He can find us in the shadow world."

"Oh, here we are again, talking of this mysterious, all-knowing man called Dorofej." Wit grimaced, pulling the sleeves up on his shirt. "The man might as well be a god, the way you speak of him." Wit's eye twitched. "Still, you are correct on this matter. The Stuhia can find anyone in Klukas if they have come across them before. Their gift of scrying supersedes the skill of the greatest oracle. He would be able to find you no matter your destination, I assure you."

"Oh. Are you suddenly an expert with the Stuhian people, Wit?" Sulanna mocked, twisting her mouth with suspicion. "Funny you have not said a word of them until recently."

"Well…I have read Tom Flitter's *Mystagogical's Forlorn Folio* and Colin Turney's *Unchanted and Unequaled*." Wit crossed his arms, leaned back like he had taken a blow to the bits, and then wobbled his head back and forth in disbelief. "Do you not know I have access to every book in the known world, Sulanna? I would have been reading about the *dragon people* long before now if I had known anyone cared to know about them. But you three keep your tongues wrapped so tight, I would not be surprised if you did not have any tongues at all. I don't know how you expect me to help."

Branimir stuck out his tongue. "No one asked for your help. We asked for one book on ancient religions, and here you still are—"

"Yes, I remember. *The Compendium of Infernal Light* by Emrys Trudgeon." Wit widened his eyes. "No other man could have gotten you that little treasure. If you don't want me, I can be on my way." He stomped the back of his foot against the earth, indicating he had no intention of budging. "You know, it is not everyday someone asks about a text not highlighting the Lightbringer."

"Czern's breath. You mustn't go anywhere," Adamus said, angling an eyebrow at Branimir.

Sulanna flashed her teeth, chiming in, "Indeed. Your input is always welcome, but our business will remain our own."

"Of course, my Lady," Wit said, nodding his head again with enough momentum to bounce his hat. "And I don't mean to pry, but anything you need to know, I can find." He winked, pointing at Branimir. "Don't get me wrong. The Kras have wicked memories, but none are as old as books. None can know how their minds have twisted their words over time."

Branimir clenched his jaw, catching another narrow look from Adamus. "Okay," he murmured, "is it decided? Are we leaving Gaetana?"

"We will discuss it more after breakfast," Adamus answered. "We should have a destination in mind before simply packing up and marching out of the gates."

"South is clearly out of the question," Sulanna said.

"Sulanna…" Adamus opened his hands, repeating himself, "after breakfast, eh? Branimir needs to get back to the tavern. He has work to do. We all have work to do."

Hanging his head, Branimir sighed. He, Adamus, and Sulanna had been trading work for lodging and food for the better part of the year.

She folded her arms. "Very well, Adamus Ebordon. But I hope you have better sense than to give me orders and expect me to simply follow."

Wit peered at Sulanna over his shortened nose.

Adamus's features turned to stone seconds before he threw his head back with a booming laugh, his beard bouncing against his chest. "Never, Sulanna. Never."

Branimir tailed the other three on the dirt path winding back through the gates, beneath the half-raised portcullis, to return to the Peddlar's Rose. The road to the inn branched into a hundred twisted routes within the city. According to Wit, the city had been built sporadically over the age with buildings thrown wherever space allowed. Built from both stone and wood, the shops and homes were as intertwined as a briar patch. The Shielded Boar sat against the smithy, like a crooked blade against the hilt. The Poppy Garden, the apothecary, was positioned so close to the cobbler the front doors would collide if ever they sprang open at the same time. The hodgepodge of mangled architecture continued from the housing district to the Highspire to the looming hold of King Gaven Frantisek.

The Peddlar's Rose sat only a few streets south of the King's courtyard, frequently full of patrons from all stations in Gaetana, common and noble alike. Yet mornings typically were slow with only a few guests descending from their rooms for breakfast.

Branimir was the last to enter the Peddlar's Rose, closing the oversized, wooden door behind him. He imagined a giant from the western island of Tundris Mor, an Ispolini, could fit through the entryway without straining the neck. He instantly caught the scent of sausage and biscuits, skimming the common room to see a handful of patrons sitting amongst the tables.

"Good morning, Master Branimir," one of the men at the table lifted his hand. Branimir forced a smile at the frequent customer named Jon Goraen, having more greying hairs on his chin than combed over his receding hairline. Although a citizen of Gaetana, he spent ample time at the inn due to marital spats. Branimir only met the wife twice prior, and neither instance was pleasant. She had a shrill whine, matching the fracas of demons.

"Morning," Branimir replied, forcing a serpentine grin.

"Will you be honoring us with your dagger throwing tonight? I came a bit too late last night," Jon said, tearing a biscuit in half.

"I do not know what Lady Gail has intended for evening festivities," Branimir answered.

Jon laughed, pushing the bread into the back of his cheek. "I'll talk to her then, and see that it is *intended*."

Branimir held the smile. Jon likely would persuade Gail, considering the amount of coin he spent at the Peddlar's Rose. Branimir care little for the spectacle he provided for the townsfolk, but understood the fascination they had with his ability with a dagger. He once entertained in a similar fashion after leaving the Netherworld while working at The Oaken Bard in Gavlok.

"I best get to balancing the books," Sulanna said, scrunching her small nose. "Lady Gail will likely have another stack of letters to be drafted by midafternoon. We all have to earn our stay, right?"

Adamus said, "And I will head to the stables to shuffle hay. Morkanfej plans to come by this morning with a fresh pair of mares, looking for a buyer." He lowered his voice. "If we plan for departure, we would make better with a couple of horses."

"You mean the kingsguard?" Branimir asked. He had not heard Morkanfej's name in weeks. He and Adamus played cards frequently after settling in Gaetana, but the man seemingly disappeared.

Adamus rumbled, "The same. I am hoping to learn more about the Uvil's advancement. We would be wise not to travel in any direction they may be scouting."

"Don't spend all of our coin, Adamus," Sulanna said.

"I know the circumstance," he replied, rubbing his thick beard. "I will only make a deal if 'tis fitting. Besides, Morkanfej owes me a debt, whether he remembers it or not."

"He owes everybody a debt," Branimir mumbled.

"I have an hour until I am needed at the Highspire," Wit said. "If it pleases you, Adamus, I will join you. Confronting a man about money should not be done without witness."

The Ariadnean grunted in agreement.

Branimir gave pause as the other three took their leave, Adamus and Wit through the front door again, and Sulanna marching to Lady Gail's study to ruffle through the stacks of papers. With a heavy heart, Branimir turned to the kitchen, snatching an apron from behind the newly furnished bar top on the way.

He swung open the galley door, the clang of a stirring spoon dinging against the pot while Meisher, the scrawny boy, began a soup for midday. Lady Gail supervised nearby, cutting dough for more biscuits.

"Master Branimir," she said, rolling a ball of sticky dough between her old, boney fingers, blue eyes bugging from under her eyelids. "I hope your morning stroll was pleasing. If I had been thinking, I would have asked you to stop for another sack of flour on your way back."

"Would you like me to fetch one now?" Branimir asked.

"No, no," Gail said with a laugh. Her dimples creased under the wrinkles beneath her eyes, nearly hiding her age. "I will have Meisher go once the soup is set. The Lightbringer knows my boy could use some muscle on those skinny legs."

"I spend a lot of time running, Ma," Meisher said. "They are skinny because I am so fast."

Gail rutted her brow, holding back a chuckle. "You run like a ruffled chicken."

Her son cackled at the joke.

Branimir gave a polite smile.

"Does a mood hold you this morning, Branimir?" Gail asked, turning the dough.

Branimir scratched his head. "I must not have slept well last night."

"Maybe your heart will be lifted to know you have a visitor then?" Gail said. "The young lass arrived early this morning while you were out."

"Visitor?"

Gail nodded. "I admit I was surprised. You and your friends have been here for some time and made no mention of friends or family seeking you out. But she did ask for you specifically by name."

"She has the prettiest eyes I have ever seen," Meisher swooned.

Gail giggled at her boy. "You have time yet before you need to be thinking of a wife. You jump into marriage too soon and you will be as miserable as ole' Jon out there."

"Who is it?" Branimir pressed.

"Oh, she may have given her name… I cannot remember. She said she came from the east," Gail said. "Maybe she is one of those Kadari." The innkeeper hooted at her own joke. She waved at the door. "I had her wait for you in the study."

"The study?" Branimir stumbled through the swinging door, his mind on fire. The Kadari had finally come to kill them. "Sulanna…"

Chapter II

The room blurred while Branimir pondered his few options. He did not have time to rush to his room upstairs to retrieve his daggers. By the time he pulled the chest from under the bed, and returned to Sulanna in the study, she could be dead. From the bar top, Branimir could see the windowless door of Gail's study, situated behind the curved staircase. The thick door remained shut beyond the scattered tables. He had no choice but to go now and discover the danger on the other side. But he needed a weapon.

With uncanny precision, Branimir scoped the room for an alternative blade, resting his eyes on Jon, who scraped absentmindedly at his breakfast plate. Branimir quickened his footfalls until he stood at Jon's table, barely peering over the edge.

The old man turned from his plate of sausage and biscuits to lift his bushy eyebrows with wonder, holding his food at bay in his cheek. The two younger men who shared the table also stopped chewing.

"Master Branimir," Jon began, gritting his teeth, the wrinkles on his face as defined as valleys pitted within the northern hills, "you nearly stop a man's heart sneaking up so fast. What can I do you for?"

"Your knife." Branimir held his hand out expectantly.

"My knife?" Jon repeated.

"The Kras has a dark look about him," one of the other men said.

Jon squinted at Branimir, lastly chewing whatever food remained in the corner of his mouth. He slowly swallowed.

"All of your knives," Branimir forcibly said, "now."

Jon's eyes bugged like a boy who had never seen war, and now faced unmatched bloodshed. "No need to make a fuss, Master Branimir." He grunted. "Go on. Hand them over, boys."

Three serrated blades, fixed in wooden handles, were hastily placed at the edge of the table. Branimir scooped them up in his tiny hands, testing the end with the tip of his finger. They held little sharpness, but would do the trick with enough force.

"Be careful now, Master Branimir," Jon cautioned, dipping his saggy chin to his chest. "Don't be doing anything you would regret come the 'morrow."

Branimir averted his eyes and covered the expanse of the common room to the study door. He ignored the fretful whispers of the three at the table, and listened carefully through the door. The hushed sounds were loud in his sensitive ears.

"Do you think anyone is going to believe such a ridiculous story?" Sulanna questioned in a husky undertone, followed by the sound of a chair dragging along the wooden floorboards. "Why did he not come instead?"

"He cannot move through his own gateway, and few others have the skill to create one," a woman answered.

"Were you not the one who betrayed him?"

"You must believe me..."

He gripped the knives in his hand, sliding one to his left while holding the other two in his right.

A thump of something heavy hit the floor, causing Branimir's heart to jump. He wasted no time, swiftly pulling the latch and pushing the door open.

The dim room, shadowed by lantern light, had no impact on Branimir's eyesight. As a Kras, he could see as clearly in complete darkness as under mid-day sun. Shelves sitting at his eye level sat on either wall, filled with books and loose manuscripts. The walls above them were decorated with amateur paintings and armaments that would be as effective in battle as a quill pen.

His instinct was to throw the blades. Yet, too many times he had killed without thought, whether against the Lilitu last year at the Ariadnean port or…the red mage… Branimir was not sure how much more guilt he could stomach.

Branimir's eyes flickered by Sulanna, who raised her head from where she kneeled to pick up a stack of books from the floor. He settled his gaze on the woman with short, dark hair, barely touching her ears, and inimitable, purple irises. She was the same woman he discovered being interrogated in the dungeons of Melkorka a year ago, but the narration of their history seized centuries more.

"Alyona," he croaked, almost dropping the knives. He held them up at waist level instead to appear menacing, if anything, remembering the beating he watched her take at the hand of Falmagon.

She dropped to her knees almost instantly at the sound of her name. The hoary shirt she wore hung loosely on her thin skin, covered partially by the faded, black cloak. "Alyona Gounari, at your service, Branimir Baran. Please, you must believe me. I have been sent by Dorofej to see you safe."

Sulanna clicked her tongue, setting the heavy books on the desk. "Her story is remarkable, and hardly believable, Branimir."

"Did she try to harm you?" Branimir asked.

"No," Sulanna said. "She had the chance, catching me unaware when I first came in here. But she has not so much as lifted a finger."

"I will not hurt you," Alyona said, remaining on her knees. "I may have done wrong many times in my life, but I have no interest in seeing the Likhyi return or Aenar destroyed."

"She claims redemption," Sulanna said. "Yet, is she not the one who followed you and Dorofej into the Netherworld? A spy for Falmagon and the Kadari?"

Branimir nodded. "She and her brother, Artemiy. Though, she was nearly slain when held at Melkorka. I watched them torture her."

"And Artemiy?" Sulanna asked.

"Dead," Alyona said, giving Bran a peculiar look, widening her purple eyes. "Dorofej said he had fallen to Marheena shortly after we fled the Netherworld. Her magic withered him away into an old man. He died protecting the Mager bloodline."

Sulanna opened her mouth to respond, and Branimir hurried to shush her.

Alyona uncomfortably shifted on her knees, and added, "I know the boy is dead too. Not only did Dorofej tell me what happened before we escaped, but I heard whispers of the events while in the dungeon."

Branimir's heart swelled in his chest. "Dorofej escaped?"

Alyona dipped her chin to her chest.

"Do not believe everything she says, Branimir," Sulanna again cautioned, moving around the desk with a noble's grace.

Branimir looked at the knives in his hand for a moment and grasped them tighter. He boldly stepped closer to the Kadari woman. Her unwashed, pastel skin seemed to pale even more under his gaze. "Tell me what you know. How did you find us?"

"Dorofej said to start asking around Gaetana about you, and well, I cannot say many Kras travel the area. Finding you was not difficult." Branimir gritted his teeth, seeing the simple logic of the explanation. He motioned for her to continue. Alyona nodded, purple eyes still wide. "Three days ago, Melkorka was attacked by Bukavac—"

Branimir interrupted. "Three days? You were at Melkorka three days ago?"

"Yes. Dorofej sent me here through a gateway, the same as he had done for you. His magic does not allow him to pass through himself, or he would be here too," Alyona replied with a steady tone.

"He was nearly dead when we parted ways," said Branimir.

"And he was restored by the Waters of Life before leaving Melkorka," she replied.

"How?"

Her eyes stayed fixed on Branimir as the thoughts poured through her lips. "Melkorka was sieged, and the dungeon walls collapsed around us. I used Koldovstvo to free Dorofej, and then Tyr pulled us to safety. The Ash Tree was not far from the castle keep."

"She has rehearsed the story well," Sulanna said.

Branimir scrunched his face, and shook his head in disbelief. He knew the Ash Tree lay within Melkorka's walls, but her story still did not add up. "Not well enough." He crossed his arms. "Why would the Ispolini help you? Why would he rescue Dorofej when he last tried to kill us?"

Alyona folded her hands, and continued, "Tyr was held captive by the Kadari too. Falmagon believed him to have killed Eisliev, and…" Alyona continued speaking but Branimir's mind clouded.

The name rang in his ears, a name he wished he could disremember. A year ago, Eisliev Kluk, always drowning in his red robes, helped capture the boy, Bohumir Mager, and took him to Melkorka—the same boy Artemiy, Alyona's brother, supposedly had tried to protect. Eisliev brutally slaughtered the boy to exact his own revenge on Falmagon, and in turn, Branimir gave Eisliev equal punishment.

Branimir could still smell the charred corpse of Bohumir withering in the flames of the cottage fire. He could still feel Eisliev's warm blood gushing around his fingertips.

His thumb picked at his fingers on either hand at the horrid recollection when he struck the thin, silver band on his left forefinger. He frequently forgot he was wearing the piece of simple jewelry, called *Faegrim*, which was not all that simple at all. He stole the magical band from Eisliev after killing him, unable to resist keeping the polished trinket. While the ring held no purpose for Branimir, it gave Eisliev the ability to control the mind of any who did not possess the power of Koldovstvo. Branimir did not like to think about how the red mage once forced him to act against his will, causing him to hurt Adamus, Dorofej, and their now deceased friend, Hanna. The thought gave him chills, thinking such a thing existed in the world, to give one being power over another.

Alyona's words pulled him from memory.

"Wait…" Branimir said, perking his pointed ear. "What did you just say?"

Alyona took a breath. "I know it does not sound believable. I know, okay? But Eisliev returned from the dead more powerful than any Kadari or Stuhia I have ever seen, with an army of Bukavac at his back. It was like the battle at Shayol Domier with Nedezhda Mager, Branimir." She pulled at her dark hair, shaking her head. "Eisliev marched on Melkorka with such vengeance…he killed so many…and now, he is coming for Kaelandur…"

Sulanna blinked with an unconvinced frown and cocked her chin. "I told you that her story wasn't anything to be believed."

"No…" Branimir's feet were frozen to the floor. "She is telling the truth."

Sulanna did not remain so fixed, nearly falling where she stood. "What?" She gripped the desk. "You mean the Stuhia *you* killed came back from the dead?"

Branimir tried to keep his hands from shaking. "When I killed him with Kaelandur, I was so angry. I didn't think. I just…"

"I don't believe it," Sulanna said. "How is it possible?"

"I have seen it before." He nodded at Alyona. "We have both seen it before," Branimir said, pulling Kaelandur from his waist belt. "The blade's power is dangerous." He gripped the handle, looking at Sulanna. "Keeping this dagger from Eisliev's grasp is the only thing saving the Ash Tree. If he gets Kaelandur, he will release the Likhyi."

Alyona stared at the dagger, unable to tear her eyes away, as though she was surprised he held the fabled weapon. Yet her words confirmed his fears. "Eisliev said as much. He aims to release the

Old-dark at the behest of Marheena. He says the living had their time on Aenar, and he brings a new age."

Branimir heard the riddle in her words. He was suddenly reminded that Marheena, the Frozen Goddess, was also responsible for telling Dorofej to create the copper dagger. "How did you and Dorofej escape?"

"Eisliev let Tyr, Dorofej, and myself leave freely," she replied in a whisper.

Branimir trembled, returning the dagger to its safe holding. "Why? Do not lie to me."

"I am not," she said, jaw tightening. Her eyes lingered at his waist and then lifted. "Falmagon and Dagmar escaped Melkorka, and Eisliev wants them dead. We promised to kill the two for him, in exchange for…"

"Exchange for what?" Sulanna raised her tone.

Alyona answered, "A place safe from suffering when the Old-dark are released to reform the world for the dead." She hurried to add. "Listen. We bought our time from death to protect Aenar and the Ash Tree. You must believe me. Dorofej was wily with Eisliev and riddled our way to freedom."

Sulanna sighed. "That much I believe."

Branimir agreed with her. "But where is Dorofej? And Tyr?"

"They come to meet us," Alyona explained, "but we must hurry. Dorofej fears Falmagon and Dagmar have already come for Kaelandur too, and Dagmar can forever find you in Klukas."

Branimir shivered. "Why have they not come for me sooner?"

"I—I do not know," Alyona said, "but they are not at Melkorka. Dagmar departed weeks before Eisliev returned from the Netherworld, and Falmagon left days ago."

"Where are we to go to escape them?" Branimir asked.

"*Iriy*," she answered.

Sulanna looked at Branimir incredulously, her eyes larger than he had ever seen. "We are meant to travel to the fabled City of the Gods. For what reason?"

"Dorofej says we must seek the gods to gain their wisdom and end this chaos," Alyona said. "He thinks they might destroy Kaelandur."

Branimir clenched his fists, realizing he still held the table knives. He tossed them through the open door behind him. They clattered in the common room, igniting a series of grunts and chairs shuffling from Jon's table. Branimir ignored the din.

"Then we go," he said.

Chapter III

"You cannot simply up and leave in the middle of the day," Gail insisted. Her dimples from this morning were gone. Her small figure held rigid in the doorway of their room, clinging to the frame as though a wind might send her reeling down the hallway. Branimir clipped his green, hooded cloak around his neck, despite her protests. "We have a room full of customers, letters to be sent, and horses to be tended. Our agreement was you would work for your room and board."

"And we have," Sulanna debated, falling back on her feathered bed to slide on her boots. "I understand our going comes as a surprise; believe me, we are all surprised. But you will be better off if we are not here."

Gail's voice cracked, the wrinkles on her face crinkling across her old skin. The innkeeper clearly did not believe her. "Your tab is unsettled."

Sulanna leveled Gail with a hard glare. "By the Nine Lands, who are you trying to bluff? I have been running your books for a year. I know exactly your worth and ours. If anything, you owe us money."

Branimir disregarded the entire conversation, sitting next to Adamus a few feet away. He watched the hero-warrior slide his steel axe into his belt loop. The weapon fit in his hands much more naturally than the reins of a stable horse.

Adamus humored Branimir with a spirited nudge. "Tis far too warm out for your cloak."

"Not enough room in my pack," Branimir said with little enthusiasm. Adamus was joyous after hearing they were leaving the inn, and although Branimir was glad to be gone, Alyona's summary of events repeatedly played through his mind. Dorofej was free. Dagmar and Falmagon were coming for him. And Eisliev had returned from the dead, because of Branimir's past ignorance.

He grazed by Kaelandur with his hand to fasten his two, well-weighted daggers at his belt. With determination, he gave each blade a firm jerk to ensure they were properly secured. He could not calm his heart from thumping against the inside of his chest. The weight of the world suddenly fell back on his shoulders.

Adamus spoke softly, "We will be fine, Branimir. Tis important to keep faith."

Branimir jumped as Gail struck the frame of the door with her open hand. Her voice stole any response he may have had for Adamus. "You are going to force me to hire those senseless mandrills back. They barely know the quill from the ink!"

"I am sorry, Gail," Sulanna said with an air of grace, once again reminding Branimir of her noble upbringing. "You knew we would leave eventually. None of us belong in an inn."

"What did that Kadari woman say to lug the three of you off so quick?" Gail's eyes flashed madly around the room. "Where is she anyhow? She strolled in and ruined everyone's day and then scamper off?"

Branimir replied, "Leave it alone, Gail. You would be better off not knowing the details."

"Don't talk to me all mysteriously, Master Branimir, after your stunt. You stole kitchen knives from patrons just to toss them across the commons!" Gail stretched out her hand to shake a boney finger. "You scared the beard right off ole' Jon's chin."

Branimir tensed his jaw, having no response.

Sulanna redirected Gail. "Alyona is preparing the horses, and Branimir is right. You do not need to be concerned about our business.

Gail clenched her teeth, keeping what words she had left trapped in her throat. Her gaze fell to Adamus. The bearded man quickly turned away from her and went back to rolling a bedroll. With a final grunt, the old woman threw her hands up. "Fine. I'll have Meisher pack up some of the leftover biscuits from breakfast. You could have at least waited until the morning."

"Thank you, Gail," Sulanna said, giving a half-smile and gesturing to the door. "If you would, please."

Gail squinted her beady eyes at Sulanna with ire, pursing her lips. Holding the grimace, she bobbed her head and shut the door. Branimir could hear her feet stomping down the hallway.

Adamus waited until the footsteps faded before saying anything. "Tis likely we will not find a moment anytime soon to talk without being overheard. What can you say of Alyona? Can we trust her?"

"Of course not," Sulanna said, snagging her leather chest guard from the bed beside her. She continued speaking, slipping the armor over her head and pushing her arm through the already fastened side. "From what I understand, she has lived as long as Branimir or longer. Time surely has given her the upper hand. We cannot know what secrets she holds."

Branimir said, "I agree. When I first met her, she was cruel at Shayol Domier. And then to learn she had tracked Dorofej and me in the Netherworld to retrieve Kaelandur for Falmagon..." His voice trailed off for a moment. "She has too long been loyal to the Kadari. I cannot think she truly wishes to serve those she has forever betrayed."

Sulanna started as soon as he finished. "Mark my words, we will see Alyona telling stories of her torture to justify her reasoning in the coming days," Sulanna added. "She will do what she can to gain our trust, and we cannot be drawn in too closely."

"What do you know?" Adamus asked, meeting Sulanna as she stood and moved to the center of the room. He took the leather strap hanging from her disconnected shoulder piece and pulled it through the adjoining buckle.

Sulanna replied while he tightly clasped the leather. "My family built their name in Eldhaft by persecuting the Crown's enemies."

"Your father is the northern Vornic?" Adamus finished with her armor and stepped back in surprise.

"Hm." She nodded. "Most know the name Maelthirren because of my father's rather vicious pursuits of seeking justice," Sulanna answered. "He bends knee to Count Vlassi in Eldhaft, who historically hungers for violence. The man is nothing like King Frantisek."

"So, your family tortures people?" Branimir concluded.

"My father persecutes those who are deemed to be unlawful, and he *extracts* the truth by whatever means necessary. I watched him torture the young and old alike when I was but a child. In some instances, he tortured the soldiers who failed the directives of Count Vlassi. In no instance did cruelty ever weaken their commitment; if anything, the soldiers became more loyal in fear of any backlash."

Adamus sighed. "Tis then as I thought it to be. You must agree we cannot go traveling across Maharia with the three of us against one Kadari. We are formidable fighters," Adamus looked at Sulanna, and then Branimir, "but we can do little against Koldovstvo without Dorofej's protection."

Branimir took a breath, his hand resting again on Kaelandur at his belt. "I do not trust her either, but by happenstance, if she is telling the truth, we cannot risk otherwise. We have no choice but to go with her."

"I think so, too," Adamus said.

"If you are not suggesting we should leave without her, what are you saying?" Branimir asked.

Sulanna sunk her long knife into the sheath at her belt, and eyeballed Adamus in equal suspense. She must have noticed something Branimir had missed. "Out with it, Adamus. What did you do?"

"After you told me what Alyona had said," Adamus cleared his throat and tugged at his beard, murmuring his words as though they were an afterthought, "I asked Wit to ride along."

"Why? Why would you bring Wit? He…he has other duties to attend at the Highspire," Branimir moaned.

"I can stomach the man," Sulanna said, "but he offers nothing but another mouth to feed."

Adamus shrugged. "Maybe so, but Alyona does not know as much. Maybe she will be intimidated by our numbers. Besides, Wit has no interest in being in Gaetana if sieged, and he has been talking for some time about needing to go to Lonemere to retrieve a manuscript or two for the library. We can, at least, share the road until Gavlok."

Branimir tensed. He had not realized they would be traveling through Gavlok. The couple years he spent working at *the* Oaken Bard after he and Dorofej had exited the Netherworld left a sour taste in his mouth.

Sulanna crossed her arms. "You told him we would take him to Gavlok?"

"Wit is not that bad," Adamus said, placing his shiny, oval shield across his back against the polished steel breastplate.

"He only talks about how great he is, and insults the intelligence of anyone he crosses." Branimir pulled his pack over his shoulder. Dealing with the snooty historian for three days and having no escape would contest with a millennium in the Netherworld. "If Alyona is threatened by Wit, we have nothing to fear from her."

"Come on," Adamus said, pulling at his beard. "A few days on the road, at least, until we can have a better understanding of Alyona's motives."

"Fine." Sulanna said.

Branimir raised his hands defensively. "I am not saying he cannot come, but if he says one more thing about how his books hold more knowledge than the Kras, I might kick him."

A soft knock rattled the wooden door of their room.

"Who's there?" Adamus asked, taking a step and reaching for the latch.

"Meisher, Master Adamus," replied the familiar voice of Lady Gail's son. Adamus pulled the door open to reveal the lanky kid balancing waterskins and several wrapped handkerchiefs in his hands. "My ma sent me to give you some food for your travels."

"Come on in, boy," Adamus said.

"I'll take it," Branimir said, opening his pack. "Set it on the bed, Meisher."

The boy did as he was instructed with a half-hearted smile, and Branimir went to work to find room in his pack. He could smell the leftover biscuits and dried sausage.

"Ma said she would have brought it up herself, but she is *too* busy in the kitchen," Meisher said. "She wanted to be sure I tell you as much."

"We appreciate your ma's hospitality, Meisher," Sulanna responded, rolling her eyes at Branimir.

Meisher smiled. "I am sorry to see you go so soon, but I guess there are grander things to see in the world than dust settling on chairs."

"Yes," Branimir said, handing Adamus and Sulanna each a waterskin before pulling the ties to his pack.

"Oh," Meisher said, "I almost forgot. You have another visitor waiting down in the commons." Branimir's heart gave pause. "He said he was an old friend."

"Dorofej," Branimir pushed himself from the floorboards to rush downstairs only to be stopped by the strong arm of Adamus.

"Hold on, Bran," Adamus said. "Did he give a name? What did this *old friend* look like?"

"Uh…he was a younger man, taller than most, with a thick mustache," Meisher replied, scrunching his brow as if trying to recall detail. "He asked for you in a hushed tone like he was trying not to draw attention. He told my ma he was the patrician. Isn't that a title among the Kadari?"

Branimir's heart sank.

"Falmagon," Sulanna hissed. "I told you we could not trust the girl."

"Careful," Adamus said. "Tis not likely Falmagon would come strolling into an inn asking questions if he was working with Alyona."

"We don't know that," Sulanna said. "Who else would call themselves the patrician?"

Adamus crumpled his beard to mustache, and grabbed Meisher's shoulder. "What did you tell him, boy?"

"Well…" Meisher's eyes were wide with panic. "I…I told him I would see if you were here. I did not say you were." The boy frantically looked around the room. "Are you in trouble? He is not an *old friend*?"

"Hardly not," Branimir said, yanking a dagger from his waistline.

"Branimir…" Sulanna started from the corner. "The commons is full of innocent people."

Branimir pulled his pack over his shoulder, and stepped out the door. "My aim is true, Sulanna. I can end this right now."

"At what cost?" Sulanna pressed. "What if you find Alyona with him? You are not going to battle two Kadari with a couple of daggers. Adamus, tell him."

Adamus let go of Meisher. "I agree this should be ended, but Sulanna is right, Branimir. What if your dagger isn't a deathblow? What if he has flasks of the Waters of Life with him?"

"Waters of Life?" Meisher echoed with wide eyes.

Adamus went on, "Even if you are successful, the kingsguard would take you to the dungeons and remove all weapons from your person, including Kaelandur. What attention will you draw when the dagger is taken from your hand?"

Branimir frowned, returning his blade to his belt. With the Likhyi embedded in the dagger and bound to him, Branimir could not pull the dagger away from his skin without considerable pain. The feeling was akin to having his flesh burning from the inside out. "I had not considered losing Kaelandur."

"We would face greater difficulty in destroying the weapon if the king were to take the weapon," Sulanna said.

Meisher paled, blankly staring at the wall between Adamus and Sulanna. "I do not think I should be listening to this. Please…just leave, and see no one is hurt."

Branimir examined the innocent boy, and then jerked his head in response. "You will need to distract Falmagon while we exit from the door."

"Not the front door," Meisher said. "Go down the stairs and through the kitchen. He will not notice you slipping behind the counter from the staircase."

"I will lead the way." Sulanna gripped the neck of her waterskin. "Adamus take the rear."

Branimir rubbed his nose as Sulanna pushed by him in the hallway. She clearly believed he might attack Falmagon, and wanted him bound between her and Adamus. Of course, his two friends could not stop him if he chose to become invisible. Yet he had no desire to risk the lives of the people in the commons, or the fate of the copper dagger he carried.

The hubbub of chatter and mugs clinging echoed as they made their way down the staircase and into the kitchen. Branimir peeked for only an instant to gain sight of the crowded commons. Gail stood over a man in a faded robe, nodding and laughing as though she were hearing a clever tale. Bran struggled to make out any features beyond the back of the head, shorn with brown locks. He could not see enough to discern the man to be Falmagon for certain, and yet he knew. The image was brief as Meisher moved himself in front of the counter to block view of Branimir and the others sneaking away.

The kitchen was empty, save the contents of the evening meal, a venison stew, cooking in an oversized pot. The three of them exited the Peddlar's Rose in a few steps with Adamus swinging the thin door closed behind them.

Without a word, Sulanna stayed in the lead, heading down the timber staircase and straight to the stables adjacent to the inn. Few people of Gaetana littered the streets, going about their business with little concern of their surroundings. Most of the citizens stayed inside and avoided summer's heat.

Branimir kept his feet forward, despite every muscle in his body wanting to turn around and face Falmagon. He took a hearty breath, glancing at the sky, full of a raging sun and absent a single cloud for shade. Sweat beads lined the base of his neck moments before they walked up to the stables.

The doors were already open with Alyona and Witigor standing inside, ready with the mounts.

Alyona crossed her arms under her breasts as they approached, hugging the light shirt to her torso. Sweat dripped down her cheek, falling to the dark cloak hanging down to her knees. "Am I to expect he will be coming with us?"

Witigor tipped his brown, pointed hat at Alyona. The few strands of his hair were barely discernible against his malformed skin. "I have already answered her question a hundred times. I understand the girl is young yet, but she is the daftest woman I have ever met." The painted horse he held whinnied next to the brown pony he also held at bay. He lifted the pony's reins to Branimir with a snort.

Alyona ignored the three horses standing behind her calmly. She glared at the historian. "I would suspect few women have stomached your company."

Wit twitched his nose, considering the argument. "Few women are worth being in my company," he concluded.

"No one is going to be appreciative of your humor, Wit," Adamus said.

"Wit-less," Branimir muttered.

"He is coming with us, Alyona," Sulanna said over him. The terseness of her tone was unmistakable. Branimir almost expected the noble woman to breach the topic of Falmagon within the inn, but Sulanna gave pause.

Branimir reached out and took the cords to his pony's bridle from Witigor. He then fastened his pack on the saddle, signifying the need for haste. Adamus mirrored him, taking his own from behind Alyona. The Kadari stood, unmoving, glowering at Witigor.

"We are losing the light," Adamus said.

"We should have waited until morning," Wit said, "when it would be cooler. We are going to burn in this heat."

Branimir gazed at the sky with the sun directly overhead. The day barely reached its apex. Wit may have been sweating more than any of them, even without wearing armor. He only clothed himself in tan britches and a grey shirt as though he were a commoner.

"We will draw a lot of attention with a large group," Alyona argued. "Every man, woman, and child will remember us from here to Eldhaft."

"And, why would we care about that?" Wit asked, cocking his head. "You trying to get rid of me?" He shook his finger at her. "You are just upset because I asked why your eyes are such a peculiar color, which I may add, you have not given an inkling of an answer. You talk and talk and say nothing at all. Just like a woman." Wit rubbed the back of his head and squinted at the Kadari with disdain.

"Mind yourself." Her nostrils flared. "I don't need to be pressed by some wiseacre for the next three days."

Branimir wondered if Alyona was fabricating her scorn toward Wit, but he agreed with her. He did not want to hear Witigor's persistent yammering on the road either. Making his decision, Bran pulled himself up on his pony and wiped the sweat forming on his forehead. "Stop insulting her, Wit-less."

Wit wrinkled his nose. "My name is Witigor. I have never met a group of people so insistent on holding onto their secrets than you."

"You obviously haven't met many people who understand the function of a secret, then," Alyona said, pointing her finger at him.

"Enough," Sulanna muttered. "We must—"

A loud commotion from the Peddlar's Rose interrupted her. Branimir spun around, hearing what may have been shouting and the breaking of glass.

"Nine Lands!" Wit exclaimed, springing back against his mount.

The horses, battle-trained, held stagnant against Wit's sudden shout, but Branimir's pony lurched with the intent to bolt down the twisting road.

"Whoa," Sulanna cried, reaching for the pony, but Alyona was quicker. The Kadari stepped in front of the pony and touched its head, calming the animal straightaway.

Wit did not seem to notice, gawking at the inn. "Should we go see if they need help?"

Adamus answered, crumpling his forehead. "No, tis not our problem."

"Nothing directed toward us," Sulanna said evenly, a hint of knowing flickering in her eye, "and not worth investigating. We have other concerns to heed."

Wit twisted his neck, gazing at each of them. The crashing grew louder from in the inn. "Wait a minute. Someone could really be in trouble. What if someone is killed?"

"Czern's breath! Then they are killed," Adamus said. "Get on your horse. We are leaving. Come on."

Alyona stepped away from Branimir's pony as he repositioned himself on the animal. He did his best to keep the suspicion of her use of Koldovstvo from his eye, but he guessed she had done something to calm his mount. Knowing Faegrim had the power to control the mind, he thought his trinket suddenly felt exceptionally heavy upon his finger. He could not help but check her hand as she neared her mare, but noticed no jewelry.

Witigor lifted his eyebrows at the four of them preparing for leave-taking, and then reconsidered the inn.

Branimir wondered if the historian believed them to be immoral because of their decision. Of course, they would not use Falmagon's presence as an argument to avoid the Peddlar's Rose, but even then, Branimir was not certain he or the others would have gone inside. Branimir knew he had changed over the years. Bygone battles hardened him. A commoner like Witigor could not understand.

"Are you coming, Wit-less?" Branimir mocked, hoping the historian would return to the Highspire.

He answered the question with a question. "Should I expect similar respects if I am to encounter danger on the road? Will I be left for the crows and forgotten?"

Alyona's reply gave Branimir's answer before he could part his lips. "Yes."

Chapter IV

Evening set, darkening the already colorless tufts of the Gaetanean Grasslands. The uniform blades had faded with the lack of rain during the warm months, threatening to soon wilt and wither. Branimir could see above the far-stretching meadow from the top of his saddle, though the grass would stand higher on him if he were walking along the road.

The frequent traffic between Gaetana and Eldhaft had stripped the road bare of grass, leaving a hardened, cracked, and uneven dirt path. Bran was sure that any wagon wanting to pass between the two cities would leave the passengers with a crick in their neck and a sore bottom. Yet he had not seen a single wagon, and only a handful of travelers since leaving Gaetana. Wit claimed they were the only ones stupid enough to travel in the heat.

Admittedly, Branimir could have refilled his water skin twice over with the sweat secreting from his face. He removed his cloak an hour after leaving the city, thinking it might keep him from passing out in the heat, but the sun only warmed his red skin. Since then, he had been unsticking his shirt from his chest so often he practically fanned himself with the fabric. They stopped plenty to water the horses and huddle in the ditch under the tall grasses for shade, but something about the temperature left them feeling feverish and exhausted.

The dark blue sky contrasted against the dark grey scattered clouds, and soon it would all fade to black. Of course, for Branimir, he could see easily enough, despite the failing light. He rode alongside Alyona in the back with Adamus and Wit leading and Sulanna in the middle.

"We should break for camp soon," Wit suggested, helplessly peering into the fading light.

"No," Adamus said. "We have Branimir to help lead us in the dark if needed, and the road will be cooler at night."

"You all have been in a rush since leaving Gaetana," Wit carped, tilting his hat. "What in the Nine Lands for? You act as though you are being chased."

Branimir bit his tongue while Sulanna answered, "We have our business, Wit. If you need to turn back for Gaetana, we will understand."

Adamus turned his head at the mild proposal, but said nothing.

Wit stubbornly grunted, showing no sign of changing course. He impatiently looked to Adamus. "Are you not going to say anything more?"

The Ariadnean patted his horse. "About what?"

"You are going to leave me in suspense about why you have suddenly left Gaetana and headed north?" Witigor pressed.

"Sulanna answered you," Adamus replied with a shrug.

"My father was silenced by my mother's commanding tone too, until he killed himself, Adamus. She never let him have a say about anything, and it drove him mad," Wit said heatedly, glaring at Sulanna under the brim of his hat. "It is not right for a woman to speak a man's thoughts, or tell him what he should think. Read Campbell Lilliard's *Women and Slaves*, and know the truth. You will fall to ruin."

"Czern's breath! You know you have my deepest sympathies for your loss, but Sulanna will hardly lead any man to ruin." Adamus forced a soft smile. Branimir wondered how long Adamus had known about Wit's loss. He supposed Adamus would feel sorry for

Witigor, but Branimir did not see it to be a fitting excuse to treat others poorly.

Branimir watched Sulanna glide her hand from the long knife at her belt to her saddle. She did not share Adamus's sympathy. "Wit, I have overlooked your slights for the better part of a year, but if you continue to insult me, I will run you through."

"You are threatening me?" Wit gawked, looking again to Adamus for help.

"I most certainly am," Sulanna said. "I would threaten anyone who vouched for the written works of Campbell Lilliard. The man was a misogynist and a pig."

Wit moved his jaw back and forth awkwardly, trying to form words. "I was only asking why the hurry."

Branimir filled his lungs. He wanted to give a suitable answer, saying they needed to put more distance between themselves and Falmagon, who had somehow come to Gaetana. Branimir longed to ask Alyona how Falmagon could have skipped across such a distance to arrive in Gaetana from Kalamaar. However, where Dorofej had supposedly aided Alyona, Branimir suspected Dagmar had somehow helped Falmagon.

Regardless, Sulanna had not breached the topic of Falmagon with Wit or Alyona, signifying the secret should remain so for now. Wit knew nothing of Falmagon in any sense, and Branimir found no reason to enlighten the historian. Besides—after giving more thought—Falmagon had Dagmar to find Branimir in Klukus no matter where or how fast they fled. Therefore, the argument was moot.

For another hour they traveled quietly until Wit broke the silence. "If we are going to travel all night, we could, at least, talk about something. Tell a story or something."

"Talk about the weather," Alyona muttered so fast Branimir thought she might have been waiting for Witigor to open his mouth so she could shut him up.

Wit scoffed, and then—out of what might have been pure spite toward the woman—he went on a tangent about the weather. "This heat belongs to the desert, not the grasslands. Maharia is known for harsh winters and mild summers. I remember, last year, everyone was talking about the warm weather; it was thick with every conversation. But these Months of Warmth have exceeded anything known to history."

"The written history does not stretch so far, Wit," Adamus said.

"Long have patterns been documented by the Anshedar, whether on animal migrations, the stars, or the seasons, and only a couple generations of study can recognize the design," Wit argued. "We have had scrolls and books detailing the weather much longer: *Moon of Next Year* by Farkas Finn, the *Fine Manual of Fire and Frost* by Saym Green, or Pap Benjamin's *Pamphlet of Lunar History*. I am telling you, something unnatural is happening."

"I agree we have seen many patterns, which have been documented. But do you not think smaller cycles could work inside of larger rotations," Sulanna spoke up, "like the gears and cogs of a water mill?"

"Ah, yes," Adamus nodded in agreement. "Tis like a story. We know every great tale has minor lessons taught within the overall story."

Branimir could see Wit tapping his saddle in thought. He turned his head to give view of the most deformed side of his face. "What evidence do you have to think the seasons work in such a way?"

Sulanna shrugged. "None. We are but mortal. You cannot think we will have all the knowledge needed to know the truth of something in our lifetime, else we would be called gods. A thousand years ago, those living hardly know what we know now."

"*The Tract of Wonderful Words* by Paul Friar," Wit said with a smile. "You are talking about his works."

"I thought you might recognize it," Sulanna said.

"You know the hour has drawn late when Sulanna begins to speak about gods," Adamus laughed, twisting alongside Wit to watch Sulanna pull back her shoulders. She may have very well flattened Adamus's nose if they had been any closer.

Branimir slowed his pony to keep distance.

Sulanna preserved her unruffled tone, saying, "I am not paying them reverence, Adamus. I am repeating Friar's argument that humans would not offer their lives up to worshipping *gods* if we were *all-knowing*. Sadly, our lifespans are too short to learn all we should." She cleared her throat, nodding her head back at Branimir. "Thus far, the Kras and their knowledge is the closest thing to godly I have found on Aenar."

Wit scoffed. "I doubt any Kras will lead you across the Kalinov Bridge to the next life. Knowledge is not everything."

Adamus roared with laughter. "And the historian betrays his profession for faith."

"Earning the name Wit-less," Branimir said with a scowl.

"I am not a fool. History helps me find my footing while alive, but what knowledge I gain in this life has no bearing on the next," Wit said, hat flopping wildly with his defense.

Adamus responded again, but Branimir cut him out to focus on Alyona riding next to him. He did not want to hear any more of Wit's insults, even if morsels of truth were hidden in his words.

Night had come, and whereas the others squinted their eyes to find the road, Alyona was watchful with wide, purple eyes. Her gaze fluttered in his direction shortly, before turning back to the road.

"Why do you stare?" she asked under her breath.

Branimir watched Sulanna move her horse further from Wit and Adamus as they continued their inquiry on the meaninglessness of their lives, and its connection to the afterlife. Noticing they were not listening, he hurried his words, "How did you calm my pony at Gaetana?"

Alyona pressed her lips together, trying to fight back a smile. She intentionally gazed at Branimir this time. "Many questions I had expected from you while we were on the road, but nothing so slight."

"I am curious," Branimir said.

"Very well," Alyona said, settling in her saddle. "You have been with Dorofej for a long while. What can you tell me about Koldovstvo?"

"We did not speak much of it," Branimir said. "I know Koldovstvo consumes life when power is spent."

Alyona's lips curved in a smile under her small nose. She assented with a hum in her throat. "The magic originally comes from the Stuhians, gifted by the gods, but has been blended with other races over the centuries as the Stuhians mixed bloodlines. Stuhians themselves do not age unless they wield Koldovstvo, whereas mixed bloodlines age at a slower rate. The Highborn, as you knew them in the last age, were not Stuhian, save Dorofej."

Branimir picked at Faegrim on his hand nervously. "That does not answer my question."

She smiled all the wider, and went on, "The limits of what a Stuhian can do with Koldovstvo is limited by imagination and bloodline." Branimir frowned at the comment, but Alyona did not give him pause to speak. "Our blood reveals the source of Koldovstvo for each of us, specifically identifying what kind of magic will steal our life the slowest. Most who manipulate Koldovstvo can access any type of elemental magic: sea, sky, fire, or stone; though some, like I said, may be stronger in its design. Other users are skilled in the intangible arts: profane, sacred, primal, or void. We each have our special gifts."

"And you?" Branimir asked.

"Sacred," Alyona finally answered. "Among many other things, I can remove fear, or provide protection, or even mend wounds from living creatures."

Branimir straightened a bit more in his saddle, leaning toward Alyona. "Like Dorofej?"

"No." Alyona pushed her hair from her cheek. "Dorofej is an aberration. He descends from the Kaligula bloodline, giving him greatest strength in void magic, altering space and time, or even thought. Yet he also wields sacred magic with an uncanny ability. He is the only Stuhia, Highborn, or Kadari—pick your term—who I have found to practice more than one intangible magic."

"How is that possible?"

"I don't know," she said.

Branimir realized his assumption about Dagmar likely held truth. If Falmagon's mentor held the same blood as Dorofej, he could help Falmagon escape to Gaetana through a gateway like that from which Alyona had traveled.

"How do you know so much about Dorofej?" Branimir asked, his words suddenly swallowed by a resonating clamor coming from up the road. He rotated with Alyona to look for the cause.

"Branimir," Adamus directed in a soft voice, stopping his horse, "the road is too dark. What do you see?" Sulanna and Wit halted their mounts on either side of him. Branimir followed Alyona's lead and stopped behind the other three, having no room on either side of the road to fan out.

"Four riders," Branimir began, his heart thumping against his chest in realization of what he was witnessing, "surrounding a male Svet in the road." Branimir looked at his companions with excitement, away from the five torches flickering further up the road. "I have not seen a centaur in so long."

"Savages," Wit said, standing in his stirrups as though it would help him see better in the dark. "He must be their property. No Svet would wander onto the main road unless he was already a slave."

"Slave…" The word hung on the edge of Branimir's tongue. "Anything else, you would like to add Wit-less?"

"Stop calling me that," Wit said. "It is Witigor, and you know it."

"No, the Svet is not a slave." Alyona interjected, soothing her mount with her hand. "He is arguing against being one with the riders. The men are unknown to him."

Wit plopped back into his saddle and rubbernecked at her. "How can you hear them?"

"Because my ears are not filled with the sound of my own rattling tongue," she said.

Wit jerked his head away from the woman, clearing his throat in contempt.

Branimir knew the distance was too great for any of the humans to hear more than muffled conversation, but Branimir, too, could hear the words. He kept his eyes forward, away from Alyona, and abridged the words. "The Svet is called Farthr. He says he is among the Crimson Sun." Bran looked to the old Crimson Sun affiliate. "Sulanna?"

Sulanna noticeably perked in her saddle, an evening breeze suddenly erupting across the highlands and rustling her brown locks. With a subtle nod, she said, "If it is Farthr, the centaur speaks the truth. We would do well to align with him against these men."

"How have you come by this knowledge?" Wit demanded, only to be ignored by the rest.

"To arms then?" Adamus said.

"First, let us see what we can accomplish with words," Sulanna corrected, directing her horse toward the increasing commotion. "I will do the talking."

Sulanna led them ever closer, down the dirt road, with Wit falling back to Branimir's side with noticeable discomfort. The historian's hands shook hard enough he could have been riding in a wagon instead of a horse's saddle.

The words between the riders and Farthr were clear as they closed the distance. The man closest to Farthr spoke in a shaky voice, waving a torch in his hand. "He may be telling the truth. Look at his crossbow and the leatherwork of the quiver. Those are not common armaments, and definitely would not be found in Svet settlements."

"He likely stole them from the last human he killed," said another. "I bet a hefty reward is on his head. We should take him back to Eldhaft, or even down to Gaetana."

"I have told you the truth," Farthr said. "I am Farthr of Brennen, retained by the Crimson Sun. Delaying my orders will have you answering to Ivarr Gauthus."

"That is the name of the man leading the Crimson Sun."

"Are you certain?"

"Yes."

"Does it really matter? Anyone north of the Dyndaer could find the name of Ivarr Gauthus. I say, he is an escaped slave who killed his master and stole his weapons."

Farthr growled as the men argued, swelling his burly chest. Branimir could see the Svet's ears twitching near his long, black mane. Farthr said, "I have not survived the face of death to listen to this drivel. Be off or wish you had."

"Something I would expect—"

"Rocher," another cut in, "others approach on the road." The man pointed at Branimir and the other four, who advanced leisurely. Each of the four horsemen shifted, waving torches in their direction for better light.

"Good evening. The Svet is who he says he is," Sulanna said, guiding her horse into the light. She leaned toward them like two old friends chatting over noontide tea, and smiled. "He is free in Maharia."

"And who are you?" the man called Rocher asked.

"Sulanna Maelthirren, also one among the Crimson Sun, and friend to all who are employed by them," Sulanna said, holding the smile, "including Farthr. I understand he may appear a bit brutish, but his services have long protected you and the people of Eldhaft."

"Maelthirren?" One of the men furrowed his brow. Two others murmured the name.

Rocher scooted his horse back, a sudden fear enveloping his eyes. "Your father is Vornic Myrthos Maelthirren?"

"He is," Sulanna said. Farthr rumbled again, air pushing through his wide nostrils, before dipping his head to greet Sulanna. "He and Count Vlassi, who the Crimson Sun has often worked in hand with, would be displeased that you have threatened such an esteemed member. Yet I would guess this is but a misunderstanding. The night is dark, and only words were exchanged."

"Indeed. Only words," Rocher agreed. He signaled the other men with his hand. "We will be on our way. Apologies to you, Farthr. We owe you our thanks to your service."

"You have no idea." Farthr snarled.

"Travel safe, friends," Sulanna said. The men turned their own mounts, heading north on the road.

When they were beyond earshot, the Svet lifted his torch toward the five of them, eyes tempering on Sulanna. "Seeing a familiar face after all this time does me well. Though, last I knew, you had abandoned your station among the Crimson Sun with Alden Forgaff. Ivarr Gauthus has a bounty on both your heads."

Wit spun hard enough in his saddle to glare at Sulanna, he nearly slid off. The historian, of course, knew nothing of Sulanna's misdirection from the renowned group of mercenaries.

Sulanna kept her poise. "Should I expect you to take me to Tamarri then, after I intervened on your behalf?"

"I have never had a quarrel with you, Sulanna." Farthr held out his torch to examine the rest of them, stopping the flame near Branimir. "I long ago rid myself of any notion of pursuing you or Alden, despite what orders were given."

Branimir stared at Farthr through the flame. He saw a glimmer in the Svet's wide eye. Sulanna must have picked up on it too. "You have recently come across another Kras," she said.

"I have," Farthr admitted, stamping a hoof against the dirt, "though not as recent as you may think. A year has now come to pass since, and many dark tidings with it."

"We aim to travel through the night to escape the heat, Farthr. Tis a long road ahead to Eldhaft," Adamus said. "If you are traveling the same way, you should share the tale."

Farthr twitched his ears. "I am. Yet I am uncertain the tale would add any light to the darkness. I survived long enough to recite the tale to Ivarr before being sent to see more perilous deeds done." He returned his gaze to Sulanna. "Deeds I have yet to act upon. I, too, have recently been sought by the Crimson Sun for my waywardness."

"So, you do not travel back to Tamarri?" Sulanna asked. "I truly did save you from an ill-fated outcome with those horsemen."

Farthr dipped his head, the horns on either side of his fawn-like ears glimmering in the torchlight. "Yes, you did. I now return to Sorod, to my tribe."

"We are really going to allow this mongrel to travel alongside us? A deserter to the most powerful company in Maharia?" Wit gaped, flinging his hat upright for a better view of the rest in the flickering light.

"Mongrel?" Branimir scrunched his face. "Why would you attack him? You do not even know him."

"I do not need to know him. My father once told me all about his kind, and it is well documented in the history books. Read *Slaves for Men* or *Friends of the Stockades* by Duras Thatcher," Wit said. "His people are all the same. Savages."

Sulanna, an identical defector, pursed her lips at Wit in consideration, as though the man's true colors—the haughty, superior rascal Branimir knew him to be—continued to reveal himself. Adamus, on the other hand, flashed his white teeth between his black beard and mustache as if the historian had just told a great joke.

Branimir could only stare incredulously at the man.

Alyona replied in a dry tone. "We are all guilty of falling from youthful oaths once ripened with wisdom. Such lessons cannot be adequately taught in books."

Wit wrinkled his scarred nose, nostrils flaring. "If I had known traveling alongside the lot of you would have brought such ridicule of knowledge, I would have stayed in the Highspire. None of you have any respect for reason."

Branimir scowled at the historian. "Wait until you have to forget what you know to save your friends or yourself. Those who defend reason have never done much more than sit and judge those who were faced with an inescapable fate," Branimir said. "For your sake, I hope you never have to come to learn that the *just* choice is not always the *right* choice."

"Well…" Witigor wiggled his head back and forth, sticking his chin up. "Just who oversees this group anyway? Who has the final say on our decisions? Sulanna? Please…" His face tightened with disapproval. "To lead this party, we need someone intelligent, preferably male, and likely me. But since I have only come along, I suggest Adamus—who obviously is the only one with any sense—makes all definitive decisions."

Branimir directed his horse away to keep himself from punching Wit in the mouth.

Adamus, on the other hand, who suddenly was overwhelmed with amusement, burst into a deep-throated chuckle, which swiftly changed into a howling cackle.

"Oh, Wit," Adamus wiped the tears from his eyes, his entire chest shaking uncontrollably with laughter, "you should really shut up."

Wit's jaw fell. "What?"

Adamus could not keep the grin from his face, distracting from the seriousness of his words. "You are going to find yourself crawling back to Gaetana if you keep at it."

"We make our decisions together," Branimir clarified.

"Clearly," Wit mumbled, drifting his eyes from Adamus to Bran. "All the same, when we reach Eldhaft, I think I will venture to Gavlok alone."

"Whatever suits you," Sulanna said in a flat tone, directing Farthr to follow her down the road. He lifted the torchlight for them to see the path ahead. Adamus and Alyona followed with Branimir close behind, and Wit, finally at the rear, who paled in shock at the sudden dismissal.

Branimir breathed easy. He wished they had left the man at Gaetana.

"Farthr," Sulanna said in harmony with the clopping of the horses' hooves, "tell me about the Kras? What has caused you to drift from the Crimson Sun?"

"I am uncertain you would believe me unless you have crossed such darkness yourself, but I will tell you all I know," the Svet responded. "Seigfeld Brecher and I were sent to explore the ruins of the Dyndaer, directed by Ivarr, but truly by the hand of Falmagon Sej of the Kadari. The mages of Melkorka believed the Old-dark were returning to the world."

Branimir's heart thudded in his chest. Falmagon had knowledge that the depletion of the Ash Tree was releasing the Old-dark. Yet he continued to kill the source of life of this world and the prison of the ancient gods. The last thing Branimir wanted to think about was the terrible evil he faced in the catacombs of Garain'l. The same evil, called Likhyi, had implanted itself into the Kras, Drak, until Branimir was forced to take his life. Now, the Likhyi lived within Kaelandur at his belt.

Farthr stopped talking to consider them. "Strange none of you ask what the Old-dark means."

"I hardly need a history lesson from an illiterate savage," Wit spoke up from the rear, his over-confident tone piercing the ear like a fine blade. "For those learned, who have read Tom Flitter's *Mystagogical's Forlorn Folio*, we know the Likhyi, as they were once called, to be the eight old gods worshipped in Aenar before time had been recorded. I recently found the eight cruxes of the Stuhian magic is also the elements of each god: sky, stone, fire, sea, primal, void, profane, and sacred. Legend tells of the Ash Tree being a prison for the Old-dark, and upon its withering will come the release of the Likhyi."

Adamus gave a weak smile absent Farthr's gaze, who scowled at the road ahead of them. "Tis something some of us know without reading a book."

"It's a tale," Wit replied dryly. Branimir twisted to see Wit glowering at Adamus.

"You believe in the modern gods," Branimir said, "but not the old?"

Wit turned to Branimir. "The gods have transformed over time with our understanding of them, but have never changed themselves outside of name."

"Your conjectures are misguided," Alyona said.

"Quite mistaken," Farthr agreed, "or my eyes, my hands, and my memory have deceived me."

"I am among the mad," Wit claimed. "You speak as though you have walked among gods and drank from the very waters surrounding the Ash Tree. You realize you are contesting hundreds of years of written research on the subject?"

"You would be wise enough to know some write history with the intent to misdirect the masses," Sulanna said. "If knowledge is power, as you press, why would anyone share the knowledge and distribute it to the many. Best to keep said information close to heart while pointing others astray."

"You are claiming the histories I read are fiction?" Wit asked, his voice like silk, captivated by the thought.

"None here would argue against the tutelage the Highspire has provided you or the other pupils. Many of your references I may agree with, Witigor, but you cannot believe all you read," Sulanna said. "A lesson my father would voice strongly."

"Hm." Wit grunted.

Sulanna refocused her attention on Farthr. "What did you and Seigfeld find?"

Farthr replied, twitching his ears, "While passing through the Dyndaer, we found a Kras and Uvil on a path to find similar answers about the Old-dark."

"An Uvil?" Adamus scratched his beard.

"Another race of ignorant sods," Witigor muttered.

Farthr growled, continuing, "I know the pairing seems odd. How they came together, I do not know, but the Kras and Uvil woman sought Shayol Domier to find the name of death. I advised Seigfeld for us to go our own way, but he refused, believing our greater numbers gave us the advantage. His thinking gives reason to why I still hold breath today; yet Seigfeld was not so lucky."

Sulanna gasped. "Seigfeld is dead."

"Fallen at Shayol Domier, along with the Uvil." Farthr said. "The Kras and I took separate paths after escape, having no bonds of brotherhood."

"Escape from what?" Branimir asked.

Farthr rested his hand on the crossbow hanging next to the bolts at his side. His hooves echoed against the dirt for several steps before responding. "I fear myself as mad as the scraggy human suggests for even saying the word, but a Likhyi."

Even when guessing what Farthr would say, Branimir's fingers bound around Kaelandur in his grasp, horrified. The Old-dark¬ had gained more power over the last year, solidifying into the world of the living as the Ash Tree deteriorated from the Kadari.

First at Garain'l, and now, Shayol Domier.

Dorofej once told Branimir that Marheena gifted the Stuhia with Koldovstvo. Yet the first *Eretik*, Nedezhda Mager, had been sent by Marheena to destroy the Ash Tree, the prison of the Likhyi. Now, if the eight Likhyi were incarnations of the eight cruxes of Koldovstvo, what would this mean to the Stuhia whose blood embodied each type of magic? Branimir's mind raced with unanswered questions.

For as long as Branimir could remember, Dorofej said Marheena, and the other gods, had no interest in men and their actions. He said no gods were good or evil, but simply were. However, Marheena's hand guided Dorofej in making Kaelandur; the Frozen Goddess incited the ruin of the world, seemingly intending to return the magic she gifted to the dragon people back to the Old-dark.

"A Likhyi?" Wit finally echoed after a minute of silence from the rest. "You expect us to believe you came face-to-face with an Old-dark? Even if such madness were true, I cannot think you would survive the encounter."

Farthr snorted. "I expect you to believe nothing. I barely believe it myself. Though I was asked to tell the tale as I know it."

"The Kras you were with knows the same?" Alyona asked.

"Better than I," Farthr said. "Wrylyc Titchen, son of Gard, son of Potap, helped lead us from the Likhyi's distortion."

Potap! Branimir nearly fell from his saddle. The name, though old, was familiar, marking a Kras he had known a millennium ago at Shayol Domier. To hear his friend secured a worthy lineage nearly brought a smile to his face.

"What do you mean distortion?" Branimir asked, clinging to the reins.

"After Seigfeld's fall, Wrylyc and I were attacked by demons in the darkness," Farthr said, "and we secured our lives. But a fog fell on our senses, like the haunting of a dream, which we had difficulty in waking. Images of what I had longed for danced in my vision as though reality for days and days."

Sulanna said, "And how did you wake from the dream?"

"I truly do not know, but Wrylyc and I slipped from the madness and escaped into the Dyndaer," Farthr grunted. He then took in a deep breath, waving the torch in his hand. "I have told what I know, the same as I told Ivarr in Tamarri."

Sulanna led her horse forward to touch Farthr's arm. "I am sorry you had to see Seigfeld part from this world. I know what he meant to you. May he and Alden find peace in their passing."

Farthr turned his head sharply. "Alden?"

Sulanna nodded. "I fear he fell some time ago in Talastein."

"No, Sulanna," Farthr shook his head. Sulanna's hand retreated to her chest with the Svet's next words. "The old kook yet lives. I crossed him upon the road two days past."

"This road! Going which direction?" Sulanna asked.

Farthr said, "North toward Eldhaft. He and I spoke for nary a minute, passing pleasantries, before he set off again."

"He is looking for me," Sulanna whispered, a smile forming on her face. She turned to look at Branimir, who responded with a wide grin. "He would search for me in my home city."

Branimir scratched his head in bewilderment, a grin plastered to his face. He looked to Adamus for an answer. "But how did he escape the Lilitu? You said the Lilitu did not keep their prisoners alive?"

Farthr replied before Adamus could form a word. "The Crimson Sun paid for Alden's release. To knowledge, they planned to deliver him to the Kadari for questioning. But Alden escaped on the road back to Tamarri."

"Who was sent to retrieve him?" Sulanna's voice quivered with her question.

"I don't know." Farthr shook his head. "But Alden made short work of them."

"He killed them?" Branimir gasped.

Farthr's ears twitched. "I heard the deaths were swift. Merciful."

Branimir could hear Wit mumbling from the saddle behind him.

Adamus grunted, speaking aloud before Wit could say anything substantial. "If we make haste, we may still find him in Eldhaft. Tis not likely he will be welcomed by any who recognize him."

"Alden is well known in these parts…" Sulanna said. "If he is looking for me, he would go to The Harper and Mug in Old Town."

"Then," Branimir said, "let us not waste any time in getting there."

Chapter V

Branimir could not help but smile at the thought of Alden traveling on the road ahead, and Sulanna had not stopped grinning since she heard the news. For hours, Branimir enjoyed listening to the high-spirited, idle banter of her and the others. Farthr and Sulanna swapped heroic tales from their days among the Crimson Sun. Adamus soon joined, reliving his tales of battle; and then Alyona matched him with her own mystifying feats against demons rising from the Netherworld. Wit, of course, would not be left out of the haughty bragging, sharing the histories of men—greater than himself—who had fought against powerful foes, as though he had warred against them himself.

"Gebereht was favored by Svathevit," Wit said, referring to the legendary hero-warrior from Ariadne, whom the God of War had allegedly blessed. The historian clicked his tongue, followed by a haughty chuckle. "Veselin's *Excursions into the Dyndaer* tells the account of Gebereht's battles fought in The Second War. He may have been the greatest warrior among the Ariadneans during the sixth century."

Branimir watched Wit deliberately pause and look to Farthr, who tensed at the mentioning of The Second War.

"You know The Second War was between the Anshedar and the Svet?" Farthr rumbled at Wit. "For forty years, we killed one another, until the Svet were beaten down by the Kadari, not Gebereht."

Wit smiled. "Oh, but Gebereht was a mighty enemy to the Svet—"

"I am not questioning Gebereht's valor." Farthr interrupted Wit. "Gebereht is remembered among the Svet much like he is among the Anshedar. The Svet respect a warrior no matter where he stands on the field of battle. But you knowingly insult me."

"How could I insult a beast?" Wit said, tipping his hat with a sneer. "Have you no control over your primal emotions?"

Farthr snorted. Branimir was certain the centaur heard far worse in his travels across Maharia, especially with his people considered as slaves among the Anshedar.

Branimir, on the other hand, already was curling his fingers into a fist.

Farthr spoke in a low voice. The strain to remain civil with Witigor was evident. "Adamus, Sulanna, and even Alyona have shared their own exploits, none of which have slighted any other here. Yet you crow about ancient wars, which you held no part in, wars that led to centuries of bondage and oppression for my kind."

"Your slavery was blessed by the gods," Witigor said, pointing his finger at the Svet. "Look what has been accomplished by intellectual minds directing those of lesser beings. Cities have been built. Governments have been strengthened. Crops and commerce have considerably expanded."

Farthr's eyes slanted at the historian. "You humans have destroyed the land. You believe your will—your way—gives light to the future. Yet I have also heard how you claim your god—this Svathevit, a mirror of the Svet God of War, Rujan—blessed you in leading my kind to servitude. Funny how your path to the future is borrowed from savages. Somehow, you humans—simple and weak—fail to see that the only reason us *savages* stand as slaves is because of the Kadari's vile magic. They won The Second War. Not Gebereht. Not any human. And, especially, not you."

"Vile magic?" Alyona raised an eyebrow more with intrigue than offense.

"Yes," Farthr said in a dry tone. "You use your power to strengthen shackles when you could instead shatter them."

Wit shouted in defiance to Farthr, while Alyona slowed her mount. "Not true! The Kadari only came in the final years of the war, after the Svet were pushed back to their so-called Holy Lands. Holy lands, I may add, that we were kind enough to allow the free Svet to hold until this very day. Tell him, Alyona!"

Alyona tensed her jaw, staring at the wild-eyed historian, and then simply shook her head. "I was not here during The Second War. I know Gebereht played a significant role in the war, as you said, but I also know the Kadari have stolen glory from the Svet before in the past."

"The savage insults your magic and you defend him!" Wit said.

"Many do use their magic for immoral reasons," Alyona said.

"Farthr speaks the truth, Wit-less. I have seen how the Kadari have robbed life and glory from the Svet," Branimir said, glad for Alyona's remark. He remembered too clearly the first time he had met Alyona, and her brother Artemiy, on the outskirts of Shayol Domier over a millennium ago. The two, and the Kadari with them, were quick to slaughter his Svet friends, Melyena Rogov and Asgrim Garoar.

Bran wondered what changed Alyona's position on the *savages*.

"Must my words be refuted by every confounding fool amongst you?" Wit glared, holding his gaze temporarily on Branimir. "Do you have no respect for written history? No! Of course, you do not. I have somehow been tossed into a party of cranks and criminals."

"Claiming Gebereht pushed the Svet back to the Holy Lands is one thing," Branimir said, "but saying the Svet deserved enslavement and death is wrong."

"You are going to lecture me on what is right and wrong?" The man ripped his pointed hat from his head, flinging accusations at each of them with equal disdain. "Two defectors from the Crimson Sun bent on finding a third turncoat, a fugitive from the Kadari, and a two-tongued Kras, who should be bending knee as much as this brutish Svet. You all deserve lashings." Witigor spit over his shoulder. "I would not be surprised to find you had absconded from the war, Adamus. How else would you get caught up with this lot of misfits?"

"Wit," Adamus scowled, stopping his horse and turning it around, "you have been warned over and over. We talked about your tongue before we left Gaetana. You go too far."

"Do I?" Wit scoffed. "Or do I speak the truth?"

Sulanna kept an even tone, pushing her brown hair behind her ear. "Wit, go back to Gaetana. Return to the Highspire."

"No," Wit said, squaring his shoulders. "I am going to go ride straight to Eldhaft, and tell Count Vlassi what contemptible itinerants approach his gate, so he can take care of you appropriately."

"You will not," Branimir said, easing up in his saddle.

Alyona circled around Wit on her horse. "The historian compromises our journey."

"Where is your sense, Wit?" Adamus moved his horse closer, leaning forward. "We invite you to travel alongside us and you answer with disrespect and threats. You really think tis possible to give insult and then attempt to deliver us into a hang noose?"

Witigor's eyes flashed. "You think you can stop me?"

"Without effort," Adamus said, then swung his leg over his horse to dismount.

Branimir moved quicker than his friend. Climbing up on his saddle, he leaped through the air at Witigor. In a fluid motion, he tackled Wit from his saddle. The historian cried out in surprise, releasing his horse's reins, flailing over the side of the animal with Branimir holding fast to the front of his shirt.

With a groan, Wit hit the rutted road. Branimir crashed into Wit's ribcage with all his weight. With a bawl of passion, Bran ignored the faint shouts of his companions behind him. Staring at the disfigured face, he punched Wit squarely in the teeth. When blood barely surfaced on the upper lip, Branimir hit him again. This time the lip split wide open.

Satisfied, Branimir stood. Adamus grabbed Branimir's shoulder and pulled him back from Wit.

"Keep the red brood away from me," Witigor cried, straining for breath. He scooted away from Branimir across the dirt, fumbling to his feet, grabbing at his bleeding nose and upper lip. "By the gods, you will all be punished for this. I swear it. I have done nothing wrong." He stumbled, almost falling over.

"And you do not know what we have done to come this far," Branimir said, trying to steady his shaking hands. He had already lost Dorofej; he would not let Witigor endanger the lives of his other friends. "You risk too much."

Adamus let go of his shoulder. "Czern's breath! I don't think you will find any argument from any here, Bran. But what do we do with him?"

"He cannot come with us to Eldhaft," Alyona said, "and he should not be allowed to return to Gaetana."

Witigor's eyes widened.

"We could see if he calms down before reaching Eldhaft," Sulanna said. "For now, take the reins from his horse, and tie him up.

"I'll do it," Farthr said, reaching for Wit's horse.

Witigor gained his balance, eyes whipping up and down the road for any sign of life, or escape. "You cannot—"

Alyona shocked the historian into silence, using Koldovstvo to pick up his body and fling him toward Farthr, who caught the scrawny human in a single hand. The centaur snarled with sharpened fangs, causing Witigor to clench his jaw with fear, twisting his head away.

Branimir watched Farthr place Wit back in his horse's saddle. The Svet bit through the reins, using one end to tie together Wit's hands. "You don't mean to set him free, do you?" Branimir asked Sulanna.

"I do not know what *we* will do with him yet," Sulanna answered.

Farthr snagged the remaining cord hanging from the bridle to lead the horse. "I can take him with me to Sorod and give him a proper education." The Svet smiled. "We could slow cook him before feasting."

Branimir twitched, knowing the centaurs had a habit of eating their enemies, as well as their own dead.

Witigor whitened. "Adamus. Sulanna. I have done nothing so grievous as to be treated this way. I thought we were friends."

Adamus shook his head, grimacing. The Ariadnean's muscles flexed, balling his hand into a fist. "Tis interesting how his tune changes at the thought of filling the belly of the Svet. We suddenly become friends again, where moments ago he wished to call us enemies to the crown."

"No," Wit said. "I would never have called you enemies to the crown. You misunderstood…"

"You would do best to stop talking," Adamus growled. Wit responded by clamping his jaw shut and hanging his head.

"Listen," Alyona said, redirecting attention from the historian, "even if we keep riding for the rest of the day and night, we will not make it to Eldhaft. The sun will be rising any time now, and we are going to need some sleep."

"She is right," Sulanna said, rubbing her sore neck, "but sleeping on the side of the road in the broad daylight will bring unwanted attention, especially with Wit bound up."

"We have put in many miles between here and Gaetana," Branimir said, choosing his words carefully. He did not want to hint anything about Falmagon being in Gaetana. Alyona should not know their late night had been to increase the distance between themselves and the Patrician of the Kadari, in case she had not been honest about her allegiances. "We may be able to afford a couple hours off the road for sleep."

Alyona gripped her animal's reins, her purple eyes watering from exhaustion. Branimir imagined the woman was completely fatigued, considering she came from Melkorka after being held prisoner in a dungeon and surviving a siege. "A couple hours would be welcomed."

Adamus said. "Our horses need rest, too. Tis early yet and the road is clear. We can take a couple hours to rest."

Farthr grunted. "I have no need for rest. I will continue my own way and take Witigor with me."

Sulanna shook her head. Branimir noticed that she eyed Alyona from the corner of her eye. "Farthr, I was hopeful you would stay among us for a while."

"I have no interest in traveling too close to Eldhaft." Farthr snorted. "I do not have a family name to keep me safe. I will make for Sorod."

"You think my name will keep me safe?" Sulanna nervously laughed. "My father rejected me from his sight two decades ago. He is the reason I joined the Crimson Sun."

"One can never know how time may heal wounds, and your name holds power still," Farthr said. "I am a Svet in a world of Anshedar. No name. No title. No power. I will be enslaved or killed without my position among the Crimson Sun."

Sulanna rubbed her hands together, looking to Adamus and then Branimir.

Bran knew what she was considering. The protection Adamus sought from Alyona was rapidly dwindling, and none of them would be able to predict whether Falmagon was already in pursuit.

Adamus pulled at his beard, keeping his eyes from Wit, and reluctantly nodded. With a sigh, Branimir dipped his head in agreement too. "What will be his fate, Farthr?" Branimir did not like Witigor, but he also did not want the Anshedar to be eaten by the Svet.

Farthr twitched his ears and looked to Sulanna for direction.

"You remember Ailin Meadhre?" Sulanna crossed her arms, glaring at Wit. A smile formed on Farthr's face as he bounced his head. "Give him the same fate, but let him roast a bit longer."

"What?" Wit screamed as Farthr grabbed the reins and began leading him away into the grasses. The historian rocked in the saddle, fighting against the restraints. "Who is Ailin Meadhre? Who is he? Nooo!"

Branimir twisted his neck for some explanation from his companions. Adamus and Alyona looked equally confused by Sulanna's sentencing. Branimir finally asked her the question. "What happened to Ailin Meadhre?"

Sulanna smiled. "He was stripped naked, tied to a tree, and left to roast in the sun until found. I suspect Wit will be back in Gaetana before the week's end."

Branimir's light chuckle was swiftly drowned out by Adamus's raucous laughter.

Chapter VI

Three and a half days passed before they reached the gates of Eldhaft in the northwest, a city of liars and thieves, as Sulanna once claimed. They lost almost a full day traveling to the city due to the heat. Several times Sulanna advised them to stop and take shelter off the road, hunkering down in the shade. Branimir worried Falmagon would gain on them, but he had seen no signs of the Patrician of the Kadari. He did wonder how far Farthr had taken Witigor from the road while traveling northeast; he doubted the historian would survive long under the sun. Despite his feelings for Wit, he hoped he was quickly found.

Eldhaft was nearly the magnitude of Gaetana, lying nestled in the Gaetanean Grasslands. Knolls rose and fell as far as the eye could see—a slight suggestion of the Hyaendi Hills further to the north. Thick grasses covered much of the land, but the locals cleared patches for farms and crops. In the midday light, Branimir could see homesteads reaching to the skyline, chock full of hard-working men in the field, animals roaming amongst their fenced cages, and children running amuck, diverted from chores by imaginary play.

Branimir wished he had the energy of the children, but the sweltering heat stole all he could muster. He barely could stay aloft on his pony. For what felt like the hundredth time since noon, Branimir wiped the sweat from his cheeks and forehead with the end of his cloak, hanging over the neck of his saddle. He then reached for his waterskin, glancing to the river running alongside the road. They had traveled near the water since the sunrise.

Sulanna must have noticed his gaze. She pointed to the water. "The Deep Run flows from the mountains in the north all the way to the ocean in the south, slowed only by the Gnyn Waters at Gaetana. You will find here, in the city walls of Eldhaft, the Gneveh Rill merges with the Deep Run to give the river enough strength to pierce through the southern lake. The sound of the rushing water can be deafening in some areas of the city. Honestly, the two rivers coming together is breathtaking."

"We should see it while we are here," Branimir said.

Sulanna rubbed the neck of her horse. "You will not be able to miss the sight. The main road through Eldhaft passes by the rivers."

Branimir gazed up to the green and gold banners hanging from the almost perfect circular stone wall surrounding Eldhaft, and took another drink from his waterskin. The banners displayed a golden horse dancing on its hind legs, wearing a crown of arrows, which Branimir mistook for strands of wheat crop at first glance.

Branimir said, "I once saw an image like that horse on the chest piece of the man we fought at Cavell. Remember, Adamus? He was with the Crimson Sun, too."

Adamus scrunched his beard, peering at the tapestry. "I remember something of it. Tis been a while, and if I recall, I drank more than I should have that night." Adamus returned his eyes to the road, stone-faced. Branimir wondered if he triggered memories of Hanna, Adamus's friend who died in battle last year. She had been with them at Cavell.

"Teodor Bacheva?" Sulanna interjected, raising an eyebrow and slowing her horse. She whispered, "I would not mention anything of it in the city. Teodor's father is stationed among the league of thieves, the Guardians of Gero. And as such, gave Teodor a considerable place in the Crimson Sun. He may have been Ivarr's most strategic asset among any in the company. Being involved in Teodor's death would not grant you any favors here."

"Great," Branimir said, remembering something more at the mention of the Guardians. "I forgot the league of thieves was in Eldhaft. They were looking for me several years ago when I worked in Gavlok. They were interested in my dagger-throwing."

"Let us hope they have forgotten your name, if they ever knew it," Sulanna said. "The Guardians believe themselves to be the very voice of Gero, the so-called god of Fertility, Harvest, and Rebirth. These men and women commit unlawful acts of violence for his exaltation. They lose so many of their affiliates to the gallows; they are frequently seeking more capable recruits."

"And why does Count Vlassi allow it?" Branimir asked.

"The Guardians do not rob or kill anyone in Eldhaft. At least, not without permission from Vlassi. Instead, they focus on neighboring cities, like Lonmere. You will find Guardians bled dry on pikes outside that city," Sulanna replied with a shake of her head. "The Guardians preach that Gero was stolen from Perom and delivered to Wolos, and so they steal from those unfaithful to Gero and deliver the goods to Eldhaft."

"Nary has a week passed, and again I hear Sulanna teaching the history of the gods," Adamus said. "Are you feeling well?"

"When you spend half a lifetime with Alden, you pick up a thing or two," Sulanna said with a frown. "I am not saying any of this is true. I am telling you what those fanatics believe. I would prefer we do not spend any more time in this cursed city than we must."

Branimir shook his head with emphasis, his thin hair bouncing against the edge of his eyelashes. "We will stay long enough to find Alden, and be done."

Alyona swept her eyes over them, reaching for her dark hood to pull over her head. She had been quiet most of the morning, watching the road intently, but finally spoke. "I agree. We must hurry to Iriy to meet Dorofej. He will be traveling with the wind; and we do not have time to waste."

The sound of flutes and harps permeated outside the walls, reaching Branimir's sensitive ears. Laughter and boisterous voices imbued the sound, as though the whole city may have been a patron-filled tavern. Branimir struggled to hear the faded trickle of the peaceful river flowing away from the city.

"A sprightly bunch, are they not?" Adamus said, steering his horse with a gentle tug, leading them beneath the portcullis. The guards gestured them through, talking loudly to one other about some evening festival. None seemed interested in any who came or left from the gates. Adamus continued, slowing slightly, "Most of the people will be prepping for harvest this time of the year, if the heat has not burnt up all their crops. Still, I suspect these people will laugh their way through starvation. I fought alongside a man from Eldhaft at Raybin. I cannot say I ever caught him without a smile. Even when the Uvil put a hooked sword into his side, he grinned like a fool."

"And yet, Sulanna rarely smiles," Branimir said with a crooked grin, stopping his pony as two girls ran by the road in front of him, laughing and holding half-made wreaths of flowers and ferns over their head. They looked up at Branimir for a half-second, giggled, and continued into the crowded streets.

Sulanna smirked, stopping her own mount. "I was born here, Branimir. I did not stay around long enough to adopt the drivel." The color from Sulanna's face suddenly drained as she examined the roads ahead of her.

"What is it?" Branimir asked, searching the streets for the cause of her distress. The road immediately forked left and right on either side of the gate, leading through buildings nearly built on top of one another. Some of the structures were homes, built behind tall wooden fences, while others were shops or taverns. People encumbered the streets. Young women pranced about with similar wreaths as the first two girls, men ambled by carrying long strips of wood, while handfuls of others laughed, danced, or talked.

Sulanna rotated on her mount to address the first guardsman found, leaning against the stone wall behind them. "What is today?"

The young guardsman smiled with oversized, white teeth filling the space between his lips, standing upright. His hand rested on the hilt of the longsword at his belt, the horse head glimmering on his chest plate in the sunlight. "Why, my lady, it is the Day of Myestera. Join us at sun fall in Old Town for dancing, drinking, and merriment. The fires will burn bright through the night." He dipped his head at Adamus and Alyona, swinging his hand in a wide arc, "Bring your husband, your daughter, and…" he looked at Branimir with hesitation, "your Kras."

Sulanna gripped the reins until her knuckles turned white. "My what and my what?"

"Your daughter may find herself with a gallant husband before the night is through," the guard said, turning his eyes from Bran to Alyona once more. The Kadari sunk into her hood, turning her purplish eyes away. The guard's words lingered. "No city can offer better men than Eldhaft."

"Come on," Adamus sniggered, drawing out the next word, "my sweetness. We should find a place to freshen up before the festivities."

Sulanna growled through her teeth, despite the flashes of color on her cheeks. "Do not push me, Adamus. My blade is recently sharpened and your neck is bare."

Adamus only grinned wider, directing his horse down the dirt path. "Where to?"

Branimir coaxed his pony forward, leaving the guardsman behind them. He personally thought she would make an excellent mother someday, but decided against mentioning it.

Sulanna took a moment before answering. "Take the right fork. We will go to Old Town to The Harper and Mug."

"We cannot stay long," Alyona pressed with concern.

"Only long enough to find Alden," Branimir repeated.

Adamus did as he was told, leading the way with Sulanna directly behind him, then Branimir, and finally Alyona at the rear. Branimir spotted a second set of walls almost immediately, dividing Old Town from the remainder of the city.

Branimir waited until they navigated through the congested street and passed under the second portcullis before raising another question. "Would anyone like to explain to me what the Day of Myestera is?"

Alyona moved her horse next to Branimir's pony, people flooding on either side of them. "The celebration is also called *Pal'ka*, honoring the marriage of the Mother of the Stars and the Lightbringer. Women yet wedded end the feast by tossing handmade wreaths into a river. They say it will foretell the future of their own marriages by whether the flowers sink or float. The holiday was once sacred, but now, it is really an excuse for excessive drinking and fornication."

"Mother of the Stars…Myestera…" Branimir wondered aloud. "We are talking about the Moon Goddess, a goddess worshipped by the Vucari."

"Yes," Alyona said, turning under her hood to look at Branimir. "The Vucari first worshipped Wolos, and then Myestera. Neither god has been revered among humans in my lifetime." She bent over, hovering above Branimir on her horse, and asked softly, "How have you come to know the skin-switchers of the far north?"

Branimir gazed under the hood into Alyona's purplish eyes. "A long time ago, before we first met, I was friends with a Vucari woman from Anaerfell. She told me many things about her people."

"Friends?" Alyona cocked her head.

"I know the Kadari believed the Vucari to be wicked creatures, but they were the wardens of the Ash Tree. When they fought you at Shayol Domier, I think they were trying to protect the tree," Branimir explained, "but the Kadari…only wanted power."

Alyona sighed heavily. Branimir could see the water forming at the corner of her eyes, unhidden from him despite the dark folds of her hood. "My father would say the Vucari are savage beasts, but I know better."

Branimir gritted his teeth. "I do not know your father, but I would guess he is the same type who would call me a demon." Branimir tugged at his hooked nose irritably, and then laid his hand back in his lap. "Yet I have met demons and devils alike, and I am nothing like them."

"No," Alyona said, "you are not."

Sulanna whipped her head around, hushing them. "Do not draw unwanted attention our way. Need I remind you, we are in Eldhaft? The guards may have their hearts set on dancing and drinking tonight, but the Guardians will not be as unconcerned."

"We are not speaking against Gero," Alyona said.

Sulanna's nostrils flared unattractively. "No, you speak of Wolos, who stole Gero, and his long-forgotten, faithful people. May I remind you of the rumors of Wolos being murdered? Those in Eldhaft do not readily forget."

"I do not see what—" Alyona started.

Sulanna growled under her breath. "Do not talk about any gods or goddesses, old or new, real or otherwise! Not until we are a hundred miles outside of Eldhaft, and even then, you best ask me first." She gave a motherly stare, and jerked her head frontward again.

Branimir hardly heard Adamus's muffled jest. "Three times."

"By the Nine Lands, Adamus," Sulanna said. "I am trying to keep our heads. And the three of you seem intent on seeing them severed."

It was nearing dusk by the time they reached The Harper and Mug. The road, although long and crowded, was a straight shot to the three-story edifice, sitting three buildings south from the double-wide bridge passing over the Deep Run. Branimir stretched on his pony to look at the water. The dark blue, rigorous river surged under the bridge, crashing against either bank, pitching into small waves. The water smelled anything but crisp, likely full of waste from the inhabitants of the city. Yet the river did remind him of the sun's heat. In that moment he abruptly noticed the fact that Alyona had been sheltered beneath her thick hood, but showed no signs of discomfort, including sweat.

Branimir forfeited his attention on the inn shortly, to confirm Alyona did not seem to be affected by the weather. Whereas the rest of the party—as well as every citizen of Eldhaft who ventured too close—reeked like the rotten mires of the Dyndaer. Alyona held no such smell.

She may be telling the truth about Dorofej, but she was hiding something.

"Afternoon," a middle-age man approached them from the steps leading up into the inn. "If you are looking for a room, I can take your horses to the stables. Chaid Paddley is the barkeep. He can see you to room and board inside."

Sulanna took the lead, dismounting and grabbing her pack. "Our thanks, Master…"

"Ayden Stansfield," the man filled in the blank with a smile, "and just Ayden, if you please. I have done nothing to deserve any title."

"Thank you, Ayden," Sulanna reiterated, handing the man a few silvers. "Please keep the horses well attended. We will speak to Chaid about a room."

Ayden clinked the coins in his hand with a smile. "Well attended, indeed."

Branimir's buttocks and legs were sore as he climbed from the saddle and grabbed his own pack. He purposely held his cloak over his forearm, blocking any view of Kaelandur at his belt. With a grunt, he took his place behind Adamus and Alyona who followed Sulanna up the solid staircase. Awkwardly, Bran attempted to rub some of the soreness on the back of his thigh. He only now realized they had been riding since the early morning without taking any time to rest.

The Harper and Mug had a worn disposition, complete with faded wood and hung oil paintings to put Lady Gail's artwork at the

Peddlar's Rose to shame. The commons were half-full of patrons, who started their drinking a few hours early. The design was like the Peddlar's Rose with the staircase against the back wall, accompanied by several doors leading into other rooms on the first floor. Tables and chairs were equally spread out through the commons, adjacent to the long bar to the left. Branimir barely took notice of a beaming woman entertaining the gathering, playing a fiddle on a corner stage, before the barkeep stole his attention.

"You have a Kras in your party?" The man known as Chaid leaned over the bar to peer at Branimir. His bushy eyebrows ran together over his nose, forming a single brow, nearly thick enough to cover his beady eyes. "I am not sure we have a bed small enough to accommodate him, but I can check with Master Berkeley. We don't see many Kras in these parts."

"That will not be necessary, Chaid," Sulanna said with a soft smile. "He is perfectly capable of sleeping in a regular-sized bed."

"Now, my Lady, Master Berkeley will want to be assured you are well taken care of while staying at our establishment," he said with a grim smile. "I would hate to be the reason your stay is less than expected."

"We hold no unreasonable expectations," Sulanna began.

"It is no trouble," Chaid insisted. "Go on up to your room. Third door on the left will sleep the four of you comfortably, even with the addition of another bed. I will speak with the Master."

Sulanna frowned. "When is supper served?"

Chaid kept the smile plastered on his face, as though painted on. His eyes fell to Branimir, blinking several times. "As soon as you are ready for it."

"We will take it in our room," Sulanna replied.

Branimir met the man's stare while Adamus thanked Chaid, and ushered Sulanna toward the staircase. He trailed behind, finally turning away from the gawking barkeep.

"What do you think his problem is?" Branimir hissed at Alyona as they climbed the staircase.

"Maybe he has never seen a Kras before," Alyona offered, looking behind them under her hood.

"I do not know I feel right staying here tonight," Bran said. "Something does not feel right. We would do better to stay camping out in the grasslands."

"Let us not start with sinister thoughts already," Sulanna replied, pushing their door open.

Branimir walked behind her, ready to respond, when he bumped into the back of Sulanna's leg. His comment was forgotten when he realized she had unexpectedly stopped.

Peeping around Sulanna, Branimir caught a glimmer of the large, low-lighted room, prepped with a water basin, fresh beds, and readied wine. Yet an aged man with white, braided hair, and a thick, curled mustache, dressed in a green suit with gold buttons, sat in a wooden chair with his legs crossed, already gifting himself with the wine. His blue eyes, akin to Sulanna, skimmed over them briefly before he took a slow sip from his golden chalice.

Sulanna rigidly suspended her chin and folded her arms under her breasts. "Father."

Chapter VII

"Quite the muddled mess you have made for yourself, Daughter. I thought the Crimson Sun would have ironed out your rough edges, but even the ways of war and death were incapable of teaching you proper reason." Vornic Myrthos Maelthirren sipped from his chalice again, eyes thick with malice as he watched Sulanna take the seat across from him.

Branimir remained at Sulanna's side, eyeing the old man with uncertainty. Adamus and Alyona piled into the room behind him. The few hanging lights around the room likely made it difficult for Adamus and Sulanna to see. Though, Bran saw the room was clear, save the old man.

Myrthos gulped the mouthful of red wine, catching a droplet on the edge of his lip with a thin finger. "And now, you return to Eldhaft to further blemish the family name, and plague an old man with your foul schemes. Oh, yes… I have a very clear understanding of what plots you have tangled yourself in with this red brood, and," he squinted at Alyona and Adamus, "these indecent coconspirators."

Sulanna moved her hands to her knees, shaking her head slightly. "Whatever you think you know is far-removed from the truth, Father."

"I think not," Myrthos said, his mustache lifting with a sneer. "Ivarr Gauthus has sent for news regarding your whereabouts more times than I can remember. And the Patrician has had a mark on that *red brood* for a year and more. Now, less than a week ago, he sent a message to every major and minor settlement in Maharia to bolster efforts to bring you both to justice. Did you not think the Guardians would see you approaching the city? You have broken the law, Sulanna. The very law you swore to uphold. You have shamed this family for the last time."

"Falmagon is the one who cannot be trusted," Branimir said earnestly. "You do not know him. You do not know what he is capable of."

"Tis the truth," Adamus said with a jerk of his head, exchanging glances with Sulanna and Branimir. "Far more is at stake than the egos of men in position."

"Oh," Myrthos said, unable to mask the mocking tone, "and I should believe an outlaw over a Kadari who saved Aenar from itself, not only fending off demons from the Netherworld, but also holding fast to the faith of the Anshedar."

"An outlaw? I bled for Maharia!" Adamus thundered, flexing his arm in restraint from grabbing the steel axe at his belt. "My brothers, my friends, have died to give men the capacity to hold faith."

"Yet you help shroud those who hold precious artifacts to save this world from demons," Myrthos said, casually placing his goblet on the floor.

"You know nothing of the nature of these artifacts," Sulanna said.

"I may not," Myrthos said, "but Falmagon has kept men on the righteous path of Dahz the Lightbringer. To truth! I trust he knows what should be done, and the Crimson Sun supports his claim."

"You seek to further yourself," Sulanna scowled.

Branimir spoke over Sulanna. "What are you talking about?" He stood up straight as he had been jerked, staring at Myrthos. "The gods have no interest in how they are worshipped or what we do to honor them. Any *truth* Falmagon told you has been to gain power."

Sulanna looked daggers at her father. "My father seeks the same power, Branimir. He is the Vornic of Eldhaft, remember? He tortures innocent men and women to gain position and privilege. Our words fall on deaf ears."

"You speak blasphemy, as I would expect from your kind. I have dealt with lawbreakers my entire life," Myrthos said. His blue eyes were haunting through the thin slits of his eyelids. "Sulanna should have known I would see through your lies. You are the sort to leave an educated scholar from the Highspire, without any account of wrongdoing, bound unclothed to a tree for your own sick enjoyment." Branimir's mouth dried. The Vornic must have noticed his changed expression. "Oh, yes. I have had the pleasure to talk at length with Witigor Sirska this morning. I have learned a great deal about the four of you, and we will find the Svet soon enough."

Branimir folded his arms to keep himself from shaking. The extra time they spent resting had apparently given Witigor time to beat them to Eldhaft. The historian had kept to his promise. "Haven't you tortured people your entire life? I am sure you do far worse than tie them to a tree," he said.

Vornic Myrthos Maelthirren took another sip from his wine with a smile.

"Where is he?" Adamus said under his breath.

"He has been given residence at my estate after your contemptible mistreatment," Myrthos responded. "Not that it matters. You will never be within arm's reach of him again."

Branimir trembled. He could punch Witigor in his scarred face. The historian was keeping him from Dorofej.

Myrthos returned his attention to his daughter. "I am sickened, Sulanna, that you have aligned yourself with these types. But you clearly have chosen your own way, despite having a father who did all he could to place you on a better path."

Sulanna shuddered, turning eyes away from him. "You discarded me with my mother."

"Your mother chose to leave," Myrthos retorted.

The tears streamed down her cheeks, stealing her strength. Her words were drawn out. "What choice did she have after what you did to Hegedus?"

Myrthos's voice seethed with anger. "You moan like a sheep, Sulanna. Your brother was a heathen, and enemy to the crown."

"You…publicly gutted him in the streets…like a swine."

Adamus roared at the revelation, pushing past Branimir to stand between Sulanna and Myrthos, protecting her like a shield. "You murdered your own son!"

Myrthos did not as much as flinch, standing to face the Ariadnean. His words dripped venom. "A fate each of you will share when I have finished recovering what information you have locked inside those insignificant skulls."

In an instant, the room became a flurry of movement. Adamus's hefty fist plowed into the under jaw of Sulanna's father, knocking him back into the rear wall, flipping the chair and dumping the goblet of wine. Behind them, the doors of other rooms in the hallway sprung open, and out poured more men than Branimir could count, all dressed in similar dark green, hooded cloaks, stitched with golden embroidery.

"No," Sulanna shouted, seeing her father crumple against the wall. Adamus moved to strike the man again, before becoming aware of the countless men rushing into their room. He spun around Sulanna's chair, pulling his axe free and swinging it at the first coming through the door.

The lithe invader rolled under the swing, springing to the side, and elbowing Alyona under the chin. She flailed back into the bed, her hood falling back, revealing her purple eyes and dark hair.

Branimir faded from view, releasing his pack, and pulling the two daggers from his belt. He dove for the first invader, stabbing a dagger into the man's leg, and then his knee. The attacker bawled for a moment, before Alyona was back on her feet. With a wave of her hand, she flung the injured man back through the door, causing several more to collapse in an attempt to catch the airborne body.

"Who are they?" Adamus shouted as more rushed into the room, pulling knives from their belts. The men moved quickly, rushing around the room, surrounding them.

"Guardians of Gero," Sulanna said, pulling herself from the chair. Her hand hung over the long dagger at her belt, but she did not pull it free. "We will not be able to overpower them."

"We can try!" Adamus growled. "Come on, Bran." The Ariadnean crashed into the circle of Guardians, his shield moved to his left arm, mid-jump, crushing a smaller, unaware man into the wine jugs sitting in the room. Adamus belted a second Guardian in the side of the head with his axe. He dropped to the floor with a gravelly groan.

Branimir reacted straightaway. He threw his dagger with deadly intent into a Guardian's chest, who was raising a dagger at Adamus's side. The man dropped his own dagger, gripping the handle of Branimir's lodged weapon. Bran skittered across the floorboards, stabbing another man in the leg, before picking up the dropped dagger and flinging it into another Guardian's eye socket.

Adamus cleaved off a man's arm, and smashed another with the shield, roaring as though he stood among thousands on the battlefield. More Guardians entered from the hall replacing their fallen brethren.

"Alyona, come on," Adamus cried, pivoting on his foot to dodge the blade of a Guardian. Branimir shadowed Adamus, looking to the bed where Alyona had tumbled moments ago. "Nine Lands…She tricked us." Adamus inhaled, his jaw falling.

Alyona Gounari had vanished. Her white shirt, dark trousers, riding boots, and faded black cloak were scattered over the bed and floor, and she was gone.

Before Branimir could process what had taken place, Adamus snarled with pain. Branimir whipped his head around to see a dagger buried into Adamus's leg. Dark, red blood already seeped through his trousers from the wound.

The Guardian who threw the weapon still had his hand extended, standing near the doorway. Branimir dashed forward, using his single dagger to slice the tendons in the back of the Guardian's legs. The man screamed and collapsed to the floorboards, only to be speedily silenced by Branimir's blade cutting through his neck.

Branimir ignored the warm blood splattering on his face, hearing Adamus cry out once more. Another blade plunged into the Ariadnean's back, causing him to sink to one knee.

"Stop this, Father!" Sulanna screeched. "Adamus! Branimir! Stop it."

"Enough." Myrthos keened with a gasping breath, grabbing at the wall behind him. Slowly, he pulled himself to his feet and cupped his jawbone. A bluish-black bump swelled beneath the lip. Myrthos's beady eyes locked on Adamus, raising his other hand to stop the Guardians. "Take him and my daughter to Harrowhal."

A Guardian behind Adamus slipped a rope around the hero-warrior's thick neck, rigidly jerking his head back. Adamus strained against the lesser might of the Guardian as the other thieves removed his weapons and bound his hands and feet.

"Run, Branimir," Adamus grated, dropping his axe to the floor. "Tis over. Get out of here. Wherever you are. Get out of here."

More Guardians advanced on Sulanna, who looked pleadingly at her father. The wrinkles of her own aged face were suddenly evident in her distress. "You truly mean to rid this world of all your children."

Myrthos scowled. "If only the gods had blessed me with children worth saving." He stomped by her, addressing the Guardians. "Someone get downstairs and block the front door. No one leaves or comes without our knowing." One of the Guardians rushed to do as bid, while Myrthos went on, calling out, "Master Bacheva?"

Branimir slipped into the corner of the room, staying cloaked with his invisibility. From the hallway, a middle-aged man with a salt-and-pepper goatee hurriedly emerged, wearing the same attire as the other Guardians of Gero. He dipped his head in respect to Myrthos. "Yes, Vornic Maelthirren?"

He recognized the name of Master Bacheva, marking this as the father of Teodor, who they fought at Cavell last year. He was the very man Sulanna had said to avoid while in Eldhaft.

Myrthos wiped his hand on his clothing as though there were something of note on his skin needing removed. "Find the Kadari woman and the Kras; they could not have gotten too far. Once found, you can bring them to Harrowhal."

"Of course," Master Bacheva said, "but I must warn you that finding the Kras will prove difficult. Their kind can stay invisible indefinitely, and can only be seen by another of their kind. And, unless we bring the Kadari down unaware, she could topple half the city on itself."

Myrthos frowned at the man, taking a moment to glance at Sulanna and Adamus having their mouths gagged. He finally said, "Are there any more Kras in Eldhaft?"

Master Bacheva paused for a moment before responding, perhaps realizing he overstepped. "I will check, Vornic."

"Good," Myrthos said. "You will also send word to Patrician Falmagon Sej. He was heading east from Gaetana. Tell him we have found what he has been looking for."

Master Bacheva hesitated. "As you command, Vornic Maelthirren."

Branimir's blood boiled at the mention of Falmagon. If he came to Eldhaft, Branimir would make sure to kill him for good, as he should have at the Peddlar's Rose.

The Guardians hauled Sulanna and Adamus from the room, Master Bacheva traipsing behind them out the door. A few more thieves fell in behind him, taking the dead from the room.

Branimir tiptoed a couple steps forward as the room emptied, suddenly halted by Vornic Myrthos Maelthirren who filled the frame of the doorway. Sulanna's father scanned the room with vigilant eyes. His voice boomed, "If you are here, Kras, you should know your friends will be dead by morning."

Branimir clutched the dagger in his hand, itching to take the man's life, pausing only with the knowledge that the Vornic was Sulanna's kin.

With a smirk, Myrthos departed, shutting the door behind him, and leaving Branimir alone in the room.

Branimir gazed at the wooden door, turning the dagger in his hand in contemplation. The Guardians would be lurking in the hallway and in the commons, and they surely would be guarding the exit leading outside. Invisible or not, Branimir could not run around the inn opening doors and remain undetected. A Guardian would notice, and then Branimir would be forced to kill someone else.

His hand reached for the doorknob, and paused. He would kill hundreds to save Adamus and Sulanna, but maybe he could find another way out of the inn.

Rubbing his chin, Branimir examined the room with the flipped chairs, spilt wine, and pools of blood on the faded floorboards. Eventually, the innkeeper would send someone up the stairs to clean the mess and he would be able to exit the room. However, by then, Sulanna and Adamus would be long gone, taken to this place the Vornic had called Harrowhal. Certainly, the whereabouts of Harrowhal was in Eldhaft, but the city was massive. It could take weeks to find Harrowhal without directly following Adamus and Sulanna.

He glowered, suddenly recognizing the room did not have a single window.

Sulanna's father had been wise in devising a scheme to capture them. Of course, Branimir placed full blame on the assiduous historian. Witigor, of course, had earwigged Sulanna's intention to stay at The Harper and Mug to start looking for Alden. Branimir speculated that Witigor had told Myrthos everything he needed to hear—having the information sought by both the Kadari and the Crimson Sun—and they ignorantly let Witigor walk right into the Vornic's hands.

From what Myrthos said, Farthr remained safe for the time being. If the centaur made his way back to Sorod, the Guardians would be unlikely to follow. They could not survive in a city of Svet.

Branimir cleaned his dagger off on his pant leg, and returned the weapon to his belt. He could not risk staying in the inn until morning. He had to rescue Adamus and Sulanna. He moved for the door again.

The creaking of a floorboard caused Branimir to freeze his movements. He heard a rustling near the bed, and slowly peered over his shoulder. To his astonishment, Alyona bowed over the bed, naked to the world, retrieving her clothes from where they had fallen.

Completely oblivious of Branimir standing invisible behind her, the pale-skinned girl hastily yanked the trousers over her thin legs, and then slipped on her boots as quietly as she could. As Alyona reached for her shabby shirt, Branimir rematerialized.

"Where did you run to?" he murmured. "Was this part of your plan all along?"

Alyona spun around into a crouch, with her shirt halfway pulled over her neck, just above her breasts. Her purple irises swelled at the sight of Branimir. She blinked and then yanked her shirt down over her torso, pushing her arms through the sleeves. "No, Branimir. My plan is to get you to Iriy as I said in the beginning. I had no idea Myrthos was looking for you, or that Falmagon was in Gaetana. Nor did I know Witigor was a fickle rat!"

"Why did you not fight with us?" Branimir accused, crossed his arms. "You could have ripped the Guardians to pieces with Koldovstvo."

"For what reason? To have my life drain away in the musty room of an old inn while thieves rained down upon us? They would have eventually killed me, or subdued me and taken me prisoner, too," Alyona scoffed.

"Subdued a Kadari?" Branimir wrinkled his brow.

"The Guardians of Gero are thick in Eldhaft. The Guardians would not have been defeated here. Why do you think Sulanna did not raise her own weapon against them?"

"Because her father was here," Branimir said. "She could reason with him."

"Sulanna doesn't care about her father, and Myrthos is beyond reason," Alyona hissed, standing upright and snagging her cloak from the bed. "The man slaughtered her brother. Believe me, she has no love for him."

"Then why wouldn't she fight to the death? Why wouldn't you? Isn't that a better fate than being tortured and killed?" Branimir protested.

"I am not going to die in a tavern bedroom, Branimir," Alyona said, pushing her short dark hair behind her ear. "My quest is to take you and Kaelandur to Iriy. We are trying to save Aenar, remember?"

"If you are going to suggest we leave Sulanna and Adamus with the Vornic—"

Alyona grimaced. "I would not even attempt to convince you."

Branimir twitched his nose, and finally kicked at the floorboards. "Tell me what happened to you. How did you disappear like that? I have never met a Kadari who can do what a Kras can."

Alyona winced. "I did not disappear…I…"

"You what?"

"I transformed," Alyona lingered, "into a bat. And I hid up there on the ceiling. In the corner."

Branimir followed her eyes to the shadowy corner of the room, barely discernible in the lowlight of the windowless room. "A bat? How?"

Alyona fastened her cloak around her neck, and then fell back to sit on the bed. "My mother was a Vucari, and my father a Stuhia. She died giving birth to me and my brother, but her blood runs through me as strongly as the Stuhian."

Branimir peered at Alyona as though he was seeing her for the first time. "So, when we were traveling on the road, you could see in the dark as well as I can?"

"I can do much like the Vucari, but not everything. I never had a…guide." Alyona turned her gaze from Branimir.

"But you killed the Vucari at Shayol Domier. You were bent on slaughtering every skin-switcher in the Dyndaer."

"I did as I was commanded. My father believed in the Kadari and Patrician Moreth, and I favored my father's teachings," Alyona said. "While they did not do everything right, Falmagon has further warped the Kadari and their doctrine." She crossed her arms, giving the indication she was growing tired of defending herself. "I told you in Gaetana, I am trying to make things right."

"I cannot believe you have the power of the Vucari and the Stuhia. You are not human at all…" Branimir's mind reeled with the possibilities.

"We all have our secrets, Branimir," Alyona said, her eyes drifting to Kaelandur at Branimir's belt, "and our burdens." She ran her hand through her dark hair again, considering Branimir. "We don't have time to chit-chat. If you want to rescue your friends, we must get out of here."

"The Guardians are still waiting out there," Branimir said, reaching for his pack and slinging it over his shoulder.

"If they are truly calling for Falmagon," Alyona said, running her hand down her face in thought, "I would prefer not to use Koldovstvo. If we should fight the Patrician, I will need every ounce of life in me to have a chance at defeating him."

"I guess burning a hole through the wall is out of the question," Branimir said.

"Okay," Alyona said, pulling her shirt off again.

Branimir stared at her naked chest. "Why are you taking your clothes off?"

Alyona pulled off her boots, and then her pants. "I am going to turn back into a bat. You will keep me inside your cloak and get out of here." She shoved her clothes inside her small pack and handed it to him.

Branimir took the pack and slung it over his other shoulder, balancing the weight. He stood toe-to-toe with Alyona, barely reaching her belly button. "They will see the doors opening and closing. Even the blind may occasionally hit targets they cannot see."

Alyona, having no shame, put her hands on her hips and cocked her chin. "You walked amongst demons for a thousand years in the Netherworld, Branimir Baran. By the Nine Lands, you can slink by a throng of thieves and down a flight of stairs."

Branimir blinked a couple times, his hands twisting incessantly around the straps of the bags hanging over his shoulder. He replied stiffly, "Very well. I guess there is no other way." The packs suddenly felt heavy. Heavier than a mountain.

Branimir stepped away as the stark-naked woman standing before him swiftly warped and wound her body—bones cracking and skin shriveling—until all that remained was a woolly, leaf-nosed bat.

Alyona flapped her wings in a circular motion, hovering expectantly in the air. Branimir watched her at the end of his hooked nose for a moment, and then he spread open his green cloak. Alyona pulsated forward and clung onto his shirt with her trifling toes. He took a slow breath, feeling her weight suspended from his attire.

"This is weird," Branimir said, adjusting the pack on his shoulder again. Alyona squeaked in response, and Branimir could only think she directed him to get on with it.

Fading from sight, Branimir moved to the door and listened, his hand resting on the latch. Footsteps passed by the door and were moving away from him toward the staircase. Taking the chance, he sprung the latch and pulled the door open, peeking into the hallway. A Guardian, as expected, paced away from him facing the stairwell. The green and gold cloak flapped behind the man with every swish of his feet.

No others were in sight.

He eased into the hallway, and firmly closed the door behind him. The bang of the wood hitting the frame clacked loudly in the hallway. Branimir sneaked away and the Guardian, who hastily flipped around, rushed to where he had been standing. The light-eyed man pulled a dagger from his belt and pressed his ear to the door.

Branimir held his breath as the Guardian gently opened the door to investigate the sound, and stepped inside the empty room. Branimir crept down the hallway, ignoring the Guardian, and began his descent down the staircase. With the packs on his back, he could not share much space with any other, especially in a close-knit hallway or on the stairwell.

Chaid Paddley disappeared from behind the bar, leaving the commons to the many Guardians who hounded around like hunting dogs rapt on startling the fox from its hole. Branimir counted close to twenty of the thieves traipsing in and out of the back rooms, a couple purposefully stationed at the exit door. Branimir would be unable to swing the door open without being stopped by the boot of either guard. Yet if he could break the large window next to the front door, he may be able to spring to the streets without being grabbed.

Alyona's hind claws scratched at his chest through his shirt as she clung to him. He resisted the urge to let go of either pack and respond to the subtle sting.

Footsteps echoed from behind him as the Guardian from upstairs approached the staircase. He twisted his neck to see the blue-eyed man start down the stairs.

"I had a door slam upstairs," he shouted into the commons. "Have you seen anything odd down there?"

Branimir scooted off the stairs to avoid colliding into him, clinging to the wall that led to the back rooms. Several Guardians met the blue-eyed thief as he reached the bottom step.

"Nothing."

"What do you mean a door slammed?"

The Guardian said, "I mean the door opened and then shut without reason. My guess is the Kras snuck down there."

"We don't even know if he is still here," said another.

"Fan out," the first one called out. "Do not leave any space between you. Not so much as a child should be able to squeeze through."

Branimir shirked back further as the Guardians throughout the commons hurried to follow the hastened command. The thieves leapt over tables and chairs, exiting the back rooms, forming a line that blocked the staircase, the barkeep, and extended across the front door and promising window.

"Draw weapons and advance," said the first. "Two of you remain by the door." In unison, the thieves jerked the daggers from their belt and took a step forward.

The Guardians kicked chairs out of the way and flipped tables. The line remained firm.

Bran scooted back along the wall. Again, the Guardians advanced, clearing anything in their path. A chair turned, landing close to Branimir's feet.

The thieves ignored the barkeep, continuing forward, closing the empty space.

Unable to find an opening in the line, Branimir turn toward the back rooms to find the thieves had left both doors standing wide open. He darted to the first doorway on his light feet, discovering what appeared to be an office. He looked for anything of use in the room. A desk, bookshelves, chairs, and…a window.

Nightfall had come.

Grabbing a paperweight from the desk, he rushed to the windowpane. As he prepared to break the glass, he noticed the simple latch. The window opened sideways. With a smile, he ignored the clashing of furniture being flung in the commons behind him. He flipped the clasp and sprung the window open.

He was free.

Chapter VIII

Branimir scuttled along the western road, veering in and out of the swarms of people—dancing and singing around bonfires blazing in the streets—who were already immersed in the celebration of Pal'ka. He snaked between the thin and fat, ducked under flailing arms, and dodged the drunk and sober alike, while darting around mindless children who senselessly changed their trajectory, heedlessly stumbling into his path. The multiple melodies from many musical instruments rebounded through the streets, especially alongside the river, where young girls tossed their handcrafted wreaths into the water, and then giggled with unrivalled delight. Branimir had not the time to gawk at the flowers floating in the water to see which floated or sank.

He remained hidden from sight, clinging to the packs over either shoulder, while Alyona, in her bat-like form, clung to his shirt beneath his cloak. He rushed for the wall and gate, marking the exit to Old Town, and away from the Guardians of Gero.

To his left were rows of shops and houses, and to his right roared the Deep Run, crashing against the shores of Old Town and whatever lay on the other side. Branimir could make out the castle keep sitting on a small rise overseeing the city, where he presumed the Count held residence. The sight told him he had exited The Harper and Mug and fled in an unfamiliar direction, but his only concern was placing distance between himself and the thieves. And then, he needed to find this place where Adamus and Sulanna had been taken, Harrowhal.

Branimir glanced to the moon, hanging like a silver coin in the sky, emitting a hoary light bright enough to dim the twinkle of the stars. Yet, as he made his way through the streets, Branimir's eyes witnessed wonders, including men forcing themselves on women—who tittered in pleasure—in alleyways and on street corners without shame. After a thousand years and more, Branimir could not understand the minds of the Anshedar, who meant to give reverence to the gods through debauchery, dancing, and fornication.

He could only guess humans believed the gods to be more of fleshly desires than anything divine. Though, as Dorofej often expounded, the gods had little care about the whims of humans.

The open gateway, leading from Old Town, pulled Branimir from his brief musing. Branimir almost expected the Guardians to be nipping at his heel, shouting to all guardsmen to close the gates, but no guards were found. Those who should have been standing watch had joined in the festival.

Branimir soon withdrew from Old Town without any taking notice of the pitter-patter of his invisible footfalls.

He sprung onto a dirt road, reaching a statue that he did not bother to examine. A bridge on his right led across the Deep Run, while his left led back to the entrance to the city gate, where he and the others entered that afternoon; and ahead lay more houses and merchant buildings than he could stomach.

Several common-folk ambled by Branimir toward Old Town. He took the moment to catch his breath, pulling his green cloak open to check on Alyona. Her nostrils flared on her triangular nose, suggestive of her anticipation, but he could read nothing of her thoughts as to what they should do next.

He whispered so only she could hear. "I don't know what direction to go. Any way could lead us further from them."

Alyona scratched at his chest again and then let go of his shirt, flapping out from beneath his cloak. He watched, as she stayed suspended in front of his nose for a few moments before taking off into the air.

"What now?" he muttered, keeping an eye on the brownish bat fluttering above him.

To the Anshedar, Alyona likely blended into the night, unseen, but for Branimir she was clear as day, swooping up and down along the city street. He raced after her down the road, staying clear from any humans heading to the festival, which seemed centralized in Old Town. Recurrently, Branimir could hear Alyona squeaking loudly into the night, causing a bothersome ringing in his ears. The humans around him did not seem to notice the riling sound, but for him, the echoing peep was maddening.

Alyona lunged back and forth for several blocks before she decisively darted into an alley on Branimir's left. He pursued her, until she finally stopped where the backstreet ended. The alleyway ran perpendicular into a stone wall; he guessed it was the opposite side of the same inner wall circling Old Town.

Alyona landed and transformed back into her human form, stifling a groan as her body snapped back into place, leaving her crouching on all fours in the dirt. Branimir surfaced from the shadows in front of her.

"Are you okay?" he murmured.

"Hm," she hummed. "You followed me. Good."

"Of course, I followed you."

She reached her hand out for her pack. He swiftly passed the bag into her hand, peering over his shoulder to look at the main road while she slipped on her clothes.

"Where are we?" Branimir asked after a moment.

"Harrowhal," Alyona replied, her feet scuffing against the ground as she stood up. "Adamus and Sulanna are being held somewhere in this building."

Branimir turned around as Alyona lifted her hood back over her head. She repositioned her dark cloak to cover her bag. "How did you find it?"

Alyona approached a wooden door in the brick wall on their left. With a flip of her hand, the door unlocked and opened. "Bats cannot see well, but they have exceptional hearing, even better than a Kras. The Guardian out front said something of the Vornic's daughter being inside. I can only assume this is Harrowhal."

Branimir pulled at his nose, wondering why he had not heard the men. Maybe he was too focused on following Alyona to pay much attention, or maybe bats did hear better than Kras.

"I hope you are right," Branimir said.

He followed Alyona through the wooden door into the horseshoe-shaped courtyard surrounding the oversized brick building that towered stories above them. He examined the several balconies suspended from the second and third levels of the building. Each window had the curtains drawn, outlined with yellow light.

In the courtyard, Branimir could hear the voices of the many Guardians walking the perimeter. "We cannot stay out here," he said softly.

"This way." Alyona grabbed his arm and pulled him along the walkway to an iron door almost directly in front of them. Again, with the wave of her hand, the door unlocked and opened, yellow light flooding the path. She crept inside with him lightly following at her heels.

The immediate hallway stretched before them for about twenty feet before venturing right. Branimir could see lanterns every ten feet on both sides of the hall, giving more than enough light for any patrolling Guardians. Alyona would not find any shadows to cling to for concealment.

Branimir was glad he would not need shadows.

He could see a set of double-doors on their left and another door directly ahead of him. He could only imagine how many twists and turns, and other doors, would be found in this massive manor.

"It is quiet," Branimir said.

"I do not hear anything either," Alyona said in a hushed tone, inching down the hallway, her feet clicking on the wooden beams of the floor. They turned the corner to find another long corridor, without any end in sight. It stretched to the far right, leading to a small incline of stairs, and then another hallway.

"This is going to take a while," Branimir said, hopelessly looking back and forth. "Can you use Klukas?"

"I cannot go into the shadow world, Branimir. My bloodline is diluted with Vucari blood." She rubbed her hands together in thought. "We only need to think about where they would hold prisoners. Likely they are being detained in a dungeon, which means they would be on a lower-level."

"That is heartening to hear," Branimir said. "That means there is probably only one way in and one way out."

"A staircase," Alyona said.

"Or a secret passage."

Alyona frowned at him. "They would want to place the entrance to the dungeon far away from any door to the outside to slow down any who might escape." She looked behind them at the door they had come through, and then to the west. "Meaning if we entered here, and the front door is that way…" she pointed down the long hallway, "our best option is to search down this way."

Branimir raised an eyebrow. "Unless…a door leading outside is also located on that side of the building."

"Then maybe we will find the door somewhere in the middle." Alyona peered at him from beneath her hood. "Do you have a better place to start?"

Branimir shrugged. "I don't."

The Kadari led them halfway down the long corridor when the left wall suddenly disappeared to an open wide foyer. Alyona stopped walking at the sound of voices echoing somewhere beyond the foyer. Branimir pressed his body against the left side of the wall and peered around the corner edge.

A candlelit chandelier hung from an elevated ceiling between two spiraling staircases on either side of the sweeping room, decorated with sitting chairs and small tables. A wide, decorative rug covered the floorboards, and along the walls stood several suits of armor on embellished stands. Beyond the staircases, Branimir could make out broad double-doors leading back outside.

As incredible as the architecture may have been, the men standing beneath the chandelier was what caused Branimir to catch his breath. The first was Master Bacheva from The Harper and Mug, the father of Teodor Bacheva, pulling nervously at his salt-and-pepper goatee. And the other was none other than Dagmar Kaligula, Dorofej's unkind grandson, who had been advising Falmagon at Melkorka. Dagmar stood a head taller than Master Bacheva, dressed in a red button-coat, black trousers, and a blood-red cloak. He was dressed as though he were a powerful noble.

"What is he doing here?" Branimir grimaced as though he might spit.

He could see Alyona only shaking her head from the corner of his eye.

"Lord Kaligula," Master Bacheva trembled, "the Vornic retired to the dungeons some time ago to begin questioning the prisoners. He is determined to discover whatever information he can before their passing."

"You should have sent for me sooner, Gaspar," Dagmar said, running his hand through his scraggly red hair and placing a hand on his waist. Branimir could see several flasks hanging from leather cords around his midsection; Dagmar carried bottles of the Water of Life. Branimir loosened the dagger at his belt, eyeing Teodor's father warily.

The liquid would do nothing for Dagmar if Branimir buried a blade in the man's skull. "Does Myrthos have the Kras?" Dagmar asked.

"Not yet," Gaspar replied, moving his hands to his sides awkwardly, settling his thumbs in his belt loops. "The Guardians are tracking his trail as we speak. He has been confined to The Harper and Mug in Old Town. The Kras cannot stay hidden forever."

Dagmar smirked. "He has found the means to stay hidden from me for the past year. I would not underestimate the red brood."

The Stuhian should have been capable of finding Branimir in Klukas. He wrinkled his brow with confusion, turning to face Alyona. The Kadari was wide-eyed and biting her lip. He asked, "How exactly have I stayed hidden?"

She shrugged, but said, "If we wait, they may lead us to the dungeon."

He replied softly, "I would prefer to get Adamus and Sulanna free first…"

"We don't have the time," she said.

Heavy footsteps echoed as Dagmar and Gaspar neared them, making way for the corridor. Alyona grabbed Branimir's shirt, pulling him back down the hall from where they had come, pulling him around the corner and out of sight.

"Falmagon will not be pleased you have sent for him and do not have Branimir. He was specific in what he wanted," Dagmar said. "Tell me, who does Myrthos hold?"

"I…thought to suggest as much to the Vornic, but my position does not give the voice to question him." Gaspar cleared his throat. "I hope the Patrician will be pleased that we have captured Adamus Ebordon and the Vornic's daughter, Sulanna Maelthirren."

"The Ariadnean…" Dagmar rubbed his neck as they turned the opposite way down the corridor. "I owe him a debt of pain. Does the Crimson Sun know Sulanna is being held here?"

"I do not think the Vornic has elected to share his daughter's discovery with them," answered Gaspar.

"And what of Alden Forgaaf?"

"No," Gaspar said. Branimir's heart skipped a beat, moving back into the hallway to follow the two men. Alden was alive and being held in the dungeon too! "We have not told the Crimson Sun of his capture either. I apologize, Lord Kaligula, I am not certain of the Vornic's purpose in withholding the knowledge from Master Gauthus."

Branimir had never met Ivarr Gauthus, but he heard his name often enough from Dorofej. The man headed the Crimson Sun, but supposedly answered to Falmagon.

Dagmar murmured offhandedly. "Do not worry about it, Gaspar. Ivarr paid a large sum of coin to the Lilitu for Alden's release. The matter is no longer a concern, but I would guess the man would be displeased to discover Myrthos hiding him in Eldhaft. If the plan is to keep it secret, be certain it stays buried."

"Alden's stay here has not been pleasant." Gaspar stopped to lead them down a narrow staircase on the eastern wall.

Branimir hurried to catch them, stopping at the top of the stairs. Looking back the way he had come, he realized Alyona was no longer following him.

Gaspar and Dagmar descended from sight, reaching the bottom of the stairs and turning right.

"Alyona," Branimir hissed down the hallway. When she did not respond, he tried once more, louder, "Alyona!"

Again, silence.

Pulling his dagger from his belt, Branimir balanced the weight in his hand. The Kadari woman vanished at the first sign of danger as she had before at the inn. Branimir did not have the time to look for her. He had no choice but to move forward and rescue his friends in the dungeon. He would start by weakening Falmagon by taking the life of Dagmar Kaligula.

He only wished he had brought more daggers.

His footsteps were silent as he made his way down the staircase, though the foreboding trek downward caused his heart to feel as though it would beat from his chest. The walls of the narrow corridor were lofty, yet uninviting. He finally made it to the last step and took a slow, shallow breath.

He listened. Nothing.

He hoped Dagmar and Gaspar had not gone behind a locked door.

At a snail's pace, Branimir turned the corner and inhaled in fear as Dagmar Kaligula stood in waiting with Gaspar several feet behind. Dagmar growled, seizing a hold of Bran's shirt, cloak, and straps of his pack in one burly grasp and hurled him into the stone wall opposite of the stairs.

Branimir's bones rattled and stung on impact, the knife in his hand skittering out of his reach. Before he could think of grabbing Kaelandur at his belt, Dagmar used Koldovstvo to lift Branimir from the wooden floorboards and back to his hand.

"Gaspar," Dagmar gleamed with a sinister glare, "you can now tell Falmagon we have the Kras."

Chapter IX

Branimir awoke with a spasm, suspended from a vertical, iron table in the corner of a rectangular room. The cold metal prickled at his bare flesh. He wore nothing, save a belt tightened just above his waist with a sheath holding Kaelandur. He remembered Vornic Maelthirren repeatedly attempting to remove the cursed, copper dagger, only to return it to Bran to stop his curdling screams.

He told the Vornic all that he knew, but what he knew was not enough. Sulanna's father wanted to know where Dorofej was located, so Kaelandur could be destroyed.

Many times, Branimir explained he knew nothing about Dorofej's whereabouts, except he was somewhere between Melkorka and Eldhaft. The answer had consistently been less than satisfactory.

The room spun out-of-focus but Branimir finally caught a glimmer of his red skin, goose-fleshed and bruised, trembling against the slab. In desperation, he lurched against the thick, pigskin straps clasping his wrists and ankles. He twisted his neck up and down to see the leather strung through slits in the iron on either side of his limbs, buckled on the other side of the table. Escape was impossible.

The soreness in his head pulsated, reminding him of the beating he received from Sulanna's father before losing consciousness. He licked the dried blood from his swollen, bottom lip. He could not even recall the questions he refused to answer.

His finger nicked at the silver ring, Faegrim, still on his finger. The Vornic had not taken the trinket when preparing him for the torture chamber.

His eyes fluttered, and he hung his head helplessly. He could not have been in Harrowhal for more than two weeks. If Alyona had not betrayed him, she may come yet. Or perhaps Dorofej if he did not meet him in Iriy, but that could be weeks or months.

"Bran-i-mir," Adamus strained from somewhere within the room.

Branimir lifted his head once more, seeing the room for what felt like the first time. His mouth felt too dry to make a response.

To his left lay Sulanna naked and destitute on a table, tied in a similar way as Branimir. Her eyes were closed with her mouth corded. She looked to be unscathed from blade or flame, but he could not remember seeing her awake since being dragged to the dungeon. Her skin had paled considerably, the flesh clinging to her ribcage. They had been given water once a day to wet their throats, but no food.

Next to her lay a table with cogs and wheels and ropes, which Branimir had grown to understand was meant to pull bones from the sockets of his victims. He tried not to look at the device for too long.

Adjacent to the rack was a large wooden basin of water, large enough to fit a human if they kept their knees tucked to their chest. And then a barrel full of what sounded like rats shrilling and squeaking, while running over one another in attempts to escape. Further yet burned a fire pit, flashing blue, orange, and red, with metal bars deeply sunk into the fiery coals. And only a few feet more, extended a table with hooked blades, knives, and other torture devices Branimir had no interest in remembering.

He shivered as his eyes fell on a metal cage hanging from the ceiling. The bald, old man, who Branimir never thought to see again, powerlessly stared back at him before turning to gaze at Sulanna on the table. Alden Forgaaf flexed his muscles against the sturdy cage, whispering prayers fervently under his breath.

"Bran-i-mir," Adamus echoed with less air.

"Adamus," Branimir finally forced the word from his throat, twisting his neck past Alden to see the Ariadnean, hanging with his hands bound from a chain above the ceiling. The iron cut into his wrists as he struggled to hold himself upright, feet dangling inches above the stone flooring. Affixed around Adamus's neck was a belt enfolding a bi-pronged metal fork with one end pushed under his chin and the other firmly pressed to his sternum. Adamus strained to keep his chin to the ceiling—his exposed body shivering with little control—to avoid dropping his head and letting the prongs pierce the soft flesh beneath his chin and chest simultaneously.

The Ariadnean could not have slept since the Vornic attached the device to him, or he would already be dead.

Adamus gulped, his Adam's apple recoiling against the sharpened points at his neck. Sweat dripped from his dark beard and mustache. "I…will be dead before long," Adamus said, quivering again, the chains rattling over his head. "Tis been an honor…to call you… friend, Bran-i-mir."

"No!" Branimir rasped, pulling uselessly against the restraints. "You must keep fighting, Adamus. Dorofej will come. Alyona will come."

"Czern's breath! She deceived us," Adamus groaned, "as Sulanna said."

"Listen to him," Alden said from the cage, peering at Adamus from over his bent nose. "You cannot lose faith. We can still survive this. The gods have delivered us from worse fates."

"My leg burns…" Adamus groaned in torment. "Even if I live…I will not…*survive* this."

Branimir cringed at the sight of Adamus's mangled leg, wholly skinned from the knee down, the muscle and sinew filleted— the rind slacking and dangling—with his blood seeping to stain the stone beneath. It was a wonder the hero-warrior had not lost consciousness.

"Dagmar will pay for what he has done to you," Alden said between gritted teeth. The old man pathetically pulled at the metal bars on his cage with a muffled roar. "Svarog will show us a way."

"The…gods…will not help us…" Adamus sighed, tears forming at the corners of his eyes and falling from his cheeks. The salty droplets soaked into his beard.

Branimir was inclined to agree with Adamus. Marheena was the one who had bid for Dorofej to make Kaelandur and wrought this evil upon them. If the other gods were of like mind, none would save them.

He wanted to know *why*? But, more than anything, he wanted to see Dorofej again.

A clang of a metal door opening recoiled through the stone room, followed by the commanding voice of Vornic Myrthos Maelthirren. "Are we awake?" Multiple footsteps clicked down the staircase from somewhere behind Branimir. "Or are we dead? Let us properly inspect our guests."

Branimir stiffened as the Vornic noisily passed by him and approached Adamus to survey the hanging body as though he were a butcher examining meat. Myrthos wore the same simple, black trousers, white shirt, and boots that Branimir had seen him dress in for the past couple weeks. But today, his hair was unkempt and unbraided, wildly hanging on either side of his sunken cheeks.

"You lasted through the night without impaling yourself," Myrthos said, running his finger down Adamus's chest admirably, "or bleeding out. No wonder they call the Ariadneans hero-warriors. I have seen Guardians die in half the time with fewer injuries. Those thieves always think they are craftier than any other." Myrthos laughed to himself, looking over his shoulder at Branimir. "Plainly not craftier than a little Kras, eh? I suspect your *friend's* stunt at the inn will keep the Guardians questioning their ability for months to come."

Myrthos tapped Adamus on the chest a couple times, eliciting a groan from the Ariadnean. "You know," Myrthos went on, reaching for the pronged instrument at Adamus's neck, "I could remove this if you would only tell me what I want to know. You would have at least a few more hours left before you…bleed out…"

Adamus peered down at Sulanna's father for only a moment before twisting his eyes back to the ceiling.

The Vornic leered for a moment, pulling at his white mustache, and then poked Adamus again. "Lucky for you, I am feeling kind today." He reached up and slanted the metal fork, giving Adamus the ability to drop his chin without inflicting a wound. "I would hate for you to die before allowing you time to consider my offer."

Alden rumbled from his cage, glaring at the Vornic hatefully. "The gods will see you punished. You rob men of their charge for your own gain. You rob them from Thrice Ten Kingdom." Alden's eyes lifted to look to the man beyond Branimir. "You will both be punished."

"Why do you not torture the old man?" Dagmar's voice lifted from the door. "He may have something useful to share with us besides menacing premonitions concerning the will of the gods. Falmagon had the Crimson Sun pay a hefty sum to pull him from Talastein. I doubt Ivarr would like his money spent without purpose."

Branimir twitched at the sound of Dagmar behind him. This was the first time Dagmar had come to the dungeon, which likely meant either the Vornic was not satisfying him, or Falmagon was close to Eldhaft.

Alden spoke from the cage in wonderment, as though the information was new to him. "The Kadari ordered my release from Talastein? Not Ivarr?" He frowned squeezing his hands around the bars of his cage. His escape from the Lilitu had been a ruse to have him captured for questioning.

"The Crimson Sun will acquire more coin." Myrthos waved off Alden, approaching Branimir. "Besides, I have no interest in a man who is compelled to commit penance for the *blessing of gods*. He knows pain in equal measure with breath. My daughter, however, will tell us many things by watching him suffer." Myrthos stopped in front of Branimir as Dagmar approached from behind. "That is, unless the Kras wishes to save his friends from such unpleasantries. He could simply tell us what you need to hear."

"Don't…Bran-i-mir…" Adamus coughed.

Myrthos and Dagmar ignored Adamus.

Branimir snarled at Myrthos. "What more could I tell you? You will not listen to me."

Dagmar grabbed Branimir's jaw, wrenching his head sideways to look at him. His bedraggled, red hair curled in every direction placing a shadow over his face. "You will tell us where we can find Dorofej, so we can rid the world of this…" he flicked Kaelandur hanging at Branimir's waist, "…cursed dagger."

Branimir tensed under the hard gaze of the Stuhia, but he still found his voice. "I will tell you what I have told him." He shifted his eyes toward Myrthos. "Kinhar ordered Kaelandur to be made. He brought the first Eretik back from the Netherworld with its power," Branimir said, returning his gaze to Dagmar's cold, blue eyes. "Kinhar wanted the dagger to fulfill his prophecy, to give power to the Kadari."

"I do not care about any of that," Dagmar said. "I do not care about the Kadari or their ridiculous adoration for the Lightbringer. I want this dagger destroyed."

"You held Dorofej prisoner, and you did not kill him," Branimir said. "Why now? You must have known he created Kaelandur."

"I may have." Dagmar sneered, clenching his jaw. "But Dorofej cannot be simply killed and the dagger be destroyed. He must be killed *with* the weapon he created. Otherwise, he would continue to *linger*." The word rolled off his tongue, leaving Branimir stunned.

He had been terrified this whole past year of Dorofej dying, while the threat was empty while he held Kaelandur. Did Dorofej know he was safe while Branimir remained hidden? What more did Dorofej hope to accomplish at Iriy?

Dagmar suddenly hit the iron table next to Branimir's head. "And I did not yet have Eisliev Kluk return from the Netherworld in pursuit of my head."

Branimir held his mouth closed. Alyona had been telling the truth about everything. Eisliev returned from the Netherworld, and sought to exact his revenge on Dagmar Kaligula. Bran did not know what blood feud bound the two Stuhian families, but Dagmar looked *afraid*.

"Now tell me where Dorofej has gone?" Dagmar asked in a raspy whisper.

"Why are you doing this? Why are you listening to Falmagon and not your own kin?" Branimir snapped back.

"You mean listen to Dorofej?" Dagmar shook his head as though the question made little sense. "Grandfather or not, he has threatened the world by making this weapon. I will not die by his hand or any other," Dagmar winced. "And if you think I grovel at Falmagon's feet, you are mistaken, Kras. Now tell me where he is, so I can rid myself of Eisliev Kluk."

"Destroying Kaelandur will not rid you of Eisliev," Branimir said, peering at the Stuhian. Dagmar had no more interest in dying than Dorofej did. Branimir hoped he could use the insight to say something smart. Yet, he struggled to find the words to persuade Dagmar. "Eisliev can only be ended by luring him back to the Netherworld, and killing him there. The same happened with Nedezhda Mager twelve-hundred-years ago. Dorofej killed her in the Netherworld to stop her from attacking the Ash Tree."

"He created a weapon that would destroy the world, but killed the demon who returned to destroy the world? Why?" Dagmar asked.

"I don't know," Branimir said. Dagmar squinted at Branimir as though he were trying to assess the truth of his words. At least, he seemed to listen more intently than Vornic Maelthirren.

"But, I am telling the truth," Branimir insisted. He hoped Dagmar would understand the futility of Falmagon's quest. He repeated what Erzebeth Navenka had told him at Garain'l last year. "The god, Wolos, was killed, leaving none to lead men after their deaths. The Netherworld cannot house all the dead." Branimir was almost shouting, hoping Dorofej's grandson was listening to him.

He had to understand. "It was two men at Anaerfell. They are the ones who did this to us."

"What do you know about my sons? How have you come to learn this?" Dagmar twisted his face with fury, spit flinging into Branimir's eyes.

Branimir struggled against the restraints, having no way to escape Dagmar's quickened temper. "I didn't know they were your sons."

"Answer me!" Dagmar screamed. The Stuhia grabbed Kaelandur from Branimir's belt and tore it away, holding it in the air away from him.

Rocking against the table, Branimir screamed until his throat burned and his ears ached. A few seconds lasted an eternity.

"Stop it!" Alden yelled at Dagmar. "You will kill him!"

Branimir's bones cracked, the feeling of flames seared through his insides. He needed to reclaim Kaelandur. His body thrashed, his head repeatedly slamming into the iron. With Kaelandur away from his flesh, Branimir would rather have been pierced by a hundred arrows and trampled by a thousand horses.

"Stop…" Adamus tried.

Dagmar pressed the dagger flatly into Branimir's left hand. Feeling the weapon back on his flesh was like having his heart restored to his chest. He wrapped his fingers around the hilt, chest heaving.

With a deep breath, Branimir said, "The death of Wolos brought demons from the Netherworld…not the dagger. Kaelandur is only a tool to destroy the Ash Tree."

Dagmar gasped, seemingly forgetting about his sons, considering Branimir's frantic words.

"The Ash Tree…is dying, regardless of Kaelandur. The Kadari have wasted it away," Branimir heaved, locking his eyes onto Dagmar. "The Old-dark are being released from their prison."

"The Old-dark?" Myrthos looked to Dagmar for an explanation. "What is he talking about?"

Alden rumbled from his cage, giving hint of his knowledge. "Svarog will not allow it."

Branimir went on, "Falmagon doesn't know what he is doing. His efforts are wasted."

Myrthos stepped forward. "How is he bound to this dagger, Lord Kaligula? Why does he continue to scream when it is taken from him? What madness have you brought to Harrowhal?"

"Some ancient evil has bound it to him, and possibly abundant knowledge in the melding," Dagmar said.

"Knowledge we can extract," Myrthos said. "Falmagon will be here soon enough. He will be pleased."

"We will see. Falmagon has little appreciation for knowledge," Dagmar muttered, standing upright to study Branimir. He straightened his grey shirt, loosening the strings around his collar. "But we would be wise to discover all the Kras knows…especially if Kaelandur's destruction truly will do nothing to save us from the demons. You will help me convince Falmagon that finding Dorofej is no longer a concern…we have wasted our efforts." Dagmar suddenly tensed his jaw and reached for Branimir's hand almost dislodging Kaelandur from his grasp. With an exasperated breath, Dagmar ripped off the simple, silver ring from his finger. "What is this? Where did you get Faegrim?"

"I found it," Branimir forced the lie, clinging to Kaelandur in his hand. Dagmar could use Faegrim to control the minds of any who did not wield Koldovstvo like Eisliev had done to Branimir at Cavell. "I do not know what it is."

"Faegrim!" Dagmar shouted, moving away from Branimir, and pulling a strange book from his pocket. The book quadrupled in size at the command of Koldovstvo, and Dagmar flipped through the pages.

"What is that?" Myrthos asked, clearly confused by most of the conversation and now this strange revelation.

"This is the Varkolak," Dagmar said, "and this ring is how the Kras has avoided me this past year." Branimir juddered at the sight of the Varkolak, a book Dorofej had transcribed ages ago, holding the mysteries of Koldovstvo and the gods knew what else. Dagmar nodded to himself as he read through a faded page in the codex. "As I thought, Faegrim keeps the wearer blocked from being found in Klukas."

"I didn't know," Branimir cried.

Dagmar shook his head, speaking through his teeth at Myrthos. "Come; let us see if Falmagon has arrived."

Chapter X

The door slammed at the top of the stairs, echoing back into the dungeon.

Sulanna stirred on the table near him, moaning softly, but still not awake. Branimir turned his neck to see Adamus had also lost consciousness. Blood persistently oozed from his battered leg.

"They will likely kill us now," Alden said, fine-tuning his position in the metal cage. He crossed his legs for comfort and folded his hands in his lap. "Fight in any way you are able, Branimir. Die with honor. For glory."

"Why? Why do you say that?" Branimir asked.

Alden angled a bushy eyebrow as if the answer was clear and Branimir were too dense to see it. "Because you have given them no reason to keep us alive. We were being interrogated to give away Dorofej's position."

Branimir squeezed his eyes shut with frustration. "And I told them the truth," he muttered, hitting his head against the iron table. "Now that Dagmar sees destroying Kaelandur will not save him, he has no reason to kill Dorofej."

Alden lifted his shoulders to his ears. "Besides keeping Dorofej from being a pain in the ass for Falmagon? No," Alden took an exasperated breath, "I see no reason they will pursue Dorofej. You have magnificently removed the target from Dorofej's back while identifying the rest of us as loose ends."

"But what should I have done? Keeping the ruse would have only left us to be tortured without reason," Branimir said.

Alden remained surprisingly calm given his words, a knowing curve of a smile dimpling his old cheeks. "We had reason before, Branimir. We were holding ourselves alive until a chance for escape or rescue presented itself. I am less certain now. Adamus is dying. Sulanna and I will be quick to follow when Falmagon comes. But you," he rubbed his brow, the fake smile disappearing, "you have the knowledge of a lifetime upon a lifetime. You have traveled the Netherworld. You have fought monsters that most believe to be only from fairy tales. Dagmar can keep you alive, picking you apart piece by piece as he unearths what you know."

Branimir shivered, his stomach tightening in fear. "Why would he do that?"

Alden answered with a rhetorical question. "Why did he leave Dorofej alive at Melkorka for the past year?"

"You heard him say he needed Kaelandur to kill Dorofej," Branimir said hesitantly.

"Whether true or not, Dagmar hungers for knowledge. For power," Alden said. "You have already proven your intelligence with Faegrim."

"No," Branimir argued. "I did not know Faegrim would keep me hidden from Klukas. I only knew…" Branimir stopped, jerking his head to Alden with excitement. "I am no longer wearing Faegrim. I…I am no longer wearing the ring."

"I know," Alden sighed.

Branimir kicked his feet as much as the binding would allow him. "No. You don't understand. I wondered why Dorofej had not come for me—why he had not sought me in Klukas. I *was* wearing Faegrim; he could not find me in Klukas, but now, he can!"

Alden spun onto his knees, eyes widening. The cage clanged, swaying from its perch in the ceiling. "Where was Dorofej? How far does he travel?"

"You have heard me answer the question many times. He was at Melkorka," Branimir answered. "If Alyona told the truth, he would have been at Melkorka only a few weeks ago. He would have to pass near Eldhaft to go to Iriy in the Shade Fells."

Alden scratched his bald head in confusion. "This Alyona woman? How did she come to find you so soon?"

"Dorofej can make these gateways that create an opening between two places, but he cannot travel through them himself. She said Dorofej made her one to travel from Melkorka to Gaetana. It is the same as how we had escaped from Melkorka last year," Branimir said.

Alden arched his eyebrows in surprise.

Branimir answered the unasked question, or what he thought Alden may have been thinking. "Of course, the Ash Tree at Melkorka would have allowed him to return to his youth right after sending her to us."

"But, if you wore Faegrim, how did he know you were in Gaetana?" Alden asked

Branimir began to give the same reasoning Sulanna had clung to for the past year, considering Dorofej sent them to Gaetana so he could find them when needed, but a more evident truth struck him. "Dorofej still could have found Sulanna or Adamus in Klukas, even if he could not see me?"

"With that thought, he would then know we are here…and he has not come…" Alden sunk back onto his bare haunches, defeat filling his eyes.

The hard truth stung Branimir's chest. He shouted in defiance. "He will come for us!"

He grimaced, scratching his bald head. His words were soft. "He may come for you eventually. The rest of us will be long dead."

Branimir's heart sunk.

Alden went on, "I am not concerned for myself. I have lived a long life serving Svarog well. For a thousand years, humans have rumored that the God of the Dead was killed, but I scarcely believed it. Yet, if Wolos has been killed as you say, I will have no guide across Thrice Nine Lands to reach Thrice Ten Kingdom in the afterlife. I will forever be perverted by Marheena's death magic, becoming one of her devils in the Netherworld." Alden's shoulders shuddered, blinking away his tears. This time was the first Branimir saw any weakness from the old warrior. Alden lifted his eyes to Sulanna. "You cannot let her die here. Not by her father's hand. Not by our enemies."

Branimir's fingers curled with determination. The hilt of Kaelandur weighted his hand. He had nearly forgotten that Dagmar left it in his palm instead of returning it to the sheath at his waist.

"I will not. We are leaving," Branimir said. "Now."

Branimir turned the copper dagger in his hands, rotating the blade downward along his forearm, gripping the sleek hilt in his long fingers. Ever so carefully, he inched the dagger up, balancing its weight above his hand, transferring his fingers from the hilt to the blade.

"You can do it," Alden encouraged, moving in his cage again to gain a better view.

Straining his neck to peer at the blade in his hand, Branimir manipulated Kaelandur further and further until the tip of the blade hung over the pigskin strapping that held his hand suspended on the table. Then, with the utmost care, Branimir kept the dagger flat against his skin, slipping it between his wrist and the leather strip. He did not stop until the blade hung passed his wrist and the hilt was back in his hand.

Alden was elated from his hanging prison. "You did it, Branimir. You did it. Quickly now."

Branimir used what muscle he had to slide the copper dagger up and down against the leather bindings. In little time, the magical blade—holding a honed edge unlike any weapon of its kind—soon began to split the strip around his wrist.

Time seemed to stand still as Branimir cut at his bindings. Soreness seared through his body, from his wrist to his stomach to his knees. The world was pain and fire. He pushed through the agony. Slicing. Cutting. Until the last thread fell away.

"Yes," Alden praised.

The strap fell to the ground, and with its release, the buckle on the opposite side of the iron table clinging to the ground. The sound echoed, and with the echo came the clang of the door opening once more at the height of the staircase.

Branimir froze.

Alden rattled in his cage, hearing the noise. His eyes locked on Branimir with intensity. He pressed himself up against the bars of his cage, his nostrils flaring. "Flee!" he hissed.

In a half-breath, Branimir twisted sawing at the leather around his left ankle, and then the right. Kaelandur tore through the pigskin like flame through flesh. Footsteps thundered down the steps like an impending storm.

"Hurry!" Alden berated.

Branimir held his breath, hanging suspended from the table by a single arm, his bare legs slipping and sliding in desperation for something to grip. He wildly slashed at the final restraint on his right hand, while keeping the blade clear of his own flesh.

"Destroying Kaelandur will not end this." Branimir listened to Sulanna's father speaking from the stairs. "Dagmar believes the Kras is telling the truth."

Falmagon's recognizable tone boomed. "By Mulafell, Branimir will say anything to keep Dorofej alive. A malady I fear Dagmar also suffers from. One that has cost us dearly."

Bran did not hear the response, slicing through the final strand of his shackles. He dropped to the floor without making a sound, and vanished from sight, clutching Kaelandur in his hand.

Branimir stayed on his toes, springing across the floor, and ducking behind the water basin. He gripped Kaelandur in his hand, knowing he could not kill either of the two with the magical dagger, or they would return like Eisliev from the Netherworld.

Myrthos was the first to exit the staircase, running a hand through his white, ragged hair. The old man paused as though he had taken a blow to the gut, gawking at the empty table where Branimir had been moments before. Like clockwork, he sifted the room to ensure the other three prisoners were untouched.

"The Kras is gone," Myrthos said, "but not far."

Branimir gulped, taking a step closer to the fire pit in the center of the room. The rods sticking from the coals glowed with intense heat, too hot for him to grip and use as a weapon.

Falmagon bounded over the last couple steps with the spoken revelation, his brown cloak flapping behind him. He dashed to the iron slab, his long, crumpled, brown hair whirling around his face. A year passed since Branimir had last seen Falmagon, and before that, an eternity. Even now, Branimir's nerves were shattered upon seeing his old Highborn master.

Falmagon struck the flat surface of the table with an open hand as though the action might make Branimir magically appear. The sudden movement caused Branimir to jump away, almost falling to his haunches.

"What is this?" Falmagon roared, balling up his fist. His other hand clawed at the stubble along his cheek and chin, his eyes maddening with rage. "Is this supposed to impress me, Myrthos?"

Myrthos stepped behind Falmagon as though the man were a shield. "The Kras must be in this room. Not only is the door above locked and guarded, but I doubt he would have left his friends. We likely caught him in the act of escape."

Branimir finally slid Kaelandur into the sheathe hanging from the belt, the only garb on his naked body. He would not be able to use the dagger against his enemies. Instead, his eyes locked on the table with the hooked blades and knives.

Of course!

"He did have the dagger on him," Myrthos warned.

"He still has Kaelandur," Falmagon glowered, whipping around to look at the room.

"Something binds him to it," Myrthos said. "He cannot be parted from the blade."

Falmagon relaxed his fist, facing the room. He directed Myrthos to block the staircase with a wave of his hand. The man once known as the Highborn Longwalker soothed his voice to what may have been a stern father suddenly trying to comfort a disobedient child. "Branimir, you cannot win this fight. Show yourself."

Branimir shuffled to the table. Two of the torture knives were possibly throwable. He grabbed them and then a hooked blade about the size of his forearm. They clinked slightly as he shuffled one knife and the awkward blade to his left hand. Expecting Myrthos and Falmagon to react to the faint noise, Branimir nosedived into a somersault toward Alden's hanging cage, clasping the weapons to his chest, and then springing back to his feet.

While Falmagon seemed oblivious to the sound, Myrthos waved a boney finger at the table, shouting, "Over there! Several of my tools just disappeared."

"What tools?" Falmagon asked.

"Knives," Myrthos stuttered. "A couple knives, I think."

"I am not playing this game, Branimir!" Falmagon screamed, his face reddening. Using Koldovstvo, he blasted energy at the table of torture tools, flipping it over. The remaining objects scattered across the floor. Falmagon moved around the table, staring beyond the fire. "Show yourself now!"

A gurgled, muffled scream across the room followed the clinging iron as Sulanna abruptly awoke. Branimir watched as she strained against the binds holding her feet and hands, her naked body arching off the table. She whipped her head sideways, her brown and grey hair clinging to her face. She glared at her father and Falmagon.

Branimir used the distraction, slinging the blade from his hand at Falmagon's head.

Falmagon howled unintelligibly, jerking to the side as the blade materialized mid-flight. The knife missed the Patrician, grazing by his ear, and unpredictably speared into Vornic Myrthos Maelthirren's eye.

Myrthos's other eye wobbled in the socket until it rested on Sulanna, who stared at him with her head reared back, suddenly frozen in silent confusion. A bloodied tear dripped from the corner of Myrthos's eye, sliding down the length of his nose. And then his body convulsed. He dropped to the dungeon floor.

Sulanna lay captivated by her dead father.

"Kill him, Branimir," Alden shouted, his head pressed against the bars.

Branimir darted back toward Sulanna, moving the other knife to his throwing hand, while gripping the hooked blade in his left. Falmagon steadied himself, pulling his eyes away from the fallen Vornic.

He did not wait for Falmagon to stand fully, throwing the other blade. Branimir gritted his teeth in anticipation for the deadly blow to fell his enemy. But Falmagon was quicker, using Koldovstvo to pull the weapon as it appeared from its route to his outstretched hand.

Falmagon whipped his head, staring at the direction from which the blade had been thrown. "You cannot win, Branimir." Falmagon raised his hand to the fire, lifting one of the heated rods from the pit. The metal glowed with immeasurable heat.

Branimir crouched, moving from his position, prepared to dodge the flying projectile. The metal bar spun in the air over the fire as Falmagon glared into the corners of the room. Branimir inched closer, promising himself that he would finally kill Falmagon. He could not be found unless Dagmar came and ventured into Klukas. He would not let Falmagon make it back up the stairs.

"You will lose," Falmagon said, his voice eerily soft.

With a wave of his hand, the sizzling metal bar flashed like light into Adamus's stomach to remain lodged in the pit of his gut. The Ariadnean, ripped from his comatose torpor, threw his head back to the ceiling and cried out until his voice cracked into a pitiful scream.

Branimir covered his ears, aghast, unable to look away from his friend. Adamus's skin singed and smoldered away, eaten by the flaming, metal rod, his insides emptying out until the makeshift weapon clattered with them to the stone floor. Completely catatonic, with a slobbering sob, Adamus convulsed mindlessly in his chains with spit and mucus staining his dark beard, until his life fled from his body.

"No!" Sulanna choked on her own scream, her muscles flexing and fists clenching in attempts to burst from her bindings. She thrashed about on the table in desperation.

Alden kicked at the door of his cage.

Tears welled in Branimir's eyes, blurring the image of Adamus hanging dead from the linked chains. He felt his face tighten, his hand hurting from squeezing the remaining hooked blade in his hand.

"Who will be next, Branimir?" Falmagon yelled, pulling another burning rod from the fire with Koldovstvo. "The old man or the woman? Who else would you have die for your foolishness?" He dwelled in the moment. "Show yourself!"

Branimir howled from the depths of his drying throat, the sound echoing from every wall, as he raced across the short expanse with his weapon held to his side. Falmagon rotated half a step before Branimir was on him.

With another cry, he swung the blade, catching the hook into the meaty flesh at Falmagon's side, just below the ribcage. Falmagon roared, losing his control over the heated, metal rod. It clanged against the ground harmlessly behind Branimir. Mechanically, Falmagon reached for the wound with his right hand while swinging his left at Branimir.

Branimir ducked under the hand with ease and jerked the weapon free before Falmagon could cling to it, ripping a chunk of skin and fat from the Patrician's belly.

Ignoring the blood spraying his face, Bran carried the arc of the pull, rotating the blade around his head to land a second blow. This time, the hooked blade tore into Falmagon's thigh.

Branimir barely heard the spine-chilling scream as Falmagon reached out his hand. A gust of wind struck Branimir in his chest and flung him into Sulanna's iron table. The back of his skull cracked against the corner surface, and the dungeon of *Harrowhal* faded black.

Chapter XI

A hand pressed firmly against the back of Branimir's aching head. He flinched, attempting to pull away, but a secondary hand grasped his forehead to hold him in place.

"Hold steady, Branimir." His eyelids fluttered while Alden shushed him. His vision was distorted, but the interior of Alden's cage was unmistakable. "I think the cut has stopped bleeding but you are going to tear it open again if you keep thrashing."

Branimir sank into Alden's arms, with no mind that the man was also unclothed. He relaxed, letting Alden support his weight. The hot coals crackled from across the room.

"Will he live, Alden?" Sulanna's voice pierced the hollow room from the table where she remained bound.

"I think he will," Alden said, easing his hand from Branimir's head, "for a while yet. Once Falmagon's wounds have been stitched, he will return with a mind for punishment." Alden physically tensed under Branimir. "I suspect he will take out his wrath on you and me, Sulanna, and force Branimir to watch."

Sulanna's words barely masked her low whimper. "Why must you say such things? Have we not already suffered enough?"

"It is the truth of it, and we must prepare for what will come," Alden said. "I have known the minds of men like Falmagon before.

He will not stop until he feels as though he has extracted justice, and righted the wrongs against him."

Branimir futilely tried to sit up from Alden's lap only to fall back and press his eyes shut. It did not stop the aching. He could feel his heartbeat pounding in the back of his skull. "Where did he go?" Branimir said hoarsely.

"Falmagon used Koldovstvo to move you in here," Alden said, "and then returned upstairs. Soon after, a couple of Guardians came and took the Vornic's body."

"Nine Lands." Branimir forced his eyes back open. He could not see Sulanna. He intoned, raising his voice so that she could, at least, hear him. "I…I am sorry about your father, Sulanna."

"Myrthos's death warrants no apology," Alden said gruffly. "You leveled the scales by ridding him from this place."

"At what cost?" Branimir shivered, thinking of Adamus's atrocious death. The Ariadnean's last moments were filled with pain and suffering.

"Adamus was already dying," Alden barked with authority, reading his thoughts.

Branimir gazed into nothingness. "I did not mean to kill him."

"You did *not* kill Adamus," Alden growled, hovering over Branimir.

"Stop." The bite in Sulanna's tone completely tore away the sobbing undertone she had moments before. "Adamus died a hero, and my father deserved much worse than a quick death. He only brought suffering to this world," Branimir heard her shifting on the iron slab, "suffering which will not soon be forgotten."

"No," Alden agreed, looking past the confines of the cage, "it will not."

Alden's words added a heaviness to Branimir's heart. In another attempt, Branimir reached for the bars to pull himself off his back. "Help me up." Alden reluctantly nodded, his flimsy white beard swaying. As Bran wrapped his fingers around the bars, Alden steadied him, holding his thin, narrow shoulders.

Branimir instinctively covered his mouth at the sight of Adamus's ruined, naked body. The skin lost its color; the blood was dark and a viscous consistency, sitting like syrup on his leg and from the wide hole in his stomach. The mutilation of his friend's body made his stomach churn; though, with two weeks from food, Branimir would have nothing to spew. Only Adamus's closed eyelids gave him a sense of serenity.

"I only wish he would be able to go to a better place," Branimir finally said, sliding his eyes to Sulanna. She, too, stared at Adamus with watered, blue eyes. Knowing the afterlife only held more pain gave them more than enough reason to weep Adamus's passing.

"We need to leave this place," Sulanna choked.

The clang of the doorway at the top of the stairs sounded as it opened and shut. Branimir reached for a dagger at his waist to find Kaelandur secured back in the leather holding on his belt.

"They did not take Kaelandur," Branimir said, gripping the hilt of the cursed weapon.

"No, Branimir." Sulanna arched her back off the table, twisting to face him and Alden in the cage. She behaved as though she might fling herself from the table if she were able. Her whisper was demanding. "Leave the dagger alone."

Branimir removed his hand, and dipped his head. He understood the danger of taking someone's life with Kaelandur. The victim would not only return from the Netherworld, but they would be more powerful and more dangerous than before. Like Nedezhda. Like Eisliev. And even if the person did not die, who knew what the Likhyi now bound in the dagger could do.

He watched the staircase, holding his breath, hearing only the descent of a single set of scraping footsteps. No voices chattered this time to give away the potential harm awaiting them. Branimir's shoulders tensed; nausea and pain fleeing from his body. In fact, he abruptly felt very aware of the reality of the dungeon. As Alden anticipated, Branimir was certain graver consequences were coming for them. In this moment, he could not help but wonder if Adamus's death was a blessing.

Yet the emergence of the purple-eyed woman from the cliff of the stairs was unexpected. She looked to have been wearing the same white shirt and black cloak from when Branimir last saw her, but now—in addition to the pack on her back—she carried an armful of gear and bags.

"Alyona," Branimir sighed in relief, pulling his face to the bars.

"Alyona?" Sulanna disparaged, arching her neck to see the woman behind her. Alyona lay all she carried to the floor, her eyes falling on Adamus at her right. She stifled a gasp, and turned her head away. Sulanna whispered with doubt, "I thought you betrayed us."

"Never." Alyona covered her mouth, her eyes daring to look at Adamus's hanging corpse once more. "I should have come sooner...I tried. I had little chance with the Guardians and Kadari combing the halls."

"Kadari?" Branimir coughed. His stomach pined from hunger. "You mean Falmagon and Dagmar?"

Alyona sniffed. "Several who survived at Melkorka came with Falmagon. A couple dozen, I think."

"How did he and Dagmar travel so fast to Eldhaft with so many Kadari when Dorofej has not yet come? Where is he?" Branimir asked.

Alyona shook her head. "Dagmar left long before Eisliev attacked Melkorka. How Falmagon came to be here..." Alyona swallowed, reaching into one of the packs and pulling out Sulanna's long knife. She made her way to the iron slab with Sulanna, purposely keeping her gaze away from Adamus. "I don't know. We can ask these questions another time. Right now, we need to move."

Alden stirred behind Branimir, moving the cage. "How do we know this is not another one of Falmagon's schemes? Branimir just killed the Vornic, you know?"

"And I killed the guards at the top of the stairs," Alyona said, raising her eyes and scoffing at the old man. She gestured her hand at the cage, popping the lock with Koldovstvo. "You must be the man called Alden, who they came here to find. Well, Alden, it will not be long before someone notices what I did, and if we are still down here, we will be dead."

Branimir creaked open the cage door, pulling at Alden's arm. "Let's go."

Alden grumbled in agreement, grabbing Branimir's arm to help lower him to the ground. Bran welcomed the support considering the surroundings of the dungeon continued to blur in and out of his vision.

Across the way, he could hear Sulanna ardently speaking to Alyona as she cut away the leather bindings. "I should not have disbelieved you." As she freed her hands, Sulanna gripped at Alyona's black cloak. "Forgive me. Please."

"Think nothing of it, and do not thank me yet," Alyona said. She cut away the last strip, handing Sulanna her long knife. She gestured to the gear and bags. "I found your things stored not too far from here, but I—" her voice trailed, turning to Alden. "I have Adamus's gear. Alden, I did not know you were down here."

Alden shuffled by the body of Adamus, steering Branimir to the bags at the base of the stairs. "I will make do. Thank you."

Weakly, the three of them rummaged desperately while Alyona peered up the stairs. Clothes and weapons were scattered as they pulled on trousers and shirts, and fastened blades and shields. Sulanna's breaths were the heftiest as she slipped on her shirt, and then the leather breastplate, which Alden soon helped her fasten much like Adamus had in the past.

Branimir felt like a stranger in his own green cloak and wooly garments. However, holding the balanced dagger in his hand returned some strength to his muscles.

"We have to leave him here," Sulanna's shaky tone pulled Branimir's attention. She stared across the room at Adamus. "I am getting tired of leaving friends behind."

Branimir placed his hand on her back. "He will not be forgotten. We have more to do if we are going to bring his spirit peace."

"He is right," Alyona said. "And you will need to be at full strength. Hold steady." She approached Branimir first, cupping his head in her hands. A familiar glow of reds and yellows swirled and swelled in her palms, sinking beneath the skin of Branimir. The gash on the back of his head mended, the strands of skin reconnecting, sealing the wound. The soreness in his muscles absconded with the hunger cramps in his stomach, and soon the dizziness and exhaustion disappeared too.

Branimir huffed in a breath of air like he had awoken from a long night's rest. "Alyona, what have you done?"

"I told you," Alyona said. "I have the sacred bloodline."

She reached for Sulanna next, and then Alden, stealing away their minor aches and fatigue.

Alden clasped the axe in his hand. "I admit, I did not think we would be able to escape Harrowhal, but you have given us a fighting chance. I knew the gods would send for aid. How will we repay this kindness?"

"Survive, and escape Eldhaft," Alyona said, leading the way up the staircase. "Let us ensure Adamus did not die for nothing."

Sulanna hurried to follow Alyona. The color returned to her face, her cheekbones tight with determination. "Let us escape this foul city."

Branimir's hand quavered around the handle of his knife, following Sulanna with Alden at his back. "Falmagon will die."

Alyona stopped at the door. "If you think you can kill him, Branimir, I will not stop you. Though our priority is to reunite you with Dorofej and Tyr at Iriy." Her purple eyes dug into Branimir. He stared back at her. He had almost forgotten the Ispolini was traveling with Dorofej. She added, "The fate of the world and the gods rests on you delivering Kaelandur. The dagger will be safe among them."

He gazed back, having no desire to argue with the Kadari, who saved them. "I understand."

Alyona cracked open the upstairs door, the familiar clang of the door echoing down the staircase into the dungeon behind them.

Sulanna whispered. "By the gods, if I never should hear that sound again."

Her voice was drowned out by the sounds of screams and the din of battle filling the halls of Harrowhal. Alyona swung the door open to give full view of the dead littering the corridors. Dead Guardians, as well as men not wearing the distinct cloaks, were strewn in all directions. Some had blood seeping from beneath their garments, and others had their skin wrinkled and blackened by flame. None gave any sign of life.

"What did you do?" Branimir asked.

Alyona's jaw tightened, listening to the roar of battle echoing in the distance. "I did not do this."

"Dorofej?" Branimir wondered, starting left down the hallway.

"No." Alyona grabbed his shoulder. "Dorofej could not have made it here yet. The distance from Melkorka is too far."

"Dagmar did. Falmagon did," Sulanna said, her weapon drawn and held at the ready. She stood on her toes, waiting for anything to barrel into the hall.

"Dagmar may have created a gateway like Dorofej to send Falmagon here," Alyona explained in haste. "Another Kadari must have been able to do the same for Dagmar; yet, the effort would have likely killed him."

"I thought you said Dorofej was the only one who could create gateways," Branimir said.

Alyona scrunched her face as though remembering her words. "I said he was one of few. Dagmar and Dorofej have the same bloodline. Their power is great, and they both touch Koldovstvo in a way unlike any I have ever known."

"As much as I am enjoying the lesson in magic and Stuhian bloodlines," Alden interjected gruffly, his hardiness returned, "We should move our asses."

Sulanna agreed. "Even if Dorofej found a way here, he will do well enough to find his own escape. If he escaped Melkorka, Harrowhal would not be difficult."

Alyona led them only a few paces down the corridor when they reached the corner leading into the oversized foyer. For Branimir, the time since he laid eyes on the extended room with the double staircases leading to the second floor felt eternal.

Branimir sprang back as a Guardian blasted through the opening; feet lifted off the ground, and slammed into the wall opposite of the foyer. His head cracked against the wall, and he fell to the ground. The expressionless gaze on his face clearly told of his fate.

"Where are you, Dagmar Kaligula? Will you continue to hide behind the weak?" a gurgled, male voice shouted from the foyer. "I did not travel from Melkorka to slaughter these swine."

"No, no, no," Branimir said, whispering to the other three. He stepped back, clutching the hilt of Kaelandur at his belt. "I know that voice. It is Eisliev. He has come to Eldhaft." Branimir remembered what Dorofej said about Nedezhda when she returned from the Netherworld. "He is drawn to Kaelandur. I cannot hide from him. I cannot outrun him."

Alyona replied in a hushed tone. "He is more interested in his revenge on Dagmar than the dagger. But, he is bound by the magic of the blade to destroy the Ash Tree. He cannot be distracted by his selfishness for long."

Alden tightened his hold on Adamus's axe.

"What do we do?" Sulanna followed Branimir's lead and stepped away from the archway leading into the foyer. "Can we fight him? Should we?"

"He is limitless with his magic," Alyona said, hearing Eisliev scream for Dagmar again. His voice rebounded through Harrowhal, lifted by the power of Koldovstvo. Branimir could hear the chandelier hanging from the ceiling shake from the reverberation. "We could not win."

From behind them, toward the dungeon, Branimir barely heard the strained words being spoken. The syllables were broken apart; the tenor uneven and grating. His vision blurred while sourness laced the inside of his cheeks. He gagged on the taste, and try as he might, Branimir mentally fought against whatever foul magic swept over him.

Yet he was powerless.

Harrowhal vanished from his sight to be replaced with the grand hallways of Heshayol in the depths of the frozen Netherworld. The memories buried in his mind swiftly resurfaced, taking hold of his senses. From somewhere in the far distance, beyond this world, he could hear Dorofej's screams.

Osiscica.

The monstrous, white snake guarding Heshayol emerged from nothingness in front of him like a nightmare, coiling and looping, a hundred times greater than his size. The snake's body must have been twice as wide as he was tall. Branimir was swift to disappear, hiding from the slimy forked tongue, slipping between its encrusted lips. The glowing black and yellow eyes searched for him, hungered for his flesh. He screamed, slashing his knife at the thick scales of the beast.

A bawl of pain pealed at his ear drums; blood colored the end of the blade. He could not see the cut on Osiscica, but he must have hurt it.

"Branimir!" someone called his name.

The snake whipped its head with incredible speed and lifted its triangular head to strike, baring fangs dripping with glistening venom. Branimir choked with fear, clinging to the dagger in his hand. In desperation, he sprang into a roll to escape the lurching attack.

A decorative rug suddenly appeared under Branimir's hands and feet as he sprung back to his toes. The sitting tables and chairs of the foyer magically reappeared before him; the staircases spiraled before him and in front of him stood the red mage, Eisliev.

Dead bodies of Guardians, Kadari, and the gods knew who else had been torn to pieces. Eisliev stood among them victoriously, his arms folded and attention on the hallway behind Branimir.

Branimir maintained his invisibility, but he could not immediately recall how he had come into the foyer. The hallucination remained fresh in his mind. He jerked around to look for Osiscica only to see Alden flail into the room by some unseen magic. The old warrior tumbled to the floor, refusing to release the steel axe in his hand. The bloodied cut on his forearm was unmistakable.

Branimir looked back to the dagger clutched in his hand, painted with crimson.

"Branimir," Sulanna cried, rushing around the corner of the hallway to join Alden. She skidded to his side to help him up. "Where are you?"

"Eisliev!" Alyona cried out, backing into the foyer with her hands crossed and extended past her chest. A blue orb of magical protection crystallized in front of her; flames licked at the gelled barrier from a concealed caster further down the corridor. Alyona dropped the protective wall to spring after Sulanna. "Dagmar is here."

Dagmar!

Branimir did not have to think long to put together what happened. Dagmar had used Faegrim on him and controlled his mind. Leaving his line of sight must have broken the connection.

He jerked his gaze to Eisliev dreadfully.

Eisliev's blue eyes glowed, causing his grey, rotting skin to fade more in comparison to his black veins. He twisted his bloodstained lips into a smile at Alyona, running a hand through his long, red locks. Branimir shuddered at the sight of the undead red mage whom he had slain at Melkorka last year.

"You have obeyed well, Alyona," Eisliev crooned. "As promised, you will have a place among the Likhyi." Eisliev's eyes dropped to Branimir, who stayed invisible. "You brought me the Kras with the dagger, too."

Branimir shuddered, stepping back from the red mage, remaining hidden.

Eisliev leered, leaning over Branimir. Red streaks of blood pulsed through the whites of his eyes. "You cannot hide while you hold Kaelandur, little murderer."

Bran's blood ran cold. He tried to ignore the fear, remembering how Eisliev had slit Bohumir Mager's throat, and tossed him into the fireplace. "You earned your death after what you did to that boy."

The evil grin did not leave Eisliev's face. "As you have earned yours—"

Sulanna's knife plunged into the red mage's belly, thrown from a distance across the room. Eisliev stumbled in surprise, gripping the hilt of the blade lodged inside his tainted flesh.

Branimir whipped around to Sulanna, who ogled at her outstretched hand from which the dagger had been thrown. Alden groaned from beneath her knee, pressed against his chest.

"Wha—" Sulanna could barely utter the word, eyes clouded in confusion. She pulled herself back from Alden to allow him to breathe.

Looking for the obvious explanation, Branimir spotted Dagmar gliding through the archway. As expected, the silver band, Faegrim, encircled the small finger on his left hand. He was using mind-control to have them attack Eisliev.

Time and space warped with Dagmar's precipitous use of Koldovstvo, a magic Branimir had often seen displayed by Dorofej. Branimir's thoughts flowed at regular speed, but the material world around him slowed with Dagmar's sway over reality.

Dagmar fluttered through the room—ignoring Alyona, Sulanna, and Alden—like a bird flying through the treetops, flickering in and out of view. Hundreds of particles of light bent around his body as he zipped from space to space across the room, advancing on Eisliev. The red mage's moldy face was chiseled in horror as his archenemy assailed without restraint.

Inch by inch, Branimir lifted his blade in preparation, knowing Dagmar would reach Eisliev long before he could raise the weapon at his creeping pace.

Dagmar ripped Sulanna's dagger from Eisliev's stomach, tearing it from his fingers with ease. With unmatched speed, Dagmar rotated the weapon in his hand and knifed the red mage in the chest twice, and then the neck, where it remained.

Branimir could only watch, frozen in time.

Eisliev gurgled, blood sloshing out of his mouth. And yet, the red mage feebly twisted his hands to release a fiery inferno at Dagmar. The flames carved through the air like clouds grazing the heavens, struggling to take shape against Dagmar's time-altering magic. The blaze distended like distorted fingers, ever eager to melt away Dagmar's sneer.

The spell abruptly dispersed as Dagmar attempted to dodge Eisliev's weaving of Koldovstvo. He dove toward Branimir—yet invisible— and Eisliev shadowed him maliciously with the fully forming fireball. Branimir acted fast, leaping into Dagmar, and plunging his dagger into the Stuhia's chest. He hung onto the handle while Dagmar thundered in agony; Eisliev's fire blistered the Stuhia's back, melding cloth to skin, the flames whipping around Branimir as he shielded himself with the torso.

Dagmar's fingers dug into Branimir's back like iron in attempts to rip him away. When he was unsuccessful, he clutched Bran closer to his chest under his surprising strength. Dagmar's howling twisted into a roar, pivoting his feet with the intent to pull Branimir into the unyielding flames. Branimir could do naught but gape at the hateful man's gritted teeth.

The sputtering fire snapped at Branimir. His yelps drowned out by a war cry from Alyona. From his peripheral, Branimir saw Eisliev's blood-spattered body zip across the room, tugged by invisible strands of air. The flames dispersed.

The red mage smashed into the rug next to Sulanna, who pounced on him, ripping her dagger from his neck to finish what Dagmar had started.

As soon as the blade was free, Eisliev flung Sulanna away from him with Koldovstvo, slamming her into a wall across the room. Branimir could hear her breath leave her lungs; while Eisliev pressed his hand over the bloody wound in his neck and attempted to rise to his feet.

Branimir yelled, booting Dagmar in the bits. With a grunt, Dagmar freed him and toppled back, thrashing his head around to make sense of what happened at the same moment that Alden tackled Eisliev back to the floor again.

Branimir landed on his back, scrambling to stand up with Dagmar feet away, and Eisliev another twenty paces behind him.

"Kill him!" Dagmar growled at Alden, gripping the dagger still lodged in his chest with his right hand, leaving it entombed in his chest. He hugged it in despair. Baring his teeth, he lifted his left hand toward Eisliev to lash out with Koldovstvo.

Alyona was quicker, slinging a fireball into Dagmar's mid-section. He intermittently howled, his lung failing from being pierced by Branimir's blade. The fire scorched the front of his torso, the flames tearing into his belly. He grabbed at his stomach with his hand, lessening the flame with his own magic. His wild eyes, now darkened with wrinkles from his use of Koldovstvo, were tinted with unmistakable fear.

Branimir searched for another weapon, only to find Kaelandur, before Alden's body crashed into him, pitched across the room by Eisliev. Alden's legs smacked Branimir in the head, taking him off his feet again, and leaving the two of them entangled on the floor in a heap. Branimir instinctively grabbed at his skull to protect himself, the weight of the human partially pinning him to the ground.

He reappeared, trying to push Alden's leg off of him.

"You cannot defeat me. None of you can," Eisliev gurgled, speaking to Dagmar more than any other. "You do not have the power. I am immortal with Kaelandur's magic. I will kill you…and then the Ash Tree."

"Immortal?" Dagmar repeated at a whisper, already nearing death. He shielded his stomach, turning his eyes to Branimir with wonder. Branimir winced under the gaze. He examined the room, seeing Sulanna crawling across the floor attempting to gain her breath, and Alyona not far away, retrieving a sword from a dead Guardian.

Suddenly, Dagmar ripped Kaelandur from its leather holding with Koldovstvo and plunged it into his own chest.

"No!" Branimir cried out, the pain instantly searing through his body with the separation from the copper dagger. His body ached from his head to his toes; the taste of metal stung the tip of his tongue. His mind swirled, stinging from temple to temple. He reached in despair for the dagger sticking from Dagmar's chest cavity.

"No!" Eisliev echoed, flinging his own arm upward and using his magic in attempt to pull the dagger to him. Dagmar grasped hold of the hilt to keep it in his heart, fighting to hold back his own yell. Eisliev's force lifted Dagmar off his feet, pulling him across the carpet.

"I…will have the…power now." Dagmar forced the words with his last breath. His hands slipped from the blade at the same moment his limp body fell to the carpet. Dead.

Branimir cringed, fire burning his insides. The room faded, threatening to leave him blind without the Kaelandur. The last he saw was Alden leaping over him toward Dagmar. If Eisliev had said anything more, they were lost as Branimir's hearing was replaced with a loud ringing. He quailed, hitting his head against the ground.

What felt like an eternity passed, and then the familiar hilt was pressed into Branimir's open palm.

He gasped, sucking air into his lungs, and wrapped his fingers around Kaelandur. Alden hung over him, his thick eyebrows arched in concern. Feeling his strength return almost immediately, Branimir rolled away from the old warrior to face Eisliev Kluk.

To his surprise, the red mage's face was fastened with shock, a curved blade erupting through his mouth from the back of his head. Alyona let go of the hilt, and pushed Eisliev to the side.

"Our odds have worsened," Alyona muttered. Her use of magic had added extra wrinkles around her eyes, but concern lining her eyes caused her to look all the older. "Kaelandur's magic will bind both Dagmar and Eisliev to destroy the Ash Tree, giving them unlimited power."

Sulanna replied, "More the reason to get to Iriy and have the gods destroy this dagger."

"Yes. However, the dagger will not end Eisliev's and Dagmar's desire to destroy the Ash Tree and free the Likhyi," Alyona said. "It will only steal away their immediate means."

Alden grumbled. "What do you mean?"

Alyona faced the old warrior. "The two will continue to seek a way to release the Old-dark, even if we convince the gods to rid the world of Kaelandur."

Branimir coughed, his throat dry. He spoke with a strangled breath. "Why would Dagmar kill himself with Kaelandur?"

"Power…knowledge…immortality…" Alden speculated with a shake of his head.

"We can hope their blood feud will keep them at each other's throats, even in death," Branimir said, collapsing to his knees next to Dagmar's corpse. He pulled Faegrim free from the finger to put on his own.

Sulanna huffed, eyeing Branimir warily. "Keep the ring close. I do not know its power, or what Dagmar did to me. But it is best no one who can touch Koldovstvo touches it, or we might kill each other."

"I will keep it safe," Branimir replied. Although he spoke of the ring, his hand rested on the hilt of Kaelandur, wondering how he could keep anything safe against the power of Koldovstvo.

"What about her?" Alden said, pointing at Alyona. "She did save us from the dungeon, but for what purpose? She did not know Eisliev had come here. And we all heard what Eisliev said about her working for him? How long would it have been before you betrayed us?"

"I would never deceive you." Alyona frowned. "At Melkorka—"

"We can trust her," Sulanna interjected. "The story was a ruse crafted by Dorofej for them to escape Melkorka." Sulanna stood next to Alyona, almost protectively. "We can trust her."

Branimir agreed, turning his eyes from Dorofej's dead grandson. He combed the room laden with the dead. "But where is Falmagon?"

Chapter XII

Branimir avoided the blood pooling under Dagmar, and searched the body until he found the ancient codex, the Varkolak. Dagmar had kept the tome magically folded with Koldovstvo to fit snuggly in his pocket. Branimir did not have the power to undo the leather casing holding the faded vellum. He pushed the small-scale book into his pocket. Dorofej would want it; he was certain.

Alyona rummaged next to him. She watched him put the ageless text away, pressing her lips together as though she were holding back her words. Returning to her work, she unbuckled the belt holding the vials of Water of Life from Dagmar and carefully slipped it off. Three glass containers shattered when Dagmar had fallen to the ground, but there were three remaining for her use.

Considering the few age lines on Alyona, Branimir guessed she would have some time before needing to restore her youth.

"Eisliev does not have anything on him." Sulanna said, cleaning her knife on his clothes.

"I found some silver on the Guardians and Kadari. And these," Alden said, handing two daggers to Branimir. He took the blades with a nod, and carefully tucked them into his belt, along with the blade from Dagmar's chest. He slipped the sheath with Kaelandur to the far side, grazing the handle uneasily. Alden added, "We should have enough coin to get us by until we reach Gavlok."

"We should get moving," Alyona said. "More Guardians will eventually arrive, and we do not need to be here. Not to mention, I have little interest in facing whatever Kadari remain with Falmagon."

"What about Falmagon?" Branimir asked, again, for what felt like the hundredth time. "With Dagmar removed, the Kadari are weakened. Falmagon was injured when he left the dungeon. We can end this right now."

Alden was the first to respond, hooking Adamus's shield over his back. "Harrowhal has a lot of space to track, but I agree with Branimir. If we do not kill Falmagon now, we will be looking over our shoulder for him and whatever Kadari remain all the way to Iriy."

"Why press our luck?" Sulanna asked. Despite Alyona's healing, Sulanna looked exhausted once more with the color fading from her skin. Branimir suspected the undue amount of death, including her father, was weighing on her. Her words clarified his suspicion. "We have already lost so many, Alden. Please...we should leave."

Alyona neared Sulanna, wrapping a hand around her shoulders like a mother comforting a child. Her purple eyes rested on Branimir and Alden. "I agree. Eisliev cleared the path but the lack of hindrance will not last. The Guardians will come. We may not be able to call this a victory, but it is something."

Branimir shook his head. "We cannot leave. We already made the mistake of leaving Falmagon alive in Gaetana, and look where it led us."

Alyona angled her brows. "I should have been told he was in Gaetana. Why did no one tell me?"

"We saw him at the inn before we left, waiting for us in the commons," Branimir tried to explain.

"But why was I not told?" Alyona asked, removing her arm from Sulanna. Only a moment passed before she answered her own question. "Because you did not trust me." She dipped her head, running a hand through her hair. "I understand."

Sulanna meekly shrugged at the Kadari.

Alden cleared his throat, gripping a spear he had found among the bodies. "It doesn't matter. Alyona and Sulanna are right. We cannot be sure Falmagon is here anyway. He may be dead already. If we go traipsing about, we are likely to become trapped."

Branimir ran his hand through his thin hair. "Fine," he finally muttered. "How will we leave Eldhaft?"

Alden scanned the room with a knowing look. "The gods have blessed us, providing a proper means to walk right out the city gates. Search the bodies for clothes unblemished with blood."

"No," Sulanna argued. "Wearing the Guardians' garb would only bring more attention when trying to leave the gates. If Branimir stays hidden, we should be able to leave."

Alyona agreed. "We have wasted enough time already. We need to go."

As Sulanna and Alyona led them from the foyer, Alden turned to Branimir, who had already vanished. "I know you want to find Falmagon, but stay with us, Branimir."

"I do not plan on sneaking off, Alden," Branimir said sternly. He added in a soft undertone. "Just promise to keep Sulanna safe. She cares about you."

The old warrior lifted an eyebrow with interest, turning his granular chin to the woman, who had traveled and fought with him among the Crimson Sun for so many decades. "I would give everything for her."

Branimir considered his words as they plodded through the bodies lining the hallway. He wondered if Alden's fondness for Sulanna matched her own toward him. Branimir had not forgotten Sulanna's confession about her love for Alden.

Eventually, the four of them reached the rear door that had first brought them into Harrowhal. Alden and Sulanna recoiled at the midday sun, while Alyona and Branimir's vision adjusted to the fluctuating light. Holding his breath, Branimir glided behind Alden, who followed the women, up the alleyway to the main road.

The southern gate, which they had entered when coming into Eldhaft, sat but a half mile down the road. Whilst the northern gate would have been much further in the opposite direction. Sulanna, being the wiser, vouched for the southern gate with the intent to walk around the city instead of through it. Grunts from Alden and Alyona suggested they agreed with her quick decision.

The four made a left and briskly walked toward the towers marking the portcullis. They only traversed half the distance when Branimir spotted the hated historian from the Highspire, Witigor Sirska, slinking into a side shop. His ugly, pointed hat bounced with as much vigor as Branimir remembered. He heard him speaking to someone in front of him as he went inside.

"I saved Eldhaft from the worst kind, I tell you. I bet they are all dead now," he scoffed. "By the gods, I am a hero." The door to the shop closed behind him.

"Sulanna," Branimir hissed from behind them. "Wit went—"

"I saw," she whispered back. "He is no longer our concern. Come on."

Branimir's blood boiled, but he followed behind his friends. Moments later, Wit fled from his thoughts and his attention was drawn to the front gate. A handful of Guardians gathered around the gate, encircling the too-familiar Ispolini.

"Tyr Og," Branimir identified the Ispolini with incredulity, turning to Alyona who stood next to him. He swallowed, drawing back. After speaking with Alyona at Eldhaft, he expected to come across the giant again, but not here in Eldhaft. The last time he saw Tyr was at Melkorka when the Ispolini had tried to kill him. Of course, the attempt was moments after Branimir had put a dagger in Eisliev's skull. "Dorofej must be close, right? You said they were traveling together."

Before Alyona could answer, Branimir heard one of the Guardians ask, "What is your business here, Ispolini?"

"I heard the Patrician talking about his kind," another said. "I bet he would be interested in seeing this one."

Tyr raised his hands, taking a step back, gazing to the road ahead—the same direction from which they were coming. "I do not want any trouble. I came looking for my friends is all," Tyr said. His blue eyes were darker than Branimir remembered under his dark red strands of hair.

"I do not see Dorofej," Alyona said plainly.

Branimir grabbed Kaelandur at his belt again, wrapping his fingers around the handle. At least he knew Dorofej was not dead. Dagmar said he had to be killed by the copper dagger.

"Come on," Alyona directed. "Tyr must have brought a message from Dorofej."

"You expect us to fight the Guardians in the open road?" Sulanna asked.

"If it comes to it," Alyona replied. "We cannot let him be taken."

"It will come to that…" Branimir started. "The moment the Guardians see us, we will be in danger. We would do better to catch them unaware."

Alden spoke gruffly under his breath. "You said to trust her, Sulanna, but this seems too much the coincidence."

Sulanna loosened her belt knife and shushed him. "I know, Alden." Her face twisted in absolute disgust, her chin shaking with immeasurable wrath. She yanked the blade loose from her scabbard and set the pace toward the gates. "Put some faith in the *gods*. I am not leaving anyone else behind. If she says Tyr is with us, we will keep him safe."

Alden matched Sulanna's step, gripping the spear in his hand.

"We should make a plan, before…" Alyona started, watching them down the street. She rattled in a frenzy. "Branimir? Where are you, Branimir?"

His words were loud enough to reach Alyona's ears as he hustled by her. "Two steps behind them."

Branimir disregarded Alyona's curses, pulling two of the daggers from his belt, leaving an extra blade plus Kaelandur. He did not have to study Alden or Sulanna to know the two were not going to wait for an invitation to the battle. Tyr, unaware, lifted his hand as though he might be waving to Alyona—the massive axe in the leather strapping on his bare back swinging with the motion—and then dropped his six-fingered hands to his skin trousers, realizing what was about to happen.

With less than ten paces, Alden and Sulanna attacked without as much as a shout.

Alden's spear ripped through the back of a Guardian's neck as Sulanna wrapped her arm around another and sliced his neck open. Branimir bounded by her onto the back of a third, stabbing the two knives into chest. The man tumbled backward with a pained cry. Branimir ignored the sound, dodging Alden, who stepped over his invisible body to thrust his spear into a Guardian's gut.

The other Guardians yelled in surprise, moving to counter. Yet, before any could pull their swords free from their scabbards, three more had fallen dead.

Tyr backed away further crying out. "What has happened? Alyona!"

The Guardians ignored him to respond to the immediate threat.

Sulanna scowled, shouting to the Ispolini. "Tyr!" She ducked under the high arc of a sword, and then stepped over an adjacent attack as a blade swung for her ankle. Branimir rolled behind her first attacker, cutting the sinew behind his knees. The guard barely made a sound before the Kras stuck him in the jugular. "Stand with us!" She deflected another blow from the second guard.

The Ispolini, his bare skin glistening in the summer's heat, looked up to Alyona in the distance, nodding with a hearty growl. He jerked the axe from his back. His roar resounded through the city street as he lurched forward and grabbed a man half his size. He hurled him back into the stone tower to the right of the gate.

"For Svarog, the Kingdom and victory!" Alden bellowed loudly, thrusting the spear into the brains of the enemy.

"We need to go," Branimir shouted among the din of battle. Sulanna and Alden did not seem to hear him. He slashed his blade against the tender skin of Sulanna's attacker, distracting the man enough for Sulanna to scoop in close with her own blade. Branimir did not see the death blow. "Come on," he started.

"Branimir!" Alyona shouted from behind him. He rotated back the way they had come to see ten to fifteen Kadari marching at them with Falmagon walking unsteadily behind them, gripping his side, and masking the pain.

"Kill them all!" Falmagon decreed, directing his small legion with a free hand. The citizens of Eldhaft, who had not already fled indoors or in-between buildings, raised the alarm, fleeing in all directions. In the distance, Branimir could hear more men marching through the streets. He suspected them to be more of the Guardians of Gero.

Alyona flung up a wide shield of Koldovstvo to defend against the lightning and fire that quickly rained down from the Kadari. The vitality of the blue field wavered against their power. Alyona's desperate voice called out for him again, carried by Koldovstvo. "Branimir!"

Tyr, Sulanna, and Alden held the battle in balance. The Guardians would not last against them.

He had to help Alyona.

With persistence, he bolted for the Kadari opposite side of the blue shield, remembering the battle on the shores of Melkorka. The mages were not like Eisliev with eyes set on Kaelandur, seeing between worlds. No, the Kadari could not see him; he could lessen their numbers with little effort if he were quick. He could save them all; he could kill Falmagon.

"Stay here," he shouted to Alyona sprinting by her. His feet were light against the dirt, kicking up dust behind him.

Her purple eyes darted where he had been in a failed attempt to see him. "We must flee," she begged over the sound of combat.

His eyes locked on Falmagon, ignoring her. Part of him knew she was being wise, but what Branimir said at Harrowhal held true. He wanted his old master to taste the bitter air of the Netherworld as he and Dorofej were forced to twelve-hundred-years ago. Falmagon single-handedly turned the world upside down, robbing free choice from its inhabitants with the Kadari, binding the living to his chosen god—his vision—his corrupt concept of perfection. Any who did not bend knee to his will were judged. And for what? The world would burn all the same with the return of the Old-dark.

Branimir barely recognized the low, guttural growl rumbling in his gullet. He was several paces from the swarm of Kadari when he let the first dagger fly at the front-line. The weapon pierced the eye socket of a middle-aged man with short, dark hair, felling him to the dirt. His Kadari brethren adjacent to him jumped at the sudden death, hardly noticing the dagger materialize in the air before slaying the unaware man.

Yet Falmagon kept them steadfast, counseling with commanding authority. "Split the ground; spill lightening; rain fire. Kill the red brood before he reaches you."

At the Patrician's command, the ground quaked and split—like a tidal wave—rolling sediment over sand. A stupefied expletive could be heard from behind Branimir, indicating Alyona had lost her balance. He did not have time to look over his shoulder; instead, Branimir had to scrabble and clamber over the roiling dirt wobbling under his feet. The buildings on either side of the city street rocked; the glass in the windows shattered.

The screams of the frightened citizens would have given Branimir pause if he would have had the luxury to dawdle. But Falmagon was resolved to slaying Branimir, even if he should destroy all Eldhaft in the effort.

Branimir jerked the remaining dagger from his waist—leaving Kaelandur in its sheath—and hurdled over the fissure forming under his feet. He slipped by the first—a woman—stabbing her mid-thigh, tearing the blade free at a downward angle; in the same breath, he impaled the man to her right in the groin with his second dagger. The harmonious squawking from the two coalesced with the other Kadari like a tuneless choir, frightfully wailing with panic.

"Kill him!" Falmagon bawled the loudest, slinking away from the Kadari, who stopped molding their magic to fan away from the two who collapsed.

"Where is he?" one screamed.

"Nine Lands," muttered another.

Branimir slipped behind another Kadari making his way to Falmagon, who slowly continued to retreat. Lightning sizzled and popped from the cloudless sky, tearing through a woman opposite side of the circle. She was dead before she struck the earth.

Branimir twisted to see Alyona back on her feet, casting Koldovstvo from a distance. Another bolt struck a man twenty feet ahead of him, ripping a fiery hole from his back to chest.

Defensive blue shields erupted around several of the Kadari.

"Run!" a man hollered, pushing a woman out of his way. "We cannot win here." The Kadari nearest to Falmagon began the excursion back down the main road, and soon the Kadari closest to Branimir started after them.

Falmagon jogged his head with anger, pulling at the corner of his mustache as his small army retreated behind him. Unable to see Branimir, he glared at Alyona across the upturned street. He lifted his hand to cast a spell.

Branimir responded without thought, hurling his dagger forty feet at Falmagon. Although he aimed for the man's head, the distance was too great. Falmagon's eyes bulged as the dagger appeared before him. He swung his hand to defend the attack only to catch the edge of the knife in his palm.

He yelled in agony, blistering with fury. Pulling his injured hand to his chest, he took one final look at the street before fleeing with the Kadari.

The echo of the marching guard on the adjacent road grew louder, halting Branimir from racing after Falmagon. He raked his eyes through the streets to see Guardians of Gero also advancing, ducking in and out behind buildings, measuring their best path to the gates. Without a doubt, Branimir knew he could catch Falmagon, but the cost would be his friends being captured and imprisoned, or even killed.

Near the gate, he could see Alden and Sulanna directing Tyr back out the gate.

He squeezed the handle of his dagger and backed away from the approaching thieves. He stepped around the two Kadari he had left injured on the ground, crawling at a snail's pace after their brethren. Bran did not stop until he reached Alyona's side.

"Branimir," Alyona yelled about the time he reached her. "We have to go."

Branimir appeared at the Kadari's side. "I know. Come on."

Chapter XIII

The sinuous river, the Gneveh Rill, trickled over the patchy rocks scattered beneath the flowing surface. The vibrant water was cool on Branimir's lips, briefly abating the hunger spasms in his stomach. Alyona's revitalizing magic at Harrowhal faded over the evening hours while they bolted north toward Gavlok. And, unfortunately, whatever food had remained in their packs had spoiled while they had been in the dungeon.

Hunger and discomfort resurfaced tenfold within Branimir's body. Alden and Sulanna did not appear to be faring much better. Luckily, the injuries they each suffered did not return as the hunger did.

"Finally," Sulanna sighed, sinking to her knees in the water. She cupped her hands and slurped the liquid from her palms. Eagerly, she fished for more water.

Branimir hummed in agreement, swooping handfuls to his mouth. Any other time, he may have found the water bitter; but, in this moment, he could not have asked for anything more refreshing. His stomach gurgled in response.

Alden collapsed on the other side of Sulanna, resting on the bank. He followed suit, taking a drink, mumbling between gulps. "The regular guard will stay in Eldhaft unless given a directive by Count Vlassi, but the Guardians will not turn so easily from pursuit."

"Neither will Falmagon," Branimir added, struggling to keep his eyes open. He blinked several times, splashing some of the water on his face to help keep himself awake. The sun setting in the west, behind the distant mountains of the Shade Fells, did not help the drowsiness. He looked at the faint peaks. Somewhere in their vastness held their destination, Iriy, the City of the Gods.

"No, he won't," Sulanna carped, hitting at the water with frustration. Her short, grey hair clung to her cheeks from the heat. "Maybe we should have pursued him like you suggested, Branimir."

Branimir jumped back, startled by Sulanna's sudden movement. An image of Adamus having his head dunked in the basin of water in the dungeon at Harrowhal played through in his mind. He had been helpless watching while strapped to the table.

"He could have killed us," Branimir said, shaking the sound of Adamus gasping for breath from his ears. His hand was trembling from the memory. He tried to steady it, continuing, "I am certain he would have. We should have killed Wit when we had the chance. He is the reason we were held captive in Harrowhal, and the reason Adamus was killed."

"I do not care for him anymore than you, Branimir, but Wit acted as I would have suspected him to," Sulanna said with a shake of her head. "He is no longer a threat to us."

Alyona joined them as Sulanna finished her sentence, scanning the landscape warily, crossing the road at Branimir's back. Tyr's heavy footfalls were close behind her. She had asked them to wait another hour before risking the much-needed drink from the river; but Sulanna and Alden refused to stay hidden in the tall grasses any longer. Regardless, the hour had grown late enough to sift most of the traffic from the road's breadth.

"We were right to leave. You would have been either dead or back in a dungeon if we would have stayed," Alyona said. "Right now, our purpose is to get Branimir to Iriy, no matter Falmagon's fate. The gods will set our feet on the right path to end this madness."

"I hope so," Sulanna said. "I do not know how much more madness I can stomach. I have seen enough death to last me a lifetime."

Alyona sighed, addressing Tyr, "You should know Eisliev will be returning from the Netherworld—again—for Kaelandur." She paused, biting her lip. "And Dagmar, too."

"Wait. Dagmar was killed with Kaelandur?" Tyr asked with a shiver, the suggestive tone in his voice was nearly insolent.

"No one is at fault," Alyona said. "He killed himself with Kaelandur."

Tyr scratched his scraggly red hair. "We will need to get to Iriy before we cross paths with either of the murderers."

Branimir snappily cut him off. The sound of Eisliev calling him a murderer rang in his ears. The color of blood filled his vision. "You are as guilty of murder as Eisliev is! You let that child be killed."

Tyr tensed, his chest flexing in restraint. He wrapped his six fingers into a fist at his side. "You do not know anything about Eisliev and I, or what we have done. I cannot say he was the most honorable, but he was my friend."

Branimir was taken back from the biting response, searching Tyr's blue eyes. His words cut deeper than he expected; he had not expected the Ispolini to attack him. Bran stumbled to find the words to ask forgiveness for his brashness. "I—"

Tyr glowered at Branimir, continuing, "Understand, I did not want Bohumir dead, but I will not be held responsible for the boy's death. Maybe I could have stopped Eisliev from slaughtering him, but from what I can tell, you could have done the same."

"You knew what he intended." Branimir's jaw trembled, smelling the burnt flesh of Bohumir. He could not shake the memory. "You did not see the violent way he slaughtered that innocent child and flung him into the flames."

"No, I did not," Tyr admitted. "But I did not throw him to the flames. What I have done is travel halfway across the world to take you into the Shade Fells." He shook his head at Branimir in disgust. The look on Tyr's face nearly made Branimir apologize, but he held his tongue. "You have the right to be angry. Believe me, no one knows anger more than me, but you best direct it to someone more deserving."

Branimir clenched his teeth, looking for a rebuttal, but his mind was mush. He attempted to distract himself by looking up and down the wide road. Of course, the path was not *completely* empty. Carts continued to rumble in the distance, identifying the coming travelers. They could not stay on the road much longer.

Alyona opened her mouth to intervene, while Alden and Sulanna stared at them with concern.

He kept her from speaking, finding the words to attack Tyr once more. "Where is Dorofej? Alyona said he was with you?"

Tyr rumbled, looking to Alyona uneasily "He was; but he was insistent on getting to Iriy."

Branimir searched the giant's face for any hint of deceit. "Instead of coming for us in Eldhaft? Why would he leave us to suffer at the end of Dagmar's and Falmagon's hand?"

"He did not know." Tyr's angled his brow. "When Dorofej and I split outside of Sorod, he said he found Sulanna, Alyona, and Adamus outside of Eldhaft. He never saw you, half pint." Tyr scratched at his head, his eyes falling to Branimir's hand where Faegrim rested. "I honestly thought you would be halfway to Iriy by now. It was a surprise that you were held up in Eldhaft."

"We had complications," Alyona said.

"I can see that," Tyr said with a frown, directing his eyes away from Branimir. He looked at Alden suspiciously. "I expect you to have more questions for me, half pint. But I, too, have questions. I recognize Sulanna by her description, but this is not Adamus Ebordon."

"Alden Forgaaf," Alden introduced himself. "Adamus is dead."

"I am sorry," Tyr said with heavy eyes. Though, he sounded almost relieved to change the topic. "I do recognize your name from the Crimson Sun." Tyr rubbed his chin. "You and Sulanna were frequently spoken of among many, including Seigfeld and Farthr."

"You are with the Crimson Sun?" Alden narrowed his gaze.

"I joined them with Eisliev after you had long been gone. We worked under Teodor Bacheva," he gestured at Branimir, "until they killed him in Cavell. You may have met his father in Eldhaft. My plan was to find Master Bacheva before the Guardians stopped me at the gate."

"You are lucky you did not," Alyona said.

An awkward exchange of disorderly facial features and unsystematic murmurs resounded as Alden, Sulanna, and Tyr jammed the pieces of their mixed histories together. Their roads were nearly as entangled as a nettle patch.

Branimir tensed with frustration, realizing the topic split away from Dorofej. His heart raced with anticipation.

He remembered the Ispolini to be rough around the edges when they crossed paths before, but he did not plan to back down from the giant. If Tyr believed Eisliev to be a friend, he may betray them, even if Alyona were honest.

After several minutes, when none of them rerouted the conversation back to Dorofej, Branimir broke up the muddled fuss. "Tyr, would you like to explain *why* Dorofej is not with you?"

"I don't have a reason, Branimir. Dorofej asked me to attempt to reach you before you reached the Shade Fells in hopes of being of some help through the mountains. He did not say why he chose a different path. Though, from your brief recount, Eldhaft does not seem the safest place for Dorofej to travel," Tyr said. "If he had crossed Falmagon, while they held you captive…"

"You mean he was saving his own skin by leaving me to die?" Branimir fumed. "That cannot be the reason."

Tyr scrunched his face with irritation. "I would be glad to tell you more of what I know once we make camp. Not all of us hide as well as others, and the road will not remain safe."

Alyona sided with him. "We need to move on anyway and find a place to rest. I am not restoring you four with Koldovstvo for the next month until we reach Iriy."

Branimir took a final drink, watching Tyr. He hoped he was not buying time to make up a better story. He hated to think Tyr to be untruthful, because, conclusively, it meant Alyona could be lying as well. The Ispolini returned the gaze, and rubbed his jawbone as though it pained him to keep his mouth clenched.

Alden heaved Sulanna up from the riverbank, and minutes later they headed west into the tall grasses outlining the road. Covering their tracks in the Gaetanean Grasslands would have been impossible if it were not for Alyona. For almost a quarter mile, she weaved Koldovstvo to realign the trampled greensward, including the wildflowers. Her hair continued to grey from the effort, but when Branimir showed concern, she claimed the magic was necessary to keep them safe. The path behind looked completely untouched.

For several miles, they walked.

Branimir's memory was overwhelmed in the silence. He thought of the Netherworld and the demons walking across the frozen wasteland. At the time, their grating and groaning was a constant ambiance that nearly drove him and Dorofej mad. As he thought of the bone-chilling sound, the noise distorted in his head, matching Adamus's screams from when the Ariadnean's leg was skinned at Harrowhal. The thought brought tears to Branimir's eyes. He had turned his head when Adamus had been tortured, unable to watch, but the pained cries could not have been ignored.

"Branimir!" Sulanna shouted. "Where are you?"

He blinked the memory away, turning around in the grassy fields to face Alden and Sulanna behind him. He must have accidentally disappeared while they were walking with Tyr and Alyona. He rematerialized. "I am here."

"You scared me," Sulanna weakly said. "Don't do that."

Branimir rubbed the back of his neck in confusion, unsure of how he had unintentionally vanished.

Alden raised an eyebrow at Branimir, and scratched his bald head. However, instead of commenting on his strange behavior, Alden changed the topic. "Once my belly is filled, I will be more than keen to travel to Iriy. I have wanted to stand before those I have given reverence; and I would like to know what path will lead me to

Thrice Ten Kingdom if Wolos is truly dead. I want to know why we should serve gods if they can be slain by mortal men." Alden took the edge of the green cloak he wore and rubbed the sweat from his brow. "Is that not the story as we understand? Two Stuhian asses slaughtered Wolos in a battle at Anaerfell?"

"Ye—yes. Dagmar's sons, so it seems," Branimir said. He found himself having difficulty staying calm since leaving Eldhaft; his heart was thudding in his chest. Still, he could recall what Dagmar said at Harrowhal. "He confirmed what Erzebeth told me at Garain'l." He jumped suddenly at the memory of the Likhyi at the old ruins.

"Are you okay?" Alden asked.

Branimir bobbed his head, taking a deep breath. "We must keep Kaelandur from the Ash Tree."

He decided not to expand on the story. Though, he knew the undead Vucari did plan to release those same brothers from their northern prison with the aid of *Lahmia,* a three-headed white dragon. He could not be certain of the full scheme, but the dragon had appropriated Branimir's shiny stone, *Ojenek,* for the quest. Erzebeth believed the brothers could be sent into the Netherworld to see the God of the Dead reborn.

Branimir understood the plot to be the only real hope of saving Aenar. Without Wolos born-again, the dead would continue to walk on Aenar, regardless if the Old-dark were freed from the Ash Tree.

Alden scratched at his scalp, and would have likely pulled at his hair if he had any worth tugging. "What would lead these men to such folly?"

"I would imagine the same vices leading all men to recklessness," Tyr offered, stamping at the ground. "Power, greed, envy…love."

"Love is not evil," Branimir said.

"Nothing is evil on its own, but in excess," Tyr said, hovering over Branimir, "all things can lead us to do what we never thought we could. I know as well as any other."

Branimir cowered under the brutal gaze of Tyr, his light, oval eyes widening. His lips parted as though he might add something more, but Alden interjected with a grumble. "Seeking to physically kill a god is not something anyone with any decency would *think* of doing."

Sulanna groaned. "Can we please not dissect the minds of gods tonight? I do not have the energy to listen to it."

Alden hummed in agreement.

In time, the tall grasses did lessen, the road between Eldhaft and Gavlok completely disappeared, and Branimir saw distant trees on the horizon. Branimir's legs started to ache around the time Alyona finally gave the signal to break for camp.

Alden was the first to sprawl out on the grass, laying out on his back, and sucking in the cooling night air so noisily Branimir could hear it whistling through his teeth. Sulanna crumpled in a heap next to him; her hand reposing over his chest. Alden tilted his head to look at her with a questioning look, but she had closed her eyes.

He turned to Branimir instead for an explanation.

Branimir did not even have the strength to shrug at the old warrior. Instead, he sat at the bottom of the hill they just passed over, and settled against the incline. Clouds blanketed out the moon with coming night, but the weather stayed as timid as it had hours earlier.

"We can build a fire once we have something to cook, but we should otherwise douse it for the night," Alyona said, removing her cloak, and then slipping off her boots. She unloosed the strings on her pants next, letting them fall to the ground. She sniffed the air. "I will go see what is stirring in the brush; I should be able to find a couple rabbits out here."

Tyr's eyes crossed, turning his head from the half-naked Kadari. "Why you must remove your clothes to hunt?"

Alden jolted his head off the ground to gawk at the nude woman, almost stirring Sulanna, who already drifted into a deep sleep. His blue eyes broadened until they could not stretch any further.

Alyona scarcely noticed, pulling her shirt off over her head. She then tilted her head at Tyr, and folded her hands under her breasts. "Really?"

"You are no more a savage than I am," he said plainly.

"Nor am I human," she said with a wry smile. "Keep them safe. I will return soon."

Alyona briskly changed from human to animal, holding their attention. Her bones broke and folded, while black, silk fur waved across her skin like a breeze rippling over water. She slumped to all fours, maintaining her balance—her hands and feet erupting into oversized paws paired with retractable claws; and then, she suddenly sprouted a long, thick tail from her back, inches above her waistline. Her neck thickened and cracked; her pale face lost its color, restructuring to parallel the visage of an oversized cat, budding the same black coat as her skin. Alyona had become a panther.

Branimir sat up to meet her brown eyes, widening beneath her cup-shaped ears. Her tongue licked at the air, and then she was gone, dashing into the tall grasses.

"By the gods," Alden said weakly, resting his head back against the dry grass. "What is she?"

Tyr replied, swallowing hard. "A skin-switcher. I thought her kind had all died ages ago."

"She does have Vucari blood," Branimir explained, eyeing Tyr with concern, "but she is also Stuhian. I do not think she holds any commitment to the Vucari or the old ways besides the skin-switching."

Tyr shook his head, blankly staring off into the darkness. He seemed to notice Branimir's concern. "My father said the Vucari were a plague to the Stuhians for a long time, but they never threatened my people. I have rarely heard stories where a Vucari could be trusted."

Alden delicately moved Sulanna from his chest. She curled into a ball, turning away from him. Her breaths were deep as she dreamed. Alden forced himself to sit up and folded his legs. "How do you know her, Branimir? Can she be trusted?" he asked.

Branimir scrunched his nose at the complexity of the question, and finally rubbed his hooked nose as though it itched. After a moment, he nodded his head, answering partially to spite Tyr's concern. "I think we can trust her, Alden."

"How long have you known her?" Alden asked.

Folding his hands in his lap, Branimir realized he never told Alden about his adventures with Dorofej in the Netherworld, his old life at Melkorka, or given him any real indication of his age. Branimir trusted Alden but did not see the need to share the over-told story, especially with Tyr in their company. "A long, long time," he smiled.

Alden accepted the answer with a simple nod. He pulled Adamus's steel axe from his belt and sat it in front of his crossed legs. Rubbing his lips with the back of his hand, he said, "I suppose we should talk about what we do next. I do not know where to find Iriy in the Shade, but Alyona said earlier the journey would take about a month. We do not have the supplies or the coin to gain the supplies to survive a month."

"We could get supplies at Gavlok," Branimir suggested.

"Gavlok is closest. Any other place would add weeks if not more to our journey," Alden replied. "We would have to backtrack and the risk of being found by the Guardians or Falmagon would only increase."

Tyr grunted. "Gavlok will not be safe. It would be the first place any of them would search for you."

Alden scratched the wrinkled skin of his scalp. "You are right, but what other choice do we have?"

"There must be another settlement between here and the Shade?" Branimir asked.

Tyr met Alden's eyes as though he were debating whether to share a secret, and then sighed. "Out there, Branimir, you will only find the whispers of myth. Most would not dare risk travel under the shadow of the Shade Fells. The woods are unexplored, the terrain is barren, and the closer you roam, the more likely you will come across demons fleeing from the Deep. Not to mention, we will be facing wyrms gliding above the mountain peaks, large enough to blot the skies."

Branimir looked at Tyr with curiosity. "What is the Deep?"

Tyr answered, "The underearth. Paths upon paths of underground tunnels twist and turn, leading to the Netherworld and beyond. And among other demons the very enemies to my people, the Witiko, pack its paths like a plague."

"You have seen the dragons and Witiko? You have been to the Shade before?" he asked. Branimir did not remember seeing anything called a Witiko when traipsing through the Netherworld with Dorofej, but the two had not exactly sat around recording every species of demon either.

"I am from Tundris Mor, an island south of the Shade Fells," Tyr paused to take a breath. He rubbed at his red hair. "My people have fought dragons for eons. And yes, I have been within the Deep of the Shade and I have battled the demons therein."

"I am not afraid of demons," Branimir said, "or dragons."

Alden cleared his throat, folding his hands back over his knees. "You have courage lost to most men."

Tyr's pitched gaze sang of admiration. "I have not come across many half pints in my life, but I must agree. I admit your steadfastness is honor-worthy."

Branimir grimaced, waving off the compliments. The Ispolini had not answered his questions regarding Dorofej, and he had not forgotten. "Can we speak of Dorofej now?" Branimir asked. "I think we are far enough from the road for you to give us an explanation."

"Certainly," Tyr said. "Dorofej and I traveled as far as Sorod when he sent me to find you."

"Why?" Branimir almost shouted, fumbling to sit up straighter against the hill.

"Wha—" Sulanna stirred with a gasp, turning over on her side in a rush.

She did not have the chance to say any more with Branimir's words flooding from his mouth. "Why did he stay at Sorod? Is he still there?"

Tyr frowned, shaking his head.

Sulanna's heavy eyes revealed her exhaustion. "Hold on. Are we supposed to head to Iriy or not? I thought Alyona said Dorofej would make it there before us." She half-heartedly eyed the area, pushing her hair behind her ear. "Where is Alyona anyway?"

"Hunting," Tyr said off-handedly to Sulanna, and then continued. "Alyona did not lie to you. Dorofej would have reached Iriy by now and will be waiting for us."

"You are making no sense," Alden muttered, running his hands down his cheeks. "You just said he was at Sorod. That is almost two weeks in the opposite direction."

The Ispolini snorted impatiently. "Sorod has a temple with a secret gate leading to Rujan. The High Priest has used this passage for thousands of years to travel to Iriy and speak to their god. Dorofej said he would use the gate to reach Iriy."

"Rujan?" Branimir jarred his memory. He completely missed the end of Farthr's sentence, recalling when Dorofej had told him about the Svet's Four-Faced God of War. But, more importantly, he remembered when he traveled through Sorod during his first trip to Maharia—a memory he often regretted—and the High Priest who consulted with the Oracle by walking through the magical, underground door. "Remember when we were on the boat to Talastein, Alden? Sulanna? One of the shipmates said Rujan is called Svathevit the Red. They say the God of War has the power to call back Gebereht from Thrice Ten Kingdom to save Aenar. Has Gebereht come back from the dead, too?"

"I do not know anything about any human named Gebereht," Tyr said.

"He was from Ariadne," Alden said, intently shaking his head as he spoke. "At least, he took the name of Gebereht during Ariadne's greatest victories. Some believe he is truly Kowin the Deathless, detained by Svarog in Thrice Ten Kingdom. He cannot be killed by any regular means; his soul is kept separate from his body in a needle, hidden somewhere on this earth."

"Are we talking about the gods again? I cannot believe I was woken up for this rubbish," Sulanna mumbled, rubbing her eyes. She turned on the three of them. "By the Nine Lands, have you three been this tangential the entire time I have been asleep? Stay focused, or I swear by the gods, I will run each of you through."

"I thought you did not believe in the gods?" Alden's mouth twisted into a smile.

"And I thought you cut your arms whenever you displeased your illusory puppeteers," Sulanna shot back with a whimsical lift of a single eyebrow.

Alden held the grin on his face. "I thought I would try something else…at least, until I know whether I have a guide to cross the Thrice Nine Lands."

Sulanna held her jaw tight to keep from smiling. "Alden Forgaaf, I said to stay on topic."

"So Dorofej fled to Iriy and left us at Eldhaft," Branimir concluded. From the time he had known Dorofej at Melkorka to their time in the Netherworld to their journey last year, Dorofej always pledged to stay alive. If the black mage feared anything, it was his own death. But Branimir would never have guessed Dorofej to leave him in a dungeon to be tortured.

"I told you, he did not know you were in danger, Branimir," Tyr said. "He was eager to speak with the gods."

Turning his gaze to the field, bright as day to his peculiar eyes, Branimir noticed movement in the field. He awkwardly recoiled, startling himself, before realizing it was Alyona. He was not sure what he expected, but quickly calmed meeting her flat expression. She tossed a handful of dead rabbits and a fox to the dirt, and then reached for her garments still lying in the grass.

"Or, he was saving his own skin," Alyona said, echoing Branimir's thoughts, while she clothed herself again. "He would be safe at Iriy from Eisliev. It is holy ground."

Sulanna squinted at the naked woman, moving her mouth with an unspoken question before snapping her lips closed.

"Listen," Tyr said, "Dorofej is at Iriy. He will be waiting among the gods. He and I spoke, at length, about the Old-dark and what you had seen at Garain'l." Tyr gave a throaty growl, organizing his thoughts. "You have been urged to make haste."

"Then we should travel back to Sorod through the gate that he used. The way is half the distance," Branimir said.

"The Svet would rip us to pieces coming into their Holy Lands," Tyr argued.

Sulanna blinked, pulling her long knife from her belt and reaching for Alyona's catch with the intent to skin their supper. "I don't understand. Dorofej made it through the gate, right?"

"If you think you can reason with the centaurs?" Tyr said.

Alden shook his head. "I don't think that would be wise."

"If we found Farthr, maybe," Sulanna muttered.

Alyona reached for her boots after adorning her other clothes. "Traveling east will only lead us into the hands of the Guardians, or Falmagon and the other Kadari. I think we stand a better chance going into the Shade."

Branimir did not see how demons and dragons were a better alternative to thieves and the Kadari.

"We still need coin. We need supplies," Alden said definitively. "We will not make it far without horses and food."

Branimir clasped his hands together until his fingers hurt, and exhaled. "We will go to the Shade. Tomorrow, we will start for Gavlok to get what we need. I have buried silver we can use for supplies."

Chapter XIV

Branimir was certain they traveled two or three times slower through the tall grasses than they might on the main road and taking the extra time to rest had not helped them cover much ground. But Alyona and Tyr insisted the extra rest would do Branimir, Alden, and Sulanna some good. In the meantime, Alyona led them, snaking back and forth in case they were being followed. The entire process had been dully slow.

Alden and Sulanna's soft tones were comforting to Branimir's ears as he marched ahead of them, and behind Tyr and Alyona. Branimir peeked over his shoulder, unnoticed by the two humans behind him, caught up in their own musings.

"I am surprised by your change of view of the Svet. At one time, every conversation about them was filled with scorn," Sulanna said, her fingers woven between Alden's as they walked. "Remember how quick you were to denounce the Svet and their Holy Lands? Now, I suspect you might even be eager to rescue the heathens."

"Farthr was a brother-in-arms. That is all that I said," Alden claimed, clearly surprised at her prodding.

Sulanna lifted her eyebrow. "Was that all? I heard a lot more in that simple statement."

"Do all women from Eldhaft woo their men by labeling their failings, or have I been furtively blessed? I promise you I have spent more time than most listing my many shortcomings," Alden forced a chuckle. Sulanna impishly glanced up at him before elbowing him in the ribs. Alden grunted, stumbling to the side, but refusing to release his grasp on her hand. He drew close again. "Alright," he said in defeat, returning the earnest gaze. "While imprisoned by the Lilitu, I had time to reflect on my limited understanding of the world. And when I was reunited with you in Harrowhal," he shifted his eyes to the horizon, speaking with a hint of humility, "I confirmed what I had considered..."

Alden drifted off, wrinkling his forehead in deep thought. Sulanna nudged him to continue, her features suddenly solemn at mention of Harrowhal. The torturous scenes of the dungeon would forever linger with them. "Tell me."

The older warrior shrugged. "I realized that we are all caged in this life. We are destined to live and die, but nothing else is truly guaranteed. Sure, faith may promise something more, but faith is not as tangible as the people who suffer alongside us. Many have suffered next to me," Alden said.

"Isn't that why it is called faith?" she said, her voice cracking. Her face flushed upon seeing Alden being honest with her. His words were counter to the theology he had defended for generations. Sulanna pulled him closer to her.

Alden went on, "You must hear me. The Lilitu do not understand the gods of Maharia; the Uvil have no account of them. The Svet worship their own, and I am not even certain the Kras would know what gods were if humans had not enslaved them centuries ago. And what about the other races of the world—living or dead—what do they believe? How about the more ancient pantheons, like the Olddark?"

"I don't know," Sulanna admitted.

Alden rattled on as though she had not said a word. "I believe in the gods. I can't *not* believe in them." Alden took a breath. "But I do not know the nature of gods outside of what men have preached. I have spent my entire life following the *trusted* words of men, who

I presumed to be wiser." Alden took a deep breath, sucking in the morning air to calm his nerves. "It is okay. I know you don't believe in them, Sulanna."

Branimir felt the urge to join them, and slowed his pace so they may gain on his position. He watched Alyona tilt her ear with interest from the far-front, but she kept her nose facing forward.

"I believe in the gods," Sulanna replied, clasping his hand between her own. "I just don't think they have done anything worth praising."

"What about your life?" Alden asked.

"A violent father, an executed brother, and with so many friends now dead…" Sulanna's voice wavered, her gaze steady on the warrior beside her. "I am not sure what good can be found in the torment."

Alden responded after a moment. "Svarog has given me too much strength in my life to turn away from him, as they might to any who suffer. But we know many routes lead to unearthing courage. The promise of glory. An oath of loyalty. The blessing of friendship. A vow of love."

An unintentional grin split Sulanna's face. She looked for an explanation for her sudden release. She turned to her crude humor. "In another life, you might tell me all *those* things are meaningless without your gods."

"And today," Alden shrugged, "In absence of any of these things, the gods do not exist; in fact, the gods may very well be *those* things."

Alyona flipped her short, greying hair over her thin shoulder, calling out to them as she skirted through the greens and yellows of the tall grasses. "Yes, we all live and die for the same truths; only the names by which we call them divide us." She yanked a strand of grass from the dirt as she cut her own path for them to follow. Her next words were mumbled, "Sad to think humans spend their entire lives trying to grasp the concept of unity, if they ever figure it out at all."

"Branimir!" Sulanna suddenly shouted. "Branimir, where are you?"

He spun around to face her, realizing he was invisible again. He rematerialized.

"I am right here," Bran said, pulling at his nose with irritation. When he had journeyed with Dorofej in the Netherworld, he spent most of his time hidden from sight. He wondered if that had anything to do with his sudden disappearing when his mind wandered. He knew he was struggling to keep his thoughts from bad memories. "I am sorry."

"How many times is that now, today? Three?" Alden asked. "Are you sure you are feeling alright?"

"I am just having a hard time focusing." Branimir bit the inside of his cheek, and nodded. "Let's keep going."

The next several hours were quiet. The five of them rested midday about two miles from a cluster of trees to the west, an equal distance from the main road to the east. Branimir could not see or hear anything in the distance to suggest danger, and Alyona too said nothing.

Yet with the silhouettes of the Shade Fells increasing in height since morning, the blotches of grass had become more sporadic, scattered across the bumpy terrain in uneven clumps. If needed, Branimir doubted they would be able to find concealment.

A few hours later, their trudging rustled up a covey of quail for an afternoon meal. Before long, they were kicking dirt over the fire and picking the greasy meat off bones. After the meal, Branimir could finally claim his strength had fully returned since Harrowhal.

Alden and Sulanna also acquired an undeniable, youthful vigor; though, Branimir doubted it had anything to do with the rest or sustenance. The two, separated by maybe fifteen years, intrigued him. They each talked to Branimir with affection toward the other, but he only recently began to understand how deeply they felt.

Never knowing love, or even affection, in his own life, Branimir had difficulty keeping his eyes from the blossoming relationship.

Alden and Sulanna fought and journeyed together for years, always bound by their duty and their undying ideologies. And now, with the world slipping from existence, they had torn down the fictitious shade of rigidity in hopes of finding something more binding.

Branimir wondered why so many looked to the horizon for some lofty meaning in their life when the answer stood so near. Life was not about discovering something new, but molding what was already had.

They were nearing Gavlok near nightfall when a sense of uneasiness churned in Branimir's stomach. He caught up with Alyona. The woman had changed since Gaetana from casting Koldovstvo. She had extra lines around her eyes, and her hair had faded; still, she appeared healthier than most Kadari who he had seen cast magic. He quickly thought of a question to ask her, even though he already knew the answer. "How many vials of the Water of Life were you able to pull off Dagmar?"

Alyona pulled her hooded, black cloak to the side to reveal the belt with the three vials hanging from the leather strappings. "I am saving them for the journey ahead."

"You think you will need them in the Shade? Tyr said we might cross demons and dragons," Branimir said, looking over his shoulder. The Ispolini had made his way back to Alden and Sulanna about an hour ago.

She lifted her shoulders, moving the cloak back across her waist. "I have not been to the Shade since before Shayol Domier. We will not find anything worse there than what was found in the Netherworld."

"But your magic was limitless in the Netherworld," said Branimir.

"It was," Alyona said, "but I am not helpless. Dorofej asked for me to lead you to Iriy for more than one reason, Branimir." He waited in silence for her to explain. She shifted her purple eyes in his direction and sighed, noticing his silent anticipation. "You did not know my father. His name was Meimer Gounari, a Stuhian from Lairhein. My mother was Erzebeth Navenka.”

“Erzebeth?” Branimir squinted at her in disbelief. “How is that possible?”

“The story of the Stuhians and Vucari would take me more than a month to explain to you, Bran,” Alyona said softly. “When my mother and father met, the two races were not warring as they have for past centuries; in fact, they had a similar task as Wardens of the Ash Tree. Birthed by Wolos, the Vucari and Stuhia kept each other balanced, having access to eternal life through the Waters of Life as long as they kept the Ash Tree protected.

“When I was nine-years-old, the Stuhians splintered away from the Vucari to gain the power we know as Koldovstvo by revering Marheena. Wolos was furious that his *dragon men* betrayed his blessings, and called for a gathering. I attended with my mother and father to Iriy,” she continued while Branimir listened intently. “Wolos’s will was absolute. Stuhians were cursed; those who wielded Koldovstvo had their life drained, and their station as Warden was stripped. The Vucari, who remained Wardens, were also punished for not maintaining the balance with the Stuhians. The Vucari who disagreed with Wolos’s will were perverted by twisted magic and turned to Vulkodlak.”

“The wolf-men and wolf-women,” Branimir said, recalling the monstrous beasts he once faced in the Hyaendi Hills. He blinked a couple times, trying to make sense of Alyona’s tale. “It has been a long time, but I do remember Erzebeth telling me about when she became a Warden and learned of the Ash Tree. I cannot say yours and her story are the same.”

“Did she tell you these stories before or after her death?” Alyona asked the rhetorical question with a knowing look. “Dorofej told me you met my mother’s ghost in the tombs of Garain’l, and even then, she aimed to correct some of what she had told you while living.”

“I don’t understand,” Branimir said. “Why would she lie?”

Alyona kicked at the ground. "She did not know she was lying in life. Death brings knowledge of the world, and magic, and the gods, which is hard to understand while living."

"How has she lived on after death?" Branimir asked.

Alyona hummed in response. "She is a Warden, protecting the Ash Tree in life and death." Alyona tilted her head, and added, "She held to her onus, abandoning my brother and me with my father after the divide between the two races. It doesn't matter. I would have chosen to stay with my father anyway."

Branimir gritted his teeth at the thought.

"My father was a good man. He is the reason I went to Shayol Domier and followed Moreth," Alyona said banally. The two passed over another hill with Alden, Tyr, and Sulanna following somewhere behind. Alyona went on, "Anyway, the Ninth Council was created among the Stuhians to fabricate a lie to keep their civilization functioning. Even today, I imagine most still think they are blessed by Wolos, even though they are the very ones who betrayed him. When the Ninth Council was created the Carian Council preceding them was slaughtered, save one."

"Dorofej. He was on the Carian Council." Branimir filled in the blank. "How old is he?"

"Old," she laughed. "At least, a thousand years older than me. That book you pulled from Dagmar at Harrowhal is his tome, dictating the ancient magics and history of the Vucari and Stuhian races. From what I can tell, Dagmar distorted much of what was written for his own benefit. I am assuming you plan to return it to Dorofej?"

Branimir nodded. "Of course. He told me he had written it. I thought the best thing to do would be to give it to him."

Alyona looked off into the grasses for a moment, not responding to the statement. Branimir wondered if she thought otherwise.

"So, why did Dorofej want you to lead me to Iriy?" he asked. "Because you have been there before?"

"Yes, and," Alyona lingered for a moment, "besides having a sacred bloodline, I can also handle more Koldovstvo than most Stuhians. Like Dorofej, I drank the blood of a dragon to gain more power."

Branimir bit his inner lip, nearly crossing his eyes at Alyona in shock.

"You surely have noticed Dorofej can do *things* other mages could never attempt?" Alyona lifted an eyebrow with a taunting smile.

"I thought maybe the flow of Koldovstvo had been diluted over time, or repetitive uses of the Ash Tree kept him from aging as much," Branimir said wondrously, running his hands through his hair. "But drinking the blood of a dragon. Nine Lands." He could not believe the secrets Dorofej kept from him. "Do you even need the vials at your belt?"

Alyona moved her cloak to the side again to reveal the Water of Life containers. "These may be the only thing saving any of us from a final death."

Branimir caught his breath. For some reason, he thought Alyona would use the Water of Life to replenish her own life, to help her funnel additional Koldovstvo during battle. He never considered that she might use the liquid on someone else.

Branimir stammered over his question as she moved the cloak back across her waist. "Would one of those flasks have brought Adamus back?"

"Not unless his spirit miraculously stayed in his body," she answered. Her purplish eyes met his. "I am sorry you lost your friend, Branimir."

The itch in Branimir's throat came quicker than he had anticipated. He may have been suffering from gaining too much knowledge at once.

He coughed and sputtered to keep himself from breaking down. "Like you, I have watched a lot of people die in my life, but nothing like what happened to Adamus..." he trailed off to find his words.

He gulped, blinking back the salty water in the corner of his eyes. "You don't often find a friend like him."

"He seemed like a good man," Alyona conceded. "I would have liked to know him better."

"He had family in Ariadne. A sister," Branimir said suddenly, pulling at his nose. "I think I will return to them when this is over and… I don't know… maybe help them if I can."

Alyona placed her hand on his shoulder. "You have a good heart, Branimir Baran. But we may not survive the ending to this tale either."

Chapter XV

The hour was well past dusk when they reached the edge of Gavlok, silhouetted along the winding river. The mediocre town did not have fortifying walls; but it was not completely unguarded. It was defended with numerous, wooden watchtowers on the outskirts. Branimir scanned the base of the towers and what he could see of the streets from their vantage point. Nothing appeared out of the ordinary.

At two-hundred paces, he kneeled, picking at the edge of his chin in thought. Alden, Tyr, and Sulanna, of course, could not see anything in the moonless night, but Alyona squatted beside him staring at the town with equal interest. Branimir talked in a shushed tone, "I hoped we would have come earlier in the day. Nothing is going to be open this late."

Alden jerked his head up and down, but did not seem to be listening to Branimir. "Do you see any of the Guardians or sign of the Kadari," he asked, gesturing to the watchtowers. "And what about the guards?"

"They have men in the towers as they should," Alyona answered for Branimir. She ran her hand through her hair, addressing Alden. "We do not have any reason to sneak into town."

"Unless the Guardians or Kadari are close, waiting to ambush us," Tyr said gruffly. "We gave them plenty of time to reach Gavlok."

Alyona scrunched her nose. "Why would either of them be waiting here? We have spent nearly five days walking through the grasslands without any sign of life. I imagine if they came to Gavlok, and saw we were not there, they would have returned to Eldhaft or even to Vucan."

"They may have thought we were going into the lands of the Svet," Sulanna said, reflecting on Alyona's argument. She rocked her head back and forth like she was physically bouncing the idea around. "Falmagon might even think we were aiming to meet Dorofej."

Branimir rubbed his brow. Even at Harrowhal, they had not mentioned anything to Dagmar, Falmagon, or Myrthos about going to Iriy. So, if Falmagon did not know they were traveling to the City of the Gods, he would not think of Dorofej using the secret gateway to the Svet's Oracle. "They have a point, Tyr."

"What tavern did you say you stayed at?" Sulanna asked.

"The Oaken Bard," Branimir said, scratching at the thin hair hanging to his eyes. "The owner is Deak Armin. His father died a year or so before I arrived, and Deak inherited the place. I never knew him to keep the doors open too late."

"What type of inn has a closing time?" Alden muttered, gripping the long spear lying next to him. "People are known to pass through at all hours."

"Gavlok has never been known for heavy foot-traffic, Alden," Branimir replied.

"He is right," Sulanna said. "Remember when we were sent to Lonmere to quell that uprising five years ago? When we passed through Gavlok, we ended up sleeping outside in the mud due to everything being closed."

Alden grunted in response.

Alyona pulled her hood over her head, sliding back behind the hill. "Staying out here for the night may be the smartest move for us, too. We will not gain anything by approaching the city this late besides suspicion."

"I agree," Sulanna said, siding with the Kadari. "We will be able to see more at morning's light when the people begin to wake."

"But they will be able to see us better, too, and Tyr isn't going to blend in with the crowd," Branimir replied with a scowl. "If anybody has come looking for us, they have likely defined us in detail. I can hide, but the rest of you cannot. If we are recognized, it will be a fight to get out of Gavlok."

"The same could be said if we go into town tonight, Branimir. We are taking the chance by being here," Alyona claimed. Branimir gave her a wayward look, suggesting he was scheming something better. She took the bait. "What are you suggesting?"

Three years ago, when he had emerged from the frozen Netherworld with Dorofej, he brought a bag brimming with coins, shiny stones, and other trinkets he gathered from Heshayol and the Tower of Eresh. The hoard of treasure he had seen were grander than anything he could have carried in a thousand lifetimes. He could not be sure how long he had sifted through the troves before Dorofej could finally pull him away. But the goods Branimir lifted from the Netherworld were special to him. Every single curio, bauble, and gewgaw. Knowing they would have to trade his riches made his chest ache; yet he had no choice if they were going to meet Dorofej.

"I have coin buried here. I will go into Gavlok tonight—alone— and get the buried silver," he began.

"How much do you have?" Alden asked.

"Enough," Branimir answered.

"What are you doing with silver buried halfway across the world from your homeland?" Alden muttered, half under his breath.

"I will get the silver," Branimir repeated, ignoring him and speaking with authority. "You know I can make it and back again without any trouble. I will come right back." He rubbed his fingers together, clicking his thumb against Faegrim. "Early tomorrow, we will send Alden and Sulanna to purchase our supplies and horses."

"And what would keep us from being discovered by the guard?" Sulanna asked, adjusting the cloak on her shoulder. "These will not hide our faces well enough."

Branimir revealed his plan with a smile. "Alyona will give each of you one of the vials to restore your youth." Alyona opened her mouth and then closed it, almost appearing wounded. She gazed at Branimir with her half-opened eyes; her concern was only outstripped by Alden and Sulanna's mutual bewilderment. Branimir breathed through his crooked teeth. "This will work," he coaxed. "No one would know them."

"I…I don't know," Sulanna hesitated.

"We may need these vials," Alyona finally said.

Tyr finally spoke up from where he had ducked down. "I agree. Using the vials now is not a good idea."

Alden's voice drifted behind her. "To be young again…"

Branimir lifted his hands. "Dorofej must be bringing more vials with him. He would not have left Melkorka without ensuring he had a way to keep his youth."

"We have to make it to Iriy," Alyona replied sourly. She probably would have put her hands to her hips if she were not kneeling in the dirt.

Branimir nodded with as much seriousness as he could muster. "I know. And that means we have to get these supplies."

"Okay." Sulanna was the first to hesitantly dip her head in agreement. A second later, Alden followed suit. Alyona conclusively pulled the vials from her belt and handed them to the humans. "We will do it your way, Branimir, but if you are going into Gavlok tonight, I am coming with you."

Moments later, Branimir vanished and was skittering across the heath toward Gavlok with Alyona tucked inside his cloak in her bat-like form. Her little claws hooked into his shirt, scraping lightly against his chest. He almost did not feel it.

With any luck, the short jaunt to grab his hidden treasure and return to the hill where the other three waited would be swift. He abstained from sharing the full account of how he had come by the coins, and besides, Alden, Tyr, and the two women did not seem to care much. All in all, he hoped to leave some of the treasure planted in the dirt.

He did not see a reason why they would have to use everything he brought back from the Netherworld.

Branimir hardly paid attention to the guards he snuck around. From those tarrying at the base of the watchtowers to those ambling down the lone street paths, not a single guard seemed concerned. They waved their torches in the dark aimlessly; their blank faces fully indicating they did not anticipate finding anything out of the ordinary.

If the guards were not tense, it could very well be that Falmagon or the Guardians had never come to Gavlok to search for them.

The Oaken Bard was not difficult to find. The long, two-story building stretched off the main road near the center of town by the blacksmith and armor shop. Interlaced logs constructed the mainframe of the inn with two large, paned windows carved into the front of the building like watchful eyes. Similar windows were spaced equally along either side of the building to give patrons a clear view outside and natural light when the establishment was open. As of now, the lights had been turned dim outside of a fireplace burning in the commons near the back wall. Branimir had forgotten about the oversized fireplace, mirrored after the old hearth fires of past days.

Branimir did not have to creep up to the windows to see inside with his sharp vision. Several bodies were moving around the fire; their voices were faint outside the building, but not so much that Branimir could not hear them.

"Holding all the power in the world, run out of our home, and now chasing a Kras across the countryside blindly," one of the men muttered before tilting a mug to his lips. "We would be an embarrassment to our forefathers. The Kadari are supposed to be ruling this world."

"We are not without power yet, Beryl," said a woman sitting adjacent to him. "Rulers across Maharia, including Kings, still turn to us for counsel while trembling in our wake.

"No," Beryl said, coughing against the liquid in his throat, and pulling at a yellow sash around his waist. "They tremble for Falmagon Sej. Not the Kadari. If they had known what we sacrificed at Melkorka to keep them safe, to keep them alive in their *precious, little* fantasies, we each would have been given lands. We would all hold the esteem of the Patrician."

"You speak dangerous words," another woman said, wrapping a fresh bandage around her thigh. Branimir recognized her as the Kadari he had stabbed at Eldhaft. Although invisible, he hunched back from the window as she continued, "The Patrician will be downstairs soon enough; it would be wise for you to change your tune."

"Falmagon is here," Branimir murmured to Alyona inside of his cloak. She squeaked in response as though he would understand the rickety noise.

Beryl harrumphed loudly from inside the building, taking another swig. "The time of the Kadari is coming to an end. We can all see that. The world is crumbling with the demons bleeding from the Crags. Dagmar is dead, and we are only a few."

"The Kadari have always battled against demons, even when our numbers were trivial," the first woman said. "And Dagmar was not always among our number."

"Kerra is right," Falmagon's voice carried into the commons room from the middle of the stairs. Branimir peered through the window pane at the Patrician. He slipped down the stairs carefully, undoubtedly favoring his many injuries. He cringed, holding his left side with his right hand, while clutching his bandaged, left hand to his stomach. "Our numbers will grow again, and we will push the Bukavac back to the Netherworld. We must only first destroy Kaelandur, which means we must rid this world of Dorofej Kaligula."

"Then why are we chasing the Kras?" growled Beryl.

"By Mulafell," Falmagon cursed, maneuvering off the staircase. "Branimir will lead us to Dorofej."

"Not if we cannot find him," Beryl said. "You had Dorofej in your grasp and he escaped. We could have put an end to this nightmare a long time ago."

Falmagon looked exhausted, dragging himself across the floor to the fireplace. "You know full well why we did not kill Dorofej at Melkorka. We needed Kaelandur, and none could have predicted Eisliev returning from the Netherworld. None could have predicted his power." Beryl only frowned at the Patrician, before turning back to the fire. Falmagon growled to gain the fellow Kadari's attention. "Dagmar is dead. We will now do what is right."

Beryl took another drink and then spit the liquid into the fire. The flames flashed higher, illuminating his face. "Too late. Branimir could be well on his way back to Melkorka by now."

Kerra scoffed, standing from her chair. She moved it to the opposite side of the fire for Falmagon to take a seat. He nodded appreciation, falling into the wooden chair while she talked. "He was seen heading north from Eldhaft. Where else would he have gone?"

Alyona suddenly scratched at Branimir's chest, stealing his attention away from the window. He peeled back his cloak to look at her brown eyes peeking back at him, taking the concealed meaning. Eavesdropping on Falmagon and the Kadari was not telling him anything he did not already know. And the longer he stayed away from Alden and Sulanna, the greater chance of them coming to look for him, leading them all to being discovered.

He hastened his steps around the side of the building, naturally ducking beneath the windows even when he had no need for the extra precautions. Before long, he reached the rear of The Oaken Board, and scanned the area. Sadly, the buildings in Gavlok were not built like those in Eldhaft or Gaetana. The spacing between each structure was wide enough that Branimir would have difficulty hiding his actions from any patrolling guards. He was invisible to the naked eye, but anybody passing by would notice a hole being *magically* dug in the hardened dirt.

He pulled his cloak to the side again to remove Alyona from his shirt, cupping her small frame in his hand. She peeped with surprise as he whispered, "Keep watch." He then boosted her into the air with his hands, and watched her flap into the air above him. She circled overhead repeatedly disappearing over the inn only to return again and again.

Branimir ignored her, effortlessly remembering where he buried his treasure. He darted to the edge of the building, faced north, and stepped heel-to-toe twelve steps. Straightaway, he dropped to his knees and started digging at the dirt with his bare fingers. The Season of Warmth kept the ground stiff, but tough skin and nails gave him the leverage to tear into the dirt with minimal difficulty. Although he did not have claws like the demons he faced, Branimir had been born to quarry stones and rocks from the underearth like any Kras. He might as well have been a child sinking their hands into a pie.

Trifling mounds of dirt piled on either side of the hole as he dug. He sank his hands deeper until he was elbow-deep and the dirt had softened, and nothing. Worry crawled into the pit of his stomach about the time his hand grasped hold of the moistened fabric.

He smiled, hearing Alyona's excited squeaks over his head. He looked up to her with a crooked grin, forgetting she could not see him. She flapped over the edge of the building out of sight, about the time he realized he had stopped concentrating and reappeared again.

The thought was fleeting as he wrenched the backpack out of the hole, hearing the clinking of his coins and gems inside. He remembered first collecting them from the Tower of Eresh and Heshayol. He had not been able to grab all he wanted, and even now, he considered how difficult it would be to go back and collect more.

"Gah!" he groaned. He barely felt the gust of wind that flung him from the ground into the side of the inn. His head cracked against the wooden planks, rattling his head. With a stifled cough, he struggled to gaze up at Falmagon, and several more Kadari, who stood triumphantly behind him.

"Branimir Baran," Falmagon said with a deep-rooted laugh, gripping his side. "The Lightbringer does answer prayers."

Chapter XVI

Branimir only had seconds to comb the sky for Alyona's bat-like form before he was dragged inside The Oaken Bard. He had been too excited about his shiny stones and lost his concentration. He could not believe he had been so stupid. The door slammed behind him before he saw any sign of Alyona. She could not have fought all the Kadari alone. He could only hope she rushed to get Alden, Tyr, and Sulanna to free him.

He frantically eyed the room, counting almost a dozen and a half of Kadari. Some bounded down the stairs while others were waiting around the fireplace. The men and women watched him with frozen grins foul enough to drain the color from Branimir's skin.

Beryl, and an equally large man with a greying beard, held his arms in iron fists, hauling him to the center of the room. The lithe woman with the dark hair, called Kerra, pushed chairs and tables out of the way to make room. A few other Kadari, who had not been in the commons room earlier, hurried to help her.

Branimir could hear Falmagon's boots smacking against the floorboards behind him; the Patrician maintained a flamboyant recoil to his step, despite his injuries. He whistled between his teeth with delight. Branimir twisted to glare at his old master, but could not see beyond the humans on either side of him.

"Marla," Falmagon clucked, "go reset the wards before we have any other unexpected company. I suspect Branimir's friends are not far away."

A grey-haired woman separated from the crowd. Depending on her use of Koldovstvo, she could have been any age. "Patrician, my apologies, but I told you I am not proficient with sacred magic."

"We are aware," Beryl barked, "or half of us wouldn't be limping around here like old geezers."

"I may have the bloodline, Beryl, but I never had a mentor," she barked, pushing around the mouthy Kadari. She shifted her eyes to Falmagon. "We do not have any more vials left to restore my life. We do not have vials to restore any of us," she said.

"I appreciate your sacrifice," Falmagon said from behind Branimir. He could hear the Patrician's voice shake, but whether from the fury of being questioned or frustration for their predicament, Branimir could not be sure.

The woman physically tensed, her eyes holding over Beryl's shoulder. "I can maintain them for another hour or two, but we should simply take turns keeping watch."

"We must risk it," Falmagon replied steadily. "Whether Branimir's friends are in waiting, or Eisliev returns for Kaelandur, we will need forewarning. Men will fail and the magic will not. Go set the wards again."

Branimir frowned, watching Marla circle around.

The door of the tavern banged shut with Marla's exit.

He turned his attention to the scraping chair near the fireplace as the dark-haired lady he stabbed in the leg several days ago pulled herself to her feet. Her blue eyes examined him like butchered meat in the marketplace. "So, this is the red brood who attacked us in Eldhaft?"

"Yes, Kveta," Falmagon grunted. The Patrician hobbled around the left side of Beryl, his hand pressed against the side of his stomach. The two men holding him tightened their grip as though they had divine knowledge of Branimir's imminent misfortune. His mouth dried as he met Falmagon's iced eyes, twinkling under his tangled, brown locks of hair.

Branimir's chin already ached from clasping his mouth closed. His heart rapidly thumped against the inside of his chest, blood pulsating through his veins. He did his best to appear brave—to mask his fear—but Falmagon held no kindness in his eyes. And Branimir did not know the words to entreat the man to reason, to forgiveness, to understanding.

Despite the few passing seconds, the time Branimir spent in the shadow of Falmagon's unblinking scowl felt like an eternity. He unmistakably wanted Branimir to grasp his power in this room with *his* Kadari. He coveted Branimir's subjugation to his will; he intended for Branimir to abandon his hope—to believe Falmagon held absolute control over his insignificant fate.

And, although panic coursed through Branimir like a drunken man's liquor, Falmagon's effort was wasted. For whether Branimir was believed or doubted, hated or loved, or caught and tortured—even to the extent of having his heart carved from his chest—he would never again be a slave.

Kveta emerged next to Falmagon, stooping over so low that Branimir could feel her hot breath on his face. "You think you are smart, knifing folks when they cannot see you? Using your devilish magic in battle? I bet you think you are a brave warrior." She sneered. "You are a coward."

"Kveta…" Falmagon started, as though he might be hurrying her along instead of silencing her.

She cut him off. "Dalibor bled out from the bits because of this little, red brood. Vladan had to be buried with a dagger still lodged in his eye socket," she growled, her thin lips trembling. "And how many of ours did he kill outside Melkorka last year?"

Again, the bearded Kadari and Beryl tightened their hold on his arms.

With a flash in her eye, Kveta pulled aside Branimir's cloak and pulled the dagger from the belt. Kaelandur stayed hanging from its sheathe around his waist. She barely looked at the copper blade, twisting the iron dagger in her hand. The sharpness of the weapon gleamed in the firelight.

Her free hand grabbed his shoulder roughly, balancing her weight to keep pressure off her bandaged leg. "Should I wedge this in your leg, your eye, or your *dear*, little bits?"

Beryl's blithe snigger robbed the air from Branimir's lungs. "Why choose only one?"

Disbelief and horror seized Bran, his timorous lip quaking with realization. He twisted against the Kadari holding him, hardly budging.

He dared to break from Kveta's ghastly expression to look at Falmagon. The twisted smile under the Patrician's mustache screamed of gratification. After Harrowhal, he realized how far gone Falmagon truly was. He once thought Falmagon, at least, considered himself decent, but nothing was left of the Highborn Longwalker.

Nothing could have readied Branimir for the shockwave of pain riddling through his body as Kveta speared him with the dagger. He reacted at instinct, thrashing violently against the two Kadari holding him hostage, his wail causing the very flames of the distant fire to waft. He could not pinpoint where she struck him at first, only knowing the pain surged from beneath his belly. The heat of the immediate wound was only diluted by the warmth of the thick blood flowing down his slender leg.

He moaned. Tears descended from his cheeks with heaved sniffles, snorting his slick snot back into his nose and off his upper lip.

Kveta twisted the blade, grating the sharp edge against his femur, isolating the dagger's location. Branimir blubbered softly, catching the saliva on the edge of his tongue, hatefully glaring at the Kadari woman.

He gagged in effort to keep his throat from closing, gasping for oxygen. He needed to breathe. He had to shake away the abysmal pain. Inhaling the metallic odor of his own blood, Branimir gazed to Falmagon and exhaled the bitter thoughts flooding his mind. "I *will* kill you! I swear it! Marheena will leave you broken and deformed!"

"I have done all I can to protect Aenar," Falmagon shouted, spit flinging from his lips. Any joviality he may have held left him. "You and Dorofej have enticed demons to plague us for giving glory to the Lightbringer instead of your pathetic, Frozen Witch. We know how you survived the Netherworld. We know how her magic even twisted Alyona and Artemiy from the path of righteousness." Falmagon's faced reddened. "I am the chosen leader of the Kadari. Kinhar chose me! Do you think you can rid me from this world? Rid me from record like the thief you are? I will be remembered as a god!"

Branimir puffed his chest, holding himself up on his one good leg, despite Kveta's bulk remaining heavy on his shoulder. He crowed with his reprisal. "I would not steal your name from history. I would tell your story to every ear. History should know you, so the hearts of men are never again rapt by such selfish delusions."

Falmagon shoved himself in front of Kveta, knocking her to the side where another Kadari quickly caught her before she fell over. Branimir rocked back with surprise only to be straightened like a sword stabbed in stone. The ire in Falmagon's eye suggested that he noticed nothing, smashing his good fist into Branimir's nose with all his strength.

Branimir's head popped back, the cartilage cracking on the bridge of his hooked nose, spurting crimson from his nostrils. He gasped, snapping his head forward as a second blow connected with his cheekbone.

Falmagon's fury was everything Branimir remembered from his subjugated days at Melkorka. "I will bleed the lies from your lips until all left to be spilt is truth!"

"You are cursed," Branimir faltered, blood dribbling from his lips.

Falmagon screamed between his grinding teeth. The Kadari around him stepped away as the tables and chairs lifted from the ground with the power of Koldovstvo, only to be smashed to the ground again. The clangor echoed in the commons room as wood splintered and cracked.

"Patrician Sej," a weak voice whispered from the top of the staircase. "Patrician Sej, what is going on down there? My customers are—"

"Master Armin," Falmagon bellowed, fastening his gaze to Branimir, "stay upstairs and remain quiet."

Branimir turned to the staircase.

Frightened whispers reached his ears, listening to his old employer, Deak Armin, urging his patrons back to his rooms while crouching beyond view. The pitter-patter of footsteps could be heard as the customers were shooed back to their rooms.

A moment later, Deak half-heartedly tried to speak to Falmagon again. "Patrician Sej, my Lord, if you could be careful while—"

"Be gone, Master Armin," Falmagon snapped, "or by Mulafell, I will have you feeding yourself the embers from your fireplace."

"Ye—yes, my Lord," Deak replied. Briefly, Branimir considered calling out to Deak for help, but the thought was lost when Falmagon brusquely closed the space between them.

Branimir recoiled as Falmagon grabbed his sore chin, wrenching his neck to a curve to force him to look at his insufferable eyes. Branimir squeezed his words through swelling lips. "What do you want?"

His head grew light from the blood endlessly leaking from his leg, making it difficult to hear Falmagon's demands. "Tell me where Dorofej has gone? Is he with you?"

Branimir faintly shook his head in Falmagon's grip.

"We can hang his feet over the fire until there is nothing left but stubs," Beryl said in Branimir's ear. "He will talk to you, Falmagon. He will remember his place."

Kveta sneered over Falmagon's shoulder. "Move aside, my Lord, and I will twist the dagger in his leg. He will know what it means to be enemy to the Kadari."

The room buzzed in agreement. Falmagon tore his hand off Branimir's face, snapping his head sideways. He leaned closer until Branimir's bloodied nose touched him. "Maybe I should let Kveta and the others finish you," Falmagon said, holding his injured hand to his stomach. "But I know how to make you talk. You will tell me where to find Dorofej. I will cut his throat. I will destroy…" he moved Branimir's cloak to the side, "Kaelandur."

Falmagon wrapped his fingers around the copper hilt of Kaelandur. Acidity touched the edge of Branimir's tongue, his stomach churned. "One more chance. Where is Dorofej?" He could do naught but shake his head. Falmagon scoffed, "Have it your way. Hold him."

He withdrew with Kaelandur in his hand, turning to face the cackling flames.

The room gyrated. The aching in Branimir's body was tenfold compared to what he suffered at *Harrowhal* when Dagmar removed Kaelandur from his being. Although he could move his eyes back and forth, and his vision was clear, Branimir's body became as rigid as a gravestone.

He cried out as his inner skeleton pulsated against his muscles. Lashing out at the Kadari on either side, Branimir snapped his teeth and slung his head, yearning to be free. His chest burned as though an inferno streamed through his veins.

With palms spread open, his howl quickly turned to a death-chilling scream; the taste of blood lined the glands of this mouth. He felt like he was being torn apart from the inside. The Likhyi was tearing him to pieces without Kaelandur near his skin.

Shadows formed at the corners of his eyes, clouding the edges of his vision; yet his other senses were heightened. He twisted his neck in time to see Kveta collapse to her knees. Her gurgling buzzed in his eardrums. It sounded as though the Likhyi was ripping her apart, too.

Despite his feverish thrashing, the bearded Kadari and Beryl dragged Branimir from Kveta's body to the front door of the inn. Although they pressed solidly against the timber, he swore he could feel the sting of lashes striking against his back.

He screeched like a diseased animal.

Falmagon sprang from Kveta, collapsing to his knee, while clinging to Kaelandur. He caught himself on his injured hand and wailed in pain. Biting his tongue, his blue eyes locked on Kveta scraping at the floorboards with her fingernails while the life drained from her.

"Patrician!" Kerra skidded next to him. "We need to get you away from here. Eisliev may be out there." She grabbed him under his arm to help him to his feet.

He grappled with her and a table to stand. "No. We need to protect ourselves," he said, barking orders. "Frang and Morgan, move away from the windows. Ailis and Sine, douse the fire." He finally hobbled up to his feet. "Beryl and Seoc, do not let go of Branimir."

Bran kicked, his fingers reaching for Kaelandur across the room, dangling in Falmagon's fingers. His throat burned from shouting; his chest may as well have been crushed by boulders. He felt himself slipping from their grasp. Without the dagger, he would die.

"Falmagon, his flesh is cracking and peeling," Seoc shouted. "We cannot hold him much longer."

"What?" Falmagon asked.

Branimir cricked his neck, tears swelling, to see pin drops of blood trickling through the pores of his red skin. Seoc and Beryl's grasp skated over Branimir's arm, his body becoming lathered in blood.

"No," Branimir cried, feeling his body judder. His vision turned pitch.

"This is not Eisliev," Kerra cried.

Screams rebounded in the commons, increasing his overwhelming nausea. The Kadari fell on either side of him, releasing his arms from their iron grips. He could not see what happened, but their death cries were nauseating. Without their support, his legs buckled from underneath him, unable to hold his weight. Branimir dropped to the ground in a throbbing heap.

From somewhere light flared on the opposite side of the blanketed darkness like the sun radiating behind the thickest of fogs.

A voice emulating the dying song of a demon rumbled like relentless thunder. Frenzied, foul laughter followed—arcane and abysmal—cackling inside Branimir's head.

He could only believe the Likhyi trapped within Kaelandur surfaced from the copper blade with timeless hatred.

The veil was lifted from Branimir's eyes, but the pain was anything but fleeting. The unyielding sting surged through him. He writhed against the inn's wooden floorboards, his own hands mechanically etching over his body like frantic maggots on a corpse. His voice had become hoarse; the smell of sulfur pricked at the inside of his nostrils. His blood dripped off his flesh.

In front of Branimir lay Seoc with his head hanging limply, neck broken, blood oozing into his beard. His dead gaze stared pass Branimir to Beryl, who sat dead against the frame of the door. Branimir could not see what killed him.

"Help." A woman's voice whispered from the base of the fireplace. With great effort, Branimir tilted his head to see Kerra sprawled among a dozen dead Kadari. Limbs were broken. Bodies were torched.

Yet his questions fled his mind, witnessing the murky mass swirling over Kerra like a storm cloud. The Likhyi.

The Old-dark's vehement undertones sprang about inside Branimir's skull. He cried out, slamming his head into the floor to knock away the vexing sound.

"Branimir!" He heard Alyona shout from outside.

"Branimir!"

"Branimir!"

Those yelling his name seemed so far away. He tried to scoot over to the window. The Old-dark's unintelligible words grew louder. From the corner of his eye, he saw Kerra's body lift into the air by an unseen magic. She scarcely wriggled before being flung through an adjacent window, her head cracking against the wooden beams of The Oaken Bard.

"By Mulafell," Falmagon cowered on his knees beneath the Old-dark with Kaelandur clutched in his hand. He pressed his head to the floor in prayer, his brown locks hanging over his face, shielding his fear. He was the last of the Kadari in the commons. He averted his eyes from the blackness, fervently pleading to the Lightbringer, "My God, Dahz the White-Clad, Protector of Man, ride swift on Mioengi wielding Mulafell, the Hammer of Righteousness and protect us from the wicked. Do not let us drift into the night without your righteous light."

The Likhyi rustled like a pit of vipers, grating like a whetstone against a sword's edge. The shade swirled and swelled above Falmagon.

The Patrician cried out louder to Dahz for protection but to no avail. In its place, Falmagon's pleas to the Lightbringer twisted into garbled, blood-curdling yells. Time bent around Falmagon, aging him decades in seconds. His hair greyed, whitened, and fell from his scalp, while his skin dehydrated and clung to his bones. The smell of rot—Falmagon's body decaying from the inside out—caused Branimir to retch, and, all the while, Falmagon continued to huskily scream for help.

No gods would come to save him. The gods would not save any of them.

The door leading outside suddenly opened. Branimir's sight was teeming by the visage of a young, dark-haired man and an equally young, light-haired woman. The man gripped Bran's cloak to pull him outside the inn. "Come on," he said. "We need to get you out of here."

He swung at the stranger's clasped fingers, feeling the heat swell in his gut, suggestive of his insides boiling. He uttered the single word, "Kaelandur."

Branimir did not see Alyona step over him and pass into The Oaken Bard. Nor did he see her use Koldovstvo to whip Kaelandur through the air from Falmagon's degenerating hand to her own. But Branimir did feel her slip it into his shaky fingers.

The grisly Old-dark faded from being the moment the dagger connected with Branimir's skin as though it never existed. Branimir wheezed like he had never known breath, the pain from the Likhyi's separation softening. The shadow in the corners of his eyes drifted, and his body relaxed against the inn's floor. Yet he could not keep the tears from flooding.

Agony crept across his body from the gaping hole in his leg to his broken nose to his aching heart. Blood oozed from every cavity of his body, seeping from his skin as though he had been stabbed a hundred times.

"Thank you," he blubbered, looking to Alyona and then the other two, quickly recognizing them as the younger versions of Alden and Sulanna. "You…you drank the vials of the Water of Life. You are young."

"And we have one left for you," Alyona said, gripping the back of his head.

"Hurry," Alden urged. "The guard will come and Tyr cannot stay hidden in the hills for long."

Branimir did not argue with him, sipping the renewing water. As swiftly as he downed the water, his body mended his muscles and settled his bones, stitched his skin and restored his vigor.

"Branimir," Sulanna said in kindness, placing her hand on his forehead. "We thought we had lost you."

Branimir could hear the rustling of movement in the inn beyond his gaze. The low rumble of Falmagon's tenor slipped across the commons like a final breath.

"He is still alive," Alden said, lifting his strong jaw. "What should we do with him?"

Branimir did not think the question really required a response, but he felt better saying the words. "Kill him."

Month of Sickle

Sixth of Warmth

1352 CE

Chapter XVII

Falmagon was dead.

"Less than a week and we will be at Iriy," Alyona said from the top of her pale horse, a few steps ahead of Branimir. Koldovstvo drained enough of her life that, absent her youth, she reminded him of her mother, Erzebeth. She definitely spoke with the same authority.

He forced a half-smile at the thought of seeing Dorofej again. He was eager to have the black mage give reason to why he hurried ahead to the City of the Gods alone.

Alyona returned the smile, continuing, "We have done the impossible, but we are not done. We should expect Eisliev and Dagmar to come for Kaelandur to finish what Nedezhda started with the Ash Tree. Remember the magic binds them to release the Likhyi."

"It has been almost a month since Eldhaft," Tyr said, plodding alongside her, his axe swinging from the strapping of his back with every step. He lifted an eyebrow under his long bangs, suggesting they had little to worry over. "And we have not seen any sign of life since Gavlok."

Branimir listened, slanting the waterskin and wetting his lips. He was careful not to drink much of the liquid. The heat had lessened since leaving Gavlok weeks ago, partly because the rapid approach

752

of the Months of Frost, but also due to their increased elevation in the mountains. They abandoned an unnamed, multi-forking river yesterday, which led them hundreds of miles from The Oaken Bard and Falmagon Sej's wan corpse. Now the five of them delved deeper into the spiraling Shade Fells with the supplies they had purchased with Branimir's silver; none could be certain when they would come upon water again.

He adjusted in the saddle of his pony. "Of course, Dagmar and Eisliev will return for Kaelandur, but Melkorka is on the opposite side of the world. We will reach Iriy long before either find us."

"We *hope* to reach Iriy first," Alyona knowingly said with a dip in her voice. "There are many exits from the Netherworld across Aenar. The Shade Fells are riddled with rumors of demons bleeding from these very mountains, crawling to the surface from their frozen pit. Nothing promises Dagmar or Eisliev will choose to exit from the Crags of Kazimir."

"We can hope they would," Branimir said. "Or, with any luck, they are locked in an eternal battle with one another."

"Have some faith, Alyona," Tyr said. He was daunting, his height stretching over seven-foot-tall, standing above the horse she rode. His large, six-fingered hands swung on either side of his bulky body as he walked bare-footed next to them. "The Bukavac may be chipping away at the Ash Tree, but they cannot completely destroy it without Kaelandur. We will have real dangers to face in the Shade. The demons are more than rumors. We cannot be worrying about ghosts chasing us down."

"We need to be prepared for anything," Sulanna murmured, twisting to look back the way they had come. Her olive skin was smooth, and flushed from the slight chill on the wind. Her grey horse strayed a hair behind Alden. Branimir looked to them. Whatever started between Sulanna and Alden after Eldhaft had been further strengthened after Gavlok. The two were practically inseparable. For many nights, Branimir had caught them slinking back and forth across camp to share blankets, but after a couple nights of forgetting to drift back to their own bedrolls, they gave up on hiding their affections.

Branimir did not think it was worth hiding anyway. He was happy for them.

"Where is the nearest exit?" Alden asked. After drinking the Waters of Life, he was hardly recognizable to Branimir outside of his angular nose and blue eyes. He may have had a receding hairline to give promise to the baldness to come, but his thick, curled hair hid most of the evidence. The *old* warrior did not have a wrinkle on him anymore; instead, his skin was taut against his youthful strength.

Alyona pointed to the southwest, specifically to a towering peak rising far above the rest in the distance. "I do not know the closest exit, but see Mount Zyem," Alyona said marvelously. "Legends say the tunnels within the hollow of Mount Zyem leads to the Kalinov Bridge, defended by Zyem. Many demons are known to spread from that mountain."

"Zyem, Marheena's serpent, the Lord of Dragons," Alden mused, gazing at the mountain in the distance.

Alyona replied, "None can pass to Thrice Nine Lands without passing by Zyem. The balance of life and death would be chaos if living men frequented the world of the dead to bring back their lost loved ones."

"More chaotic than now?" Sulanna smiled, blue eyes sparkling. With a month now gone since Adamus's death, or even her father's— which she would not mention—Branimir was surprised by Sulanna's attitude. Whether credit was given to her newfound youth or Alden's company, she had seemingly found solace.

Alyona snickered with amusement, keeping her head on the landscape ahead.

Branimir bit the inside of his cheek. "If we suspect Eisliev or Dagmar will come by the Kalinov Bridge, we will not have any chance of defending against them here."

"No, we could not defeat them in open battle," Tyr said, as he walked, rubbing Alyona's horse with care. "We would run and hide."

"I cannot hide from them while holding Kaelandur," Branimir said softly. Most days, he kept himself from speaking to Tyr. Although, he had come to believe the giant was genuine in his effort to help, like Alyona. Branimir remembered the Ispolini to be an ignorant brute, but he could not ignore Tyr's loyalty—considering how he defended Eisliev, despite the red mage's clearly evil motives.

Still, he hoped Tyr had changed his allegiances. Branimir suspected they all changed in some way since starting this adventure, whether for the good or worse.

For instance, what they had gone through at Harrowhal and at Gavlok should have been enough to break Branimir, to leave his mind as bruised and bloodied as he had been himself. His nerves had undoubtedly been rattled, leaving him with a pounding heart, racing thoughts, or suddenly vanishing or reappearing without thought. Yet, in the past week, he found some comfort. Surely, he should have been looking over his shoulder for Dagmar or Eisliev. He should be terrified.

But Falmagon was dead.

Since reuniting with Tyr, Branimir had undoubtedly wondered why the giant supported the red mage. The two clearly were not cut from the same cloth. Unable to satiate his curiosity, he turned toward Tyr, and asked, "How did you meet Eisliev Kluk?"

Tyr grimaced, the large axe on his back bouncing in rhythm with his footsteps. "My father and Eisliev had been in an alliance together for some time, scheming against the Kadari." Tyr scratched at his head, swelling his chest with a breath. "I trusted my father. He had always been a bit mad, you know? But I trusted him."

"So, he led you into an alliance with Eisliev?" Branimir concluded. "He had you scheme against the Kadari?"

Tyr rocked his head in agreement. "He believed the God of the Dead had been killed and we needed the Stuhians to be safe from the demons. Eisliev's price was Dagmar's head. I agreed to go with Eisliev to kill Dagmar to maintain my father's alliance."

"And now, Dagmar and Eisliev are both dead-ish," Alyona said, interrupting Branimir's interrogation, "and we need to be ready for them. I would expect them to come from Lonmere, where Branimir and I slipped from the Netherworld several years ago. The path is less known, especially by the demons, but he would find it. He would have a better chance of closing the distance on Kaelandur than trying to cut us off."

Alden gasped with sudden clarity, reaching over his horse and tugging on Branimir's cloak. "Your courage makes sense, now. You were with Dorofej in the Netherworld for all those years. No wonder you fear so little." He looked to Sulanna as he leaned back; lifting an eyebrow as though he had discovered a great secret. She simply shook her head at him.

Branimir tried to smile. He was terrified of losing Dorofej, who would die with Kaelandur's destruction. His only comfort was that he would die too, and accompany Dorofej in the life hereafter, even if they were warped into demons.

For another half mile, the clopping of hooves against the softened, unkempt grasses and uneven rock were all to be heard. The size of the mountains expanded on either side of them.

They journeyed through a natural crook in the mountain, which may have been a wide river at some time in history, stretching miles wide. The Shade Fells showed no sign of retreating from the heavens, obscuring the horizon as though they were a boundary to the edge of the world. Signs of vegetation dwindled considerably as the number of broken boulders and smooth rocks lined the uneven path.

Branimir reached for Kaelandur at his belt, unable to erase the grimace from his face. He had no understanding of why or how the Likhyi escaped from the copper dagger and attacked Falmagon. He remembered the fear and the pain, but he could not place how such a thing was possible. He carried Kaelandur on him for a year without any display of such godly power.

Now, with the understanding that Eisliev could come around any bend in the road, he wondered if the Likhyi would abscond from the dagger once more. His heart told him the Old-dark waged war against Falmagon, because the Patrician had aimed to destroy the Kaelandur.

Eisliev Kluk, on the other hand, intended to unshackle the old gods from their eternal chains. Branimir would bet having Kaelandur taken by the red mage would be a welcomed notion by the Likhyi.

And if Bran were parted from Kaelandur, he would die.

He pressed Alyona to tell him more. "Will we be safe at Iriy?"

Her silence gave his heart reason to quicken, and he nearly repeated the question. But before he was able, Alyona replied, "Iriy is holy ground, meaning the dead would be kept from treading there, but I cannot pretend to know the will of the gods."

"But you have been among the gods," Branimir said. He noticed Alden sitting up straighter in his saddle at Branimir's comment. Sulanna also seemed intrigued by this information, pushing her mare a step closer. Neither must have been listening to him and Alyona's conversation when traveling to Gavlok.

"I was a child," Alyona said distantly. "I barely knew who I was; let alone who the gods were."

"But are they magnificent?" Alden asked.

"The word does not quite live up to the feeling you have when standing with them," Alyona said.

"Real gods?" Sulanna questioned.

"Yes." Alyona said simply.

Alden turned and grinned at Sulanna. His boyish grin nearly cut his face in two. "I told you they were real, Sulanna."

The clacking of the pony's hooves melded with those of the other horses as they ventured in the shadow of the mountains. Tyr tirelessly stomped along beside them. The dim sun from the morning faded to overcast, as it had been the night before, with an occasional light drizzle.

After a while, they stopped to let the horses rest and eat, and then set off again.

It was not long before Alden was tugging at the small curls on his dark beard in thought. "Something has been bothering me. I understand Dorofej hopes the gods will help us. But what more can be done?"

Alyona petted the mist from her brown horse's mane with her fingertips, swaying back and forth in her saddle. "The gods will give us counsel on Kaelandur and the Likhyi," she said.

"What does that mean?" Sulanna asked. "We require more than simple words. Will they destroy Kaelandur?"

"I believe that is what Dorofej intends for them to do," Tyr said. "Why else would we come all this way?"

"No." Branimir pulled at his long nose. "That cannot be it. Marheena told Dorofej to make Kaelandur. I cannot see why she would direct him to create something only to destroy it when asked."

Alden practically threw his hands in the air. "I don't understand why Marheena would have him make the dagger to begin with. What did she hope to accomplish?"

"I have asked the same question," Branimir admitted.

"Maybe it is a test of faith," Tyr said.

"I could believe that, maybe. But I don't see the gods killing Dorofej, or Branimir," Alden responded to Tyr, adjusting the long spear at the side of his saddle. "If Dorofej was commanded by the gods to make something, and he did, why would he be punished? Why would they let Branimir die when he has done so much to save this world?"

"Well, I am comforted that I have *not* died yet. But I have this feeling in my stomach telling me the gods have little concern whether any of us do or not," Branimir said.

"That is terrible," Sulanna said.

"Maybe they don't, but they surely don't want to die any more than we do. The Likhyi would destroy everything, including them, right?" Tyr asked with a grunt. "Are they not all-powerful and all-knowing?"

Alden ruffled his beard. "Again, Tyr is right. That has to weigh on their minds."

"Assuming they are mindful of anything," Sulanna said. "Dorofej may want them to bring Wolos back from the dead? Can they do that? I mean, they are gods."

Branimir frowned. If Wolos returned, the dead would no longer flood from the Netherworld, meaning Kaelandur would no longer be needed to destroy the Ash Tree. But Erzebeth planned to have the two men at Anaerfell bring Wolos back to life. If the gods returned the God of the Dead, Branimir would have given his shiny stone, Ojenek, away for nothing. "No, I don't think they would do that either."

Alyona snickered from the front. "No, they would not bring Wolos back. They may have the power to restore him, but the gods cannot be responsible for the mistakes of men."

"They created us to be capable of making mistakes to begin with," Sulanna muttered, seemingly frustrated for having her idea so easily rejected. "I would think they are partially responsible."

Branimir scratched his head, repeating the question to Alyona. "So, what is Dorofej hoping to achieve at Iriy?"

"Maybe he hopes they will destroy Kaelandur," Alyona said. "I cannot be certain, but I know the gods will tell us how we can stop the Likhyi."

Tyr suddenly stopped Alyona's horse with his hand, pointing in the distance at the rock-strewn terrain. "Did you see the movement up ahead?"

Branimir edged his pony forward, along with Sulanna and Alden on their horses, eyeing the distance. He did not see anything, but his pony stepped back nervously as Alden jerked loose the spear from its holding.

"What is it?" Branimir asked.

Tyr rubbed his hands against his skin trousers, and then removed his large axe from the leather strapping against his bare back. His dark-blue eyes narrowed. "Witiko."

"Demons?" Sulanna reached for her long knife. "How many? Where?"

"I do not see it now," Tyr said, looking to the sky and squinting. Branimir followed his gaze. Twilight had come quicker in the shadow of the Shade Fells. "We should find higher ground and make camp. Who knows how many roam these parts of the mountains?"

"Does that mean there is an exit from the Netherworld nearby?" Branimir asked.

"Not necessarily," Alyona answered, continuing to peer across the landscape ahead.

"The Deep runs through the Shade Fells," Tyr said, referencing the many tunnels of the underearth he had told Branimir about. "The Witiko call them home, and they are numerous."

"But the dragons keep guard over the mountains, usually lessening their numbers on the surface," Alyona added. "From here on out, we will need to be watching for either, and take equal precaution."

Branimir trembled with the onslaught of another gust of wind, unmoved by Alyona's dire warning. Nothing would stop him from reuniting with Dorofej.

The clouds dispatched and a full moon had risen before they settled around the fire. The evening was cool enough that the flickering flames were a surprising blessing. Branimir pulled his green cloak up around his shoulders and scooted closer. Tyr sat on his left, while Alyona scanned the darkness for the Witiko to his right. Alden and Sulanna huddled under a blanket together on the opposite side of the fire, blocked by the roiling smoke.

Tyr's voice came without invitation, diving into his tale again as though he had onus to share the full of it until their ears bled. "After Melkorka, Dorofej and I moved with haste, thinking you would reach Iriy long before we could. We expected to fight the Kadari, demons, or even the Crimson Sun. Yet nothing deterred us from Melkorka to the edge of Sorod. He went to Klukas many times to see how far you had gone, but he never could see the half pint."

Branimir could feel Tyr's eyes on his skull, but did not meet his gaze.

"I remember you mentioning as much before," Sulanna said. "He would not be able to see Branimir while he wore Faegrim."

"Ah," Tyr said. "I thought as much."

"But he could see the rest of us, and therefore, he could gaze on Branimir?" she added.

"No," Tyr replied. "Branimir always remained hidden with Faegrim on his finger, even when Dorofej found the rest of you. Luckily, I knew something about Faegrim from the time Eisliev carried it in his possession. It did not take long for us to think Branimir picked it up, but I was not certain." Tyr paused for a moment. "Do you still have the ring?"

Branimir nodded, watching the fire.

"Were you wearing it when you were being held at Eldhaft?" Tyr pressed.

"For a time," Branimir replied, eyeing the Ispolini curiously. "Why?"

Tyr explained gruffly. "As I said, I separated from Dorofej before you reached Eldhaft; but even if he did not see you, he should have found everyone else in Harrowhal."

"Unless Dagmar used Koldovstvo to block any of us from being found in Klukas," Alyona reasoned, scraping her foot against the dirt. "I heard him and Falmagon talk about the ability many times."

"I see," Tyr swallowed. Branimir glanced at him from his peripheral. Tyr clenched his chin as though he were expecting an explanation of how they may have escaped Dagmar's schemes. When none elaborated, Tyr said, "I suppose that explains it then. I thought Dorofej would meet us on the road."

"He seems to have chosen to stay at Iriy. We would have crossed paths long before now," Alden said.

Branimir gritted his teeth, remembering how Dorofej originally fought with Falmagon about going to the Netherworld, fearful of dying, or the many times he escaped death, whether using Moreth's skull or the Ash Tree. In all their time together, Branimir repeatedly heard Dorofej's confession about how he sought to live more than anything else. For all his bravery, Dorofej was a coward when facing the grave.

"The thought baffles me," Tyr said. "He undoubtedly cares about each of you. You can see it in his eyes."

Branimir stared into the fire. And, although his words sounded unforgiving, he could not say he was angry with Dorofej. "Yet he fears death more."

The smell of rot stung Branimir's nostrils an instant before a gangly, ash-grey monster howled and rushed into the camp behind Alden and Sulanna. Branimir cried out as the demon sprinted on two legs, jumping with outstretched, clawed hands. He had no time to respond, reaching for his weapon while attempting to spring to his feet.

Tyr similarly struggled next to him.

Alyona shouted spinning around, to face the beast bounding for Alden; her hands were already rising defensively. She hastily weaved Koldovstvo, whipping the flames from the campfire around the demon like ghostly hands, and pulled the monster through the air to the searing fire.

The movement was so quick, Branimir had barely jerked his dagger from the sheath at his belt.

Branimir fumbled, scooting away from the thrashing Witiko, while acknowledging the massive size of the demon, its length as long as Tyr was tall. The lanky beast floundered in the flames, screeching, until the color faded from its bulbous eyes. The death-howl of the beast echoed against the mountain sides.

"By the gods," Alden pulled Sulanna close to him, skimming the darkness around them. "I barely heard it until it was on top of us."

"We will be alright," Alyona said, taking a breath. "The Ispolini have fought these demons for ages. Tell them, Tyr."

Tyr growled under his breath, kicking the rotting limbs hanging beyond the campfire's edge. "I know the Witiko well. One or two are easy to defend against. They are mindless beasts, attacking anything they can eat." Tyr covered his nose from the smell, his dark-blue eyes filled with fury. "But, out here, I would not be surprised if we cross larger droves."

Branimir returned his dagger to his belt, shaking his head at the giant and his so-called soothing words. "Tyr, you should take first watch."

Chapter XVIII

Branimir often heard the demons from the Deep at night, howling and screeching against the frigid wind; but, for the next two days, none of them saw any sign of the Witiko.

The path leading to Iriy had become arduous. Their mounts fought to keep footing on the loose rocks, which had long since rolled down from the enfolding crags. Even now, Branimir clung to the saddle as his pony lost its foothold, scrambling its hooves to keep pace with the larger horses.

He huffed in surprise, eyes fixated on Alyona ahead of the company leading them up the mountain. He tightened his thighs so he would not topple off the animal.

Tyr, who walked next to him, reached out and snagged the bridle of the animal, holding it steady with his incredible strength. "Careful there, girl," he whispered, calming the animal. "We will find a break up ahead."

The pony whinnied as Branimir repositioned himself, leaning his weight forward. "Thanks, Tyr."

Tyr's blue eyes met Branimir's. "The trail will level out once in a while, but it will not get any easier."

Alden grunted behind them as he, too, steered his horse up the difficult incline. Sulanna encouraged him to push through.

Tyr added, "The longer the mounts can carry you along, the better. You would exhaust your legs trying to keep balance. You do not want to be tumbling back down the mountain."

Branimir was sure Tyr had less difficulty than most climbing alongside of them with his thick legs.

He cricked his neck to look behind them, quickly realizing how far *up* they traveled after leaving Gavlok. His perception had been skewed by focusing on the road ahead, seeing little except the wall of the Shade Fells. Yet gazing across the expanse of Maharia articulated the truth of how far they had come.

He could see no signs of civilization from where they were positioned. The landscape was painted with yellows, oranges, and greens, coupled by the blue and white sky. He did not see any signs of plowed fields, or cropped woods. Yet he could see the wild grasslands nestled between the scattered forests; he could see the rocky knolls they journeyed beyond, dwarfed at a distance.

"That is beautiful," Branimir said.

"Very," Sulanna said, swaying on her horse. "I imagine few in the world ever have the chance to see a sight like this. Maybe fewer would fight amongst themselves if they could."

"Bah! If you think that is something, you should see Tundris Mor," Tyr pointed over Mount Zyem, ever-expanding to the south. "You cannot reach the islands of the Ispolini without going around the Shade, but the venture is worth the labor. Our isles are as much a part of the Shade as the crags we are crawling through. And when you climb to the tops to see the world," Try breathed, shaking his head in memory, "you really see Aenar. The ocean. Maharia, Haemus Mons. The land stretches for thousands of miles in all directions."

"I have never been to Tundris Mor," Alden said, "but you must be stretching the truth. No offense, but look at the size of Mount Zyem. If you can see anything beyond that mountain, you would be soaring across the sky with Dahz in his chariot."

Tyr grinned. "I may exaggerate, but not to boast. Lofty memories keep my hopes high and my mood mended, much in the same way parents speak about their children."

Sulanna said, "Alden and I traveled through most of the North and never met an Ispolini. The fact you journeyed across the continent and joined the Crimson Sun is beyond strange."

"I imagine before you crossed over, most the world thought giants to be legends," Alden chuckled.

"Some continue to think so," Tyr laughed, keeping his hand firm on the bridle of Branimir's pony. Branimir noticed Tyr stealing a glance at him. "Others think the Ispolini are monsters or demons. It is a difficult thing to live in a world where others are afraid of you for looking different."

"Why did you leave your home?" Branimir asked.

"Bah!" Tyr hesitated, shuffling his bare feet over the rocks awkwardly. He did not give any sign that the rocks were hurting the soles of his feet, but then again, the Ispolini did not seem to be affected by much. In fact, the cold mountain air hardly made his bare skin pimple gooseflesh, whereas the rest of them kept adjusting their cloaks to keep warm. Branimir saw the muscles in his neck and back noticeably tense before he answered the question. "The story is complicated. My home is the heart of Mount Dvargen, the city of Almdalir. The law of the Ispolini works similarly to those in Stuhian lands." He nodded at Alyona near the front, who had not bothered to engage them. "You are familiar with the Stuhia?"

Branimir shook his head. "Not really."

"Oh," Tyr said, angling his brow. "Well, the government is made up of a Council of Elders who lead the people and enforce laws. My father, Enlil, was an Elder until…" Tyr fidgeted, making a six-fingered fist in his right hand. "…until I was banished from my home after the death of my mother and sister."

"You killed them?" Branimir asked with shock.

"No, no," Tyr said, forcibly shaking his head. "Nothing like that. But I did kill someone who insulted their honor. It is not something I like to talk about."

"You did right by them," Alden said from the rear.

"I like to think I did, but that day I became an outcast to my own kind," Tyr said. "I should have been cast into the lava pits and left to burn. Instead, I was sent to the Deep."

"To wander with the Witiko?" Branimir asked, directing his mind off the idea of being thrown into scorching lava.

"Yes," Tyr replied. "I crossed a few Witiko while in the tunnels. Some I killed, and others I avoided. We would be blessed by the gods to not cross them again before reaching Iriy."

Eventually, as Tyr promised, the path straightened and flattened between towering escarpments. Alyona directed them to give the horses a rest, and they gathered to eat what dried food they had in their packs. Branimir was discouraged at the scarcity found in his own, but even more frustrated with how light his waterskin had become.

He sat down next to Alden, who hurried to move his spear to the side and make room. The warrior bit into a piece of dried meat, and scratched at his head of black hair.

"You would not believe how ridiculous you look to me, Alden," Branimir said, crossing his legs.

"I can imagine." Alden beamed his white teeth, chewing steadily in the corner of his mouth. "Sulanna has poked at me many times regarding my beard and hair. Ha! You know I had been bald so long, I almost forgot I ever had hair."

The thought made Branimir giggle.

Alden gestured to Sulanna unsaddling her mare. "I will not argue that I have changed how I think over the past month, but people hear you differently when you aren't as wrinkled as a rotten prune," Alden said, holding the smile.

Branimir unwrapped his dried bread, shaking his head at the warrior. "I could drink the full of the Waters of Life and I would look no prettier."

Alden flattened his gaze, leaning over to study Branimir's face, knowing he had drunk the last vial. "Your skin looks…smoother," he offered.

Branimir pushed him away with a laugh. "Save your compliments for when I have lived to be five-hundred and have need of it."

Alden lifted his bushy eyebrows. "Do the Kras really live to be so old? Naturally, I mean?"

Branimir nodded, taking a bite of his food.

Sulanna approached, digging in her own bag for rations, her dark hair whipping about in the swirling winds. She paused her rummaging to pull the fabric of her cloak around her. "I remember the cold of the mountain in Lonmere," she said, "but it has been so long. And to think we still have a couple weeks until the Season of Frost."

Alyona and Tyr were not far behind. Neither seemed concerned by the cold chill as though their bodies had been built specifically to withstand the frigid weather. Alyona checked over her shoulder at the horses tied together as she spoke. "We will be marching into snow by tomorrow, if not tonight. I would suspect the weather is going to drop considerably by nightfall."

Branimir widened his eyes at the prospect of sleeping among the barren terrain. "We would freeze to death."

"I will create a fire with Koldovstvo to keep us warm," Alyona offered. "We will not need much to keep the magic aflame."

Tyr grunted. "We should find a cave for shelter. I hope we can find one hollowed enough to hold the fire, but without any deeper paths."

"No, we do not need the Witiko coming upon us in the night," Alyona said. "Then again, we must keep watch for Eisliev or Dagmar. With limitless magic, they could gain on us, and we do not want to be caught in a cave only to have it come crashing down on our heads."

Alden frowned. "Maybe we should just travel through the night and continue to Iriy."

"Maybe," Alyona said, biting her lip. "Branimir and I may do well enough if we abandoned the horses, but the rest of you would struggle on the path."

"We should not abandon the horses," Tyr said. "If you plan on leaving Iriy, you are going to want them. We have hundreds of miles stretching between us and civilization."

"And the gateway to Sorod?" Branimir asked.

Tyr shook his head. "Bah! I do not think the centaurs would be favorable of us appearing in their underground temples. We would be disemboweled and roasted."

"Well, that is pleasant," Sulanna muttered. "Sounds like we have the choice to risk the road or holing up. Considering we know the road is a hazard even in the light, and we have not seen any warning of Dagmar or Eisliev, we fortify ourselves in the rock."

Alden dipped his head, chewing the dried meat.

Alyona bit her lip, glancing in a circle for objections and found none. "Our days are growing shorter in the shadow of the mountain. We may have a few more hours. Let's see how far we can make it until dusk."

Soon, they were winding through the mountain path sliding and slipping across the rocks. The slope of the mountain tilted, and although the path was wide, Alyona had to lead them in a zigzag to give the horses enough traction to stay afoot.

Tyr maintained his hold on Branimir's mount, helping guide the pony. The giant breathed heavily as though he may have been physically lugging the pony up the side of the mountain. His muscles bulged from his chest to his back with sweat layering his skin despite the damp cold.

Branimir opened his mouth a few times to caution the Ispolini, but chose to refrain. He did not get the impression Tyr was going to back away from aiding him.

The sun faded into the west about the time the path leveled again. A valley appeared to the north with what promised water and vegetation, but the drop-off was so steep, they would have killed themselves going down or never would have found a way back up. Branimir could hear Alden and Sulanna murmuring similar realizations behind him.

Alyona heaved with exhaustion at the front of the line, but continued forward on her horse, muttering something about a few more miles.

"We should…" The smell of decay stopped Branimir from finishing his sentence. He jerked his head to the mountain ridge opposite of the valley, catching sight of Alyona already swinging off her horse with a warning shout.

From the shadows, bursting from an oblique fissure in the side in the rock, rushed the too-familiar, ash-grey monster. Standing as tall as Tyr, the long-limbed beast had blue, bulbous eyes with skin dried across the length of its frame like a rind splitting over rotten fruit. Bone and muscle surfaced along the body where the flesh had decomposed.

Tyr sneered, unstrapping his two-handed axe to intercept the demon. But Alden was the quickest to respond, flinging his spear over Branimir's head with deadly accuracy. The perfected point tore through the temple of the monster, knocking it sideways off its feet, and leaving it dead, skidding over the rocks.

"Witiko," Tyr growled stomping toward the mountain as though he might tear it down with his hands.

His voice was met with the ringing howls erupting from the opening. The demons from the Deep burst through the crags with gurgling growls and rippling snarls. Alyona extended the first's blood-hungry roar, lifting it in the air with Koldovstvo and flinging it behind them into the valley below.

A second, third, and fourth fled from the hole.

Branimir swung off the pony about the time it twisted to bolt from the impending battle. Branimir vanished from sight and pulled his dagger from his belt.

In two large leaps, Tyr reached the next Witiko in line, swinging his axe to slice the demon across the chest. Bluish blood spurted, but the beast hardly noticed. The Witiko swung clawed hands at Tyr, baring sharpened fangs.

Branimir twisted around the Witiko, barely standing above the knee, and jabbed his iron dagger into the back of the knee. The Witiko kicked wildly with a howl, but did not fall. Sulanna ran on the opposite side, slicing her long knife across its belly and releasing its innards.

The smell was as horrid as the tombs of Garain'l.

Tyr roared in the face of the Witiko, hitting it with the handle of his weapon and felling it to the dirt.

Branimir turned from Tyr and followed Sulanna into the midst of the Witiko horde. Alden's heavy footsteps thundered close behind him.

"For Svarog, the Kingdom and victory!" he cried.

Sulanna ducked the wild swing of the giant monster, stabbing the creature on the inside of the thigh. Branimir slid on the rocks beside her, attacking the knee ligaments once more. The Witiko screeched in pain, spraying spit with its furious roar. Sulanna ignored the sound with the tenacity of a seasoned warrior, jamming her knife into the under jaw and through the brain.

Alden, armed with Adamus's steel axe, threw his weight into the next Witiko, lifting the beast off the ground and hurling it into the rock. The warrior then flurried his attacks with a deafening roar, hacking and slashing the refined blade into the monster's meaty flesh.

Rasping cries rang against the rigid rocks, and across the lowly vale. Branimir whirled between the many Witiko, sieving between his friends, lending his service where he could. He felt crippled, equipped with the single dagger, but the demons were dwindling and none of them had dropped.

Tyr noticed Alyona aging behind them. He shouted to the rest of them. "Give Alyona some relief." She flung fire and frost from the edge of the drop-off behind them, her hair greying in patches and skin wrinkling from the use of Koldovstvo. Without a weapon, she was limited in her fighting power against the Witiko. Branimir was certain that changing into the panther would leave her more vulnerable against the quick demons.

Alden and Tyr retreated to form a barrier in front of Alyona. Before Sulanna could join them, a Witiko emerged from the drove, striking her in the chest with the back of its oversized hand.

"No!" Alden shouted as she slammed against the rocks with a hollowed groan.

The Witiko advanced on her with outstretched claws and incalculable speed, saliva dripping from its pointed fangs. Not worrying about the aftermath, Branimir slung his dagger and struck true. The blade cut through the back of the Witiko's head. Yet, where the one fell, three more rushed to overcome Sulanna.

Branimir darted to Sulanna, materializing halfway across the distance. She attempted to scramble to her feet, gasping for breath.

Tyr took off from the opposite direction, abandoning Alyona, noisily shouting at the Witiko as though it might draw their attention. He held his axe in front of him like a battering ram, his face wretched in fury. The Witiko's raucous roars out-pitched those of the Ispolini as they closed the distance.

"Get up!" Alden shouted. He flung his axe, splitting the face of one of the demons. The Witiko crumpled to the rocks, and Alden sprang for the spear still sticking from the first Witiko's skull. "Get up!"

The ear-splitting roar at Alyona's back sounded seconds before the black-scaled dragon swooped up from the depths of the vale, colliding against the cliff's edge. Alyona dove from the space, rolling shoulder over shoulder to escape the wyrm.

Rocks crumbled and cracked under the beast's mass. Its long tail swished like a snake over the expanse.

Branimir did not have time to lay eyes on Tyr or Alden, hardly capable of processing the sight of the dragon, as he slipped in the loose rock, falling to his knees at Sulanna's side. The dragon had three crescent-shaped heads swaying forebodingly, its massive, weather-beaten wings flapping strongly as it balanced on two of its hind legs. The two muscular, front legs were tucked near the wings. The screech released by a single head was enough to make Branimir grab his sensitive ears. When the second two heads echoed the sound, Branimir's heart threatened to stop beating.

He would never forget the white dragon, Lahmia, but the black dragon before him made her seem a molehill compared to a mountain.

In desperation, Alden's renewed command came as a faint, frantic wail. "Stay down." From the corner of his eye, Branimir saw the warrior jerk the spear free from the Witiko's corpse. He barely lifted it to his waist before fire fell from the dragon's gullet.

The flames pierced through the darkness, igniting the two Witiko in mid-step. More demons rushing from the rock turned to retreat, shrieking in pain. Their howls were cut short in the sudden fiery death. Branimir could only watch with Sulanna in wonder as the horde of demons burned. His face heated, stealing away the ice in his veins.

"Keep to the ground," Alyona screamed at them through the crackling flames. "It is Torn'ash, the Father of Serpents. He is protecting us."

The skin of the Witiko sizzled and frothed, melting away with the cold of the mountainside.

The dragon brought down its front legs, smashing a demon beneath its massive foot, the claws digging into the earth. One of the heads whipped around to release fire breath again on the host of Witiko. Their decayed skin liquefied against their bones; the dragon fire was all-consuming.

Branimir twisted his neck to see Tyr holding firmly to the ground like Alyona commanded. Alden, too, had chosen to lay down his weapon and cling to the rocks.

A rumble from the black dragon's throat ended the second spectacle of dragon breath, leaving the route littered with burnt corpses. The dragon then kicked off the rock, flapping its wings all the harder to soar into the sky.

As it lifted, a fleeing Witiko was snatched up in the strong jaws of one of the heads. Torn'ash snapped the body in half, raining the bluish blood down over them, and then turned away from the mountain side. The remaining pieces of the final Witiko crashed against the ground around them.

Branimir dared to stand, covering his head protectively, watching the beast ascend over the valley. "I don't even know what question I should be asking."

Alden rushed to Sulanna, pulling her to her feet. They held on to one another, shadowing the wyrm with their eyes.

"Bah!" Tyr stated, pulling himself to his feet. "I never thought I would see the day a dragon swooped in to protect a mortal."

"I told you the dragons protected these mountains from the demons. Wolos may be dead," Alyona said. "But his servants are not."

Chapter XIX

The elevation of the Shade reached the clouds. The silvery vapor relentlessly eddied across the frost-covered rock for the next three days. The mountain pass widened once more with the disappearance of the low-cut valley, leaving boulders and rocks with few scattered bushes. Alyona dispersed the few edible snowberries when found, but for the most part, little food was unearthed.

The sky was almost constant smoke, reeling from white to grey to black. Flurries flounced with few actual snowfalls, leaving drifts of snow as tall as Branimir accumulating on either side of the road. He had taken note that Alyona stopped them more frequently to rest the horses, feeding them what little grain remained in the saddlebags. The mounts thinned significantly since purchasing them at Gavlok; Branimir hoped none would die before reaching Iriy.

Branimir pondered over whether they would slaughter his pony for meat when Tyr announced, "At last, we have arrived."

"Nine Lands," Sulanna said breathlessly to his left. Her mare snickered, its nose aligning with Branimir's pony.

Wordless, Branimir beheld Iriy, the City of the Gods. The mountain path had all but evaporated, splitting open into a wide-reaching dale. In the center erupted a rock-strewn summit, stretching hundreds of feet into the air. Iriy covered the entire mount, built in nine layers, crowning in a circular, archaic fortress. Branimir could see the vertical, white-stone columns erected at the zenith of the stronghold.

He could identify the ramparts sectioning off each area of the city, glimmering majestically. Spherical domes of hundreds of buildings and rectangular towers with triangular overhangs were proportionally ranged at each level. Being hundreds of feet beneath Iriy meant Branimir could not fully gauge the size of the archways, cloisters, and walkways, but he suspected a wyrm as large as Lahmia could saunter through in comfort.

The heavens miraculously cleared from all signs of storm, the sun almost seeming close enough to touch; the warmness sinking into Branimir, stealing away his hunger and fatigue. He dared to think of removing his cloak and sopping up the sunlight. But before he could act on the thought, he was distracted by the red stags and hares, partridges and wildcats, and foxes promenading through the fields. Trees with low-hanging fruit and bushes laden with berries and nuts crowded the gorge.

"Do not eat or drink anything without invitation," Alyona said, climbing down from her horse. She unfastened her cloak and tucked it into the straps near the saddle. She then turned to the others expectantly, purple irises flashing, running her hands through her hair. "Let your horses roam and replenish their energy. The saddles will not be a burden to them here. And leave your weapons." She considered Branimir with concern. "Bring Kaelandur."

He bit at the inside of his cheek, but Branimir did as instructed. In tune with the others, Branimir swung off his pony, removed his cloak, and tucked his dagger into the saddlebags. Kaelandur remained sheathed, dangling from the leather belt around his waist in full view.

Tyr handed his two-handed axe to Alyona with his leather bindings. She hooked the weapon to her own horse so it would not become lost.

The mounts wandered into the grasses and trees with the other animals. They moved as though they had freshly awoken, and had not just journeyed halfway across the world.

"How far is it to the top?" Alden asked, stepping away from his horse. Sulanna found her way to his side, interlocking her fingers in his hand.

"Half a day," Alyona said. "But we have to be allowed through the front gate first."

"Allowed?" Branimir wrinkled his brow.

Before Alyona had a chance to respond, a light flashed in the dale so bright and brilliant, Branimir may have thought they had been staring into pitch a moment before, even under the vivid sun.

"Bow," Alyona commanded, dropping to a knee, and hanging her head. Tyr followed suit beside her, crumbling to both knees and placing his head to the softened earth. Alden released Sulanna's hand, taking a large step and pressing a fist to his chest.

Sulanna delayed her kneeling, along with Branimir, but decidedly stooped next to Alden while mumbling unintelligible words of wonder under her breath.

Branimir, on the other hand, shielded his eyes from the brightness perforating his senses. Dawning from the pure light, painted in whites and yellows, emerged a golden-haired goddess of immaculate splendor. Although she had the features of a human, she stood as tall as an Ispolini. Her light-blue eyes penetrated through him, ignoring his kneeling friends. Immediately, his heart swelled with infinite love and kindness, as though every sorrow ever known had been washed away from the abysmal pit of his very soul. Grief and regret and mourning fled from his mind like frost from flame.

She divinely touched his very essence with an absolute love he had never known; in this moment, Branimir deliberated if he had never known real love. The rareness of her expression dimmed all other notions—lust, appreciation, and even friendly adoration—which mortals pretended to know. He was dazed; engrossed to the degree that he did not notice when she skated across the greensward to loom over him.

Her white gown, festooned with golden flowers, flowed at her heel. With each footstep, Branimir swore he could hear bells playing like a distant song. She advanced, unnoticed by the others, and hovered in front of Branimir. Her thin lips arched into a smile, and although he heard her melodic intonation in his head, he knew she did not outwardly speak.

'Waiting for you, we have been, Branimir Baran, son of Hrani. I am Lada, the Mother.'

She dipped down giving full view of the ears of grain braided in her long, golden hair. Never had he felt so full of peace. As though she could read his every thought, she gave comfort.

'Here, you are safe. Here, you walk where mortals fear to tread, in the footpath of the gods. Here, you endure till the end of your tale.'

Lada delicately handed Branimir a rose, red as an angry sunset. From whence she had drawn the flower, Branimir could not say. He took the stem with a trembling hand.

'Go forth into Iriy and be at peace.'

Branimir hugged the rose, watching as Lada faded from sight. With her withdrawal, a sudden weight fell onto his heart; he pined to return to her presence. He could only think she resided somewhere within the white walls on the summit.

Tyr gasped in response as if he had just taken his first breath of life, gripping the grasses under his fingers. He pulled himself to his knees, staring wondrously at the magnificent city above them.

Alden spoke in bewilderment. "Lada, the Lady of Flowers, and the Mother of the Gods. I cannot believe it."

"It is real," Sulanna said, her buttocks falling to rest on the heels of her feet. Her hands slid from her sides to her belly, shaking her head. The water surfacing glittered against the sunlight.

"We must go into Iriy," Branimir said with a shaking voice.

The other four were slow to return to their feet, each stricken with different emotions.

Alyona was the first to look to Branimir, tears flooding the ducts of her eyes. She used the back of her hand to wipe her face. Branimir believed the tears were from gladness, considering what he experienced with Lada. Yet Alyona's frown did not bespeak of any joy.

She dipped her head at the rose in his hand. "You have received Lada's blessing, and the key to the front gate. We have been permitted to enter Iriy."

"Not all of us," Sulanna said with a shaking voice. She stumbled to her feet with Alden rushing to her side. His action suggested he understood her words better than any, squeezing her with as much strength as he could muster. His muscles flexed as though he were wielding his weapons in battle, fighting for every delicate breath.

The two fell into a silent embrace for several seconds while the other three gazed in question.

"What do you mean?" Branimir asked. "Why could you not come after all you have done to bring us here? If anything, you have sacrificed the most."

Sulanna gazed into Alden's eyes longingly, and when he finally nodded his head, she answered, "Lada told me that I am with child, Bran. Alden and I have helped bring you to Iriy but we must go start a new journey."

She turned to Branimir, eyes riddled with torment.

Branimir broke into a smile. "No apologies from either of you. I wouldn't ask you to come any further."

Alden squeezed Sulanna in his hands, his own tears falling to his thick, black beard. He pulled back and turned to Branimir to make words, but stumbled trying to keep his lip from quivering.

"I know," Sulanna said to him, wrapping her arms under his and pulling him close.

Branimir said what he could only imagine was on Alden's mind. "You have spent your whole life living for the gods, and now, upon arrival, you are given another path." Branimir gritted his teeth, looking up at the *old* warrior. "Few men are committed to their beliefs. Few, if any, ever get the chance to question the gods and be presented an opportunity to be given answers."

"No," Alden interjected, gathering his strength. "Too many men are unbent in their thinking. They question gods because they have no sense to question themselves; and when replied to, they alter the answer to fit their foolish delusions." Alden steadily looked at Branimir. "Their narrow *beliefs* bring dishonor to their *life*. I will no longer be the man who saw my life a burden and dishonored it."

"Alden," Sulanna said, touching his cheek with her hand.

Her soft tone did not quiet him. Alden finished, "*Few* men have the heart to *father* their children. They rush to war, or into politics, or to seek some other misfound glory, forgetting their legacy lies in their blood." He tensed his jaw, shaking his head with purpose. "My child will know their father. My child will know life is a gift."

Branimir flew forward and wrapped hands around Sulanna and Alden. He felt their hands on his back to return the embrace.

"You will forever be missed," he said.

Sulanna replied, "We will remain here in the dale for a while, Branimir. We may still travel together on the journey back to the east."

Branimir let go, looking back to Alyona and Tyr. "I do not know where my road will go from here."

"We will wait for an answer," Alden said in kindness. "For now, the City of the Gods awaits Branimir Baran."

"I hope to see you when we are done." Tyr said, clasping Alden's smaller hand in his own. "If not, take care of one another."

"We will." Sulanna returned his hearty smile.

Bran's fingers grazed across Kaelandur at his belt like a shadow, seeing his friends for what felt like the last time.

"Come, Branimir," Alyona said, placing her hand on his shoulder to pull him away. "We need to go."

Alden and Sulanna stayed behind to settle in the dale while Bran and the others trudged to the base of the center peak. No road marked a path to the entryway to Iriy, but Branimir did notice the grass they traipsed across appeared untouched after they passed. Alyona led them around the side of the rock to the entrance.

Around the side of the mountain, they soon came upon the great gate. Twenty-foot pillars topped with stone effigies first caught

Branimir's attention. The sculptures were chiseled from stone resembling men and women wielding swords and staves, mallets and axes, and crossbows and spears. Branimir could see reflections of many races in the depictions: Stuhians and Anshedar, Ispolini and Lilitu, Vucari and Svet, and, finally, the Kras.

At the edge of the final two columns, the grass disappeared and a stone pathway, wide enough for twenty horses to march down, led to an incline of nearly sixty stone steps. The double-doors at the top of the staircase were almost forty-foot tall, made from iron and steel. The doors were firmly placed in a stone archway fixated into the side of the mountain. Whatever walls were built for Iriy remained on the summit beyond these doors. Branimir was almost afraid to think how many steps they would find on the opposite end.

"Nine Lands," he mumbled, tilting his neck as far as it would go. "Who built this?"

Tyr answered. "I imagine the gods."

"No one knows for certain," Alyona said. "Though, I have often wondered if Iriy is this magnificent, what more could Thrice Ten Kingdom have to offer."

Branimir licked his lips in admiration. "After Lada, I am starting to think our ability to dream is trifling to what really exists."

"We are lucky to be limited in our thinking," Tyr said with wide eyes. "We do worse enough with what we know."

Alyona ran her hand through her greying hair, studying the door.

A ghastly, womanly form with shimmering green eyes, like emeralds, materialized on the steps without warning. She floated in mid-air, solemnly gazing at them as though she were making sense of where she had come, or how she had gotten there.

"Erzebeth!" Branimir recognized her immediately from the last he had seen her at Garain'l. "Why are you here?"

The skin-switching Vucari, Erzebeth Navenka, blinked away the glossed-over look, focusing on Branimir first with a knowing smile. The pale green light emitting from under her skin dimmed as she floated down to the bottom run of the stairs to meet them.

"Branimir," she acknowledged in a flat tone, "you have come to Iriy. Yet you still carry Kaelandur. Who have you brought with you? I do not see Dorofej Kaligula in your company any longer."

"He is inside," Branimir explained.

Erzebeth nodded, half listening. She turned her neck first to Tyr, who slowly introduced himself with a look of confusion. He clearly knew Erzebeth was not a goddess. "Tyr Og, son of Enlil, from Almdalir."

Her face stayed like stone until turning to Alyona. Even as a ghost, the look of dread swept over Erzebeth's face. Her faint memory seemed to rush back to her, even without Alyona's words.

"Alyona Gounari, daughter of Meimer, from Lairhein," the Kadari said, squaring her shoulders.

Erzebeth swooped down to Alyona, reaching to touch her face. Alyona pulled away from the embrace, leaving Erzebeth's hand to fall back to her side. "My daughter," Erzebeth said, "you should never have been a part of this terrible tale. Meimer and I never wanted this for you. You were meant to stay safe in Lairhein."

"I know what you intended," Alyona said bitingly. "You sought to live forever to serve Wolos. You left Artemiy and me alone to find our own way."

Branimir remained frozen, watching the two. Tyr, also, seemed uncertain how to respond. He shuffled at Branimir's side.

Erzebeth backed away from her daughter, though her tone stayed defensive. "The Ash Tree *needed* protection. It still does."

"We *needed* a mother. You do not know how father ridiculed our Vucari blood. You will never know the heartache of a daughter abandoned…" Alyona blenched with a shake of her head. She snuffled, staring Erzebeth in the eye before finally turning away. "It does not matter anymore. My father is dead. Artemiy is dead. You are dead. And I am left behind to do what must be done."

Erzebeth tensed. "I am sorry, Alyona. I thought I was doing the right thing." Erzebeth blinked, searching for whatever words would bring her daughter comfort. She looked to Branimir, and sighed.

"No matter how we elect to live our lives, we always seem to be burdened by the choices we did not make."

"Tell us why you are here, and then be gone," Alyona demanded, her voice cracking.

"Very well," Erzebeth said grimly, turning back to face Branimir. "I hoped you found a way to rid yourself of Kaelandur. It must be destroyed so the brothers at Anaerfell can begin their quest. The threat of their saga being undone by Kaelandur is too great. Destroy it so this world may still be saved."

"What are you talking about?" Tyr growled at her riddlesome words.

"I have done as I promised Branimir in Garain'l," Erzebeth said. "Wolos is dead and waits in the Netherworld to be rescued. Lahmia has set free Tyran and Drast Kaligula from Anaerfell to see the deed finished. They will undo their mistake and re-birth Wolos."

"They have Ojenek?" Branimir asked.

Erzebeth nodded. "They need your stone to see the task done. I will be joining them soon on the Kalinov Bridge to help guide them to Wolos's prison."

"Can it be done?" Tyr asked, looking to Alyona for answers. "Can two mortal men march into the Netherworld and resurrect a god?"

"They are not ordinary men," Erzebeth said. "They are dragon-men."

Tyr ran his hand through his red locks. "If Wolos were to be brought back to life, he would be able to lead the dead from the Netherworld. Aenar would be safe again."

"Zyem will tear the Kaligula brothers to pieces," Alyona said, turning back to face her mother. "They will not be allowed to pass over the bridge. Marheena would not allow it."

Erzebeth said. "We will see. Though, Tyran and Drast will undoubtedly fail if Kaelandur is plunged into the Ash Tree and the Likhyi are released."

Branimir gripped the hilt at his belt, and began making his way up the staircase. He gripped the rose given to him by Lada in his other hand. An orange light seared between the double-doors as they opened on their own. Branimir gulped. "Then let's go ask the gods how to destroy Kaelandur."

Chapter XX

Branimir could not guess how much time had come and gone since they entered the gate and started up the never-ending staircase. Not only did the sun stay at its apex over the City of the Gods, giving constant warmth and light in every crevice, but also something kept his stomach from hunger and his body from exhaustion. Every time his foot lifted and fell, his body seemingly had forgotten he repeated the same movement a hundred times before. In the beginning, the mundane climbing had been a game; but after a couple hours, he lost interest in playing. He stopped counting the stairs after reaching the thousands. Yet he felt no aching in his back, legs, or feet. Bran supposed he should be thankful for being away from the snow and wind on the mountain pass, but the monotony was wearing on him.

"You would think," he said, after several hours, "with all the magic in this place they would find a quicker way to the top. I bet the Svet's gateway takes them straight to the top of the peak."

Alyona ambled along behind him, responding with a dull tone. "Close. You arrive on the seventh tier, near the temple."

"Nine Lands. And no one thought to put one of those gateways at the bottom of these stairs?" Branimir asked, gazing at the rocky wall on either side of them. He was certain a dragon could fit on the staircase without discomfort. Which did not matter much, considering the dragon could fly to the peak of the mount.

Tyr held the smile on his face, climbing besides Branimir on the right. "Bah! Can you imagine when we go back down to leave? I bet we will lose our minds going back down these stairs." Tyr swung his giant arms back and forth as he climbed. Branimir hardly noticed he had six fingers anymore. "How about if we were to arrive through the doorway up there? And then, when we went to leave, we were faced with *this*? At least, we know, right?" Tyr rumbled, peering over his shoulder for an instant. The bottom of the winding staircase could no longer be seen. "I might consider flinging myself down the steps, or simply lying down and rolling. Maybe the gods will spare me if I crack my head."

Alyona's dry tone answered the unasked question. "No, they will not."

The smile faded from Tyr's face. "Well, I will not try to sprout wings and fly then."

Branimir looked at Alyona worriedly as she tread beside him on the left. Her mood had been sour since meeting her mother. She kept quiet for the most part, except when she had a stinging remark aimed to steal away their mirth.

He tried to rationalize Alyona's anger. He remembered, early on, when he first met Erzebeth in Arkaim. She always presented herself as having a mind for survival. From what Bran knew of Alyona, she likely shared this same trait with her mother.

"If you would like to turn into a bat, or something, and fly to the top, I could hold onto your clothes. You don't have to climb all these stairs with us," he offered.

"Yes, I do," she muttered, rubbing at her small nose. "I am not able to change forms here. Not only is it forbidden, but it is also impossible. We cannot wield any type of magic, even Koldovstvo."

"Really?" Branimir rubbed his chin in thought. The silver band of Faegrim touched the edge of his cheek.

Alyona pressed on. "Climbing the steps is supposed to show your resolve. Demonstrate your dedication to the gods."

"Because traveling a thousand miles through wind and snow, and facing demons along the way, is not enough," Tyr joked.

Branimir smiled, pulling at the edge of his nose. "Wait a second. If it is to test your will, why do the Svet get a gateway leading to the top?" he asked.

"Have you ever seen a centaur try to meander up a flight of stairs?" Tyr hooted with laughter. The image danced in Branimir's head, forcing him into a fit of laughter. One wrong footing and they would be sliding and stumbling back to the bottom. He imagined the effort of snaking up the stairs would be tenfold for a Svet.

Alyona smirked, walking on by them.

Tears touched the corners of Branimir's eyes. He leaned down to hold onto a step to keep from falling, doing the best to stifle his giggles. "Oh, it was funny, Alyona," he said. She ignored him. Shaking his head, Branimir cleared his throat to be more serious. "So, if Eisliev were to attack the City of the Gods, he would not be able to use Koldovstvo?"

Alyona shrugged. She clenched her fists, caught up in her own thoughts. Branimir noticed Tyr put a bit more space between them. Alyona did not seem to notice. Her tone was grave. "Eisliev cannot come here, Branimir. He has significant power because of Kaelandur. But Kaelandur was made by Koldovstvo, and Koldovstvo is controlled by Marheena."

Branimir piped up with excitement. "So, the gods would kill Eisliev if he came to Iriy? We should have led him here."

Alyona raised an eyebrow in confusion. He was, at least, glad to see a different emotion from the woman. "No. The gods would not do anything of the sort. This is sacred ground." She lastly relaxed her face, trying to find a way to explain. "He simply could not come to Iriy. You may never see Eisliev again if the gods can rid us of Kaelandur."

Tyr dared to open his mouth again. Though, his tenor had lost its joviality. "What do you mean?"

She replied, "Eisliev does not have any purpose on Aenar without Kaelandur. He was sent here by Marheena to release the Old-dark from the Ash Tree by using the dagger. If he cannot break the chains, I would hope he would return to the Netherworld."

"Hope?" Tyr questioned. "From what I can gather, there is no place in the Netherworld for him. He will more than likely terrorize Aenar with his unchecked power."

Alyona frowned. "Pray it does not come to that."

Hours came and went before the three of them reached the top of the stone stairs and the second gate, which only stood a hair shorter than the first. As before, the rose in Branimir's hand proved to be the key to Iriy. An auburn light illuminated through the center crack and soon the massive iron doors creaked open to allow them entrance.

Alyona steered the way, unwavering in her task to take them to the top of the summit. Tyr, who had never been to Iriy, ogled alongside Branimir, examining the splendor of the city.

He could not steal away his gaze from the exhibition of exaltation.

The double-doors opened to a three-tiered, stone fountain sitting in the center of an extended walkway. Branimir could not help but stare at the craftsmanship. The stone had been chiseled to reflect a man wearing a crown, tipped with nine flames, kneeling in the swirling pool. The crystal blue water sprouting from the top of the fountain dropped forty feet to sift through the man's hands before returning to the rippling water. He did not see a single chip or scratch in the fountain, nor a single flake of dirt or dust.

"What is this?" Branimir asked in awe.

Alyona stopped for a moment, twisting her head. "The gods in all their *glory* are no strangers to vanity. This is Perom, the Thunder-Bearer, the Creator. He rules here on Iriy while Svarog remains in the Kingdom. Naturally, he would be certain the first image seen in Iriy is one of himself."

"The Creator? I had always wondered who made the Kras," Branimir said.

"Perom made every race, Branimir. Did your people never teach you your origins?" Tyr asked. Branimir shook his head, thinking of how his people had their history stripped from them by the Highborn in centuries past. Tyr gestured at Perom's crown. "Nine flames for the nine races on Aenar: Anshedar, Vucari, Stuhia, Ispolini, Svet, Uvil, Lilitu, Arkono, and the Kras."

"By the Nine Lands," Branimir muttered, gawking at the bold chin and fiery gaze of Perom. "I do not even know all of those different people." His rotated around to gaze at the city from the top of the spiraling mountain down to his feet.

Branimir nearly jumped when he realized the paved stone under his feet had been hewn with as much care as the fountainhead. Portrayals of animals running among forests and fields had been carved the length of the path in all directions.

Alyona ambled off to the left. "This way. These gates are staggered out along each wall on each level. It should not take long to reach the top, and then we can speak with Perom."

Tyr rolled his eyes, grunting, "Bah! You act as though rushing through Iriy might grant us an audience quicker. The gods will surely do things in their own time, as they always have. Let us relish in this place. It will be a story we will want to tell someday."

Branimir did not miss the heavy look in Alyona's eyes as she looked over her shoulder. She half-nodded, but started walking.

His gut told him that Alyona was holding back from saying something more. Chewing the inside of his lip nervously, he followed her, determined to not disrupt their walk anymore.

Alyona ignored the ivory temples and stone shrines built into the rock. Multiple archways had been cut out, laden with peculiar vines growing from the stone. Under them were entrance ways leading into the rock, beckoning Branimir to explore. His tongue quivered with wanting to ask what lay beyond each ingress; yet he said nothing and kept his feet behind Alyona.

The three of them trudged along through five more iron gates. Each rise gave way to what may have been grander sculptures of the gods and goddesses in their many known triumphs. Branimir begged to ask questions of the tales told through the sculptures, but again, he stayed quiet and simply marveled. He knew of a few select deities in the pantheon from those he journeyed alongside, but rarely had the time to hear the tales in their entirety.

But here, in Iriy, the history of the cycles and creation were mesmerizingly displayed to withstand the test of time, forever to be speculated upon. Walking along the streets was like strolling through antiquity.

As the orangish light seared through the seventh gate and the doors swung open, the red rose given to him from Lada dispelled from his fingers into ashes. He looked at his empty hand in bewilderment. "I thought we had two more gates to pass through before reaching the top."

Alyona guided them through the door. "We have reached the echelon of the lesser gods. I suspect we must wait here until Perom gives us permission to advance beyond the next gate." She cleared her throat in annoyance. "I thought he would be more eager to see us, considering the fate of the world is at stake."

"I am telling you, the gods do things in their own time, Alyona," Tyr said plainly.

"I know that, Tyr," Alyona snapped. "But this is not a normal instance."

Branimir precipitously turned about, looking through the wide streets and chiseled structures. Everything they crossed by had been beautifully created, but none filled the streets to know the greatness. "You are right. Where is everyone? Why has all this been created if none are here to appreciate it?"

Alyona swallowed her irritation. Her tone suddenly held as much awe as regret. "Many Stuhians and Vucari once lived here together in days long past, but after the Stuhians sought the power of Koldovstvo, everything changed. You may consider the divide to be the first breaking of the world, when mortals and immortals were no longer welcome in each other's company." Her eyes filtered down to Kaelandur at Branimir's belt, despondently shaking her head. "Aenar will not survive a second breaking."

Movement in the road caught Branimir's eye. Based on Alyona's abrupt silence and Tyr's sudden kneeling, he knew they also saw the same sights. Though, Branimir had no inclination of falling to his knees.

A hundred paces away approached three figures. The first was a beautiful woman, taller than Alyona, with high cheek bones and long, red flowing hair. Her gown of gold and purple flowed across her frosty skin. The second, standing as tall as Tyr, had the body of a man, dressed in greens with gold lining, but had the head of a stallion. Branimir hardly had time to gawk at the strange being before he noticed the angled horse ears flip against the brown, stringy mane hanging down his back; the creature's black eyes reflected at Branimir. The horse-man reached out to touch the other man, clouded in black robes, with tufts of blood-red hair bursting from the edges of the hood. His icy eyes attuned to his surroundings along with the redheaded woman.

The three stopped in whatever conversation they may have been sharing along with their casual footfalls down the street.

"Dorofej," Branimir whispered, hardly recognizing the young, black mage, standing between the unnamed god and goddess. Branimir, in his excitement, scarcely noticed the divine light emanating from beneath the woman and horse-man's skin. He ran to embrace him, leaving Alyona and Tyr stooping on the paved stone. "Dorofej!"

A foolhardy grin split Dorofej's face as Branimir wrapped his arms around the waist of his old friend, almost knocking him off-balance. Dorofej patted Branimir on the back lightly, speaking in soft undertones. "Welcome to Iriy, the City of the Gods, Branimir Baran. At last, you have come; and Kaelandur, you have brought."

"I am so sorry we did not come to save you at Melkorka. I wanted to," Branimir said with batted breath. "I cannot believe you lived."

"Give it any more thought, you should not," Dorofej said, pulling back to study Branimir. "I say, we have both had exceedingly difficult circumstances, yes? But, to the future, we must keep our attention. More difficult decisions are yet to come, I am afraid."

The horse-man whickered behind Dorofej, stealing away Branimir's long-winded response, and his question as to why Dorofej had come without him.

"I know," Dorofej said in response to the creature, a hint of sadness in his tone. He folded his arms from beneath his robes.

The redheaded woman folded her colorful gowns and glided closer to gaze at Branimir. Her long, pale fingers reached for him from under her wide sleeves; her touch was as cold as icicles against his cheek. Time slowed as she traced a fingernail from his chin to his eye, her emotionless eyes locking onto him. Branimir was spellbound, transfixed on the center pitch of her iris. He braced himself against a lucid vision dancing in front of him like images in a fire. Beyond her eye, he thought he saw the warped Ash Tree, its roots severed and limbs burnt black. The tree's color faded, sitting in gurgling waters under grey clouds. The luscious vines and fruits once ornamenting the Ash Tree had decayed, oozing slime and death. The stench of its rot clung to Branimir's nose. The familiar screeching of demons echoed.

And then, the image was gone, and only the woman lingered. She withdrew her finger, but a thought surfaced in Branimir's head.

'Speak again, we will, Branimir Baran. Learn, we will, if a world broken by the spirit of men may be saved by those thought the slighter.'

A burst of flashing light like the sun whipping through a crown of treetops pronounced the woman's sudden exit. The horse-man disappeared with her.

Branimir dizzily grabbed his head, hearing Alyona and Tyr whispering behind him. He looked to Dorofej for an explanation. "Who was that?"

"Ah," Dorofej said, seemingly unaware of the revelations that had been dancing in Branimir's head, "that was the honored

Marheena, Goddess of the Netherworld, and her brother, Gero, the God of Trickery, Harvest, and a number of equally dreary titles."

Branimir's chest tightened at the thought of the Frozen Witch, the Goddess of Nightmares, touching him. She may have cursed him. "Marheena?" he gulped. "Being in her presence was nothing like when we met Lada."

"You would have seen Lada in the dale, yes?" Dorofej smiled with amusement. "A sweet thing she is, but she does like to enchant mortals with her charm and beauty."

"Next time you see Gero," Branimir added, "you should tell him what evils the thieves guild in Eldhaft does in his name. They killed Adamus, Dorofej."

Dorofej rested his hand on Branimir's shoulder. "Care what men do in their name, the gods do not, Branimir. Told you this many times, I have, yes?"

"But they dishonor the gods," Bran said. "The thieves kill for Gero, the Kadari for Dahz, the Svet for Rujan, the Ariadneans for Czern, the Vucari for Wolos..." Branimir ran out of breath.

"Only themselves do they dishonor," Dorofej replied, cutting him off, "and whether their actions are fated, or not, will be determined when death comes to them, yes? I say, death has its purpose but only if we restore balance."

"What do you mean?" Branimir asked.

Dorofej did not answer. Tyr spoke aloud, approaching first with Alyona at his rear. "Branimir, you ought to show respect when you are in the attendance of the gods. Not all will take kindly to you running amuck."

The black mage grinned at the sight of the Ispolini and the Kadari. Branimir did not need any other sign to finally give peace to the thought that Alyona had been truthful with him about her purpose.

"Done the deeds you both have, I could not," Dorofej said, his blue eyes swelling with gratitude. "Not only do I give my many thanks, but through your actions, I hope the world will, too."

"We will see," Alyona said dryly, her purplish eyes meeting Dorofej's with strain. Branimir noticed Dorofej wrinkle his wide nose in consideration, noticing Alyona's disagreeable mood. Certainly, Dorofej could see she withheld words from slipping off her tongue.

"I say," Dorofej reached for his beard to tug only to find his clean-shaven chin, "what news do you bring from the road?"

Alyona answered, placing her hands on her hips, "The Kadari have been cleansed from Aenar. Falmagon fell at Gavlok. Any remnants are scattered like dust in the sand, but the worship of Dahz will fade less eagerly in the lands of men."

"Told me of their defeat, Marheena did," Dorofej said, blinking. "Roaming the Netherworld, Falmagon is, already being twisted into a devilish wraith, bound to death." He pressed his thin lips together in certainty.

Branimir's throat tightened at the thought. "That is horrible. I cannot say I wish that fate on any man, no matter how evil."

"Wish it on him, too, I would not," Dorofej shockingly claimed. "And, an afterlife Falmagon eternally deserved, it is not." The black mage shook his head. "I fear Dagmar's fate was not so grand, yes?"

"Dagmar fell at Eldhaft, by his own hand…" Branimir said. "He used Kaelandur."

Dorofej did not appear surprised. "I say, his wrath will be greater than Eisliev's. Fortunately, according to Marheena, drifting through the Netherworld, Dagmar still is." He slowly uncrossed his arms. "But what of Eisliev Kluk? Somewhere on Aenar, he is."

"We sent him back to the Netherworld when we escaped Harrowhal," Branimir replied. "We have not seen him again."

"Strange, indeed," Dorofej said. "Expected him to pursue the dagger tenfold, I would have."

"As did I," Alyona said. "Is he not in the Netherworld with Dagmar?"

Dorofej shook his head. "No."

Tyr frowned. "What reason would keep him from chasing Branimir and Kaelandur? His desire for Dagmar's blood shadowed him into the afterlife, but with his enemy dead, nothing should hold him back."

"Would he return to torment Dagmar in the Netherworld?" Branimir asked. "He never did exact his revenge with Dagmar taking his own life."

"For certain, I cannot be." Dorofej rubbed his chin as though he missed his beard. "The pact made with Eisliev at Melkorka was inexplicably upheld by Alyona, yes? Agreed to help slay Dagmar and Falmagon, the three of us did; and done, it has been."

Branimir rattled his memory, recalling what Alyona said about Dorofej talking their way out of being killed at Melkorka. "Does that mean if the Old-dark are released and destroy Aenar, the three of you will be spared?"

"Hm," Dorofej grunted.

"Only if Eisliev holds up to his end of the bargain," Tyr muttered.

"I do not understand why you would make such a deal with him, Dorofej," Branimir said. "He could not have killed you anyway. Dagmar told me you could only be killed with Kaelandur."

Dorofej scratched his nose, looking to Alyona and Tyr with sympathy. "Yet, kill these two, he would." As though a thought unexpectedly gripped his senses, Dorofej pulled back his robe and revealed a vial hanging from a leather loop on his belt. Branimir caught sight of several other vials too. "I say, Alyona, you have aged considerably since last we met. A vial, saved for you, I did."

The black mage handed the Kadari the flask of the Water of Life. She reached out and took it with an appreciative smile, clutching it to her chest. "Thank you, Dorofej."

"Now," Dorofej shooed them with his hands, "go wander about and find a place to rest, yes? Branimir and I have much to say before we speak with the Thunder-Bearer."

Dorofej tapped his lips with an anxious tick while Tyr and Alyona gracelessly accepted their forced dismissal and continued down the road. Branimir watched them only for a second before turning back to Dorofej, who watched him with enough intensity to shatter the ground at his feet.

"Will they come with us when we talk to the gods?" Branimir looked for a place to tuck his hands, and finally hooked his thumbs on his pants.

Dorofej hummed in his throat, suggesting he did not care if they did or not. "Searched for you many times in Klukas, I did, and always hidden from me, you were. Whilst in Melkorka or traveling to Iriy, discover your whereabouts, I could not." He raised his red eyebrows knowingly, stepping closer. "*Even* when I walked along Sulanna or Farthr on the opposite side of the veil, see you among them, I could not."

Branimir pulled the silver band from his finger, and handed it to Dorofej's already reaching hand. "The ring is called Faegrim. I took it from Eisliev after his death at Melkorka. He used it to control my mind when we were in Cavell before they took Bohumir from us." Branimir let go of the piece of jewelry, feeling a sense of loss. The ring had not been with him as long as Ojenek, but it unknowingly kept him safe for the past year. "It was not until Dagmar found us at Eldhaft that I learned Faegrim also kept me hidden from Klukas."

"A blessing that you had it, yes? Right about this trinket, Tyr had been," Dorofej said, rolling the circlet in his finger in wonder. "I say, many artifacts were made in the ageless days before the Stuhia learned of the dangers of mixing magic with the mundane. Unaccounted and forgotten, many still are."

"You mean that you do not know all of them?" Branimir asked with a half-smile. He supposed part of him believed that Dorofej knew everything.

"Know of Faegrim, I did not," Dorofej said. "Knowing what more may lie in the folds of time, I cannot say. Yet a shield to ultimately defend against our fates would be welcomed, yes?"

Branimir nodded, not missing the unnerving tone. "I also have brought you something more," Branimir said, reaching into his pocket. "I took this from Dagmar after he had fallen. Your book, the Varkolak." He presented the magically folded book, currently the size of his hand. With Koldovstvo, the book could be unfolded to be a weighty tome, brimming with Dorofej's recorded secrets.

He reached to touch the book and then withdrew with a satisfied smile. He curled his fingers into a fist, pulling his hands behind his back to keep himself from taking the volume. "A thief, you should have been, Branimir. Ever clever and wise, you truly are." Dorofej grinned, taking a breath. He scanned the statues and chiseled stone walls that surrounded them momentarily before continuing. "You keep the Varkolak until there is need, yes?"

Branimir crumpled his brow. He did not understand why Dorofej would cling to the newly acquired Faegrim while discarding his sacred text. Though, he had been around Dorofej long enough to know one question would only lead the black mage into riddles which would rarely lead to a sensible answer.

Bit by bit, Branimir tucked the Varkolak back into his pocket.

With a self-assured smile, Dorofej motioned for him to follow. His red hair bounced with each footfall as they headed toward the eighth gate.

"Will Perom see us so soon?" Branimir asked.

"Perom?" Dorofej repeated. "Oh yes, we will go see the Thunder-Bearer straightway. But eventually meeting with Svarog, the Grandfather of the Gods, we will be. From Thrice Ten Kingdom, he has come, to grant you audience, Branimir."

"The gods must be concerned about the Old-dark, if Svarog is coming all the way to Iriy, right? Alyona told me that Perom usually rules of Iriy, and oversees Aenar," Branimir said.

Dorofej hummed in his throat, not giving a clear answer to Branimir's question. "Keeper of Kowin the Deathless, Svarog is, and whether to release Kowin back into the world of the living, he must decide. I say, the Likhyi give him reason to consider doing so."

"Alden spoke of Kowin," Branimir said. "He said that the God of War had the power to call back Kowin to fight."

"He does," Dorofej said, "but bless the request, Svarog must. An easy decision, freeing Kowin, it is not."

"You are telling me that the God of War has already asked for Kowin's release then," Branimir said.

"Indeed, Svathevit has," Dorofej confirmed, "and your witness to Svarog will weigh heavily on his final decision, yes?"

"Why mine?" Branimir asked in shock. "Why should I give balance to the mind of a god?"

Dorofej looked down at Branimir with reverence. "I say, a fair question to ask. But even when asking, a humble heart, you have exposed; and the answer to the question, too, we have found."

Branimir breathed deep and scratched at his thin hair. He did not think he was so kind that he should sway gods in their thinking. Any mortal, by definition, did not have the wisdom of gods; and thus, they were ill-equipped to make godly decisions.

"Ah." Dorofej scratched at his head, seeing the eighth gate ahead of them on the path. "Time, we are wasting. I say, the tale of Kowin the Deathless, you must know, yes?" The black mage hurried his speech before Bran could reply. "Alive, he is not; yet, neither is he dead. The magic Kowin wields is effortless and eternal like that of the Old-dark, yes?"

"He wields Koldovstvo?" Branimir asked.

Dorofej moved his mouth without words for a moment, searching for the best way to explain. "Kowin the Deathless *is* Koldovstvo. If the Likhyi were one, he would be the deadly amalgamation, yes?"

Branimir worked a finger in his ear. He must have misheard. His mouth dried. "Then why would Svarog consider releasing him on Aenar?"

The black mage went on, "The capacity to trap the Likhyi back into the Ash Tree, should they escape, or another prison, he has. Yet..." Dorofej gritted his teeth, his voice like ice, "if the Ash Tree dies, the Likhyi escape, and our gods die. Rule absolutely over Aenar, to forge the world however he would see fit, Kowin could, yes?"

"That is terrible!" Branimir finished. "How could we defeat such power?"

Dorofej tilted his chin, arriving at his point. "Neither blade, nor fire, nor anything natural can kill Kowin. Hidden is his soul, inside a needle, which is in an egg, which is in a duck, which is in a hare, which is in a chest, which Svarog has buried somewhere in this world," Dorofej said. Branimir scrunched his nose at the babbled explanation. Dorofej said, "Control over Kowin, Svarog has, as long as he holds power over the soul; but, if ever Kowin must know death, the needle must be broken."

Branimir grabbed Dorofej's robes, stopping him outside the eighth gate. The Stuhia turned to face him, holding more fear than Branimir had ever seen in his old master. "Why are you telling me this, Dorofej?"

The black mage clenched his jaw, pulling a red rose free from beneath his robes and holding it to the gates. The magical light separated the double-doors. As they opened, his voice trembled, "Remember, you must. Promise me, you will remember."

Branimir hesitated, letting go of Dorofej. "I promise."

Chapter XXI

The streets of Iriy remained empty. Branimir's chest swelled with sorrow considering the size and beauty of the City of the Gods, and then comparing it to the haunting silence that inhabited the place. Nowhere could he find yelling merchants, laughter or conversation, or even the sound of shuffling feet. Iriy was dead.

Dorofej guided them to the Great Hall of the Gods, *Koranitsa*, sitting on the edge of the zenith. Branimir turned from the sanctuary to look at the peak of Iriy. Branimir could see the final gate and the utmost level beyond the circular black wall, separating them from the top sphere of the summit. Somewhere beyond the wall awaited Svarog, the Lord of Lords.

Dorofej's words stuck with Branimir, suggesting the High God of Wisdom sought his counsel. Though, Branimir could not imagine what he might say. He simply wanted Kaelandur destroyed and the world saved. He supposed the gods had the power to make Aenar right again. Branimir wished he knew why they had not already; they surely did not need his permission.

Dorofej promised he would speak to Svarog soon. But first he was to be presented before Perom in Koranitsa. The enclosed sanctuary was positioned just east of the eighth gate, towering over all other edifices on this sphere. Branimir was certain he could have seen the magnificence of Koranitsa while standing at the base of the mount, but nothing could compare to standing so close.

Koranitsa had twenty-seven, ivory columns, standing thirty-foot tall, around the building, with a single, stone archway leading directly into the building. Sculptures of five gods were built at equal height of the columns, guarding the front of the temple. Branimir had seen similar images of the statues before in other places in the world to know who the figures represented.

From left to right, in a row, he first recognized Dahz the Lightbringer, with his pointed beard, grasping his hammer, Mulafell. Second in line, crouched Czern, the Grey-Clad, wearing his stone crown, *Maelifell*, and carrying his scythe, much like the statues found at the catacombs in Garain'l. And then, Perom stood with his thunder-axe held above the nine-pointed crown, depicting the races of his creation. The fourth was a beast with horns, three times thicker than the hilt of sword, balanced on hooves, and holding a spear like a shepherd's stick. Branimir could only guess the god to be Wolos, God of the Dead, and Protector of the Eternal Spring.

The final god, he could not place with the long, curling beard reaching his knees. Wings sprouted from the god's back, and, in his hands, he carried a long horn and trident.

"Who is that, Dorofej?" Branimir asked as they approached the effigies.

"Strega the Powerful, Ancestor of the Nine Winds, and Defeater of Marheena," Dorofej said, folding his arms inside his black robes.

"Strega's Deep," Branimir said with a smile, referring to the waters surround Maharia. "He is the god who governs the sea."

Dorofej dipped his head. "Mm. Seafarers would say his might is vaster than the other four, yes? But the measure of one god against another is but another way mortals divide each other, listening little to simple reason, even when told otherwise time and time again." Dorofej expounded on the thought. "Without each part working to be whole, the body cannot function. In the patterned skein, a thread each mortal is, and unraveled they have always been. I say, mortals are untiring in their effort to pursue war instead of peace, disagreement instead of harmony, hate instead of love, or opposition instead of friendship. Fearful, I am, that the world was never meant to be mended while mortals inhabit it."

Branimir swallowed. "If our flaws lead us to the breaking of the world, why would Perom create us to be imperfect?"

Dorofej ascended the steps to the temple. "I say, you cannot know real love without first loving imperfection. The appreciation of beauty may be fleeting, but never will you grasp a greater sense of meaning in this life, whether mortal or otherwise, yes?"

"I think I understand," Branimir said.

Dorofej smiled, gesturing for him to follow. "Come."

Whereas the sun shined endlessly over Iriy, giving light to the streets, the inside of Koranitsa did not have any such lighting. Of course, Branimir, barely noticed the change, examining the room without difficulty.

The room was as large as he imagined, capable of holding hundreds of people. More columns were positioned equally around the edges of the grand room, much like the twenty-seven outside the temple, to hold up the vaulted ceiling. He almost expected the ceiling and walls to be painted with grand colors and images of the gods, but they had been left completely blank, colored a whitish grey. The center of the floor, however, was decorated with patterned colors that did not make any sense to Branimir. The purples and reds, blues and greys, and yellows swirled and overlapped in exhausting complexity. Time did not seem to wear on anything in Iriy.

"Wait much longer, we should not," he said.

Branimir took Dorofej's word and followed him to the center of the room.

Five hours later, he and Dorofej retired to sitting positions on the floor. Branimir walked the inside perimeter of Koranitsa several dozen times until the mind-numbing task had worn on him to the point he thought he might cry from absolute boredom. He spent the last hour tracing the colors on the floor with his fingers, while

Dorofej sat cross-legged against one of the far columns with his eyes glazed. He could only assume Dorofej entered Klukas, but what he had gone to observe, Branimir could not guess.

If time were a weapon, the gods wielded it with perfection. Branimir had no rational defense against time. Due to the enchantment of Iriy, he was kept from knowing tiredness, or hunger, or any bodily ailment. Instead, he had been abandoned in silence with his rootless, banal musings. His mind wandered, thinking of Alden, Sulanna, Adamus, and so many others. Many traveled with him over the ages, and now, most had been lost or forgotten. He did not want to remember any longer; he did not want to be waiting in this abandoned temple. At this point, he would have welcomed a headache to add a bit of zest to this sapping reality. Yet he had no choice but to endure.

"By the Nine Lands, it must be dull to be a god," Branimir muttered. Even at a whisper, his voice rebounded off the stone walls of Koranitsa.

Dorofej stirred with a grunt. "I say, what is that? Come, have they?"

Branimir poked aimlessly at the painted colors under his stretched-out feet. "No, Dorofej. My apologies for waking you."

"Quite alright," Dorofej said, adjusting his robes around himself. "Perhaps, something of import, I can share with you to pass the time."

"Tell me why you did not come to meet me on the road, and you rushed to Iriy without me," Branimir said finally, his hands shaking with anticipation. "Why did you send Alyona and Tyr, but never come yourself?"

"Clear, I thought the answer was," Dorofej said, folding his hands in his lap. "I say, it was too dangerous to be near you with Eisliev, Dagmar, or Falmagon in pursuit."

"You were afraid of dying?" Branimir accused.

Dorofej's blue eyes widened with surprise. "Afraid of death, I no longer am, Branimir. For a long while, I have been, but we all must die, yes?" He swallowed, attempting to form his next words.

"Rightly fastened to Kaelandur's fate, my life is, but yours is not. I say, if I had come for you, and was struck down, you would have fallen with me."

"You stayed away from me to protect me?" Branimir asked in disbelief. "I could have still died apart from what happens to Kaelandur."

"True," Dorofej conceded. "Yet, another threat on your life, I would have been."

Branimir wrung his hands together, watching Dorofej carefully. The black mage had been eager to share knowledge with Branimir since they reunited only hours ago, whereas before, Dorofej always kept his secrets well hidden. Either he had an awakening at Melkorka, or he believed he was going to die. Branimir hoped it was the former. "What would have happened if Falmagon would have won? What if he destroyed Kaelandur and killed us?"

Dorofej sighed, readjusting himself against the hard flooring. "Many things, I am afraid. Erzebeth may still have my great-grandsons attempt to resurrect Wolos, yes? But, continue to weaken the Ash Tree, Falmagon and his Kadari would have, which would have strengthened the Old-dark until the success or failure of Wolos's re-birthing."

"But the Old-dark¬ could not have been granted their full freedom," Branimir said.

"No. Not unless another means of destroying the Ash Tree came into existence, yes?" Dorofej replied. "But Falmagon's closed-minded teachings would have continued to infect the hearts and minds of men, ridding them of free will for his own gain. Some may consider the Kadari to be righteous in solely aligning mortals under the Lightbringer; but, inhumane, I believe it to be." The black mage gestured to the temple they sat inside. "Many other paths exist for mortals to explore, yes?" Dorofej returned his hands to his lap. "Come, what else?"

"Um," Branimir scratched his head. "Tell me about the Old-dark."

"Ah, yes," Dorofej said. "A topic worth exploring in more detail, yes? Eight Likhyi, there are, who were long ago trapped in the Ash Tree by Kowin the Deathless at the direction of the gods found in the modern world."

"The Old-dark are gods, too?" Branimir asked.

"What the Likhyi are precisely, I cannot say, but believe them to be ancient gods, some do," Dorofej said. "I say, the same could be said of Kowin the Deathless; though, what he is exactly, I also do not know."

Branimir pressed. "What do you know about the Likhyi?"

"Remember Kowin is Koldovstvo, yes? Still, a manifestation of each of the eight cruxes of Koldovstvo, the Old-dark are: void, primal, profane, sacred, fire, sky, stone, and sea. Elements of the world, these are," the black mage said, rubbing his pointed chin. "Profane, the Likhyi was, who we encountered at Garain'l, and void, the Likhyi was, who Farthr had said to have found at Shayol Domier."

Branimir hesitantly touched Kaelandur at his belt. The Likhyi who ruled over profane magic was trapped within the blade.

Dorofej continued, "Where the others may be emerging, I wish I knew; though, no defense do I know to shield humanity from their wrath. Know the extent of their strength, I do. For, fed by one of these elements, each Stuhian man or woman's bloodline is, giving them a taste of the power of the Likhyi."

"From Marheena?" Branimir concluded with a raised eyebrow. "Marheena took the power of Koldovstvo from the Likhyi, and gave it to the Stuhians."

"Hm. Well, different traits of the Likhyi, each of the prevailing gods possess. I say, whether it be creation, or magic, or the turn of seasons, the gods see the phases of life completed," Dorofej paused, finally nodding, "but yes, through Marheena, the Stuhia spring their magic. All Stuhians can touch the primary elements of fire, sky, stone, and sea; but, allotted only one of the secondary elements, we are. The strength of our blood determines the amount of life drained from our being, yes?"

Branimir narrowed his eyes at Dorofej. "Alyona told me the Kaligula bloodline is bound to void magic, and yet, you also use sacred magic. Are those both not secondary elements?"

"Yes, they are," Dorofej said, a smile forming at the corner of his mouth. "I say, when I still sat on the Carian Council—when I had begun transcribing the Varkolak—I sought to complete the dragon-blood ritual to heighten my power. Though, seek an ordinary dragon, as many might, I did not. In secret, *Zywey*, the gold-plated dragon, I slaughtered, and her sacred blood, I consumed." Branimir stared in amazement at the black mage. Dorofej returned the gaze with endless interest, and then rolled his eyes. "Pleased by the slaughter of his precious Zywey, Wolos was not."

"I would think not." Branimir frowned.

Dorofej closed his icy blue eyes, leaning his head back against the column. "Young and restless, I was. If I had known about the *Alatir Stone* before, I would have sought it instead, yes? Forever, it keeps you safe from disease and injury and aging."

Branimir's jaw dropped at the prospect of another shiny stone, brimming with magic. "Do you have the Alatir Stone now, Dorofej?"

He kept his eyes closed, despondently shaking his head, speaking mellifluously, "Located somewhere in the Netherworld, it is. Searched for the stone, I did, while we trekked about the frozen wasteland, but never was it revealed to me. Perchance, Zyem holds it at the Kalinov Bridge, yes?"

A crack of lightning near the entranceway knocked Branimir back on his buttocks in fright, and even sent Dorofej scuttling away from the door leading outside.

Suddenly, none other than Perom, the Lord of Aenar, appeared from the thunderbolt, standing nearly twenty-foot tall with his thunder-axe held over his head at an arc. His eyes crackled like thunderclouds, his face like stone; even his pointed, copper beard beneath his silvery hair appeared unyielding. He shielded the exit to the outside street, his dark skin rippling with muscle, scrutinizing Branimir and Dorofej beneath him. The nine-pointed flamed crown on his head fervently burned. Branimir could do little but stare in awe, his skin prickling.

The moment should have remained staggering, but Branimir's attention was drawn from Perom. Dahz, the Lightbringer, emerged from a gateway forming from the stone wall, riding on his sun chariot, Mioengi, pulled by the oversized goat-stag with flaming feet and fiery eyes. In a fluid motion, he bounded from the back, clutching Mulafell, while sending the chariot flying across the temple through a gateway arising suddenly on the other wall. Flames rippled from the corners of his eyes, standing at equal height of Perom.

Branimir cowered away from the celebrated god of the Kadari only to bump into Dorofej.

From the opposing wall, where the chariot exited, materialized Strega, God of Wind and Water, from bristling smoke and cloud. His long, white beard rolled across the floor in front of him, running the length of the floor, causing Branimir to briskly scoot the other way. He flipped the trident in his hand, the ethereal weapon's ends emerging and disappearing through the walls of the sanctuary without making physical contact. He, too, reached the towering heights of Koranitsa— standing thirty-feet tall—bespeaking of his divine presence.

And then came Czern, the God of Darkness, hobbling through the door, maintaining the appearance of an old man with a wrinkled face. He outwardly ignored the other gods' intimidating stances, locking his eyes on Branimir. He hobbled forward with his scythe, using it as a walking stick, remaining wrapped in his bulky, grey robes. His stone crown, Maelifell, sat crooked over his brow as though it had been placed there in haste.

Czern opened his mouth as though he might speak first, but stopped, and wrinkled his nose. He blinked several times, raising a single white eyebrow with a sense of confusion. He seemed to have forgotten how to form words with his tongue.

In the next breath, the other gods and goddesses rallied in a circle behind Branimir. Dorofej eased to his knees next to Branimir, identifying them as they appeared.

"Myestera, the Mother of the Stars," he said, as a dark-haired woman emerged next to Dahz, yet standing at equal height as Czern. Next to Perom materialized another woman, older and in simple clothing. She, too, appeared as a human might, standing humbly before him. "Mokosh, the Weaver," Dorofej identified her, while motioning for Branimir to respectfully stay at his knees. "They have nearly all come, yes?"

Behind them surfaced Marheena, the Frozen Witch, and Gero, the God of Harvest, tilting his stallion head to better see Branimir. Neither needed an introduction. Branimir balanced himself on his shaking knees, turning his eyes away from Marheena. The vision of the dying Ash Tree she placed in his mind left a lasting image.

Lastly came Lada, the Lady of Flowers, in a flash of white glory. Her golden hair flowed behind her with every step she took, bouncing delicately against her white, floral-patterned gown.

The room vibrated with divine power, a low hum ringing in Branimir's pointed ears.

Lada, standing at the height of an Ispolini, glanced over the room at the other deities. The gods did not speak as mortals might, but imprinted their thoughts on Branimir's mind. Sometimes more than one thought would fill his mind at a single time. Strangely, Branimir inherently could identify who spoke, even though not everyone made a signifying gesture.

First spoke Lada, her voice like ringing bells, *'Grievously pressed, we have become. Let us speak plainly as to not confuse the mortals. Be certain your words are known in their tongue.'*

'Present, some still are not,' Perom rustled, his authoritative disposition clear among the other gods. He peered down at Lada. *'Ever late, grows the hour. How much longer should we wait?'*

'Easy, Thunder-Bearer,' mocked the Lightbringer, his voice booming in Branimir's head like horse's hooves. *'Cleansing the mortal does not require Svarog to be here.'*

Perom's face did not reflect his annoyance, but his voice was biting. '*I speak not of Svarog, but of Svathevit the Red. The judgment must be undisputed.*'

Dorofej kept Branimir hunched over with his right hand, peeking through his red locks at the gods. Branimir stayed stooped, while trying to make sense of the conversation.

'*Svathevit has given his sanction,*' Marheena said, her voice cracking like breaking ice, '*else he would not have brought Kowin to be birthed back into the mortal world.*'

'*A mistake,*' Strega mumbled, his white beard waving over his chest as though a breeze blew beneath the stringy, white hairs. Several of the other gods murmured in agreement, while others simply mumbled nonsense.

Marheena spoke louder, '*We must hurry. The wards protecting Iriy are failing.*'

'*What of the Protector of the Eternal Fallows?*' Czern blinked several times, clasping his lips together in a pout. '*Should we not postpone till his homecoming?*'

'*Wolos is dead, Czern.*' Dahz growled, the fire in his eyes igniting. He began speaking before Czern had time to finish the thought. '*Time for your games, we do not have, brother.*'

Czern adjusted the stone crown on his head. '*He may not be pleased to return and find we made a judgment before his rebirthing.*'

'*We cannot give pause and see whether the mortals will resurrect him,*' Perom said definitively. He folded his arms across his chest, the thunder-axe held firmly in his hand. '*You steer the dialogue away from the dispute, Czern. Let us find unanimity quickly and be done.*'

Dahz addressed the gods and goddess, '*I remind you, a ruling on Branimir Baran, son of Hrani, and his unnatural bond to the Likhyi, we give. Be swayed by the fate of the forged weapon, you should not be.*'

Marheena neared closer behind Branimir. '*We need no reminder, Protector of Men. We are not moved by mortal desires. We have not the capacity.*'

Lada's voice purred, pressing them to conclusion, *'The Old-dark has fated Branimir Baran to an untimely, mortal death for his nobility. All in favor of overruling this mortal's bound fate, and re-weaving his life-thread to foster further goodness, speak now.'*

'The Likhyi yet have the power to command fate,' Strega said. *'No argument is there to be had.'*

'Bound to the Old-dark, Branimir Baran, son of Hrani, should never have been,' said Mokosh.

'Remember the grace of the prevailing gods, he should, until death touches him naturally, or comes for us all,' spoke the Lightbringer.

Branimir's mind swirled with the resounded consonance of additional statements, speaking positively of saving him from Kaelandur's fate. He rose slowly on his knees in confusion. Only now did he begin to understand what was happening. He looked to Dorofej for an explanation, but the black mage stayed on his knees, eagerly nodding his head.

This was the real reason Dorofej had come early to Iriy; he had pleaded for Branimir's life.

"You will not destroy Kaelandur?" Branimir spoke aloud, regarding the many gods in their magnificence. "I came to Iriy so you might rid us of this cursed dagger destined to break the world. My life means little in comparison!"

'Kaelandur is not for the gods to remedy,' Perom thundered from above him.

Branimir's mind reeled, dumbfounded. He had come all this way and the gods would do nothing to help them. They would let the world crumble.

'Decided, it has been,' Dahz, the Protector of Men, said with a boom. *'Myestera, purge Branimir Baran of his burden, so we may leave. Kaelandur's magic has weakened the city. The red mage breaches the gates.'*

Branimir twisted in fear, making sense of their words.

The dark-haired Moon Goddess, who Branimir heard much about from Erzebeth in ancient days, glided across the stone flooring and then kneeled at Branimir's side. Her wide eyes met his, filling him with a sense of tranquility that he was unsure he had ever felt before. Perhaps, a long time ago, in the arms of his mother he had felt so serene. Branimir could not be for certain. But he knew the agitation that tightened his chest only moments ago lifted from his body, and quickly drifted to a distant memory.

She hummed a song as elegant as an evening's breeze, soothing him until he wanted nothing more than to lay his head down to sleep. Yet as he peacefully slouched over and closed his eyes, her hand caught his chin, holding him against her lap. Myestera leaned into him, caressing his cheek. Her hand was as soft as a mother's kiss. Without rhyme or reason, Branimir nuzzled into her embrace.

The throbbing began in the back of his skull, trailed down his spine, and churned in his stomach. Surprisingly, he was unflustered by the sharpness burrowing somewhere inside of his skin. The pain was genuine—as real as what he had went through in Harrowhal or The Oaken Bard—and he held no concern.

When the primordial scream tore from his gullet, he believed the sound to have come from a dream. He may have juddered in Myestera's arms; he may have thrashed. He may have bled.

When he opened his eyes again, the recollection regarding the Likhyi being peeled from his essence was a waning thought. Myestera returned him to his knees, and rose to her feet. Her singsong voice echoed inside his skull.

'No longer will you share the fortune of Kaelandur, Branimir Baran, son of Hrani.'

Chapter XXII

Golden light flashed. The Great Hall of the Gods was emptied as swiftly as it had been occupied, save Branimir, Dorofej, and Marheena. The Goddess of the Netherworld lingered, without a word, in the dimness of the temple, watching and waiting, like a looming storm.

Branimir looked at her from the corner of his eye, his hand shaking against the hilt of Kaelandur. He could not understand why the Frozen Witch would stay behind, unless she wanted to kill him now that he had been saved. Warily, he twisted around searching for Perom, or Dahz, or even Strega to demand answers to his questions, but no, the only uncouth deity left was Marheena.

In truth, he feared the Seamstress of Nightmares; she simply touched him and forced him to see the decaying Ash Tree. He did not want to think about what other terrible images she could force into his head. Yet the thought of her holding such power over him only added wood to the fire burning inside of him.

If anything, she was the most blameworthy for all that had befallen him and Dorofej.

Since Melkorka, her schemes left the world on the brink of destruction. Branimir fought Nedezhda and Eisliev, who she sent back; he battled against her hordes of undead, and her battalions of demons. He survived the frozen Netherworld, and he would survive her in this moment, too.

Despite her divinity, and her reputation for malice amongst mortals, Branimir's fury beat against the inside of his chest. He quivered with untamed anger. His vision turned crimson, as blood red as Marheena's flattened hair, clinging to her pale cheeks.

Yet, before he could say a word, her thoughts became his own. She whispered to him as sweetly as a thief might before stealing a coin purse. *'Promised you we would speak, I did, Branimir Baran. Make haste, for time is fleeting.'*

Branimir fumed. "You have made a mistake. You all have made a mistake!" he screamed. "Call back the Thunder-Bearer and the Lightbringer! Bring back those who can make this right. You must destroy Kaelandur before the Ash Tree falls."

"Branimir..." Dorofej started, rising from the stone flooring with a lenient smile. "I say, no mistake has been made."

He did not listen to Dorofej. He could not listen to Dorofej. "The gods must take Kaelandur. Take it and shatter it into a thousand pieces. Save us!"

'Take Kaelandur, I cannot. The dagger is from the world of mortals, crafted by mortals. No more can I touch the dagger than the dagger can touch me.'

"Take it," he repeated. "Please. You are a goddess." He could not believe what she was saying. He blinked the water from his eyes. "You must destroy the dagger."

Marheena flowed tranquilly, closing the distance between herself and Branimir. The gold and purple gown rippled with her rapid movement. She tensed her cheek bones and entered Branimir's mind again.

'Branimir Baran, eliminating the peril of Kaelandur, and giving shape to this world, rests with you and Dorofej Kaligula. The gods script the pages of history; never do we give precedence to what has not yet come to pass.'

"Nine Lands, you don't!" Branimir barked, his inflection demeaning, staring up at the Frozen Witch. He twisted his sadness into further ire. He jerked Kaelandur from his belt, holding it daringly close to Marheena's chest, despite her warning that it could not touch her. "*You* commanded Dorofej to craft this dagger. *You* guided the world to its death! And now, *you* refuse to make amends with those you have wronged with your devilish plots!" Branimir screamed, his voice echoing off the stone walls. Marheena only watched him with utter serenity. He howled, "My friends died because of you!"

Dorofej began to say something to Branimir, but he could not hear it over Marheena's reverberating tone. In fact, he was sure Dorofej stopped talking mid-sentence as though Marheena hushed him partially through whatever he might have been saying.

'Mistake the gods, you do, Branimir Baran. Preserve the wax and wane of the finite, we do: the succession of time, and seasons, and life and death. The Kaligula bloodline unbalanced the scales, and parallel again, they must become.'

"You think the Likhyi will return balance to the world again?" Branimir curled his lip in disgust. Marheena's expression was emotionless. Branimir shook his head. "The Old-dark will cleanse the world of everything you have created."

'As we once cleansed it of all they had created. Sacrifice must be made to keep balance.'

Branimir slowly lowered the dagger to his side, gazing into Marheena's blue irises. His words were more of realizations than questions. "You do not care if you die. Being forgotten means nothing to you. You…you are not truly a part of this world."

'To die is to be bound by time, and therefore, to be mortal. The gods cannot die; the gods are time.' Marheena echoed her reason. *'Either Wolos should be unbound or the Likhyi released.'*

"You rule the Netherworld!" Branimir shouted. "You could release Wolos at any time."

'Imprison him in death, I did not. Mortals made their choice, and now, they must decide if they deserve to stay upon Aenar.'

"You mean Dorofej and I must make a choice," Branimir said, gritting his teeth. "I understand Dorofej's kin have upset the balance of the world, but why must the burden be put on the two of us?"

"I say," Dorofej said, clearing his throat, "one of us must make a choice, Branimir. Kaelandur must be ended, yes?"

"No," Branimir said, turning to Dorofej, "you cannot die." His nose twitched, fighting back tears.

Dorofej's blue eyes watered as well, nodding his head so that his shaggy, red hair bobbed against his ears. His thin lips struggled to form the words. Although Dorofej looked young, Branimir could see the old man with a tasseled beard sadly looking back at him. His icy blue eyes reflected the hearth fire's flame that had long ago given heat to forge Kaelandur. Dorofej never quailed as he now did. His accented tenor quaked with dread. "I have never loved death, but a mistress I must still lay with, she is."

Branimir grabbed his head as though it might withhold his sorrow. He shouted at Marheena. "He cannot die! You cannot keep me from Kaelandur's fate and forsake Dorofej to share it."

Marheena leaned forward, the chill from her body prickling at his skin. *'At Dorofej Kaligula's behest you were shielded from this fate, Branimir Baran. The gods have elected to award his appeal; do not be wasteful of his faith in you.'*

He could not speak at the confirmation of the revelation. Dorofej brought him to Iriy to have the gods heal him from the curse of the Likhyi.

"Branimir," Dorofej said pleadingly, "trust in Erzebeth, we must. She goes to Anaerfell to lead my kin to the Netherworld to give rise to Wolos once again, yes? I say, our tale ends with the destruction of Kaelandur. Saved, the Ash Tree will be."

"Unless they fail, and Marheena entices another to make a weapon to set the Old-dark free," Branimir said. "You would have ended your life for nothing."

"A chance, we must take," Dorofej said. "Without balance, the world will forever be inundated with demons."

"You do not have to die, and Kaelandur does not have to be destroyed. We are safe from Eisliev in Iriy," Branimir argued. "We could stay here indefinitely, or, at least, we could wait to see if

Wolos is reborn. Alyona said he could not step foot inside of these walls—"

The temple flashed with a fiery blue light, illuminating a path to the door leading outside. Immediately, Branimir was forced to his knees by an unseen power pulling him down by the shoulders. At first, he thought Marheena or Dorofej had grabbed a hold of him, but they, too, had dropped to their knees by the same force. With a startled cry, Branimir covered his eyes from the sudden brightness, peering between his fingers as three shadows emerged from the glow, transforming into human figures, as tall as giants.

Although three stood, Branimir could only look upon one. Once his eyes fell on the High God, he could not steer them away, nor did he have the desire. Even without introduction, Branimir knew the god to be Svarog, the Grandfather of the Gods, the Lord of Lords. The recognition came from somewhere deep within his being, potentially known before his own creation.

Svarog, his eyes shrouded in a golden blindfold, cocked his head at them as they knelt. His white beard shamed the long beard of Strega, folded and tied so many times that the hair may have reached across the expanse of Aenar. In his right hand, he clutched a fistful of flaming spears, burning as bright as the blaze silhouetting his white and yellow robes.

His imperious, orotund timbre fell from his lips—unlike the lesser gods, who shared their thoughts in the minds of mortals— and crashed against the walls of Koranitsa as though the very stone could have bled his word and will. "The *Hall of Iredale* is devoid of mortals bearing witness, and the hour has passed. Svathevit the Red has implored for Kowin the Deathless to return to Aenar to stay the balance. Alas, I can see the charge of Dorofej Kaligula has yet to be fulfilled. Will it be so, Branimir Baran, son of Hrani?"

Branimir shook on his knees. In the distance, he thought he could hear the cracking of stone, thunder felling, and wind rustling as strong as the northern gale. Svarog shadowed over him, even at a distance. The sound in Branimir's ear amplified as though the sanctuary let loose the din from the columns holding it sturdy. Branimir felt disoriented, still unable to see those who stood with Svarog, and completely incapable of looking to Dorofej and Marheena. He stammered incoherent words, scarcely understanding what was being asked of him.

As though Svarog saw his confusion, he clarified the task to Branimir. "The magic of Kaelandur will not allow Dorofej Kaligula to die by his own hand. Will you rid him of it, Branimir Baran, son of Hrani?"

Branimir squeezed Kaelandur in his hand, realizing Svarog never wanted him to bear witness with his words, but by his actions. "No!" Branimir bawled. "No, I will not! I will not kill him."

Svarog's tone flattened, gazing blindly at the ceiling through the golden wrapping over his eyes, "Kowin the Deathless will remain in Thrice Ten Kingdom until Dorofej Kaligula's soul resides in the Netherworld with his brethren in the afterlife."

Branimir suddenly could turn his eyes from the Grandfather of the Gods, to see the corpse of a half-dead man, skin rotted and peeling, chained on Svarog's left. The eyes were sunken into his skull; his cheeks had decayed to the degree that Branimir could see the putrefied teeth in his enflamed, bloodied gums. The chains rattled around his wrists and ankles as he shifted, sneering at Branimir. Kowin the Deathless, adorned in his faded, crimson armor and dual-side swords with decorated hilts, billowed smoke from his mouth as Svarog raised his hand with his ordinance. Without warning, Kowin turned to ashes, disappearing from the temple.

"Be certain the Deathless stays caged until the appointed time," Svarog directed the man on his right. The God with Four Heads, Svathevit the Red, showed as bright as a morning sunrise. He made no motion to indicate he heard Svarog, keeping the same emotionless expression on all four faces on each side of his head. His fierce gaze missed nothing. His blood-red cloak draped over his shoulders, swirling in an untamed breeze, from some distant world beyond the temple. His magnificence was only lessened by Svarog's overshadowing glory.

Svathevit disappeared in a flash of light, taking Marheena with him from Branimir's side.

Svarog folded his arms in what Branimir believed to be displeasure. "The sacredness of Iriy wanes in the presence of Kaelandur and the Likhyi within, diminishing the protective wards. The power of the Old-dark grows stronger as the Ash Tree fades." Branimir attempted to debate Svarog, but found his mouth would not open. Svarog went on, disregarding him, "Although, the Ash Tree cannot be fully abolished without Kaelandur, the chains holding the Likhyi will fracture, giving them a greater bearing on the mortal world."

"I will not kill Dorofej," Branimir finally forced between his clenched teeth.

Svarog turned away. A blue light deepened around him to pull him back to the Beyond, to Thrice Ten Kingdom. "Iriy is no longer a haven. Eisliev Kluk has come."

The High God of Wisdom and Fire was swallowed whole by the divine light, leaving Dorofej and Branimir kneeling against the stone of Koranitsa.

The gods had abandoned them.

Chapter XXIII

The paved streets under Branimir's feet quaked as they sped from the Great Hall of the Gods. The entire mountain shook with such intensity, Branimir wondered if the city of Iriy would collapse to the dale below. In the distance, he could hear the crack of lightning and the fracturing of rock. Along with the clamor sounded the low-rumbling roar of demons rasping and growling on the lower levels as they marched up the mountain. The beginnings of a war had reached the gates.

"I don't understand." Branimir faced Dorofej in the arching shadow of Koranitsa. "Iriy should have been safe from Eisliev and the demons. Why have the gods forsaken us?"

"Kaelandur's magic and the power of the Likhyi have weakened the city, yes? And causes to battle against this inescapable doom, the gods have not. The Likhyi and the gods are cut from the same cloth, yes? I say, the Old-dark already have begun to destroy the fabric of this world, even when partially caged," Dorofej said, the irritability unmistakable on the edge of his tongue, "and they begin with the destruction of Iriy. Hear nothing from the gods' wisdom, did you? Men invited this calamity, and men must either remedy the mistake or embrace it."

Branimir ran his hands through his hair, pulling at the thin strands with aggravation. The city around him, in all its magnificence, would crumble, because he brought Kaelandur to its gates with the Likhyi trapped inside. The gods were supposed to help him. "You and I were not the ones who killed Wolos. Why should we pay for another's mistake?" he asked.

"Every action is worthy of consequence, yes?" Dorofej rhetorically asked. "Speak of good and evil, or right and wrong, I do not; but about what naturally occurs. The fields, forests, and streams are upset for centuries by a nation's cultivation, yes? Our children and our children's children are impacted by the wars of their fathers, yes? Can one man's hate not squelch the love of another? For eternity, the faults of one man can become the burdens of another." The city of Iriy pitched, nearly knocking Branimir to his knees. Dorofej grabbed him by the shoulders, jerking him close. His words were as water dousing flames. "The question is not *why you and I*, but *why are more not* seized at knife's edge? For, in every choice we make, we should think of ourselves as pressing a dagger to our brother's chest, and then see whether our selfishness has wounded the heart."

"I will not wound you, Dorofej," Branimir said, his words garbled. "I would give my last breath before I would see it done."

Dorofej sighed with exasperation, letting go of him. The black mage looked over his shoulder, listening to the demons marching toward the eighth gate. "I say, Eisliev will no longer be kept from Kaelandur. Re-balanced, the scales of the world must be. You must take my life, Branimir, and destroy Kaelandur, yes? Give mortals another chance to find their way. Win this battle, we cannot."

Anger flared—more than anger—but he hammered it down. He wanted to scream until his throat bled so Dorofej might hear his resounding response to the harrowing solution. He forced breath through his nostrils in attempt to release steam from his inner ire. His answer emerged as a choked whisper. "No."

Dorofej tried again. "Branimir—"

"We will flee Iriy and find another solution, even if I have to travel back to the Netherworld and kill Eisliev with my own hands," Branimir said hastily. "We need you, Dorofej. I need you."

"Branimir! Dorofej!" Alyona shouted, running toward them from further up the road. She appeared to be coming down from the highest spire, appearing as young as she had when they first met at Gaetana months ago. She had clearly taken the vial of the Water of Life that Dorofej had given her.

Tyr trailed right behind her, his eyes wide with concern as the sound of the approaching army grew louder.

Alyona stuttered to a halt feet from them. "Eisliev is attacking the city and has brought half the Netherworld with him. How is this possible?" She looked at Dorofej for an explanation. "Iriy is sacred ground. This city should be untouchable by the hand of death."

"Enfeebled the consecrated wards, the primal Likhyi in Kaelandur has," Dorofej explained. A deafening crack sounded from the gate behind them, the iron and stone splintering.

"That is impossible," Alyona said disbelievingly. "No one has ever marched on the City of the Gods."

"Nine Lands," Branimir muttered, turning to face the walls. He suddenly realized an inescapable truth. "Sulanna and Alden are still down below. We must—"

Tyr halted his words. He could not keep the sadness from his deep tone. "Nothing is left down there but demons, Branimir. We could see the entire dale from the summit above. It is lost."

"They may have escaped," Branimir said, taking a step backward as though he might leap over the mountain's edge to search for his friends. He looked at Tyr and Alyona for any sign of hope. The shared looked between the two plumbed the depths of despair.

"Only one road leads in and out of Iriy," Alyona replied.

Branimir gritted his teeth and turned away. How crude would the gods be to give Alden and Sulanna the blessing of a child, only to have them hacked apart by the undead hours later.

"It cannot be," Branimir said stubbornly, pointing to the top of the summit. "How did you two get up there without a flower from Lada to open the gates?"

Tyr answered, "Lada came and took us to the Hall of Iredale. The ninth gate was not sealed when we returned just now. But, Branimir, we did not see Alden and Sulanna here or there."

"Maybe Lada took them somewhere else," Branimir said in a brittle voice. "She must have."

The gateway behind them split, pieces falling away as something struck it repeatedly. The unmistakable layer-upon-layer of frozen skin reaching through the crevice was clearly the giant, demonic Bukavac tearing through. Tyr reached for his two-handed axe on his back only to remember he had left it below with Alden and Sulanna.

Dorofej redirected them. "Weapons, we do not have."

"But we can wield Koldovstvo with the weakening wards," Alyona said.

"Wield Koldovstvo, I will not." Dorofej scowled, shaking his head. "We only have a single route to end Eisliev's assault, yes?"

"No," Branimir glared at the black mage. He could not believe that Dorofej would refuse to fight.

"What is he talking about?" Tyr asked.

"He wants us to kill him so Kaelandur will be destroyed," Branimir said with frustration. Tyr reeled back in disgust at the proposition. Branimir was glad to see the gut response from the Ispolini. The roars of the demons were growing louder. "We must find another way. We can defeat Eisliev."

Dorofej's eyes pleaded for understanding.

"We cannot kill you, Dorofej," Tyr said in agreement, turning to Alyona who shuffled her feet, considering Branimir's words. Tyr hesitated. The gate behind them would not last much longer. The giant winced at his own words, "If you are certain, why do you not kill yourself?"

"He cannot," Alyona answered for him. "For Kaelandur to be destroyed, he must be killed by the blade, but the magic of Kaelandur will not let him."

"By the Nine Lands," Tyr groaned, looking at his own hands. "I have killed before…"

"No. I will do it. It should be me," Alyona said, acknowledging Dorofej with respect. She rubbed her hands against her pant legs and then reached for Branimir. "Give me Kaelandur."

Branimir shook his head. "I said *no*." He stepped away from the Kadari. Behind her, stone fell from the gate in several large chunks, crashing to the ground. It burst into smaller pieces, scattering across the street.

Bukavac squeezed through the gate. Branimir had almost forgotten the massive size of the beasts, standing twice as tall as any human with brawny arms equally thick as his own lithe body. The bodies were colored like snowfall with blue-grey eyes brightly lit like gems. A smaller army had taken Melkorka from the Highborn twelve-hundred-years ago; Branimir could not fathom how the four of them could defend Iriy.

"Kill them!" he heard Eisliev shout from somewhere beyond the gate. "Bring me the dagger!"

The first to surge from the opening clutched an iron sword between its three fingers and thumb, roaring with fanged teeth. More emerged from behind the Bukavac, carrying axes and maces, forged in the Netherworld.

"Run," Tyr ordered. Before Branimir could say a word, the Ispolini turned to meet the monstrous demon. Springing forward, he raced to intercept the Bukavac.

Despite the Bukavac's larger size, Tyr was built for war even when he held no weapon; his physique glistened in the sun's light. The demon swept the sword blade in an upward arc with aim to cut Tyr in two, but the Ispolini was light on his feet, spinning at the last second to dodge the attack. He then hooked his arm under the Bukavac's leg and pulled up with a growl. The demon roared, flailing the weapon wildly before crashing onto his back.

Tyr rolled over the demon, crushing the demon's arm to the stone, and ripping the sword free from its grasp. The giant maintained the momentum, rolling completely to his feet in a fluid motion, crouched at the ready. The Bukavac hastily reached over to slash at Tyr with its clawed hand, only to catch the sword's edge. The bluish-blood spurted with the severed hand. The Bukavac's cry turned to a gurgle as the demon's own sword plummeted through the mouth, the iron point chinking against the paved stone on the opposite side of the Bukavac's skull.

Alyona joined Tyr in the fight, flinging fire and ice at the demons who rushed from the gate. Their screeches and howls echoed through the city streets.

Branimir stepped back as another crashed into Tyr, using its body as a weapon. The giant stumbled back a step, ducking the secondary attack as the Bukavac swung an axe for Tyr's head. With his own battle cry, Tyr kicked with his bare foot into the demon's stomach, and then spun on his heel to slice the sword across the beast's chest. The Bukavac screeched its death cry and collapsed.

"We have to help him," Branimir said, reaching for Kaelandur. He had no other weapon to wield. Tyr was already lifting the sword against another Bukavac.

"No, Branimir," Dorofej said. "*Kaelandur* has only one life left to take, yes? Kill these demons, or Eisliev with it, you must not." The weapons clanged with as much ferocity as two armies fighting instead of one against hundreds.

Alyona shouted at them. "This place was not meant to withstand a siege. We will die here."

"Then we need to go somewhere else," Branimir urged.

Metal on metal rang as more Bukavac advanced from the gate. Tyr had slain another demon or two, but the numbers would soon be overwhelming. Almost twenty beasts pushed through the gates with hundreds more at their back. Tyr Og swatted at them, barely deflecting their attacks with the sword.

Alyona cried out, dropping fire from above the horde of Bukavac. The flames threatened the space near Tyr. "Where can we go?" Alyona asked.

Branimir looked around with frustration. "Sorod!" he lastly exclaimed. "Sorod can be our escape."

"Beyond the demon army, the gateway to Sorod stands," Dorofej said, pointing at the Bukavac pushing through the gate.

Alyona agreed. "He is right. We would have to miraculously push through them to even reach the gate. But you might escape if you are not to be seen."

He could hear Tyr snarling in the backdrop among the Bukavac. Alyona shouted, throwing stone. Already, she had wrinkles forming near her eyes.

Branimir shook his head, recalling his encounter with Eisliev at Harrowhal. "If I am holding Kaelandur, Eisliev can see me, regardless of whether I am invisible."

"Again, only the one option stands, yes?" Dorofej pressed. "Kill me, and then flee from Iriy."

Branimir's roar of frustration melded with Tyr's sudden cry of pain as an axe caught him in the lower thigh. He fell to the ground, swinging the sword riotously at the oncoming demon horde. The Bukavac with the axe circled him, avoiding his flailing sword. Blood flowed from the leggings he wore; the gash cut to the bone. As he swung his sword at the Bukavac, another demon plunged a sword into his side.

"No!" Alyona screamed, flinging fire at the first, only to have another take its place.

"We must hurry," Dorofej cried.

"Give me Kaelandur, Branimir," Alyona whispered. She reached for him. The marching footsteps were as loud as thunder. The Bukavac were coming for the dagger.

"No." Branimir pulled back.

"Give it to me, Brani—" Alyona was silenced, ripped through the air by the unseen magic, and flung into the statue of Perom guarding Koranitsa. The sickening crack of her head hitting the stone could not be missed.

Branimir gasped.

"No," came the voice of Eisliev Kluk, stepping from the throng of demons, his red cloak flowing at his heels. Eisliev's light blue eyes blazed with intensity. He raised a finger, devoid of color, grey as death, at Branimir. "I will take Kaelandur."

Tyr cried out at the sight of his old friend, swinging his weapon to catch the still attacking Bukavac in the knees. The demon fell to the ground and Tyr scrambled over him to jam his sword into the monster's chest.

Another Bukavac with an axe advanced.

"Tyr!" Branimir cried out.

The giant spun around soon enough to catch the blade in his chest. He immediately spurted blood, swinging his sword aimlessly at the Bukavac. The demon backed away, leaving the axe lodged in Tyr's torso.

With a grunt, he pulled his sword behind his head and flung it with both hands. The blade ripped through the frozen chest of the retreating Bukavac. The demon screeched in surprise, descending to its knees. No doubt, the monster would die, but Tyr had left himself vulnerable. He tugged at the axe in his chest as more Bukavac advanced.

Branimir tried to rush forward but was caught by Alyona's hand. The first Bukavac loomed over the giant, pulling back his iron sword. Tyr, bloodied and already dying, yelled with defiance. The sword's end ripped through Tyr's throat, silencing his protest.

Branimir turned from the sight, tucking his head into Dorofej's shirt, as the blade was pulled free and the giant slumped over.

"No other choice, do we have. I am sorry, Branimir Baran." Dorofej backed up the steps to the sanctuary.

Branimir saw Alyona fall limp on the ground behind him. Everyone he knew was dying.

"My sincerest apologies, Dorofej Kaligula," Eisliev said, his blood-stained lips twisting into a smile. "I appreciate you and this Kadari killing Falmagon. He will be a fine addition to my demon horde. But I am afraid there will be no place for you in the next world as we had agreed." He laughed to himself. "Though, I promise to keep you alive until the Likhyi have been freed from the Ash Tree. I believe that is a fair trade considering the horror your bloodline has not only set on my own, but now, the world."

The black veins beneath Eisliev's grey skin darkened, lifting Alyona's drooping figure from the stone steps. He twisted her with a sneer, while the Bukavac at his back waited for their command.

"Stop," Branimir weakly begged. Fear gripped his heart. The world would break.

"I cannot say Alyona will last, Dorofej," Eisliev smirked, drawing out his words, dropping his gaze to the black mage.

Dorofej took a breath, falling back to his haunches, sitting on the steps in defeat. Never had the face of the Stuhian been etched in such shade. He gulped, pulling up the dark sleeves of his robe. Faegrim caught Branimir's eye. "I am sorry, Branimir. When it is done, you disappear. You run."

Branimir had not the time to make a sound, and all the foreboding ridding his heart of courage fled from him. The world became a dream, unrecognizable to Branimir. Something deep within him stirred, screaming at him that nothing was real. Yet he could not help but embrace the state of sentience, brimming with light and love.

A mirage of all who knowingly forewent their own paths to follow Branimir overlapped in his mind like pages being flipped through in a book. The countless benevolent words and kind embraces; the many gentle smiles and altruistic passions. Thousands of words spoken, and battles won, and moments shared overwhelmed him. He could think of nothing else. Laughter occupied his ears. Admiration filled his thoughts.

Eisliev's voluble screams rocked Branimir back to reality, the pleasantries of his hallucinations evaporated. The temple of Koranitsa faded into focus. The statues of the powerful gods overseeing the perfectly-spaced, stone steps, brushed with the ever-brooding blood. The crimson shade matched the color dribbling from the end of Kaelandur, grasped securely in Branimir's hand.

Dorofej's lifeless eyes stared past Branimir at the cloudless sky. The black mage was dead.

"No!" Branimir's shriek was prolonged, echoing off the stone, forever meant to linger across Iriy. His voice cracked painfully in his throat. The salted tears burned from the corner of his eyes to the depths of his nostrils. He was drowning in his own sorrow. "No! By the gods, no!" Pain trickled against his temples, forcing him to his knees. Kaelandur slipped from his fingers, falling to Dorofej's bloodied robes.

Branimir could not believe Dorofej would have been so cruel. He used Faegrim to force Branimir's hand.

"What have you done?" Eisliev bellowed, dropping Alyona, and storming forward. He whipped Branimir around by the jacket. Bran crashed against Dorofej's body with Eisliev looming over him. Fire furiously flared behind his eyes. "You have fated the world to endless death without reprieve. Never again will there be peace!"

Branimir could not make a sound, his soul shattered by the evil he had done. Dorofej's blood soaked into the back of his thin shirt. Feeling the inevitable warmth, his vision blurred with tears.

The din of the Bukavac growling and snarling gave a clear warning of Branimir's imminent death. No doubt, Eisliev would be certain he followed Dorofej to the afterlife to be warped into Marheena's demonic army.

Eisliev fumbled around Branimir, finally pulling the copper dagger from the stone steps where it had toppled. As though he hoped against hope, he held the blade in his open palm studiously watching Branimir from the corner of his undead eye. At first, his face etched with confusion, but then the inevitable happened as foretold.

Kaelandur dissolved into ashes, flowing from his hand into nothingness. The remaining slags fluttered across the stone of the temple as though it had never been.

The black, billowing fog surfacing with Kaelandur's destruction was unexpected. An unholy darkness spread over the expanse above Eisliev and Branimir with gale-force, stretching as far as the first ranks of the Bukavac, violent and untamed. Branimir struggled against the unfathomable force, noticing the demons milling in the streets, several withdrawing through the eighth gate. He wiped his eyes with his sleeve, staring helplessly at the mass collecting above him.

Finding his strength, Branimir cricked his neck to see Alyona stirring near the statue of Perom. He rolled off Dorofej to his stomach, shielding his eyes from the swirling darkness above him. With what resolve he could muster, he crawled for the Kadari.

Eisliev cried out, stooping back from the ethereal form. He shouted as though he were speaking to a voice only he could hear. "I have not failed. Do not renounce me!"

A blast of energy, along with the strident thunderclap, propelled Branimir face first into the stone steps, cracking his forehead open. He groaned, blood straightway gushing down into his eye.

He swayed, lightheaded, swiping the blood down and across his cheek. "Alyona," he forced the name from his mouth. His throat swelled as though he had not spoken for days.

"The Ash Tree will perish!" Eisliev screamed in desperation. "I promise you! You will be freed!"

Eisliev's words turned to wails as the darkness corkscrewed into a downward spiral into his wide-open mouth. The red mage's petitions fell to distorted sobbing as his body convulsed under the power of the profane shade. In a breath, the skin molded into the remnants of a corpse a thousand years old, reduced to nothing but rotten remains. Eisliev Kluk had been defeated.

The Likhyi had come.

Chapter XXIV

Branimir shook the Kadari woman with both hands, praying she was not dead. "Come on, Alyona. Wake up. Wake up, please."

Eisliev's decrepit carcass had become little more than a pile of brittle bones and corroded flesh. Branimir could not ignore the smell of the decay, more rotten than all the demons in the streets of Iriy. He repeatedly looked over his shoulder to ensure Eisliev did not return from death while attempting to rouse Alyona.

"Alyona." He shook her again.

The Likhyi above him, a pool of darkness hovering over the streets, blocked out the sunlight meant to forever shine over the City of the Gods. Branimir could still see well enough down the streets— enough to see the Bukavac swaying hesitantly behind their now dead commander—but the Likhyi's bleakness reminded Branimir how terrifying it had been in the tombs of Garain'l when he first encountered the Old-dark. His heart raced in remembrance of the fear. The Likhyi had stolen his sight with the impenetrable pitch of its ethereal form. He did not want to experience blindness again, nor did he want to experience the same fate as Eisliev—and Falmagon.

Branimir wanted to flee Iriy, but he did not want to disappear and leave Alyona behind.

He hit her across the cheek, feeling the sting against his own fingertips. "Alyona!"

She stirred slightly but gave no sign of waking. The blood on the back of her head had dried. He could feel the soft flesh rising from where she had struck the statue of Perom with her skull.

He needed her to be okay.

The Likhyi's darkness broadened and descended, roiling over the stone, sifting through the demon ranks. The Bukavac gnashed their fangs at the empty air as the mist consumed them. Their ice-blue eyes darkened as though they were possessed by some irrefutable force. Branimir shuffled closer to Alyona, horror-struck. The beasts turned to him at unspoken command and raised their weapons at the ready. The clinking of their weapons chilled his blood.

"Alyona," he hissed.

The mist of the Likhyi continue to expand, unyielding, reaching over Eisliev's body toward Branimir. He swore he could see ghastly fingertips forming from the swelling vapor.

He backed away until he practically sat on Alyona's chest, his back pressed against the stone foot of Perom's statue. As the Likhyi neared the tip of Branimir's hooked nose, a blooming radiance vented from the doorway of the temple as luminous as the first light of dawn. The rays struck the Old-dark's ghastly hands, causing it to recoil from Branimir.

Branimir jerked to the strange light, half-covering his eyes, to see a silver horse appear in the doorway with a rider on its back. The animal was led unconcernedly from the doorway, halting just above the steps to oversee the demon army and Likhyi. As the yellowish glow gently subsided, Branimir saw Svathevit the Red, the God of War and Glory, sitting atop the hoary mount. The four faces on either side of his head remained expressionless, as they had in the temple earlier. His blood-red cloak fluttered behind him, draped over the haunches of the horse. The esteemed god of the Svet, pulled a glimmering blade from the sheath on his back, and held it out to the side.

At first, Branimir thought Svathevit intended to hand him the master-blade. But then the undead warrior exited from the temple behind him. Kowin marched to the stairs, the blue dots of his sunken eyes barely visible, snatching the weapon from Svathevit's hand. He slipped the blade into the empty scabbard on the right side of his belt as though it were a key being inserted into its lock. Then he cocked his neck and reached for the two scabbards on his left, pulling loose two straight-edged blades. He twirled the left blade to hold it upright in his hand, while testing the weight of the other in his right.

The chains at his wrists and ankles unfastened and fell away from his decaying skin. Smoke roiled from his lips. With satisfaction, he lifted his hateful gaze to the Likhyi eddying above them as a storm cloud might.

Svathevit spoke in Branimir's mind with the dominance of the divine. *'Svarog has given way for Kowin the Deathless to stay the hand of the Likhyi until mortals have revealed whether balance can be regained. He shall return to Thrice Ten Kingdom once their failure or triumph has been determined.'*

A roar spewed from the hundreds of demons in defiance, signifying the displeasure of the Old-dark, their new imperious master. Kowin shortened their battle cry, waving his hand, using Koldovstvo, flinging the front line Bukavac a hundred paces back into their own kind.

The demons wrestled over one another in a fitful attempt to hurriedly return to their feet, to wage war against the unforeseen threat.

Branimir had nowhere left to scoot, but he still shirked back against the statue as Kowin stomped down the steps with purpose. The crimson-colored, steel breastplate seemed to deepen in its redness.

He did not pay any attention to Branimir, engrossed on the reassembling Bukavac. He was uncertain if the man was alive or dead, god or mortal, friend or enemy, but he carried himself as though he were unstoppable.

Branimir grabbed at Alyona's face, pulling at her desperately, while his eyes stayed forever fixed on Kowin the Deathless.

Like a snowstorm, the Bukavac collided with Kowin, fanatically devoted to the Likhyi hissing with irritation in the sky. Nothing could have prepared Branimir for the heroic battle which ensued before him. Iron and steel clashed, sword against axe and spear tip. Kowin moved with trained proficiency, unaffected by his old age or decomposing skin. He ducked under blades, and stepped over polearms, using his two whirling swords to parry and then pierce when an opening broke in the demon's attack. Skin was cut away and guts spilled; blue-tinted gore gushed and sprayed. The Bukavac, standing a head and a half taller than Kowin, soon began to amass at his feet.

The death count was incalculable. And, yet, more demons rushed from the eighth gate to attack Kowin. The rumble of the Likhyi intensified as the Old-dark¬ beckoned his newfound army to eliminate the warrior who had been sent to deny its emergence. Branimir could not hear the Likhyi's grating tone any longer—now separated from Kaelandur—but the swollen, curling fog cast a shadow darker than all the Shade Fells.

"Branimir…" Alyona coughed, pulling at his leg. "Get off me. I cannot breathe."

Branimir sprang from the Kadari, falling on his knees next to her. "You are alive. Nine Lands, you are alive." He grabbed her by the shoulders to move her, ignoring the death cries screeching around them.

"How am I alive?" She lifted her neck to see the battle raging in front of them. She pulled herself up. "Is that Kowin the Deathless? That means…" She gasped, seeing Dorofej's body sprawled across the stairs. "Oh, Branimir…No…"

Branimir did not follow her gaze. He could not look at Dorofej's corpse.

She weakly looked up at Svathevit, who remained seated on the silver horse. He watched everything around them with his four faces. The face on the right side of his head, skimmed Alyona and Branimir, but he said nothing.

Kowin stole Branimir's attention, bellowing with fury, running his sword through a Bukavac's chest. Kicking the demon from his blade, he then lifted his hand and released a stream of fire into the demons. Orange and red flames lashed through the ranks of the beasts. The skin of the demons ignited in an infinite blaze, causing them to thrash back with screeches of agony.

Branimir gaped in shock, noticing the festering skin stretching from his cheekbone to his jawbone begin to patch itself together. Threads of flesh stitched up and down the side of his face, while the fire burned and the lives of the demons were stifled.

With a gritty grumble, Kowin unleashed a greater inferno with Koldovstvo, crying out the louder. And then, as if showing the extent of his power, he used his magic to rip the statue of Wolos from the front of the temple. With little effort, the thirty-foot tall statue was hurled into the demon legion. The stone shattered against the bodies of the Bukavac. The curled horns, and hooves, and the stone spear of Wolos wrecked into the horde, breaking bones and crushing skulls.

Branimir also noticed the statue pummeled into the wall and the gate, sealing the entrance and their exit. The Bukavac on the opposite side could be heard crashing into the stone in attempt to break through and pursue Kowin at the behest of the Likhyi.

Kowin roared with power. With every demon life taken, Kowin's body regained the time taken from its essence. The rot and decay disintegrated from his skin, replaced with the thriving color of life and vivacity.

His eyes were no longer sunk. His skin no longer hung loose from its bones. His muscles swelled to reflect their impressive strength. Kowin the Deathless was being renewed.

"Branimir, we have to get out of here," Alyona said, struggling to her feet. "Kowin cannot be trusted. We cannot be here when he has finished with the Old-dark. There is a reason he was held prisoner by the gods."

He looked at Alyona in confusion but dipped his head in agreement. He thought Kowin fought for goodness and righteousness. He eyed Kowin uneasily, standing upright with her.

Kowin surged forward, cutting his sword through the remaining Bukavac in the street. The demons screeched and bawled, defenseless against his swords.

"How will we pass by him? Where will we go?" Branimir asked, reaching for Alyona's shirttail.

The Likhyi rumbled loud enough to deafen his words, declining toward Kowin. The swelling, black cloud only made it a few inches before Kowin spun on his heel and lifted his hand. A blue, shimmering field of force rapidly formed beneath the Likhyi, spreading a distance great enough to envelop the darkness. Like water trapped in a bottle, the Likhyi sloshed around inside the magical shield, attempting to break free. Kowin gritted his teeth, his dark hair and blue eyes reconstructing with his flush skin until he nearly looked fully human. He appeared to be an Anshedar male, never to have known death.

"Branimir," Alyona murmured, pulling at his shoulder.

He turned around and stopped, facing the thigh of Svathevit. The God of War climbed down from his horse and approached them without word. He now hovered over Branimir and Alyona with his eternal, silent expression. His horse neighed behind him like a meek warning.

Svathevit grabbed them.

The flash of light was dazzling, and suddenly Branimir found himself clear of Kowin and the dead. He blinked several times, identifying the perfected carved stone beneath the shining light of the sun. Svathevit had taken them to another level in Iriy.

Bran steadied his feet, feeling Svathevit's hand holding fast to his shirt behind him. He chose not to struggle. The God of War's voice echoed in his head.

'Your share in this tale has expired, Branimir Baran, son of Hrani, and Alyona Gounari, daughter of Meimer. Here, you will find

safe passage to Sorod. Beware the path of honor and glory; death awaits. For glory. For Rujan.'

With a shudder, Branimir twisted on his heel to face Svathevit, but the god vanished with his last words.

"Where are we?" he turned to Sulanna. The sounds of battle echoed close by.

Alyona pointed at a shimmering stone wall ahead of them, shaking her head. "Svathevit has brought us to the seventh level. This is the ingress to Sorod."

Alyona ran a hand through her dark hair, looking in the direction of the eighth gate. "The world has not been saved; if anything, it has only become more dangerous with Kowin the Deathless venturing back from the Beyond. His power is only stayed by Svarog stowing away his soul. If he were ever to discover its resting place, he would wield more havoc than the Likhyi combined."

"The Likhyi have not been stopped either," Branimir said with frustration. "The demons at Melkorka will keep hacking away at the Ash Tree until another weapon is forged to break it completely. The Old-dark have only been hamstrung by Kowin." Branimir irritably clenched his hands into fists. "What have we truly done? Has this all been for nothing?"

"No. Kaelandur is destroyed," Alyona assured. "This tale started with Wolos's death and will end with his rebirth. Our journey is but the pages between the covers of a book. We have given the brothers at Anaerfell the chance to save Aenar."

Branimir took a breath and scratched at the thin hair on his head. "You are right. Erzebeth will see the dragon-men to the Netherworld and Wolos reborn."

"Do not worry, Branimir. I do not think our tale is over," she said.

"Far from it," he agreed.

Alyona stared at the gateway with concern. "Though, the Svet will not be pleased to find us in Sorod. If we are seen, the centaurs will likely string us up for their evening meal."

“Best we are not seen then, yes?’ Branimir asked slyly.
Alyona grinned. “A bat then?”
Branimir returned the smile and disappeared.

ABOUT THE AUTHOR

Joshua Robertson was born in Kingman, Kansas on May 23, 1984. A graduate of Norwich High School, Robertson attended Wichita State University where he received his master's in social work with minors in psychology and sociology. His bestselling novel, *Melkorka*, the first in *The Kaelandur Series,* was released in 2015. Known most for his Thrice Nine Legends Saga, Robertson enjoys an ever-expanding and extremely loyal following of readers. He counts R.A. Salvatore and J.R.R. Tolkien among his literary influences.